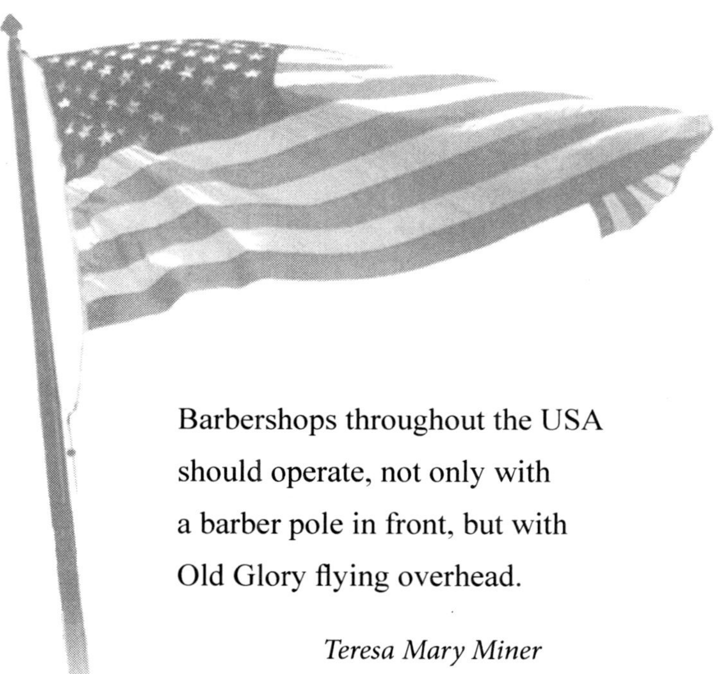

Barbershops throughout the USA
should operate, not only with
a barber pole in front, but with
Old Glory flying overhead.

Teresa Mary Miner

Written in Loving memory for
Richard Bruce and Betty O'Dell.
Glenn William and Consuelo Martin.

Lady Behind the Chair

by
Teresa Mary Miner

Lady Behind the Chair

Comments:
Contact Teresa Mary Miner
Email - teresamminer@gmail.com
www.facebook.com/ladybehindthechair

The Lady Behind the Chair is a fictional novel based on events that happened over years behind the chair. All names have been changed and any reference to real people, historical events, is coincidental. All places are used fictitiously and the author's imagination has shaped them to fit the story.

ISBN: 978-1-941069-19-6

Published by ProsePress
75 Red Maple Drive,
Pawleys Island, South Carolina 29585

www.Prosepress.biz
proseNcons@live.com

ACKNOWLEDGEMENTS

The earliest brain storming of thoughts and ideas for this novel came to mind in Garden Grove, California inside a tiny apartment. The ideas that day were hand written on two sheets of white paper and put into a blue envelope and addressed to the author. Early the next morning the letter was taken to the United States post office and was stamped as registered mail, dated March 15, 1983 and then stamped and sealed and addressed back to the author. This is called a "poor man's patent." After that all ideas, thoughts and story lines concerning this novel were all handwritten and put into shoe boxes by the author. Then put away in a closet. The shoe boxes multiplied.

Many years later the author Teresa Mary Miner felt passionate about beginning the work of piecing a manuscript together. So on the date January 5, 2003 she called a friend, Notary public-Miss Enid S. Vella to come to her barbershop business to execute a California All-Purpose Acknowledgement for Title of Novel "Lady behind the Chair." With her thumb print safely on the new document her ideas of the novel were forming.

In the month of January 2005 Teresa boarded a plane headed to Myrtle Beach South Carolina with shoe boxes in suitcase. She would stay there alone, in her sister Irene Ann Martin's condo on the beach, and form a manuscript using a computer for the first time. The author says thank you to her sister.

Author Thanks:

March 2005 Miss Kelly Shorey proof reader editor from Myrtle Beach, South Carolina edit the first very rough draft.

February 2007 the manuscript was sent to William Greenleaf literary services out of Rio Rancho, New Mexico.

March 9, 2007 the manuscript was sent back from William with hopeful changes and ideas towards a better way to write.

Beginning October 2011 manuscript edited by McKean Nowlin of Myrtle Beach, South Carolina.

Summer of 2014 In-depth editor- at Large- Caroline Evans/ stareditors@gmail.com

APPRECIATION TO

Bill Inman client and accountant through the years.

Gingerose Miner of Corona California my hairstylist and confidant.

Evelyn Ester Langenberg deceased in 2007 age 82. Thank you for support.

Esperanza Hope Conroy deceased 2014 age 90. You were blind and paid for someone to read manuscript in 2005. You appreciated this story. I thank you my darling Aunt.

Michael Hetzer Author in Myrtle Beach, S.C. for words of encouragement 2005.

June Weikle, Author in Myrtle Beach, S.C. for knowledge of this profession.

To my dear friends for their friendship:

Sue Moderegger Barber, my dearest listener.

Golden West College, CA. Professor Sandy Smith of vocational education in Cosmetology.

Golden West College, CA. Professor Nancy Viele of vocational education in Cosmetology.

Master Barber: Mr. Augustine "Augie" Souza: deceased 2014. Owner of The Real Barbers College, Anaheim Ca.

Master Barber: Bill Martin Owner of Royal Barber College 1981 in Anaheim Ca.

Chiropractor Myrtle Beach, S.C. Dr. Carole A. Martin

Gary Stephen O'Dell and Larry Bruce O'Dell.

Michele Marie O'Dell and Crystal Patricia O'Dell.

Mr. Darrell A. Miner for this long traveled journey.

Nidia M. Colomer de Saca, M.D. Psychiatry in Chino, Ca. After finishing this task, I am forever grateful to you for bring me back to reality and Out of the complex, "Rabbit Hole".

Contributors on Art work for book cover;
Teresa Mary Miner, photography director.
Crystal Patricia for trust and endurance.
Artist for painting of book cover by the gifted and talented:
"June Blanco;jun.blanco@yahoo.com."

Robert T O'Brien, Publisher and owner of Prose Press Pawley's Island, S.C. and author of a must read novel,"The Toppled Pawn."

I shall be forever grateful for my two brothers:

Michael Glenn Martin. And Dr. Patrick Martin who so graciously assisted me with hours that turned into months and years. Your interest and encouragement throughout this process would not have been accomplished without both of you.

Finally but not least, to You the readers!
I hope you enjoy the story.
Most important that you are inspired to find your path in life,
No matter what life throws at you.

I am pleased and humbled to have lived long enough
to see this work published.

Best wishes from Teresa Mary Miner.

CHAPTER - PAGE NUMBERS

Family Tree

The O'Malley Family:

Barney ~Father
Isabel~Mother
Peter~ Eldest Son
Morgan~ Eldest Daughter
Noah~ twin Son
Casey~ twin Son
Emma~ final Daughter

O'Donnell Family:

Rick~ Father
Betty~ Mother
Dean~ Eldest Son
Luke~ Final Son

Dean and Morgan O'Donnell Family:

Noelle~ Eldest Daughter
Cathleen~ Final Daughter

Barber Clients

Tom~ Businessman
Christopher~ 'Chris' Police Chief
Lucky~ 'Lawrence'~ Parolee
Firefighter
Blackie~ Outlaw Biker
Victor~ Professional Baseball Player

Barber Clients - Continued

Jon Pierre~ Cruise Ship Pastry Chief
Mr. Fang ~Businessman from China
Dino~ Quiet Man with Celebrity Daughter
Antonio~ Delivery Newspaper Man to Self-made Millionaire
Doctor Jared~ Dentist
William~ Accountant and Taxman

Morgan's Childhood Friends and Acquaintances:

Lucy~ Childhood Neighbor to Carmelite Nun Sister Amelia
Sara~ High School Classmate
Gina~High School Classmate
Peggy Wilson~ Babysitter for O'Malley Children
Warren White~ Child Eye-witness to Motorcycle accident to Prison Inmate

Morgan's Teenage Years and following years:

Rusty~ Loyal Friend and Vice-President of Car Club
Georgia~ Rusty's Mother
Damien~ Car Club President

Torres Family ~Friends to Noah

Tootsie~ Plump Jolly Woman Friend
Johnny~ Guy Friend of Rusty
Tina~ Neighborhood Charismatic Older Teenager Girl

Continued on page 326

Good listener
or closet therapist?

- Ruby Sue Tootser

Baby's heads have no hair,
Old men's heads are just as bare;
Between the cradle and the grave,
Lies a haircut and a shave.

- Samuel Hoffenstein

"When love and skill work together,
expect a masterpiece."

- B.J.Palmer

Chapter 1

After lingering for ten minutes in the lobby of the tallest and newest hotel in Anaheim, California, Morgan finally pushed the elevator button. Moments later, the doors opened to reveal a full cast of complete strangers of all nationalities dressed in business suits. Almost all were men and she was alert to the fact that most of them turned to look at her as she stepped through the doors.

"Why would they not take notice of me?" she thought, smiling. After all, she was wearing her favorite high-priced vintage outfit that she had found in a Beverly Hills thrift store. She looked like a 1940s movie star in her tight, black-pinstriped, high-waist, side-button slacks, sheer white blouse, and small jacket. She wore black 1940s platform heels fastened around her ankles and red toenail polish peeked out of the peep toes. Crimson red lipstick matched her nail polish. A spiraling wave of black shiny hair fell just above her shoulders.

Morgan remembered that she knew this new hotel was going to be famous for business meetings way before the hotel had broken ground. A few years ago she had the pleasure of giving a haircut to one of the head honchos on the building's supervisors' committee. The purpose of her being there today concerned the future of her barbershop.

Morgan was not enthusiastic about this meeting, but after five years of arguments they had finally persuaded her. The year was 2003, and she was 48 years old. The elevator stopped at the top floor. The doors opened, and she was not surprised to see her attorney Mr. Kennedy standing there wearing a navy blue suit, black tie, and white collared shirt. His thinning white hair was slicked back, and his silver eyeglasses sat deep upon on his nose. It comforted her to see him, but she did not show it.

He looked her over as she exited the elevator. "Please don't misunderstand me, but you look lovely this morning," he told her. "Something is different about you."

Her answering smile produced two endearing cheek dimples. "Thank you. I'm not wearing my white barber coat."

He smiled sweetly. "In all these years I have only seen you maybe twice without that white coat on."

Morgan followed closely as he walked down the long, blue-carpeted hallway that smelled and looked like royalty. They stopped at a door, Mr. Kennedy turned the gold-plated handle, and the two of them walked in.

At the long table in the middle of the room, eight men in expensive suits sat on both sides of the table. They all stood up when the door opened. A stack of documents waited on the table. Morgan overheard two men whispering: "Is that her? Is that the lady barber?"

She made no eye contact with any of the men, but she said out loud to her attorney, "We all know why we're here. Can we just get this done?"

The men in suits all sat down. Morgan put on her black-ribbed eyeglasses and started to sign several documents alongside a California notary public officer who stamped and wrote his signature, too. An hour later, she took her eyeglasses off and slowly put them into her vintage black velvet eyeglass case and carefully closed it. The meeting was over.

One man stood up and handed her a check. His face and smile reminded Morgan of a Smurfs cartoon character. "How does it feel to be a wealthy, happy, smart woman?"

Morgan took the check, looked at it, then folded it carefully in half and put it in her wallet. Slowly, she raised her head, looked up into the Smurf in the suit, and smiled. "Sir, I *am* a happy, smart woman, and I have always had more fortune than money could buy."

With poise and dignity, she stood up and looked at each man's face. Seriously and with a breathless voice that was nearly a whisper, she told them, "Gentlemen, this has never been about money. This has been about tradition. My disagreement with you has *only* been about preserving one of southern California's great landmarks. Now, if you all will excuse me, I do not want to be late for work. I have clients waiting."

Chapter 2

Twenty minutes after the meeting ended, she approached a street sign that read Magnolia and made a left-hand turn. Immediately, she made another left into the business driveway. There were two cars already parked in the front. Three men were standing outside in front of the glass door, and when two of the men saw her, they waved and smiled. She waved back as she drove past them to the parking lot in the back.

The parking lot was full. Morgan pulled her brand new, black Ford SUV into the empty parking space with a sign that stated, "Reserved for Owner of the Mustache Barbershop." She remembered how pleased she was that she had taken the time and money to invest in her own private parking spot. Two other signs were in the front of the shop that said, "Parking for Mustache Barbershop customers only." She had paid one hundred dollars for each sign. It was an expensive investment but well worth it.

Before getting out, Morgan searched inside her purse for her favorite Christian Dior red lipstick and silver compact powder. She reapplied her make-up using her rear-view mirror. She tossed her thick black hair and carefully rearranged the two silver combs that held it up. Reaching back inside her purse, she took out the tall delicate bottle of White Diamonds perfume. She lavishly sprayed the fragrance all around her neck and cleavage, wrist and elbows. She carefully placed everything back inside her purse. "OK, sweetheart, it's show time," she whispered to herself.

She grabbed her red leather shoulder purse as she got out of her car and put the strap over her left shoulder. With a quick pace, she clicked the button to arm the SUV alarm and walked around the building to the front door of the barbershop.

When she reached the front of the barbershop door, she looked into the men's eyes and said, "Gentlemen, I'm sorry I'm late; the traffic was horrible. Please give me a moment." She smiled innocently at the men and fluttered her eyelashes as she quickly shoved the silver key into the lock, opened up her shop door, and went inside.

As the door closed behind her, she began to perform the opening routine that she had done thousands of times: disable the alarm system and flip on the light switch. She noticed how chilly it was in the barbershop, so she turned the thermostat dial up to 72 degrees. Looking up to the ceiling vent, she paused for a moment to wait for it to turn on. It started up.

She walked down the long hall to the stainless steel double-door refrigerator and opened the doors. The refrigerator was packed full of bottles of water, sodas, and beer with an assortment of cheese, lunch meats, fruits, and candy. She even stocked chocolate diet drinks for her favorite truck driver who was always trying to lose weight but was unsuccessful in part because he would always drink three cans. Looking at the well-stocked refrigerator, Morgan felt satisfied to see it full and ready to offer to any of her clients free of charge.

Morgan walked back up the hall to her desk in the front of the shop and took the blue bank bag full of money from her tote and put it in her classic petty cash box and then put the stainless steel box back inside a deep drawer in her oak desk. The money was the change she would need during the day. Looking down at the cash, she felt proud that she'd kept a nostalgic feeling in the shop over the years. Televisions, credit cards, computers, and cell phones were not used in her barbershop.

Giving the answering machine a glance, Morgan was not surprised to see that a lot of people needed a haircut. She knew there was no way she was going to be able to answer all of those calls that day. She looked down at her full appointment book, read the various barber services she would be performing that day, and felt content.

As she walked over to one of the closets, she took a deep

breath to relax herself and smiled as she opened the door. It almost embarrassed her to feel so happy from seeing the seven starched white barber coats, fresh from the dry cleaners, in the thin, tall closet. She carefully removed her little black jacket and placed it on a wooden hanger. Then she took out a crisp white barber coat. It reminded her of the owner of the dry cleaners who never charged her for dry cleaning because they traded services. For the past twenty years, she gave him haircuts and he dry cleaned and starched her coats. She sat down and pulled off her vintage shoes to put on her comfortable black clogs.

As she zipped up the coat, she smelled the scents in the room and relaxed as she became aware of the comforting and familiar aroma of men's cologne and hairspray that hung in the air.

Studying herself in the mirror with her white coat on, she felt transformed into a barber both physically and mentally.

She looked around her haircutting station. Everything was perfectly in place and ready for business. Going over to the stereo, she turned it on so jazz music filled the room. She went to the front window, pulled up the blinds, and turned the "open" sign around.

Just before opening the front door, she said her routine prayer to herself. "Dear Lord, I need you to help me not to be judgmental to any of the men who come through this door today, and help me to be kind and understanding. And please let me stay in the moment and not think of the meeting this morning."

Taking a deep breath, she opened the door. "Please come in."

Chapter 3

Three men walked through the front door as the telephone began to ring. Two of the men sat down and one began to pace back and forth. Morgan reminded the group, "Don't worry about the phone. The machine will get it."

With a smile, she looked at her appointment book, "Tom, you're first." As Tom got into the barber chair, she looked to the other men; only one was familiar to her. "Chris, can you hang my flag outside, please?" she asked sweetly.

"Sure!" he answered and quickly got up from the chair. She handed him the perfectly folded United States of America flag.

Morgan grabbed Tom's card from the filing cabinet and took it with her to her station. She read:

"*Tom wears a Full Crown haircut 3 ½ inches on top. Watch the two cowlicks on the left side/Clipper only across the back of the neck, the taper coming out near the lower tip of the ears.*"

Tom sat in the barber chair with a big frown on his face. Morgan turned to him and placed the black-and-white striped chair cloth over his business suit. She put a white paper neck strip around his neck and closed the neckband of the cloth.

He was his usual barking self. "Why are you opening up so late again?"

Morgan knew Tom very well. He really was a sweetheart but oh, what a spoiled brat! He was just an early bird kind of person and preferred having his hair cut very early in the morning. She knew he continued to seek her service for only one reason: she gave him a perfect haircut.

"Tom, I'm sorry that I was late today."

"Woman, your hands are going to wear out because you

still have not hired more barbers. You need help in here," he complained.

"No, I have not replaced the other two barbers yet," she replied patiently. "It seems no one knows how to use a straight razor properly these days."

Tom looked at Morgan, nodding his head in agreement.

After washing, rinsing, and drying her hands thoroughly, she turned back to him. "Now Tom, please relax and just enjoy your haircut." She put on her black-framed eyeglasses.

Tom never preferred his hair to be washed; it took too much of his valuable time. However, he was respectful enough to come in for a cut with freshly shampooed hair, so all she had to do was take a water bottle and fill it with warm water to dampen his thick, coarse, salt-and-pepper hair.

With total concentration, Morgan began the contour haircut skillfully with the shears and thick black comb. With her strong fingers, she pulled the hair straight up and cut a perfectly straight line. After the top was completed, she began the right side and cut the hair in a circular fashion from the right side all the way to the left side in a diagonal rotation to the bottom of his neck.

Tom continued to chat about his work and politics. As Tom talked, Morgan remembered how she had taught herself a long time ago to stay quiet, just listen, and answer with few words while she worked on a client. She had learned that many of the men never really cared about her opinion anyway and just wanted someone to listen as they talked.

More than a few preferred a haircut without any conversation at all. Morgan learned not to take it personally because that was just the way God made some men. Most men were selfish: their way or the highway. They were lazy when it came to communicating their thoughts. With this type of man, she did not initiate conversation. Instead, she catered to their mental needs and that kept everyone happy with little or no drama – most of the time.

She ever so gently blended in the bottom of his neckline with the thinning shears and a black, thin, taper comb. She knew if she used those scissors improperly it could tear up beautiful, healthy strands of hair, as well make the hair look horribly stringy.

She stepped back from the chair and looked at his haircut from the view of the mirror. She was not satisfied: the back neckline was not perfect. Picking up the silver electric clipper with the taper comb, she gently sculpted it just a tiny bit more.

Satisfied, she carefully unsnapped the neckband of the barber cloth that lay over his clothing. She grabbed the small red clipper edger and lightly cleaned up Tom's long neck hairs that hid beneath his collar, around the inside and outside of his hairy ears, long nose hairs, and unruly eyebrows.

Pulling out a hot white towel from the steamer, she tossed it from hand to hand until it cooled down just a little. She placed the hot towel on Tom's neck and massaged his neck with firm hands for five minutes over the warm towel. She felt his neck loosen up and he finally simmered down and stopped talking. Carefully, she picked up the straight razor and properly honed it, put it under the faucet to get it wet and, with the tip of her thumb, lightly touched the blade along its edge. It did not stick. The razor was sharp and ready to work.

After gently pulling off the cooled towel from his neck, she applied warm lather near the back of the neck and the outline of each ear. With great skill, she used her German straight razor and meticulously shaved his neck but was careful to stretch the skin of the neck and took great caution when she shaved close to his four protruding moles. Morgan checked the length of his sideburns by using the large mirror facing him. They matched perfectly.

Once she finished, she took a new hot towel, opened it, and sprinkled after-shave tonic on it. Folding the towel in half, she gently placed it on his smooth neck, and let it sit there until it was completely cool.

"Oh, that feels wonderful," he moaned.

Morgan knew Tom was pleased. Smiling, she took one last face towel and placed it under cool water. She wrung it out to clean Tom's face like he was a newborn baby kitten. Then she stood in front of him and slowly moved her body very close to his without intruding, close enough that she knew he could smell her perfume, like a rehearsed dance. She very carefully wiped up the leftover lather from around his ears and lightly washed off his forehead, nose, cheeks, and under his chin and chubby neckline. Tom moaned again.

Unhurried, she took the last towel off his neck, poured a generous amount of men's cologne on her hands, rubbed them together, and splashed her hands against his face, cheeks, under his jaw, and lastly along his neckline.

"Boy, do I feel like a million bucks," he said as Morgan pointed the barber chair in the direction of the door. She carefully removed the chair cloth without getting any loose hair on his blue suit and said, "Sir, you're all finished, and I apologize again for being so late."

Tom got up from the chair, reached into his pocket, and took out his wallet. He pulled out three twenty-dollar bills and shoved them into Morgan's hand.

"Honey, keep the change. You did a fabulous job as usual. See you in three weeks, and don't be late." He hurried toward the door. She looked down at the money that he had shoved in her hand.

A few moments later, Tom walked back into the shop. His footsteps were loud. "I forgot to give you this." He shoved two beautifully wrapped small boxes in her hands that still held the cash. "You are going to love these. My wife picked them up for you while we were vacationing. One is from Paris and the other from Capri. Hey, I've got to get out of here; I'm late for a very important meeting." He rushed toward the door.

With a raised voice, Morgan said, "Tom, stop." His footsteps immediately stopped at the door's edge. As she walked across the waiting room, the other clients busied themselves reading or looking out the window.

Not smiling and with a low, stern voice she said, "Tom, you have insulted me this morning. To begin with, you never said thank you for the haircut. And I don't appreciate anyone shoving money in my hands." She put her hands on her hips. "I'm afraid that you're going to be late for your important meeting this morning because I'm going to write a thank-you card for your wife, and I would appreciate if you waited for it."

The attractive fifty-year-old executive looked into her fiery green eyes and took a deep breath. "Thank you, madam, for the haircut, and yes, I will wait for the card."

Tom followed Morgan back to her desk and stood in silence. Sitting down, she pulled one of her specially-made thank you cards that showed a train emblem. They were neatly stacked in the cubby compartment of her desk. Opening the top of a thin, small, long box, she took out her gold dragon fountain pen and with perfect cursive handwriting, she wrote:

Dear Marilyn,

I am writing to say thank you for taking the time during your vacation to think of me. I am grateful for your thoughtfulness and appreciate the time you spent to find me these lovely spoons.

Sincerely,

Morgan O., Lady Barber

After gently slipping the card into an elegant chocolate-brown envelope and sealing the back with a fancy gold monogram stamp, Morgan wrote on the front: *To Marilyn.*

Standing up, she handed the envelope to the man who was waiting patiently. Tom's face softened and he said, "I will hand this to my wife as soon as I see her. Thank you again for the fine service, and I'm sorry I was so rude."

With calmness, she looked deep into his dark brown eyes and spoke to her client of fourteen years. "Thank you, Tom, for the spoons. You know how I appreciate them. By the way, stop being such a smartass." They grinned at each other. Morgan walked over to him and they gave each other a firm, respectful hug. She patted him on the back. "Now get out of here and make it a good day."

When she got back to her desk, she smiled humbly as she looked at the tiny, beautiful, wrapped boxes adorned with black satin bows. She remained calm and did not show how thrilled she was to receive more spoons for her grand spoon collection. She thought to herself, "Oh, my God, they came from Europe!" Quickly, she opened a drawer and placed the little delightful packages safely away.

Morgan looked down at her schedule, called for Chris, and pulled his file from the cabinet.

Christopher was the police chief of their city. Morgan had been his barber for more than twenty-two years. As Chris got up to sit in her barber chair, she thanked him for putting out her flag. Glancing at his card, she dated it. "Hey, you're two weeks late. I was getting ready to call the police. I was concerned about you."

He smiled. "I appreciate that you were thinking of me. It's just been busy at the station."

After making small talk about the city's crime, they talked about his family. It was his twentieth wedding anniversary, and he was debating on taking his wife on a cruise.

"Don't give it another thought. Here, you can use my phone." She quickly took the telephone from the wall and handed it to him. "Do you have the cruise line number with you?" she asked.

His eyes were wide. "Well yes, but I..."

"No buts. Call now," she insisted.

With a firm look on her face, she sat on her barber stool with arms crossed and waited. He got out his wallet, fussed with his credit card, and made the call. He hung up the phone, smiling widely.

"Well it's a done deal; the wife and I are going on a cruise. Thanks Morgan, I am sure I would not have done that so soon. I'm a big procrastinator."

Smiling softly, she replied, "I know you're a procrastinator, but look, you did it. The two of you deserve to have a romantic cruise. Twenty years of marriage is a big deal, and you're such a good husband."

Getting up from the small barber stool, she walked over to the sink and washed her hands. Chris looked at a train magazine while Morgan cut his hair in comfortable silence.

For the past twenty-two years, she had given Chris the exact same haircut. Many times Morgan had wished she could give him a new look, but she knew that would never happen. Chris was a creature of habit. When the service was completed, Morgan stood to the side of the chair and waited.

"May I have the mirror?" Chris asked. She handed him the large hand mirror. He checked out the back of his hair and asked, "Can you please make the back tighter?"

Morgan grabbed the silver clippers and patiently faded the back neckline shorter. "How is that?"

He looked in the mirror. After a long moment, he gave a studied approval. "That's great. Thank you."

Morgan repeated the routine neck shave and hot towels. After splashing the cologne on her hands, she briskly slapped his cheeks, ears, and neck, and carefully removed the chair cloth. Pointing the barber chair to at door, she said "You're finished, my friend." Quickly she washed her hands again.

Chris waited at Morgan's desk for her. With his head cocked to the side, he motioned her to follow him. They stepped outside.

"What's up?" she asked.

"Do you know that guy sitting there with all the tattoos?"

"No," she answered.

"Are you going to be okay?"

She grinned. "Thanks for being so concerned but have you forgotten that I have been a barber in this neighborhood for twenty-three years? You know quite well this is not a mall shop. Many men come in here with tattoos, and most of them come in here after being released from your jailhouse. Now stop worrying. I will see you next month."

"Where is that stun gun that I gave you for Christmas?"

"It's in my desk in the top drawer."

"Well, put it in your pocket," he ordered. "And remember where that alarm button is. In two minutes a patrol car can be here!" He winked reassuringly.

Then he looked up at the gloomy sky. "Hey, do you know there's a big storm coming?" "Yeah, at dinner last night my dad was saying that southern California is going to get hammered by a freak autumn storm."

Chris looked concerned. "You had a little flooding here last year, right?"

Morgan nodded. "Yes, we sure did."

"I have to stop by the fire station after this, so I'm going to have one of the firemen drop by a couple dozen sand bags."

Morgan smiled at the concerned chief. "I appreciate that. Thank you."

"Thanks again for the great haircut," he said.

They hugged each other as close friends do and she watched as he drove off in an unmarked police car, waving goodbye.

Chapter 4

As Morgan walked back into the shop, she thought, "I had better leave the door open a little since I don't know this man. Damn, I hate that Chris made me paranoid." She kicked down the door-stopper to leave the door partly open and walked back into the shop past the man who was sitting and looking at a magazine with his legs crossed.

Stopping at her desk, she looked down to the appointment book. While she was there, she inconspicuously slipped the black 3.8 million-volt stun gun out of the drawer and into her barber coat pocket.

Then she looked up and said, "You must be Lucky?"

He looked up from the magazine and said, "Yeah, that's me. I came in here three weeks ago and you were busy. You said no walk-ins and that I would need an appointment, and you handed me a business card. So I called your place and was surprised that I had to wait three weeks for a damn haircut."

She did not remember his face. "Sorry about that. I am short-handed right now. It seems everybody needs a haircut at the same time. I understand how inconvenient that must be for you. Please come in."

When he got up from the chair Morgan was surprised to see that he was such a tall man. Standing, he was well over six feet tall and weighed at least 250 pounds. With his shoulders slumped and his head tilted down, he walked over to the barber chair and sat down.

Morgan guessed his age to be around thirty-five years old. He was wearing a crisp, new, white, short-sleeved shirt, new dark blue Levis, and black tattoos covered his wrists and arms.

She took a black, large barber cloth out of a drawer. As she stood behind the barber chair and placed the chair cloth over her new client's clothes, she could see that he had black, thick, letter tattoos on the back of his neck. Before starting his haircut, she walked in front of him and faced him. Looking into his eyes, she noticed they were an intense blue that looked older than his years and that his face was very pale.

"Hi, let me introduce myself. My name is Morgan. May I ask why you choose this barbershop?"

"Yes ma'am," he replied. "Well, I did time in prison with Warren White. Warren and I buddied up because we were both robbers and caught up in that crap cocaine. Anyway, good old Warren told the other men and me stories of what great haircuts and shaves he got here at the Mustache Barbershop. Warren bragged you were not a beautician but a real man's barber. He would tell stories about how the beautiful woman barber used hot steam towels and shaved with a real, old-fashioned straight razor. I've been dreaming about this moment for seven years."

"Oh, is that right?" Morgan smiled.

"Yeah, and Warren said you were famous for doing the best flat-top haircuts in the whole wide world."

With a big grin, she asked, "Well, what else did Warren say?"

"He said to say hello and to tell you he hoped you were living a good life."

"It's such a coincidence that we are talking about him. Just the other day he crossed my mind. It has been years since I last saw him."

"Well ma'am, it's like this: Warren went and robbed two banks, that darn son of a gun. He got bored and hit a third one. That time he got caught. He is serving three consecutive terms of nine years a piece on each bank robbery."

Morgan's face grew serious. "I'm not surprised to hear about his sad troubles. Warren never robbed for any other reason other than the adrenaline rush it gave him."

"How long have you known him, ma'am?"

"Warren and I crossed paths when he was a skinny, fifteen-year-old thief, breaking into cars. He was a sweet kid who had a mother who worked nights and an absent father. His life was living on the streets. We became friends after he witnessed a horrible accident in my neighborhood many years ago."

Morgan put her glasses on. "So, you would like to have a shave and a haircut?"

Lucky grinned. "Yes ma'am, I sure do."

"What kind of a cut do you want?"

"A flat top," he said, still grinning.

Morgan's face became serious again as she lifted the headrest at the top of the barber chair and asked Lucky to lift his feet off the bottom step of the barber footrest. The chair reclined back easily. "You can put your feet back on the chair footsteps now," she said after the chair had reclined.

With warm water, she moistened her hands. Next, she lathered them up with a bar of soap, massaging as she washed her hands up to her wrist, top and bottom, between fingers, and beneath her fingernails. Twenty seconds later, she rinsed her hands well and was ready to proceed after drying them with a clean towel. After taking another clean towel and tucking it in around his neck, she applied warm lather to his face and neck. "This is going to be a tough shave," she thought to herself. "His face is sensitive with extremely coarse beard stubble."

Lucky was lying with his eyes closed and Morgan could see that he was deeply inhaling her perfume with his hands in a fist. She guessed that he had not been this close to a woman in some time. However, that did not bother her one bit. After years of working behind her chair, dealing with men was one of the things she knew exceptionally well.

Using her barber brush in a rotary motion, she lathered his face for three minutes. Lucky moaned, "Oh God, I love this."

Morgan watched as he moved around in the chair and became restless. Then he smiled widely and he opened up his eyes.

She dropped the lather brush she had in her hand into the shaving cup. Quickly and gracefully, she snatched up her razor. With a snap, it opened. She was sure that Lucky saw her long, shiny, glistening, sharp, German straight razor in her hand. Immediately, his smile turned into a frown. He closed his eyes and gulped.

Sensing that Lucky understood how serious her profession was, she carefully put the opened razor down within reach. She applied a thick, hot steam towel over his entire face, careful not to cover his nose, and stropped the razor.

Minutes later, she removed the towel and re-lathered the beard generously with warmed baby oil. After a moment, she wiped it clean. She placed a piece of lather paper across his chest. Finally, she picked up her sharp razor and began to shave on the right side of his face.

Once the right side was finished, she stropped the razor again.

"Sir, how are you doing?" she asked.

There was no answer. Lucky was asleep. Glancing down, she saw that his hands and arms were now relaxed and resting on her wooden barber chair arms. She smiled.

"Now I can work peacefully," she told herself.

Gently she re-lathered the left side and continued the shave. When she finished she applied a new hot steam towel. After five minutes, she lifted the towel and saw that his face was a little pink. She rubbed on a cooling cream and with a light touch but gentle pressure, she massaged his face and throat for several minutes. She rinsed a new towel under the cool water and wrung it out then applied it lightly on his smooth face.

As the cooling towel comfortably sat on his face, she grabbed her small, fine-point, sharp shears and shaped the top of his wild eyebrows and used a small razor to clean up between the brows and on his thick nose hairs. "This is quiet challenging," she thought to herself as she removed the nose hairs.

Looking down at his clean face, she smiled because he was still fast asleep. It was no surprise to her; she had watched hundreds of men sleep through the entire shave procedure. Morgan yawned and stretched as she walked away from the chair to go look at her appointment book. She looked up at the clock and decided to let him sleep for 15 more minutes.

Sitting down behind her desk, she noticed that Lucky was wearing brand-new, expensive, white tennis shoes. It saddened her as she wondered if he was going to stay out of jail long enough to get those shoes dirty. She had done many haircuts for men who had just come out of the joint, and she knew it was just a matter of time before most of them went back to their familiar territory.

Morgan thought about the prison system and it made her sick to her stomach because she knew it made the men dependent on the state and they became institutionalized. They knew no trade and lacked the discipline to make it on the outside. Many were not hard criminals, just lost men who became hooked on drugs to escape their hopeless reality. Oh sure, she knew of a few success stories but not many. She filled a card out with his name on it and recorded what service she performed for him and the date. Looking over at the clock, she saw that his time was just about up. She stood up.

Her accountant walked in the door. William grinned, and as always he looked in a hurry and was wearing a formal dark-gray suit. He handed over a large white envelope. "Your taxes are done." He smiled.

With a quiet voice, she asked, "How much do I owe you this time?"

"Forty dollars and a free haircut."

William had been her friend first, then accountant. Fortunately for her, they had met while she was a student in barber college. She handed him the cash. "See you in a couple weeks." He pointed to his attractive, thick, white hair that was already in need of a haircut.

Then it was time to wake up Lucky. Over the years, Morgan learned how to wake men up. The main thing she learned was not to stand close to the barber chair. Some startled awake, moving their arms and kicking their legs, especially the deep sleepers.

With her voice lowered, she called twice, "Wake up, Lucky." He still snored, so she pushed his left arm. Sure enough, he woke up, startled, kicked his legs up, and his hands went back into fists. "Shit, ma'am, did I knock out? I haven't been able to sleep since I got out of the joint eight weeks ago."

Morgan replied with a smile. "It's perfectly fine. You're not the first man to sleep during a shave. It is a relaxing service."

After pulling the barber chair back up into the sitting position, Morgan gave him the traditional flat-top haircut. She followed all her usual procedures with steam towels and razor work on his neck and slapped the manly cologne on his face, ears, and neck. While she took the cape off him, she asked, "May I ask you how you got the name Lucky?"

His eyes sparkled with excitement. "It's like this: when I was a kid the first time that I got into trouble, I stole a bicycle out of a store. The police officer saw me, and I ran. To get away from him, I climbed up a building. I ran to the other side, and I jumped off the building. To my surprise, there was another police officer waiting for me on the ground. He grabbed me and asked me my name. I told him it was Lawrence. The police officer said to me, 'Lawrence if I were you, I would name yourself Lucky. You are lucky to be alive.'"

Carefully, she took the cape from his clothes and smiled, "Yes, you were lucky."

As they walked to her desk. Lucky pulled out his wallet, "Lady, how much money do I owe you?"

"For a hot towel shave and flat-top haircut, you owe me thirty-five dollars."

Slowly he took out the dollars and began to count his money. Morgan edged closer to him and saw that he would only have two dollars left after he paid her. She did not like the fact that he would be broke after paying her.

"Lucky, I am going to make you a deal. I need some help around the shop. If you take the trash out to the dumpster for me, wash the inside of the front windows, and sweep down the outside front of the barbershop, then we will call it even. Do we have a deal?"

Lucky smiled gratefully. "Yes, lady, we do. Thank you."

While Lucky did the chores, Morgan was able to sit down and return four phone calls from the answering machine. The front door flew open and an attractive Vietnamese young man walked into the shop.

She looked up and smiled. "Hi, Sam."

Sam smiled. "Good morning, boss lady."

Right away, he picked up the already full stainless-steel hamper, took it to the back of the shop, and began to do laundry. Morgan stopped and thought about Sam for a moment. He had always been so respectful. Smiling now, she remembered the moment he began to work in the shop he had innocently called her by the name "boss lady."

About 1:30 that afternoon, the fireman Chris sent over walked into the shop. He asked Morgan where she wanted him to put the sandbags. Morgan went outside and showed him the spot just as it began to sprinkle. Lucky and Sam immediately assisted the firefighter with the bags.

When Lucky finished with the chores, he went over to Morgan to say good-bye and express gratitude. "You are a real nice lady. This is the best I have ever looked in my life. I feel like a new man. Thank you again."

Morgan looked at him thoughtfully and said, "Lucky, I don't want to intrude, but I would like to say something personal to you."

"Okay," he replied.

She looked into his eyes that were much too young to have so many deep lines surrounding them. "I want you to know that years ago I suffered severe depression and loss. It was a brutal time. I almost surrendered to it. Some days it can still be a battle." She paused. "The only way I know to live my life is by getting out of my own head and trusting in God. And most importantly, I learned a trade."

Lucky was quiet. Moments later, Morgan was pleasantly surprised when he made deep eye contact with her for the first time. They looked for a long time into each other's eyes.

Finally, he spoke. "Please, don't laugh." He put his head down then raised it up to her. “I’ve always wanted to be a florist. I have been in and of the joint since I left the farm at 18 years old. Every time I got locked up, all I wanted to do was read books on flowers and plants. I know them well; they calmed me down.”

“Let me think,” she said softly. She turned around to her files and pulled out the F file: Anaheim Florist and Nursery Garden and Plants Center.

The top of the card said “OWNER.” She sat down at her desk and pulled out one of her special stationary papers with the train emblem on it and picked up her fancy dragon fountain pen. Quickly, she wrote a small letter. Then she put the letter in one of her chocolate brown envelopes and sealed the back with her usual monogram stamp. She turned the envelope over and wrote *To Tomo* with the address. On another piece of paper, she wrote the exact details for the city bus directions to Mr. Tomo’s landscaping business on the other side of the city.

“If you are really serious about changing your life, go to this man and hand him this letter. He is my longtime friend. I assure you that you will begin to work for him tomorrow morning. He will teach you everything about the plants and flower business and more. But you must never be late to work because he would fire you immediately.”

He stared at her in amazement. “You are serious?”

She smiled. “Yes. And please address him as Mr. Tomo.”

Morgan handed him the envelope and paper with the address and directions. “Introduce yourself to Mr. Tomo with your birth name, and until he gets to know you, wear a long-sleeved shirt. Leave your past behind. Good luck Lawrence.” They shook hands.

After he walked out, she went over to the front glass window and watched as Lawrence stood up straighter and walked with his head held just a little bit higher.

Chapter 5

After Lawrence left the barbershop, the hours passed quickly. Morgan changed the music in the shop from country to jazz to classic rock; she knew the type of music most of her clients preferred.

Sam stayed busy cleaning the bathroom and doing things for her in her private office. He polished furniture, wiped down all the mirrors in the shop, and dusted.

Later in the day, she gave a regular haircut to a sweet, quiet man who had been her client for years before his daughter had become a world famous rock singer. Morgan respected Dino's privacy, so she never asked about her. Instead, they made small talk about his grandchildren.

Next to come in was her Latin-Irish client. He came by for a trim and facial-shave every week. Antonio was a self-made millionaire. He wore his shiny black straight hair proudly below his shoulders.

Morgan had given him a haircut, shave, and facial almost every week for the past fifteen years. He trusted only her to trim the ends of his luscious hair. For these services, he paid Morgan one hundred fifty dollars every time to show her his appreciation. He had an incredible life story that began with his career as a newspaper delivery boy. For many years, Antonio had been lonely. He was a single father who was raising five daughters, and he enjoyed telling Morgan about them. Part of the reason he paid her extra was not only for the trust he had in her but also because she allowed him to be what he valued most: a father telling stories about his daughters.

After applying the facial mask over Antonio's face, she placed a warm towel over his eyes and left him alone in the barber chair to rest. As she sat behind her desk and watched him sleep, she reminisced about a life-altering time for him four years earlier.

Antonio had come into see Morgan. When she had finished with his facial, shave, and hair trim, he had asked her a question. "May I discuss something personal about my life with you?"

"Of course you may," she had answered, sitting down on her barber stool in front of him and giving him her full attention.

"I am painfully self-conscious in discussing this, but it seems that I have fallen in love with a much younger woman, twenty-three years younger. She has two small children of her own. What do you think people will think?"

Morgan had thought for a moment. "Who cares what people think? If you are in love with her then don't waste any time."

It was two months after that conversation when Morgan, along with one hundred other guests, stood and witnessed Antonio and his shy young wife exchange marriage vows. Morgan smiled now because the young woman he married was not only beautiful and lovely, but she turned out to be a charitable and compassionate woman.

After Antonio walked out of the shop, a man with a difficult beard walked in. Blackie was the vice president of a well-known outlaw motorcycle club. Twice a year he traveled two days on his bike to come see her. He looked intimidating in his colorful vest with black lettering; however, to the woman barber who knew him well, he was simply another intense beard trim. Blackie would not let another barber get near his precious "Van Dyke" black beard. Morgan knew not to offer him anything to drink but a cold can of Coke; he was a recovering alcoholic of ten years. He was proud that he had also stayed out of prison for ten years.

It took Morgan more than forty minutes to detail the difficult beard because she had to correct the shape of the mustache and detail the shape of his neck and cheek area with her straight razor. It was a challenging, artistic job.

Blackie was generous with the tip he left on Morgan's desk. Then he enthusiastically demanded that she come out and look at his newest baby. "Come outside to the front, I want you to see my new Harley-Davidson. My baby is a beauty." He smiled with pride. "My bike was on the cover of Biker Magazine for Bike of the Year."

She followed him outside. Sure enough, it was an impressive Harley-Davidson with a masterful paint job. Blackie took a magazine out of one of the saddlebags. "Look I'm standing next to the bike, and there's your beard trim! You're famous, too."

They both laughed. "Oh, my God, you're so crazy!" she exclaimed.

After Blackie roared away on his motorcycle, Morgan's dentist rushed in to schedule his appointment for the following week. "Here Morgan," he said, "I just made this batch of beef jerky; this is the one you like, not so hot." Dr. Jared placed it on her desk.

Morgan smiled at Dr. Jared. He had been giving her homemade jerky for years. Dr. Jared had been the only dentist to care for Morgan's teeth. She had bartered haircuts for special dental work many times.

"Thank you, Doc, for the beef jerky. I hope it's as good as the last. My dad and I gobbled up the last batch."

The dentist smiled with a burning Cuban cigar in his mouth. He bragged, "This batch is even better than the last."

Morgan giggled because he always said that.

Doc walked to the edge of the barber door and turned and said, "Missy, don't forget to schedule my appointment for a hot towel shave and haircut two weeks from today."

Right away, Morgan went to her appointment book, put his name in the correct day, and scheduled his time for an hour so he would not be rushed through a whirlwind appointment.

Finally, her last client was done. Exhausted, she walked with Victor to her desk. With effort, she flashed him a smile. He told her, "Thanks again for the great haircut." He pulled on his golden-brown leather jacket.

Morgan walked over to the dark-skinned good-looking man who could have passed for a movie star. She reached up and straightened his collar. "There now," she told him, "You look handsome."

The professional baseball player gave Morgan a hug. She could always sense that Victor's hugs meant a lot more than friendship. She gently pushed Victor away.

He smiled as he inhaled her perfume, and his eyes narrowed on her. "I'll see you in three weeks, and be sure to write my name on your calendar book." He handed her a hundred-dollar tip. She took the money, began to count out his change, and handed it to him. He handed the money back to her. "Keep the change." Then he said, "Follow me outside, I want to show you my new ride." They walked out to his new red 2003 Jaguar XJR. He opened the door and she looked in.

"Nice," she said. As she relished the smell of new leather, she smiled.

Victor's smile was electrifying. His teeth were white and perfectly straight. He quickly planted a kiss on her neck. Like a hot tiger, he purred, "I guess I can't talk you into going for a ride. Can I?"

She grinned and said, "You guessed right. If I ever got into this car, I may never want to get out, especially with you in it. Now be a good friend. Get out of here, and go home to your wife."

Victor cupped his huge left hand on Morgan's chin and kissed her lightly on both her cheeks, then lightly on her mouth, and whispered, "You are still so beautiful."

Placing her small hand over his huge hand that was still holding her face, Morgan teased him. "And you, my friend, are still a handsome snake charmer." They hugged this time like good friends then she had to push him firmly away. He got into the exquisite sports car and she watched him drive away and waved.

When she returned to the shop, Sam was dusting the nearby chair. "Boss lady loves the baseball player?"

Morgan smiled at Sam. "Are you spying on me?" She laughed lightly. "No dear, I don't love the baseball player in a romantic way."

"Boss lady, may I ask how many years you have been cutting

Victor's hair?"

With a peaceful smile she said, "I was his barber years before he made the cover of Sport Magazine and was named Player of the Year. He was in high school." She went behind her desk to put the change away, and she remembered something.

Looking at Sam, she said, "I want to tell you a story. Many years ago, when I had only cut Victor's hair four times, his haircut cost six dollars and each time Victor would tip me a one-dollar bill. Well, the next time after I finished his hair, he handed me ten one-dollar bills. I gave him back three dollars for change. Boy, was he mad at me! He put the three dollars back on my desk and told me to give him back the ten dollars. I did."

She paused, smiling. "Victor looked at me that day and said, 'Morgan, my father is a waiter, and he taught us never to assume you get a tip. So this time you will not get a tip from me because you assumed I would give you one.' He gave me six dollars and left angry. I never thought Victor would come back to me for another haircut, but he did. And I was grateful to him, because he taught me never to assume anything."

Sam looked at Morgan thoughtfully. "Wow, that was an important lesson for you to learn. Thank you for sharing it with me."

Morgan looked at Sam. "What is it? You are looking at me funny."

"Boss lady, I know you are tired, but all my work is done. Can you please cut my hair?" He smiled and showed off his beautiful white teeth that had a small gap between the two front teeth.

Morgan laughed out loud. "Of course you can have a haircut, but first, go outside and get our flag."

Sam hurried outside and took the flag down. When he came inside the shop, he said. "It's windy out there."

Morgan frowned. "Yeah, it was windy when I went outdoors to say good-bye to Victor."

Eagerly, Sam got into the barber chair, and he sat perfectly still as Morgan cut his hair. She left the top section and crown area longer, and she put a men's classic firm-hold styling gel into his hair and slicked it forward and pulled it spiked up. It was dramatic and edgy look. She carefully lathered his neck, shaved it with the straight razor, and applied a hot steam towel. Finally, she slapped the cologne on his neck and his cheeks.

When she looked at him in the mirror, she grinned. "Do you remember the first time I cut your hair?"

His smile was big. "Yes I do! You said I looked like someone had put a bowl on my head and cut around it!"

They both doubled up laughing. Then Sam caught his breath and said, "And the truth is that that was how my father cut my hair: with a bowl on top!"

"I can picture that bowl on your head," Morgan giggled. They looked at each other again and loudly laughed with pure pleasure.

Morgan followed Sam outside to watch him walk home. He lived two blocks away from the shop. "Be careful walking home, and tell your father that I said hello."

"Boss lady, are you forgetting that I just had my 18th birthday? I am a grown man. Yes, I will tell my father that you said hello."

Morgan tapped the top of his gelled spiked hair. "Oh goodness there is so much gel on this hair that a tornado couldn't move it."

Sam smiled. "Thank you, boss lady."

Standing outside, she looked up; there was something very odd about the sky. There were unusually dark, almost black, storm clouds forming, and the wind was beginning to kick up stronger. It looked a bit scary. She looked at her wrist watch: 7:00. The cold wind blew through her hair and up under her white coat. She shivered as drops of rain began to fall on her head. Morgan went inside and turned the sign in the window over to closed. She went to her desk and got her key ring, and she locked the old glass door. Closing the blinds, she let the feeling of exhaustion roll over her from the long day.

Immediately her thoughts went to her home and loving family: Her father Barney, aged 80, her respected German housekeeper/personal assistant and best friend Ann, who was now 71, and her two intelligent, quick-thinking laborers, Miguel and Jose, who both lived on her property.

She grabbed up the white telephone on her desk and dialed. It rang twice. A voice answered, "Hello, this is Barney."

"Dad, this is Morgan."

"Well, hello daughter, how has your day been today? Tell me all about it."

She was not smiling. "Dad, I had a busy day. I don't want to sound rude, but I really need to speak to Ann."

Barney said, "Honey, she is right here. We are all in the kitchen eating. Me, Ann, Miguel, and Jose are eating spaghetti and meat balls." She held the telephone tight as she heard Barney say, "Ann, Morgan wants to talk to you."

"Hello, Morgan. This is Ann."

Morgan's voice was firm but calm. "Ann, I want you to put me on speaker phone."

"Okay, you are on speaker now," Ann said.

Morgan was glad they were all together. It was easier to speak to all of them at the same time. "Good evening, everyone. I want you to listen carefully. You all know there is a bad storm brewing. I just have a gut feeling this one is going to hit hard. Just to be safe, I want Miguel and Jose to close the shutters on all the windows on our main house as well as your small house. Miguel, I want you to go to the four-car garage, and you know where all the covers are to cover the vintage vehicles and the motorcycles. Cover everything up.

"Jose, pull down the storm shutters in the garage. Bring the patio rocking chairs and anything else you see that needs to come inside into the garage. Please do this as soon as I hang up. Do you understand?"

At the same time, both Miguel and Jose said, "Yes."

Morgan said, "Okay, thank you both."

Sitting up straight in her chair now, she said, "Dad, please stay inside. I don't want you to go outside to help the men. Ann, please gather the emergency box from the attic; the candles and matches are up there as well. Dad, you know where the four heavy-duty industrial flashlights are under the kitchen sink. They all have new batteries."

"Should the men bring in the generator?" Barney asked.

Morgan smiled. "Yes! I forgot about that. I will stay in my shop until the storm blows over. Oh, and I want all you to stay together. Miguel and Jose can bunk in the downstairs guest room. I love you all, and please take care of each other."

Ann said, "Morgan, we will all be fine. Please, just take care of yourself. Barney wants to talk to you now."

"Okay, thank you Ann," Morgan replied.

"You're welcome."

Barney said, "Daughter, thank you for being so stern this summer on putting up those storm shutters. Sorry I gave you such a hard time. I guess the weather is changing in southern California."

Morgan smiled. "I love you, Dad." As Morgan hung up phone, she thought, "I'm surrounded by the most extraordinary people at home and here at work."

Chapter 6

Anxiety consumed Morgan. She pulled her purse out of her desk drawer and took out her wallet. Taking another deep breath, she felt the dread of the secret she carried. It was a secret that she had been keeping from her dad, faithful housekeeper, and all of her clients, as well her loyal worker and friend Sam. She did not even tell her two adult daughters who resided in other states.

Slowly, she took out the folded piece of paper. With an ache in her heart, she unfolded it and read it again. It was a check made out to her. Morgan had sold her business name and the building and the property the shop was on. The amount was much more than a profit; she had made a generous fortune because the land she sold was now prime property near a famous amusement park in Anaheim, California. Everything in this area was expanding. Morgan folded the check again and placed it back inside her wallet.

Glancing down at the calendar, she saw that in thirty days the shop would belong to "The Corporation." The shop had originally been established in 1920 and was the first barbershop in Anaheim. The first clients had been from the hard-working farming community of around five thousand people. Morgan was the fourth owner. For five years, she had said no to the notion of selling. As the years flew by, Morgan had grown tired of the drive back and forth to her country home. The insane freeway was much too crowded. Most of all, she was discouraged trying to find dependable people to work for her.

She was a smart businessperson, and the corporation had finally made an offer that even she could not refuse. Morgan fully understood that she had become a famous barber in her time, which had given her respect and joy, but she was no longer enjoying her business; it had all become a struggle.

With her hands folded in her lap, she thought about the meeting. It made her sad that signing all those documents meant she would never see her romantic dream of the old-fashioned establishment becoming a National Landmark Museum Barber Shop; a place where adults and children could come to visit and understand the history of the barber profession.

Reclining back in the desk chair, she looked at her hands. No one knew she was in constant pain. Her hands had been active and busy over the many years, cutting and clipping, washing and shaving. They were still extremely strong, but they were tired. She pulled them up to her face and spoke aloud. "Hands, you have done me well through the years, and I thank you." Looking down to her feet, she slipped off the black leather closed-back clogs and said, "Feet, I also thank you for all your service to me."

Morgan remembered that she had neither the time nor self-indulgence to complain about her aches and pains. One of the many lessons she learned at the beginning of her career was to keep quiet about herself. Her father had warned her repeatedly, "Daughter, you will never make any money if the people hear you complain. They come to you to tell you their woes and tales, not to hear yours. Believe me, most men go to the barber just to get a damn haircut without any bullshit."

Feeling more pains of anxiety than physical pains, she rose up from the straight, antique desk chair and began to pace the room. She put on one of her favorite CDs; the piano music and drifting strings filled the room and calmed her. With her arms folded close beneath her breasts, she walked from room to room. The barbershop was full of many memories and the physical representations of those memories were everywhere. All of them had been gifts from her clients. Many of them represented significant parts of American history. One such gift was a painting of Indians fighting cowboys with a train sitting in the background. While staring at the unsigned artwork, she walked across the room and pushed open the heavy, squeaky, office door.

Some of the postcards and letters she collected were neatly taped on the back of the door. All were thank-you notes from people who had come into the shop; they sent postcards from all over the world. Morgan had kept almost every note sent to her over the years. There were several boxes of them. Not one letter was unopened or went unanswered. She always took the time to read them all and mail back a handwritten thank-you note. Their gratitude embarrassed her. Humbled by it, she often thought, "I am only giving them a haircut or a shave." Picking a letter that was on the back of the door, she took her black-rimmed eyeglasses from her barber coat pocket and put them on. She read the letter from Mr. Fang:

> *Dear Morgan, I was in a deep depression the morning I came into your barbershop. I was in great mental and physical pain. You sensed that I was in distress. You sat down and listened to my sad story about the death of my beloved wife. You cared and felt my heavy heart. You treated me like an ordinary broken down man. I am back in my country of China, and I will always be in gratitude to the Lady Barber who sat and talked with me. It was because of you that I did not end my life. I had a loaded gun in my briefcase of which I had all intentions on using. I give you my personal phone number and address. You are a welcome guest in my home anytime.*
>
> *Sincerely,*
> *Mr. Fang*

Smiling, she remembered him; she did think he was only an ordinary man. It was only years later that she learned he was an important international executive from China and one of the wealthiest citizens there.

Fear overflowed her heart and mind as she restlessly thought about the dramatic change that was about to happen in her life. Her heart began to pound faster. The barbershop was such a large part of her life, her soul. She thought, "If only these walls could talk." This had been her small separation from the outside world. Morgan glanced around the large, crowded office space. There were organized wooden boxes that were overflowing with small packages – gifts from grateful customers. All the packages were collectible spoons.

Only Sam was allowed in this private space of hers. He was the one who made sure that every spoon received was logged in a large, leather-bound notebook as well as her thank-you cards for each. Sam also made sure all the books that piled from the floor to the ceiling were in order and stacked perfectly. Some of the books were autobiographies of the lives, loves, and legends of the world's most admired women and men, other books were about the history of the United States, world religions, and maps of the world; she had read all of them.

Other shelves showed stacks of railroad and train magazines. She loved trains even though she had only been on one short trip to Santa Barbara by herself on the Amtrak. All the magazines were arranged in chronological order and were years old. On the walls hung unique clocks that Sam had taken the time to set. In one corner stood a combination floor safe; it caught her eye and made her remember the check in her wallet. She took it out and slipped it safely into the slot.

Making her way over to her small, private wine cooler, she took out one tall, cold wine glass and a bottle of wine. Before opening it, she read the label, "Chapoutier La Mordoree Cote Rotie 1997." The wine was a gift from a client who had come from France. Jon Pierre was a famous pastry chef on cruise liners. For years he had shared stories of his exciting life while Morgan cut his hair.

Morgan remembered the last time she saw him. It was the day he brought her the bottle of Cote Rotie. He had told her of a beautiful woman he had met on the last Hawaiian cruise. Her name was Chantilly; she was 15 years younger than he was. She worked on the Hawaiian cruise ship as a server. He was so in love with her sweet innocence and dynamic smile and her carefree attitude on life. He even made her a German chocolate ten-tier cake for her birthday aboard ship. He adored Chantilly. He told Morgan, "I am going to divorce my selfish wife and marry my sweet lady. I am in love, finally, with all my heart."

Sadly, as most affairs turn out, his wife found out about his cheating. The wife was firm in telling him that she would not grant him a divorce because of her religion. Jon Pierre went back to live with and be faithful to his wife. A year later when he missed his young lover again, he searched for her everywhere. Unfortunately, he never found Chantilly. Later, he heard rumors that his beloved lover had moved on with her life with a broken heart and had made a new life off the cruise ships. The last time Morgan saw Jon Pierre, he walked like a broken, ill-fated man.

With melancholy thoughts of Jon Pierre, Morgan uncorked the French wine and poured it into the tall wine glass. Aloud she toasted, "Here is to you, my friend. Perhaps you should have divorced and lived a beautiful life with Chantilly." She swallowed a large amount down. The taste was the finest she had ever had; she licked the drops off her lips. The red was so dark it was almost purple, and it had aromas of black raspberries and roasted herbs. "Oh, my God, this is delicious!" she exclaimed.

As the night went on, the rain fell harder. Outside, she heard the unfamiliar growl of thunder and lightning that sounded like gunshots. The howling weather made her comfortable with her decision not to drive home tonight. California drivers did not know how to drive in the rain; they certainly did not slow down. The roads would be slick, slippery, flooded, and dangerous. Then she realized that this was an ideal opportunity to spend one last night in her shop while it was still hers. With her evening settled, Morgan decided to pour herself another glass of the wonderful wine. She savored the taste even though she drank it faster than normal.

In the part of town where the barbershop was located, no one was allowed to spend the night in their business. It was dangerous at night because of the crime in the city. This actually meant very little to Morgan because she had been spending the night there off and on for years. There were many times the barbershop had been a safe haven for her. The lights inside the shop had to be off during the night so no one would know that she was inside the building. In the closet, Morgan found three vintage candleholders with the candles and matches. After they were lit, she placed two of them throughout the shop and kept the third to use while she walked around turning off all the inside lights.

Now she needed to pull out the sofa bed that was in the office. Amused, she looked at the assortment of pillows that covered the sofa. They were her handiwork. The needlepoint was exquisite. As she moved each pillow, her hands lovingly graced the tops of the embroidery stitching and she gave each one a little squeeze. One had a delicate pink rose and said in small letters, "Be Thankful." Another was cream-colored with tiny floral designs and the letters read "Open Your Ears." Next was a red ladybug with medium letters that said, "Secret Keeper."

Familiar thoughts flooded her mind as she remembered when she first learned to needlepoint. It had been a laborious craft to master. The first two years of her barber career, the embroidery canvas saved her from boredom. It had helped her hands stay busy while she sat next to her empty barber chair, waiting for customers.

Her German barber instructor Mr. Gable had warned her, "Don't leave your chair unless you go to the bathroom. Bring your lunch to work. In order for you to build up a clientele, you must be with your chair. The people will go sit in another chair if you are gone. However, if you get them in your chair the first time and give them a perfect haircut, they will always come back to you." That is exactly what she had done.

After moving her pillows and a few of the boxes to the front of the shop, she was able to pull out the bed. Standing on a small stool to reach up to the top shelf of the closet, she took out a large plastic bag and unzipped it. She took out the cream-colored thick quilt, white bed linens, and two soft white pillows and began to make the bed.

She wasn't sure but thought the wine and the final sale of

the shop had made her feel extremely fatigued. With low energy, she went over to a small chest of drawers in the office where she kept extra clothes. Bending down, she opened the top drawer and pulled out a pair of lacy lavender panties and a long, white, cotton, embroidered nightgown and matching robe. Morgan pulled the nightgown up toward her face and smelled it, smiled, and then lightly touched the soft fabric. "Oh my goodness, it's been a while since I have worn this and it still smells fresh." Morgan was always particular in what she wore and nighttime was no exception.

Sitting on the edge of the folding couch bed, she warmed up each foot by stretching the foot up and down and around. Focusing on the bottom of each one, she made circular motions and stroked both up and down and side to side. They were sore and tender to the touch. She whined loudly from the pain.

"Get moving, I need to wash up," she thought as she stood up and gathered her stuff. Morgan dragged herself through the long, dark hall with her lit candleholder. It was dark in the back of the shop where the washer and dryer and all the store supplies were. As she approached the bathroom, she looked to the right into the shop storeroom and over to the small window that was high above. It had black security bars across it and no window covering. While she listened to the rain falling and to the sound of the wind screaming, something hit the window with a loud crash and made Morgan jump.

She walked into the bathroom very much in need of a bath. She unzipped her barber coat and let it fall to the polished black and white ceramic tile floor and then she unbuttoned the front of her white blouse. Reaching around her slim back, she easily unhooked her white lacy bra, and it too slumped to the floor.

She grabbed the stopper and put it into the deep porcelain sink. While the sink filled with hot water, she removed her pin-striped black trousers, carefully unbuttoning the side buttons, and she folded them in half neatly. They carefully went to the floor along with her pink lace panties. Turning off the faucet, she reached under the sink for the stack of clean, white towels.

As she stood up, she was aware of her reflection in the long, gold, antique mirror that hung perfectly on the wall. It had been a long time since she had seen her full nude image in a mirror. Unconsciously, she had begun to cover herself with a towel. A moment later, the towel dropped and Morgan stared at her naked body. Whispering, she teased herself, "You look beautiful in candlelight. I am aging rather well."

Tenderly, she touched her almost flat belly around and around, and when both her hands moved softly over her ample breasts, she lifted them up and massaged them all around because it felt so good to get her bra off; she felt free. Then she let go, and they fell back into place. "You two girls used to be higher," she teased her breasts.

Morgan slowly turned her back toward the mirror then she stopped and only turned her head long enough to glance at the engraved art word that took over both her shoulder blades and consumed all the area between as well as down toward the small of her back. A moment later she turned away, unable to continue looking at the extreme exotic design. It began to flood her mind with memories.

She flashed back to the exotic Chinese artist who did the piece that took one year to complete. He called himself Sun, and the last time Morgan had heard from him was ten years previous. Sun had sent her the dragon fountain pen that she used almost every day. He had also sent her a gold collector spoon from Singapore. His letter said, "My city is so small that it could be toured in three days but to see all the highlights of the underneath city would want you to stay many days longer. Hope you come for adventure one day. My tattoo business every day is new and daring." Knowing that Morgan loved to learn and read, he had sent her a beautiful book that told all the history of Singapore and its economy. She treasured that charming book while reading it through one long, hot summer.

Slowly stepping closer to the mirror, she studied her reflection more. She looked deep into her green eyes. Morgan whispered, "Sweet child, is that you in there?" She put her small, strong hands to her face and traced the little lines around her eyes and mouth with her fingers.

Morgan had never understood why people said she was beautiful. She felt pretty but definitely not beautiful. Her olive skin was flawless, and she had a warm smile with lips that were full but not pouting. When she laughed, it was whole-hearted. The first thing that caught people off guard was her expressive eyes. Often she heard men say, "You look at me like you could read my mind."

Morgan pulled the combs out of her shoulder-length black hair, and playfully tossed it back. Without rushing, she quietly began her bathing ritual. She grabbed a bottle of baby oil, poured a little on a ball of cotton, and removed her black eye make-up. With another cotton ball, she removed the bold red lipstick. Then she lathered her face and neck with soap and rinsed well.

She bent to place towels on the floor to protect it from water. She wet a new washcloth with hot water, rinsed it out, and washed her neck and breasts. Then she washed under her armpits and then her arms. "How good it feels to get the smell of the client's hair and men's cologne off my body," she thought. Taking her time, she sat on the toilet seat cover and tenderly washed her feet.

At last, she stood up and grabbed the little pitcher off the top shelf and filled it with hot water. Morgan lifted up the toilet seat cover and sat down. She spread her legs wide apart and then slowly poured the clean water over her private body. It felt so refreshing. Standing up, she dried her body, and then generously applied talcum power under her arms and between her legs.

"Well, who said a bird bath isn't fun," she thought. Feeling clean, she slipped into her nightgown and panties then cleaned up her mess.

Chapter 7

Carrying the candleholder, she closed the door of the bathroom. The loud noise of rumbling thunder reverberated through the shop. The heavy rain had turned into a massive thunderstorm. She ran over to the front of the barbershop and peeked through the blinds.

The inside windows had misted up so Morgan wiped the windows clear with her hand. As she did so, a large tree branch hit the window with a crash, causing Morgan to jump. Thankfully, the branch did not break the windowpane. Lightning blazed across the sky, followed by more threatening sounds of thunder. Morgan ran to the closet in the back of the shop. She grabbed an armful of large towels and placed them against the bottom of the front glass door, though so far no water had seeped through the cracks.

"Thank God that the firefighter, Lawrence, and Sam put the sand bags in front of the shop to protect it. Without those bags, there would have been a flood of water through the door. Even though the barbershop will not belong to me for much longer, I don't want anything to happen to it now," she thought.

Standing alongside her barber chair staying very still, she listened to the rain and thunder and she lovingly stroked the strong wooden arms of her faithful friend. She spoke to her chair in a comforting voice, "You are okay, girl." She hugged the chair. "You and I have been through some tough times before. Don't be afraid, it's only water." With her eyes closed, she listened to the storm screaming uncontrollably while her arms wrapped around her beloved barber chair. When she came out of her reveries, she hurried back to her office, grabbed a wool blanket, and went back to her chair and covered it carefully. Still not satisfied, she grabbed a huge canvas tarp that the painters had left in the back. Morgan stretched and pulled the heavy canvas over the top and down to the floor under the base of the chair. It looked covered to her satisfaction – secure and safe.

Morgan glanced sleepily at the array of clocks on the wall; it was 10:30. “How can it be that late?” she wondered. Sweetly, she patted her barber chair and whispered, “Time for you to go to sleep, missy. You had a long day, too.”

Exhausted, she walked into her office. The sofa bed looked so inviting. She gently crawled into the bed and pulled the warm comforter up around her shoulders. Just as she was drifting asleep, she heard a scratching and opened her eyes. “Now what is that?” she muttered.

She reached for the flashlight that was by her shoes. It wasn’t there. “Where was it?” she said to herself. Fumbling around, she found it and switched it on. With the ray of light shining, she searched all around the walls and ceiling with her heart racing. “Oh, my God, there it is!” she exclaimed. She leapt out of the bed, opened a small drawer, took out a pair of vinyl gloves, and put them on. She stood up on top of the bed.

Behind the dusty books on the middle shelf, she saw the long tail of the rat. Swiftly, she grabbed his tail with her right hand, the flashlight dropping from her left hand as she took hold of the back of his neck. He turned his neck, looked at her, and they both screamed.

With perspiration beads forming on Morgan’s forehead, she crawled off the bed and walked to the burning candlelight to look directly into the rascal’s beady little eyes.

“Well, you fat little bastard, you scared me half to death,” Morgan said to the rat. She walked to the front of the shop and looked at the intruder. “I sure hope you can swim, now go home to your family, get going.” With a big push, she shoved the fat rat through the mail slot of the front door.

Morgan took off the gloves, washed her hands, and wiped her face. Finally, she was able to get back into bed. She snuggled under the covers then laughed heartily and thought, "Oh my goodness, I can't wait until tomorrow when I can tell my dad and Ann about this rat episode. They will get such a kick out of it."

Chapter 8

Morgan woke up and looked at the clock: 4:30 a.m. Lying in her warm bed, she listened to the sounds of the intense weather. Her first thought was to call Barney and Ann but she knew it was much too early. If the storm continued there would be no way she could open the shop for business. "Oh, I'm not going to worry about it," she said to herself and then stretched her arms up around the back of her head and rested them as she snuggled into her soft pillows. She looked around the room, happy to be there. From the bed, she could see into the other room. The reflection from the candlelight was dimly shining on one particular very tall wall that once had been a loft and it caught her attention.

This wall faced her hair-cutting station. Hung in perfect order on the wall was a display of collector spoons. Many were behind glass cabinets; all the spoons were on antique spoon racks. The spoons twinkled and glistened, reflecting the effort it took to keep them that way. Morgan felt grateful to Sam. One of his many duties was to keep the collection in perfect order. He had to do a lot of polishing to keep them shining.

Morgan smiled as she remembered him as a 12-year-old boy and recalled the day he came into the shop. Drained of energy, she had been resting in her desk chair after doing more than 13 haircuts and dreading the next task of tidying up the barbershop. She had fired the last kid who helped her; he had done a half-ass job. Then unexpectedly a young kid on his bicycle opened the shop door and very politely asked, "Hey lady, I am tired of watching TV. I need a job. Do you have any work for me?" That very moment he started to work for her, his first job. Morgan trained him well and taught him good work ethics. She showed him how she expected the chores to be done. If he did not do a good job, then she had him do it again. He washed the windows inside the shop and polished all the mirrors. Sam kept the train collection free of dust. She paid him fairly and if she saw that he worked harder, she would give him extra cash. The boy had become an excellent worker.

One year after she hired Sam, he said, "Boss lady, I never knew my mother." He frowned. "My father said the last time I was with her, I was one year old."

This caught Morgan by surprise. "What happened to your mother, Sam?"

"My mother cried every day to go home to her family so one day my father sent her back to Vietnam. She never came back."

"Oh, that's so sad for you," Morgan had said.

"Oh, not too sad," he had replied. "I am lucky to live in the United States, and I am an American citizen. I have a good job and I go to a good school." They had both smiled and nodded in agreement.

After that conversation, Morgan let her guard down and grew closer in trusting Sam. Clearly, he was a lot smarter than most boys his own age, she figured.

Looking up at her spoon collection, she remembered a time when she knew where the first 200 spoons had come from. Back then, she could relate the story of each one. That was not the case now. She smiled, knowing that there were more than 784 spoons in her collection and all 784 spoons had come from some place in the world. All the locations had been noted in the brown, leather logbook. The male clients, their wives, and children had brought her spoons as tokens of appreciation for her friendship over the years. Even some strangers had heard about her collection and had just dropped off unusual, nameless spoons in her mailbox. Since Morgan did not know who gave her those spoons, they hung in an exceptional glass cabinet appropriately recorded in the logbook as "Orphan Spoons Find a Home."

Sam had learned that collector spoons were purchased in remembrance of the time a person visited a special vacation spot. They could be from someone you had met, or who lived on the other side of the world, and this person wanted you to remember them. All of the collector spoons were engraved with the name of a state in the United States or a country. For Morgan, these spoons were a special reminder of where her clients came from and where they had traveled. Many times Morgan and Sam had simply passed the time by dreaming of traveling to all those places someday. When the barbershop was not busy, they would sit together, study the world map, and search for the places each spoon had come from.

Morgan was pleased that Sam was always eager to learn and that he had been a good student all through school. He excelled on the wrestling team, as well. It had really helped, she knew, that she had never allowed him to play video games in her shop and that there was no television.

The rain outside continued to pour. She had grown accustomed to the peaceful, steady rainfall. Morgan snuggled into her pillows and looked directly to the spoons that glistened. "The most amusing thing about my collection is, in all these years, no one has ever asked me why I started to collect the spoons. Not one of my clients or employees or even Sam has ever asked about my own childhood or my life before I became a barber," she thought to herself.

With great joy and simultaneous unspeakable heartache, Morgan had nowhere to go, so she closed her eyes and thought back about her life and the journey that had brought her to where she was today.

Chapter 9

1966

The O'Malley family had quite a busy household in 1966. Isabel and Barney were a lovely, devoted couple raising five children. They showed thoughtful affection to each other as well as their children. The oldest boy, Peter, was 14 and kind-hearted, with light blond hair and a strong jaw like his father. Next, there was Morgan who was 12 years old but closer to 13. She was carefree girl without any worries. Her hair was thick, almost a blue-black color, and she had distinctive green-hazel eyes. The twin boys, Noah and Casey, were 8 years old and energetic. They were full of curiosity and blessed with curly red hair, blue eyes, and freckles. The youngest, Emma, was the little drama queen and at 5 years old had acquired a skill for crying on cue. Emma looked more like her mother with black eyes and straight, dark-brown hair. Her skin tones matched Morgan's; it was a delicious rich light brown. From the day Emma was born, Morgan called her baby girl.

Morgan knew Isabel relished being an early riser because there was only one bathroom in the modest home and it was next to Morgan's bedroom. Every day she would hear or see Isabel go into the bathroom, up early before anyone else. She would shower, dress, and neatly comb her long, black hair into a thick ponytail. An hour later, her mother would make coffee and boil water for an oatmeal breakfast most days, but occasionally it was truly a treat for the family to wake up to stacks of pancakes or French toast. Morgan thought that maybe that was why Isabel always smelled of maple syrup.

Mother always greeted everyone with cheerful smile. Her

favorite color was yellow and she had four yellow cotton aprons that matched her backyard garden's roses. The vase on the kitchen table was full with beautiful, warm, butter-gold Floribunda roses. They had a strong, sweet licorice and spice smell. The sunlit influence was apparent on the walls and blended warmly with woodwork painted in gold. Unfortunately, mornings were not as pleasant for Barney. Always in a hurry, he would gulp down his coffee barely taking a breath and gobble up his breakfast. He wore a navy blue mechanics service uniform. By the time the children were coming to the breakfast table, he was on his way to the door. Always before walking out that door, he would stop and wait for each of the five children to line up by the front door so he could kiss and hug each one of them. "Be good for your mother and your teacher," he would say lovingly yet sternly to each child. Then he would kiss Isabel smack on the lips. "I will be home in time for dinner," he always said with a wink.

Barney's trade was an automobile repair brake mechanic. It took him one hour to travel to downtown Los Angeles from their home in Novella and an hour to come back. Novella was a small suburban city in Los Angeles County, not far from Dairy Vale which had hundreds of dairies, 100,000 cows and 106, 000 chickens within its city's limits.

Morgan's favorite breakfast was then and still was today, apple-spiced tea served with a little milk and honey and hot oatmeal completely covered with brown sugar. She remembered the beautiful authentic Mexican platters that Isabel loved. The platters' place was in the middle of the long oak dining room table that was always covered with a white lace tablecloth. The platters always overflowed with bananas, cantaloupes, pineapples and oranges, apples and grapes. The other vibrantly colored platter was full of Mexican sweet bread and Irish tea scones and soft, fluffy biscuits. There were two delicate, glass-covered butter dishes and two small silver-rimmed glass jars, one full with cinnamon pear jelly and the other strawberry jam. Milk and orange juice were served from white glass pitchers that had once belonged to Barney's grandmother in Ireland. The milk and creamer were delivered by the milkman from Dairy Vale in glass bottles. Large, fresh, brown eggs, sweet cream, and unsalted butter were delivered as well.

Growing up, Morgan had always assumed that every family was Mexican-Irish. As an innocent child, she just thought that on every kitchen stovetop there was a black, cast-iron round plate to warm tortillas as well as a dark brown crock-pot full of homemade, creamy Irish potato soup on Friday nights for dinner. In later years, Morgan realized her dear mother was forever trying different recipes in an attempt to honor her husband's Irish heritage. Isabel was a creative cook and alternated all the meals between the two ethnicities. The family would eat meals of bangers and potato pie. There would be herb and dumpling stew, and apple and custard pies. On St. Patrick's Day, Isabel served a huge pot of corned beef potatoes and cabbage. Morgan did not like to eat the cabbage nor did she enjoy the smell, but she said nothing.

Other days there would be meals of cheese enchiladas. Leftover roast turned into an easy taquitos recipe covered with guacamole dip that was made from ripe avocados and sprinkled with a generous amount of grated cheese and sour cream and salsa smothered on top. That dish was Morgan's favorite.

On Friday nights it was the custom for the entire family to be together. Barney and Isabel would roll the rugs up on the front room floor and put it behind the couch. With help from the children, they would move all the furniture to the side of the room to make plenty of room for dancing. Barney loved to dance. He would put on Irish records and teach all the children how to dance the Irish jig to his music, keeping his upper body controlled with straight arms and quick, precise movements of the feet.

Then it would be Isabel's turn and she taught the kids to dance the Mexican hat dance to Mexican music. It was so much family fun that some Friday nights didn't end until midnight.

Television was viewed in the living room with the entire family sitting together. They watched "The Ed Sullivan Show" every Sunday night, but at 9 p.m. on Sunday night was Morgan's favorite because "Bonanza," the television western series, came on. Thankfully, Barney liked that. Morgan would fantasize that she lived on that ranch with the Cartwrights and that she was Ben Cartwright's only daughter and they would ride horses and the stagecoach together.

As a child, Morgan had one doll, Cathy; she stood 24 inches tall, with a one-piece stuffed vinyl body. She was completely original down to her white stockings and black, shiny, high-heel slippers. Cathy was dressed in ruffles and pink chiffon with a purple sash. She had silver stud earrings, and big blue eyes with curled eyelashes. Her lips were ruby red, and she had long blond curls. Peter would tease Morgan about that doll every day. "You are too old to play with dolls. You act like a sissy girl." Then Morgan would give in and play with him. They would play marbles for hours but Peter valued his enormous baseball card collection the most.

Finally one Saturday morning Morgan had had enough of him teasing her. When Peter asked her, "Sister where are my baseball cards? I cannot find them. I've looked everywhere!" Morgan looked at him squarely in the eyes and said, "I sold them to the kid down the street."

Peter just about passed out. "No, I can't believe you did!"

"Well you got one thing right, I didn't sell them. But if you tease me one more time about Cathy, then I will for sure!" Never again did Peter tease her about that doll.

Chapter 10

All the children in the O'Malley house attended Catholic school. Morgan remembered that in seventh grade she had been on the honor roll. Her entire report card was straight As. One particular evening sometime after eight, she had finished two hours of homework and sat at her bedroom vanity quietly and in deep concentration as she looked at herself in the oval mirror. Counting to herself, she was up to 44 strokes brushing her long hair. In some magazine, she had read that girls should brush their hair 100 strokes every day so it would become shiny.

Isabel walked into her bedroom. "Sweetheart, can I talk to you a moment?"

"Sure mom, come on in. I am almost finished brushing my hair." Morgan smiled happily.

Isabel stood there for a few moments, not saying anything. She finally sat on the bed facing her daughter with her eyes cast down. She nervously folded her hands then unfolded them repeatedly. Morgan noticed the strange behavior and put her hairbrush down. They sat there in silence for a while.

Isabel finally looked up with sad eyes. "Morgan, I am taking a job at the private hospital. I will be working as a cook in the kitchen. They will be paying me 2 dollars an hour."

Morgan was shocked. "So this is for sure?"

"Yes, and it has all been arranged but I have not told your father yet. The woman down at the church helped me get this job; she is an important person at the hospital. The money your father makes is not enough for the education that I want for you children. And this is a lot of money."

Quietly, Morgan asked, "I don't understand. Mother, why are

you doing this? You have always been home. And who will take care of the children?"

Isabel looked deep into her daughter's eyes without blinking. "Morgan, you are old enough. I am going to put you in charge of the little ones while I am gone. All of you are in school now; so you will help with the children after school."

Morgan was speechless and began to fidget with her pajama button.

Isabel was unable to hold back her tears. "I'm so sorry, my darling girl," she said, trembling. She stood up and began to leave the room. Stopping at the door, she turned. "I am going to prepare a schedule for all of you to stay on during the week." Isabel took a deep breath. "Now don't look so sad. It should not be that difficult without me here. I'm happy I will be working as a full-time cook. It works like this; it's called a split shift. I will work in the mornings from 9 a.m. to 1 p.m. Then I will come home. Then I go back to work at 4 p.m. to 8 p.m. But I do need to tell you if I work a few Sundays they will pay me double."

Tears were streaming down Morgan's cheeks. She was still unable to speak.

Turning from the door, Isabel rushed back into the room and pulled her daughter to her feet. She wrapped her arms around her young teenage daughter. Morgan looked at her mother's face that was almost crushed with tears, and she threw herself into her mother's arms and the two hugged each other hard. Isabel cried like a little girl into her daughter's arms. After a time, Isabel finally let go. "It's not what you and I want, but this is also for the children."

"Mother, I will help with everything. Please stop crying," Morgan said with a strong face.

After Isabel settled down and stopped crying, she tucked Morgan into bed and covered her with her favorite pink blanket. Softly she closed her daughter's door.

Pulling the covers up over her head so no one would hear her, Morgan sobbed hard into her pillow. She knew that soon her life as she knew it up to that point was about to change.

Chapter 11

It made Morgan anxious to be inside a small space for a long time. She remembered how skittish she felt about going into the red, oak, thick, handcrafted confessional booth one particular day. It had been about four months after Isabel had left the house to go to work.

Pulling the thick, heavy door open, she went inside. Very gently, she knelt down on the padded kneeler in the dark confessional booth and faced the black screen with her hands folded in prayer, her eyes closed. Then she heard faint whispering coming from the other side of the screen; the priest was speaking in an annoyed voice. Right away, she began to pray harder so she could not hear what the voices were saying.

At once, her heartbeat pumped faster as she heard the small window door in front of her slide open. Now there was only the black screen between her and the priest. It was her turn. The priest recited a prayer and then she began.

"Bless me Father, for I have sinned." She made the sign of the cross. "It has been three weeks since my last confession and I accuse myself of the following sins. I threw away a cold fried egg sandwich that my mother made me for lunch. I copied a few answers for the math test from the boy sitting in front of me. I ate meat on Friday. I ate two bites of ham. I did my sister's homework then lied to my father about it. I broke my mother's favorite teacup; I lied to her about it because I was afraid to hurt her feelings." She squirmed on her knees, restless, then took a deep breath to continue. "One more thing, Father, only one time, I did not fast before communion. I took a drink of milk and ate a bite of bread when mother was not looking. I was hungry. That is all, Father."

There was silence for a moment, then the priest asked in a stern voice, "How old are you?"

"I am 12 years old, Father."

"Then you are old enough to know that it is a sin to waste food, and to lie to your parents is a very serious offense against God. God is very mad if you do not fast before receiving holy communion. There are church rules. You must not eat any food or drink any liquids except for water twelve hours before you receive the host. Now please say the act of contrition."

Morgan bowed her head and began to say the prayer aloud. After Morgan said the prayer the priest said, "Now, for your penance, you will say the ten Hail Mary prayers and five Our Fathers so that you will grow in self-restraint."

"Yes, Father."

"I absolve you of your sins in the name of the Father and of the Son and of the Holy Spirit. Now go in peace, my child." The slide window closed.

Morgan left the confessional box. She went to the left corner of the church and knelt down on the solid oak, padded prayer bench. Looking up to the picture of the Blessed Mother Mary, she bowed her head in respect. Then she took out her First Communion light blue oval plastic rosary beads, and made the sign of the cross and began to pray. She was sorry that she had made God mad. Morgan was concentrating in prayer when her teacher came up behind her and tapped her shoulder. Sister Margaret was an old nun with a weak chin. "Young lady, it is time for you to go back to class."

Morgan whispered to her, "I'm sorry Sister Margaret, I can't go back. I'm not finished with my penance yet."

"For every five minutes that you are late you will say ten Hail Mary prayers," the nun whispered angrily then turned and left.

Without turning around, Morgan nervously fidgeted with her rosary beads and listened as Sister Margaret's shoes click-clunked loudly on the hardwood floor as she hurried out of the huge cathedral. She was just beginning to get up from the kneeling position when the priest came out of the confessional.

Immediately he walked to her. "Are you the 12-year-old girl who was just in my confessional?"

Morgan nodded. "Yes, Father."

"Well, where do you think you are going? There is no way that you can be finished with your penance."

"But Father Alexander..." Morgan tried to explain.

The old thin priest interrupted. "I am speaking, not you child. You are a very disobedient girl, and you are going to be punished. Come with me." Father Alexander grabbed Morgan's arm and pulled her into the back of the church and up the steep stairs to the priest's private office. He unlocked the door and shoved Morgan into a straight wooden chair. "Wait here."

The priest took out a key ring full with brass keys and locked the oak office door. Morgan sat there in complete silence in disbelief of what had just taken place. The room was full of antique statues of saints and the picture of baby Jesus in the Blessed Mother's arms. "How could this old priest be so mean with this beautiful picture of the baby Jesus right here in his office?" she wondered.

The door opened suddenly. In came the old priest with a frown and following behind was Sister Margaret. "Yes, this girl needs to be disciplined," Sister Margaret growled. "She falls asleep in class, and her homework has become sloppy. Three times she has missed assignments. A few months ago she was an A student and now she is a C-minus student. Perhaps she is playing at home instead of doing her homework!"

Morgan looked at the two of them. Of course, she knew why she was not doing well in school. It was because she had so many chores to do at home. Helping with the children demanded her time. Mother was not at home. The responsibility of all of it had been so much more than Morgan could ever have imagined. Nevertheless, she just sat there, rolled her eyes, and did not utter a word.

The nun and the priest turned to talk to each other in whispers and nodded in agreement. "Stand up miss," the priest told her. "Now put both of your hands out, make a fist. Do not move those hands." Morgan stood up. She stretched out her arms and made a fist.

A thick ruler appeared from somewhere and Sister Margaret held it in her hand. She smacked Morgan's knuckles hard on each fist three times. Morgan cried out. "Stop it. That hurts!"

After that outburst, the priest reached over and slapped her cheek. Father Alexander grabbed Morgan's wounded hands and said, "Now you will remember to pray when you are told to and your grades had better improve. You make God very angry because you are so disobedient and today you will have no lunch. Instead you will stay in the rectory until school is over."

The nun went up to Morgan's face and glared fiercely into her eyes. "Morgan, you will improve your grades and never ever fall asleep in my class ever. Are we understood?"

Morgan showed no tears to the two of them. With her jaw clenched tight and her face swollen and red, bowing her head, she answered, "Yes, Sister Margaret. I understand." To the priest she said nothing nor did she make eye contact with him.

Father Alexander yanked Morgan by the arm and took her to a very small room with a cot and toilet. "Stay here," he said. "Pray for God to forgive you."

With her face and hands aching, she sat silent on the cot. The heavy door closed. Tears streamed down her cheeks. She felt shameful, misunderstood, and angry.

A while later, the door opened a little bit. A young priest stood there, Father Paul. He put his finger on his lips and motioned her to be quiet. "Hush." As Father Paul came closer, Morgan could see that he was clearly upset. Father Paul handed Morgan a cup of water and a piece of chocolate and he gently hugged her shoulder. Without a word, he was gone.

That evening, Morgan lied to her mother when she had noticed her daughter's hands and swollen cheek. "What happened?" Isabel demanded.

"I was playing volleyball and that ball just kept hitting my knuckles and then the volleyball smacked me in the face."

Immediately Isabel put Morgan's hands in ice water and gave her an ice pack for her face. "Did you tell the nuns about your injuries?"

"No Mother," Morgan said. "I did not want to bother them, there are so many children that they are busy with."

"Follow me; I want your father to see your hands."

Isabel took Morgan into the living room to see her dad. She began telling Barney what happened. He looked up from his newspaper, and looked at her hands and said, "You better get some ice on those knuckles. You'll be fine." Then he noticed his daughter's red mark on her cheek and said, "Well, it looks like the ball hit you in the cheek, too. Volleyball is a tough sport so you had better keep your eyes open. It's getting late go help your mother make your sister and brother's lunches for tomorrow." He put the paper back up in front of his face.

Morgan looked over to Isabel; she was standing next to Barney's recliner chair. Isabel asked her daughter one last time: "Don't lie to us. Are you sure that's what happened today at school?"

Without so much as a blink, Morgan looked directly into Isabel's eyes and said, "Yes, that is the truth."

Morgan went into the kitchen and put an ice pack on her hands. Soon after, Isabel and Morgan began to pack the five brown paper bags for the children's lunches. They made sandwiches of white bread smeared with mustard, sliced bologna, and cheese with lettuce and tomatoes. Isabel put an extra slice of bologna into Morgan's sandwich. They wrapped the sandwiches tight with wax paper and put them in the refrigerator for tomorrow. Morgan took five oranges, sliced them in four, and wrapped them tight. Then she wrapped up a bar of Jamoncillo candy in every bag. Isabel took a bite from one candy and shoved another piece into Morgan's mouth. They both laughed together. "Very yummy," Isabel said, smiling. With a red pen, Morgan wrote the name and room number on each child's bag.

As more months passed, many changes happened in the O'Malley home. Isabel became friends with a woman from work.

The woman taught Isabel how to drive. After that, Isabel passed her driving test. Then Barney bought his wife a 1964 Ford Falcon four-door station wagon. Isabel was no longer taking the bus to work.

Another day that stood out was when Isabel had marched into their home with a new fashionable, short haircut. No one in the house could believe it when she walked it. "Mother, what have you done to your beautiful long hair?" Morgan asked in disbelief.

"I cut my hair like Elizabeth Taylor," Isabel said proudly.

That day marked a slow decline between Isabel and Barney. Morgan and the children listened to their parents arguing loudly behind closed doors that night. Barney was shouting. "Why do you make decisions without asking me first? You are never home! I hate that you went to work and I don't like your haircut. Our life together has changed." Isabel stopped trying to fight back. The shouting stopped.

Another year flew by and Morgan knew her mother had changed and was becoming independent. Barney became a man of few words. In the evenings after he came home from work, he would go outside and do yard work or fool around in the garage. After dinner, he would read the newspaper. He spent less time with his children.

Morgan often wondered why her father slept in his chair many nights. Later she learned Barney had been adding vodka to his orange juice. It seemed that the life that she had known as a child was gone forever now that her mother had gone to work and made new friends.

One night Morgan was putting away the last of the clean dishes around 7 p.m. It was no surprise for her to hear Isabel shuffling to find her coat. This time, she noticed that Isabel had new high-heeled shoes on with stockings. Isabel was going to a Monday hospital meeting, which was held once a week, even though Monday's were her nights off from work.

Morgan watched disappointed as Isabel put her black trench coat on and go over to all her three smaller children. She kissed them on their foreheads. "Now mind your manners. Listen to Morgan and Peter. They are in charge. I want you in bed on time." She smiled happily as she hurried out the door then she turned and playfully shouted. "Hey, Peter, my darling son. Be sure to help your sister get the children to bed, and don't forget to take the trash out!"

After the door closed, Morgan looked over at the lovely Mexican platters on the dining room table that were only full with bananas. Gone were the homemade breads and desserts. The beautiful butter dish was there but empty. There were only memories of the delicious homemade meals every morning and evening. Now Isabel only cooked on the weekends and maybe twice a week and put leftover dinners in Tupperware. It was interesting how the modern world had brought TV dinners and store-bought bread and margarine in plastic bowls into their home. Frankly, it seemed so long ago that mother didn't have a job.

By 8 p.m. Morgan still had not begun her own homework. She helped her twin brothers get ready for bed and she made sure that their school clothes had been laid out for morning. Noah and Casey loved their older sister. They did anything Morgan told them. They were such good boys, so full with laughter. It seemed that she spent more time with them than their mother did. In the evenings, Morgan always said prayers with the twins and Emma before she turned out the light. Before Morgan went to sleep, she would go in their room and check on them.

Emma's room had originally been a storage space but Barney had made it into a tiny bedroom so the two girls could have some separate space. The arrangement did not make Emma happy. Halfway through most nights, she made her way into Morgan's bed. Unlike Morgan, little Emma was very sloppy. Every school night Morgan would sneak into her 7-year-old sister's homework papers and arrange all of it neatly.

Peter's simple life had changed also. Every morning at 5 a.m., he would wake up because he had a newspaper route. He delivered newspapers on his bicycle before school so there was not much time for him to help his sister. However, he certainly did manage to find the time to tease her. Hiding behind the furniture, he would scare her to death!

Morgan loved Peter. She looked up to him because she saw a responsible young man who was not a wimp but a trooper. He studied very hard for good grades and he took care of himself. He did his own laundry and ironed his own school shirts and slacks. The only gap was that there was no communication between Peter and his parents. Life had forever changed in the O'Malley home.

Chapter 12

Morgan remembered a very specific Saturday morning one summer. She was in the backyard hanging clean, wet clothes up on the clothesline with wood-spring clothespins. Out of nowhere, she heard the kids yelling for her.

"Morgan come quick!" Casey screamed. "You have a special letter."

"You won something!" shouted Noah.

Dropping the wet clothes into the wicker basket, she ran into the front yard. "Do I have a letter? Is it really for me?" Her eyes were huge with excitement. "I've never received a letter before." She stared at the postal worker, who teased her. "This letter is for you, if you are Miss Morgan O'Malley." He smiled and handed her a pen. "Sign this please." Then he handed her the letter. "I hope it is good news!" He grinned as he hurried back to the delivery truck and took off, waving at the children.

Isabel came outside as Morgan and the children waved good-bye to the mail carrier. Morgan eagerly opened the letter. She read the letter aloud to Mother, Emma, Peter, Casey, and Noah who surrounded her.

Dear Morgan,

This is to notify you that you have been granted a scholarship. You have passed all the qualification testing at a very high standard. You have been accepted as a freshman to Saint Catherine Catholic Girls Academy. Report to my office for an orientation meeting, uniform fittings, and meet with counselors and staff and receive books. Your appointment is on August 15, 1968. Congratulations.

Sincerely,

Mother Superior, Sister Mary Bernadette
God bless you in Jesus Christ's name.

Morgan was in shock and was unprepared for her mother's reaction. Isabel jumped up and down and started to cry tears of joy. With her hands raised up toward heaven, she thanked the Lord.

The boys began to tease Morgan. "You're going to be a nun," Noah chirped.

"Morgan's going to be a nun," Casey chimed in.

Emma joined in teasing her. "Does that mean I can have your record collection?"

Embarrassed, Morgan ran into the house, the screen door slamming behind her. She rushed into her bedroom and shut the door. She sat on the bed and read the letter again. Then she thought about her best friend who lived next door.

"Lucy, are you there? Lucy!"

From the house across the graveled driveway, a blonde-haired girl with long, wavy hair came to the open window. "Hi Morgan, what's up?"

"Did you get the letter from the academy?"

"Yeah I did," Lucy smiled. "I was accepted. What about you?"

Morgan smiled. "I was too."

They both giggled. Lucy's face was peaceful. Morgan knew her friend had always wanted to be a nun. Lucy had planned on going to the all girls' high school ever since Morgan could remember.

Morgan sat on the bed in disbelief. Never in a million years did she think she had done so well on the tests. The examinations had taken six hours and she had hurried through it all. Isabel opened the door and walked into her daughter's room.

"What is it, honey?" she asked her daughter as she sat next to her. "Isn't this what we have wanted all our lives for you? You have always wanted to go Saint Catherine; perhaps this will be your preparation for the Carmelite Order."

"But I don't know." Morgan tried to talk.

Isabel interrupted her. "Maybe you will be a teaching sister.

The children will love you because you are smart and the Lord gave you a beautiful face so the children will pay attention to you. We are blessed that you won the scholarship. We are a middle-class family. Your father and I could never afford to send you to this private school; this is a sign from God." Isabel wrapped her arms around her daughter. "I am so proud of you, sweetheart."

"Yes, I know that you are proud of me, but what about the kids? If I go to this high school I won't be home until much later."

"We will hire a babysitter for a few hours during the week. Don't worry, it will all work out."

Later that night as she was alone in her room Morgan sat on her bed and flipped through some teen magazines. No one knew how much she loved looking at hairstyles. She loved the men's haircuts so much more. She whispered to herself, "I wish I could be a barber. What fun!" Shyly she grinned to herself then put the magazine back under her bed.

Before she fell asleep, she tiptoed out of her room and went into the twins' bedroom. They were both asleep. She kissed each one on the forehead and made sure they were covered. Then she went into Emma's room, kissed her sleeping face, and tidied up her school papers. Satisfied, she walked softly to her room. Before she fell asleep, only three things raced through her responsible young mind: Noah, Casey, and Emma. How would they do without her?

Morgan and her mother reported early for their scheduled meeting at the academy on August 15. Morgan had changed twice that morning before finally settling on a white, short-sleeve knit top and narrow gray pencil skirt that touched right below the knee. Morgan's body had developed over the summer so Isabel had taken Morgan to buy bras. To both their surprise she was a D cup now but Isabel was completely unconcerned about her daughter's maturing body.

Morgan knew today was the special day that Isabel had dreamed of for her since she was born. Both Isabel and Morgan sat in the waiting room at the office at Saint Catherine Catholic all-girls high school for the Mother Superior.

Finally, the secretary called Morgan's name and said, "Please follow me."

Isabel stood up to go with her daughter, but the secretary politely stopped her.

The secretary said, "I'm sorry, at this time Mother Superior only wants to meet with your daughter."

"Oh yes, I understand." Isabel sat back down.

As Morgan walked away, she turned back and glanced at her mom. Isabel sat straight with pride radiating from her face.

Walking into the wood-paneled office, Morgan was pleasantly surprised when she saw a beautiful, angelic older woman wearing a traditional nun's habit. The nun immediately stood up. In a low voice she cheerfully said, "You must be Morgan; it is lovely to finally meet you."

Morgan smiled and said, "Thank you."

"Please sit down," said Mother Bernadette. "I have been reviewing your papers. You had some of the highest tests scores of any incoming student this year. I want to congratulate you, my dear."

"Thank you, Mother." Morgan smiled widely.

The two of them went over the school enrollment papers and classes for the next hour but Morgan did not have the heart to tell Mother Bernadette that she wanted to learn to cut people's hair. Instead, Morgan was placed into science, history, English, and geometry classes.

The Mother stood up, came around the oak desk, and said, "Morgan, I want you to understand all blessings come to us through our Lord. Unlike your friends in the world, Christ helps and strengthens us. He is a kind God. The God that I know is slow to anger. He will never abandon you when you are troubled or distressed. I want you to remember that always."

"I will remember, Mother Bernadette," Morgan said. "She is so kind, unlike the other old nag nun from grade school," Morgan thought to herself, already in love with this nun.

"All right, my child. Now it is time for you to go and be fitted for your uniform." The nun came around from the back of the desk and hugged the newest member of the school.

Isabel was waiting anxiously for Morgan and smiled as she came out of the room and stood up.

"It's uniform time," Morgan sarcastically told her mother.

Side by side, the two women walked across to the other side of the school. Isabel whispered, "Did I hear a little sarcasm in your voice?" Morgan shrugged her shoulders.

Morgan stood still as she was measured for a school uniform. She was 14 years old and not entirely pleased to wear another uniform. The dress code consisted of one blue-gray, plaid, pleated skirt; white, short-sleeved, round collar blouses; a navy-blue, knitted vest; and one gray tie. The blazer was navy-blue wool with a flat, polished brass button. The shoes were white Oxfords, worn with white knee socks or white shoe socks. Nylon stockings were not permitted. The bra and undershirt were to be white. Only plain white cotton panties with a pair of cotton bloomers over them were allowed.

Morgan was handed the rules and regulations handbook. Immediately she went to the section in the book and read about make-up. "Not even light lipstick!" she whined.

"Hush up," Isabel commanded. "The nuns will hear you!"

Morgan grumbled to herself, "Jeepers, so many rules."

Chapter 13

Three years passed quickly at Saint Catherine's. Morgan excelled in high school and life at home had become a nice routine. Peter and Morgan were playful, nurturing, and loving to Noah, Casey, and Emma. The 21-year-old babysitter, Peggy, was reliable and kind to the children.

At the end of Morgan's junior year she and the other students sat in silence in the auditorium as Mother Bernadette walked up to the microphone. She bowed her head in prayer and made the sign of the cross. Every nun and student in the auditorium did the same. In the traditional custom, the prayers were said. Later with a proud, robust voice, Mother Bernadette encouraged the girls to participate in a summer program that would prepare them for becoming nuns. They would live at the retreat house and assist the Carmelite nuns during the coming summer months and have the opportunity to learn a useful trade.

As Morgan passed by the table with the enrollment papers, she took one.

Three weeks later, Mother Bernadette had a meeting in her office with Morgan. "This is for you. Congratulations." She handed her an envelope. Morgan read that she was accepted into the nuns' 11-week summer program living at the retreat house.

Morgan showed Isabel the letter when her mother got home from work that night. Isabel took a deep breath. "Well, we want you to be a nun. This will be a good thing. Somehow we will manage without you."

On the night Morgan was packing to leave for the retreat house, Emma was being a brat. Every time Morgan put a piece of clothing in her suitcase, Emma took it out.

"Now stop it," Morgan scolded her firmly.

Emma raised her voice. "I don't want you to go to the stinking nun house!"

Morgan sat next to her sister. "Baby girl you are 9 years old. You are a big girl now. And your babysitter Peggy will help you with your homework."

Emma put her arms around her sister. "I've never been without you." Her big eyes overflowed with tears. "I don't want you to be a silly nun. You just want to leave our house the same way that mommy did."

Looking back into Emma's sad eyes Morgan knew it would be hard on her sweet sister when she left. Calmly, she tried to explain. "Emma this is the time to find out if I really want to be a Carmelite nun. I love you with all my heart."

Emma arms were folded across her chest and tears streamed down her cheeks. Morgan put her arms around her sister and whispered, "I promise when I come back home you and I will spend a lot of time together. There will still be a few weeks before school starts up again." She wiped Emma's cheeks with a tissue. "You can sleep in my bed while I'm away. And you can sleep with Cathy." Morgan began to tickle her sister. "You are such spoiled baby girl!" Morgan jumped up and took her favorite doll Cathy from the top shelf to her closet and placed her in Emma's arms.

Emma smiled and gave her sister a big bear hug. "I promise to take care of Cathy. I know how much she means to you."

Morgan got up. "Come here. I have something else for you."

Emma followed her to the closet. Morgan got on her knees and searched far back in the closet behind her shoes. She reached for a small blue box. Then the two sisters sat on the closet floor cross-legged, facing each other as Morgan opened the box. Emma's eyes were huge as she saw a stack of one-dollar bills inside. "Where did you get all this money?"

Morgan winked at her sister. "Remember all the ironing I was doing while mommy was at work?"

"Yes," Emma replied.

"Well, no one noticed that I was ironing shirts for the rich lady neighbor down the street."

Emma pointed to the silver, blue, and turquoise money clip with the butterfly on it. "Where did you get that? It's beautiful."

"The lady gave it to me for doing such a good job." Morgan smiled.

Now Emma was happy. "Oh Morgan, you really have a good secret!"

"Do you think it's possible for you to help me keep this our secret?"

Emma's face became serious. "Oh yes. I promise, sissy. I promise not to tell anyone."

Morgan counted out five one-dollar bills. "This is for you." She handed her sister the money. "This is enough money for you, Noah, and Casey to buy plenty of ice cream until I come home. Surprise them with this money after I am gone. Okay?"

Emma smiled and said, "I will and thank you sissy."

Next Morgan showed Emma the rest of the money. "I'm going to leave this money in the box. Only use this money if there is an emergency. Do you understand?" Emma nodded. Then Morgan put it away back in the secret place. "I have one more surprise for you. You may listen to all my records while I'm away."

Emma looked delighted and jumped up and down. When she stopped, she looked suspicious. "Do you promise to spend more time with me when you come home? Can we go to the beach and walk in the sand? Will you roller skate with me?"

Morgan smiled. "Yes. I promise that we will walk on the sand and swim in the ocean and roller skate until we get blisters on our feet."

Emma smiled, her cheeks dimpling. She grabbed a blouse off the bed and lovingly looked into her older sister's green eyes. "I will help you." Together, the two girls quietly packed the suitcase.

Later, from inside the car Morgan waved back to her family and watched as Peter stood straight and tall with no smile. He was holding Emma's hand whose chin began to quiver, then the tears streamed down. Noah and Casey looked heartbroken. They were unbelievably brave young boys who not did sob but soon they had eyes full of tears. Isabel stood with a face full of pride and a small smile.

Morgan looked over to Barney as he said, “Daughter, they will all be fine, it’s your turn now.”

As the car drove away from the house, she turned around to look through the backseat window glass. Her eyes met Peter’s and they locked stares. Peter nodded yes and showed a small grin to his beloved sister. Tears streamed down Morgan’s face.

Chapter 14

Morgan looked for Lucy as soon as she arrived at the convent. When they found each other, Lucy said, "We are roommates!" They rushed to their room and began to unpack. Morgan was equally excited when she found out she was to go into the nursing program. It was exciting to see if she would be a nursing nun.

After two weeks, the head nun called Morgan into her office. Sister Agatha had a cream and peaches complexion with a sprinkle of freckles. She quietly sat next to Morgan and explained to her that she did not believe that nursing was Morgan's calling. "You talk too much to the sick patients."

Morgan, being so good-natured said, "I am sorry, Sister, it's hard for me to keep quiet." The nun smiled. "I have an idea. Let's try the laundry room for now."

Morgan was disappointed, but she said, "Okay, Sister, I can probably be of help there, I helped my mom with laundry for years."

After two weeks, Sister Agatha called Morgan into her office again. "Dear," she said, "the laundry room is not for you. You are just too fast and you are making too many mistakes. You are mixing up the colors."

"I forgot to tell you that I was color blind," Morgan told the nun.

The nun smiled. "Well, that explains that."

Morgan was bothered. "Sister, what am I going to do?"

"Well, I talked to the other nuns and we have an idea."

"What is it, sister?" Morgan asked eagerly.

"How about the bakery?"

"I helped my mother bake in our kitchen. I can try it. Maybe

I can be helpful there."

After two weeks, Sister Agatha found Morgan again. "Come follow me to my office."

Morgan knew the routine with the nun coming to get her. She said to the nun politely, "Okay Sister Agatha, are you going to tell me I don't fit in here?"

The nun smiled sweetly. "No dear, quite the contrary. You are doing a wonderful job in the bakery. Now we need your help somewhere else. We have a bakery open to the public; it's near a big factory outside of the retreat house."

"When do I start?" Morgan replied without hesitation.

"Tomorrow morning," Sister Agatha smiled.

At 6 a.m. the next morning, a small private white bus waited while Morgan stepped in. The bus driver drove her through the opened convent gates and out into the city. He stopped on a street that had a few family storefront businesses. "The bakery is over there." He pointed to the brick building across the street.

Morgan stepped out of the bus and felt uncomfortable in her gray uniform. She straightened the wrinkles of her skirt with her hands the best she could. She felt the strands of her hair to make sure none was flying out of her ponytail then she swiftly walked toward the bakery. As she was walking, she passed by a large spiraling barbershop pole and it caught her attention. "I wish that I were going in there to work," she thought to herself as she stopped and peeked through the window. Two older barbers in white jackets waved to her, she waved back, and they all smiled. A few steps later, she reached the bakery door, opened it, and walked inside.

A very jolly, chubby, black woman with a big smile said to her, "Hi honey! From the looks of that uniform you must be my helper from the convent. My name is Josephine. Now put on that gray apron, we have to begin working."

Quickly Morgan tied the old gray apron on. Josephine said, "I understand you know how to bake cookies and bread. But now girl, you are going to learn to make Josephine's famous yummy doughnuts."

Without looking up Josephine quickly explained how she wanted things to be done as she took out several ingredients. Impressed by the quick movements of Josephine's experienced hands, Morgan watched how she worked. In a short time, Morgan had the hang of it.

Side by side, the two women filled dozens of doughnuts, which were stuffed full with raspberry, lemon and custard filling. They frosted cake doughnuts with thick white, strawberry, and dark chocolate frosting and sprinkled dozens of white frosted doughnuts with coconut and chocolate sprinkles.

Josephine looked at the clock and said, "Oh my, child where has this morning gone? It's almost 7:30. The men will be lining up soon." Hurriedly, she went to the window and turned the closed sign around to open. She had already made several big black pots full of hot, strong coffee. It had been Morgan's job to fill up all the little stainless steel containers with creamer and to fill all the glass containers with sugar. Both women put clean, white, starched aprons on and tied them neatly in the back. Morgan went to the bathroom and brushed her hair back into a neat ponytail, then anxiously waited for the customers. Josephine turned on the small transistor radio and R&B music flowed through the room of the bakery. Never before had Morgan worked with music playing. Marvin Gaye's, "I Heard It Through the Grapevine" was playing. "Being with Josephine is fun," Morgan thought happily.

Just as Josephine had said, the men began to line up for their coffee and doughnuts. They were hard-working men who came from the airplane factory. It was halfway through the morning and Morgan was pouring a cup of the black coffee into a 12-ounce paper coffee cup. She awkwardly over poured it, spilling it all over the clean counter top. "I am so sorry," she said to the man.

"Oh, that's okay," he said, "Accidents happen."

She hurriedly grabbed a nearby terry cloth towel and began to wipe up the mess. She was so busy she hadn't looked up into the stranger's face. When she did, she saw a handsome young man. His golden-blond hair swept across his forehead. His eyes were the bluest eyes Morgan had ever seen. Instantly she felt shy.

Morgan had never looked into a young man's face that way. Her heart pounded faster and she turned red in the face.

"Hey, you got a uniform on under that apron?" he teased. "Where are you from? I've never seen you here before. Are you one of those convent girls?"

She saw that he had the whitest teeth and deep dimples when he smiled. Nervously, she grinned back at him. "You ask too many questions." She blushed red. "Take this coffee before I spill it again."

As Morgan reached his hand to take his money, he touched her hand lightly and then squeezed her bare hands. He did not let her go. "Damn, you're cute." He looked right into her eyes.

Again she blushed as she thought, "Wow, this guy is really cute. I've never seen such gorgeous blue eyes." Breathlessly she said, "Thank you, have a good day. Quickly she pulled her hands away from him.

After he left Morgan went to the back of the bakery to the big stainless steel sink and began to rinse off the large doughnut trays.

"Girl, that boy could not take his eyes off of you!" Josephine laughed. "Are you sure you want to be a nun?"

"Oh you are so silly, Josephine." Morgan smiled, blushing red again.

Morgan worked at the bakery the rest of the summer. Casually, she would look up at the faces of the men who lined up in the morning, hoping to see the young man with the outstanding blue eyes only to be disappointed. She wondered what happened to him.

The weeks flew by and the summer program had come to an end before Morgan knew it. "Thank you for everything, Josephine. I had the most wonderful time working here with you."

"Oh, child," Josephine said, "you just come here and give me a big hug. I'm going to miss you. Sweetheart, I am going to pray for you that you are making the right decision on becoming a nun. And if those nuns get you they're very lucky!"

"Thank you for everything," Morgan said. "I love you Josephine." They hugged tightly.

"Now go, child, before I start to cry. Go on now," Josephine said. Then with one last look at Morgan she lovingly said, "Child, never change your sweet self." Josephine pointed to her own heart.

Back in the convent room, Morgan waited for just the right time to give Lucy the present she had kept hidden. They were both sitting on their beds when Morgan jumped up and mischievously said, "Lucy, I have a surprise for you."

"You have a surprise for me?" Lucy grinned. "What is it?"

"Close your eyes and open your hand." Morgan carefully placed a small wax paper package in her hand. "Open your eyes."

Lucy opened her eyes and unwrapped the wax paper. To her delight, saw the most delicious-looking, chocolate-dipped doughnut.

"It's filled with lemon, two scoops, and I made it myself just for you."

Lucy looked sheepishly then said, "I don't think I should eat this. You know, it's Saturday night and we are supposed to fast before communion tomorrow morning."

"It's our last night here and I've never brought you anything from the bakery. No one will know but you and me," Morgan goaded her mischievously.

Lucy looked at the delicious doughnut again.

"We only had chicken corn chowder soup and a bread roll for dinner. It's okay," Morgan urged again.

Lucy looked at Morgan, looked at the dessert, and gobbled up the wonderful treat. All that was left was the chocolate all on her face and hands. Morgan ran to the bathroom and grabbed tissues for Lucy to wipe herself clean.

"Oh, Morgan, that was delicious. I want another one!"

The two girls laughed hard. Just then, they heard the sound of the nuns walking down the hall ringing the bells, which meant all the girls in the dorm were to fall on their knees and immediately begin the ritual of evening prayers.

Sister Agatha peeked into the girls' room. "I heard noise coming from this room. What are you two up to?"

"Nothing, Sister Agatha," they said at the same time.

The nun smiled. "All right then, you two girls begin your evening prayers."

They both smiled as they dropped to their knees

Later, the girls were in their single, twin-size beds, and Lucy asked, "Are you still awake, Morgan?"

"Yes," Morgan said.

Lucy whispered, "I can't wait until we can live here."

"Are you serious?" Morgan asked.

"Yeah," Lucy continued. "When I am at home with all my family it's hard to hear God's call sometimes. By being here and just listening to the silence, it's easier. I hear Him clearly."

Morgan was quiet for a moment. "You really love God and I know you want to be a nun. I'm going to be so sad when we aren't best friends."

Lucy got out of her small bed and walked over to her best friend. "I don't want to be alone."

Morgan pulled the thin blanket back, Lucy crawled into her bed, and covered them both up. She held her friend close and whispered, "You have been my friend since we were 4 years old, and we will be best friends forever no matter what life brings to us."

"Promise?" Lucy asked.

"Promise," Morgan answered.

The two friends hugged each other as they fell asleep.

The last morning at the retreat house, the girls were up, dressed, and at the Sacred Heart Chapel waiting the priest to begin mass at 6 a.m. An hour later, the rosary was recited and Mother Bernadette gave a touching vocational speech. Finally, it was time to line up and go to breakfast.

More prayers were said at the breakfast tables while the postulant nuns served the hot chocolate and orange juice. In silence, Morgan inspected the young pretty women who were serving. They were dressed in white. She knew they were on their way to taking their final vows to dedicate the rest of their life to the convent. While the young nuns served hot bowls of oatmeal and baskets of hot rolls, the twelve girls ate in complete silence, as expected. Morgan knew Lucy was always more hungry than her, so she slipped Lucy her breakfast roll underneath the table when no one was looking. Nudging Lucy under the table, they smiled at each other as Lucy grabbed the roll. The two girls had to keep their eyes cast downward so they would not laugh.

Chapter 15

Morgan sat in the lobby of the convent, staring out the big bay window. Now it was past one hour she had watched all the girls leave with their parents. It was 1 p.m. but there was no sign of her parents.

With black shoes clicking loudly on the hardwood floor, Sister Agatha walked down the hall and up to her. Morgan smiled as looked over to the beautiful Carmelite nun who had been so kind to her this summer. The nun looked regal in a beautiful white cloak over her long black habit.

"Morgan, your brother Peter called and he said that there was a problem with the family car. He said would you please take the city bus home."

"Okay. Thank you, Sister Agatha," she said softly. Picking up her suitcase, she began to turn toward the door.

Sister Agatha called her name quietly. "Morgan."

"Yes, Sister."

Sister Agatha walked to Morgan. "I want to tell you what a pleasure it has been to know you and I wish many blessings to come your way. You are a sweet, smart young lady."

Morgan curtsied to the nun respectfully. Then without delay she plunged closer and hugged the beautiful nun tight. "Thank you, Sister. God bless you."

She walked outside reluctantly through the black iron gates and on to the front road of the convent and waited for the bus. While Morgan sat in the bus, she had a weird feeling in her gut. Staring out of the bus window at the many cars passing by her intuition felt a hunch that something more than the car was wrong. When the bus stopped, she felt disappointed to see that there was no one waiting for her.

As she walked home, she looked to the houses that lined the streets that were so familiar. They looked so much smaller now that she had been away. She skipped up the three cement steps to her home, overjoyed to greet her family. Putting down her suitcase, she dashed from room to room, calling out names. "Mom! Lucy! Casey! Noah! Peter? Where is everybody?" she called aloud. No answers, no voices. A cold chill came up her back and she fidgeted with her coat button and her heart began to race. She made her way to the backyard and found Barney sitting in the garden area alone under the big oak tree in a wicker rocking chair with his head down.

"Daddy, what are you doing back here? Where is the family?" She smelled the distinctive smell of alcohol. Then she saw the almost empty pint of Popov vodka lying by his shoe. She got down on her knees in front of him and grabbed both his hands. "Daddy please! What is going on? Where is the family?"

Slowly Barney pulled his head up. She saw that his face was red and swollen from crying. His words slurred. "My girl came home." Immediately he pulled her close and she put her arms around him. This was the first time Morgan had seen her father cry. She was heartbroken and confused as she held her father close.

Finally, he began to gain some control over his crying. Gently, she pushed him away from her. Her throat tightened. "Please tell me, what's wrong?"

They looked into each other's eyes. Barney slurred, "There was a horrible accident last night..." Tears streamed from his eyes. He began to cry again.

"What are you talking about? What accident? Tell me please!"

He cried. "Casey and my baby girl." Again, he cried out and said, "Oh, my God!"

Peter walked into the backyard and ran to his sister. She stood up and faced her brother. "Peter, what happened to the children?"

Peter held on to his sister's arms. With tears streaming, he softly said, "Last night mother and dad went out to a dinner and movie. I was at a baseball game. Peggy was here babysitting. They all got bored so Peggy took Noah, Casey, and Emma for a walk to the little store by the dairy across the railroad tracks for ice cream. There was a horrific accident." Peter began to weep.

Chapter 16

The thunder roared angrily from outside and the discharge of the lightning against something outside sounded like an electrical blast of explosion. The outburst snapped Morgan out of her daydreaming. Her mind came back inside the barbershop as the rainstorm continued to hammer southern California.

Morgan stopped reminiscing about the past. She stood up from the bed and paced the long hall of the barbershop like a caged animal. Back and forth and back and forth she strode. "It happened so many years ago and yet I remember it like it was yesterday," she said aloud. She felt lost in a delusion, even more like a hallucination caught between the present and her past.

Frantically, she ran to the front window and looked outside. The rain was on a rant and the trees were swinging back and forth. Looking across to the highway a car was flipped upside-down, caught underneath several trees and power lines. She went away from the blinds. Feeling claustrophobic, she ran to the bathroom and searched around underneath the bottom cabinet of the sink. Finally she found the small bottle of Xanax. "Oh, my God, thank you." She got water and popped two tiny pills in her mouth and swallowed fast. She hadn't had to take those pills in a year.

Pacing the hallway again she thought that weed would have calmed her down but she stopped using that a long time ago, especially because it was not legal. "Why in the hell did I stay in here tonight? I could have driven home," she thought to herself. "The meds are not working!" she told herself as she panicked and paced back and forth. She ran her fingers again and again through her long hair. Again, her memories tried to consume her. "Please help me, Lord, to calm down."

She tried to stop the memories but she knew it was hopeless. Those beautiful innocent children became angels that day years ago. With her arms crossed close across her bosoms she continued to pace. "Why? Why? Why? It's so unfair! Wrong! Wrong!" she shouted out loud.

Reaching her arms straight up to the ceiling toward heaven, she cried. "My arms have been empty without you all these years. We had so much more to share my brother and baby girl. I have lived my life without your love. Oh, my darlings, I should have been home that summer."

With quiet steps, she moved close to the safe on the floor, sat down and entered the combination. The safe door swung open.

Morgan opened it up wide and searched far in the back for a gold envelope. She found it and brought it with her to the bed. Plopping in the bed with the candlelight near, she opened it and took out the newspaper clipping. She read something that she had not looked at in more than thirty years.\

A fire Saturday night in a detached garage destroyed the structure. Two kids and one woman killed in the southern California fire. Firefighters were called in to the location. A water-tender truck was called in because there was no water fire hydrant in the area. The initial cause of the fire was described as a gasoline leak that ignited when vapors reached a propane heater in the small area. After dousing the flames firefighters found the bodies inside. The neighbor across the dirt field heard a huge explosion. He said, "It shook my house. I thought it was an earthquake until I saw the flames. Then I called the police." The victims were local residents. Casey O'Malley, age 12 years old; Emma O'Malley, age 9 years old; and Peggy Wilson, age 21 years old.

After staring at the old fragile paper, she folded it in half again and placed the newspaper clipping back in the envelope and put the envelope back in the safe. Morgan watched the safe door click shut. She shivered now and felt cold as she remembered what Noah described.

"Peggy had been teasing us about a scary homeless man living in that old garage all summer. He had one arm and a black eye patch and one ear. So that night they all crept into the house except for me. I was too scared. Then Peggy must have lit something for light. It all happened quickly. There was a huge ball of fire explosion."

Morgan thought about how hard it had been on Noah. For many years, he felt guilty for being alive. Morgan felt wet tears stream down her cheeks. After all the years, she finally cried the tears that were far back in her mind. "My beautiful brother and baby sister. I miss you."

She hopelessly went back to the bed. Listening to the pouring rain and left with memories, she felt like a captive in a prison. She had no restraint over her memories. She reached over to her purse and took out her blue rosary and quietly prayed on the bed and asked God to help her. For a long time she remained still. The meds began to work. She breathed deeply as she calmed down.

With her eyes closed, she knew it was happening again. She snuggled deep under her comforter and did not fight it; she surrendered and went back in time.

****

She remembered one of the few things about the funeral service held for Casey and Emma was the long procession of automobiles, which seemed endless. Inside the Catholic church, she had stared at the two small white caskets that lay side by side. Emma had a blanket of tiny pink roses on top. Casey had tiny blue roses. Isabel had insisted on the small caskets even though there were few remains inside. Morgan had forced the vision of what was inside the coffins from her mind by praying to the Blessed Mary repeatedly in her mind. Her conversation with God was as if He were her only friend in the world. The prayers had calmed her. It had been such an unusual feeling that came over her in the church that day. It was the first time she felt calmness in the presence of death though unbeknownst to her then it would not be the last.

Isabel wore a black satin and laced veiled funeral hat that covered her face, and Morgan wore a black lace mantilla that fell to her shoulders. Both women wore tailor black dresses and black shoes. "Ave Maria" then "Amazing Grace" played on the pipe organ while the Catholic nuns sang the songs. Morgan remained strong and regal in bereavement as she stood next to Isabel with a tight grasp on her mother's small waist to keep her on her feet. Isabel's weeping grief echoed throughout the massive cathedral. Barney stood between his sons Peter and Noah, his arms cradling both of them.

Morgan remembered more about the following day because the O'Malley family wore the same clothes when they attended the funeral for Peggy Wilson, the babysitter. It was quite understandable by all when the O'Malley family left as soon as her service was over without speaking to anyone.

Morgan pushed forward and stayed busy in the weeks that followed. Senior year in high school would be starting soon. She spent most of her time with Noah. He was a sweet boy but he was much more serene and quiet after the accident. Morgan knew how helpful the psychiatrist had been with him, trying to make him understand that the horrific accident was not his fault.

A month later, Isabel and Morgan sat talking. "Mother, I think we need to put the children's things away," Morgan said quietly and as gently as she could.

"Why should we?" Isabel looked concerned.

"It's just too sad and I feel it's important to pack away their belongings so that when we are all stronger it will all be stored neatly. Then we can look at everything again. I am so sad with all the kids' stuff here knowing they are never coming back! It's tearing me up and I know that it's tearing you apart."

"All right dear, maybe it will be good for all of us to put things away. Can we please leave their coats in our hall closet? I need to be able to smell my children." Morgan hugged her mother.

Right away, she went and brought both Emma and Casey's coats and hung them in the hall closet. Before she closed the door, she smelled the coats and yes, they did smell like the children. With sad eyes, she closed the closet.

Early the next day, Barney took Noah to a baseball game and Morgan and Isabel and Peter began an almost impossible project. Soon after they left the house, Isabel put on her favorite Latin albums performed by Vicky Carr. As soon as Morgan heard the music play she knew how much this music gave her mother joy and today it gave her strength. Peter and Morgan did not understand much Spanish but they both looked at each other and smiled. Peter had said many times, "Music reaches the soul even when you don't understand the language." They all knew how much baby girl Emma loved to hear Mexican music.

Without speaking, they began to meticulously fold and wrap with tissue paper each piece of clothing that belonged to Casey and Emma. They folded underwear, T-shirts, blouses, and school uniforms. There were Halloween costumes and Christmas outfits as well as Easter outfits. Dresses, slacks, and shoes of all kinds were piled neatly in pairs on the bed. On the dresser were stacks of Emma's ponytails, barrettes, and headbands, handkerchiefs, hats, and socks. There were two umbrellas, two raincoats, and two pairs of tall yellow vinyl rain boots. They threw nothing away. Another box included storybooks, puzzles, dolls, one baseball glove, balls, and one bat. Another box had about two hundred photos.

Isabel and Morgan agreed to leave Emma's dresser top alone. They did not touch her hairbrush, Raggedy Ann doll, or hair barrettes. Morgan put her doll Cathy on the dresser also.

They did the same for personal belongings on Casey's dresser. His comb, wallet, and baseball cards were left untouched. No framed pictures were packed or moved.

Isabel was crying softly as she delicately packed up her deceased children's belongings. Morgan was in tears too as she listened as her mother repeated again and again, "My babies are in heaven."

Hours later, they took a break and Isabel cooked quesadillas in warm tortillas with bacon, cheese, and butter. Then Peter brought in the tall ladder, climbed up to the attic door, and pulled it open. He and Morgan climbed into the attic together to move other treasures from the past away to make room. Morgan saw that her strong, handsome brother looked miserable. He shot a fearful, sad glance back to her and they hugged without words.

The two women handed him box after box that were marked with the names Casey O'Malley or Emma O'Malley.

Peter called out from the top of the ladder. "How are we doing ladies?" Morgan stood there with her hands placed on her hips and said, "Peter, I need to get one more thing!" Quickly she hurried into her room and looked at the records that were neatly in their album covers. The record collection reminded her so much of Emma. She had loved the Beach Boys, The Carpenters, Smokey Robinson, Diana Ross and The Beatles. She went and grabbed a box. Gently she passed the fragile records up to Peter in the attic with thoughts of Emma's laughter and how they danced to the music.

Peter was about to come down from the attic when Morgan remembered one last thing. She went into her closet and found the small blue box. All the money was still there when she opened it. Tears flowed down her cheeks like a waterfall when she remembered her sister's final words to her. "I will keep your secret."

"My sister was a remarkable girl," Morgan thought.

The small blue box with the money went into the box with the records. Morgan sealed the top with tape and beautifully wrote the name "Emma O'Malley's music" in cursive writing. Isabel stood behind her, watching the final box go away. The women held on to each other as they both wept hard and shared their grief.

Chapter 17

Three weeks later, school was getting ready to begin and Morgan knew that life would have to go on. Being so devoted to Noah and refusing to leave him meant she had missed some important pre-school meetings at Saint Catherine's high school the week before. Moreover, she had not attended mass in weeks. She was tired of going out in public; people who knew the family tragedy always came up to her to say how sorry they were. The last time she had attended mass was for the children's funeral.

The first day of senior year was mandatory at Saint Catherine's to attend the church service one hour before school began. As usual, Morgan had fasted the usual twelve hours before the service so she could receive the communion host. When she walked toward front of the chapel, she saw her friends Sara and Gina eating a doughnut and drinking sodas in front of the church. She stared at her friends. "I can't believe that you're eating before mass!"

"So what, we're going to communion in an hour," Sara said.

"You're eating now? I'm confused."

"I think you missed the meeting about the church's new rules," Gina said calmly. Then she got closer to Morgan. "I was at the children's funeral with my family but I couldn't get close enough to you to say, I'm so sorry." The girls hugged.

Then Sara put her arms around Morgan's shoulders. "I was there too with my family. We are all so sorry too. My mother is devastated and we are all praying for you and your family."

All three girls had tears trickling down their cheeks. They wrapped their arms around each other and shared a strong group hug.

"Yes, it's bizarre," Morgan said after a moment. "I still feel like the children will be coming home one day." Then she let go of the girls and looked at them. "I really can't talk about them anymore. I hope you girls understand." The girls nodded.

With a serious face, she changed the subject. "Gina, what's going on with the church?"

Gina had a bitter sound in her voice when she spoke. "I guess you haven't heard that our Holy Father the Pope has made some unconventional changes. We don't need to fast twelve hours before communion. Now it's only one hour."

"Remember when we heard the rumor about the mass being changed to English not Latin anymore?" Sara chimed in. "Well, it's here this year. And can you believe confession is changing? We will have general absolution of our sins. This means we don't need to go into the confessional box to confess our sins individually. The priest will give us absolution during mass with the parishioners." Sara's eyes showed no warmth. "My mother said it's happening because there is a shortage of priests."

"Or maybe an experiment?" added Gina.

Morgan was flabbergasted. "How can someone change a tradition?"

"The Pope and the Vatican can do whatever they want," said Sara. "Times are changing, my mother said they changed these laws because the church needs more Catholics. They want to be more modern."

The bell rang and the girls walked together into the chapel. After mass, another bell rang and they went their separate ways to class. Morgan walked into her first-period class. She sat down and in walked another bombshell.

Gone were the Carmelite nuns. A new order of nuns was teaching at the school. The nun who walked into the classroom was dressed in a white blouse and a knee-high, navy-blue skirt that was nothing the traditional nun's habit. Morgan was blown away by the nun's headdress; the custom veil was gone. The short dark-brown hair had nothing covering it. The only thing on her that conveyed that she was a nun was a small cross pinned on her blouse.

Dazed, Morgan did not hear her name called. The nun repeated, "Morgan O'Malley would you please come up to my desk?"

Morgan walked to the front of the classroom and as she looked at the woman's face she was surprised to see that the nun had light pink lipstick on.

"This is your schedule," she said, as she handed Morgan a piece of paper. "You may call me Sister Helen." Uneasily, Morgan answered, "Thank you, Sister Helen."

Morgan barely got through the entire day of school, as every class was the same. There was not one traditional Carmelite nun left in the school. Even the classes were more unstructured. There was a lot more unscheduled time. Students were placed on an honor system which meant they could get the class work done in the class, or they could take the schoolwork home. There were no more deadlines; as long as the work was finished by the end of the semester and all tests were passed, that was all that was required.

The surprises just kept on coming. Students were allowed to wear light lipstick and casual make-up on campus. There were no rules about wearing a t-shirt under the blouses, no more bloomers under the skirts, and it was not a rule to wear white underwear. Another treat for students was Friday was free dress day. The students did not have to wear uniforms.

Morgan felt anxious and uncomfortable without the structure. Up until the death of her brother and sister, her life had been controlled and structured.

Two weeks later, quiet as a mouse, Morgan stood with the small group of girls waiting to be car-pooled. Listening to the girls chatting about the great new changes made her queasy. "How could they be so unconcerned? Have all the years of tradition been pointless and meaningless?" she thought to herself. She felt faint and her stomach began to hurt. She felt so out of place, and for the first time in her life, she questioned her feelings about the church. "How could a mortal sin be changed?"

Morgan thought about her home life. It was depressing. Isabel did not embrace the new changes in the church and in fact, she ignored them. “The changes in the church have come from evil demons that did this for profit.” Isabel continued to be a traditionalist. These days she spent most of her time caring for aging priests and nuns in a private convalescent hospital who were all, like herself, traditional Catholics.

Morgan’s brothers had fallen into busy schedules. They were occupied with lots of activities. Peter was busy with sports and his first year at the local college. He also worked part time at the local market.

Noah had made a life outside of his own home spending hours with the neighbor family down the street who included him in all their family trips. The family had five kids and they went camping and boating almost every weekend. Morgan knew that the family Noah was spending so much time with was a fun, loving family and she knew they loved Noah. The Torres family had come into Noah’s life at a very good time.

Life was not happy for Barney and Isabel. Sadly, Morgan watched Barney withdraw. He had the same sweet smile, and was agreeable, but he went to work and came home and relished in becoming an extremely quiet man.

As months passed, Morgan became very lonely without her sister. There were no more sounds of Emma’s voice. No more sounds of Casey laughing and teasing. The sound of death was a quiet one, she learned. There were times she would go outside and sit on the porch alone and indulge herself in daydreams. She would close her eyes and see herself with Emma running on the beach, jumping in the cold ocean, splashing about, and laughing. Those thoughts that had once given gave her tears now gave her comfort. She was beginning to feel how blessed she was to have had the younger children in her life. Nothing could take away the cherished memories.

To make things worse, her friend Lucy had not returned to Saint Catherine’s for her senior year. Lucy’s grandmother had paid the expensive tuition for Lucy to go to a very prestige boarding school run by traditional Carmelite nuns. Lucy was going to finish her senior year there, then prepare to become a nun.

The day before Lucy left for the private convent they sat down on the green lawn by Isabel's rose garden. Lucy talked to Morgan about Casey and Emma and told her how much she missed them, too.

Suddenly Lucy's face had a mischievous look, "I am going to show you something." She took out a shiny razor blade.

Morgan was surprised. "Where did you get that?"

"I got it from my father's razor."

"What's it for?" Morgan asked.

Lucy smiled. "Just watch," she told her friend. "We are going to become blood sisters."

Morgan watched as Lucy sliced the tip of her own finger. Then, she quickly grabbed Morgan's hand and cut the tip of her finger.

"Oh, that hurts," Morgan cried out. Then the two girls started laughing together. They rubbed their bleeding fingers together.

"There," Lucy said to Morgan. "We will be blood sisters forever. Now there is one more thing that I want to do before I leave for the convent school."

"What's that?" Morgan asked.

Lucy took out two cigarettes and a book of matches and one can of beer out from her jacket pocket. "I took these from my dad; he would die if he knew." The two girls giggled.

"Wow, girl you are sure full of surprises. Come on, let's go walk down the street to the park, no one will see us there." The girls walked hand and hand down the block. When they reached the park, they climbed up to the top of the roof of a building. "No one will see us up here," Morgan promised.

"How did you find this spot?" Lucy wanted to know.

"Emma and I used to climb up here and tell our dreams to each other and just talk about stuff," Morgan said sadly.

The girls had never smoked a cigarette or drank beer, but when they did, they laughed and coughed. Both agreed beer tasted bitter, but they drank every drop. They sat on the rooftop and looked out across the lawns and out to the city.

"I am going to tell you a secret," Lucy said, looking straight into Morgan's eyes.

Morgan laughed. "A secret. What secret? Tell me."

"Well, you know how your brother Peter and I have always been friends."

"Yes," answered Morgan.

"Peter came over to my house last night. He wanted to wish me luck and say good-bye so we went for a walk. We walked over to the little league baseball park and we somehow ended up in the dugout."

"What were you guys doing in the dugout?"

"Hush," Lucy said, as she put her hand over Morgan's mouth. "Let me tell you something, the next thing I knew we started kissing, French kissing."

"You were kissing my brother!" Morgan was surprised.

Lucy nodded. "I felt light-headed, it was wonderful. We kissed for an hour."

Morgan gasped.

"It was never planned. I just couldn't catch my breath it just happened. And I didn't want it to end."

Morgan was stunned. "Did anything else happen?"

Lucy was hesitant, "I, hum, I let him touch my breasts and he was gentle. Then he wanted to go under my sweater but I stopped him and grabbed his wrists. I told him to stop. It was hard for me because it felt so good. He was a gentleman. He stopped. I mean, we both stopped. It was difficult. Then he told me that he loved me."

"Do you still want to be a nun?" Morgan asked in disbelief.

Lucy smiled. "It was lovely to kiss Peter. I have always had a crush on him. I love him, only not enough. My calling to be Carmelite nun is stronger than my feelings for Peter."

"Are you sure?"

Lucy nodded. "Yes, I'm certain and please don't judge me. I know that I was supposed to stay pure."

Morgan took a hold of her friend's hand. "I would never judge you." They smiled to each other and made a promise to take that secret to their graves and to be blood sisters forever.

Emotion dripped from Lucy's soft voice. "Please tell Peter that I will cherish that moment for the rest of my life and tell him not to stay angry with me for leaving. My road is to serve our Lord." Then Lucy whispered into Morgan's ear. "It felt awesome." The girls giggled. Lucy hugged her friend. "Thanks for smoking the cigarette and drinking the beer, now I have a taste of the worldly life."

Morgan looked over to the view of elegant maple trees that overtook almost every diminutive residential yard. In the distance, she could hear the sounds of dogs barking. Casually, her head turned toward Lucy. "Life is mysterious. I think you were born to be a Carmelite nun."

Chapter 18

Soon after Lucy left for the Catholic boarding school a lot of excitement came into Morgan's life. It all began with a young woman who moved into the neighborhood. Tina was energetic, bubbly, and flamboyant. She was a year older than Morgan and in college. She was obsessed about the current trends in make-up and hairstyles. Morgan thought she was silly but Tina made her laugh.

One day Tina begged Morgan, "Please let me fix those bushy eyebrows of yours. I can't stand to look at them another minute."

Morgan was unsure. "I don't know. I'm scared. Do you really know what to do with eyebrows?"

"Yes, I do. Trust me. You're going to look adorable." Tina already had the tools needed on a small tray. There lay one pair of shiny silver tweezers, a tiny pair of eyebrow scissors, and a tiny comb.

"Okay, just do it." Morgan finally gave in. She put her head back on the pillow on the bed and Tina began to pluck away. "Oh, MY GOSH that hurts!" she yelled when Tina pulled the first lash.

Tina ran into her kitchen and came back into the bedroom with a bowl of ice cubes. "Put this on your eyebrows. It's going to numb it." Impatiently, Tina waited a few minutes. "Okay, let's get this done!"

Twenty-five minutes later Tina showed her a small hand mirror and said, "Now isn't this better?"

Morgan looked in the mirror. She couldn't believe the improvement. Her eyebrows were arched and not shaggy. "Now can I do your make-up?" Tina asked.

Morgan frowned. "My mother would not like any of this, but do it. I want to see what I look like with real make-up on."

"Morgan, you have the most beautiful eyes and perfect mouth, you just need to have some more color like the girl on the magazine cover. See, look at her." Tina showed her the magazine then began with a sharp brown pencil lip liner like a pro. She outlined Morgan's lips first, and then she put a cream-colored lipstick on, then shiny lip-gloss over the lipstick. With a pale cream color, she put the eyeshadow on and then added brown eyeshadow to the crease of her eyes. The part of her eye closest to her eyelash she applied with black liquid eyeliner. Steadily she applied the thin strip of white eyelash adhesive to the fake lash and then placed it on top of Morgan's lash. "Now try not to blink your eyes a lot until the eyelash glue dries," she instructed. Next Tina took a black eyeliner pencil and rimmed underneath the bottom lash. She patted liquid make-up carefully on her nose and cheeks with a small white make-up sponge. Then took a thick soft blush brush and dabbed a rosy blush color on the apple of her cheeks. "Now smile." Then she added just another dab of blush.

Begging like a little girl wanting a piece of candy, Tina asked, "Can we *please* do something with your hair?" They both giggled when Morgan nodded her head yes.

Tina took a rattail comb and teased Morgan's hair then attached a shoulder-length fake piece of hair on the top of her head. Then she combed more hair over it.

"Is that a wig?" Morgan asked.

Tina laughed. "No, this is called a hair piece and it makes your hair look full. You are so lucky because we have the same hair color." Tina worked on Morgan's hair a long time. Finally finished, she said, "Close your eyes and hold your breath." She sprayed a lot of hairspray on it. "Open your eyes and go look in the big wall mirror."

Morgan could not believe her eyes. She looked so grown up with the black eyelashes and the big hair.

"You look like a young Elizabeth Taylor. No, you look like

Sophia Loren!" Tina squealed with delight.

Morgan cried out, "You're crazy!" The two girls laughed with delight.

"Gee whiz Morgan; I wish you would go to the college dance with me tonight. It's held on our campus in the auditorium. This rock band impersonates famous bands. They play all kinds of music, rock, pop, and soul. I'm so psyched about it."

"No, I can't," Morgan said.

"Why can't you?" Tina demanded.

"I don't think I should go. I've never been to a dance before and mother expects me to be home soon. And besides that I told you that I was thinking of becoming a nun."

"You have to be kidding me. Are you telling me that you have never been out dancing?" Tina could not believe it. "I don't know a lot about this nun stuff but I'm sure nuns need to have fun too! You need to start chillin' and get your groove on."

"I don't have anything to wear," Morgan said with her eyes cast down.

Tina had a gleam in her eyes. "That is not a problem. We are about the same size, except your boobs are bigger than mine." She giggled, but Morgan blushed.

Tina opened her double-mirrored closet doors, and Morgan could not believe what she saw. There were so many clothes. When Tina opened her dresser drawer, Morgan asked, "Are those all your bras?"

"Yes, why do you ask?" Tina wanted to know.

Truly embarrassed, Morgan whispered, "I only have two white ones, I've never seen such beautiful bras before."

Tina smiled, "Well sugar pie, now you have three bras, pick out any one that you think will fit. By the way, all the bras are push-up bras. Don't ask me to explain what a push-up bra is, just put one on."

"Before I do that, can I use your phone?" Tina handed the white princess phone to Morgan. Isabel answered the telephone after the third ring. "Hello?"

"Mother, is it okay if I go to the movies with Tina? I won't be home late."

"Sure, have a good time," Isabel answered drowsily.

"Mom, are you feeling okay?"

"Yes, honey, I'm fine. Your father and I are watching Lawrence Welk and we just ate our TV dinners. Have a good time." She hung up the phone.

Morgan held the fancy white phone in her hands and felt that Isabel did not care about anything these days. A brave, warm feeling came over her. Looking up to Tina she said, "What am I going to wear to the dance?" Morgan still had her school uniform on.

Tina smiled. "We must find you a hot dress." She disappeared into the closet and came out with a twinkle in her eyes. She held out the dress to Morgan. It was a very short, hot pink umpire dress with a low-cut scoop neckline. The price tag was on and it read $35.

"This dress is so short!" Morgan exclaimed.

"It's an umpire mini dress."

"Oh, I can't possibly wear this out." Morgan looked skeptical. "I would feel naked, it's so short."

Tina thought for a moment then went over to the white small dresser and brought out a package of Beige Beauty mist pantyhose. "Here, put these on. You will feel more covered up."

Morgan took the stockings out of the package and felt them. "I've never seen anything like this, so silky soft. How do you put them on?"

"It's quite simple," Tina smiled. "Sit and put your foot inside and pull them up your legs and all the way up over your panty."

Morgan rustled into the glossy pantyhose. They fit perfectly and so did the little pink dress. Tina handed her a pair of platform shoes and Morgan snuggled her feet inside. "Wow, we are the same shoe size, too!"

Tina hurriedly got dressed in a flowery dress that was almost identical to Morgan's dress, but she wore black pantyhose with black knee-high boots. By the time they left the house, it was already dark.

Chapter 19

While they walked toward the college, Tina talked endlessly, explaining to Morgan how to be hip. "They don't serve booze because it's an 18 and over dance. Be cool if you see some of the dudes sneaking booze in, just look the other way. Make sure you don't take a drink if someone offers it to you because it might be laced with drugs. Okay?"

"Why would anyone put a drug in a soda?" Morgan asked innocently.

"I don't have the time to teach you all crap in the world so just listen to me. No more questions."

"Okay, no more questions. I'm just so happy to be out and dressed up."

As the girls approached club, Morgan pulled on the back of her short dress to make sure it was covering her butt. Feeling the height of her hair, she wondered if the hairpiece was going to stay put. She was nervous as she looked down to her overflowing bosoms. The push-up bra left little to the imagination.

When they got to the auditorium, it was a remarkable sight. There were more than fifty kids their age waiting to get in. The girls were all lined up in one line. There was no one dressed conservatively. Some of them were wearing mini dresses, others longer maxi skirts or hot pants and all the colors of the rainbow were in that line. Morgan had never seen girls dressed up like this; it seemed like anything was in style. Some had a little make-up on with their hair straight; others had gobs of make-up on and big hair. She could feel the energy in the room as soon as they walked through the doors. They walked into a huge room with hardwood floors that glistened.

On the stage, the band consisted of four guys wearing black leather jackets and skinny, tight, leather pants. Their hair was longer than Morgan had ever seen on a man. One person was playing a keyboard. They all had electric instruments. The drum set was impressive with colorful lights flashing and painted in orange and yellow-red.

Everyone in the room appeared cheerful and energetic. The music was blaring from four giant speakers on the small stage. In addition, there were huge speakers placed throughout the room. Lights were flickering on and off in illuminating colors.

Morgan stayed close to Tina as they walked briskly through the large room. Several young women and men called out "Hey Tina, what up?" She watched as Tina said hi to all her friends. Everyone hugged.

Glancing around the love-filled room, Morgan was nicely surprised to see everyone hugging each other. Tina was swinging her hips from side to side and swinging her arms all around. Morgan laughed, thinking Tina looked like a chimpanzee.

At that very moment, a young man with long red hair grabbed Tina's and Morgan's hands at the same time. "Let's dance, babes," he said, smiling from ear to ear. Looking over his shoulder he yelled to his friend, "Come on, I have blazing hot chicks."

The lights in the room were turned down now so it was difficult to see the cute slim guy with dark blond hair walk over; he was grinning and happy too. His hand clasped on to Tina and away they went into the dancing crowd. Morgan yelled to the red-headed guy who was holding her hand, "I don't know how to dance!"

He smiled at her and yelled in her ear. "Just do what I do." He started moving his body around and Morgan copied him. She started laughing. "I am hopeless."

The red-headed guy yelled into her ear again. "Listen to the music, can you hear that bass guitar? Feel the drums. Listen to the keyboard."

She watched him and the other kids bop dance. It was all about bending your knees and moving your body hard and quick. Everyone was doing their own thing and some couples were stepping moves together. Others were dancing, lost in their own heads. The strange, upbeat music filled her head. At first she felt awkward, but in no time, she found herself lost in the sounds of the loud instruments.

Again, the red-headed guy yelled in her ear. "This is the Funky Chicken, it's a crazy dance!" Morgan tried to imitate him with both hands tucked under her armpits to make wings and flap down on the beat while kicking one foot out then back in, and then doing the other foot.

"This sure is not the music I grew up with," she thought. "This is no Lawrence Welk champagne music." She barely restrained herself from laughing out loud but a giggle escaped her lips.

Hours later, the music stopped and the lights flickered off and on.

"What's going on?" Morgan asked Tina.

"They're telling us this is the last dance."

With a grasp of her hand, the red-headed guy pulled Morgan away. "Come with me." He took Morgan through the crowd and they approached the front of the stage. Morgan watched as the band got ready to perform the next song. They sang a song called "I Just Want to Celebrate." The feeling in the room was electrifying. There were chills and goosebumps on Morgan's arms as the crowd cheered and the music was happily intoxicating. The red-headed guy yelled in Morgan's ear. "Can you dig it?"

Just then, the cute blond guy who had been dancing with Tina all night walked up to Morgan and shoved a little piece of paper in her face and a pen. He ordered, "Morgan, give me your phone number."

"Well, I don't usually give out my home telephone number to strangers." She blushed. He persisted, "We aren't strangers. I'm a friend of Tina's. Give me your phone number!" Morgan scribbled her phone number on the backside of the paper. Tina walked up and grabbed Morgan's hand. "Bye bye, guys. I have to get Cinderella home. We are out of here."

The two girls left the dance and hurried home. They were

laughing and talking about how much fun the dance was. Morgan was so happy. "Oh Tina, I had the best time, thanks for taking me. I never knew how much fun I was missing."

Tina smiled. "All right Catholic schoolgirl, you better go inside now," she said as they arrived at Morgan's house.

"What about your clothes?" Morgan asked, tugging at the mini dress.

"The clothes and shoes are yours, kid. My divorced parents buy me so much stuff. I have tons of clothes and they will buy me more. See you tomorrow." Morgan watched Tina disappear down the street in a hurry.

As soon as Morgan stepped inside the house, she felt a twinge of guilt from lying to her parents. With narrow eyes and mischievous look on her face, she took her shoes off and tip-toed past Barney. As usual, he was snoring asleep on his recliner chair.

Softly, she walked down the hall into her bedroom and closed her bedroom door. Quietly she took the platform shoes and hid them and the dress and undergarments in the back of her closet and pulled on her pink cotton nightgown. She snuck into the bathroom to take off the make-up and eyelashes and used her mother's Ponds cold cream to wash the make-up from her face. It was a challenge to get the hairpiece out and it was a job to brush the hairspray and knots out of her wild hair.

As she was coming out of the bathroom, Isabel was coming down the dark hall. "Is that you, Morgan? I did not hear you come in."

Morgan hid the hairpiece behind her back. "Yes, Mother it's me."

"How long have you been in?"

Yawning, Morgan answered, "I've been a sleep for a while Mom, I just woke up to go to the bathroom." She kissed her mother on the cheek, "Go back to bed."

"Okay, honey, sleep well," Isabel replied sleepily. Then Isabel sniffed. "Hum, do I smell hairspray?"

"Tina sprayed some on my hair. Good night."

Chapter 20

A week later on a Saturday, Morgan had just finished a shower when the telephone began to ring. Then it stopped so she ignored it but then it rang again. Annoyed, she wrapped her wet hair in a towel and picked up the receiver. "Hello?"

"Hi, can I talk to Morgan?" It was a male voice.

Morgan answered, "This is her."

"This is Rusty; I met you the other night."

"I don't know anyone named Rusty. How did you get my phone number?"

"You gave it to me on a paper at the college dance. Don't you remember?"

Morgan had to stop for a moment and think. "Oh yes, that's right." She had forgotten that she given out her home telephone number. Thankfully, he had no way of knowing that this was the first time she had given out her number to a guy.

"Tell me where you live," Rusty blurted.

"I'm not allowed to have guys come over to my house."

"Why? I want to come over to see you."

"Rusty," Morgan said, "I don't even remember what you look like it was so dark."

"Well, I am tall, about 6 feet, I have blonde hair and blue eyes, and I'm cute. Can I come over? Please." He had a silly laugh and Morgan started to laugh with him.

"You're funny," she told him.

"No, I'm cute *and* funny. Where do you live?" Rusty was persistent.

Morgan gave him her street address. "You can come over at three today."

"Okay, see you then." They hung up.

A half an hour later, the front door bell rang. She still had her hair wrapped up in a white towel when she opened the front door.

With a very silly laugh the guy said, "Surprise! It's me, Rusty."

Standing at the doorway was the cute, freckled face, red-head with long hair. He was a little plump and most definitely was not six feet tall. He was the fellow who had shown her how to dance and had grabbed her hand and taken her to the front of the stage. Morgan was so shocked and started to giggle.

"You are not the one I gave my phone my phone number to. I wasn't expecting you." She smiled.

"Oh that's okay," Rusty grinned. "I took your number from my friend, he was the handsome blonde guy. Anyways, I'm here now and did you know I only live a couple of blocks away, can you believe that? Is that just too cool, can I come in?"

Morgan unlocked the old screen door. "I guess so. Come on in."

Rusty followed Morgan into the kitchen. Looking around the kitchen, he asked, "What smells so good?"

Morgan smiled. "Chili beans with hamburger meat and bacon, my mother makes them every Saturday morning."

"Boy, does that smell good." Rusty said as he went over to the big steamy black pot sitting on the stove. He stood staring at the pot of beans and smelled the aroma. Morgan looked over at him. "Rusty, are you hungry?"

He licked his lips. "I'm always hungry. My mother never spent much time in our kitchen."

"Well then, today's your lucky day, you are going to eat the best chili beans in the whole world." She went over to the cupboard, took out a big white ceramic bowl, and filled it to the top with the tasty beans. She also gave him white rolls with butter and a tall glass of milk and placed everything on the yellow chrome kitchen table.

Rusty sat on one of the four yellow, round-back vinyl chairs with chrome legs. He glanced around the kitchen and said,

"Wow, your family must like the color yellow." Just then, Noah walked in.

"Rusty this is my brother Noah." She looked at them both. "Pardon me guys while I finish getting ready for the day."

Noah smiled and then he served himself a bowl of the hearty bean soup and sat down at the table. When Morgan walked away, she overheard Rusty say, "Noah, is your sister always so polite?"

Noah answered, "Yes."

Twenty minutes later Morgan walked into the kitchen looking natural with just light pink lipstick on and her black hair combed straight.

"You sure did look different at the dance with all that make-up and hair. Hey how old are you anyway?" Rusty asked.

Laughing, she said, "You thought I was one of the college girls. I'm a senior in high school."

He nodded. "Yeah, you did look older, but I don't care. I like your personality that's all. So don't get any funny ideas that I'm here for any boyfriend stuff. Got it?"

She smiled. He was a sweet guy but definitely not her boyfriend type either. "Got it!"

"Hey, you want to go to a movie?" Rusty asked.

Looking at Noah, she did not know what to say. Finally, Noah said, "Sure she can go to the movies, she never goes out." He took three bucks out of his wallet and gave it to her. "This is my lawn mowing money. You can pay your own way in. And don't worry about mother, I will speak to her."

As Morgan and Rusty walked together through the main entrance of the house, he looked around at the living room and to the right side of the room. There was a beautiful old tall Victorian bookcase that held statues of saints instead of books. Looking at the religious statues, he asked her, "Is your family into religion? Do you worship the statues?"

Morgan explained. "The Bible forbids idol worship. The statues are just a simple reminder of all the holy persons who have sacrificed their lives for their Christian beliefs. It's kind of like keeping photographs in your home to remind you how much you love your family."

She points to one. "This statue was my great-grandmother's. It's the Sacred Heart of Jesus. And this one belonged to my father's grandmothers. This reminds us of Saint Michael the Archangel."

"These are awesome. You can see every detail." He looked at Morgan and smiled. "You are cool. And you have a unique home."

Looking into his eyes, she knew this was not the time to tell her new friend about her family tragedy. She remained quiet.

That day was the beginning a good friendship between Morgan and Rusty. He treated her like a younger sister. They would go to the movies on Saturdays or they would just sit on the porch in front of her house drinking lemonade and talking. He soon learned all about her going to Catholic school about how maybe she was going to become a nun like her friend Lucy.

One day on the porch, he reached over and tousled her long dark hair. "You can't be a nun, you're too pretty, and nuns don't have a figure like you!"

She laughed. "You're so silly; you don't know anything about Catholic nuns."

"Yeah, I do," he said. "They have no sex and they have no freedom. What a drag."

Her eyes became soft and she whispered, "Rusty, the Catholic Carmelite nun's life is a lot more serious than going without sex. They dedicate their entire life to praying for the world and living without worldly possessions. They spend their time giving service to the needy, poor, uneducated, and dying. That is what my friend Lucy will be doing with her life. Lucy had a call from God to follow Jesus Christ more closely. She felt it as a child."

Rusty looked into her eyes. "Wow, that takes a gutsy woman." He took a breath. "Since you have been so upright with me, can I be honest with you and ask you a serious question?"

She nodded.

"Morgan, do you feel you are capable of living that nun life 100 percent?"

Chapter 21

It was early October in the afternoon and Morgan lay stretched across her bed doing homework when she heard a horn honk. She got up and looked out the window. To her surprise, it was Rusty. He saw Morgan from the window and hollered, "Come out here."

As she approached him, she looked closer, "Rusty, where did you get this truck?" The truck was a 1965 Chevy pickup truck painted with flames on the hood. A big American flag was painted on the side of each door. Morgan loved it. "It's so different than anything I've ever seen!" she said as she walked around the truck.

"Yeah, this baby is my new toy. It beats walking. Don't you remember this guy? He is the guy from the dance."

Morgan had been so preoccupied looking at the hot truck that she hadn't even noticed him. With a smile she said, "Yes, of course I remember you. You gave my phone number away."

The guy introduced himself, "Hi Morgan, I'm Johnny. I grew up down the street from Rusty. I used to date Tina. Sorry about that, but Rusty made me do it. He thought you were a lot older." They all laughed. Rusty came close to her back and pulled her ponytail. "Hey, Morgan, do you want us to pick you up after you get out of school?"

She pulled Rusty away from Johnny and from the truck. "I have always been in a car pool. If my mother ever found out she would have a heart attack."

"Oh, come on," Rusty said. "You need to have a little fun in your life. All you do is go to school, do homework, go to church, and watch a movie occasionally. Come on, I promise not to make a scene. Please let us pick you up."

The silence of her seriousness ended with a giggle. Finally, she smiled. "Rusty you're crazy. All right, you need to be there at three o'clock and park by the statue of the three angels." The two guys drove off with the stereo blasting, waving goodbye to Morgan.

The next day at about two-thirty in the afternoon Morgan looked up at the clock and began to get fidgety at her desk. She was nervous about the boys picking her up after school. During lunchtime, she had gone to find Sara. "What you think about me going home with the guys? I usually go home with you and your mom."

"Well, I wish it were me and I wasn't going home with my mother. I will tell my mom that you had to stay late and that you are going home on the bus. No big deal. Don't worry, Morgan, I'll cover for you," Sara had said.

"I hate to lie," Morgan had said as she looked to the ground.

"If it makes you feel any better I am doing the lying not you. Just go and have fun. For goodness' sake, you are a senior!"

Three o'clock came and as planned, Morgan walked to the far back parking lot and waited in front of the statue of the angels. It was not long until she saw the boys coming in the truck. Rusty got out, opened the door, and said, "Nice uniform. What's with the white shoes?" She felt embarrassed but at the same time happy. She hopped in the truck and slid into the middle of the seat between Rusty and Johnny.

"Please," Rusty begged, "can we cruise the school parking lot? We've never been to an all-girls school and there are so many girls. Can't we just check them out?"

She thought a moment. "All right, but don't say anything to anybody."

"I promise, we'll be good, it's all cool." Rusty smiled.

The red truck with the American flags did not exactly get lost in the crowd of the school's parking lot. It stood out like a sore thumb. They received even more attention because Rusty had the newest stereo equipment available installed in the truck. The whole parking lot full of people could hear Jimi Hendrix blaring on the car stereo. The truck with her in the middle seat became the topic of conversation that afternoon.

"Let's go around the parking lot one more time," Rusty pleaded.

"No. Let's get out of here, there's the principal," Morgan pointed. Sure enough, there stood the new principal. She was a nun with a short haircut and no veil. She spotted Morgan like a hawk and wrote her name down on a sheet of paper.

Morgan enjoyed the ride home with the guys. Listening to the stereo in the car was fun. They stopped at The Dairy King for a chocolate-coated waffle cone flooding over with vanilla ice cream. Rusty pulled his truck into Morgan's driveway. He let her out on his side and she stepped out of the truck. The moment Morgan's feet hit the gravel driveway she heard her mom shout, "Morgan, come in this house!"

Morgan was surprised that her mother was home. Embarrassed, she thanked Rusty for the ride. Slowly she walked into her house. Rusty jumped back in to the truck and took off.

The door closed. "Mom, did you really need to yell at me in front of my friends?"

Isabel was angry. "Morgan, you need to understand something. First, it's a good thing that I came home early today, or I would not have been here to answer the telephone call from Saint Catherine, and second, the principal told me that you were in the school parking lot riding around in a truck, creating a disturbance, and that you will be on suspension."

"Mother, there was no scene, the boys just had the radio volume turned up a little, that's all."

"No, Morgan, that's not all." Isabel's eyes were blaring red. "Not only did you leave with those boys, you did not notify the school of the changes. You were supposed to get written permission from me or your father if you are leaving in someone else's car. Morgan, I do not understand your behavior. You have never broken rules. I don't even know my own daughter." Isabel began to cry.

Morgan paced the living room and fidgeted with the button

on her blouse. She turned to Isabel. "Mother, I am seventeen years old, and this was the first time that I have ridden in a car with guys." She continued pacing.

Isabel sat down on the couch. Morgan went to her, sat next to her, and looked directly to her. "Mother, I had fun. They even took me to The Dairy King and we laughed and ate ice creams. There were other teenagers there. Everyone was cheerful and joking, I had fun. That is all it was. You are making too much out of this ride home!"

Isabel stopped crying. She got angry and her face turned red. Standing up, she looked down at her daughter and clasped her hands together. "Well, so you think I am making too much out of this. You are the only living daughter that I have, and you are out joy-riding with a couple of boys. I am going to tell you something, young lady, you are in trouble at school and you are going to be on restriction here at home. You have a vocation to fulfill when you graduate from Saint Catherine. You and Lucy will be together in the convent. Daughter, beginning right now you are not allowed to leave our property, except to go to school, for the next two weeks. Now go to your room!"

Morgan looked at her mother. Never had she heard Isabel raise her voice to her; she walked to her bedroom and closed the door. She faced the window from her bed and looked outside to the back yard garden. Everything looked the same as it had for years yet everything inside had changed.

At that moment she knew how deeply the death of her brother Casey and sister Emma had made an impact on all their lives. It was a harsh reality. Morgan's mind was filled with thoughts of Isabel. How heart-breaking it must have been for her to endure losing two children.

Chapter 22

A few weeks later on a lovely Saturday morning, Morgan was watering the front yard lawn in cut-off blue jeans and her brother's white tee-shirt tied at her waist. Her long hair was neatly combed in a high ponytail. She turned when she heard the loud noise of a horn honking. There was Rusty.

Happily, she turned the water off and ran over to his truck. "Rusty, it's good to see you. I haven't seen you for two weeks."

Rusty looked toward the front door of her house and said, "Tina told me about your restriction. Damn. I didn't mean to get you in this much trouble just for picking you up after school. Is your mom home?"

Morgan smiled. "Mom's not home. There is no need for you to be worried about her. She is a sweetheart; you just don't know her. Are you in a big hurry?" Rusty shook his head no.

"Let's sit in your truck. I need to explain something that I should have told you when we first met."

They sat in the truck in the front seat and Morgan began to explain the accident with Emma and Casey. By the time she finished telling him the tragic story, they were both in tears.

"That's a terrible thing to happen. That's sad for the kids and the babysitter. Now I understand why she's so strict with you."

Morgan nodded.

Rusty grabbed Morgan's wrists. "You need to get out and have some fun. I want you to meet some of my friends, they'll like you."

"Oh, Rusty is that all you ever think about? Fun?" She smiled.

"Yes," he said. "I love to have a good time, and you act like an old woman."

"I will be off restriction on Friday."

"All right then, I'll be here on Friday night to pick you up, and tell your mom that we're going to the movies. Tell her that Tina is going along too. So she will feel comfortable that the three of us are together. I think this time I will pick you and Tina up at her house so we don't make your mama nervous."

"Okay," she smiled warmly at him. "Thanks for being such a good friend." She began to get out of the truck.

"Morgan, you didn't say anything about my new Harley-Davidson tee-shirt. Do you think it's cool?"

Morgan smiled. "Yes, I think it's cool. What does Harley-Davidson mean?"

With a shocked face, Rusty shook his head. "I don't know whether to laugh or smack you on top of the head. It's a damn motorcycle. The best bike in the world."

With a laugh, she shoved his arm. "Okay don't get so excited. Now I know what a Harley-Davidson is."

Rusty had a serious face, then he laughed. "You really don't know much about the world."

Morgan got out of the truck and waved good-bye. After showering, Morgan picked a knee-length skirt with a black and white plaid pattern and white cotton blouse with embroidery lace details. She applied her make-up to look natural and combed her hair into a French twist. Then she slipped her feet into comfortable, black leather, low-heeled sandals. She grabbed her small black leather clutch purse as she left.

She walked to the nearest corner bus stop. While she waited, she hoped that no one recognized her. She was embarrassed to be taking the bus so she stood with her back to the street and her head faced down. Finally, the old city bus stopped in front of her.

She settled into a seat and looked out the window. After a time, it slipped her mind how far her destination was. She looked at her wristwatch; she had been riding the old rattling bus for an hour. At last, the bus drove by the familiar corner. Morgan reached up and pulled the dirty white cord to alert the bus driver of her stop. As soon as the driver heard the buzzer, he pulled to the side of the street at the next bus stop. He pushed a button to open the bus doors. Morgan was already standing up and had begun to make her way up the aisle of the bus to the open doors.

"Thank you sir," she told the bus driver and stepped out.

The big city bus drove away. Morgan's stomach felt queasy as she looked around and began walking. So much had happened since the last time she stayed here. Turning the corner, her attention went to the ivy that blanketed the tall walls. Today, they looked taller than their seven feet. The security rails looked colder than ever. At the front entrance, she pushed the buzzer. The voice on the other end said quietly, "Hello, do you have an appointment?"

"Yes, I do."

"And your name please?"

"Morgan O'Malley."

The black security gates swung open. Morgan smiled as she smelled the scent of the roses. There were more roses in bloom now than when she had been here during those early summer months.

"So much has happened," she thought again as she walked along the narrow dirt paths. She pushed yet another buzzer.

The soft voice said, "What is your name please, and who are you here to visit?"

"I am Morgan O'Malley. I have an appointment to visit Mother Bernadette."

The small iron door opened wide. Morgan walked in. She entered the room and passed a small table that held a beautiful crystal vase full of red, white, and pink roses. Quietly, she followed the unfamiliar nun who ushered her down a long, dimly lit hallway. They reached a door and the nun knocked softly. She opened the door and announced. "Mother, Morgan O'Malley is here."

"You may go in now," the nun stepped aside.

Morgan walked in and over to the beautiful old nun. Respectful, she got on her knees and bowed her head, and kissed the soft hand of the woman who was waiting to see her.

"I am so happy to see you my dear child, it has been much too long."

"Oh Mother," Morgan immediately began to weep, "I have missed you so much."

Mother Bernadette pulled Morgan up from her knees. "Come here and sit with me, child." Mother Bernadette sat on a stiff brown leather chair. Morgan sat facing her on another matching chair.

"My dear child, what is troubling you? Why are you here?" Mother Bernadette asked gently.

Morgan studied the familiar face; her heart was so happy to see her friend. She searched Mother Bernadette's eyes; they were as wise as she remembered. "I missed you so much, Mother. Everything that I knew in the church has changed. Our mass isn't even traditional anymore. All that I learned to know and believe in has changed. My religion was such a comfort for me. I never questioned it. I never questioned the laws or the sacrifices we had to endure. Now the school has changed. There are women teaching us who do not even resemble nuns. It is all so bizarre to me. I was raised to hold the nuns on a superior level. I adored and respected them because of their humility and sacrifice to be traditional unlike the world."

Morgan began to weep. Mother Bernadette handed Morgan some tissues. She took Morgan's soft young hands into her own hands and stroked them so very gently.

"I am going to tell you I did feel the changes coming in the church but I had no warning that I was going to retire. I woke up one day, I was the principal of our dear high school, and then the next day I received a letter from The Vatican. The letter said we shall be replaced with a different order of nuns. We moved from the convent at Saint Catherine's back to our retreat house here. The letter had no explanation. We were told that our teaching order was to retire here for now and we are to spend our days in prayer and nursing."

Morgan looked into the eyes of the Mother in confusion. She could hardly believe what she was hearing. "Oh, I am so sorry.

How could the church do this to you?" Morgan was horribly disappointed and her face blushed with anger.

Both women sat in silence as they held each other's hands. Finally, Morgan broke the silence and whispered, "Mother, I have come to see you because my entire life I have been raised to believe I would become a nun. I don't want to disappoint my mother. It is so confusing."

Morgan talked at length about the tragedy of Casey and Emma. Mother Bernadette listened.

"Why doesn't our Holy Father change the laws so the priest can choose to be married? There are so many rumors about some priests and I know some priests are horribly mean. I'm still so confused about the fasting laws and that the mass is not said in Latin. Was everything I was taught to believe in just a fantasy?" With eyes wide, she looked at the nun. "What should I do?"

Mother Bernadette took a deep breath, looked into Morgan's eyes, and calmly said, "Child, you must remember, we must not blame God for the actions of what the world does. For me, becoming a Carmelite nun was not a decision I struggled with. Without a doubt I wanted to serve God, to serve the church, and serve mankind in love." Mother Bernadette paused. "The church, I am afraid, will someday suffer because they have tried to keep man from going against nature. I dedicate my life to praying for the salvation of souls. Morgan, you are a bright young woman and you have your whole life ahead of you. Perhaps you are not being called to serve our Lord as a sister. Only you can hear that call. Please, you must not be angry with our Lord Jesus Christ for the tragedy of your brother and sister. We have no right to question our Holiness or The Vatican. We must obey."

"But, Mother Bernadette," Morgan tried to speak. The Mother Superior silenced Morgan with her hand. "Go search your heart, my dear, and I will pray for you with all my heart."

A bell began to ring. The Mother Superior stood up and so did Morgan, still holding on to each other's hands.

Mother Bernadette whispered to Morgan, "Live your life to the fullest, go and experience God's great world. Do not do something unless you do it properly with all of your heart, otherwise do not do it. With every season there is change."

Morgan looked back into Mother Bernadette's eyes. "Are you happy, Mother?"

"My child, a person can only gain happiness with a love-filled heart. Therefore, the answer to your question, yes. I am completely happy."

Just at that moment, another bell rang, the door opened, and the same nun stood at the door and beckoned Mother Bernadette. "I must go now. Our time is done." Then she looked into Morgan's eyes and said, "Will you pray for me?"

Morgan nodded and bowed her head to respectfully kiss the Mother's hand. The Mother Superior touched Morgan's cheek and then she turned to leave.

"Mother Bernadette, I love you. I will pray for you."

The lovely 71-year-old Mother Bernadette walked out of the room slowly with her head bowed down.

Outside, walking back toward the front of the convent door, Morgan glanced over to the Carmelite nuns. They stood together in two lines ready to go into chapel in silence. When the nuns began to go inside, she recognized Sister Agatha, the nun she spent time with at the retreat house. Sister Agatha waved and smiled with her same peaceful face.

Morgan waved back and wished she could be as happy as these nuns were. "Could I ever be so content?" she wondered.

She knew that these women had chosen to live in poverty with few belongings. Morgan knew their simple routine. After attending mass in the chapel, they would eat a simple breakfast. After that, they would return to their small bedroom, which resembled a cell, to pray more. The nuns humbled themselves and did all this with a positive attitude.

On the bus ride home, Morgan sat motionless as she gazed out the cold, dirty window. She thought about the visit to the convent as she watched the lines of the road zoom past. As the bus drove into Morgan's neighborhood, she wished that she were somewhere else. Her heart felt so heavy she could barely breathe.

Her mind was buzzing full of uncertainty. She reached her arm up and slowly pulled the cord to notify the driver that she wanted to get off. The bus pulled over to the next stop where an old bench was waiting. The doors of the bus opened and the bus driver waited for someone to get out off his bus. Then anxiously he turned around to look at the few people sitting in their seats. No one moved. The bus driver with the big belly, thick round, eyeglasses, and black thinning hair got agitated and angrily pushed the bus doors closed. He drove back out into traffic. Morgan had slouched down in her seat. She had decided not to get out.

Finally, after thirty minutes she did get off the bus. To clear her mind, she walked the long distance back home. At last, her anger subsided when she came to a barbershop and stopped and peered into the window. The thought of a simple lady barber career strongly played in her thoughts. The white barber coat was so distant from a nun's habit.

Waking past the barbershop, she looked across the street to the public library. "I am so ridiculous I am out of my mind," she scolded herself as she crossed the street and walked inside. As soon as she entered the library, she asked the librarian, "Excuse me do you have any books on the history of barbering?"

The woman looked through a thick catalog and wrote down some number. "There is one book on the subject."

Morgan found the book, sat down, and began to read the first page.

> *"The profession of barbering is one of the oldest of the world. Razors have been found among the relics of the Bronze Age 3500 B.C. Barbering was introduced in Rome in 296 B.C. For more than a thousand years they were known in history as barber-surgeons because they assisted Christian clergy in the practice of surgery and medicine.*
>
> *"It was a custom of the barber-surgeon to use a white-cloth bandage to stop bleeding after surgical operations and do blood-letting and dress wounds. Later they pulled teeth.*

This blood-stained bandage would be hung outside where this practice was performed to dry out. For more than a thousand years, they were known as barber-surgeons.

"This blood-stained bandage became recognized as the emblem of a barber-surgeon profession. Years later, this was replaced by a painted wood pole of red and white stripes.

"The United States pole often appears to have blue in the pole. This barber pole symbol represents red is for blood, blue for venous blood vessels that carry blood throughout the body and up toward the heart, and white depicts the bandage. Others argued it was colored to pay homage to represent the USA national colors."

"Whatever the disagreement, the blue was added. The barber pole is a symbol that is universally recognized as the sign of the barbershop and that a licensed barber is ready to serve."

Morgan sat there and read the entire detailed book that detailed the history of the rise and fall of the barber profession as well as the science and procedures of barbering. The effect it had on her was overpowering. She closed the book and immediately put the book back on the shelf where it belonged. This knowledge was fascinating to her. Dramatically, she vowed to herself, "I will trust no one with the inner desire of my heart."

Chapter 23

Morgan knocked at Tina's front door. The front door opened and Tina looked surprised to see her friend standing there looking sad. "Come on in," she said to Morgan as she held the door open. Morgan went in and told Tina all about the trip to the retreat house. Tina listened as she smoked a cigarette.

"Honey, you need to lighten up. You are carrying the problems of the world on your little back with this Catholic nun thing. You are going to the party with Rusty and me, aren't you?"

Morgan sighed. "Oh, I don't know. I don't know any of your friends."

"Yeah, you do. You know Rusty, he will be there and everyone else is friendly. Trust me, you are going to have a cool time. One thing though, you can't go to a party dressed like a secretary."

"These are the same clothes I wore to visit the Mother Superior."

Tina took a drag from her cigarette and blew the smoke out. "Wow, you are in a bummer mood. We need to fix that right now."

The two girls went into Tina's bedroom to change. Morgan called her mother and said she was going to a double feature movie.

After a while, Rusty pulled up into the driveway, jumped out, ran around to the other side of his truck to open the passenger door. He smiled as the girls walked over and he carefully helped them up into the truck. He stared and grinned at the red hot pants that they were both wearing. He climbed in and put an eight-track into the cassette deck. Smokey Robinson's soulful voice filled the air. Rusty was such a perfectionist he adjusted the balance on the system so the music would sound just perfect. The girls grinned. As Rusty drove away from their neighborhood, he looked over to the girls. "Damn, I'm one lucky guy to have the two foxiest girls in my truck."

"You've got that right," Tina agreed cockily.

Morgan looked at Rusty. "You are sporting a new hairstyle tonight."

Rusty grinned. "Yes, I am. I call it my rockabilly hippy look."

Sitting in the front seat between her two best friends, listening to soulful sounds on the stereo, and watching the light bar attached underneath the cassette player and the dashboard made Morgan happy. Smiling, she touched her hair, for Tina had put another hairpiece in her hair as well as the fake eyelashes.

Rusty shouted across Morgan to the other side of the truck. "Hey Tina, we finally got our girl out of the house for some fun!"

Tina laughed. "Man it's about time, the kid has been depressing me." Tina tickled Morgan and they all began to laugh. Rusty drove for 45 minutes. He pulled the blinker shift down to make a left-hand turn at street sign that said, "Welcome to the city of Pacific Gardens." Rusty pulled into a driveway that was full of parked cars. All the spotless cars were custom painted with custom leather interior. Many were lowered closer to the ground. She saw several Harley-Davidson motorcycles with extended front ends parked side by side on the lawn. Still more custom trucks were parked in the back empty lot.

Although Morgan was prepared to go to this house party, she just assumed the people there would look like the ones at the college dance. She was dead wrong. Her green eyes changed to hazel in surprise. So many handsome guys were just hanging out in front of their cars, smoking and talking. All the guys wore matching royal blue drag racing jackets that had the words "Nite Owl" embroidered on the back.

It was a little overwhelming for Morgan to see these guys who wore dark blue rugged Levi's bell bottoms that fit tightly. She felt a little shy to look at them. Most of them had such muscular bodies. Their hairstyles were combed to a ducktail in the back and blow-dried into a pompadour style on top, kept neat by gobs of hair spray. Rusty wore a hairstyle that looked like no one else's. His was slicked back at the sides and pumped up at the top. He took it to the extreme with the back of his hair worn just above his shoulders.

Rusty helped the girls out of the truck. He took out his comb and looked in to the side chromed mirror to touch up his already perfectly combed red hair. He told the two girls, "Don't forget, if you want a ride home, we leave at 11 o'clock. I don't want Morgan's mom on my ass!"

"Okay," the girls said in unison.

Morgan tugged at the thick white belt that was holding the red, hip-hugger hot pants in place. Tina grabbed Morgan's hand. "Just be cool and enjoy the party. Stop fidgeting." They all started to walk up the paved driveway. Rusty stopped walking and said, "Wait a minute, I forgot something."

They watched him run back to the truck and grab his blue club jacket. He smiled as he took it off the hanger. With great care, he slipped it on. Then he ran back to the girls. "Let's go party!"

Rusty led them to a small house that was behind the big house. The music was loud as they walked through a crowd of young people who ranged in age from 15 to 20. Morgan was walking close to Rusty. She read the logo above his front top pocket jacket. With a sudden feeling of amazement she said, "You never told me that you were the vice president of a club."

He smiled and teased her. "Sweet thing, there's a lot you don't know about me." He patted the bottom of her chin. "Come on, I want you to meet the lady who helped my mother when she had no work. She's a good friend of my family."

They walked through the dimly lit living room through the small crowd and to Morgan's surprise, there sat the prettiest and fattest woman she had ever seen wearing a leopard print shift. Rusty leaned over and kissed the fat woman's rosy cheek. Rusty nudged Morgan over. "This is the lady I was telling you about. This is Tootsie."

Morgan saw that the fat woman's make-up was perfectly applied. She wore heavy black eyeliner and dark blue eye shadow though her blue-green eyes were bloodshot. Her hair color was a bright red shade that perfectly matched her lipstick and nail polish. Her hair was combed into a very high beehive and looked like it hadn't been washed for days.

"This must be Morgan O'Malley, the Irish Catholic girl who wants to be a nun, come here so I can get a real good look at you. Well, you sure are a looker!" Tootsie's words were slurred.

Morgan put out her hand. "Hello."

Tootsie grabbed hold of her hand and smiled. "Well the little lady has manners! Now that is real nice. Don't be bashful when you are in my house. Lots of drinks are in the fridge." Tootsie picked up a basket of Kentucky Fried Chicken. She took out a big piece and begun to busily chomp down.

She gave Morgan a hard pat on her bottom and began cackling loudly. "Rusty, get your ass moving. Go serve our new chick a cup of strawberry wine and damn it, dance with her!"

Rusty opened up the big white refrigerator; it was full of cheap wine in different flavors. There were bottles of Ripple Red and Boone's Farm Strawberry Hill. Rusty poured Morgan a cup of wine and she took a sip from the paper cup.

"Do you like it?" he asked.

"This tastes like Kool-Aid."

Music was blaring from speakers in the back yard. "What is that sound?" she asked as she peeked through the window into the backyard.

"Santana."

Morgan smiled. "I know this music; it has had a Latin salsa beat. I'm half-Mexican and I love it."

"You're right, Santana is mixed with salsa, rock and blues, and African rhythms. This is their third album. 'Santana 111.' If you like it so much you can have my album. Come on, let's cruise out to the back and see what's up."

In the enormous backyard, there were cheap old Christmas lights that lit up the trees. Several large black stereo speakers were set up by the driveway. A guy stood there with a multi-colored scarf wrapped around his head with long, wavy hair lying on his shoulders. His shirt looked like a woman's blouse and he had a big turquoise moon pendent necklace on. He was in charge of playing the music.

There were stacks of eight-tracks on a fold-out square table. Next to the boom box player was a young woman with blond hair wearing a thin purple headband across her forehead. She stood relaxed and looked free from care.

Surprised at the dress the girl wore, Morgan could not stop staring at it. It was covered in a groovy paisley pattern that had light pink, red, yellow, and white. Her tights were pink, and glossy white vinyl boots reached to her knees. She was handing the man in the scarf the eight-tracks.

"Who are they?" Morgan asked, pointing.

"A couple of hippies," Rusty answered.

Morgan was absorbed in the occasion. Four large trashcans were full of ice and beer. There were teenagers dancing, some alone, some together, all were doing their own thing, no one was dancing as a couple. There were more young people sitting in folding chairs on the lawn placed in a circle. They were joking, drinking beer, and having a good time. Nearby a small group of girls were standing together smoking and laughing.

Tina waved to Morgan, and told the other girls standing with her, "There she is! There's my friend. Come over here, Morgan."

Rusty stayed at the table looking at the eight-tracks. Morgan walked over to the girls and immediately smelled an unusual scent.

"What is that smell?" she asked.

A tall handsome guy with nearly white hair answered. "It's weed."

Morgan turned around and looked at him. He was wearing the familiar blue jacket. His jacket said, "Damien President."

Tina introduced them. "Damien, this is my friend Morgan. She grew up in the same neighborhood as you and Rusty."

"It's nice to meet you, Damien." Morgan said. He checked

her out first then he offered her the joint. Morgan declined. “No, thank you, Damien, I don’t smoke cigarettes.”

Damien looked at Tina. “Is she for real?”

Tina nodded.

Damien said, “This is weed, you know, marijuana.” He held the thin joint up to Morgan’s face.

“I don’t care what it is. I don’t want any,” she said, beginning to feel uncomfortable.

The other girls standing beside Tina started to snicker at Morgan. Damien said, “You don’t know what you’re missing sweetheart.”

Innocently, she smiled. “I would like to have another cup of strawberry wine, though.”

Tina started laughing and hugged Morgan. “So you dig the wine! That is totally groovy.”

Damien smiled back at Morgan. “Come on, let’s go into the house and chill with Tootsie and get you some wine.”

With a firm grip, Damien held onto Morgan’s hand. Despite the packed crowd they made their way into the house. He led her into the kitchen and filled her cup up to the rim.

“You better be careful, this strawberry wine has a kick to it,” he warned.

“I like it!” she said cheerfully.

Damien laughed. “Okay, whatever. So, how long have you known Rusty? If we live in the same neighborhood, why haven’t we met? And how do you know Tina?”

She licked her lips from the drops of wine. The wine took the pressure off. “I’ve lived in the neighborhood all my life. I have gone to Catholic grammar school and now I go to an all-girls Catholic high school. I live on the street where Tina moved into two months ago. I met Rusty when Tina took me to her college dance. Rusty is a good friend. And no, I didn’t know what weed is, but now I do.”

With one hand on her hip, she looked directly into his eyes with a smug smile on her face. “Is the interrogation finished?”

Damien moved closer to her. “It’s my job to know who comes

to our house. I don't trust outsiders. I do not trust cops. But you must be okay, or Rusty wouldn't have brought you." Then Damien's face went from serious to a smile. "You talk smart. I like that."

Damien sat Morgan right next to him in the front room on the couch opposite Tootsie.

Morgan began to feel lightheaded due to the influence of the wine. She leaned into Damien's shoulder. Tootsie had begun telling the people in the smoke-filled room funny stories about when she was a teenager and everyone was laughing. Morgan casually looked around the room.

Her eyes focused on a guy who was asleep on the floor in the corner. His sandy blond hair was perfectly combed into a pompadour and the back was a detailed ducktail; his head was faced down so she could not see his face. Beefy, muscular arms were folded across his chest.

She pointed. "Damien, who is he?"

Damien laughed. "That guy is another one of Rusty's friends; he collects people like most people collect pets. Rusty was on his way home from the Colorado River in Arizona when this dude was hitchhiking. His bike broke down. Rusty dragged him over here to party with us a year ago. He rides one of the Harleys outside."

"Why is he asleep?" Morgan asked.

Damien whispered in her ear. "He drinks too much booze, smokes too much weed, and he does other stuff."

Suddenly someone yelled through the doorway. "Damien, you need to get out here now. There's a fight!" Damien jumped up. "Stay here," he said to Morgan. All the people in the house ran outside to see what was happening. Morgan stayed put. She was left inside the room alone with Tootsie and the person passed out on the floor.

Then the guy woke up. He stood up and stumbled over to Morgan. He fell on the couch and passed out again, this time with his head on Morgan's lap.

Morgan did not move.

Tootsie found it amusing and began laughing. Then Morgan tried to budge him. Finally, she got his head out of her lap and she moved away from him and stood up.

He turned his face toward her. She gasped. "Oh, my God, I think I know you."

Tootsie yelped. "You do?"

As soon as Morgan recognized his face, she crouched down in front of the couch. She took his chin in her hand and looked at him again. He was the person from the bakery. He was the person who she had spilled the coffee on that morning. Morgan's heart pounded hard as she looked at him. She could not believe it was him.

He was much more handsome than she remembered. His stubble face was badly in need of a shave. Morgan tried to sit him up; it was impossible to move him he was so heavy.

"Tootsie, what's his name?"

Tootsie yelled out; "His name is O.D."

"Tell me why he isn't waking up?"

Tootsie laughed loudly again. "Pills, weed, and Jack Daniels. He likes popping little red pills."

Morgan said, "I don't understand why he takes pills? Is he sick?"

Tootsie began to laugh even louder. "Honey," she said, "what planet have you been living on? He takes pills to get high! O.D. is his nickname for overdose."

Just then, the crowd began to come back into the house. The music began to play loudly again and Rusty found Morgan. "Come on." He took her hand. "Let's dance."

Morgan followed Rusty into the kitchen and he poured her another cup of wine. Other people were dancing in the cluttered kitchen. Rusty and Morgan danced along to the sounds of Marvin Gaye, Smokey Robinson, and Santana.

When they finally stopped dancing, Morgan was drenched with perspiration and Rusty's shirt was soaked with sweat. "Morgan, you wait here while I go find Tina. It's time to leave." Rusty dashed out the door.

Morgan was exhausted from dancing and drunk from the wine. She stood alone in a daze for a moment then her thoughts went back to him. She walked back into the front room and stood in front of him. He was stretching out his arms and waking up.

O.D. opened up his blue, bloodshot eyes and the first thing that he saw was Morgan's face. He rubbed his eyes and shook his head, wiped his mouth, and looked again. "Hey, I know you?"

Morgan did not have a chance to answer. The opportunity went by when a tall blonde girl jumped on his lap, began to put her hands underneath his tee-shirt, and started rubbing on his chest.

Morgan's heart sank low as she looked away. She was so relieved to see Tina and Rusty. "Party's over," Rusty said. Arm-in-arm the three of them left together out the front door.

On the ride home, Tina asked Morgan, "Did you have a good time?"

Morgan smiled. "I had so much fun. Thanks for inviting me, you guys."

"I saw you looking at my sleeping beauty friend," Rusty sniggered.

"No, I wasn't."

"Yes, you were," he teased her. "And you sure did enjoy the wine."

They all laughed. Morgan felt light-headed and in high spirits. Rusty stopped the truck in front of Morgan's house.

Morgan got out and Rusty looked at his watch. "Wow, we made it just in time. Your mom won't be upset." Then he said, "Do you want to meet that dude?"

Morgan shook her head no. She started to walk away, and shyly she turned back, "What's his name?"

Rusty laughed quietly. "Dean O'Donnell."

Chapter 24

Morgan sat cross-legged on her brother's bed and watched as he folded the last pieces of clothing and placed them carefully into his gray suitcase.

"Well, it looks like I'm all packed," Peter said.

Isabel came into the bedroom and handed Peter a very full brown paper bag. She held a white lace handkerchief to her face to wipe away tears. "Son, I packed you your favorites, meat loaf sandwiches and blueberry muffins. Here is a thermos of apple juice."

Peter took Isabel in his arms and held her for a moment. "Mother, stop crying please. I want you to be happy for me. Thanks for all the food." She left the room in tears.

"Is this really what you want to do?" Morgan asked.

"Without a doubt," he answered cheerfully. "I'm excited, Morgan. Just imagine me in Ireland."

"Oh, brother, but you never even met these people."

"It's going to be a blast. I am going to college in another country. These people are father's family." His grin was wide.

Morgan looked disturbed. "Oh, I wish you never got into that exchange program. You are going to be so far away."

Peter sat on his bed facing his sister and took a hold of her hands. "The grim fact is that I am dying here in this house. I can't breathe and I will not live my life here any longer. I just can't take mom and dad being so sad all the time."

She put her head down and then looked up into her brother's eyes. "Is this about Lucy?"

His eyes faced downward. "How did you know about me and Lucy?"

"She told me. She told me everything."

"Then you know that I was her experiment before she went into the convent school."

"No, you were not her test." Morgan stood up. "She told me to tell you how she felt. Lucy had tears in her eyes when she said to tell you that she cherished that moment with you. And she said to tell you not to stay angry with her, because her road in life is to serve the Lord."

Peter's face softened and he looked grateful. "Thank you for telling me."

"Are you in love with Lucy?"

"Very much so," he answered sadly.

"I thought you were. You are a good brother, Peter. You will find a new girl and have children. I know that you love this town too much not to come back. But I understand you need to get away."

Peter kissed his younger sister on the top of her head. "I'm going to miss you most of all." They hugged.

Morgan helped her brother carry his food while he carried his suitcase to the car. Peter looked so handsome in his new double-breasted gray suit. Barney looked sad as he waited behind the wheel to drive his son to the airport.

Noah hugged his brother. "I wish I was going to Ireland with you brother."

Peter smiled. "Your turn will come, Noah."

From the front porch, they waved their goodbyes to Peter. Isabel stood in between Morgan and Noah. The three of them held on to each other as Isabel cried out, "Please do not leave my son, my son!" Tears gushed down from all their cheeks.

Chapter 25

A few days later, Morgan wanted to surprise her mother by having the house cleaned for her. Isabel had started working on Saturdays, so now Isabel and Barney never spent much time at home. Noah was away again camping with the family down the street. She wore the same worn-out, cut-off blue jeans, and an over-sized white shirt that was tied at the waist. As usual, her hair was pulled into a high ponytail. The only make-up she wore was a little bit of pink lip gloss.

She placed a record by The Osmonds on the record player. Morgan kept herself busy cleaning, vacuuming and polishing the furniture. It always helped her forget the loneliness she felt without Peter and Lucy around.

There was a sound of loud motorcycles from the street and then there was a knock at the front door, followed by more brash knocks. She went and opened the door. It was Rusty, and Dean was with him. Both guys wore sleeveless denim jackets with white tee-shirts and tight Levis, with black bandannas tied across their foreheads.

Morgan was shocked to see both of them there on her porch. "What are you guys doing here?"

Rusty laughed and asked with his sheepish little grin. "We missed you. Can we come in?"

She held the door open for them. "Come in." She was so relieved that she had cleaned up the front room.

Rusty sat on the couch. Dean sank down into Barney's comfortable old chair and he crossed one leg over his knee. Morgan did not make eye contact with Dean at all; instead she talked directly to Rusty. "You are full of surprises. Now you own a motorcycle?"

He laughed. "There's a lot you don't know about me," he teased.

She smiled. "Yes, I'm beginning to find that out."

Rusty and Morgan talked about the party and about what a character Tootsie was. Then Rusty told Morgan what happened when he took Tina home that night.

"That bitch slapped me because I wouldn't come into her house and screw her. She was all over me like a cat in heat. I told her NO and that is when she smacked me. I wasn't about to be one of her boy toys."

Morgan was clearly upset. "I can't believe that she acted like that!"

In a casual way, Dean said, "Tina probably doesn't want you to know what kind of girl she is. It's no secret – she's a slut."

Morgan glared at Dean. "How can you be so sure? Why would you say that?"

"Believe me," he answered. "I know that airhead's reputation very well. She's screwed three of my friends. Johnny dumped her when he caught her screwing around. Besides, why are you so uptight about it? You need to get real."

Morgan sat there in silence. She was trying to digest all that she just heard.

Dean got up from the chair and looked over at Morgan, then he looked away. "I'm going outside for a smoke."

Rusty stood up. "Hey look, we didn't come here to get you upset. I think it was a good thing you found out about Tina. She's got a bad reputation."

Morgan was quiet. Then she said, "Okay."

Her first impulse was to shut the front door and not to talk to the guys anymore but instead she walked to the edge of the door and stood there.

Dean threw his cigarette down and stomped on it and she saw that his face was mad. The two guys whispered to each other.

"What are you two talking about?" she asked.

Rusty got on his bike and started the engine up. "I'll be back in a few minutes." He took off down the road.

Dean looked at Morgan, was quiet for a second, then he finally blurted out, "Hey I didn't come all the way over here to talk about Tina. I came here…" He stopped in the middle of the sentence. He tried again. "Morgan, do you what to do something with me, you know, go out?" He smiled and took a deep breath. "Would you like to go on a date with me to the movies?"

She was stunned. "A date," she thought. "Did he just ask me out? I don't even know him."

With a deep breath, she said, "All right, I will go out with you. Can you please pick me up in a car? I don't ride on motorcycles and you need to meet my mother before we go out."

She turned to go into her house and then she turned back. "One more thing, you need to shave because my mother is strict."

"Rusty clued me in on your mom; I need your phone number."

She hurried into the house and wrote her number on a small piece of notepaper with her name. Then went outside and handed it to him. He was sitting on his motorcycle with the engine on.

Rusty pulled up when Dean took the paper. He smiled. "You got her phone number. Cool."

Quietly she stood there and waved good-bye as they sped away. She walked back into the house, shut the front door, and leaned against it. She clutched her chest and fell against the back of the front door. "Did this just happen? Did Dean ask me out? And I really said yes!" She screamed in delight. "My very first real date and it's with the guy from the doughnut shop!"

She sat on the couch, remembering Emma. Tears welled up in her eyes. "I wish my sister were here to share this moment with me." Then she thought about her mother. "Isabel will just have to understand that I have a date with Dean O'Donnell." She hugged the crochet sofa pillow.

Chapter 26

Patiently Morgan waited for Dean to call. Finally he did, after two long days. Attentively she listened to his every word. He spoke softly, "So are you excited to go out with me?"

"You're very sure of yourself," she told him.

He laughed. "Yeah, you really like me, don't you?"

"Just a little bit," she teased. After a little more light conversation, they agreed on what time and day they would go out.

Saturday night, Isabel sat in the living room and watched her daughter come into the room. "Mother, how does this look? Do you like this black skirt?"

Isabel said, "Yes that's fine."

Morgan was unhappy. "No, I don't like the skirt, I should be more casual, I'll be right back, I'm going to change into slacks." Just as she left the room to change, the doorbell rang. Quickly, she opened the door. Dean stood there with a devilish smile; he was freshly shaved, and he had a short-sleeved, starched, buttoned-up blue sport shirt on that matched the color of his eyes. She noticed he had gotten a haircut. His sandy blond hair was combed perfectly back in a pompadour except for a strand of hair facing forward. His sideburns were perfectly shaped to the bottom of his ear. He was wearing brand new tight creased Levi's. He looked like the movie star James Dean.

When Morgan smiled, both of her cheek dimples showed, and she locked eyes with Dean. They stood there staring at each other. Isabel watched the two then finally got up and walked over to them.

She extended her hand to Dean. "My name is Isabel O'Malley.

It's nice to meet you."

He took her hand and shook it softly. "It's a pleasure to meet you, too," he smiled with white teeth beaming. "Well, I can see where Morgan has gotten her good looks from."

Isabel blushed. Then with a stern, pitched voice she said, "Dean, I want my daughter home by 11 o'clock. Sharp. Do we understand each other?"

He smiled and nodded curtly. "No problem, Mrs. O'Malley, your daughter won't be late. It's been a pleasure meeting you."

Isabel grabbed her daughter's white sweater and handed it to her, "Here don't forget this, you'll need it later." She kissed her daughter on the cheek and whispered, "Be home on time."

They walked outside to a blue 1966 Chevy truck.

"This is as close to a car as I have," he told her as he opened the truck door for her. Morgan went to get into the truck and Dean pushed her up. "You're short."

"No, I'm not. I'm five foot five."

Morgan got into the truck and waved good-bye to her mother who was standing on the front porch. Dean immediately turned on the radio to a rock 'n' roll station. He pulled out a cigarette and offered her one. "No thanks, I don't smoke," Morgan answered cheerfully.

He looked at her closely as he lit his cigarette; she wore a light pink, cotton, sleeveless blouse and a black skirt, with a touch of pink lipstick. Her smoky eye make-up was carefully applied and she wore her long black hair down with spiraling curls.

"Tell me something. At the party house, you looked like a low-rider hair chick. Now you look like a 1940s chick with your style. What's the story, what group are you in?"

She thought about his question. "Well I like vintage hairstyles that look natural. But then when Tina came into my life, she got me hooked on trying different clothes and hairstyles. I don't have any particular group. How about you, what 'group' are you in?"

"I'm a low rider slash biker. I live to ride my bike and I love low rider cars."

When they pulled into the drive-in parking lot, Morgan

was concerned. "Where are we? I thought we were going to the movies?"

He looked at her. "Haven't you ever been to a drive-in movie before?"

"No."

"We watch the movies from our car, in a big parking lot. With a giant screen, it's cool."

"Really? An outside movie?"

"Have you ever seen the flick 'Love Story'? It's been out since 1970."

"No. But I do remember girlfriends talking about the movie in my sophomore year."

"They show the old flicks here."

Slowly he drove the truck into the lane for that movie. They waited in a line behind other cars. Finally, it was their turn to pay the attendant who waited in a small room with a cash register. They pulled up to the drive by window and he handed the attendant one dollar.

"What about our snacks?" she asked.

"Yeah, there's building here with a snack bar." He smiled. "It's called a concession stand."

It took him three attempts to find the perfect parking space. Morgan watched as he rolled down the front window of the truck halfway and then he hung the speakers on his side. "Come on; let's go to the snack bar."

They walked to the concession stand and he held her hand tight. "What do you want to munch on?"

"Everything," she laughed, "I'm starving." She grabbed a bag of popcorn and a hot dog, and a large Pepsi, and a Hershey's chocolate bar. He did the same. They both put lots of mustard on their dogs.

They walked back to the truck. The movie started and Morgan started munching down her snacks. She loved seeing the movie on the big screen and she told him that it was so fun to be in the truck. They both were enjoying the movie though it was romantic and tragic. Tears began to flow down Morgan's cheeks and she cried into her hands near the end.

Dean looked at Morgan, and without any warning, he moved Morgan's hands away from her face and then he leaned over and softly kissed her. Then he kissed her again.

She sat still without moving a muscle. It was so unexpected. The five-second kisses took her breath away. Dean leaned closer to her and he took her face in his hands and tenderly wiped her tears away. Then he took his finger and traced her lips. He whispered in her ear, "Do you know how to French kiss?"

She shook her head no.

"Do you want me to teach you?" he asked her quietly.

Bashfully, she nodded.

Awkwardly, she turned her head and accidentally bumped his forehead. They both giggled and it made her feel more relaxed when he she heard him laugh.

"Close your eyes and put your head back," he whispered.

Gently he kissed her closed lips playfully then he put his full mouth on hers and with his tongue, he prodded her mouth to open. She moved back, he moved forward, and lightly his tongue went inside her mouth to explore. She tried to hold herself back from the pleasure she was receiving. Feeling out of breath she took her mouth away from him. Seconds later, they found each other's mouths again. Finally, she broke away.

At that moment, his strong hands lightly stroked her neck, shoulders, and arms. He closed his mouth and devoured her eagerly, his soft lips kissing all over her ears and neck. She got lost in the moment and did not resist. By the time Dean pulled away from Morgan, she could barely breathe. Her heart was beating fast. Embarrassed of her actions, she looked away from his eyes. Then she noticed that the windows of the automobile were steamed. Her hand touched the window.

Quivering, she asked him, "How long were we kissing?"

"Not long enough, but we need to stop now. Let's get out of here and go for a walk." He bolted out of the truck and immediately lit up a cigarette.

They walked down the isle of the parking lot. "Did I do

something wrong?" she asked shyly as she looked up to his flushed face.

"Don't get so excited sweetheart, you did nothing wrong. You are a very good kisser." The two of them walked up to the restrooms in silence.

Morgan waited patiently for Dean to come out of the bathroom. When he did, she saw that his hair was wet and slicked back.

"You okay?" she asked.

"I'm fine. Just hot, that's all."

They walked back to the truck hand in hand without a word. They got into the truck. Without looking at her, he said, "It's time for you to go home."

Dean drove Morgan home in silence. The only sound came from the music playing on the radio. Morgan watched the road. The truck turned the corner to her street. Dean parked the truck a few houses down from hers. He kept the engine running, and then he turned off the headlights.

He leaned over and this time he kissed her harder, and she kissed him back. "I really like you," he said. She breathlessly whispered, "I like you too."

He turned the truck engine off and got out. He went around to her side and opened the door for her. Slowly, they walked down the street to her house, very close with his arm around her shoulder. Dean looked at his watch, "We're just in time." They kissed again, this time a very quick, sweet, soft kiss.

"Good night," he whispered in her ear, "I'll call you tomorrow."

"I'll be waiting," she answered, breathless.

The door opened wide and the porch light came on.

He chuckled. "Looks like your mother is waiting up."

Morgan teased. "Of course she's waiting up, she's worried about you!"

Chapter 27

Three months after Morgan's first date with Dean, she was having a difficult day at school. It was a struggle to concentrate on schoolwork. Her mind continued to drift to thoughts of him. Before Dean, she was able to sail through her classes effortlessly. Now she was no longer an A student but a consistent C and sadly very close to D in science class, which used to be her favorite class.

She doodled Dean's name on her notebooks in all her classes. By early December, they were going steady. She was devoted to him.

Once a month it was Morgan's turn to dust Saint Catherine's chapel. After she wiped the saints' statues down she knelt down in front of the cross at the altar to pray. "Lord, please help me to slow this relationship down. I realize I am not going to be a nun. Please help me to find myself. Please Father God, help me to settle down and study. Amen."

She began to stand up then went back down on her knees. She remembered about her friend Tina. There were rumors of Tina having an abortion and then leaving town with a military man. "Dear God, bless Tina in her life. Amen." On the way out from the chapel she dipped her right hand into the holy water basin and blessed herself with the sign of the cross.

She walked home slowly. She heard the phone ring the moment she walked up the porch steps of her house. Tired, she collapsed on the nearest chair in the living room and ignored the phone. A few minutes later, the phone began to ring again. After six rings, she got up to answer the black receiver.

"Hello?" she said.

Dean's voice was stern. "Hello, my ass! Girl, where have you been? I have been calling for over an hour."

"I stayed after school today," she said calmly. "It was my turn to clean the chapel."

"Damn it," he said. "You need to call me from school when you are going to be late. I need to know where you are at all times. And I need to buy you a car."

"And where are you going to get that kind of money?"

"I will get another job. Baby, I have big dreams for us, you and I are going to travel. We are going to visit all the campgrounds in all the national parks in the whole United States. I'm going to take you places you never even dreamed of."

"I've missed you all day," she said, giggling.

"Yeah?" Dean said. "I have a big surprise for you tonight."

"What is it?"

"Now I told you it's a surprise. I want you to dress special and dress warmly," he cautioned her. "It's going to be a cold night."

"Dean, I don't think I can go out with you tonight. I need to study for a science exam. I'm struggling with these courses and I can't fail."

"There will time for you to study after tonight. I will pick you up at 7:30. Be ready," he commanded. He didn't wait for her to answer and hung up the phone.

Later that evening, Morgan closed her books and put away her study notes. She put the top back on her yellow fluorescent marker and pushed the pile away. "There is so much more to memorize," she scolded herself.

Obeying Dean's instructions, she stood up to get ready for "the surprise." She slipped on a cream-colored turtleneck over her head and pulled on a pair of white bell-bottoms. In the closet, she found three-inch platform shoes that were in the back of her closet and put those on. She paid extra attention to her hair, putting the fluffy black hairpiece in and back-combing it to make it look very full. It took her twenty minutes to put on her eye make-up and glue on the fake eyelashes but this time she decided not to use eyeliner.

Morgan went to the small hall closet and grabbed her black and white wool coat. Never before had she looked at it the way she did tonight; it looked worn and shabby. Running her hand across the tailored collar she felt the black and silver buttons that ran down the front of the worn coat. Just then, the doorbell rang. She threw the coat on as she ran to open the front door.

Dean stood there in a shiny black, soft lambskin bomber jacket and perfectly creased Levi's. Morgan felt self-conscious in her tweed coat. He hugged and teased her, "Where did you get that coat, from the Salvation Army?" then immediately saw that she was embarrassed. He hugged her tighter, "Baby, I'm only teasing, come on we are going to be late."

An hour later, they drove into a lovely, upper-class neighborhood. It looked like a street from out of a country magazine. Thick, overflowing oak trees lined both sides of the street. It was so unlike the small, simple suburban neighborhood she lived in. These large homes were nestled sweetly on large green acre lots. Dean stopped and parked the truck in front of a massive green and white country style house.

"We're here," Dean told Morgan with a grin. "This is my parents' house."

Morgan was stunned. "You want me to meet your parents? This is your home?

Dean grinned. "Yeah, this is the pad. And consider yourself special because I have never brought a girl home to meet my folks. This is your surprise."

Dean's house had towering red and yellow roses that lined the entire length of the long, cement driveway. The tall driveway gates that lined the front perimeter of the surrounding property had beautiful outdoor lanterns that glowed like starlight to lead the path. Morgan had not expected to see that Dean lived in a neighborhood like this. When they got out of the truck, she immediately smelled smoke. She smiled. "Your house has a fireplace."

When Morgan walked nearer to the driveway, she saw the delicate white Priscilla curtains that adorned the front bay window. The charming house was lit up and looked inviting.

Before they walked up to the house, Dean took both of Morgan's hands and pulled her toward him. She put her arms around the waist of his soft jacket. He bent down and kissed her tenderly on her forehead, the tip of her nose, and then her mouth. "I want my parents to meet you," he whispered.

Chapter 28

Morgan and Dean walked the long driveway with clasped hands. "First, I want you to see this," he said.

Dean walked over to the three-car garage door and pulled opened one of the heavy doors. With the flip of a switch, the whole garage lit up. She stood there speechless when she saw the inside. There was so much biker gear and equipment. Laid in separate piles were motorcycle parts, all kinds of metal scraps, and tools. In the middle of this disarray was an astounding sight. It was a Harley-Davidson motorcycle engine and an extended front end that was completely unassembled, a motorcycle skeleton body, and three tires, one small, and the other two thick and huge.

There was an overstuffed, black leather, high-back seat sitting off to the side. In one corner of the garage, carpet pieces were piled high. Chrome parts for the motorcycle were stacked in another corner. Dean let Morgan take it all in.

"I'm building my own bike; it will be the hottest trike on the street," he finally said proudly.

"I can see that," she quietly said. "Do you know how to put this all together?"

He smiled. "You bet I do."

A woman's voice yelled from the house. "Dean, is that you out there?"

He went to the edge of the garage door and yelled back. "Yeah it's me, mom, we'll be right in." Morgan began to walk out of the garage and stumbled over some of the parts. Dean caught her as she began to fall. "Honey, you need to watch your step. Let's get out of here."

They left the garage and Dean pulled the door down. They

ventured around the home past more gardens of flowers and went through the sliding glass doors and into a huge family room with massive vaulted ceilings. One section of the room had four over-stuffed blue cozy chairs. Beside each chair was a beautiful pine wood accent table; each table boasted a delicate Tiffany-style lamp. Each one of these small tables had a fragile china dish full of candy. On one of these cozy chairs sat a red elm wood basket that overflowed with balls of rolled yarn and knitting needles. A lush gray and pink wool knit blanket was draped over the arm of another chair.

Facing the Zenith television set and fireplace was a long, comfortable-looking blue and green flowery couch that had a long coffee table in front of it. That table was cluttered with boxes of Girl Scout cookies and magazines and a couple of books and a two-pound box of See's Candies. To the side of the room was an oversized, rustic pine office desk also cluttered with stacks of business papers, boxes of cookies, newspapers, and mail. In front of the desk was a brown leather desk chair with a heating pad on it.

Morgan looked to the far right of the room, where, up three steps, there was another opened room with no doors that was home to an impressive antique pool table.

Morgan walked back to the fireplace. One entire wall that surrounded the fireplace was made of beautiful rocks and stone. Four deer hooves held up two salvaged wood logs that made rustic-looking mantle shelves that held family photos. She noticed the side of an opposite wall had a custom-made double-locked cabinet that displayed a large collection of rifles and hand guns which were enclosed with stained glass. Morgan thought the house looked just like the ranch house in "Bonanza." "Am I imagining this?" she thought to herself.

Just then, a man pinched her arm and Morgan jumped. He smiled at her and said, "My name is Rick, I'm Dean's dad." Rick's eyes were even bluer than Dean's. He wore a very full-waxed blonde handlebar mustache and had a full head of blonde hair. Immediately Morgan liked the way he smiled and stood. He overflowed with confidence.

"Hello. I'm Morgan," she said, extending her hand. Rick shook it, and then moved a little closer to her and kindly put one arm around her shoulders. With the other one, he pointed to the fireplace. "It seems to me that you are enjoying my masterpiece. Do you like our fireplace?"

"It's beautiful." She still could not take her eyes off the wonderful stonework.

"Yes, it is beautiful," Rick bragged. "It took me years to find the right rocks and stones. I collected them from the mountains, streams, and the desert. People thought I was a crazy man because I searched for them no matter where I went. Then I would bring them home and pile them in the back of our property. My collection did get a little out of hand." He laughed. "The neighbors started calling me the rock man." He laughed aloud again while he twisted the end of his mustache.

"Yes, that's right," a cheerful woman's voice answered.

Morgan turned around. There stood a woman with a warm smile and deep dimples on both of her cheeks. Her short, light-brown hair framed her face. She wore stylish silver eyeglasses, black stretched slacks, and a white short-sleeved shirt. Her body type was plump and not more than five feet, two inches tall. She walked over to Morgan with a smile that was contagious.

"Hello Morgan, my name is Betty, I'm Dean's mom." Betty hugged her. "Rick didn't even tell me his little secret about what he was going to do with the rocks. He said it was a surprise." She laughed heartily and Morgan could see the pride in her eyes. "I left one summer to visit my sister and her family in Truckee, California. I came home to this magnificent masterpiece."

Rick playfully walked over to her and hugged her waist. "You see every rock has a place, it fits just perfectly. I planned this for years."

Dean walked in with a piece of chicken in his mouth. "And who helped build this masterpiece?" They all started to laugh because Dean had barbecue sauce all over his face.

Morgan watched as Betty and Rick engaged in conversation

with their son. She could immediately see that they deeply loved him. She was surprised how young his parents were in comparison to her own. Dean playfully kissed his mother on the cheek and teased her. "What are we having for dessert? When are we going to eat? I am hungry now."

"We are having homemade apple pie, and we will eat as soon as your brother gets home. He is stopping by the groomer to pick up our dogs." She turned to her husband. "And my love, I made you your favorite, tapioca pudding."

A few minutes later the side door near the kitchen opened. In ran two little dogs barking with an attractive teenage boy with blonde shaggy bangs following close behind. He had the same features as his mother with large dimples that came along with his wide smile.

"Well, who do we have here?" he asked playfully, looking at Morgan.

Betty smiled at her son who was two years younger than Dean. "Come here dear; I want you to meet Morgan. Morgan, this is our youngest son, Luke."

Luke smiled as they shook hands. "It's nice to meet you, I've heard nice things about you."

"Hi," Morgan replied as she bent down to pet the dogs that were sniffing her legs. They smelled freshly bathed and each had a hair bow tied on them.

Luke knelt down. "Fritz is the black poodle in the blue bow, and he has very bad eyesight. Missy is the blonde cocker spaniel in the pink bow, and she is very bossy."

"Oh they're so cute!" Morgan said as she knelt all the way down and let the two barking dogs jump all over her.

Betty laughed. "Oh, they are my loves. And Fritz follows Missy everywhere. They are inseparable. Enough of the dogs now, it's time for dinner! Let's go into the dining room."

Morgan followed Betty into the cluttered kitchen and examined all the yummy smells. On the stovetop there were three skillets sizzling with food. One black skillet had a two thick ham steaks frying with a thick piece of pineapple place on top.

Another skillet had fat chicken breasts sizzling, and yet other had a large porterhouse steak topped with sliced onions. On the countertop next to stove were homemade drop biscuits piled high in a bread-warmer that had a basket weave design with wooden handles. Next to that sat a yellow casserole dish full of creamy au gratin potatoes.

"Everything looks delicious," said Morgan. "Betty, can I help you with anything?"

"No, thank you dear," she answered. "Please go into the dining room. I will serve the food; I don't want anyone in my kitchen. Go sit with the men."

Morgan walked into the dining room and sat at the long table with a beige tablecloth and lovely flowery china place settings. Morgan sat down as Rick explained, "I just heard my wife order you out of the kitchen. I'm the guilty one for telling her when I first married her at seventeen that she was not to work outside our home. I told her that all she needed to do was to take care of the home, her husband, and our children. And that's the way it had been for the last eighteen years."

Betty brought the food from the kitchen into the dining room and sat down. "Well, don't make my life seem so boring. When our sons were in school, I belonged to PTA and the Boy Scout club. And of course I still have my girls' night out with my bingo club and my hobbies." She giggled.

"We are a busy family that enjoys camping trips. Dean and I love to hunt deer." Then Rick glanced over to his sons and frowned. "Luke never had the taste for hunting. Now Dean does not want to go on many camping trips because he always wants to be with his hard-nosed biker friends."

Betty snapped at Rick. "Richard, let's not start on that subject again. We have a guest."

Rick stopped talking.

During the next forty minutes, Morgan was amazed with this small family's behavior at the dinner table. In no time, she figured out why Betty had cooked three different meats. These men were spoiled rotten. Dean ate chicken. Luke preferred ham. Rick was served the delicious steak and onions. When Luke asked for the catsup, Betty got up immediately to get it. Dean wanted more butter and without the least bit of hesitation, she got up again. Rick wanted more milk so Betty poured it.

Rick and Dean started talking about hunting. Morgan listened quietly as Dean asked for a new rifle for his 19th birthday and promised his father that he would join him on the next hunting trip. Luke was pleasant but Morgan could tell that he did not give a hoot about hunting. Instead, he talked to his mom about his coin collection and about how he was trying to find a certain coin.

"Is anyone ready for dessert?" Betty asked. All three men said, "Yes" in unison.

Morgan offered, slightly rising from her chair, "Can I help you?"

Betty waved her off. "No thank you," she said, and disappeared into the kitchen. She came back into the room with apple pie and tapioca pudding. She left again for the large glass bowl of whipped cream. Morgan was not used to having someone serve her.

The end of the meal also frustrated Morgan as she watched all three of the men get up from the table and leave their seats without picking up their plates. Betty immediately began to clear the table. Dean went around the table and reached for Morgan's hand. "Come on pretty baby, let's go for a walk."

"No, I want to help your mother clear the table," Morgan said quietly yet sternly.

Dean insisted. "Mom doesn't want any help. She likes to do things her way."

"I wasn't raised like this. I wouldn't dare leave without helping," she told Dean.

Without making eye contact with anyone and without permission to help, she began to clear the dishes. Betty never told her stop.

The men left the room. After she helped clear the table,

Morgan walked around the dining room and looked at all the collectibles on the shelves. There were tiny china teacups piled on top of each other. Six vintage spoons that hung on a small wooden spoon racks caught Morgan's eye.

"Can I hold one?" she asked Betty.

"Of course," Betty smiled.

She reached for one that said Disneyland. "They are heavy!" she exclaimed.

"Yes, these spoons are sterling silver. I bought that spoon just two years after Disney opened the park." Morgan smiled. She picked up another that was in the shape of a tree and looked old. Betty explained it was from Yosemite National Park in California. Another was from Yellowstone National Park in Wyoming, another from Zion National Park in Utah and still another from Redwoods in California and then there was one from Oregon.

"They're wonderful," Morgan said. "Why do you have these?"

"Well, dear," Betty explained, "they are my little reminders of the places that I have traveled to. Except for Oregon, that was a gift. I am sure when the day comes when I die they will end up in the trash. They are of no value to anyone except to me. Just my little collection."

The spoons fascinated Morgan. She had never traveled anywhere but she had dreams of traveling.

Dean came back into the dining room and grabbed Morgan by the shoulders. "Mother, can I borrow Morgan now?"

"Yes you can, but bring her back." Betty smiled.

"I promise." Dean grinned.

Lightheartedly, Morgan put her old coat on. She thanked Betty for telling her the wonderful stories of the spoons and for dinner and gave her a hug.

Dean and Morgan strolled down the wide street, crunching down on the brittle leaves that were piled on the sidewalk. Morgan loved the many tall magnolia trees that lined this part of the walk. Dean held her hand tight, kissing it over and over. "I grew up in this neighborhood," he said happily, "but I don't think I have ever held a girl's hand walking down this street since I was 10 years old." They both laughed. An old couple was sitting out on their porch drinking lemonade and they waved to Dean. Dean and Morgan waved back as Dean yelled from across the street, "Mr. and Mrs. Stevenson, this is my girlfriend, Morgan!" They smiled and waved.

They walked for a few minutes more then out of the blue he picked her up and swung her around. He whispered, "I want to kiss you all night long." He kissed her again all over her face and mouth. Morgan could hardly catch her breath. She managed to stop him from kissing her by pushing him away. "Dean! We need to sit down and talk. Please!"

He stopped and pulled her down on the grass. She looked into his eyes. "Dean, you don't know me. You don't know how I think, or what my passions are. Or what I want in life."

He smiled. "Well, tell me. Baby, what do you want?"

She took a deep breath. "I know I'm not cut out to be a nun." She blushed then her face became serious. "I want to go to junior college for two years and learn more about psychology. Then I plan on going to barber college. I have never been anywhere but the convent and Catholic schools. I have never been out of southern California. And I don't want to have a child until I'm in my 30s. I took care of my sister and brothers most of my life. I don't want to be a suburban housewife. I want to travel and see the world."

For a moment, Dean didn't say anything. Then he smiled and laughed, "You are making me dizzy with all this career talk. Why a barber? That is just plain crazy. Only men do that type of work. Women belong in a beauty shop, not the barber shop."

"When I was a little girl, I would go to the barbershop with my dad and brothers. I love the smell. I would listen to the men talk about religion and politics and I would watch the barber do flat-tops and shaves with the straight razor. I know that it sounds crazy but I love the barbershop. You are the first person I have ever told this to. I never even told the nuns at the convent or my mother."

"Okay, slow down," he told her. "Woman, you sure have a lot brewing in that beautiful head of yours. You are exhausting me." He grabbed her hair in his hands and ruffled it. "I've got a better idea than college. Doesn't it sound more fun riding free down the highway with me on my Harley, and making love every night?"

He started to kiss her again. This time he kissed her on the back of the neck and around her ears softly and blew gently in her ear.

"That tickles," she giggled then she tried to move away, embarrassed.

"Don't move," he told her.

He stood up then moved and sat behind her and with gentle fingers he massaged her neck and shoulders. Then he touched the small of her back and rubbed the top and sides of her waist. He moved back to the small of her back and massaged her more. Breathlessly she whispered, "That feels good."

Dean told her, "You are my beautiful baby doll. I will promise you after we get married I will support us and you can go to college. I'm going to take care of you, baby."

Morgan stared at Dean. He was so handsome. He had on a very tight blue sweater that was the color of his eyes. The way his blonde hair fell across his forehead reminded her of a little boy. Her heart was beating fast. She reached over and lightly touched his well-sculpted arms with her fingertips. Without making eye contact she said, "Don't be so sure that I want to marry you."

"Is that right?" He teased. "Well, you're a virgin, and if I want to have sex with you, it looks like I had better marry my little Catholic girl." Then without hesitation, Dean took Morgan's face in his hands. "Morgan, I figure that we will get married as soon as you graduate from high school. I want to make love to you every night for the rest of my life. I have the biggest throbbing for you. I can't wait much longer."

Morgan turned red. She put her hand over his mouth. "Hush now, you silly boy. Let's go back to the house."

She got up and ran down the street. Dean ran after her. He caught up with her in front of his parent's house and he picked her up and swung her around again. He pulled her as close to his body as he could. "Morgan, my heart is pounding hard." He took her hand and placed it on his heart. "You're an angel, I've never felt this way about any girl. Baby, you take my breath away when I look at you. I love you." He did not kiss her this time; instead he gently outlined her face with his large strong hand. Then he kissed her eyes and said, "You make me what to reach up to the sky and steal the stars and hand them to you."

Tears were in her eyes. "I love you, but I'm scared. I'm only seventeen."

Chapter 29

The next school day, Dean picked her up after school. He was on time and she did not have to go home in the carpool with Sara's mother because Isabel had given him permission to pick her up. She got into the truck and he kissed her right away. "Babe I've got a surprise for you. We are going over to visit Rusty's mother. She wants to meet you."

"Oh, I'm so excited! I've heard so much about Georgia from Rusty. He told me that she owns three taverns and a motel and a billiard joint!" She smiled.

Dean grinned. "Yeah. And she's been curious about you."

Rusty was outside wiping down his motorcycle and stood up when he saw his friends. Morgan got out of the truck and hugged him then Dean and Rusty shook hands.

"Morgan, I thought it was time you visited my home base and met my mom. Come on in," Rusty said.

They walked into the front room which was unlike anything Morgan had ever seen. The high ceiling was painted cream and the walls were wallpapered in an exquisite Chinese Chinoiserie floral pattern. A round, ruby red brothel-looking chandelier hung from the ceiling. Luxurious, overflowing, satin, striped sheers covered the windows. The thick shag carpet was red. The antique lamps were red velvet. The half-moon antique couch was overstuffed and covered in soft gold velvet. A large gold-framed bevel mirror hung on one wall. The glass coffee table in front of the couch held the most beautiful centerpiece, a candelabra holding nine twelve-inch white candles. Somewhere from another room Frank Sinatra music was playing.

Morgan was astounded when Georgia walked into the room.

She was the sexiest woman she had ever seen. Morgan had expected to see a typical mother like her own and was surprised to see Georgia wearing a low-cut, tight, black, shiny top with her bosoms almost spilling out. She wore black satin hot pants. Her shoes were black, knee-high, shiny leather boots that had spiked high heels and she had the most beautiful, long, feminine legs that Morgan had ever seen.

The hairstyle she wore was very high and blue-black in color. The make-up she wore was perfect yet extreme and her eyebrows were perfectly arched. She wore so much jewelry that she sparkled like a disco ball.

Morgan looked over at Rusty. "You did tell me that your mother had six children and four grandchildren, right?" she whispered behind her hand. Rusty winked and nodded. Then he smiled and said louder, "Mom, I want you to meet Morgan."

Georgia walked over to Morgan. "Well hi baby girl! So you're the Catholic girl my son keeps talking about." She looked at Rusty. "Son, you didn't tell me how beautiful this girl is. She's adorable. I'll be damned. So you wanted to be a Catholic nun? Now that's something you don't hear every day." She gave Morgan a great big hug. "Now come here on the couch and sit with me. I understand that your family lives a few blocks from us, so tell me about yourself."

Morgan was nervous at first as she began to talk then she could not stop chattering. She told Georgia how she first met Rusty on the telephone. She told her about the Catholic school she attended and all about Dean and his parents. Georgia was a very good listener, nodding and keeping her eyes on Morgan as she talked. After 30 minutes, she looked at her watch. "Honey, it was a pleasure to meet you, but I will have to go back to work soon." Then she turned to Dean and Rusty. "You guys get out of here and leave us two women alone. I want a few moments alone with Morgan."

Rusty and Dean both said sure and went out the door.

Georgia looked directly into Morgan's innocent eyes. "Are you in love with Dean?" Morgan nodded fervently.

"Honey bunch, I want to you to be careful with yourself because I know him very well. Dean was a good kid just like Rusty. They played baseball together and everything was just fine until the hippies and the drug culture appeared. And there went my boy and Dean, experimenting with weed and all the rest. I wish they would have just drunk whiskey." Georgia laughed and shook her head. "I'd hate to see you get hurt."

Morgan gently took Georgia's hand. "I will be careful. Thank you for caring."

"Baby girl you should go grab a pencil and paper and write this down! I was 14 years old when I fell in love with my children's father. I was married and pregnant at 15. After I gave birth to our six children he left us for another woman. And when he left us all behind it cut my heart into pieces. The pain was so hard that I felt I could not go on another hour. It was a hard thing to recover from. I had many children to feed because the son of a bitch disappeared to Alaska. So then I learned to look like this." Georgia pointed to herself and laughed loudly. "I had to work very hard to support my six children. The reason I'm telling you my story is so you consider taking it slow and think about marriage. It's a big commitment for a man. Now I really have to go work. It was nice to finally meet you."

Chapter 30

As the weeks passed, Morgan got very attached to Dean's parents and brother. Before she knew it, Christmas time had arrived. Dean opened the front door to his parents' house and Morgan followed behind and they walked into a Christmas fairyland. It looked like Santa's home. Traditional Christmas music flowed throughout the house. Morgan could see how elegant and tasteful Betty had decorated. Morgan walked into the kitchen and found Betty in a green holiday Christmas apron. There was hot apple cider cooking on the stovetop and Christmas mugs sat on the counter top with cinnamon sticks in them. Homemade pumpkin bread and apple pies were cooling by the open window on the kitchen counter.

Morgan walked over to the counter top that had ingredients that graced the top near the butcher block. She got excited when she saw the ingredients were for Divinity candy. There was sugar, light corn syrup, 1/2 cup of water, two egg whites in a small bowl, a small bottle of vanilla extract, and wax paper sitting on the butcher block. "Betty, you are making my favorite Christmas candy! I learned to make this one day from a lady named Josephine."

Betty was thrilled. "Does that mean you would like to make the candy?"

"Absolutely!" Morgan answered.

After the candy was prepared, Morgan made sure to walk through the lovely home. Each light switch and plug had red and gold glitter covers. All the windows had fake snow sprayed on them and there were silver bells and silver reindeer ornaments hung everywhere. Colorful crystal beads and toy soldiers hung on all the shelves throughout the house. The Nativity scene was hand-carved out of cedar wood and was displayed on top of an antique table with a white lace tablecloth. All the tables in the house were covered with red-lace tablecloths and tall white candles in gold holders. Hanging on the fireplace mantle were homemade personalized Christmas stockings. There were even two stockings hanging for the dogs. The wonderful rooms oozed with vanilla- and cinnamon-scented candles, their smells filling each room in the home. Pine wreaths hung on all the doors. It was amazing to see the display of love that went into this holiday decorating.

Suddenly, Rick jumped up out of his desk chair and grabbed Morgan sweetly and kissed her. "What's that kiss for?" she asked, surprised.

"I kissed you because you are standing under the mistletoe!" Rick looked at her surprised face. "Do you know what mistletoe is?" He pointed to where the small flower bush hung from the ceiling.

She blushed. "To be honest with you, I don't know what that is!"

Rick explained the tradition. The whole family laughed and then Morgan did too. "Oh, Morgan, you are so darn sweet," Betty said.

Morgan walked into the pool table area. Display trays covered the delicate, authentic, English lace red tablecloth. There were silver trays full of assorted homemade cookies. Betty explained that every year she baked dozens of Christmas cookies for her family, the neighbors, and her friends at bingo. Morgan picked up a gingerbread man to look at him more closely and gently put him back. Her favorite was the Santa Claus cookies because of how beautifully detailed they were. It looked like Betty had spent hours making them.

"Please have one dear," Betty urged. Morgan looked carefully at the delicate cookie and then said, "Oh no, they're too beautiful to eat."

Betty finally convinced her to eat the Santa cookie and

Morgan savored every bite. Then she walked over to the enormous Christmas tree that was opposite the fireplace. "We drove to the mountains to get this one," Rick said proudly. The tree was the tallest she had ever seen in a private home. The elegant decorations were amazing. There must have been a hundred ornaments on and the twinkly lights were red, green, blue, and gold. On the very top sat an antique angel ornament with beautiful outstretched wings.

Morgan felt so overwhelmed by the beauty of the home that she went over and hugged Betty. "Your family is so fortunate to have you." Betty smiled and shook her head no. "No dear, I am the one who truly gets the pleasure for doing all these things for my family. It's that simple."

Dean came in and sat on the couch next to Morgan. Moments later Betty set before them a tray of delicate sliced apple-banana cakes filled with raspberries and garnished with confectioners' sugar on top, two red Christmas mugs full with hot apple cider and a cinnamon stick, and two white folded cloth dinner napkins that held a silver dessert fork and teaspoon tucked inside the napkin. Morgan sighed happily.

Chapter 31

On Christmas Eve Morgan was at her own home. She dressed in a red velvet, long-sleeved, empire dress that hit two inches above the knee for midnight mass. It had tiny white pearls that adorned the neck and the V-shaped empire waist. Her legs looked glossy with sheer suntan pantyhose. Her black sandals had a three-inch block heel and sling-back ankle straps. She wore her hair in a classic 1940s fashion. Morgan copied a photo from a magazine that explained the details on how to achieve a pin-up front hairstyle in victory rolls with the back worn down in loose, soft curls. Her eyes were again made up in a dramatic, smokey look with black fake eyelashes and eyeliner only lining the top lash. She put on her new red lipstick and sprayed Rive Gauche perfume on each wrist and behind both her ears.

It had always been an O'Malley tradition to attend the midnight service but this Christmas was different. She went into her bedroom, picked up the two gifts that she had wrapped the night before, and placed them under the small Christmas tree in her living room that only had a few red and gold ornaments and one string of colored lights adorning it. She had bought her mother a soft grey sweater with matching gloves. No other gifts were under the tree. Isabel had left one Christmas gift on Morgan's bed for her to open.

Morgan had opened the gift the night before and to her delight inside were the most beautiful sky blue rosary beads she had ever seen. Isabel had written a loving Christmas card the best she could with words like, "Never forget who you are. And remember to set a proper example of a good Catholic woman to the world."

Tears began to stream down Morgan's cheeks as she remembered past Christmases. She envisioned the ghosts of Emma and Casey dancing around the Christmas tree, laughing and teasing one another.

Immediately, she stood up and went into her bedroom. She searched through her bottom dresser drawer. Carefully, she uncovered a small, cream-colored quilted box and pulled it out. Lifting the top, she saw two small photos of Emma and Casey. Then she saw a large picture of the entire happy O'Malley family standing in front of the house. Morgan was holding baby girl Emma in her arms.

Morgan pulled all the pictures out then she went back into the living room and placed all the pictures beside the Christmas Nativity scene set that was exhibited on the dining room table.

Plunking down on the sofa, she sat back. Nostalgic homesickness growled in her stomach and heart-wrenching thoughts from the past crowded her mind. Her heart yearned for Emma. Once again, she closed her eyes and remembered Emma's sweet laughter. She thought about Casey, the harmless troublemaker with a cute smile. "Oh, I miss Peter and Noah!" she said aloud.

Sitting there, she looked at the letter on the table and grabbed it and read it once more. The letter was from Noah four months ago. Peter had sent a one-way ticket for Noah to join him in Ireland. Noah was extremely happy living there and the letter said he had no intention of returning home.

The letter had really pushed Isabel over the edge and she was devoting all her time now to helping the elderly. She was never home. Not even tonight.

Then Morgan's thoughts drifted to her daddy. Months ago, Barney had packed up all his clothes in a gray suitcase and moved into a small, one-room apartment. Morgan knew he spent many hours reminiscing in his rocking chair and looking out the window into the alley view that the apartment overlooked. He worked few hours.

Morgan planned to visit her father on Christmas Day and

take him his gift, a new wallet and belt.

The doorbell rang. The noise startled Morgan out of her reverie and she jumped. It buzzed again. "Oh my goodness, I had almost forgotten about him," she thought as she glanced over to the wall clock and smiled. He was on time.

Morgan opened the door. She appreciated that Dean had taken the time in choosing what to wear. He was wearing gray flare-leg slacks and a classic white, long-sleeved button-down shirt, and a thin red tie. Dean laughed when he saw Morgan looking him over. "Yeah, dammit, don't even say anything. I know I look like a Catholic school dude." He laughed lightheartedly and walked right to the mirror and checked himself out. He touched up his perfectly combed pompadour hairstyle.

Morgan stood there and smiled. Dean turned and looked her up and down. Taking a firm grasp of her arm, he said, "You look beautiful."

She looked at him and her eyes sparkled like starlight. "Every love song I hear reminds me of us."

He kissed her softly. "Do you know what my favorite time of the evening is every night?"

She shook her head no.

"Baby, it's when my bedroom phone rings at exactly 9 o'clock. Your voice is my goodnight lullaby." He began to kiss her and she stopped him.

"Watch out, you will mess my red lipstick."

"Baby, I know you've had tough times with your family, but I want you to know your arms will never be filled with anything but love." He took a look around the sad room. "Let's go now."

They walked into the huge Catholic cathedral hand-in-hand. Morgan was so proud to be walking into her church with her handsome boyfriend but she was a little concerned that he wouldn't be able to handle the length of the service in church, two long hours. It was a very traditional Catholic celebration. Just communion alone would take thirty-five minutes, as almost everyone received communion at Christmas time.

Morgan smiled when Father Paul walked into the church to

begin the service. When their eyes met, Father Paul smiled at her. She was pleased to be in the presence of a priest that she deeply respected. Father Paul began his sermon about the Christmas nativity. The music began and the whole congregation stood up. Morgan picked up the songbook and opened it. She shared it with Dean and they sang. Morgan was extremely impressed with Dean; he stood up, knelt down, and stood up again then sat down and stood up again with the rest of the congregation. A few times, he made a funny face at her with a wink and whispered in her ear, "My knees hurt." They both giggled.

They stood very close together. Morgan felt her heart racing each time that Dean put his arm around her waist. Just the touch of his arm pressing against her own made her quiver. It was hard to pray with her gorgeous boyfriend standing so near. She felt her face flush each time she looked up at him.

Finally, she forced herself to pray. "Dear Lord, please watch over my brothers and keep them safe in Ireland. Help me to get through another holiday without Emma and Casey. Please Lord, help my parents to heal from our family tragedy. Most Sacred Heart of Jesus, graciously hear my prayer. Amen."

After mass had ended, Morgan and Dean walked over to the classic blue 1964 Chevy Impala. Dean beamed with pride; the car was an early Christmas present from his father and mother.

"Isn't this ride beautiful?" he asked.

"Yes, it is," she answered as he opened the door for her.

The interior was red leather and in perfect shape. "Just don't get too comfortable in this car, because I have a news flash for you. When I finish the trike you are going to learn to love riding!"

Morgan was tired and quiet; it was almost 2 a.m. She did not bother to answer. She got in the car and he closed the door after her.

Dean hurried around the car, opened up the trunk, and fidgeted with something. Then he slammed the trunk down. Morgan looked over to him then she turned away. She just assumed he was looking for his cigarettes. He got into the car and looked over at Morgan. "Morgan, will you marry me?" he burst out.

Dean shoved a small soft white box in her hand. Completely shocked, she did not speak as she slowly opened the box. Inside was a beautiful, antique-style white gold engagement ring with a marquise-shaped diamond and a matching wedding band.

"Oh, my God, it's beautiful," she quietly whispered.

Dean explained. "I know we've only been going out a couple of months but you turn 18 next month and you graduate in June. That will give us six months to be engaged and plan our wedding."

Morgan was speechless.

"Baby, I love you. Will you spend the rest of your life with me?" He looked into her green eyes and he cupped her chin in his powerful hands.

Looking deeply into his blue eyes, gently she reached behind his head, drew him close to herself, and kissed him lovingly. "Yes, I will marry you."

Dean yelped. "I've got the belle of the ball!" They both laughed together. She said, "You're crazy, you know that?"

Going closer to her, he nuzzled her neck and began kissing her. He whispered, "You look like a beautiful yummy cupcake."

"A cupcake," she giggled. "Dean, does everything about me remind you of food?"

He laughed hard. "Yes, because I want to gobble you up." Again, he started to kiss her.

Morgan pushed him away. "Dean O'Donnell, you start this car at once. We are in the church parking lot!"

On the way home, Morgan quietly stared at the ring. Finally, she had the courage to ask him. "Sweetheart, how you could afford this expensive ring?"

"I took the money that I've been saving up for the last two years. I was going to buy another Harley bike, but I found something better to spend it on."

He took a long drag of the cigarette and blew out the smoke. Then he looked over at her. "I want you to belong to me."

Chapter 32

Celebrating Christmas Day at the O'Donnells' home was more than anything Morgan could have imagined. Morgan was greeted by Betty as she walked up their porch steps. "Merry Christmas, sweetheart. I just returned from my church service ten minutes ago. You are just in time. Come in please."

Traditional Christmas music was playing on the stereo and the fireplace was blazing. The home felt warm and cozy.

"Come into the kitchen dear, I am preparing an old family tradition of classic eggnog." After she prepared the Christmas treat Betty poured it all in a beautiful crystal punch bowl and decorated the edges of the delicate bowl with Christmas candy canes. Then she placed the long silver ladle in the bowl. With extreme care, Betty picked up the punch bowl and asked Morgan to bring in the tiny punch glasses. They went into the family room and placed everything on the already crowded table of prepared foods. Betty served both herself and Morgan a cup. They both sipped the delicious treat and then Betty filled up both herself and Morgan another glass before all the men came in to serve themselves. "Isn't this delightful?" Betty giggled. Morgan nodded with cream on her upper lip. Betty handed her a linen napkin.

Once everyone was seated on the couch, Rick began to hand out the most extravagantly wrapped Christmas presents she had ever seen. Morgan was uncomfortable as she was handed gift after gift. Dean and Luke stacked the boxes at her feet as Betty encouraged her to be the first one to open gifts. "Come on dear, let's see what you have in those packages." Morgan could see how overjoyed Betty was to have a future daughter-in-law.

The first gift was wrapped in red paper with a red velvet

ribbon. Morgan carefully untied the ribbon and wrapping paper. Inside was a fabulous white faux fur coat that was mid-length with a silky lining. It also had a full fluffy collar that could be worn up or down.

She was astounded. "Oh my goodness, this is the most beautiful coat that I have ever seen! Is this really for me? It's so soft." Morgan ran her hands up and down the inside of the jacket.

"Try it on, sweetheart!" Rick urged. She stood up and Betty helped her put it on. "Oh, you look beautiful," Betty cooed.

Morgan was speechless but finally managed some words. "Thank you. It's so beautiful." She hugged Betty then Rick.

"Open this," Dean said once she had sat back down, the beautiful jacket draped across her lap. The next present was wrapped in silver paper with a huge red ribbon. Inside was another coat, this one a genuine black leather motorcycle jacket. Dean had her stand up and put it on. He had the jacket specially tailored to fit her. Dean had guessed her size so he was especially proud when she slipped the tight leather on and the zipper went up easily. Dean winked at her approvingly. "You can wear that on the bike."

Satisfied, he gave her another present. "Open this." She opened the lavender paper with white ribbon and pulled out a traditional, double-breasted front, fully lined, leather trim beige trench coat. It has front belted cuffs, flap pockets, and a shape-defining belt. "Oh gosh, I love it!" She hugged Dean tight.

There were so many gifts to open. She received two long, maxi-flowered print skirts along with two halter-tops and two colorful, printed peasant blouses and a cute lavender print tunic blouse with a very scoop neckline. Next, she opened four pairs of designer Levi's; two were boot cut and two were bell-bottoms. She had never worn a pair of Levi blue jeans before. She read the size of one of the Levi's, and whispered to Dean, "I'm not a size 6."

"You'll be able to squeeze into them." He grinned back at her.

There were still more packages to open. There was a pair of leather, thigh-high biker boots from Dean. Morgan looked at the boots, and then put the lid back on the box in a hurry. Dean laughed when he saw her turn red.

Then she opened a medium-sized gift wrapped in green paper and black ribbon. It was a pink suitcase. "Unsnap it," Betty said. When Morgan looked inside, she saw the suitcase had pink satin lining and was full with Lancôme and Chanel perfumes and Avon nail polish in assorted colors. There were also bath powders, Avon bath oils, and several bottles of bubble bath. There was a white bath brush, and a white cloth hair bonnet. Morgan jumped up and hugged Betty. "Thank you!"

Next she unwrapped a small red gift. Inside was a pink and white polka-dotted cosmetic bag full with assorted colored lipsticks and lip polish gloss.

Now was the time for Morgan to open her last gift. It was wrapped with gold paper and adorned with evergreen holly leaves, and Christmas ornaments and gold Christmas bells. Betty was excited for her to open this last one. "Just one gift left Betty giggled in delight."

Morgan smiled as she unfolded the gold tissue paper from the box. Inside was a beautiful knee-length, soft blue, chenille bathrobe and a sweet blue nylon chiffon nightgown and matching blue slippers.

"I love you all so much," Morgan sighed. She went over and hugged Betty again as the tears rolled down her cheeks, and for the first time in a while, they were tears of joy. Morgan walked over to Rick and kissed his cheek and she giggled when his big-waxed handlebar mustache brushed against her cheek. She hugged him tight. "Thank you all for being so kind to me."

She hugged Luke and thanked him for the peasant blouses. Luke sweetly smiled and said, "I love you, sis-to-be."

Playfully she teased him back. "I love you too, brother-to-be."

Dean said, "All right honey, get over here. He's held you long enough." Morgan sat on the couch very close to Dean. She watched her wonderful new family exchange their Christmas gifts. There was so much laughter and teasing as the sons and father opened their traditional gifts of socks and underwear and half a dozen tee-shirts and several pairs of pajamas.

Luke laughed. “Mom, when are you going to stop buying us underwear and socks?”

Dean chimed in. “Come on, Mom is still going to be buying us underwear when we’re old.”

Betty laughed heartily with her sons, because every year she bought them the essentials then the big gifts came later. Dean had already gotten his classic Chevy car. Luke had received an equal amount of money in saving bonds.

“Go ahead Dad,” Luke said. “Open your gift. It’s from me, Dean, and mother.”

Rick grinned. “All right.” He untied the velvet black ribbon and carefully unwrapped the red paper. He opened the box and inside there was a large pipe with a smooth bowl rim covered with dense bird’s eye grain. The hand cut stem was incredible. Rick’s face lit up. “Well, this is a well-thought-out gift!” He cocked his head when he smiled and twisted the end of his handlebar mustache. “Yes, indeed a very well thought-out-gift. Thank you, family.”

“Mom, it’s your turn,” Luke said as he handed her a small gift. “This is from dad, me, and Dean.” In no hurry, Betty gracefully tore open the silver paper and undid the light pink ribbon. She opened the white box and there lay an authentic pearl necklace and matching pearl earrings. “Well, for goodness’ sake.” She blushed, smiled, and walked over to her husband. “My love, will you help me with these?”

Rick stood up and fastened them carefully around her neck. “Honey, the boys and I went to the jewelers together to pick out this gift for you.”

“I love you and thank you my darlings.” She kissed her husband and then went over to her sons and kissed them both.

When the family was all done opening their gifts, Morgan opened her black and white checkered purse. “Now it’s my turn to give you all a little something.”

There were four small wrapped gifts and she handed one to each of the family members. Luke opened his first; it was a particular stamp for his collection. Rick received a mustache comb and wax. Betty opened a book of poems and Dean opened a box of Old Spice cologne.

Rick told Betty, "Well, my darling, it looks like we are getting a very special daughter-in-law."

"I agree," she told her husband.

The rest of the morning was busy. Several of the neighbors stopped in to visit, coming in and out of the house with all sorts of delicious plates of foods and desserts. Even the Jewish woman Shirley from across the street came over for a short visit and brought over her favorite harvest plate of cabbage filled with ground beef in a sweet and sour sauce called holishkes with a platter of apple strudel to share.

Rusty and Damien stopped in for a while early that afternoon. They both wore red Santa hats and their blue Nite Owl club jackets. As soon as they said hello to everybody they headed for the food. Everyone laughed when Rusty loaded his plate up with mashed potatoes, oven-roasted turkey, and gobs of gravy.

Morgan showed off her engagement ring to the fellows. They teased Dean about losing his freedom. Morgan watched quietly as the three close friends played a few games of pool.

When Dean left to go to the bathroom, Rusty stood close to Morgan. "Are you happy?" he asked her quietly.

She smiled. "You know I am, and I owe it all to you." She kissed Rusty on the cheek. "You introduced me to Dean and I will always be grateful." She hugged her friend tightly.

"Morgan, have you really thought this over?" Damien asked. "Maybe you two should be engaged for a year then see how it goes then get married."

Dean walked into the room just then and looked at Damien. "I don't think my business is any of yours. Understand?"

Damien smiled and raised his hands up. "Understand."

Rusty chuckled to lighten to mood. "All right people, we are on to the next stop. Thanks for the grub. Come on, Damien we're out of here."

Rusty turned to Morgan. "I almost forgot to tell you. I saw

Barney walking down to the liquor store this morning. I picked him up and took him home. He is a nice guy but very sad. He talks about the old days."

Morgan thanked Rusty for giving her father a ride then she ran to Dean. "Oh my goodness, I need to leave. I forgot about my father!"

Betty overheard Morgan. "What are you talking about? Did I hear you say something about your father?"

"Yes, my father lives alone and I really need to leave and go to him."

Then Morgan explained to Betty a little bit more about the situation with her parents. She had no sooner finished the story than Betty hurried into the kitchen with Morgan right behind her. Morgan watched as this amazing woman filled containers with biscuits and butter, slices of ham and salad, homemade cookies, and a big piece of pie. She filled a thermos with hot coffee.

"Now go to your father and feed him. Tell him we're looking forward to meeting him."

"Let's go, Morgan," Dean said as he pulled her away from his mother.

Dean and Morgan said their good-byes to everyone. They drove to her father in Dean's new Chevy and Morgan wore her new white fur coat.

"Oh Dean, I love your family. This was a wonderful Christmas Day. I feel like I'm in a dream with the all the gifts."

Dean reached over and tapped her arm. "All right, calm down and take a deep breath. You need to understand that you deserve all of this and more, sweetheart."

She snuggled up next to him in the car. "I love you and your family." She kept looking at the engagement ring on her finger as they drove to Barney's.

Morgan knocked three times on the door of the apartment. There was no answer. She looked over to Dean. Without saying a word, he hit the old door hard, and then he went over to the dirty window. He banged hard on it repeatedly and yelled, "Barney, you in there?"

Slowly, Barney opened the door halfway. "What do you want? Who is it?"

Morgan pushed open the door. "Dad it's me, Morgan."

"Oh, hi honey, how's my girl? It's so good to see you." Morgan gave him a hug. Barney has uncombed black hair and graying temples. He was wearing light khaki Dockers with a blue zip-up fleece pullover, and he smelled of vodka.

Morgan kissed her father on the cheek. "Merry Christmas, daddy." His face was all prickly. "How long has it been since you shaved?"

"Stop complaining, I wasn't expecting company. Come on in and Merry Christmas to you."

Morgan and Dean looked around the modest room. It was not dirty, just untidy, dusty, and old. There was a small couch and his recliner chair. In the corner of the room was the faithful 1947 Zenith porthole console television. In the simple kitchen was a wood table with two chairs. Two stacks of newspapers were stacked on the floor. Beside the recliner was his old 1940s English leather trunk. The straps were undone and the top opened. It was full to the top with family photos and souvenirs.

Morgan scolded her father. "Dad, have you been looking in that trunk again?"

Barney nodded, then he started in. "Do you remember when Emma tried to make toast and it burned?" He started to chuckle.

"I do remember that dad," she said quietly as she closed the top of the trunk. "Come here." She went over to the kitchen table and began to take the food out of the paper bags.

"What's all this?" He smiled and then he looked over at the good-looking young man as if he had just realized that Dean was there. "So you must be Dean. Morgan told me about you."

Dean looked closely at the tired, run-down man who looked older than his fifty years. He held out his hand to Barney and gave him a firm handshake. Barney smiled a charming Irish smile. "You have a strong grip there, son." Dean returned the smile.

Morgan arranged her father's plate and served him a cup of very hot coffee. Barney mumbled, "Dear, you don't have to go to all this trouble for me. I'm not hungry."

Morgan took a deep breath. "Please sit down. Dean's mother sent you over a Christmas feast. All the food is homemade, including the apple pie and cookies. Please eat it while it's warm."

Barney sat down. "Okay, I'll eat if that makes you happy. I sure don't want anyone to go to all this trouble for me." He began to eat.

Morgan fussed in the kitchen while Dean turned on the TV. Barney hungrily ate every single bite that Betty had packed. He drank the hot coffee and then he even asked for the generous piece of pie. "This is a feast for a rich man. This is the best meal I've ever eaten." He smiled sweetly. "I'll save the Santa cookies for later."

Morgan and Barney talked and talked. She told him everything about the O'Donnell home and the Christmas presents that she had received and about her engagement ring. Then she told him about their wedding plans.

"Morgan, I promise you that I will be at your wedding. You stop worrying about me. I give you my word I won't drink booze."

"All right daddy, I will stop worrying about you," Morgan said. "Now, I have a present for you in my purse." She jumped up, grabbed her purse, and sat next to Barney. She took out a small box and handed it to him.

"Aw, I sure did need new a new wallet and belt." He hugged his daughter and said, "Thank you dear."

When it was time to leave, Dean helped Morgan on with her new white coat. They all hugged. Morgan looked at her father and said, "Merry Christmas, Daddy."

Barney rubbed his full tummy and yawned sleepily. "Merry Christmas kids. Tell Betty she's a wonderful cook. Just like my lovely Isabel was before she went to work."

Chapter 33

After the new year, preparations for the wedding were in full swing. Betty and Morgan and many of their chosen friends helped in the process of planning. After some persuading from Morgan, everyone was in full agreement for a Catholic ceremony.

It was quiet Friday evening when Morgan answered her bedroom telephone. "Hello?"

"Hi dear, this is Betty. How are you doing tonight?"

"Hi Betty, I'm fine, just finishing up some laundry and studying for my finals on Monday. Is anything wrong?"

"Oh no, nothing is wrong. Well, I'm calling to have a serious talk with you. Do you have the time now, dear?"

Morgan sat down on her bed. "Yes, Betty I have time. Tell me what's on your mind?"

"I really want you to make an effort to sit down and talk with your mother as soon as you can. She really needs to be a part of this wedding planning. I know you two have been disagreeing but you are your mother's only daughter. She has been through a difficult journey in her life. She's had to deal with not only losing her children to the accident but her sons to Ireland also. Please will you promise me that you will have a conversation with her and be kind and open-minded? I like Isabel very much and I respect her feelings."

"Yes, Betty I promise I will talk with my mother tonight."

Later that evening, Morgan found Isabel at the kitchen table. "Mother, I think we should discuss plans about my wedding."

"I would love to discuss your wedding, Morgan. I'm sorry that I have not been in a cheerful mood." She looked down at her hands then up into Morgan's eyes. "I need to let go of the dream

I had for you to become a Carmelite nun." Then Isabel smiled at her daughter. "I am getting used to the idea of marriage."

Isabel had her faithful black Bible sitting on the kitchen table. "I would like to give you some suggestions on the wedding mass and I…"

Morgan interrupted her. "Mother, I'm so happy that you're inspired to think of these things. You don't need to ask me what I think. You may choose any verses you want for the ceremony. I'm thrilled that you want to be involved."

"Thank you," Isabel said calmly. Then she looked directly into her daughter's eyes. She hesitated a moment before she continued. "There is one more thing I want to discuss with you. I feel that this is a good family that you are marrying into but I do feel it is so important that Dean attend the Catholic pre-marriage classes."

Morgan frowned. "Oh, is that really necessary?"

Isabel was firm and spoke softly. "Yes, it is necessary for him to understand the meaning of our faith, and how devoted you are to the church, and that your children will be raised in the Catholic faith. Please, honey, this is something I insist."

Morgan shrugged her shoulders. "All right Mother, I will discuss it with Dean. Oh, I almost forgot one more detail!"

Isabel looked concerned. "What is it?"

Morgan's face was very serious. "I want Father Paul to perform my wedding ceremony. No other priest will do."

"I agree," Isabel said.

"I love you and I promise not to disappoint you. Dean will take the classes." They hugged.

The next evening Morgan was at the O'Donnell house having dinner. After the meal, Rick and Betty decided to go out to enjoy a movie. Morgan knew this was the perfect opportunity to talk to her fiancé. They sat in the living room as Dean flipped through a biker magazine.

"Okay, here goes," she thought to herself, taking a deep breath. "Dean, we need to discuss a final detail before our wedding. We must attend Catholic pre-marital marriage classes."

Dean looked up from his magazine with raised eyebrows. "How long do these Catholic classes last?"

She hesitated. "Well, uh, for two hours and for six weeks, one day a week."

Dean freaked. "For two hours, you've got to be kidding!" He stomped outside. Morgan sat and waited. From where she sat near the window she saw him smoke one cigarette then another. Then he turned and walked back in the house with an expression of resolution. "My ultimate object is only to make you happy. Let's do this Catholic gig and get it over with," he said.

She ran over, jumped up, and hugged his neck. "I promise this will be all worth it. I will be the best wife. You will see."

"Well, after all this you had better be." He took her in his arms and kissed her soft lips passionately.

Chapter 34

Dean went with Morgan to each of the Catholic pre-wedding classes. He never complained.

Morgan managed to keep her nose to the books and completed the requirements to graduate from senior year. Her grade average was commendable and she received a certificate of great achievement. The graduation from Saint Catherine was bittersweet. Morgan knew how much she would miss her friends. Several of the girls had discussed college but she remained quiet during those conversations. In her life, every detail was being finished for her wedding. Eight weeks after her high school graduation she would be an 18-year-old married woman.

Once a week, Dean and Morgan would go for a drive in his blue Chevy car, which now had a new a stereo system and a color bar light just like Rusty had in his truck. They would go to the boulevard and cruise the long highway back and forth alongside all the other low-rider cars. They would meet up with the club friends wearing the blue Nite Owl jackets. Morgan looked just like all the other girlfriends of the other members. Her hair was combed into a beehive very high. She wore the eye make-up and the wispy black eyelashes.

Morgan and Dean had a regular routine. When they were finished hanging out with their friends, Dean would drive them to the City Park. In this area, parks were a rare luxury. He had found a special place to park his car that was hidden behind large lilac bushes and camellia bushes. The fragrance from the sweetly scented bushes filled the air. The overflowing oak trees surrounding the area were romantic and luscious and a view of the lake could be seen through the branches. They could hear the sounds of the ducks and geese chirping in the background and splashing about. Morgan had been delighted when he had first taken her to this hidden area. It was so private. She knew that it was the perfect place for them to talk about their future together.

One particular evening the weather was warm and Dean had brought along a bottle of wine. He poured it carefully and filled up the paper cups. Morgan loved the taste of strawberry wine and Dean waited patiently until she finished the cupful. "You're too uptight about this Catholic stuff. You take everything so serious. This wine will relax you. Here, have some more." He filled her cup again.

Chugging down the wonderful strawberry wine, she burped and giggled. "Excuse me," she smiled and placed her head back against the car seat. "Okay, I'm relaxed now." She giggled again. Dean leaned over and kissed her.

Morgan pushed him away gently. "Sweetheart, I want to talk to you about our marriage and our commitment to each other and our life together." She smiled at him. "Please," she begged. "Tell me your thoughts and feelings."

He kissed her nose. "No baby, we have the rest of our lives to talk." He kissed her mouth again and soon his hand went under the neckline of her halter-top and skillfully he pulled the bow tie lace.

She pulled away and scolded him. "I can't believe you just did that!"

He whispered in her ear, "It's all right, it's no big deal. You're okay, my baby kitten." He did not move away from her; instead, he gently touched her strapless bra and caressed her as he whispered in her ear, "Oh, my beautiful doll." He lovingly licked her neck and gently kissed her ear.

It was such a crazy, wonderful feeling that Morgan completely lost the ability to move his hands away. She did not move and she did not ask him to stop.

He whispered and made it quite clear: "If you want me to stop, tell me, and I will. What do you want me to do my love? Tell me."

Morgan breathed deeply, closed her eyes, and helplessly whispered, "Don't stop." He kissed her full mouth. She felt like she would faint.

"Baby doll, do you like this?" he asked.

She purred, "I do."

After a few moments, he was aware of her heavy breathing. Sly and quick, his other rugged hand went gently under her pleated skirt and up between her closed legs. He stopped at her thigh. She was lost in the moment, captivated by Dean's kisses. She purred, "Oh, my God, this feels wonderful." Then she came to her senses and firmly grabbed his arm. In a long breath, she said. "Please stop, Dean."

They were both panting with yearning for more, but with all her strength, she begged him, "We must wait until our wedding night. We cannot disappoint our Lord. Everything must be perfect."

Dean slid to the other side of the car seat. She reached behind her back and retied her halter-top. Then she straightened her skirt and fussed about with her messy hair. He watched her, frustrated.

"This isn't fair. I want you. I've waited months for you. I want you now! Morgan, I will die if I can't have you now!" he yelled. He moved to her side of the car seat and began to kiss her neck again. "I want you now, my love," he pleaded.

She was silent. For a long moment, she stared out the window of the car. She turned her head back and looked into his eyes. His blue eyes pierced her soul. She reached over and took his hand. Gently, she placed it under her skirt and whispered, "Just touch outside my panty, and do nothing else."

With a graceful hand, Dean patted across her belly button back and forth. Then his hand gently stroked across her most intimate private spot and stroked it gently. She moaned breathlessly.

"I'm touching my soft cookie," he whispered.

She was breathing harder. "You've called me a cupcake and now a cookie?"

"Because everything about you is sweet."

Morgan sighed. "I can't wait to be your wife." He grabbed her hand and placed it on his throbbing ache.

Firmly, she moved her hand and yelled, "It's time for us to stop, now!"

Dean gulped. He wiped the dripping sweat from his forehead. "Girl, I have never met anyone who has this much self-control."

Morgan face was blushed. Trembling, she reached over and held his hand. "I was taught self-respect. But don't think for a second this is easy going for me, either."

Chapter 35

"Mother, I'm fine," she told Isabel. Isabel continued to fuss with her daughter's white lace veil. "Dear, I want you to look perfect." Morgan stopped her mother from fussing and grabbed her hands. She whispered, "Mommy, stop worrying."

Isabel looked into her daughter's eyes. "Daughter, please forgive me for not always being there for you. I have not managed well." Isabel began to tear up. She took a deep breath and continued slowly. "The truth is it was I who always wanted to be the nun. Will you forgive me?"

"Mother, forget about it," Morgan said softly but sternly. "We have a new wonderful loving family and the start of a new life. Let's enjoy the time we have right now." The two women hugged.

As they parted, Morgan giggled. "Maybe if I have a daughter she will want to be a nun." They both giggled together.

Isabel wore a Georgette princess tank dress with vines of flirtatious crushed sequins and the skirt was full. She looked lovely in black. She wore two-inch high-heel sandals that had sparkling rhinestones trim and tiny silver bows.

Morgan remembered what had taken place in the bridal store when they bought that gorgeous dress. Betty had overheard Isabel telling Morgan that she could not afford the dress or the shoes, and insisted on paying for everything. Betty told Isabel, "It's only money. We surely cannot take it with us when we die."

Isabel began to fuss again with the lace of the veil. Morgan softly urged, "Go and find your seat in the church and relax. I'll be out soon." Isabel nodded and left. Morgan was grateful to be alone with her own thoughts. Observing her reflection from the mirrored wall, she nervously prayed. "Dear God, help me to be a good wife and lover to my husband. Bless our marriage. I trust in you, Father God." Once again, she stared at herself and turned around, admiring the luxurious fabrics. "I look like I should be in a fairy tale!" Her thoughts were interrupted by the knock at the door.

"May I come in?" Betty asked.

"Yes," said Morgan.

Betty was cheerful. "I wanted you to see my dress. After all, you are the one who choose it."

Morgan smiled at Betty and remembered how difficult it had been to find her future mother-in-law the perfect dress. Unlike Isabel who was petite and took the first dress she tried on, Betty had tried on many. She had been about to give up when Morgan saw a dress on a rack in the bridal store. Grabbing it, she had rushed to Betty in the dressing room and insisted she try it on. It was a short-waist three-quarter sleeve jacket with gorgeous satin lapels and accented with caviar beading and a tiny straight line of baby pearls. The deep marine blue skirt fell just below her ankles. Underneath the jacket, she wore a blue satin tank top. It was an exceptional outfit.

"You look amazing," Morgan told her mother-in-law to be.

Betty walked over to Morgan. "You are beautiful. Sweetheart, before the wedding begins I have one more surprise for you."

The beautiful young bride smiled. "Another surprise, how can that be possible?"

The door opened and two handsome young men walked in and said, "Surprise!" Peter and Noah ran into the room and threw their arms around their sister.

Morgan could hardly catch her breath. She cried out, "Oh, my God, my brothers! You're here. But how? When did you arrive?"

"Rick and Betty paid for our tickets from Ireland," Peter said. "We have been staying with them."

"We wanted to surprise you, sis," Noah chimed in. The three of them hugged tight in a huddle.

The nun organist began to play on the gigantic pipe organ and the classic piece of "Arioso" by Bach's Cantata No. 156 wafted through the halls.

At that moment, Barney walked through the door and greeted everyone. "The wedding is about to start," he said.

Morgan hugged her brothers one more time and said, "Go find your seats."

As promised, Barney was sober and in good spirits. Playfully, he turned around in a circle so Morgan could see the tuxedo that she chose for him. Looking handsome; he wore a black double-breasted tuxedo with a white formal shirt and a black bow tie.

"Daughter," he said, "I feel like the president of the United States!"

Morgan giggled. "No Daddy. You look more handsome." Barney put out his arm and waited for his daughter. She put her arm through his.

Then Rick appeared at the door in his tuxedo with a smile that glowed. "I have come for my lovely wife." Betty walked over to him.

"Rick and Betty, how can I ever thank you for bringing my brothers?" Morgan asked them.

Rick grinned. "Just give us grandchildren someday," and Betty teased, "someday soon." Everyone smiled.

Though it was a traditional Catholic wedding, Morgan and Dean had tried to keep it as simple as possible. Of course, that had proved to be impossible as Betty O'Donnell and her bingo friends and Isabel O'Malley and her church friends had other ideas. All of these women had decorated the church themselves. Every pew had decorations of garlands of scented lilies, ribbons, and bows. Rose petals were spread on the altar steps.

The altar was adorned with dozens of white, long-stemmed roses and dozens of purple dendrobium orchids. A unity candle stood to the side of the altar.

Morgan had asked her two best friends from Saint Catherine's high school to be in her wedding. Sara and Gina were dressed in long pale blue flowing gowns with a black waist sash. Both girls wore their hats tilted forward over the left side of their faces. These handmade blue hats had a wide, oblong rim and white flower clusters and ribbon on top and were quickly becoming a topic of whispered conversation among the guests.

Dean's brother Luke escorted Gina up the aisle then Damien escorted Sara up the aisle. Rusty was Dean's best man. He wore a pure wool single-breasted three-button tuxedo, with a black bow tie. He had the two wedding rings in his pocket and he had been fidgeting nervously with them all day.

Even Lucy, Morgan's best friend and neighbor, had been granted permission to attend the wedding from the convent. She had not yet become a nun. She was still a postulant, meaning she had another two years left to go before she would become a fully ordained nun. Lucy was Morgan's maid of honor. She wore a deep blue satin flowing gown with a black satin sash. Her hat was a display of the most gorgeous white feathers that attached French netting veil around her face. She looked like a delicate English delight.

"Moonlight Sonata" by Beethoven began to play on the organ. The nun played it strong and rich. As the song finished, everyone turned to watch the bride walk down the aisle. To all 125 guests' surprise, there was no bride walking through the closed door.

Chapter 36

Isabel turned around in her seat and looked over to the back of the church doors. The wood swinging doors were closed. Dean wiped his forehead and nervously looked to his parents, who remained calm.

Behind the closed doors, Morgan was unable to move. Standing like a fragile figurine, she was as still as a statue. Barney was calm. "Talk to me, daughter," he said.

A group of thoughts concerned Morgan. "Daddy, I'm terrified. I can't move." She looked for reassurance from her father.

"I've never known one person who didn't get a little jittery before they got hitched. It's a big step. Honey, you are just having a panic attack. Take a deep breath."

Morgan did just that. She took a deep breath in and then let a big breath out. Then she did it again. Just then, a Carmelite nun from the balcony rushed down the back stairs. It was Sister Agatha. She walked over to Morgan with affection and warmth. "Are you getting a butterfly in your tummy?"

Morgan nodded.

"That's a natural feeling. Now the organist wants to know: Are you getting married or what? Get moving. You are keeping Mother Bernadette as well as your future husband waiting." The nun winked sweetly.

Morgan smiled at Sister Agatha and to her dad. "Okay. Start the music please." The nun dashed back up the stairs.

The doors opened wide. Beautiful organ music blared. The "Wedding March" by Miranda played and the guests stood up, delightfully stunned when they saw Morgan walking down the aisle in a white, strapless gown. The bodice was graced in beadwork and the delicate embroidery attached was a long regal train adorned with lace and hundreds of tiny seed pearls. The headpiece was a sparkling comb that featured clustered pearls and bugle beads and crystal accents. The detachable three-layer waist length white shimmer veil held scattered rhinestones and pearls. Even her white satin shoes were lace and pearls. She held a bouquet of white roses.

The walk down the aisle was slow as Morgan and Barney were careful when they stepped on the trail of satin cloth that covered the long aisle's tiled floors.

As they reached the altar steps, Father Paul asked, "Who gives the bride away?" Proudly Barney answered, "I do." Barney had tears in his eyes as he handed his daughter over to Dean.

Dean wore a pure wool single-breasted notch lapel black tuxedo with a black bow tie. His hair was combed perfectly in a ducktail. He looked extremely handsome and serious but his face broke into an adorable grin as he took Morgan's hand and guided her up to the altar to face the priest.

Father Paul wore a white robe. He gave a greeting and an opening prayer then recited the Gospel and the Homily, followed by more prayers. Then with the assistance from the altar boys, they took the white double extra-large rosary and placed it around both the groom and bride. This was to symbolize their union before they took their vows.

The priest began the rite of marriage by inviting the couple to declare their consent to be married, which they did by stating their marriage vows.

Rusty lightened up the serious event when he fumbled for the rings that were stuck in his suit jacket. Everyone in the church giggled.

Morgan's hand was shaking when Dean placed the ring on her left ring finger. He quickly and firmly steadied her hand. Then the priest did a blessing and the vows were said sincerely and according to tradition.

Then Mother Bernadette sang "Ave Maria." Her classically trained voice brought tears to the eyes of all the guests. Morgan closed her eyes and smiled with thoughtful thanks to Mother Bernadette to sing in public.

After the song ended, Lucy went over to Morgan and helped move the veil from her face so she could receive communion from Father Paul. Because Dean was not Catholic, he did not receive the communion host; instead, the priest blessed Dean with the sign of the cross on his forehead. The rest of the guests who were Catholic came up to the front to receive communion. More prayers were said afterward along with some Bible verses. Then the rosary was removed from the couple.

Mother Bernadette stood up in the balcony and slowly walked toward the organist again. She took the microphone and sang the "Irish Wedding Song" by Ian Betteridge. The song was purposely selected for Morgan's Irish heritage. Morgan was delighted when Mother Bernadette sang again. She knew what a tremendous event it was to have Mother Bernadette sing twice.

As Mother Bernadette finished her beautiful song, Morgan stood up and walked over and knelt in front of the beautiful statue of the Blessed Virgin Mary at the right of the church. She prayed in silence with Lucy and both maids of honor at her side to help with the long train. When she was done praying, she got up and genuflected and Lucy handed her the long-stemmed white roses. Morgan took the bundle of roses and left them at the foot of the Blessed Virgin Mary's feet.

She returned to Dean's side.

Father Paul faced the couple and prayed over them. Sister Agatha stood up and went to the microphone and sang, "We've Only Just Begun" by The Carpenters.

Father Paul finally said to Dean, "You may kiss the bride." Gently, Dean pulled back Morgan's veil and lovingly kissed her with all-embracing passion. The song finished and in a loud, proud voice, Father Paul announced, "May I present Mr. and Mrs. Dean O'Donnell."

Chapter 37

The wedding reception took place in the back yard of the O'Donnells'. Rick and his gardeners had had plenty of time to prepare for the special event. He had meticulously landscaped the lawns to looked as green as a golf course. Hundreds of flowers were newly planted and matched the wedding party theme of blue and yellows. The hedges and trees had been pruned. A beautiful oak-colored dance floor was rented and brought a distinct dazzle to the wedding event. Hundreds of blue and yellow balloons were tied everywhere.

Multiple white canopies had been set up for shade on the warm summer day and 150 white chairs and 19 long tables were placed in perfect order and covered with golden yellow linen tablecloths and adorned with silk blue and white floral arrangements.

None of the food was catered. Instead, Betty and Isabel had made plans with all their friends to help prepare the wedding foods themselves. Additional white tables had been set up for the food that many of their friends had volunteered to help prepare. Plates of petite fancy sandwiches of sliced roast beef, turkey, and ham were piled high. Others platters held crab puffs and chicken and beef kabobs marinated in sauce. Deviled eggs and tomato bruschetta was stacked beautifully on dozens of cold trays, along with a variety of cheeses and crackers to satisfy everyone. Large pots were full to the top with chicken and rice casseroles. There were four deep stainless-steel pots full with Isabel's famous bacon, hamburger, and chili beans.

Summer salads set on ice bowls were all on one individual table. The two large bowls of a distinctive corn salad that mixed with chunks of tomatoes, onion, and fresh basil vinaigrette was a big hit. Watermelon salad sat in four large bowls. It was combined with watermelon cubes, feta cheese, black olives, and onions with lime juice and mint with olive oil drizzled on top.

Morgan had gone back to the bakery where she worked during her time at the retreat house in her junior year of high school to give a wedding invitation to Josephine weeks before the wedding.

"I will come to you and Dean's wedding on one condition," Josephine had said. "That I design and make your wedding cake."

The classic seven-tier white cake was adorned with blue and yellow flowers on a white butter cream frosting. All the flowers were hand-painted and tiny strings of pearls strung delicately along the entire length of the cake. When Morgan saw the cake, she hugged and told Josephine how much she loved her thoughtfulness. A porcelain cake topper graced the top, a "swept up in His arms wedding couple figurine."

All around, people continued to mix up and talk endlessly. Morgan's Saint Catherine's school friends were there as well as some nuns who had received special permission to attend. Many of the Nite Owl's car club friends and their dates and Dean's motorcycle friends came. Some folks were professional friends of Dean's parents and Isabel's church friends. Many of Rick and Betty's relatives and friends also attended and Barney's friends from his job came, as well. Georgia, Rusty's mother, walked into the party and surprised everyone by donating two cases of the best sparkling French champagne.

The celebration lasted for hours. First, Rick's favorite Big Band music played. The band was friends of the O'Donnells' and they sang songs by the best singers from the 1940s and '50s. Everyone danced to Duke Ellington, the Glenn Miller Band, and Tommy Dorsey.

Then after two hours, that band got down from the platform and another band came up on the platform. It was the four, long-haired musicians Rusty had been lucky enough to find from the college dance one year ago. They performed music from The

Eagles and The Beatles and Smokey Robinson. Not one guest was sitting; everyone was up and having a great time dancing.

Rusty walked up to the platform and grabbed the microphone. "I want to dedicate this next song to Dean and Morgan from yours truly, The Nite Owls. This is for all you low-rider oldies, enjoy this song, from Mr. Allen. It's called 'Nite Owls.'" The band began the song and the club members went crazy. They grabbed their girls and danced the slow dance proudly. So did Dean and Morgan. They played it three times in a row, then the band played a Latin rhythms and blues number from Santana and Morgan even got Isabel on the floor to dance the salsa with her.

The party went smoothly except for Tootsie, the 300-pound woman friend of Rusty and Dean. She had been brought to the party in a van and was the first time in several years that Tootsie had left her home. Morgan hugged her and was happy to see that she made the reception. "Baby doll, I wouldn't have missed this party for nothing!" Tootsie shrieked.

Tootsie got drunk and it took several people to get her back into the van. Morgan walked to the back of the van and peeked in. She saw Tootsie trying to sit up. Lightheartedly, Morgan laughed and thanked her for coming. "You're awesome, I love you sweetie pie! You're much to pretty to be a nun! And good luck keeping Dean corralled!" Tootsie laughed widely.

Hours flew by as the dancing and drinking continued and soon it was time for Dean and his bride to cut the cake. Proudly, Dean put the silver cake knife in his wife's right hand. With great masculinity, he put his hand over Morgan's hand and together they sliced through the bottom layer of the cake together. They cut one slice. Dean fed his wife a bite and surprised everyone because he was gentle. Distant sounds of the crowd cheering gave Morgan courage. She fed Dean and teasingly pushed the cake into his mouth, smearing it on his face. The crowd cheered. More music began to play and people started dancing and celebrating once again.

A moment later, Dean whispered in Morgan's ear. "Let's get out of here. I'm done with the party. Are you?"

"Yes," she answered him. "I need to go change my clothes."

"Well hurry up." He kissed her tenderly on the mouth. "I want to be alone with my wife."

Morgan found Betty and Isabel. They helped her out of her wedding gown and she changed into an elegant satin, sky-blue, empire mini dress.

"What about all the gifts?" Morgan asked Betty.

"Don't worry about them," Betty answered. "You kids can open everything when you come home from your honeymoon."

As Morgan followed Dean toward the car, she looked out onto the street and was shocked to see all the low-rider cars and motorcycles lining both sides of the street. Dean and Morgan waved good-bye to everyone as the guests threw rice at them. The young couple got into Dean's blue Chevy. The car had "Just Married" written all over the window and five strings of tin cans tied to the fender.

Chapter 38

While Morgan waited inside the Chevy, she thought, "I am probably the happiest girl in southern California. Our wedding turned out perfect." With calculated eyes, she watched Dean take the new fancy suitcases up the stairs at the hotel and rush back to the car for his wife.

"Out of the car," he said as he opened the door for her. Morgan froze. This was the first time she had ever been to a hotel. Dean grabbed her wrists anxiously. "Come on, baby." He directed her to the stair. As soon as she reached the top of the stairs with no warning, he picked her up in his arms and she threw her arms around his neck. He carried her through the open hotel door. Then he passionately he kissed his wife and put her down.

The beach-inspired room took her breath away. The luxury beachfront room was spacious and decorated all in white. The sliding glass doors and windows had overflowing cotton drapes and transparent, lightweight sheers tucked inside. Contemporary classic furniture filled the room and a modern electric fireplace was tucked into the corner.

She walked over to the glass doors and pulled the drapes back. There was a magnificent view of the ocean just steps away. She could feel her heart beat as she stood there.

"Come here. Put your hand on the bed," Dean urged.

She put her hand on the king-sized bed and it started to move. "What is this?"

He laughed. "It's a water bed and you are going to love it." He patted the top and told her to get on top. Morgan climbed onto the waterbed and the bed jiggled. "This is crazy. I love it!" she giggled.

Dean rushed to open his suitcase and produced a rare whiskey that was a gift from Rick. Dean read the bottle to Morgan proudly. "Jack Daniel's Sinatra Select." He opened the bottle and put only two ice cubes into small 4-ounce crystal glasses and poured them both a drink. He swirled the whiskey around the ice. "Drink this," he told his lovely young bride.

In silence, Morgan put the beverage up to her mouth and smelled it. "Drink it," he urged her again. She drank a sip and was quite surprised by the taste. Then she took another little sip. She watched her husband down his whole drink in one gulp. Morgan took her glass and did exactly what he did. She coughed then wiped the tiny drops from her mouth. She actually liked the bold taste full of oak and caramel-vanilla and spice. It was intense yet smooth.

Dean laughed loudly. "You like it, don't you?"

She smiled. "Actually, I do."

He poured them more whiskey over ice and they both drank the whiskey down. Morgan coughed a little this time as her face flushed red. She went over to the big glass sliding door and out to the ocean front deck. Suddenly her arms went up like a playful child. "Come on, let's go for a walk barefooted on the beach!"

The two of them walked down to the beach arm and arm with Dean still in his black tuxedo slacks and white shirt and her in her blue dress. "Let's see," Morgan teased her husband. "I'm 18 and you're 20. In thirty years I will be 48 and you will be a handsome old man of 50." She looked at Dean lovingly. "Do you think that we will still be in love?"

Dean picked up Morgan and swung her around. He yelled out. "More! We will love each other more. I promise you."

They ran through the water and sand, playing and splashing each other like two kids. At last, they ran back up the stairs to their hotel suite with her dress and Dean's slacks soaking wet.

Dean said, "I'm going to start the water. Would you like to take a bubble bath?"

"Sweetheart, the last time I was in a bubble bath was probably when I was seven."

"Stay here," he told her.

She sat in a white wicker chair near the double bathroom doors as she watched Dean go into the large white tiled bathroom. He filled the huge tube with water and poured a small amount of bubble bath inside the tub. Then he lit the ten white pillar candles that were placed around the enormous sunken tub. He took a large white towel and placed it on the sink. Then he brought her suitcase into the bathroom and laid it on the foldable luggage rack.

"Morgan, you can come in now." She walked in and smiled. "Thank you."

"Enjoy, baby." He handed her another glass with Jack Daniels and ice then closed the door.

Morgan took her wet clothes off and they dropped to the floor. She got into the tub full of bubbles and from the buzz of the whiskey, she felt as though she were floating. About half an hour later, Dean knocked gently on the bathroom door. "Baby, it's time to get out."

"Okay," she answered. She climbed out of the tub and grabbed a large, soft towel.

Dean knocked on the bathroom door again, opening it a little bit. "Morgan, there is a wedding gift for you in the small closet. I want you to wear that tonight."

She dried off and went the closet to find the surprise. She unzipped the thin black hanging garment bag. Hanging inside was a silk, red, low-cut, sequin-beaded chemise and next to it hung a tiny pair of red silk G-string panties with rhinestones on the back. There was also a satin white garter belt, a pair of white silk thigh stockings, and high-heel silver slippers in the bottom of the bag.

Morgan could hear her teeth chattering. Then she scolded herself. "Why are you so frightened?" Then she looked down to her suitcase and opened it. Neatly stored there was the two-piece beautiful peignoir bridal nightgown set. It was a white satin and lace floor-length flowing nightgown and robe. Her mother Isabel had bought this for her for this very special occasion along with white ballerina slippers.

She eyed the beverage that Dean had left for her. Picking it up in hurry, she drank down the entire Jack Daniels for courage.

"Time to get ready," she said to herself softly. She rubbed a little scented oil all over her body and slipped into Dean's choice of a bridal nightgown. She took her time pulling the petite rhinestone string panty on and then she took the garter belt and fastened it around her waist. Sitting on the edge of the bathtub, carefully she pulled the thin silk stockings up to her thigh and buckled them up to the garter belt one by one. She slipped her feet into the alluring heeled slippers and they fit perfectly.

The vanity mirror caught her reflection and reminded her of her hair. It was still very bouffant from the beauty shop. She unclipped the cascade of curls attached to the top of her hair, unleashed her long black hair, and shook her hair free. It fell down to her shoulders. Nearby was her white satin purse so she grabbed it and took out her make-up bag.

She applied pearly pink lipstick and brushed a little blush on the apple of her cheeks. Next, with steady hands she took the black eyeliner and lined her eyes. Lastly, she sprayed perfume all over. Stepping back from the mirror she stared at herself. She turned around and looked at her backside then to the front again. "I have absolutely no sensibility left," she whispered.

She looked around the bathroom nervously and spotted the long white terrycloth bathrobe hanging on the back of the closet door. She put it on and tied the belt tight. Then she looked down at her left hand where the wedding ring diamonds shined. Smiling, she nodded her head and whispered again. "You are a married woman who is about to lose her virginity." She breathed in and she breathed out. "It's time to be with the man who loves me."

When Morgan walked out of the bathroom, she saw that Dean had turned the fireplace on and had more drinks ready. There were another five scented rose pillar candles lit throughout the room. The drapes were open just enough for her to see the view of the ocean; the sun had not gone down yet. The bedspread was pulled back and only the crisp white sheets were showing. The long, white, goosedown pillows were laid across the top of the king-sized waterbed. The radio played rhythm and blues music that filtered the room with soft and sexy soulful sounds.

"Where are you, Dean?"

"I am out here, baby, on the deck."

Morgan blushed when she saw Dean without a shirt on. He had a masculine, chiseled body with six-pack abs.

"What's that smell?" she asked. She watched as her husband took a long hard drag from a thin cigarette. Now she remembered that was the same smell at Tootsie's house. Dean was smoking weed.

"Come here, baby," Dean called to her.

Morgan went out to him and he sat her down on his lap. "I see you found the thick robe." He put the tiny cigarette to her lips and told her to inhale. She hesitated for a moment. Dean whispered in her ear. "Come on, baby, inhale this." She did and coughed.

He smiled. "Do it again. This time do it slow, and see how long you can hold the smoke in your mouth."

She tried, and then she coughed more. "I'm no good at this."

With his unaffected ease, he told her forget about it. He took the joint away from her and put it in the ashtray. "Morgan, you are so damn cute." Gently he kissed her neck. "Come on, let's go inside. You don't have to smoke any more of this shit. I need to take a quick shower." He walked into the bathroom and didn't bother to close the door.

"Did he leave the door open purposely?" Morgan thought to herself as she sat in the white wicker chair and watched when he went in the bathroom. Uneasy, she sat quietly and watched Dean unzip his still damp tuxedo slacks. They dropped to the floor. He slipped his briefs off and then he looked over to Morgan and winked.

Morgan was right; he had left the door open knowing she would look. Dean proudly enjoyed displaying his masculine body. She sat back and shifted around in the chair as she watched her husband come out of the shower. He dried himself and kept his back to her and she stared at his tush, which was round, full, and well-defined. Morgan thought it looked like a beautiful hard biscuit.

As only Dean could, he strolled into the bedroom with a white towel tied around his waist. As they caught the sight of each other's eyes, he teased her. "Well, my beautiful wife, it looks like you are relaxed. How are you feeling?"

"I'm happy."

He had a satisfied grin. "That's a good thing."

Morgan loved the way Dean stood straight and tall, looking so clean and fresh with his hair wet. All the hairspray was gone. He handed her a drink and they finished their Jack Daniels before the ice even had a chance to melt.

He pulled his towel off quickly and slid under the white sheets. "I want you to go to the other side of the room for me," he commanded softly.

Slowly she stood up and walked to the other side of the hotel room.

"Now, I want you to untie the robe and take it off."

The white robe fell to the ground.

In a quiet voice, he said. "Baby, turn around for me, slowly."

She did.

"Now don't move. I want to admire you."

She did not move.

"Now turn around and walk to me slowly."

Slowly, she walked over to the bed and began to take the high-heeled slippers off.

"Leave the shoes on."

"Okay."

He got up from under the sheets, laid her back on the waterbed, and looked at her intently. "Every part of you is perfect." He began by kissing her ankles and calves and thighs then slipped her shoes off. Morgan never made a sound.

They kissed for what seemed hours. Dean grabbed the KY lubricant from the nightstand and gently put it on her private part and then on himself.

He kissed her again and finally he got on top of her. His mouth nuzzled her neck and ears with more kisses. The first time he took her, it hurt her though he tried to be as gentle as possible. When it was over, Dean immediately got up from the bed, hurried into the bathroom, and brought her back a very warm washcloth. Devotedly he placed it between her legs and cleaned her.

An hour later, he could not leave her alone. They started to kiss and made love again. The radiance of his masculine scent intoxicated her brain. This was her husband, she belonged to him, and he belonged to her. All five senses overwhelmed her. She found herself consumed by sight, taste, smell, touch, and sound.

All night long she experienced feelings and pleasures she never knew were possible. The night was full of irresistible moaning from pleasure. He was a skillful, unselfish lover. It surprised her how much she enjoyed being touched and how much she enjoyed touching him. Love making came natural to her.

Exhausted and completely satisfied, she turned over and closed her eyes as the sun came up. The last thing she heard was Dean pulling the drapes closed. The last thing she felt was Dean's protecting arms wrapped around her waist.

For two days and two nights, they ordered food from room service and they never left the hotel room, not even for a walk on the beach.

Chapter 39

Finally, the newlyweds left the beach hotel room and began their two-hour ride home. Morgan did not tell her husband that she felt lightheaded and nauseous. She simply assumed it was from drinking the alcohol that she was not accustomed to and from the lack of sleep.

"Baby, do you want to stop at the new mountain amusement park?"

"Of course, I love roller coasters and it's been years since I've been on one," she answered cheerfully.

Holding hands, they walked through the theme park and Dean saw a cart which held a full tray of tempting red delicious candied apples. He bought two and handed one to his wife. They both gobbled them up. "Come on," he said as he pulled Morgan toward the big wooden railed roller coaster. After the ride and without any warning, she belched into the nearest trash container and then threw up.

Dean took off his Harley-Davidson headband and used the handkerchief to help Morgan wipe her face and hands.

"I don't know what's wrong," she looked into her husband's eyes for an answer.

"Don't worry about it. We need to get you to a bathroom. The candy apple made you sick, I shouldn't have given it to you before we went on a fast ride." He put his arm around her shoulders. After searching, finally, they found a bathroom. Morgan rushed to a toilet and threw up again.

"You know I think I must have had a rotten apple," she told Dean as they walked to the car.

"It's okay," he said. "You drank a lot of booze and you are not used to that. That might be it."

They got in the car to drive home and he had to pull the car over to the side of the road several times for her to throw up. At one point, he even helped her hold her hair back as she got sick.

Dean stopped at a gas station. Morgan listened from inside the car when he called his parents from the pay phone. "Mom, she is really sick. I don't know what to do." He sounded frantic.

Once inside the car he told Morgan in a husky voice, "We are going to my parents' house."

Rick and Betty were waiting at their front door. Dean carried Morgan in his arms from the car into his old bedroom and laid her on the bed. Morgan said, "I'm so sorry. I don't know what's wrong." Then she turned very red in the face, sprang out of the bed, ran to the bathroom, and threw up.

As Morgan was washing her face in the bathroom, she overheard the ending of the conversation between her husband and his parents. Dean asked his parents if it was okay if they stayed with them until Morgan felt better. Rick said, "Of course son, go get your suitcases." Morgan felt relieved.

Early the next day, Betty cooked chicken soup with bouillon cubes, vegetables, garlic, onions, and rice and brewed ginger tea for her daughter-in-law. "I'm very concerned that you're not getting better. You look awful pale. I think you are rundown from the wedding and caught a flu bug."

Barney, Isabel, Peter, Noah, and a few close friends came over to the O'Donnell home and they watched Morgan and Dean open thoughtful, personalized wedding gifts. Isabel brought over a homemade delicious pineapple upside-down cake that dazzled with fresh pineapple rings stuffed with maraschino cherries, drizzled with warm butter, and melted brown sugar. After dessert, it was time to say good-bye to Noah and Peter.

Morgan was inconsolable. "I've scarcely had a chance to visit with you brothers. I am going to die from a broken heart. I don't want to say good-bye!" The three of them clustered together tightly.

Peter tried to speak but he choked up. "Sister, I want you to make sure you write us letters, pictures, and the lot, and we will promise to send back."

"Sis, you would love Ireland," Noah said. "The land is beautiful and green. The people are fun. I know one day you will come and visit." Overcome with grieved emotion the three clung so tightly to each other that they almost clawed. Morgan cried until her eyes were swollen and very red.

Rick and Dean stood at her side out on the lawn and Betty had her arms wrapped around Morgan. They waved good-bye to the family as Barney and Isabel drove the brothers to the Los Angeles International Airport. Terror crept through Morgan's spirit as darkness wrapped over her own mind with the silent wonder. "When will I ever see my dear sweet brothers again?" With great difficulty, she remained on her feet.

Chapter 40

The following week, Dean moved their suitcases and wedding gifts out of his parents' home and into their freshly painted two-bedroom apartment.

Morgan tried in vain to get the apartment in order, but it was hopeless; she had to lie down several times a day due to lightheadedness. Every morning she woke up early to fix Dean's breakfast of bacon, eggs, and coffee, but the smells just made her feel worse and she would vomit yellow bile. After seven weeks of weeks of this with no signs that her condition was going to improve, she made an appointment with her childhood family doctor.

"When was your last period?" Dr. Wilcox asked her once they were in the exam room.

She struggled to remember. "The week before my wedding, I think."

He frowned. "I want you to go into the bathroom and pee into this small jar. I am going to run a test on you. There is a possibility that you may be pregnant."

"I can't be pregnant. I just got married. And I have faithfully douched each time after we had intercourse and we used condoms." In contemplation of her stupidity, she looked down to the floor. "Most of the time we use condoms," she mumbled.

The doctor shook his head disapprovingly. "Oh my, that old wives' tale! Just to make sure you understand, douching after intercourse does not prevent pregnancy, and condoms break. Having intercourse without protection creates pregnancies and diseases. Humm, who told you about this douching fable?"

"My mother."

He snickered. "Well, that explains a lot. That woman is a strict Catholic and she does not believe in birth control. Did she have any conversations with you about birth control pills or condoms before you were married?"

"Very little," she sighed.

"Please go into the bathroom so we can do the test. I will have the results for you in less than an hour."

Later that afternoon Morgan drove herself home in the blue Chevy. She had to pull over to the side of the road to throw up but made it home and ran straight into the bathroom to get sick again. She threw her head down on the toilet seat and began to cry in despair. "I feel so ashamed and stupid for not learning more about birth control. It never occurred to me that I could get pregnant so easily," she cried.

She felt anxious about telling Dean the news. She forced herself to get up and applied her make-up then got dressed in a pink cotton blouse and blue hip-hugger Levis. She pulled her hair back into a neat ponytail and approached the mirror satisfied.

She went into the kitchen and began to prepare his favorite foods: a thick ham steak, store-bought biscuits, a baked potato loaded with butter and sour cream, and Jell-o for dessert. As usual, he came home on time, walked in the door, took Morgan in his arms, and kissed her. "Baby doll, spending time with you is the highlight of my day." Then he sat down at the table and wolfed down his dinner, not noticing that she just played with her food and only took a few bites.

After dinner, they made love in the living room on the big beanbag chair on the carpet. When it was over, Dean left to take a shower. He came back into the room and he joined her back down on the beanbag chair. Morgan let a few moments pass before taking a deep breath.

"Honey, I need to tell you something."

"No, don't talk. I want to make love to you again." He began to kiss her neck.

"Dean, I'm pregnant."

His face went blank. "You're knocked up?"

"If you mean I'm pregnant, then yes! I went to the doctor today and he confirmed it."

"Shit," he said. He leapt up like a tornado, pulled on his Levis, and went out the front door to smoke a cigarette.

Troubled, she stood up and went into the bathroom. She turned on the warm water and watched the stream of water begin to fill the bathtub. She tried to brush her teeth but the taste made her nauseous. She threw up in the toilet then sank down into the tub. She closed her eyes and put her head back on her bath pillow. As she soaked, she mentally began to wash the stress of the day away and took small, deep breaths. Soon she felt her body relax.

Dean came into the bathroom and sat on the floor beside the bathtub. His face looked exhausted. "How do you feel about being pregnant?"

Her eyes searched his face. "I'm happy I'm pregnant with our baby even though this is definitely unplanned."

"I am taking the blame. I should have used condoms every time. Your Catholic religion insists on no birth control but we should have been better prepared." He looked down and mumbled, "It's too damn soon."

She began to weep.

Dean's face looked like a convicted felon found guilty of a punishable crime. He gulped. "We'll manage."

"Leave the bathroom and shut the door. I need my space," she ordered.

Chapter 41

Four weeks passed. Morgan woke up and immediately felt queasy. She ran to the bathroom and threw up yellow bile. Dean had already left for work. Morgan knew he was scared to wake her up because of her sickness. As she sat there on the toilet, she frowned while staring at the piles of overflowing laundry that were stacked in the corner of the bathroom. She looked at herself in the mirror and saw the dark circles under her eyes and pale skin. She staggered to the kitchen, opened the cupboard, and saw no clean glasses. The dirty dishes were overstacked in the kitchen sink so she grabbed one and rinsed it out under hot water. Then she refilled it with cold water, drank a sip, then swished the rest in her mouth and spit it out on to the dirty dishes.

Her glance moved to the beautiful wedding gifts that were still in their boxes. Then the phone rang on the kitchen counter in front of her. She sighed, reached for a kitchen towel, and placed it over the white telephone.

As soon as she managed to get back into her bed, she had the urge to urinate again. "Again!" she complained, and marched unhappily into the bathroom. She peed and threw up again, then she felt dizzy and had a headache.

Finally, she was back tucked inside her bed. The room was dark. Suddenly, she heard a persistent knocking coming from her apartment door. "Go away," she said under her breath. The door knocks stopped.

Then she heard banging on the bedroom window. A woman yelled. "Morgan, open up the door at once!"

After a long delay, Morgan pulled the covers back and crept out of her bed. She reluctantly went over to the window and pulled the dark blue drape back. Betty stood there with her arms folded across her chest. Without a smile, Morgan closed the drape then slowly went to the front and unlocked the door. Betty stood there with a look of sadness and disbelief in her eyes.

Morgan never spoke a word. She looked at her mother-in-law then she turned away and rushed back to the bathroom to vomit more, followed by dry heaving.

Betty stood at the bathroom door. Morgan looked up at her. "I'm worse; I'm not getting any better. I can't even keep water down." Then she grabbed the toilet seat and dry heaved again.

Betty knelt down on the bathroom floor beside her very sick daughter-in-law. She took Morgan's head and brought it close to her own body. She held her tight and spoke to her with tears in her eyes. "You are not going to lose this baby. I am not going to lose you. I have waited a lifetime for you, my daughter. I had an eerie premonition that something was wrong but I tried to give you and my son privacy. Thank God I came over here today. I am taking you home with me."

Betty rocked Morgan in her arms. Then she got up and put a washcloth under the hot water faucet. She wrung it out and washed Morgan's face. Then she found a hairbrush and began to brush her long hair.

"That hurts," Morgan cried out.

Betty stopped. It was impossible to get through the tangles so she put a cloth rubber band around the long hair to get it out of Morgan's face. Then she helped Morgan into the bedroom and laid her on the bed.

Morgan watched Betty as she looked around the dark, cluttered room. There were dirty Levi's and work clothes that belong to Dean piled on the carpet and chair. The smell from the trash can was foul. Betty found a suitcase in the closet among more soiled clothes and she began to fill it with a few items. She grabbed a blanket and pillow from the bed and pulled the suitcase with her other arm. "I'm going out to my car. I will be right back for you." She disappeared.

With great effort, Morgan dressed herself in a dark blue velour sweat suit and white canvas sneakers. Waiting for Betty, she sat at the kitchen table surrounded by clutter, empty containers of junk food, and fast food. "I'm finally getting out of this dreadful, dreary dungeon," she thought.

Betty came back into the kitchen area and Morgan watched how angry Betty's face had become. Betty shoved the trash to the side of the table and sat down. "I'm going to have a mental breakdown, so ignore me." She proceeded to write a note and left it on the table. "Morgan, I'm going to use the bathroom. I will be right back, sweetheart. Then we will leave."

Morgan picked up the letter and read:

Dear Son,

I have taken Morgan home with me. Your wife will not return to live in this soiled apartment. So begin at once to pack up everything. You can store everything in one of our garages after you have washed all these dirty clothes! Both of you will live with us until our grandchild is born. I am appalled with your behavior in this situation. You could have a least helped your wife to keep your home cleaned. We did not raise our son to live this way. I am disgusted with your behavior. The mother of your baby is very sick! You should have told us sooner. You are lucky that your father was not here. I Love you but at this moment, I am enraged and most serious!

From, Mother

The following week Betty drove Morgan to the doctor after Morgan found blood spotting on her panties. She still felt faint and nauseous.

A nurse with a mild case of acne and somewhat creepy voice called out her name. "Morgan O'Malley?" Morgan followed the grim nurse through an old wooden door that was shouting for a coat of paint. They went into a small waiting room with flowered wallpaper that had begun to peel. Morgan warned, "I'm going to throw up. I need something to get sick in." The nurse raised her shoulder blades as though she did not care. Morgan threw up on the hospital bed that was lined with white sanitation paper. "I warned you," she said to the nurse with little emotion.

Annoyed, the nurse cleaned up the mess. Then she came into the room with a small trash container. "Here, use this. The doctor will be in soon."

After that, Morgan waited alone. She wished that Betty had come in but because she was only her mother-in-law they would not allow her into the room. "Foolish rules," Morgan thought.

At last, the preoccupied Dr. Wilcox walked into the room. "How are you feeling today, Morgan?"

"Not doing so well." Then she dry heaved into the trash can.

"Hum," Dr. Wilcox said. "Let me see what she wrote down." He looked over the papers he had on her chart. "This is a rare situation with the morning sickness lasting all day and night. Not good. And the spotting? Not good. Too, be honest with you there is a chance you will not carry the baby full-term. This will be a difficult situation. Not much to do now except for wait. And stay in bed. I will see you next month." Then he left the room.

Morgan told Betty what had happened with the doctor on the drive home. Betty said, "That damn doctor has no empathy at all." Then she drove into a parking lot of a medical supply store and told Morgan to wait in the car. After a while, Betty came back into the car with a portable potty, a suitable pail for Morgan to get sick in, a small basin, and special therapeutic socks. Then she stopped at a drugstore and came back to the car with a small table fan and a bed tray.

For days, Morgan laid in her dark room and listened to Betty's woman friends talk about her.

"This girl will never go full-term."

"If this baby lives then it will be a weak child."

"She should have aborted the baby."

"Weak women lose their life giving birth."

Morgan switched the fan on high to drown out the negativity.

As the months passed, Morgan had to stay in bed. She was nauseous and vomited daily, but there was no choice but to go forward under those circumstances. Betty tried to keep her spirits up. Most days Morgan received new gift packages to open. There were lots of beautiful elegant Egyptian cotton pajamas, panties, and cotton bras. Betty changed her daughter-in-law's pajamas daily. Morgan had several lovely maternity outfits to choose from but she avoided those clothes until it was necessary to dress up for doctor's appointments.

Each day the women stayed on a daily routine. Betty would cook hot cereal in the mornings, sit by the bed, and spoon-feed Morgan even though Morgan could only take a few bites before spitting it up in the pail. They both had discussed and hoped that perhaps some nourishment was getting to the baby. Then they walked around the backyard garden. At lunch, then again at supper, Betty patiently fed her bites of toast and Jell-o or soup and then they'd take another walk.

Every morning, cheerful Betty asked, "How are you feeling today, my darling?"

Morgan always gave the same answer. "I feel like I just got off the merry-go-round at the park and it went too fast."

Morgan slept up to seventeen hours a day. Once in a while she opened her eyes and Dean would be sitting there by her bed. He always looked sad and mad.

One day he yelled. "I just don't understand this. Why are you so sick? I've seen other pregnant women and they look happy and fat. I can't stand seeing you this way. This is total bullshit!"

Morgan lost her patience with Dean that day. "I never expected any of this to happen to me. No one knows why I'm so sick. You were never in love with me! You only wanted me because I was a virgin! I never even wanted to have a baby! This is your entire fault. I'm only eighteen years old. I just graduated from high school! None of this was my plan. In spite of this horrible vomiting, I'm dealing with it. That's more than I can say for you, Dean O'Donnell!"

It took so much energy for her to holler at Dean. Inside, she acknowledged the fact that he was tired of her just being sick in bed but she felt he wasn't being compassionate. Too weak to care about Dean's needs, she just turned over on her side and closed her eyes.

Dean got up and slammed the bedroom door, and then the living room door slammed shut, and then she heard the load roar of the motorcycle when he drove off. "He is such an ass and so selfish," was the last thought in her mind before she belched into the trash pail at the bedside. Weakly, she fell back to sleep.

Twice a week, Morgan listened to the water pour into the big white porcelain tub. Betty prepared a bath for her with warm water and her homemade peppermint bath salts made with Epsom salt, sea salt, and drops of peppermint oil. Betty undressed Morgan, helped her into the warm water and soothingly bathed her with a natural bath sponge. Then Betty filled a big water pitcher and poured water over Morgan's long hair over and over again. The pail was always within reach in case Morgan had to throw up, which happened on occasion.

One particular Wednesday morning, Morgan stood up from the bath for Betty to dry her and caught her reflection in the long mirror. Dark circles concaved her eyes. She had lost so much weight that she looked frail, but she looked past that to see the progress of their difficult pregnancy effort. Her tummy was beginning to show an expanding bulge, like she had swallowed a small bowling ball. Morgan rubbed her tummy. Betty nodded and said, "The baby is growing."

That day changed everything. Morgan envisioned her own heart and her baby's heart beating strong inside her body. Lying in bed that day she knew that the darkest tunnel she was trapped in had finally sprung a trifle of light.

Chapter 42

The last month of her pregnancy seemed to linger forever. At last, the day came; she went into labor in the morning. By the middle of the night, they were in the car.

"For heaven's sake, you are driving too fast!" Betty warned her son.

"I'm sorry mom, I'll slow down," he said.

"I'm going to get sick." Betty held out the trusted pail. Twice Morgan used it.

When they reached the hospital, Morgan was immediately put into a wheelchair. After being settled in the small hospital room, a nurse instructed Morgan: "You are not allowed to get out of the bed except to go to the bathroom. Push this button so someone will come in here to help you."

Hours went by and her back began to hurt so much from the bed that she could barely stand the pain.

As more hours passed and Morgan's pain grew, she screamed at the nurse. "I'm just going to die!" A sharp labor pain came, then another. She held her stomach that felt as tight as a ball. It was the worse cramps she had ever felt.

Dean strolled into the dreary hospital room and she yelled at him. "It's because of you that I'm in this pain! I will never have sex again!" Then she screamed again, "This is bullshit!" Her body went into the fetal position. The pains were sharp, intense, and deep.

Morgan overheard Dean talk to Isabel at the entrance of the room. "I have never heard Morgan use profanity."

"Don't worry about it. Contractions would make even the saints swear. She doesn't mean a word of it."

Isabel came in and sat with her daughter. "You are a strong woman. I am proud of you and this will all be over soon."

Morgan glared at her mother, "You never prepared me for this. You never talked to me about sex. Never!"

"I'm sorry," Isabel whispered.

A nurse walked into the room. "This will sting," she said coldly.

Morgan turned her head right away. The needle pierced her skin and veins to allow the tiny catheter to maneuver into the vein. It was attached to flexible tubing that ran to a bag that held fluids. Immediately the IV dripped its magic of liquids into her body. "The fluids will help with your dehydration," the nurse said, then looked at Isabel. "It's time for you to leave."

Isabel kissed her daughter's cheek. "I love you, and Betty and Rick and your father all love you. Everyone is in the waiting room now."

"I love you too, mommy," Morgan whimpered.

After Isabel left the room, everything started happening very quickly. Another nurse walked into the room and put on a glove and told Morgan, "Open up your legs wide." She inserted her fingers into Morgan's vagina then reported, "She's eight fingers dilated." One nurse left the room.

Morgan started to dry heave. She could not lift or turn her head because the pains were steady and powerful and her lower back was killing her with pain. She screamed, "Please give me something for the pain!" A nurse said, "In a few minutes, you will get a spinal block injection."

Morgan was scared. "What's that?"

"A needle will be inserted into your lower back through a membrane surrounding your spine and an injection fluid will block the pain. You may feel some pressure and a sting from the needle but it doesn't hurt much."

Dean was standing at the doorway. The nurse said, "This girl should have had some training classes about childbirth. She knows nothing."

Dean shook his head. "I'm sorry, we both don't know much.

My wife has been in bed for nine months. She's been very sick and to top it off she's never been in a hospital."

"Well then it's going to be tough ride for her."

"Please!" Morgan screamed. "Please, I beg you to help me. Dean, it hurts so much!"

He rushed back to her side. "Baby, it will be over soon. It's killing me that I had to watch you suffer all these months and now this."

She looked into her husband's frightened eyes and whispered, "I'm so scared."

Just then, two nurses rushed into the room and ordered him to leave. The door closed.

Ten minutes later, they gave her the spinal shot then Morgan was flung onto a gurney. The wheeled hospital stretcher was moved into the operating room.

Morgan cried aloud, "I want my husband!" A nurse in a mask and vinyl gloves firmly said, "No husbands allowed in the delivery room."

Quickly she was wheeled on a hospital gurney bed down the hallways. Then she was put onto the operating room table. The shot had worked because she could not lift her legs. They had to lift and put her legs in the steel stirrups. Morgan leaned forward and touched the stirrups because her leg stuck. They were ice cold.

Now she faced a mirrored wall. The room was freezing and she started to shake. The two nurses left the room and for a couple of minutes Morgan was alone. She felt no more pain but she stared at her opened legs that were strapped down and felt scared.

The nurses walked back in with masks and vinyl gloves and aprons on. They both opened up Morgan's thin legs and strapped them in the steel stirrups and then they strapped her arms down.

Morgan was terrified. "I want my mom," she begged. "Please get Betty." She wept.

A nurse said, "I told you no family in the operating room. Now be quiet."

When the nurse poured water between her legs and began to shave all her pubic hair off, Morgan vomited onto her hospital gown. Then one nurse roughly splashed red ointment between her legs to serialize her. Angry tears rolled down Morgan cheeks. No one told her that giving birth would happen like this. She felt unprepared and helpless. The room felt colder. She turned her head to the side of the pillow, started to dry heave, and threw up on the hospital gown again.

Then the doors flew open and a black nurse charged into the operating room. She tore her surgical mask off after looking at Morgan and shouted at the other nurses. "How long has this child been in labor?"

"Twenty-two hours," someone answered.

The black nurse yelled, "What the hell is going on here? Clean up this vomit! Get this woman cleaned up now!" She glared across the room at the two young nurses and shook her head. "There will be a mandatory meeting after this birth." Then the tall nurse went over to Morgan's side and in a comforting, self-assuring voice, said, "My name is Bessie. I am the head maternity nurse and you do not need to be frightened any longer. I am right here beside you."

Immediately and quietly, the two other nurses swiftly changed Morgan's gown, wiped her face with cool water, and changed the top sheet.

Bessie fluffed up her pillow and ordered one of the other nurses to get a warm blanket, which Bessie put across her chest. Then she looked between Morgan's fragile thin legs. She muttered, "Honey, you're as thin as a rail." She put back her white mask on and protective gloves and felt between her legs. You are at 10 centimeters and you're going to crown soon." Both the other two nurses left the operating room.

Bessie spoke firmly and softly to her. "Child, you came this far you're going to have to get your strength up and push, push like you have never done before. You need to help Mother Nature get that baby out of you so you need to listen to me. I don't want you to push until I tell you. Then I want you to push with all you have. Understand?"

"Yes," Morgan said.

Bessie took off her mask again and smiled at Morgan before getting a serious look on her face. "I know you can't feel anything, your body downwards in numb. Do what I say. Otherwise, old Dr. Wilcox will use the big forceps and pull your baby out like a calf is being pulled out of a cow. With force!" Morgan nodded, understanding what Bessie was trying to tell her.

Bessie nodded once then put back on her surgical mask and stood next to Morgan's head, brushing her hair away from her face with her strong hands. She put her arm around Morgan's shoulders as Dr. Wilcox walked in with gloves and a mask on. "Is she ready?"

"She's very close," Bessie said.

Morgan was terrified but Bessie looked right into Morgan's eyes. "You are not a child, you are going to be a mother. You need to help your baby be born. You have to get tough. I know you feel weak, but I know that you have one good push in you." She ordered her in a loud voice, "Now you push, child! Push now!"

Morgan's face was pale. Collecting all the little strength that she had left, she began to push harder. Then she lay back, exhausted. The doctor turned to grab the nearby forceps.

Bessie thundered, "Give me one more big push. Now push!" With all the strength that she could muster, Morgan's face turned red and with a rock-hard push, the doctor dropped the forceps from his gloved hands and caught the baby. "It's a girl!" he announced.

Miraculously, a baby cried. An instant later, Morgan heard a buzzer going off and her eyesight shut down. The room went black. Through the darkness, she narrowly heard Bessie say, "We're losing the mother." Immediately someone shoved an oxygen mask on her face. Morgan passed out.

Chapter 43

After twelve hours of deep sleep, Morgan woke up in the hospital room. When she opened her eyes the first thing she saw was Dean sleeping in the chair next to the side of her bed. Bessie had spent her shift time off at Morgan's side. When she saw Morgan open her eyes, she stood up and softly whispered, "Morgan, are you awake? Can you hear me?"

With expressive eyes, Morgan uttered, "The baby?"

Dean opened his eyes and bolted out of the chair. Bessie stood back to give the young couple room. He smacked into the side of the bed rails and tripped over his shoes on the floor but clumsily took Morgan's hands. "Oh, my God! Baby doll, you're awake." He lovingly touched her face then he tenderly kissed her hands. "You've been asleep for hours; damn you had a tough time giving birth." He attempted to explain the complications. "You had low blood pressure, and your body went into shock!" Then he stopped. "I don't want to talk about that bullshit anymore." He kissed Morgan's forehead. "Our daughter is a beauty just like her mother." His head went down and he buried it in her hands. "Baby, I promise to be the best damn husband to you. I will be a good father. I'm stepping up to the bat. I'm in the game now."

Morgan looked at her husband's face. There were dark circles under his eyes and his blond hair was all shaggy and his face was unshaved. She was proud of her husband for not bailing out on her at the hospital. He had stayed throughout the whole ordeal. She smiled at him.

"What do you think about the name Noelle?" he asked her. "It's a good Irish name."

Morgan smiled. "I love it." She yawned.

From the dim corner of the room, Bessie stepped forward and gently placed her hand on Dean's shoulder. "It's time for you to leave now. Your wife needs rest." Without a murmur, he left.

Morgan finally reopened her eyes hours later. She looked around the hospital room and saw no one. She glanced over to the window and saw that it was dark outside. She wondered how long she had been asleep. Then Bessie appeared at the door and walked over to Morgan. "Well, it's about time you woke up. How are you feeling?"

"I am so grateful the birth is over. That was tough."

Bessie smiled. "I have a surprise for you." She walked back to the doorway and waved to a nurse who was waiting nearby. Immediately a small baby bed on rollers was wheeled into the room. Bessie reached down, picked up the baby gently, and handed her over to Morgan. "This is Noelle. Now, you are extremely weak. I am allowing you to be with your daughter for a few minutes. Do not unravel the blanket. She just fell asleep."

"Okay," Morgan said.

Bessie walked out of the room. Morgan felt awkward holding the tiny bundle then cautiously unwrapped the white blanket confining her baby. She began to examine her infant, touching each tiny wrinkled finger and toe. Gently she squeezed her chubby thighs and felt her delicate arms. Without hesitation, she unfastened the baby's diaper. "You're perfect," she whispered. "My sweet darling angel, you grew in my body. You are my miracle angel." She pulled the baby's legs up toward her and kissed all over the tiny feet.

Noelle began to cry. Morgan was startled at how loud the cry was. The baby was turning red.

Bessie walked back into the room with a frown. "Oh my goodness, look at this, I leave you alone for a few minutes and look what you did!" The baby started to cry louder. "This girl has lungs," Bessie said cheerfully.

Morgan was relieved to see Bessie smile. "Oh Bessie, I never knew a baby could cry so loud."

"Oh, you sweet child, you have a lot to learn, but it will all work out with patience and love."

Morgan tried to explain why she had unwrapped the baby. "I wanted to see if my child had all her fingers and toes."

Bessie waved her hand. "There's no need for you to explain these things to me. I have given birth to my own six children. Believe me child, I understand."

"Bessie, I'm in a lot of pain."

"Yes, I imagine you are. Right now I'm giving you ice packs for the swelling down below."

Bessie took a big hospital ice pack, wrapped it in a white towel, and placed it between Morgan's legs. "I'm only going to give you aspirin for your pain because you are going to start nursing."

Bessie handed Morgan a small paper cup with one pill in it and a glass of water. After Morgan gulped it down, she handed the glass back to Bessie.

"Now I want you to open your nightgown and unhook the front of the nursing bra you have on." Morgan did.

The baby was crying harder. Bessie took Noelle from her mother, put her back in the little crib, and began to wrap her up tight in the blanket so she looked like a little burrito. She handed the screaming baby back to Morgan and then she helped her adjust the pillow under her arm and the baby's body.

"Are you comfortable, Morgan?"

"Yes, I am but I'm nervous."

"That's natural." Then Bessie gently shoved the baby's mouth toward Morgan's breast. She showed Morgan what to do and reminded her about a few details of breast-feeding and the benefits for both mother and baby. Noelle latched on to the nipple on the first try. She stopped whimpering and began swallowing. Her little pink ears were wiggling. Soon it was time to take a break. Morgan naturally slipped her finger gently in the corner of the baby's mouth to break her suction. Bessie showed her how to burp her. Soon after, Noelle was happily suckling on the other full breast. Morgan was quiet. Softly she watched her baby girl and touched her cheeks with the tips of her fingertips.

Her breasts were tender from the sucking and it was a relief when the baby began to stop. Morgan blocked out any pain and instead concentrated of the beauty of her healthy baby girl. This was her miracle child. The milk began to drip from the side of the baby's cheek and Bessie said, "She's satisfied."

Bessie took the baby and put her into her crib. "We are going to the nursery. You get some rest." Rolling the crib toward the door, she stopped and turned. "I admire you, Morgan. You are going to be a nurturing mother. It comes natural for you. It's not often that I have the pleasure of seeing many women who can nurse their baby this easily. Many mothers never want to try. You are an amazing, strong girl.

"Now I want you to look over to the tray at the left of your bed. There is a list of foods for your meals. Select any choice that you feel like eating. Remember we talked about food choices you may and may not eat while you are breast-feeding. When you are finished, ring the buzzer and the candy striper aid will be in to take your order. You will be able to eat as soon as the kitchen gets your requests." She left.

Morgan grabbed the paper. Hurriedly she circled the food choices, then rung the buzzer. The young teenage girl with a striped uniform walked into the room and took her order. Morgan waited 30 minutes. The same teenager walked back into the room with a tray of food covered by a silver cover. "If you need anything, just ring the buzzer." She left.

Morgan sat completely still. It had been nine very long months that she suffered with the nausea and vomiting. Slowly, she uncovered the plate and grabbed a fork and knife. She was starving as she cut the tender steak. She took a small bite, afraid of what was going to happen. She waited to feel nauseous. Nothing happened. She took another bite. Tears rolled down her cheeks as she took her time eating the warm steak, the perfect fluffy baked potato, and a hot buttered biscuit. She looked over to the two small, unopened cartons of milk. After minutes went by, she said aloud, "Okay, here I go, I haven't been able to drink milk in like, forever." Slowly, she tore opened one carton of milk and poured it into a glass. She drank down the entire glass. After a huge burp, she sat still and waited for the queasiness. None came. Immediately she opened the other waiting carton and poured more milk. She swallowed all of it and she waited. "It's okay," she told herself. "Noelle is born and it is a miracle she is a healthy baby girl! All the months of suffering are over. No more throwing up!"

Chapter 44

Four months passed. Morgan walked into the bedroom and laid her sleeping daughter on the bed. She opened the double closet doors and looked up to the top shelf. She grabbed a coat hanger and used it to try and jiggle a white box loose. Unable to reach it, she went over to the other side of the bedroom and pulled an antique wood chair over to the closet. She stood on top of the chair to reach the back on the top shelf. She got it down, opened it up, and searched through the box of clothes, pulling stuff out and tossing them on the carpet. There they were. Smiling, she grabbed the brand new size 6 pair of Levi's that Dean had bought her last Christmas. She pulled them on and zipped them up with just a small struggle. Reaching through several sweaters, she finally decided on a powdered blue one. Morgan looked at herself in the mirror, smiled again, and said aloud to her baby. "Just wait until your daddy sees me in these Levi's." She knelt down beside the box and carefully folded all the clothes tossed on the carpet and put them back into the box. Looking around the room, she saw that everything was in order and there was nothing more to do. A moment of boredom begun to oppress her until her glance instinctively sought out her baby. She crept quietly over to the bed and cuddled up close to her daughter.

The window was opened slightly and she watched the breeze blow the white curtains. Morgan looked beyond the curtains and stared out at the blue sky that held the morning sun. The baby began to coo. Morgan watched her beautiful daughter's alert eyes and then turned her on her tummy. With boundless love, she kissed every little finger on Noelle's hands. "Do you ever get tired of me kissing you? Well, I just can't stop. I adore you, my precious baby doll." Noelle pulled her head up and smiled back at her mother and giggled as Morgan touched her velvety cheek. Noelle supported herself on her arms and lifted her head and shoulders off the bed. Eventually she rocked, kicked, and flipped over. The baby's smile consumed her heart and again she smothered the baby's chubby arms and legs with more than enough kisses. Then Morgan laid her head down next to her daughter and listened to the happy voices of the neighborhood children playing outside. She thought of her life now.

With each new day, she knew she was feeling stronger. They were living with the O'Donnells and there was no hurry to move out. These days were incredibly happy; Betty and Morgan were overcome with joy with Noelle. They were both up together in the middle of the night when the baby was awake, and they both slept when the baby slept. All their meals were together. They even had two beautiful matching rocking chairs that they rocked back and forth together, taking turns passing the child between them. Morgan and Betty believed that Noelle was a true miracle. Every moment was a precious joy for them. The two women never complained when she cried, which some days was often. Instead, they would laugh, giggle, and talk about everything.

One day Rick had teased Betty in front of Morgan. "Honey, you need to stop cooking for her. What you need to do is to start teaching her to cook."

Betty had just chuckled. "Oh Rick, that's nonsense. There will be plenty of time later for my daughter-in-law to learn to cook, and besides I love to spoil my two girls." Morgan had watched as her father-in-law turned and looked at Betty and then Noelle and finally herself. For a long moment, he had gazed into each of their faces, as if to carry the memory forever in his mind. He spoke softly to his wife. "All right my love, spoil our girls." He smiled. "Our daughter Morgan has given me the greatest gift of life, our granddaughter. And I know these baby days don't last forever." He bent down and kissed Betty, Morgan, and Noelle each on the forehead. "We are living the memories that our lives will be made from."

The times were not that simple for Dean. Morgan could sense his restlessness, especially on Friday evenings. Many Fridays he would beg his wife, "Come on, Morgan. Let's get out of here and go to a party. Let's get drunk and have some fun. I want us to get crazy. I want you to ride on the motorcycle with me."

Morgan got upset and embarrassed when he said things like that. "Dean, you know that I can't drink alcohol while I'm breast-feeding. I can't leave our baby. Why can't you stay home this weekend with me and your parents? Do you have to go out every Friday and Saturday night?"

After dinner that night, Morgan handed her husband the baby. Then she went into the bathroom, applied fresh lipstick and perfume, and touched up her hair. She wondered if Dean had noticed that she was wearing her new Levi's.

It meant everything to Morgan to have her husband home. Every morning he left the house at 6 a.m. to go to work at the airplane factory. He had a new job in a different department so he was meeting new friends. He never came home before 6 p.m. Then there were the late Tuesday and Wednesday evenings when he walked in at 9 p.m. He never spoke to his wife or parents about his day, he just watched the television or worked on his bikes in the garage. He had become a solemn and silent man who paid little attention to his wife, or the baby laying in his arms, or his parents.

When Morgan came back from the bathroom, Noelle was fussy. He handed the baby back to Morgan and got up and started pacing around the pool table then darted out through the back glass doors like a missile. The next thing Morgan heard was the sound from the engine of the motorcycle. With the baby in her arms, she rushed out the back door.

"Where are you going?" she asked him angrily. "I thought you were staying home with us." Tears flooded her eyes. "It's after nine o'clock!" Dean drove off down the driveway and into the street without a word.

Morgan ran into the bedroom with her baby daughter. Dean

was an ass. He was selfish and terribly immature. She sat on the bed crying, furious, embarrassed, and hurt. It felt as if he had kicked her in the gut. She buried her face into her baby's body and wept.

It was 2 a.m. when Dean came home. Morgan pretended to be asleep. He kicked off his boots, took off his Levi's, and climbed on to the bed. He fell asleep almost instantly and started snoring loudly. He stunk of cigarettes, weed, and beer but from his hair Morgan could smell something different and began to panic. "What is that smell? Could that be perfume?"

After a while, she got up, tiptoed over to Dean's Levi's, and took out his wallet. She tiptoed into the bathroom and closed the door.

"I should not be doing this," she scolded herself as she stood looking at the black leather wallet that she bought him for his birthday. She held the wallet to her breast then put it on the counter top. With a deep breath, she began to take everything out, not knowing what she was looking for.

She came across a carefully folded-up bar napkin and unfolded it with hesitation. It said "Topless Silk Gentlemen Club." She turned it over. There was a girl's name with a phone number. "Oh, my God!" She put her hand over her mouth and began to cry. Her heart sank. She stood there for a while and stared at the napkin. After a few moments, she folded the napkin and slipped it back into his wallet along with everything else. Her mind was sickened with thoughts about her husband's behavior. She felt violated to think that Dean was in a topless bar and having conversations with another girl. Her mind flashed thoughts of wicked, perverted images. The images burnt in her heart as she bitterly reopened the wallet, took out the napkin, and threw it into the toilet. Then she sat on the seat and peed into the toilet and then she flushed it. She stood there and watched it go down the drain. Morgan tried to compose herself by washing her hands and face. Finally, she opened the bathroom door. Rick was standing there and he startled Morgan!

"Are you okay, sweetheart? I heard noise over here." He

looked at her face. "You are crying? Your face is red and swollen."

"I'm fine Dad," she answered. "Go back to bed." She tried to pass him in the hallway, but he stopped her.

"Daughter, I know something is wrong." Then he noticed his son's wallet in her hand. Morgan's tears started to spill from her eyes and Rick put his arms around her. She cried into his chest.

"Dad, why is life so deceitful?"

He was slow to answer. "I don't have the answer for you. I just know the devil is delightful in wrong doings." He took her chin in his hand. "Hush now child, Noelle needs a calm and cheerful mother. Don't let my immature, selfish son take your loving spirit away."

Uneasily, Morgan quietly got back into bed with Dean. He woke up a little, put his arms around her, and drew her close to him. He muttered, "I love you baby." His stench breath was nasty as he began to kiss her neck. Morgan put her arms around her husband's head and pulled his head down to her breasts. She caressed him as a child while he fell into a deep sleep. Tears rolled down her cheeks and she listened to the beating of her heart. "Love is complicated. Love is pleasurable and it makes me weak," she thought in the darkness as her passionate tears trickled down her neck. "This feels more painful than those labor pains." She stroked his hair and repeated again and again: "Tomorrow unfaithfulness will go away." She nuzzled her husband's face into her full breasts and wept.

Chapter 45

So many thoughts were brewing through Morgan's head the next morning, but she said nothing to her husband. Morgan knew she had to find a way of staying focused on her new daughter as well as find time to figure her marriage out.

The next day she spoke to her mother-in-law. "Mom, do you think I need to give Dean more attention?"

"Yes, you do need to spend more time with your husband," Betty agreed whole-heartedly. "I'm thinking maybe you and I have been so involved with Noelle now he feels left out." Betty took Morgan's hand and sat her down at the kitchen table. She went to the pantry and brought out her homemade lemon scones and placed each one carefully on a glass plate. She went over to the refrigerator and took out the small container of her special raspberry cream. Then she went to cupboard and brought out two tea cups. "I think it's time for some afternoon lavender tea. I just bought this new organic tea and it's supposed to be for relaxation," Betty said as she moved around the kitchen. She dropped the velvet purple tea pouch into the cups and added the water, poured just a little milk from the antique creamer bowl, and she took the little silver tongs, grabbed several sugar lumps, and dropped them gently in each delicate blue floral cup.

Quietly Betty sat and picked up the silver spoon and stirred her tea thoughtfully. "Morgan, men are about food, sex, sports, politics, sex, hobbies, more sex. Men are competitive and they all think they don't have enough money." Both the women chuckled. "And if you're lucky you will become his buddy, and later most of us strong women become their mothers. I honestly believe men never grow up. They are very needy as well as selfish."

They giggled a little. "How do you know so much, Betty?"

Betty put her spoon down. "Oh my dear Morgan, I've spent the last 20 years with my husband and two sons. And before this, it was my father and four brothers. You can't give Dean too much freedom to be alone. Men just can't deal with a lot of free time. Alone time gets most of them into trouble with alcohol, drugs, gambling, and then there are very lonely women in the world who try to steal husbands from their families. Those women have no virtues. I've been married long enough to know not to give my man a long leash. My sweetheart and I have had our share of struggles." Betty does not smile and then removes her silver eyeglasses and puts them on the table as she wipes tears that have spilled from her eyes. Betty took Morgan's hand and patted the top. "Dear, I have spoiled my guys, all of them. I knew it was going to be tough on my sons if they got married. Quite honestly, I knew it would be so much harder on their wives. The only excuse I have for spoiling these men is very simple; I love them so much. There is nothing I wouldn't do for my men. I'm sorry for you because I've made Dean lazy and spoiled rotten. Dean pretty much has gotten anything he asked for and as far as Luke is concerned, I saw as a child he enjoyed his stamp collecting but he also liked to play poker. I looked the other way. Now he loves playing cards for money. I never made him converse with me enough. I should have forced both of them to share their feelings when they were younger."

Morgan got up from the chair and hugged Betty. "I love you so much, mom." The two women hugged harder. "Thank you for sharing this private information with me about you and your family. Maybe this will teach me some good sense."

A few weeks later, Morgan, Dean, and Betty were watching TV on a Saturday afternoon. Rick walked in to the room and encouraged the whole family to go for a ride to the Dairy King to get ice cream. Rick and Betty got into the front of the truck while Dean, Morgan, and the baby got into the attached camper. Twenty minutes later the truck stopped. Rick and Betty stepped out of the cab and walked to the back of the camper to let the family of three out. When Morgan got out of the truck, she was surprised. What she saw was a long cement driveway lined with beautiful yellow and red roses. To the left of the driveway sat a large white house with a big front window and an oversized front porch with a white rocking chair. An enormous old maple tree was overflowing in the middle of the well-manicured lawn.

Rick handed Dean a single key. "Son, this is for you and your wife. This is your home. Go in and enjoy your married life."

Dean took the key and his eyes were wide. "Dad, are you serious?"

Rick's face was full of pride. "Yes, this is your house."

Dean put his arms around his father. His hug was so strong that he lifted Rick right off the ground. Betty stood by on the sidewalk holding a handkerchief to tears of joy.

"Son, now go see if that key fits!"

Dean walked up the porch steps and put the key into the door lock and it turned. Morgan stood on the bottom steps waiting with Noelle. Dean turned around and looked to his wife and baby. "Come here, girls!" he yelled.

Morgan hurried up the steps. He picked up Morgan with their baby in her arms and carried them both through the doorway, smothering them with kisses.

Chapter 46

The next few months were constructive, full of creativity and productive activity.

Betty, Isabel, and Morgan took pleasure in decorating the spacious two-bedroom house. Noelle's was the first room to be decorated. There was no question of money because there was no telling Grandmother Betty no. Hours were spent deciding how they would decorate the baby room. However, Dean had made it perfectly clear to both his mother and mother-in-law that he was going to be the one who decorated his and Morgan's bedroom.

After a month, the nursery was complete. Morgan stood in the doorway quietly as Betty and Isabel chatted excitedly about their handiworks. Morgan surveyed the room with painted lavender walls and the classic white crib. It looked fit for a princess with tall white crib bumper, and the crib skirt was white with tiny lavender bows that flowed to the ground. A whimsical butterfly purple, lavender, and white mobile was suspended from the crib's edge. There were two changing pads and several soft crib sheets and fleece baby blankets. Morgan had fallen in love with a five-drawer white dresser the moment she saw it in a magazine, most of all because it was a perfect solution for the baby's needs. It was a changing table and later it became a chest for a little girl. A large baroque antique mirror hung on the all that had roses carved throughout the frame.

There were bunny-stacking bins for the diapers and an airtight white diaper container for soiled diapers. Morgan smiled as she went over to turn the night lamp on and looked at the lavender and white nightstand with the adorable children's frog lamp with a fluffy trim shade. Smiling again, she looked over to the window cover that Isabel had finally decided on. It had taken Grandmother Isabel a week to decide on the delicate white lace curtains that had designs of intricate butterflies against a simple mesh background and butterfly edge detailing. Her fingers ran over all the detail in the curtains, and she sighed happily.

Just then, Barney walked in to house. "I have a surprise for you Morgan," he said as he walked in with natural wood rocking chair with new white cushions.

"Daddy, it's beautiful! Where did you find this?"

"I was walking the neighborhood and a very old lady had just put this outside for her garage sale. I bought it." He smiled. "This rocker comes with history. The old lady said she had rocked ten children on this fine chair."

All the women fussed over the wonderful rocker that fit perfectly into Noelle's room.

About a week later, Dean came out of the shower with nothing but a white towel wrapped around his hips. His hair was dripping wet as he went to find Morgan in the kitchen. She was wiping down the sink.

"Hey babe, that was the best dinner," he said, coming up behind her.

"Honey, it was just macaroni and cheese."

Dean leaned in closer to her. "Baby, you make the best mac and cheese." He took Morgan in his arms.

"Dean, I've got to finish cleaning."

He didn't stop. He kissed her back and reached over and moved the crystal salt and pepper shakers from the Nantucket wood kitchen table. He pulled the beautiful antique crochet table cloth from the table and threw it to the floor. He quickly pulled Morgan's tee-shirt top off above her head. He saw her pink lace bra and smothered her in kisses.

"Dean, please. The baby is about to wake up."

"No she's not; I peeked in on her when I got out of the shower. She is snoring." He grinned. "I love you baby, I want you now." He pulled off her Levi's and pink panties. They fell to the floor. Quickly he pulled off his towel and laid it out on the table then got on top of the table naked. "Come here," he whispered. Morgan's head was spinning. She was excited yet bashful. All she could think about was they were on top of the new table where they ate. She held on to Dean's massive arms as they made love with brawny emotion. Morgan soon forgot all about the Nantucket kitchen table.

"Well, I sure got me a hot little lover," he said after they were both satisfied. "You are such a good girl." He patted her butt and smiled. "I've got a really big surprise for you, baby. Get dressed."

Morgan threw her clothes back on. She bundled Noelle up and out the door they went.

They drove to a hippie store that was painted purple and black. Dean had Morgan lay on twelve different style of waterbeds until they decided on one. He picked out a huge king-size dark wood frame waterbed with an enormous matching dark wood frame mirror. It came with two matching side night tables and two purple and yellow lava lamps. To top it off, Dean saw a mink leopard print plush bedspread and black satin sheets that he had to have. "This is a sex machine bed and you are my sex kitten," he whispered to his wife, putting his tongue skillfully inside her ear. The power of his words made her blush.

Once all the rooms were decorated, their home was beautiful. It had a brown leather furniture set in the living room that Morgan lovingly maintained. Everything was immaculate and organized. Most days she made sure that fresh cheerful flowers were kept in vases throughout the house. She did try to learn how to cook to please Dean, but she burned and overcooked a lot of recipes.

The relief was that she was good at baking. Large chocolate cookies were packed with semi-sweet chocolate chips. Dean's favorite was chocolate peanut butter fudge brownies, drizzling with warm chocolate syrup.

They entertained Dean's friends some weekends and Morgan learned to become her husband's pal. She learned to shoot a rifle and handgun. It was a bit of surprise to Dean that she was good. He told her several times, "Wow, you have a good aim at targets."

Many nights they went to Georgia's bar and played pool. Dean was so impressed with Morgan's billiard playing that he ordered her a custom pool stick that had an artistic image of a tiger inlaid on the butt of the stick.

Morgan tolerated Dean spending long nights in the garage. He was forever tinkering with his collection of motorcycles. He had collected a 1934 Harley Davidson and a 1962 Harley Davidson Panhead along with the unassembled trike. On some of those evenings Morgan would put Noelle in her warm bunting outfit and they would spend as much time as they could with Dean in the garage. Morgan would spend time polishing the chrome bike alongside her husband. She knew that Dean was smoking weed because she had found his stash hidden in the garage in an empty coffee can but she chose to ignore it. She also paid no attention to the fact the Dean could never finish one project. He collected old bikes and attempted to get them put back together but never quite finished.

One night, Morgan spoke up. "Dean, I want to talk to you about something important."

"What now? Do you want to plant more flowers or something?" he teased her. Then he got up, went over to her, messed up her hair, and smothered her with kisses all over her face. She couldn't stop him from tickling her because her hands were full of chrome cleaner.

Finally, she stopped laughing and became serious. "I want to; I want to…" she stopped.

"You want to what? Spit it out!" he demanded.

"I want to go to school," she blurted.

He looked up at her. "School, what for?"

"I want to go to barber college, to be a barber," she said softly.

He frowned at her. "Oh, my God, I thought you forgot about all that bullshit!"

With a deep breath, she went on. "Dean, please be quiet and listen to me. I cut your hair and Rusty's hair and I give all your friends haircuts, beard trims, and mustache trims. Even your mother says I'm a natural, she says I am the only one who ever gave her a good haircut. I'm good with the clippers. I want to get my master barber license."

"That's enough, Morgan." Dean's face grew stern. "I allow you to cut hair and trim beards here in the privacy of your own home. Wasn't it I who bought you the clippers and scissors for your birthday?"

He walked out of the garage and lit up a cigarette, but after three puffs he threw it on the ground and stomped it with his boot. He went over to his wife and messed up her hair. "Now I told you when I bought that crap for you that it's just a home hobby and nothing more. I don't want to hear about this barber shit no more. Read my lips, no barber school. You belong home with your baby and taking care of me."

She was silent.

He went over to her and crouched down to where she was sitting. "Babe, I take care of you. You are not going anywhere. No career. Understand?" He took Morgan's face in his hands and kissed her mouth hard. "Now, who's the daddy? Are you my baby girl?" He lifted up her chin to him and held it firm.

Gratifying him immediately, she answered, "You're the daddy, and I'm your baby girl." Satisfied, Dean walked away and the conversation ended. But Morgan knew it wasn't over. Inside, she was screaming. *Dean, it would be nice to hear you say that you're proud of me for wanting to go after my own dreams, that you want me to go to barber school and graduate and be successful. I wish you could completely support me and tell me to go for it!*

Morgan kept those thoughts to herself.

Chapter 47

Noelle was busy playing in her gated play area one afternoon with Morgan by her side in their beautiful backyard. She had already weeded the flowerbeds; her roses were in full bloom. The lawn was mowed and looked green and lush. Morgan got bored. Sitting there, she looked at the uneven shrubs that grew all along the backside of the property wall, which separated her yard from the neighbors. Morgan went into the garage and brought out the big pruning shears and the electric trimmer that Dean used for the trees and a step stool. Moving from here to there, she began to trim the shrubs starting on the top and working downward. Two hours later, she stepped away and looked up the beautiful geometric shapes she had created. She wiped the sweat from her face as she talked to Noelle.

"Noelle, someday Mommy will go to school and learn to trim lots of shaggy beards." She grabbed Noelle from the playpen and twirled her around.

On other afternoons, Morgan would take her daughter for walks in the stroller and sometimes they would go on the bus to the other side of town. Morgan loved to spend time downtown. Her favorite pastime was to sit on the bench outside the busiest barbershop in the city. She loved to watch the skilled barbers perform flat-top haircuts and hot towel shaves. She especially took pleasure in watching them use the straight razor. Over time, she memorized their every move. The men barbers were accustomed to seeing her out there. They would smile and wave at her and she would wave back from outside the window. She was too shy to go inside and talk to them.

One day she was so entranced watching the barbers she forgot all about the time. She and Noelle almost missed the last bus home. Sure enough, Dean was home and waiting at the front door for her. He was furious. "Where have you been?"

"We went for a bus ride to the park. I lost all track of time."

"Oh, you are so full of bullshit! One of my friends said he saw you and the kid sitting in front of that damn barber shop again! The dude said you sit there for hours. I told you before, stop wasting time going there. I don't want you sitting in front to that goddamn shop again! Do something more useful like learning to cook or clean out the closets. Do you understand what I'm saying?"

Too exhausted to defend herself she said, "Yes, I understand."

Morgan sat on the front porch the next day with Noelle in her lap and analyzed the predicament she was in. She did not have a car nor did she know anything about a bank account, nor how to write out a check. Dean did all that. In addition, she had no way of knowing what bad habits her husband had. At 19, she found that she had nothing in common with girls her own age. She would be at a party and overhear the girls talking about college and their cars and activities at their jobs. Very few girls her own age had a child. Everyone who lived in her neighborhood was older.

The circle of people she was surrounded with all smoked weed. She tried to smoke it, but she hated the way it made her feel – lazy with no ambition, stupid, and hungry. She swore to herself that she would never get hooked on the foolish drug. She would smoke it only to appease her husband and relieve the boredom and trapped feelings that would come over her. Weed decreased her anxiety.

She still had passions, like going to mass on Sundays with her daughter and playing with Noelle and watching her learn to walk and shopping for adorable outfits. She also loved to spend quality time with Betty and Isabel. But what she considered her greatest accomplishment so far was how she had read and studied the skillful art of making love to her husband. She did what he loved her to do to him and she did get much pleasure from their love-making. Morgan could make Dean see stars and beg for more. Ultimately, she knew this was the one power she had over him and it made him stay home at night.

Chapter 48

A month later, Morgan was trembling in desperate disbelief and pacing back and forth across the dark living room. She felt like a raving maniac. Never had she felt so betrayed. It was four in the morning. "Damn, where had everything gone wrong?" she kept questioning herself. Why? was the only question in her heartsick mind. Finally, she heard the motorcycle pull into the driveway. The front door opened and he staggered in. The front door shut quietly and immediately she switched the lamp on.

"I want a divorce," she yelled at him. "I will not allow you to disrespect me and my daughter this way. We will not live this way."

"You can't get a divorce. Have you forgotten that I went to the classes with you? Catholics don't divorce." He guffawed as he walked past her.

She stood firm in front of him with her arms folded across her breasts. She stood her ground and did not let him pass. "This time you're dead wrong. Rusty called me tonight. He said he saw your bike parked in front of a motel. He called here to see if someone STOLE it!"

Dean said nothing. Tears streamed down her face. "You're cheating on me, I just know it, and the church recognizes adultery as a reason to divorce. Your parents bought us this house to have a home together. This isn't just a crash pad for you. Now get the hell out of my home!" She opened the front door and threw out a box of packed clothes and a pair of biker boots.

He tried to justify why he was late. "Hey, wait a second Morgan, you don't understand, you are overreacting. The chick didn't mean anything to me. She just needed a ride to her room, her damn car broke down, that's all."

Morgan shook her head and raised her hand to stop with the excuses. "Dean, I've had enough. Anytime you want sex you are supposed to get it from me. This is your sick problem, not mine. I want you to leave. We don't have a marriage. You've betrayed our love."

Dean hung his head down. Morgan stopped talking and she looked at the door then at him and opened the door wide. She crossed her arms again and managed a half-smile. "You just want a cheap thrill. Something is wrong with you, bastard! You can't keep your dick at home! Well, my eyes are wide open. Get out."

Dean stared at her then unwillingly walked out the door.

She locked the door then fell to her knees sobbing. "Oh, God how could You let this happen? I can't believe this he did this." She cried.

Moments later, she heard the baby crying. Frantically she dashed to Noelle, took her in her arms, and held her very close. "Mama," cried Noelle. Morgan sat in the rocking chair in the nursery and rocked her daughter until the pale morning light invaded the room.

Two weeks went by; Betty came to the house to pick up Noelle for the weekend. Betty knew they were having problems because she told Morgan that Dean was sleeping at her house. Morgan put the eight-month-old baby in Betty's arms and said, "Mom, please. I don't want to talk about anything. Just please leave it alone."

"I'm sorry, honey," Betty said sympathetically. She quickly turned toward the door and took her granddaughter with her.

The following night there was a knock at the front door.

"Morgan, it's me. Please open the door."

She heard him through the door and yelled, "Go away."

Dean persisted. "Honey, I just want to talk, that's all. I want to talk to you. Open the door please."

Morgan had just finished taking a long, relaxing bath. She had on a long red flannel robe and nothing else. She had just started a fire in the fireplace. Her hair was wet. As the knocks continued, she clutched her fingers nervously.

With great force, he knocked again. "Baby, I just want us to talk."

The last weeks had been miserable for her. Her throat felt strangled. With a fearful grip, she found herself unlocking the door and pulled it open.

He fell to his knees at Morgan's feet and grabbed her ankles and started to cry. "I'm so crazy for you. I'm a stupid fool. Baby, I will never hurt you again. You're my dream girl; you always have been and always will be." She actually felt him trembling. He wept, "I'm so sorry for hurting you." He pulled his wife down to the carpet and said, "I love you." His face was wet with tears.

Fighting back her own tears, she made an effort to resist him. She couldn't believe she had opened the door and let him in. She was dizzy with emotion and his tears made her defenseless and weak. Softly, she whispered, "Hold me, my darling." Frantically he grabbed her with his massive arms so tightly that Morgan had to gasp for air. A moment later, he broke their embrace and he buried his face in her neck and wept more.

"Dean, you hurt me so much," she shuddered.

With his strong hands, he took her face gently and kissed her tears, her eyes, and nose. "I love you baby, only you. Morgan, I want to come home. I beg you to forgive me."

He kissed her mouth deeply. At last, she broke away and with both her small hands, she took his face. "Dean, you are my whole life."

Dean reached into his jacket pocket and took out a small package. He sat back down next to Morgan and snapped a small blue velvet box open. The room had little light, but in the dim of the glare, Morgan saw diamonds.

"Can you understand what I have been telling you? I only love you." Dean took out the 14-karat white gold diamond tennis bracelet, placed it on her wrist, and closed the clasp.

Morgan gasped. "It's beautiful. But where did you get the money to buy it?"

He put his hand gently over her mouth. "Hush," he said. "I

sold one of my antique motorcycles. You deserve this and so much more."

Morgan stared, amazed at the diamonds. All she could think about was that he sold one of his beloved bikes to buy a gift for her. They sat in silence and she became aware that there was no movement or sound in the room except for the breathing of her and Dean. They sat facing each other but she did not look to his face. She thought about the day he proposed marriage to her and spent his motorcycle money to buy her wedding rings.

In time, she crept over to him and straddled her legs around his waist. Facing him, she looked at the face that held her heart. His blue eyes overpowered her self-esteem and she made the first move. Eagerly, they began to kiss. Instinctively, Dean left her mouth and he guided her robe wide open and consumed both her breasts lovingly. He lay her down and dropped his mouth down to her tummy, purring as he sweetly licked and kissed her belly button. Lovingly, he caressed her knees and devoured her mouth-watering thighs with his mouth. Gently he pressed her legs apart and whispered, "I adore you."

Morgan's emotions were out of control; she loved and hated him at the same time. She was aggressive and angry and raw with desire, emotions she had not known before. Dean and her spent hours in a marathon make-up sex session. They were panting, sweaty, and satisfied when they finally walked to their bedroom.

Reluctantly, Morgan woke up after she was disturbed by the sound of a dog barking in the distance. With the early morning light peeking through the crack of the drapes, she looked over to Dean. His blonde hair was messy and it reminded her of the first time she had seen him without the pomade hair-sprayed style that he usually wore. With her finger she brushed away the soft strand of hair that lay across his face and inhaled deeply. She remembered the night before and was convinced the worst of Dean's infidelities were behind them now. Quietly, she pulled herself out of the waterbed, the mattress rippling as she left.

She put on her red robe and heard her stomach growling. She was famished. She looked at the bracelet that was still on her wrist; it looked more beautiful this morning than it did last night. Carefully she slipped it off and placed it back into the velvet box and snapped it shut. Then she went into the kitchen and turned on the small radio. Cher was singing.

She took out bacon, eggs, milk, butter, and strawberries and plopped it all on the counter top. Out of the pantry she grabbed pancake mix, bananas, and powdered sugar. She grabbed the Crisco oil and greased up the griddle. Within 30 minutes she had whipped up his favorite breakfast. She arranged one plate with fluffy pancakes smothered with butter and dripping in warm maple syrup topped with thin sliced bananas and berries and sprinkled with just enough powdered sugar. The other plate was piled high with crispy bacon. The two white china plates went onto the wood tray with two tall glasses of cold milk. As she was about to lift the full tray, the scent of vanilla filled her nose. She began to screw the top back on the small bottle of flavoring when she got an idea. Smiling, she took the little brown bottle and dabbed a little of its liquid on the points of her wrists, between her breasts, behind her knees, behind her ears and in the bends of her elbow. Inhaling it now, she got a burst of energy and, remembering last night, she was convinced that the troubles in her life were over.

In the corner of the kitchen, her eye caught her new cataloged Bettie Page shoes that were still in the box. She went over to the box and slipped the shoes out of the white tissue paper. She admired the gold sequin peep-toe pumps with the three-inch heels and black velvet bow detail. Carefully, she slipped them on. As quick as lightning, she got another thought. Hurrying across the room she opened a drawer and took out the crisp Manhattan socialite gold apron, a wedding gift. Morgan had never used it. Quickly she dropped the robe she was wearing to the floor and tied the thick apron around her waist into a bow at the small of her back, and then she tied the gold thick ribbon at the top of the neck bib. She felt mischievous standing there naked with only shoes and an apron on.

The tray was heavy when she picked it up. She marveled at

the sight of all the food and laughed lightly. "Maybe I am a good cook!" she thought to herself.

When she walked back into the bedroom, Dean was sitting there propped up against the pillows. "Wow, you really are amazing. Thank you, my love," he said.

The two of them devoured the pancakes, feeding each other throughout the meal. Satisfied, Dean reached over and in a deep voice he said, "Please get rid of these dishes and come here."

Without hesitation she put the tray of empty dishes on the nearby night stand. He pulled back the black satin sheet and reached over and untied the apron string around her neck and she crawled back into the bed with him.

Chapter 49

Two days later, it was time for Dean to force himself away from Morgan to go to work. Betty had kept Noelle for two days more and told her daughter-in-law that she was so pleased to hear that her son had moved back into his home. Just two days later, Morgan was pouring herself a cup of coffee. As soon as she smelled the coffee aroma she had to turn and run to the kitchen sink to throw up. Instantly, she knew she was pregnant.

Morgan did some serious thinking for about a month and finally decided to go to a new female doctor she read about in an article in the local newspaper about natural childbirth. Morgan went to her previous doctor and insisted on getting copies of all her medical records. When she got them, she immediately sent them to the new doctor's office with a letter about the difficult pregnancy she had previously endured.

Three days later, her telephone rang in the kitchen. She answered the phone and talked a while. When she hung up, she smiled because she had made an appointment for the following day with the natural childbirth doctor. During the drive to the office, she had to have Dean pull over to the side of the curb and stop the car so she could throw up. He smoked while he waited.

"Damn, I should have used rubbers." He looked sad.

"It's not your fault," she insisted. "I'm not blaming either one of us. It just happened."

Dean was still pissed. "Yeah, will the Catholic church be smiling if you fucking die giving birth?"

It wasn't hard to find the medical office; it was painted blue instead of the usual white. Twenty minutes after arriving, Morgan went alone into the exam room. She sat there in the familiar white paper exam gown. This time held on to a small brown paper bag in case she got sick. The door flew open and Morgan was happily surprised to see a pretty young female doctor. Her dark red hair was pulled back in a thick braid. She wore a harbor blue scrub top and matching scrub pants. Extending her hand to Morgan, she said, "Hi Morgan, my name is Dr. Madison."

Morgan sat up after the examination. Dr. Madison smiled, "You can get dressed. I will be right back." Morgan dressed quickly and sat on the chair for the doctor to return. She felt like she was reliving an old nightmare as she threw up in the brown paper bag.

Dr. Madison returned to the room. "I've studied your charts from your previous pregnancy and after checking you today, I am wondering if this pregnancy is going to give you a difficult time like the other before. It seems to me that you were extremely lucky with your daughter's birth. This time you may want to think about your choices in not having this baby. You are very early in the pregnancy and you may choose to abort."

"No, doctor, there is no choice, I am Catholic."

Dr. Madison smiled understandingly. "All right then, I strongly recommend that after this pregnancy that you get a tubal ligation. This should be your last pregnancy." The young doctor sat down in the nearby chair and explained in detail what the procedure was for the female sterilization. "I would like you to think all this through, okay Morgan?"

Morgan stood up too. She reached out to shake Dr. Madison's hand. Holding on to the strong gentle hand she said, "I will think about getting my tubes tied in the future but what I'm most concerned about is having this baby. Please, I need your help to get through this pregnancy. I really want my daughter to have a brother or a sister."

"I will do my best," Dr. Madison smiled. Then her face grew serious. "And we will try to figure out why you get so horribly sick. You know that I am a holistic doctor, which means you will have to do things as natural as possible. Okay?"

Morgan nodded her head in agreement and smiled. "Yes, that's fine with me. Now where's the bathroom?" She put her hand up to her mouth. "I'm going to throw up." No sooner had she said those words, she did throw up in the brown bag. Dr. Madison patted her back with a concerned look on her face.

Chapter 50

Dean's brother Luke surprised the family by enlisting in the Navy. Morgan was the second person he called on the telephone to share the news; Betty was the first and she was not entirely pleased. He was leaving on a ship to go overseas for nine months, maybe longer.

The day before Luke was to leave, Betty and Morgan went shopping. They bought an adorable sailor outfit for Noelle, who had finally mustered the courage to walk. They found a matching sailor top and maternity white bell-bottoms for Morgan and a sailor top for Betty. They were too excited to stop for lunch before Rick drove the family together in the pickup camper to the pier to wish Luke farewell. After the others in the family had said their good-byes to him, it was Morgan's turn.

Morgan looked at the breathtaking view of the shores of southern California as the wind slapped her back. When she turned back to Luke she said, "I'm going to miss you so much. You look so handsome in your white uniform!"

He grinned. "I will miss you too, sis."

"It's unfortunate that Dean did not go into the service."

"Yeah," Luke agreed. "At least two years in the service would have taught him some discipline." He grinned again. "My brother is a lucky man to have you and Noelle and now another baby on the way. You look good pregnant even though you're thin." He smiled at her fondly.

"You think so?" She laughed while rubbing her extended tummy. They both laughed then Morgan hugged him. "I will pray to our Lord to keep you safe."

He hugged her back and whispered in her ear, "Please take

care of Dad and Mom for me. Nine months is a long time."

Morgan looked right into Luke's eyes. "I know it's a long time. This baby will probably be crawling the next time I see you. And don't worry about your folks, I will be right here with them."

She tugged at his arm. "I almost forgot. Please remember to send my first collector spoons from Japan." Suddenly she felt sad. "I envy you. You get to see the world."

"I will remember to send you the spoons and I will send post cards. You can see the world through my eyes. I love you."

"I love you, brother."

Morgan and the family waved goodbye to Luke. They stood there until the enormous ship was no longer in their sight. Morgan listened to the sad sounds of Betty crying as Rick held his wife in his arms. It reminded her of when her brothers left for Ireland and how Isabel carried the same pain. Dean never said a word after he had hugged his brother. He wore his black leather jacket with the collar cuffed up and his pompadour hairstyle had so much hairspray on it that the wind was completely ignored. He just stood there against the truck and smoked his cigarette, looking at the ocean.

Chapter 51

The months crawled slowly for Morgan. Some of her days were worse than others; she would vomit for hours. She bore her suffering with little complaint, staying in bed for days upon days. For the second time, she was appreciative for the faithful help from Betty and Isabel. The two of them took turns caring for dear Noelle, herself, and Dean.

In her eight month of pregnancy she received the telephone call from Dr. Madison, who wanted to see her immediately.

The next morning Morgan was in the medical office though she did not feel well.

Dr. Madison smiled. "It's good to see you." She sat down in front of Morgan in the examining room. "I have just come back from a vacation in Boston. While I was there I visited with my medical teacher who is now retired. He has studied your medical case. I want to try a new therapy treatment on you. I want to start you on injections of vitamin B12 shots and B6. It's kind of a cocktail mixture. The needle is a bit long and it will burn a little going into your hip. You may get some diarrhea at first but I think you can tolerate it. I believe if we give you injections twice a week this will make you stronger and help with the nausea."

"Is it a risk to the baby?" Morgan asked.

"At this point I believe this a plus for you, as well as the baby. You are anemic and have low blood sugar and are underweight."

"Then let's do it."

Dr. Madison gave her the shot in her hip before doing the examination. Afterward she said, "Everything looks fine. My advice to you is to really concentrate on relaxing. I want you to meditate with calming music and to perform breathing techniques and to light candles in the evenings. Oh! I almost forgot to remind you. Before you leave today I want you to stop at the nurses' station and sign up to begin the natural birth classes."

The injections worked. Over the course of the coming weeks, Morgan put ten pounds on and was feeling strong. At the natural birth class Dean and Morgan learned that Dean would be allowed to be in the birthing room with his wife so long as he attended every class with her.

Every night Dean would put music on, lie on the floor with his wife, and practice the breathing and relaxing techniques. He would sit behind Morgan with a large pillow in his lap and she would lie in front of him with her head resting on the pillow. They looked at the small clock on the table nearby and for a full minute Morgan would breathe in and out slowly. They would practice for half an hour.

The next evening Dean smoked a joint as Morgan sat staring at their records. "Hey, what the hell are you looking for babe? You've been in front of those records forever."

"I'm searching for something. I know it's here." Morgan sat on the floor on her knees in front of a large stack of record albums in front of the record player: Aaron Neville, Otis Redding, Seals and Crofts, Foreigner, Stevie Wonder, The Carpenters, Creedence Clearwater Revival, Sonny and Cher, Jimi Hendrix, Dolly Parton, Bobby Darin, Diana Ross, Bread, Eddie Holman, Chicago, Aretha Franklin, B.B. King, Luciano Pavarotti, The Eagles, The Philharmonic Orchestra, Billy Holiday, Smokey Robinson, Loretta Lynn, and Patsy Cline.

She shouted, "I found it!"

It was a dusty album. She dusted it off and put it on her classic portable record player.

"Oh shit, what's this?" Dean wanted to know.

"It's a record I bought years ago, it's soothing sounds of nature and thunder and ocean waves. I used to listen to this in my bedroom when I was a kid." As if a dam had busted loose, streams of tears poured down her cheeks. "The music would calm my sister down and put her to sleep. I haven't thought about

Emma in a while."

Dean went to her, put his arms around her, and hugged her tight. Then he teased her. "Baby, no wonder this music put little Emma to sleep. This could put a herd of elephants to sleep." She stopped crying and started to giggle. She looked lovingly at Dean. He always had a way of making light of a serious situation.

Days and weeks passed; the inevitable was approaching. All month long, Barney drove Morgan to her scheduled appointments. He enjoyed driving Dean's decked out blue Chevy.

"Thanks a lot dad for being here for me and driving me to the doctor." Barney winked at his daughter. "It's my privilege," he said happily.

"Morgan O'Donnell," a yawning nurse called once they were in the waiting room.

"I will be right back," she patted her father's hand.

Morgan followed the nurse, undressed, and waited.

"I'm having a lot of backaches and heartburn," she told Dr. Madison as she laid on her back. She knew her doctor well enough to know it was unusual for her to be so quiet. "You can sit up now," she told Morgan finally as she took the examining gloves off and washed her hands. Dr. Madison looked at the nurse who stood in the corner of the room and said, "I would like you to go and bring Morgan's father back in here." The woman left and minutes later returned with a concerned Barney. Dr. Madison did not sit down on the nearby chair; instead, she told Barney to sit. Then she stood directly in front of her patient and her father and said, "I want both of you to listen to me very carefully. Unfortunately, the baby is not in position and has not turned." She took a deep breath then she reached into a drawer nearby and pulled out a book with pictures. She pointed to the first page and pointed to a presentation. "Morgan, you are going to deliver a breeched baby. A breech birth is the delivery of a baby rear end first. For reasons not fully understood, almost all babies settle into a head-down position. The baby is upside-down in the uterus, and the head will lead the way during the birth process.

"Unfortunately, some babies do not cooperate. Your baby is

being uncooperative. Your baby is in the Frank breech position. The buttocks lead the way out of the uterus, and the legs are folded in front of the body, called a Frank breech. Delivery from the breech position poses far more risks than delivery head first. The delivery head first is called the vertex position." Dr. Madison took a breath. "Are you both with me?"

Morgan and her father nodded.

"I'm giving you the worst information first, so bear with me. The biggest part of the fetus's body is usually the head. If the head fits through the mother's pelvis, then the rest of the fetus's body should slip out easily. Now if the fetus is born bottom first, it is possible that the body will fit through the mother's pelvis, but the baby's head could get stuck at the chin level. This condition is known as the trapped head, it is very dangerous." She paused. "If the baby is born from the breech position, the skull does not have a chance to change shape to fit the pelvis, and it is even more likely to get stuck. If the baby's head is trapped, the possibility of injury is high. Once the baby is born, the umbilical cord usually stops pulsating just as it would during a normal delivery. This cuts off the oxygen supply from the mother to the baby.

"If the baby's head is still in the uterus, the baby cannot breathe on its own. Therefore, it is essential to deliver the baby as quickly as possible. The life-saving attempts to deliver the baby's head can cause injury to the baby's neck or head, resulting in permanent handicaps. In extreme cases, if the baby cannot be delivered within a few minutes, the baby might die. Obviously, it is critical to avoid a breech delivery with a trapped head. There is no way for us to know the size of the baby's head. So we will just have to wait for the birth."

Dr. Madison looked directly to the both of them. "How are you doing so far?"

Morgan's face was pale. "I feel faint."

Immediately Barney got up. "My daughter needs a cold towel."

The doctor went to a drawer and took a clean cloth, rinsed it with cold water, wrung it out, and put it on Morgan's head, who was now lying down. "Morgan, I estimate that your baby's head is not oversized and most likely not much bigger than Noelle's. I estimate the baby not being much bigger than seven pounds. There should be no problem with the head getting stuck. I do not recommend a Caesarian section. That operation would be appropriate for you if you were having a bigger baby or a premature baby. At this time, that surgical procedure carries more risk for the mother. I would recommend for you to choose the natural breech vaginal delivery. Your baby seems to be in a favorable breech position and at a perfect weight. I have successfully delivered five babies this way." Dr. Madison smiled with confidence. "You need to make a decision to have a natural birth or a Caesarian section, which means cutting through your lower belly and uterus to deliver your baby that could also put the baby's or mother's life or health at risk."

Morgan sat up and looked at her father. "Doctor, I need to get some air and I want to take a walk."

"That's fine, take plenty of time; I'll be in my office waiting for your answer."

Dr. Madison stopped at the doorway. "Oh, one more thing, Morgan, if you decide to do this. I would like the breech birth to be filmed for a documentary for future medical students. This birth will be the first natural breech birth filmed in this hospital. Certainly, you don't need to this. Nevertheless, I am asking."

"Will my husband still be allowed in the delivery room with me?"

"Absolutely he will," Dr. Madison smiled.

"Come on, Dad. Let's go outside and walk."

They walk unhurried to the outside grounds. Morgan said nothing to Barney for a while. He held his daughter's hand tightly as they took a long walk. Finally, she looked over to Barney. "Dad, I have learned so much from the education classes about natural childbirth. I never knew all this stuff when I was pregnant with Noelle. The classes have taught me that giving birth is natural and I need to trust my body."

They come to a bench, sat down, and stared at the children

playing across the street at the park. "This baby is strong, kicking all the time inside of me, this baby wants to be born."

Barney searched his daughter's eyes. "Morgan, this all boils down to one thing and that is do *you* have confidence in your doctor? Do you trust this young woman's opinion? Do you trust that she knows what the hell she is talking about, all this natural stuff? That's what I'm saying."

Troubled, Morgan went to find a pay phone to call her husband at work. Morgan put the coin in the telephone and then she dialed the number. She listened to the third ring, the voice answered, "Hello?" Quickly she hung up the telephone. She decided not to tell Dean now.

Drenched in sweat with parched lips she walked back to her father. "Come on Dad, let's go back inside."

They made their way to Dr. Madison's office. "Doctor, I have made the decision for my baby. Whatever you think I should do, I will do. I trust you, and I…" she gulped, "I give you permission to film the birth. Just make sure I have my lipstick on." Then Morgan searched the doctor's eyes. "When do you think this will happen?"

"Since we will not induce this labor, we can only wait on Mother Nature. I'm betting within the next couple of days."

Dr. Madison walked Morgan and Barney down the hall to the entrance of the front door. "Remember to practice all the relaxing breathing techniques that you have learned. Breathing correctly is the key to handling pain and anxiety."

Later that evening Dean finished his shower and Morgan handed him a beer. "So what's up with the doctor visit today?" he asked.

Morgan thought about what Mother Bernadette had told her once: "God never gives us more than we can handle." With a very deep breath, she explained the situation to her husband. Dean was somber as he commanded, "Let's go to sleep. I'm sure you're tired."

Chapter 52

Two days later, Dean and Morgan were at home watching a movie. Morgan had not told her husband that she had been feeling cramps since early that morning. Looking at the clock, she began to chart her contractions in her mind. She was determined not to go the hospital early this time because she knew she would have to stay in the hospital bed as soon as she got there. This time she told herself she was in control of this situation. As she watched the movie, the pains became a little stronger. Instead of panicking this time, she breathed and visualized her body as it was preparing to give birth.

After the movie ended, she whispered to Dean. "Honey, I am in labor."

She watched him dart to the bedroom and bring out her packed grey suitcase and daisy patch diaper bag. He placed the bags by the front door and threw the couch pillows on the carpet. Quickly he went to light all the candles and he slid a cassette of Stevie Wonder into his black cassette player on the nearby cart. "I'm glad Noelle is staying with my parents," he said softly.

Morgan was aware how nervous he was, as she watched him go into the kitchen to find his small bag of weed. He lit up a joint and inhaled deeply. Feeling calmer, he walked back into the front room with the joint and lay next to his wife on the carpet. Morgan got a sharp pain. She did her breathing and he put his hand on her tummy while they timed the contraction.

"Wow, that was amazing," he said. "That felt hard."

Morgan looked over at him. "Hand me that joint."

Dean was surprised. "Are you sure?"

"Yes, this is going to be the longest night of my life. I am going to deliver a breech baby naturally. And we will be filmed!"

She inhaled one deep hit, held it in her lungs for a few seconds, and then she exhaled and coughed ferociously. Then she hit the joint again. Seconds later she raised her voice. "Oh my goodness, here it comes again. I am getting another pain." She handed the joint back to Dean and said, "Please take that weed out of here or I am going to smoke more of it, get it out of the room now!"

Quickly Dean took the joint of the room and he came back in and decided to light the fireplace. Minutes later, Morgan whined, "Dean, another one's coming."

Dean got on his knees behind her shoulders and supported her. He told her in a soothing voice, "Okay, breathe, just breathe honey." They both exhaled and inhaled together. Morgan placed her hands on her tummy and watched it go up and down as she breathed through her stomach instead of her lungs. Dean had learned in class how to time the contractions. "You better get comfortable because we are going to be here for a while; the contractions are now far apart."

Morgan surprised him as she began to laugh. "I'm hungry."

"What, are you kidding?" he asked her.

"No, I'm serious. I want pizza."

"Are you crazy? You just got the munchies from smoking the weed, remember what the class teacher said – do not eat food in labor."

She started to laugh and then begged. "Can I please have a piece of pizza? Now!"

"Okay, okay!" He got up, went into the kitchen, and rustled through the freezer. Morgan watched him moving about the kitchen getting the pizza. He turned the oven on and slid the pizza in.

Thirty-five minutes later Morgan was wolfing down three pieces of pizza. "This is the best pineapple sausage pizza that I ever tasted. Now I want a soda."

Dean got annoyed. "You know that you are supposed to only drink water, clear liquids. That's what they told us at the class."

"I don't care; I want a cold bottle of soda now. Please." She showed him a flirtatious look.

Unwilling, he got up and went to refrigerator and came back with the bottle of soda.

She took a sip and said, "Awhhh," that quickly turned into an "owwwww! Dean, here comes another one. Oh, my God this hurts!"

He looked at Morgan and in a stern, comforting voice said, "I want you to concentrate and breathe and stop focusing on whining!"

She looked up at him after the contraction passed. "Okay. You're right."

One long hour went by and she was having contractions five minutes apart that lasted 60 seconds each.

He finally got up and said, "We are out of here, I'm calling the hospital."

Dean drove through the pouring rain cautiously. Morgan's pains were strong as she stayed in a deep concentration with her breathing. They arrived at the hospital and Dean hurried around to the other side of the car door to help his wife out. Opening the car door, he was surprised to see that she was not moving.

"Baby, come on, get out of the car." He grabbed her hand and she began to cry.

"I'm scared Dean. Oh, my God! I remember what it was like the last time I was here for Noelle's birth. It was horrible and cold, and this baby is in a bad position for birth. What if our baby gets stuck? This baby may die! This is my fault; I should have had a fucking operation! I must be insane to do this naturally."

He bent down to her and knelt on one knee. "Listen kid, the last time I heard you curse like that was with Noelle's birth. Baby doll, everything is going to be all right, we are doing this together, and our baby is coming out just fine. Our baby won't get stuck. Trust your doctor. Trust in God."

Dean picked up his wife in his arms and carried her into the hospital. He rushed into an open elevator. Morgan felt protective with her arms around his neck and her head against his muscular chest. The elevator doors opened at the maternity floor and they were pleasantly surprised. Standing there waiting for them were their birth coaches from their class, three women were there to film the occasion and a wheelchair for her to go into that had a soft purple padding. Dean carefully put her in the chair.

"Another pain is coming and it's hard." One of the women kindly whispered to her, "Relax and breathe." Obeying, Morgan quickly closed her eyes and began her breathing.

As she was being pushed by a nurse, she was led in through the doors of a birthing room. This was another sweet surprise. It was far from the appearance of the horrible operating room where Noelle was born. This was a cheerful room with the walls painted in a soft greenish aqua, not white. More nurses were waiting for them. None of the nurses were dressed in traditional white uniforms. Instead, they were dressed in pastel-colored scrub suits and caps. Morgan smiled; the colors were calming.

A jolly, chubby woman behind a big movie camera asked, "Morgan, are you ready to be a film star?"

Morgan weakly smiled back at her. "I hope to get an Oscar trophy for my performance." Another hard contraction hit. Looking around the room she could not see her man. Anxiously, she asked, "Where's my husband?"

"Your husband went to change clothes," a voice told her. Ten minutes later, Dean made his entrance looking attractive and sanitary. He rushed to her side wearing blue hospital scrubs, his shoes were covered in paper booties, and he had a blue scrub hat on. Calmly, he brushed his hand against her trembling arm. "Breathe baby."

Like a soldier, she kept in total concentration during each hard contraction, controlling her breathing. She did notice how a nurse gently pulled her legs apart and put them into the stirrups, not hooked on with straps.

"I'm going to give you a small bikini cut." She placed a plastic sheet under her body then poured a little warm water and gently shaved a small amount of pubic hair. It was done in two minutes. And then the same nurse placed a soft warm blanket over Morgan's chest and abdomen and then a cooled washcloth over her forehead.

Dr. Madison walked in wearing a cheerful pale yellow scrub suit and matching cap. With a seriously honest face she said, "Morgan, this your big finish. I do not want you to push until I say so; I just want you to continue breathing. I want you to search your mind for imageries of water. Peaceful waters."

Morgan closed her eyes and contemplated those imageries. Devoutly she breathed, outstretching her hand instead of making a fist. A big pain came and unexpectedly something came out of Morgan. It was a bowel movement. Immediately the nurses changed the sheet and replaced it with a fresh one. Quickly a nurse bathed her with warm water. Morgan was so embarrassed.

She apologized quickly, "Oh, I am so sorry." Her face turned scarlet red. With a disappointed face, the doctor said, "What was that all about? You were instructed not to eat after your labor began."

Dean had turned his face away from the messy scene but bravely said, "It's my fault. She was hungry, I fed her pizza."

"All right," the doctor said, and dismissed it.

The contractions started again. The doctor turned to the women behind her and said, "You may turn on the camera. This is the grand arrival."

A bright camera light came on. Morgan did not even notice the camera for she was so busy breathing and she did not notice that there were more than 10 staff persons in the room to witness the birth.

The doctor became concerned but calmly she talked out loud during the entire procedure. "The mother is not opening wide enough. The baby's bottom is right here. I can see the baby is a girl. I am going to do an episiotomy now. I don't want the mother to tear. There is no time for a numbing shot." With quick and steady movements, Dr. Madison took a sharp instrument and said, "I am now making the incision straight down between the vagina and anus to assist the virginal birth."

Dean was standing behind Morgan, holding her up in a crouching position with a pillow; they were in such concentration in breathing together. Morgan did not scream. The breathing rhythm had put her in a trance. She did not feel the cut at all. The two of them were completely focused; they never took their eyes off each other. Dean kept telling Morgan, "I love you so much, I am so proud of you baby doll, just breathe." He held on to her shoulders now and she could feel his support as she held on to the soft padded side rails of the bed.

Morgan heard Dr. Madison command, "Morgan, the baby is coming. Push, push, and push now."

Dean also chimed in. "Push hard now, honey, go for it! Push hard." With all of her might, she did! The baby girl was born butt first but she slid out perfectly.

"The baby is born!" Dr. Madison said.

Seconds after the baby girl was delivered and still in the hands of the doctor, a nurse handed Dean a pair of scissors and was told to cut the umbilical cord. He did and everyone in the room clapped.

Morgan observed the doctor carefully as she handed the baby over to her health care team and she surveyed the team's actions. The baby's nose and mouth was cleared from the amniotic fluid, and the creamy coating on her skin was washed off. Immediately her breathing, heart rate, color, muscle tone, reflexes was assessed. Her weight was six pounds, seven ounces, and she was 19 inches long. An identification bracelet was put on her ankle that matched her mother's. An ointment was put in her eyes to prevent an infection, and her footprints impressions were made. At last, the newborn star was placed in a diaper, wrapped in a blanket, and handed to Dean.

Tears flowed from Dean's eyes as he held his daughter in his huge hands. He was already informed to expect to see the baby with little red marks dented on her forehead from her toenails. Her legs were straight up from being in the breech position but in a few weeks they would naturally relax. The baby girl cried very softly, she had no red blotchy skin. She looked peaceful with a perfectly shaped head full of dark hair. Dean took the baby to his wife and put her on her mother's chest. The two bonded skin to skin. Morgan smiled weakly. "Oh, my beautiful miracle you have made quite a dramatic entrance." Lovingly, she lavished her baby's tiny face, arms, and fingers with kisses. The video camera was turned off.

A few minutes later, the doctor instructed Dean to kiss his wife, pick up the baby, and walk to the nursery. Then Dr. Madison dismissed almost everyone in the room. She had one nurse stay to assist. She was getting prepared to perform the mini-laparotomy surgery. Morgan was having her tubes tied; this was a permanent method of birth control. She was hooked up with an IV pain medication and the doctor gave her an injection with a needle to numb her. In silence, Morgan listened to them chatting; they were utterly absorbed in the procedure. Tears came to Morgan's tired eyes. The pain medication had worked. Exhausted she spoke thoughtfully but clearly. "Thank you, Dr. Madison, for everything." Morgan passed out into a peaceful, much-needed sleep.

Chapter 53

Eighteen months later

"Noelle, you must not give your sister any more cookies. I don't want chocolate on her dress."

"Oh mommy, it's okay. Sissy loves cookies," Noelle said with a smile.

Morgan crossed the living room and wiped the chocolate from Cathleen's face, careful to keep the wet washcloth away from her new outfit.

Noelle and Cathleen wore beautiful matching Laura Ashley pink corduroy jumper dresses. Morgan smiled at the two adorable girls.

"Slow down, Cathleen, you are going to fall." No sooner had Morgan said that then she did indeed fall. Quickly, Morgan picked up the little crying girl who was still holding on to the half-eaten cookie. Comforting her she thought about how this delicate child had kind of skipped the crawling and went straight to standing up. She surprised everyone by her vigorous determination. She was an early walker so naturally, Betty insisted that Cathleen wear the best Stride Rite classic white high-top leather baby shoes. She was concerned about her ankles. Betty had said, "I have never known a child to walk so soon. We need to protect her little ankles."

"Mommy, we go to the park!" Noelle persisted.

Morgan knew her daughter well. At three-and-a-half years old, Noelle was independent and sensitive. She was a cheerful child who had talked early.

"Mommy, where is Daddy? Daddy coming to church? Daddy going to park? I want Daddy."

Remaining tolerant, Morgan said, “Noelle, I don’t know why you ask me all these questions. I’ve told you a hundred times, Daddy never goes to church with us. Daddy works very hard for us. This is his special day to go ride his motorcycle. This is Daddy’s day.”

Noelle made a sad face. “Mommy, I don’t like Daddy’s bike.”

Morgan smiled. “I think I agree with you.”

Noelle went to her mother and held on to her tightly. “Mommy, I love you.”

Morgan looked down at her watch. It was time to go. Lifting Cathleen in her arms she gathered the children’s stuff and grabbed her purse and off they went out the door. She put Cathleen into her stroller and the three of them made their way to the end of the street to the Catholic church. They followed along behind the crowd and found the church pew on the left-hand side of the aisle where they sat every Sunday. Morgan thought about her marriage when she glanced around the church and took notice of the other men walking into church with their families. She wondered if Noelle noticed this, too. “Dean was home all the time until Cathleen turned one,” she thought. “He even came to church with us occasionally on Sundays. Then he reverted to wanting more space.”

She knew Dean was spoiled. He did what he wanted. By now, she had learned to accept the way her life was and she knew better to agree with him than to disagree. It made life so much easier for their daughters if she just accepted his routine to have his time alone.

They were in no rush to get home after the service ended. Noelle was amused trying not to walk on the sidewalk cracks and Cathleen was asleep. Morgan thought about the priest’s sermon as she pushed the stroller: “Being true to yourself means to act in accordance with who you are and what you believe. You cannot love anyone else until you love yourself. Be who you are. Have the courage to accept who you are, not as what someone else thinks you should be. Recognize and develop your own unique talents.”

Deep down in her heart she knew there would come a day when she would have to take a stand about developing her own talents. But that day was not today.

"We are going to the park now!" she cheerfully declared to Noelle. "And then for a surprise we will have a picnic on our living room floor!"

Her daughter grinned.

Chapter 54

1976

Determined to become a better playmate to her husband and for the sake of their daughters, Morgan had abandoned all negative thinking. Dean would not stay home so she decided that she would give it her best effort and take a trip with him on the Harley-Davidson. For days, she watched as Dean and Rusty rebuilt the old classic 1965 custom-built chopper trike with the extended front end.

She noticed they thought about her this time. Rusty had found a better, more comfortable seat for her to sit on and Dean recovered it with soft, black leather. Rusty built the black leather luggage compartment that connected to the back of the trike.

"Morgan, get your ass over here and take a look at this." Rusty was so proud. "Look what I built you. This compartment is waterproof so you can put all your emergency stuff, water, make-up, clothes, purse, all that shit. I know how you worry about details."

She smiled and kissed him on the cheek. "Rusty, thanks for thinking about me." When she turned and walked back into the house, she overheard Dean talking with Rusty.

"I am so damn determined to make her like riding, all I want is for her to chill out and dig the chopper. More than anything, I want her to be a biker like me and feel the freedom of the open road," Dean said.

Rusty smirked. "I hate to sound like a hard ass but you've got your work cut out, friend. I know your old lady well enough to know her life is not the road. Morgan has never been like you and me. We both know you can't push her into doing things she don't like. Good luck to you, dude."

The day before the trip Morgan told Dean, "I'm nervous about the weather." They would be riding into cold weather up to Big Bear Mountain and would stay in a cabin for two nights. "I don't want to complain about being cold. I have the leather boots and leather jacket that you bought me a couple years back. But I think I need more warm clothes."

"Then baby, we are going shopping!" He grinned.

That moment they left for the Harley-Davidson store. Dean personally selected every piece of clothing that Morgan would wear. He picked out the black stretch pants and the sexy pair of black leather chaps. And he picked out three long-sleeved Harley-Davidson shirts.

"When the weather warms up you will be taking the jacket off. So you need a few tee-shirts." He went over and picked out gray motorcycle goggles and a pair of Harley-Davidson black leather gloves and two Harley tee-shirts for her.

The first day of the trip was difficult for Morgan. She had ridden throughout the city on the bike a couple of times but not this long of a distance. The wind was violent and harsh across her face. She wore no helmet so her hair was combed in a tight bun, but it soon became unraveled and tangled. Her arms ached from holding on tightly to the sides of the seat and then around Dean's waist. To top it off, he did not ride at a leisurely pace; instead, he hungrily devoured the road, passing trucks and automobiles on the crammed freeways.

In the early afternoon of the second day, the road took on another meaning for her. The landscape had changed so much that Morgan began to enjoy the beauty of the mountains. The smell of the air was clean, fresh, and pure. She closed her eyes and smelled the fresh pine scent and began to feel more confident in her seat.

On the custom motorcycle, the seat in the back was wider and put up just a little bit higher. So Morgan's legs were father apart and wrapped securely behind Dean's mid-back. It felt as though the motorcycle, she, and Dean were as one. At times, she was aroused as she felt the harmony and the vibration from the bike.

And then all that changed.

In an instant her feelings changed to fear and panic when the road changed. As a passenger, she depended entirely on Dean's skill in driving, and his skill was speed. When they rounded a bend, she never knew what to expect. She became a little nervous going through the canyons; there were the smooth curves and then the tight corners and it felt like they would tip over at times. To make matters worse, the wind went crazy again with no remorse as it smacked against her face and slapped her with chapped cracked lips.

She finally yelled at him. "Slow down!"

Dean slowed down and went off the road on an uncharted trail. Satisfied with the isolated location, he stopped and took Morgan in his arms. Caught up in the moment, they stripped down to nothing. Morgan was shivering when they feverishly made love in the remote area by the stream and on a large round rock.

Hiking down to the stream, Morgan washed up by pouring cold water all over face and body. Carefully she slipped her lavender bikini panty and matching lace bra on, and pulled the white tee-shirt down over her head. She turned around and found her husband standing there up higher on the slope, fully clothed, smoking a cigarette, and staring closely at her.

"You are grinning funny, do you have a secret that I don't know about?"

"No," he replied. "I'm just checking out your luscious headlights." Morgan blushed.

Suddenly he grinned broadly. "Hurry up and get dressed before I decide to love you up again."

Thirty minutes later Dean rode past a small town. Morgan was surprised when he turned into a dirt road and then made a U-turn. Driving them back toward the town, he stopped and parked the bike directly in front of an old barbershop.

He got off the bike and drew a pack of smokes from his jacket pocket, fired up a cigarette, took a deep drag and said, "Go in and say hi to the barber."

"You mean I can go in and you won't mind?" She couldn't believe it. "Are you serious?"

He grinned. "Yeah, go on in before I change my mind." He helped her off the trike.

Slowly Morgan headed to the shop door. She stopped and turned around to look at Dean. He nodded his head to give her permission again to go inside. She pulled the heavy glass door opened and walked in.

"Howdy," the man said. "Can I help you?"

She walked over to the old barber who wore an immaculate white barber coat and sported a handsome white mustache and perfectly white left-parted hairstyle.

"My name is Morgan and I am going to be a barber someday," she said.

"My name is Heinz. Welcome."

Heinz watched as she walked over to look at his barber tools.

"Can I pick this up?" She pointed to the long scissors.

"Sure help yourself, you can pick up any tool that you want, young lady," he said.

Smiling, she picked them up one by one. Then one shiny straight razor caught her eye. "Can I pick up the razor?"

"Yes, but be careful. It's very sharp."

Morgan picked it up and opened the blade. "I have a straight razor but not as nice as this. I taught myself to use it."

"That was a difficult undertaking," the barber replied with a grin.

Morgan asked Heinz lots of questions about haircuts and trimming beards. Then there was a loud knock at the window of the glass barbershop. It was Dean.

"That's my husband. It's time I go." She smiled. "May I hug you?" She embraced the old man.

"Don't give up your dream of your career. I've been a barber for 40 years and I have loved it. I hope you will be a lady behind the chair. Good luck."

When Morgan walked over to her husband, she threw her arms around his neck and whispered, "Dean, I love you so much." She began to ramble on about the barber and his tools. "Heinz has been a barber for 40 years and he's loved every minute of it. It takes him six minutes to do a flat-top. He has a straight razor from Austria! He called me lady behind the chair."

Dean interrupted her. "That's enough now, babe. I'm over all the barber bullshit talk, stop getting so carried away. Now put your goggles on and get back on the bike."

The bike's engine blared on and she put her arms around Dean's shoulders and bravely asked, "When do you think I can start barber college?"

"We'll talk about it after Noelle and Cathleen are both in school and I don't want to hear another damn word about it until then. Do you understand?" he said with a raised voice.

"Yes my love," she happily answered.

Morgan's body thrust back deep in to her seat as the bike rapidly took off. She felt a feeling of triumph that she had never felt before and it was not from the motorcycle ride. Deep inside her mind, she repeated the barber's kind words to her that would become an incentive to her distant dream.

Chapter 55

Three days later they arrived at the freeway off-ramp that led to Rick and Betty's home. Morgan thought about the excitement of the last three days and grinned. She was proud of herself for undertaking the intimidating danger of riding on the Harley.

Dean drove directly through a yellow light that turned red in traffic. In a split second, her joy changed to danger. She held on tight to her seat. That incident reminded her that he drove too recklessly with a need for speed.

She could not wait to sit down with Rick and Betty and tell them what it felt like to ride on the Harley through the mountain roads. One word she knew they would like was, "challenging." She thought about the expression that would be on Rick's face when she told him about his son taking her to the little barbershop. She knew it would be full of complete happiness; he knew how badly she wanted to be a barber.

With a quick right turn, Dean circled the bike into his parent's driveway. To Morgan's surprise, there were many groups of neighbors and strangers standing around in the yard and huddled in the street talking. Their neighbor, Shirley, walked over to them.

"Dean, I need to tell you something. It's about your father." Shirley held a handkerchief in her hands as her fingers fidgeted with the fine white lace.

"What's going on?"

"It's your father. He was just rushed to a hospital in an ambulance. Your mother, bless her, rode with him."

"Oh, my God, what happened to my father?" Dean shouted.

Putting the handkerchief to her face, Shirley blubbered, "It's the spinal meningitis. Your dad had another attack. You daughters are safe with Barney and Isabel so you should go quickly."

Morgan sat rigid on the back of the bike as Dean turned it around. Dean looked at her. She looked at him. They said no words. He drove the motorcycle very quickly to the hospital.

One hour later Morgan sat in a stiff cold chair across the room and watched as her husband stood by a hospital window that was half opened and chain-smoked. He had returned from seeing his father ten minutes ago and had not said one word since.

Betty walked into the waiting room white as a sheet and she collapsed into the nearest chair. Morgan rushed to Betty and put her arm around her. "Mom, what's going on?"

Weakly Betty looked up into her daughter-in-law's eyes. "Morgan, you may go in the room with Rick. There isn't much time left."

Dean dropped the cigarette on the ashtray, rubbed it out, and went to his mother. When he put his arm around her quivering body, she began to cry. Dean ordered, "Morgan, go in and see Dad."

Morgan slowly pushed the heavy door open. She walked past patients being wheeled by gurneys down the cold hallway. Nurses passed by with their heads down as though they were lost in their own thoughts. She gazed inside rooms as she walked by them and saw sick, frail people with scared looks on their faces. She noticed a sickening smell that wasn't quite urine or stool. The stench made her shield her mouth and she felt the need to gag.

She rounded hallway after hallway until she found number 227. The door was closed. She placed her hand on the door, took a deep breath, and pushed it open. Hesitantly, she walked into the room with only one bed inside. The light was faint. Immediately she noticed that the horrible odor was in this room also. She walked to the side of his bed. Rick's chest was going up and down as he breathed hard with loud rhythms. The only machine he was connected to was a heart monitor. Morgan looked down at his pale face and saw that his closed thin eyelids had blue veins. She touched his cheek and it was hot with fever. With her left hand, she rubbed his arm and it felt clammy. Her eyes overflowed with tears. With her index finger, she outlined his handsome handlebar mustache.

Her heart sank and she whispered, "Dad, I love you so much. Please don't die. I haven't thanked you enough for everything you have done for me." She made the sign of the cross on him and then on herself. Closing her eyes, she folded her hands in prayer. "Dear Heavenly Father, with a heavy heart I come to You. Oh, God please heal Rick. He is the glue that keeps our family together. I pray for healing. Please don't let him die." She bowed her head in reverence.

Several minutes passed. She stood there holding on to his hand and then she felt his clammy weak hand grasp her own. "Oh Dad! It's me, Morgan, can you hear me?"

Rick opened his eyes and whispered, "Morgan, I'm very sick and I think I'm dying. I want you to make me a promise."

"Yes, Dad." She moved closer to his mouth to hear.

"Promise me that you will be a friend to my wife and to both of my sons for the rest of your life. No matter what life brings to all of you."

"I promise."

With a great sigh, he looked at her and blinked as tears flowed from his eyes. "My greatest regret in life will be not being involved with the lives of my granddaughters or future grandchildren. Will you promise to teach them that the most important fact in life is how you treat your family and your neighbors?"

"Yes."

Rick looked into her eyes. "When you become a barber, you be the best."

Tears rolled down her cheeks. "I promise I will, Dad."

The hours passed that day very slowly in the hospital room. Rick spoke one last time to Betty. Morgan sat in the corner of the room and felt she was in a daze, paralyzed and stunned by Rick's condition. She watched Betty as she lovingly stroked her husband's arms and spoke to him softly. Dean moved nervously in and out of the room. Dean and Morgan were standing by

Betty's side when Rick took his last breath.

Luke had made several telephone calls from overseas after he found out about his father's condition. Morgan had picked up the telephone on most of the calls and helped him make the decision to wait to come home until the funeral service. "Mother will need me," he had said.

The funeral was large because Rick was so young. He was only 44 years old. He had so many friends and work colleagues who attended. It was almost unbearable for Morgan to sit in front of the coffin while holding both her daughters. Nevertheless, she maintained her poise out of respect for Betty, who looked reflective and strong throughout the ceremony. When the casket shut down and closed, she collapsed and wept into the arms of her sons.

Luke returned overseas after the funeral.

The week after the funeral it was heartbreaking to hear Noelle crying repeatedly, "I want to go to heaven to see grandfather. Why did he die? I want my Grandfather Rick."

Cathleen was still too young to speak out her thoughts but Morgan knew she was heartbroken. Cathleen would stand at the front door of Betty's home and just wait for her grandfather to drive up. "My Papa? Want Papa," she said over and over.

One morning, exactly five months later, Morgan was visiting Betty's house. She heard Betty calling for her from the master bathroom. "Morgan, come here please."

Betty was sitting on the vanity chair in front of the large silver mirror. Her bra was half off with one of her breasts exposed.

"Dear, please come here and feel this." Betty took Morgan's hand and had her touch her left breast. "Can you feel that lump? It's under the left breast to the side of it."

Morgan touched the breast. She sighed. "What is that? It's so hard and big it feels like a golf ball. How long have you had that?"

"The first time I felt it was after Cathleen was born. It was tiny. I thought it would go away and I forgot about it. Then I felt it again when Rick was ill but I put it out of my mind. I thought it would go away. But today I felt it and it's so big."

"I can't imagine what that could be. Perhaps it's a boil or pus, but you need to see a doctor, Mom."

Two weeks later, Morgan found herself alone and frightened in a waiting room in the same hospital Rick had died in. Dean had not come and Morgan did not blame him. She understood why he chose not to be there. Luke was still overseas. Noelle and Cathleen were with Isabel and Barney.

The surgeon to whom she had already been introduced stood in the hallway. It was Dr. Olson. He walked over to her in the lobby and said, "Morgan, can you please come with me into my office? We need to speak."

Morgan followed him into the small office space. She listened as he explained Betty's situation. She could only concentrate on the three words the doctor said, "We have the results from the biopsy. The tumor was malignant. It is cancer. We are going to have to do a mastectomy NOW. We are going to remove the complete breast and remove whatever else is an intrusion."

Morgan stood there in total shock. The doctor put his arm around her. "I am so sorry." He excused himself to go to the operating room.

Morgan went into the women's bathroom and rushed into the nearest stall and threw up in the toilet. She dropped to her knees in the stall and she touched both her own breasts. The tears broke through her closed eyes and rolled down her cheeks. She felt a sharp pain in her mind. Betty's pain reverberated throughout her own body. Morgan could feel complete compassion as she envisioned the knife on Betty's body and she felt the pain. Her heart felt inexpressible grief. She wept uncontrollably. "Why? What is cancer? Oh, my God, help her!"

Three days went by. Morgan hungered for everything to be a nightmare that she would wake up from and it all would be gone.

Then they received news that Betty would be released from the hospital in one week.

Morgan began to pack a couple of suitcases for herself and her two daughters so they could move into Betty's house and help take care of her.

Noelle watched as Morgan packed. "What's wrong with Grandmother Betty?"

"Grandmother is healing from her operation," Morgan replied calmly.

"Why are we leaving?"

"Because Grandmother Betty needs us."

"Mommy, is Grandma going to heaven with Grandpa Rick?"

Morgan took the child into her arms. "No, honey. You must not think that. Grandmother is very sick. She just needs our love and smiles to get well."

Noelle smiled and jumped into Morgan's lap and grabbed her face with both her little hands. "Mommy, I know Grandma Betty will get better, I know she will. Tell me again, how long we stay at Grandma's house?"

Morgan drew her daughter near and stroked her hair, smiled at her beautiful innocent face, and said, "As long as Grandma needs us."

Chapter 56

Less than two months later, Morgan felt as though she were back in that bad dream. She was sitting in Dr. Olson's waiting room, once again alone with the thoughts that the radiation and chemotherapy did nothing except make Betty's hair fall out and make her sick all day.

Dr. Olson appeared solemn when he entered the room and sat down. His eyes never left her face. Morgan looked straight back into the concerned eyes of the handsome, clean cut, middle-aged doctor who was wearing a tan cotton suit with a striped gold-brown tie. His words echoed in her mind as she listened to the information that he was telling her concerning Betty's health.

His voice firm and clear yet compassionate. "Betty is resting now. She asked me to talk to you." Dr. Olson clasped his hands together as he spoke. "When Betty had her breast removed, it was a very bad deal because she waited so long before she came here. And you know it had spread to her lymph nodes?"

"Yes, I know that and I know you told us it was a gamble with the chemo and radiation. So what's going on, tell me?" Morgan insisted.

"Betty's cancer has metastasized, which means it has spread throughout her body, it is aggressive, and it may eventually go into her brain."

"What does this mean? I don't understand how cancer can spread so quickly. How did this happen?"

"It means that there may come a time she will not know you, or anyone for that matter, and she will become childlike and her body will lose its ability to function. She has maybe two to five months to live; we have no way of pinpointing her exact time left.

We just don't know how the cancer will affect her. All we have left now is to keep her comfortable." He paused. "I am so sorry to give you this horrible information. Cancer is mysterious and puzzling. Betty has excellent medical insurance. We will be able to place her into a comfortable nursing home until the end of her life. Betty told us that she has done all the legal paperwork and that you will make all her decisions on her behalf concerning her health and well-being. I need for you to sign these admitting papers for the nursing home."

Morgan's eyes studied the stack of papers that were lying in front of her on the desk, and then she looked at the pen in her hand. She looked up at the dark-haired man and she could feel his compassion. She fussed with her blue sweater buttons and tidied her long ponytail. "Doctor, I need a moment to collect my thoughts."

"Take all the time you need, I will be back in a little while." Dr. Olson walked out.

Morgan collapsed into the back of the chair and stared at the white tiled floor. She made no attempts to move. In the distant background, her attention drifted to the sounds and smells in the hospital that were now much too familiar. She closed her eyes and let her thoughts drift through scenes of the hospital. The cafeteria was nearby, which smelled of rotten eggs and Clorox. She pictured the gift shop with the annoying, older saleswoman who wore black-framed cat eyeglasses. Next to that was the lab that smelled of antiseptics. Sick individuals went in that room to get their arms wrapped with a tight tourniquet, get stuck with a needle, and watch their blood get sucked out only to go into specimen tubes. She envisioned the pharmacy with the long line of sick people coughing and sneezing, some folks in wheelchairs and walkers, so many suffering victims desperately waiting for their prescription medications to give them hope.

She looked back to the admitting papers on the desk and thought to herself, "I hate cancer." She put the pen to the paper to sign, then her mind ran skipped back in time when she was in the retreat house and the nuns placed her in the nursing home hospital. She had hated that place. All the nuns whispered and tiptoed around the patients who were waiting to die. The rooms were freezing cold; supposedly, it kept germs at a distance. All the windows were shut tight. There was no fresh air. The forgotten bedpans and stains on the sheets and the sick people pleading for attention were so vivid in Morgan's mind. And she remembered how she was instructed not to begin a conversation with the dying.

Her tears streamed down her cheeks. She found it impossible to wrap her head around the words she had just heard: "Betty was dying and dying fast."

As exhaustion rolled over her, Morgan started to reason with the situation. "This is not the time to feel sorry for myself nor Betty," she thought to herself. "This is the time to focus and accept our fate." She submitted to the fact that her best friend in the whole world needed her and depended on her.

Morgan stood up and went to the window. Looking up to the blue sky with fluffy gray clouds, she thought, "I am so mad at you, God. Are You so busy that You have no time to help this woman? You grabbed Rick. Why are You taking Betty from us? She is only 42 years old. Dammit!"

Emotionally drained, Morgan's mind flashed memories upon memories like piles of photographs. She remembered Betty's courage throughout Morgan's pregnancies and the struggles they shared together. There was the first Christmas she met Rick and Betty and how they spoiled her. Of course, who could forget the meals and the cookies and cakes, biscuits and tea, and her great big laugh that was so incredibly contagious. And above all in Morgan's mind was how Betty handled herself with courage and strength of character when Rick died.

Morgan prayed aloud. "Lord, give me the strength that I need to face this tragedy. The pain and the fear are impossible to bear. Lord, please give me the strength I need to be strong for my young daughters. I feel weak and afraid. Only You, Lord, are powerful enough to give me courage to walk beside Betty throughout this trial. Lord, I demand that You give me guidance and the wisdom to see this through and I will do Your will. I am pleading with You to help me now." She closed her eyes and made the sign of the cross. "Amen."

Going back to the table, she sat down and took a deep breath. Opening up her purse, she pulled out her make-up bag and dumped the stuff on the desktop. She grabbed her gold compact and powered her blotchy red face gently; next, she applied shimmer eye shadow to her swollen eyelids, she lined the top eyelash lid and bottom with black eyeliner and then added mascara. Gently and skillfully, she applied raspberry-colored lip-gloss. After one last look in the mirror, she was satisfied. Attentively she put her cosmetics away and patiently waited with her hands folded on the table.

When the doctor returned he was in surgical scrubs and looked busy. "Morgan, did you sign the admitting papers?"

Morgan glanced down at the papers as she tugged gently at her long ponytail. Her face became peaceful. "I'm not signing the papers." She handed the papers to the doctor. "The only rational thing I can do, Dr. Olson, is to take my mother-in-law home to her house so she can die in her own bed. I will take care of her."

There was a moment of silence. Then Dr. Olsen shrugged his shoulders. "Is this really what you want to do? Watching someone die can be a difficult thing."

With her eyes jam-packed of wisdom and a steady voice, Morgan said, "Doctor, watching someone trying to be born can be a difficult thing also!"

Chapter 57

While Betty was still in the hospital, Morgan made decisions and alterations to her mother-in-law's home. With the help from a small cancer organization in town, they moved out the familiar bedroom furniture and moved in a hospital bed. The organization helped her with a wheelchair and anything else needed in the bathroom to make Betty's personal needs comfortable. Morgan was determined to make their life in Betty's home as normal as possible. She and Dean packed more clothes for their children and themselves, as well as most of the children's toys.

Morgan made time to sit and make the dreadful, uncomfortable telephone call to Barney and Isabel. They both withdrew and regarded the tragedy in drowning silence. Next, she called Peter and Noah who were still living in Ireland and each of them responded in the same way, with few soft words full of heartbreak.

Luke called from overseas. Morgan could not tell him the horrific news and handed Dean the telephone. He took the phone, went into the other room, and closed the door.

Emotionally, poor Dean had shut down. Daily after work, he would come into the bedroom to see his mother and sit with her for 15 minutes. After that he would pace around the house or play for a while with his daughters. Then he would lie back on the couch and try to watch television. Like clockwork he would say, "This is so insane; I can't stand what's happening to my mother. I got to get out of here." He would take off on the bike and be gone for a while. Morgan never scolded him. He always came home sober and he would just go to bed and sleep for hours.

The rest of the world disappeared. Every moment that

Morgan was awake was about Betty. Making her comfortable was Morgan's only concern.

Morgan realized that if she remained calm, her daughters did, too. Staying busy and on a routine was a necessity. Day after day with the help of two close woman neighbors, they busied themselves with cooking, baking, and cleaning. Betty's house was spotless and vases were full of fresh flowers.

One day, Dean brought home a used children's table and two chairs; it was rectangle and natural wood. He refurnished it, painted it pink, and put Winnie the Pooh stickers on the table and chairs. Morgan explained to Noelle and Cathleen, "You are big girls now, so you may eat all your meals in the bedroom with Grandma Betty." The girls squealed in delight.

Morgan also learned that if she kept easy listening music on the radio that it kept Betty less agitated and the children calm. Most days, Betty enjoyed watching her granddaughters play house with their baby dolls and pull-along alphabet blocks, and the children's favorite game, which was Hungry Hungry Hippos.

One day Morgan was out in the back yard garden cutting long-stemmed roses; her basket was full of colorful yellow, white, and red roses in several shades. With Cathleen by her side, Noelle rushed to meet her with her little hands on her hips. "Mommy, the lady closed the drapes in Grandma's room."

Sprinting from the yard with the children following, Morgan went to the dark bedroom and asked, "Who closed the drapes?"

There were two women sitting there both wearing their best Sunday clothes. They had never visited before.

One woman blatantly said, "I closed the drapes. I thought Betty could rest better without the sunlight."

Morgan stiffened. "No, these window covers must always be kept opened; we only close them at night." She rushed and opened them up and the sunshine flowed through the room. "I NEVER want Betty in the dark! Do you understand me?" The women nodded. Noelle, Cathleen, and Betty smiled wide.

Morgan took care of Betty as though she was her own child

Betty could still walk but very slowly so Morgan insisted she get into a wheelchair when she took her out into the garden to watch the girls play. Morgan thought God must protect children for they only asked once about their grandmother being in the wheelchair. They just adapted to the situation and Noelle stopped asking when she was going home.

Morgan loved to watch Cathleen climb onto Betty's lap, kiss her grandmother, and ask her to play with her. Cathleen would take a spoon and begin to feed Betty, saying, "Grandma, you the baby and me the mommy." Betty would just laugh and eat the pretend food. Cathleen would always wrap the homemade red crochet shawl around her grandmother's shoulders and giggle. "Me take care of Grandma." Betty would laugh more and say, "Yes, Cathleen you take good care of me."

In Morgan's observations, it was particularly sweet that neither child fought nor teased the other; it was though they were little angels. Morgan kissed and hugged those girls over and over and she knew they were on this uncharted journey with her. Almost daily Morgan would weep and grieve in the shower, but not in front of her daughters or Betty.

One early morning, Betty woke up and called Morgan to her. "Honey, I know that I don't have much time left, but I want to ask a big favor from you."

"What is it, Mom?"

"Can you please indulge me one last request?"

"I'll try."

Without restriction, Betty clearly said, "Dear, I want to visit my best friend in Pecos, New Mexico. Her name is Nina. She is part Apache Indian and Spanish, we went to high school together. I haven't seen for 24 years. She lives a simple life and lives in a village tucked into a river valley. She never travels, but we have spoken on the telephone, and have written letters and sent photos through the years. I want to touch her face and tell her that through the years she gave much-needed support. I want to tell her good-bye and to give her a gift, my red heart crocheted shawl. Sweetheart, will you take me to see her? Let's take the children and go on a road trip."

Morgan was stunned at her request. All that slipped out of Morgan's flabbergasted mouth was, "I will need to think about it."

Chapter 58

In the evening after dinner, Morgan discussed Betty's request with Dean. He was supportive. "Go for it. Mom and the girls and you will love the trip. I would drive you all, but I won't be able to take off of work."

Morgan contemplated for a moment. "You know, I think you might be right. We could use a change of scenery."

"My dad would be proud of you, Morgan. He never did get to drive that awesome motor home. Remember, Dad bought it before he died. You'll be the first to drive it."

"I know," Morgan said pensively. "What am I to do if Mom gets really weak on the trip or worse, dies?"

"Morgan, this is her request and you are honoring it. She knows what's against her. Mom's no dummy and neither are you. It should be fine. If anything happens, God forbid, you drive to the nearest hospital."

It took one day for Morgan and Dean to pack up the motor home. They packed medical supplies and oxygen, the wheelchair and children's toys.

The night before the trip Dean and Morgan were in the motor home going over the food and beverage supplies. "Mom has great car insurance so you have free towing if there's an emergency," Dean said, putting paperwork in the glove compartment. "Okay, I think you have everything you need for this trip, now come here. I want to show you something."

Morgan followed her husband to the back of the motor home. He opened a top cabinet. "Baby, I'm going to give you this." He showed her a silver cigarette holder and flipped it open. "This is some good weed, just one joint."

She looked at the cigarette case and got angry. "Oh, come on Dean, you know I hate that stuff, it makes me stupid. I don't want it."

With a serious face Dean said, "There might come a time that you are going to need this weed. You're under a lot of stress with mom and the kids. Don't argue with me Morgan; just remember that this joint is here." He closed the cabinet.

At daybreak the next day everyone in the house was awake. Morgan dressed the girls in comfortable matching yellow sundresses. Then she dressed herself in a delicate flowered lavender peasant blouse and denim shorts with white tennis shoes. She went in the bathroom, brushed her thick black hair, and combed it into a side over-the-shoulder braid. Both Noelle and Cathleen wore matching pigtail braids with yellow ribbon tied at the bottom.

Then it was time to get Betty dressed. Morgan walked over to her bedroom and was pleasantly surprised to find the drapes were open and the room was full of sunshine. Betty sat on the bed facing the lovely sun. Betty had dressed herself. She wore a peach blouse and white ankle pants and white sandals. Over her very thin hair, she wore a colorful turban scarf and little silver earrings.

"Mom, you look beautiful!" Morgan was overjoyed.

Betty smiled. "Thank you, my dear."

Slowly they walked outside and were pleased to see Rusty.

"Now don't you girls stop and pick up hitchhikers along the way," he teased, and they all laughed. He handed Betty a box of oatmeal cookies and said, "This is for you."

Betty smiled. "My favorites. Thank you."

He looked into Betty's face. "I love you and you know you're my second mom, right?"

"I love you too, Rusty," she said softly as he hugged her tenderly.

They all waved to each other when Rusty and Dean left on their motorcycles for work.

Morgan was nervous when she got behind the wheel of the

motor home.

Betty giggled. “My husband would be proud of you and me.”

Looking over to Betty, Morgan smiled. “Mom, I feel as though we have been set free out of a cage.”

“I know,” Betty giggled again. “This is wonderful. We are two drifters off to see the world, a least New Mexico. Now let’s hit the road!”

Three hours later without complaining, Betty swallowed two pills of morphine, went in the back, and went to sleep. Noelle quietly entertained herself playing with her dolls. Cathleen was asleep. Morgan looked at her watch and she knew time was a necessity. She did not know how much time Betty had before the cancer would possess more of her body. She drove steadily, stopping once to gas up and to eat lunch. Later, Morgan parked at a truck stop and closed her eyes to take an hour nap.

Driving through Albuquerque was beautiful, rural, open land and huge sky. Betty was excited to be close to her friend’s home. Her friend Nina had mailed them a map and Betty read directions as Morgan drove. Arriving in Pecos, they left the freeway and went on to the country road. The country road became a mountain road full of tight turns and Morgan was extremely cautious driving her precious cargo.

At last she arrived at the mailbox that had a tall, outdoor bronze mounted light attached to it. Underneath the mailbox was a posted sign: “Welcome O’Donnells.” In the distance was an old, large, rustic cabin protected by cottonwoods, evergreens, and willow trees. Morgan drove toward the cabin and honked. Instantly, a petite, attractive woman with deep wrinkles and long, straight, black hair with streaks of gray came out to greet them. Nina waved as she scampered up the dusty roadway and she was at Betty’s side in time to help Betty out of the vehicle. Without words, the two women embraced.

Right away Nina led Betty to her bedroom that she had prepared. Betty slept with Nina in a big comfortable bed that was covered with a beautiful colorful Indian quit. Along the side of the bed was Betty’s oxygen equipment waiting patiently if needed.

After Morgan was in bed, she could not sleep, so she lay quietly in a room with her daughters. Through the walls, she listened to the two friends laugh and share story after story about their lives. Nina made a living with her own business, selling all sorts of moccasins shoes and high top moccasin boots. Morgan learned later that Nina's heritage had bequeathed her plenty of land.

The next day Morgan left Betty and Nina alone. Noelle and Cathleen were getting restless so they all put on their new moccasins, gifts from Nina, and they went to explore the Indian museum. They saw many handicrafts mastered by the tribal members, beadwork, leatherwork, painting, and pottery.

In the evening, Morgan walked alone to the end of a trail that stopped at the edge of a very steep, heavily forested slope close to the mountains. She sat and watched the fast river flow from the highland down swirling through to the lowlands. The ridges were rugged and there were caves on the side of the mountains.

Five days passed. On the last night, Morgan was lost in her thoughts outside when she felt a hand on her shoulder. She turned and looked up. It was Nina. "I was concerned about you. The moon is rising and it will be dark soon."

Nina sat down on the ground next to Morgan, snuggled up next to her, and talked gently. "Rocky Mountain elk, Bighorn sheep, golden eagles, mule deer, all share these mountains. Here, use these binoculars and look there, you should see mule deer bucks." She pointed the way.

"Yes, I see them. Oh, they're beautiful."

Nina smiled. "They are beautiful, and I am concerned about our wildlife. The people come to the campground and are ignorant, feeding them the people food. The animals' digestive systems are very sensitive and it kills them."

"That's sad," Morgan said.

"Yes. I did not come to you to talk about the animals; I am deeply concerned about you. So many people walk with broken hearts after they lose loved ones."

Morgan looked into Nina eyes. "It's hard."

Nina put her one hand on Morgan's cheek kindly. "God has given you a gift."

"What gift?" Morgan asked.

"The gift of memory." Nina pointed to her own heart and then to her head. "This is where your memories are stored of all your beloved ones."

Chapter 59

The next morning, they were all up at sunrise. The well-behaved, comfortable children were in beds in the motor home when Morgan heard Nina say her last goodbye to Betty. "I will see you again, friend, in the land of peace and plenty, where there is neither disease nor death." They hugged. Nina wore the beautiful red crocheted shawl.

Without one word, Morgan began the long drive home. Betty looked very sad to leave. Morgan suggested she lie down in the back with the children and watched closely as Betty took more morphine pills. Her mother-in-law slouched down and covered herself in between the children and fell asleep.

For three hours, Morgan drove with the radio turned off in perfect silence. Her mind was quiet, free from noise or commotion.

The time came to stop for gasoline. While she filled up the tanks, the wind blew strong and drops of water spilled from the sky. By the time she reached the freeway it was pouring. Ten miles later, it began to snow light snowflakes. Grateful to see a recreational vehicle camping sign, she drove to the exit and drove off the freeway carefully. She found an empty parking spot and pulled in.

She woke everyone up. "It's snowing!" she told her family excitedly. Morgan bundled the girls up and took them outside to play in the clean snow. Betty watched from the window of the motor home. They were having fun outside when Morgan looked to the window and saw Betty take more morphine pills.

Morgan went to the motor home and ordered Betty, "Put your jacket on and come outside with us."

"I can't. I don't have the strength."

"Yes, you do," Morgan said.

Betty managed to climb out of the vehicle. Morgan, Noelle, Cathleen, and Betty laughed. For a moment, they were all little innocent children at play.

Two hours later, they were again settled inside, nice and dry. Everyone was fed. The little girls were tired out from the snow and were asleep. Morgan had quietly climbed onto the side bunk area. She closed her eyes.

At first, she could not make out what she heard but soon she heard it again. Betty was moaning with pain. Morgan quickly got out of the bunk bed.

"Mom, what's wrong?"

"My bones ache and I'm having trouble swallowing."

Morgan looked through the window and saw it was dark. It was definitely too dangerous to drive tonight. Struggling, Betty stood up and went off to sit in the front seat of the motor home.

"Oh gosh, these pains are worse," Betty moaned. Quickly, Morgan cut in half two more pills and handed them with a cup of water to Betty.

"Mom, do you think you can swallow these?"

Betty took the pills and water and struggled. "No." Weakly she handed the pills back.

Morgan went to the kitchen area of the motor home and crushed the pills. She placed the chemicals on a spoon and went to back to Betty. "Here, take this with the water."

Struggling again, Morgan helped Betty force the spoon full of morphine down her throat with a little bit of water. "Mom, when we get home I will call Dr. Olson and ask him for liquid morphine."

"Good idea," Betty nodded.

Morgan left Betty to check on her daughters in the back of the motor home. The girls were sound asleep, so she crept in and covered them up snuggly and gently pulled the wood divider shut. As she turned around, she remembered the marijuana that Dean had left in the top cabinet. Quietly Morgan opened it up and had to smile. That stinker had put a bottle of Jack Daniels there with two of her favorite small old-fashioned glasses.

To her surprise, there was also a white envelope, two artificial white silk roses sitting on one cassette tape, a bag of York dark chocolate-covered peppermint patties, and a lavender-scented candle in a terracotta jar. Next to that was the silver cigarette case and a lighter.

Morgan opened the envelope:

Hi Baby,

If you are reading this letter that means my mother is suffering. I am suffering too. The sky is black and there is no sunshine when I hear the word cancer. I am separate from the four of you by hundreds of miles but know my heart and head is right there with you. You have the heart of an angel. We are all lucky to have you in our lives. I realize my mother is your best friend, I know you hurt. You are not alone. You are a strong woman. This reefer and whiskey should lighten things up for you and Mom. I love you even more than the day we first met.

I love you baby,
Love Dean

Morgan went to the small refrigerator, took out ice, and watched as the square ice cubes fell into the glasses. "I will be strong, Lord. Let me be joyful for Mom."

Morgan walked with determination to the front of the motor home with an armful of stuff. "How are you feeling, Mom?"

"I've had better days," Betty said.

Morgan got busy. She delicately set the deep dashboard with a white linen cloth with the white roses and she lit the candle. "This is all from your thoughtful son; he thought we needed to relax."

After getting comfortable in the leather driver's seat, Morgan poured a small dose of the whiskey into her glass, took a sip of the woody smooth taste, and then she took a big gulp.

Betty looked down at her glass and then took a sip. "You know, Morgan, I'm not supposed to mix the morphine and alcohol. I could die." They both looked at each other and in that moment they both started giggling. Then Betty clenched her chest. "I'm in tremendous pain."

Morgan remained calm. "Mom, we are going to listen to this tape that your son made and we are going to smoke marijuana to ease our tension." Morgan snapped opened the case and took out the joint.

Morgan put the tape in. They waited until they heard Billie Holliday's voice come through. Then Morgan flicked the lighter and lit the joint. She inhaled deep and held it in as long as she could, then she exhaled slowly and knew this was special weed because it did not make her cough as much.

She looked to Betty. "Mom, never in my life could I have imagined what I am about to say." She paused. "I want you to take a hit."

Betty giggled. "Oh, sweetheart, you are so silly, I've never smoked anything but cigarettes but what the heck, I'll give it try." She inhaled the joint perfectly.

Then Ella Fitzgerald's velvet voice started singing the jazz blues as Morgan lit the joint up and took another deep hit with Betty. The two women put their mellow heads back against their seats.

"I love her."

"I love her, too."

The music changed and Bobby Darin started to sing. At the same time they both shrieked, "I love him!" They began to laugh uncontrollably.

The next song was Otis Redding. Again, at the same time they squealed, "I love him."

"I'm going to pee my pants!" Morgan said, laughing. "I'll be right back Mom; I'm going to check on our sweethearts." Morgan got up and went to the bathroom and then she glanced at the precious girls who were thankfully still asleep. Morgan grabbed the bag of peppermint chocolate and the box of oatmeal cookies.

Betty put a piece of peppermint on her tongue and waited for it to melt. Morgan drank more whiskey.

A new song came on. "This is Lester Young and Count Basie's band," Betty said. "He is the king of the clarinet and saxophone. Dean knows this is my favorite."

"Mom, how's your pain?"

"I'm doing pretty darn well. Pass me a cookie." She managed to eat one tiny bite and washed it down with a slug of the whiskey. Morgan munched on a cookie and walloped more of the Jack Daniels.

"Mom, can you imagine that for the rest of my life I will remember these moments with you?"

Betty giggled. "What is the world coming to? I'm a stoned, intoxicated, dying woman." Then she looked at her daughter-in-law. "Sweetheart, when you remember these precious moments you will smile all through your life and for that I'm happy."

A complete comfortable silence came over the women. Betty reached over and took Morgan's hand and they sat looking out into the darkness of the night.

After a while, Betty broke the silence. "My little collectible spoons have meant the world to me. And the Oregon spoon is my most cherished one."

"What's so special about Oregon?" Morgan asked.

Betty had a twinkle in her eyes. "Would you like to hear a true story?"

Morgan nodded.

"My dear mother was born in 1885 and 16 years later she had an arranged marriage to a man who never spoke much, my father William. While waiting on my father to put gasoline in his new car she got out of the car to stretch her legs. There was a small store nearby so she walked over. When she peeked through the window, she noticed a fancy silver spoon. The silver spoon had the word "Oregon" engraved on it. Mother walked into the store and purchased the spoon and placed it in her pocket. Well as I said, my father was not a talker and after three hours of complete silence my mother became very lonely. All of sudden she reached into her coat pocket and she felt her Oregon spoon. Well, Oregon became her dearest friend and it gave her comfort because every time she looked at it or touched it took her blues away.

"The Oregon spoon was a remembrance of Oregon and of the family that she had to leave behind."

Morgan smiled. "Oh, that's such a lovely story."

"My mother held on to that Oregon spoon until the end of her life in 1967. Then it came to me."

The two women stayed up late in the night, and laughed more and told each other their most secret thoughts and wishes. They cursed at life's thorns and praised its beauty. Morgan placed pillows around Betty and herself and covered them snugly. The full moon filled their view out the windshield. Time filled the dark and they stopped talking.

After a long while, Betty leaned over. "I hope the spoons give you courage, peace, and hope through troubled times and I hope your troubled times are far apart."

Morgan put her arms around Betty and held her tight. "Why is God punishing us?"

For a while, Betty was quiet again. "God is not punishing. Be thankful that I will be joining all our loved ones soon in heaven. My darling girl, this is a good time for me to say thank you for being the daughter I didn't have naturally. I love you dearly and my spirit will be with you throughout your life."

Chapter 60

Two weeks after they got home from New Mexico, Morgan found herself remembering a definition of time she'd read once in a dictionary. "Time is what keeps everything from happening at once."

Rick had died in February. Six months later it was July 1976. Morgan was 23 years old.

Betty refused to keep the oxygen mask on her face. "No more," she said weakly.

Morgan remembered a conversation they'd had in the motor home. Betty had said, "When the time comes, let me die a natural death in my home in my warm bed." Morgan took away the oxygen and rolled it to the other side of the room.

The time had come for her little girls to leave and go stay with Grandmother Isabel. Before they left, Morgan sat down and had another talk with her daughters and explained the best way she knew how as to what was happening to their Grandmother Betty.

Before the girls left for Isabel's, Noelle sat on Betty's bed. "Grandma, talk to me."

"I love you," Betty mumbled.

"You tired, Grandma?" Noelle asked.

"Yes, honey," Betty managed.

Noelle's mouth started to quiver. "Grandma, I love you."

With deep, hard breathing Betty whispered, "Noelle, I will always be right there." Then she put her hand on Noelle's heart.

Morgan took Noelle off the bed, then she picked up Cathleen and put her on the bed. Cathleen sat on the edge of the bed facing her grandmother. She was quiet and calm when she took Betty's fragile hands and kissed them. "I love you, grandma."

Betty closed her eyes. Cathleen kissed her grandmother's hand again and then she turned to Morgan. "Down, mommy."

Cathleen stood on the carpet. "Grandma go to heaven."

Noelle nodded. "I know."

That night they left with their other grandparents and the house grew quiet.

Luke called from overseas. There was a lot of static on the line and they had a hard time hearing each other. "Sis, I'm trying to get home as soon as possible. They're letting me fly out by the end of the week. Please tell my mother I love her." He hung up.

That night Dean stayed in Betty's room while Morgan took a break to eat a little something in the kitchen.

When she came back, Dean said, "I'm going to sleep. I will be right there on the couch. If you need me just holler." He kissed his wife on the forehead.

Morgan sat in the white rocking chair and began to pray holding her blue rosary.

Moments later she heard a quiet, "May I have some tea?"

Morgan jumped up and went to Betty. "I will go and make you some warm tea right now."

Quietly she tiptoed past Dean and filled the teakettle with water from the faucet. Firmly she placed it on the stove and turned on the gas. Right away, she neatly prepared the tray with the saucer, the china teacup, a tiny silver spoon, and white cloth napkin.

She stood there fidgeting with the buttons on her pink pajama top and then fidgeting with her long ponytail as she waited for the water to boil. She picked up the prepared tray and slowly made her way back to the bedroom.

She immediately noticed that Betty was out of bed. The tray dropped out of her hands and slammed to the carpet. Running to the bathroom she turned the brass handle of the door. It didn't turn, so she jiggled it but it was locked. She knocked then pounded on the solid wood door. "Mom, open this door!" she screamed.

Dean ran into the room. "What the hell is going on?"

"Your mother has locked herself inside the bathroom. I can't hear anything. We need to get in there now!"

Dean pounded on the solid wood door with both fists. "Mom, open the door!" There was no sound. "Dammit! Open the door!" His face went red. He opened the closet door and put on Rick's steel-toed boots that had never been thrown away. "Get back," he ordered Morgan. Then with all his might, he kicked to the side where the keyhole was mounted. Nothing happened. Using a front kick, driving the toe then heel of his boot again, the wood began to splinter, then it broke loose. He pushed the door open and rushed inside. He looked at the closed shower door and pulled it open. He looked inside then he stepped back and gasped. "Damn. Come here, Morgan."

Morgan's heart was pounding hard as she rushed in.

"She's in there." Dean pointed to the shower.

All the bathroom cabinets were opened wide and toiletries were tipped over and thrown all about, toilet paper was trailed everywhere. She got to the shower door and peered inside. "Oh no!" she said in fright.

Betty was huddled over in the corner of the large shower. Her pajamas were doused with shampoo, and her hair, face, and arms were covered in shaving cream foam. Toothpaste was sprayed on the tile walls of the shower and white body powder was spilled everywhere. She was banging on the tiles, whispering in the voice of a little child. When she saw Morgan, she screamed, "Get away from me, doctor!"

Quickly Morgan looked at Dean."Get out of here now. I've got it handled."

He stepped back. "Are you sure?"

"Yes, your mother would not have wanted you to see her this way. Please leave!"

Dean left.

Morgan knelt down in front of the shower and calmly said. "Betty, everything is fine. Sweetheart, do you know who I am?"

With a distracted expression of fear, Betty whispered, "I want my mommy. I'm afraid of the doctor," she cried.

Morgan saw that her fists were clutched tight. "Betty, I'm your mommy. I'm here to help you my baby girl." She reached out her arms, Betty grabbed them, and Morgan crawled onto the hideous shower floor. As she rocked Betty back and forth she could not understand her addled speech.

As Betty's rage subsided, Morgan asked, "Sweetheart, can you open your hand?"

She shook her head no.

"Please open your hand for mommy," Morgan whispered.

Betty opened her hand and revealed a packaged razor blade. Morgan took it from her and placed the blade carefully away on top of the nearby window ledge.

"Baby girl, we are going to take a shower and get you all pretty." She pulled Betty up and adjusted the water to warm. Morgan saw that Betty's face softened but she was still shaking. "You are such a good girl," she told her as she pulled off Betty's pajamas and washed her hair and rinsed all the bathroom articles off her body. She washed her face with a washcloth and was careful not to get anything into her eyes and mouth.

The two of them got out of the shower and Morgan dried Betty and wrapped a thick white towel around her. She opened a bathroom drawer and took out a clean blue flannel nightgown and pulled it down over her head and fussed with the arms. Betty giggled and said, "Mommy, you are all wet."

Morgan stopped and looked down at her soaking wet pajamas and slippers. "Well, it appears that I am wet." She looked at herself in the mirror with her hair dripping and she started laughing and so did Betty. Morgan kissed Betty on the forehead. "You sit right here and be a good girl while I get out of these wet things." Quickly she slipped the wet pajamas and slippers off and tossed them into the shower. With that done, she rushed to the closet and found herself a fresh white nightgown of Betty's and put it on.

Morgan reminded herself to just breathe as she turned back to the bathroom. Betty was patiently waiting on the vanity chair where she had left her.

"Sweetheart, I'm going to dry your feet now." Morgan knelt down and began to reach for her foot when Betty reached up and took a hold of her hand and stopped her and said, "Morgan, what are you doing?"

"Mom, do you know who I am?"

"Of course I know who you are. Why? What's going on? Tell me the truth."

"The cancer is affecting your brain. You are becoming childlike and you had a razor blade in your hand and you got into the shower and..."

Betty interrupted her. She took hold of her hands. "Now I want you to listen to me. You and I talked about what could happen when this viper rattlesnake got in my head. I trust you."

Morgan started to cry and she held on to Betty's legs. "I love you so much. I don't know if I can watch you suffer any longer. I can't take it anymore!"

"Oh, yes you can. God never gives us more then we can handle. You push forward." They lovingly looked into each other's eyes.

Together the two women walked out of the bathroom, leaning on one another. Dean was at the other side of the bedroom waiting. Together he and Morgan helped Betty back into bed. Five minutes later, she threw a cup of water across the room and wanted out of the bed again. Betty was gone and the child was back. "Doctor, I want out! I want out!"

Dean sat on the edge of the bed and tried to hold her down; she was strong and forceful. Morgan stood there watching. She thought for a long moment. "Hold her down. I have an idea."

She ran to the huge linen closet and pulled out white cotton sheets. Quickly she reached to the top of the shelf and felt around; she found the long pair of black scissors and grabbed them. Gathering everything into her hands she raced back down the hall and into the bedroom. She laid the sheets on the carpet, spread them out, and began to cut the expensive cloth in long strips.

"She wants out of this bed bad," Dean said.

"Yes, I know she wants to get up, but she can't. Betty is a child now. The cancer had entered her brain and she doesn't know who she is or what she is doing, she could very easily harm herself or us."

Dean watched as his wife pulled up the side rails of the bed and easily managed to spread Betty's legs apart, then in a gentle yet secure way she tied down both of Betty's legs to the side rails of the bed. No sooner than those legs were tied when Betty tried to untie them and she screamed, "I want out!"

Dean assisted Morgan in silence as she placed pillows under her arms for comfort. Then she secured both her arms to each side of the rails. Morgan explained: "Your mother thought this might happen. She warned me what to do. Most of all she was afraid if we could not take care of her properly then the visiting nurse would take her away from us. I assured her that she would not be taken from her home." Morgan placed a cold washcloth on Betty's forehead and a crisp yellow sheet over her body.

For the first time in months, Dean took his wife in his arms and held her. They both watched Betty as she laid there. Dean said, "I think the straps calmed her down. This is horrible watching her suffer; she is so young. I hate cancer."

Morgan involuntarily closed her eyes then flicked them open and with fire in her voice said, "The whole wide world hates cancer." She kissed Dean's mouth and then she broke free from his embrace and walked over to the side of Betty's bed to watch over her.

Unexpectedly, Betty's face had turned slightly purplish and her breathing had changed. Morgan moved toward her face and listened to the rattling noise coming from the back of her throat. At that moment, she remembered that same sound when Rick was near death. Morgan's lips quivered but she stayed strong and did not cry. Promptly she untied all the ties that had restrained Betty and gently rubbed her arms.

Quiet moments passed. Betty opened her eyes and they flashed straight into Morgan's eyes. Morgan held her hand tightly and whispered, "Mom, it's time to go and I will walk with you as far as God lets me. Don't resist. You're almost home."

A peaceful, angelic look took over Betty's face, and gracefully she bowed her head up and down and smiled as her body stiffened and with one last breath, her tender heart stopped beating.

Dean held his mother's body and cried. In the distance, a telephone rang from the other room. Morgan left Dean to answer the telephone.

"Hello?" She could barely breathe.

"Hello sis, it's Luke." There was static on the line. She could hear a downpour of rain. "How's my mother?"

Breathing hard and clutching her chest, she paused. It was hard to speak. She frowned. "Mother just died."

Chapter 61

1979

Countless changes occurred after Rick and Betty O'Donnell passed away. Dean and Luke had received a plentiful inheritance.

Morgan stood with Ann at the edge of a country highway next to Noelle and Cathleen waiting for the children's yellow school bus.

"I appreciate all that you have done for us this last year," she said looking at Ann, her live-in housekeeper and nanny.

"Thank *you*, Miss Morgan," Ann replied.

Ann had winter-white hair that matched her milk-like skin. The housekeeper who lived with Morgan full-time was a large woman, around 45 who held a small sense of humor. But she made up for the lack of humor with reliability, her love of children, and patience. Standing there at Morgan's side, she wore a conventional black uniform dress with a crisp starched white bib apron and black polished shoes.

"The bus is coming!" Cathleen said excitedly.

"Mommy, I will make sure Cathleen eats her lunch; the second-graders and third-graders have lunch together," Noelle said.

Deeply touched by Noelle's concern, Morgan reached over and kissed her on the cheek. "Thank you for being such a good big sister."

The bus stopped. Cathleen was holding her mommy's hand tight and then she let go. "'Bye Mommy." She looked up to Morgan with big, cheerful eyes.

Morgan smiled but her bottom lip quivered.

The yellow school bus doors opened and in a moment both

girls were waving good-bye from inside the bus. Bravely she stood there waving with a smile to show her daughters support. She and Ann walked back up the dirt hillside road up to the new house that Dean had bought from his inheritance. The house was built on three acres of land. It was a custom 5,600-square-foot, five-bedroom, five-bath, plus office-study residence on the outskirts of the city overlooking Orange County, California.

Fidgeting with the buttons of her white sweater, she walked onto the spacious front porch where Betty's two white rocking chairs sat. Ann followed behind her as they walked through the wrought-iron doors. They walked in to a covered tower entry, formal living room and dining room, and an enormous gourmet island kitchen with a sit-down bar. Outdoors was a massive covered patio, kitchen, pool, and spa. Out back was the small, two-bedroom guest house where Ann lived.

All the doors that led outside were white French doors that opened out. The windows throughout the front of the house were extremely large picture windows that maximized the lake view.

"Ann, I'm going out back for a while. Please go ahead and tidy up the girls' rooms."

"Yes, Miss Morgan."

Morgan walked outside down the gravel-winding paths that were flushed with blooming flowers. It had been weeks since she had gone into Dean's space. She was still fidgeting with her sweater button when she walked into the custom four-car garage. It was filled with stacked stuff wherever there was space. This garage had more stuff than Rick's garage could even have handled.

She flipped the stereo switch on and she heard the song "Stand By Me" by Ben E. King. The familiar music filled the room. She walked over to the Kenwood stereo system where stacks of music tapes laid nearby and saw uneven stacks of Playboy magazines, Penthouse and Girl Next Door magazines, and Easy Rider motorcycle magazines.

All around the garage she viewed the early memories of their life together. Arranged in the corner of the far garage she looked at the living room furniture from their first house. The leather sofas and chairs made Dean a comfortable garage-den.

Morgan thought about how she and Dean had become a source of mutual support to each other. They argued seldom, respecting each other's space. They were more like close friends.

Loneliness was an unpleasant feeling she knew well. A constant source of irritation to her was that Dean spent hours in his garage and in bars while she had spent most of her time concerned with the welfare of her children and decorating the inside of their home.

She walked over to the far corner of the massive garage where nothing was conventional. There was the pool table that Dean wanted, an expensive antique Victoria pool table. Hung from the ceiling was a Victorian pool table lamp and standing on the wall was a custom Victoria cue rack where rare pool cues hung.

The door opened up. "What are you doing in my cave?" he asked.

"Today was Cathleen's first day of second grade."

"Yes, I know that," he said.

"I want to talk about barber school."

His eyes glared red. "This is bullshit. You have everything you will ever need. You have a beautiful home with no mortgage, a new car bought with cash, a housekeeper, and yard service. You are set for life. You don't ever need to work. Why in the hell are you bringing this up now?"

With fury in her eyes, she uplifted her voice, "No! YOU have everything you need and want. You don't work, you live off your parent's inheritance; all you care about are bikes and having fun. You don't have any ambition in life. You promised me that after Cathleen began school it would be my turn. You promised and that was a year ago."

"Well doll, that was before my folks died. Besides, I don't remember promising you jack shit!" The expression in his eyes was mean.

"You're lying! You promised I could go to school and I'm going!"

He grinned. "I run the fucking cash around here. I'm not giving you one cent."

Morgan's eyes narrowed. "You don't have to give me your precious money because your mother was smart. Betty knew that you would do this; she left me more than enough tuition money for my career. I've waited this long thinking maybe you would want this for me. I was dead wrong." Turning from him, she started to walk out. Then she turned back around and faced him squarely. "I'm going to fulfill my heart's desire. Just the way your brother did. Luke had no problem moving to Japan and starting his own computer business."

Chapter 62

Three days later at 9 a.m. sharp she stood in front of an elegant, historic building located in the heart of Los Angeles, California. With a deep breath, she pushed open the glass doors that read, "Mr. Steinway Master Barber College." She walked over to the reception desk. There stood a tall slender handsome Latino man who wore a Long Van Dyke beard design and a perfect medium tapered haircut that favored a middle part. "May I help you?"

"Yes. I have an appointment. My name is Morgan O'Donnell."

"Hello, my name is Mr. Gable." He extended his hand and they shook hands firmly. He handed her four vanilla-colored papers.

"Do you have a pen?"

"I do," she answered.

"Please sit there and complete these forms. One is an enrollment statement. The others are questions on barbering." He points to a small desk and chair that were waiting in the corner.

Morgan read the questions over and was immediately thankful to Ann for going and bringing her the textbook on barbering from the library. She finished the paperwork in twenty minutes and stood up to take the forms to Mr. Gable. "I'm finished."

"Well, that was fast. Thank you. Please go and sit back down." He read the papers over and then disappeared through the mahogany doors with the glass privacy panel.

From where Morgan sat, she overheard a conversation from behind the wall. Mr. Gable was talking to another man. "She finished this within 15 minutes and I expected to see several wrong answers concerning her knowledge about the art of barbering. I am quite surprised to see that each question is correct and answered most intelligently and she has excellent penmanship. And, you know what that means; she might be a detailed barber."

A man in a German accent said, "That is good. This means she came prepared. Please give her the basic test. Let's see if she has any skills."

Within seconds, the door opened and Mr. Gable waved to Morgan to come in. As soon as she went through the door, it shut hard behind her and nervously she jumped. She viewed the white and black porcelain tile floor that looked almost too clean to walk on. The room was a long, narrow room divided in half by a narrow walkway. There were low ceilings and bright fluorescent ceiling lights. Black framed mirrors hung on every wall. In each corner of the room, huge traditional barber poles swirled. There were more than 30 barber stations.

Mr. Gable said, "Morgan, I presumed you understand that in order to attend this college you must pass the basic technique of barbering?"

"Yes I do," she said.

"You may work in this station."

She observed a black barber chair with a black and white pin-striped cloth folded over the right side of the arm. On the back wall was a barber station that included a black shampoo bowl, four electrical outlets, and two towel hampers. The ample cabinet's doors were opened and showed a dozen perfectly folded white shampoo towels and a row of barber towels that had a blue line down the front. On the white counter top was a clear bottle that was marked Water and a Marvy jar that was full to the top with blue disinfectant liquid. The neck dispenser had white strips ready to use. Next to that was a warm electric lather machine.

On the white counter top one shiny straight razor, a jumble styptic pencil, and a Badger shaving brush laid in order. Three black barbers' combs and three brushes lay in the next row. Hanging on the wall next to the barber chair was a wood clipper holder, which held four different sized clippers.

"Morgan, I want you to do one basic haircut." He motioned

to a teenage boy who was sitting close to get up. The young man sat in the barber chair.

Very calmly, Morgan went to her purse, pulled out one pair of scissors, and laid them on the counter next to the combs. She went to the sink and washed her hands. Then she put a white strip around the patron's neck and wrapped the barber cloth over his clothes. Her hands shook when she grabbed a comb to put into the sterilizer jar. She was not sure if she had used the correct comb.

Picking up her 7/5-inch scissors and comb, she examined the mop of hair in front of her. Her hands shook so hard that she should have cut her fingers. She did not. What she did do was concentrate and find her rhythm with the haircutting. Her fingers, comb, and scissors became one. She felt like she was playing a musical instrument, her fingers and hands flowed throughout the haircut. With her mind only on the cut, she felt a peaceful and composed.

It was time for the final edging. She hesitated and her forehead broke into a sweat as she decided which clipper to choose. She decided on the small red clipper. Cautiously she proceeded to line up the neckline and both side burns with the red clipper. Next, she lathered his neckline and side burns. Then she picked up the straight razor it glared shiny in her eyes. Slowly she shaved the young man's neck with quick strokes and outlined the sideburns. She washed her hands.

"I'm finished," she said.

Mr. Gable looked closely at the box cut haircut with the tapered neckline and side burns that matched. "Impressive," he said modestly. "Now come along." She followed him to the office door. He knocked lightly on the door.

"Come in."

Mr. Gable announced, "Morgan O'Donnell." Then he left.

A man sitting behind a big oak desk walked around to her and gracefully extended his hand. "Hello Morgan. My name is Mr. Steinway, please have a seat." Then he went back to his seat.

Morgan sat. Her knees knocked against each other nervously.

Gazing around the room, her eyes locked on a unit that had three long shelves crowded with hair cutting trophies and the wall behind it had pictures of Mr. Steinway with celebrities and politicians.

"I see you are taking notice of my wall of fame. Don't let that impress you; it was a long time ago." The pencil-styled black mustache looked perfectly straight when Mr. Steinway smiled.

Shyly, she glanced at his flattering haircut. A Marine flat-top showed a blocky effect on a perfectly straight line at the top. She knew it was so much more than the buzz cuts she had done at home.

"You are observing my flat-top haircut. Do you like?"

"Yes sir, I do, it's the most excellent flat-top I have ever seen."

"Mr. Gable is my barber and it takes him a roughly 10 minutes to do this procedure."

Morgan whispered, "10 minutes!"

"There is a camera over there." He pointed. "I watched you perform the haircut. The shear and comb work was very good. You do know how to hold a straight razor, but you don't know a thing about honing and stropping a razor." He smiled. "Correct speed, grace, and technique will come naturally with practice. Have you had formal training anywhere?"

"No. I've learned everything I know from standing in the streets looking at the barbers cut hair through a window. Then I practice what I've watched on friends at home," she said.

Mr. Steinway rested his chin on his fist. "Interesting, you have watched from the streets. Well, you have a light hand and magnificent fingers and great coordination." He paused. "Morgan, let's get to the point. I have not had much success with women completing the requirements for State Board. It was three women out of thirty-five the last time I checked. To have a desire to be a barber sounds like a lot of fun, when in reality it takes discipline and repeated practice to perform barber services. Much of barbering is mental as well as a skill. It requires an excellent listener as well as superior hair-cutting."There was silence in the room. Then Morgan said, "I am disciplined, courteous, and I am a good listener. I was a very good student in high school." She paused. Then her eyes narrowed. "I love to cut hair and shave men. I love the straight razor, I taught myself to use one. I have wanted to be a master barber all my life."

Mr. Steinway grinned. "The profession of barbering is one of the oldest in the world. My school has a fine reputation for training students to be master barbers. Morgan O'Donnell, you will start training here next semester.

Chapter 63

Two weeks later, the leather saddle bags were packed with just the basics: tee-shirts, underwear, one pair of shorts, and a light jacket. Morgan dressed in a tight pair of Levi's torn at the knee and a yellow bikini top with a yellow tee-shirt over it. Her long hair was pulled tightly back in a ponytail with a black bandanna tied around her head and forehead. She was pulling on her biker boots when Isabel and Barney walked into the house.

Isabel looked at her daughter with a concerned face. "Honey, are you sure the area is safe where the two of you are camping? I've heard awful stories about the Kern River from my church friends. I just don't understand why Dean doesn't take you on a nice vacation to Santa Barbara?"

Morgan smiled and reassured her mother. "Mother, don't worry; Dean won't let anything bad happen to me. He wants us to have a good time before I start school."

"Isabel, stop being so dramatic," Barney agreed. "These two young people need time alone."

"Thank you, Daddy." Morgan hugged both her parents. "I'm so happy Dean is finally accepting the fact that I'm going to have a career. I must be a good sport and ride the bike with him. I love him so much."

Dean yelled from outside. "Come on, let's go!"

He jump-kicked the Harley-Davidson engine and it screamed loudly. Noelle and Cathleen came running to Morgan and she bent down to kiss them both.

"Have fun and be careful mommy," Noelle said.

"And hold on tight!" Cathleen said.

"See you all in three days." She waved goodbye.

No sooner had they turned the corner on the road than Dean pulled the bike over to the side of an empty lot. He looked around and saw that no one was lingering around. He pulled out his wallet and took out a tiny folded piece of foil paper, a razor blade, and a cut straw. Then he opened the foil and there was white powder in it. Skillfully and carefully, he divided the powder into two straight lines. He told Morgan, "Here, snort this."

"You have to be kidding, Dean! You know how I feel about cocaine. It's not for me."

He kissed her neck. "Hey, just this one time party with me before you start that school." He begged. "Pretty please baby?"

Unwillingly she took the short straw to her nose and inhaled half the line. The powder burned going up into her nostril and she swallowed hard. She watched Dean do his line plus the rest of hers. "That's good shit."

With an intoxicated, excessively happy face, Dean kissed his wife smack on the lips then said, "We're out of here."

Morgan thought about the early years with Dean as they rode. She was not an innocent girl anymore. As they headed down the highway, she felt guilty for leaving her daughters but that thought did not last for long. As the effects of the cocaine took over her mind, she felt very alert and warm inside. It was amusing, she thought, that her husband never had a clue that she had figured out where he kept his stash. Dusting the outside bar one day her hand had gone under the edge. There was a loose panel and there was Dean's precious uncut cocaine hiding along with weed and cash.

She snuggled into her leather seat and wrapped her strong, young legs in a hard embrace around Dean. "This is a beautiful day and I love you," she purred in his ear. Dean patted her thigh as they zipped by traffic. At the Interstate 5 they went east on Highway 178 to Lake Isabella. Whipping off the freeway to the Kernville exit, they continued around the lake until finally they crossed the bridge and found the campground by the river.

The day was hot and muggy. The area was a fairly secluded spot near sandy river beaches on undeveloped national forest land. There was no fee or rules. Fifteen bikes were parked side by side along the off road. There were bikers partying, swimming, dancing, and cooking. Music was blaring from somewhere. Dean parked the motorcycle with the others.

As Morgan got off the Harley, she felt a tug on her shirt. She swirled around.

"Howdy," Rusty said. He gave her hug.

"Wow, I haven't seen you forever!" Morgan hugged him tight.

Then Damien came behind her and hugged her too. "It's about time, girl."

"I know it's really been a long time. I'm so happy to see you both," she said.

Rusty pulled out a fat joint. "Have a drag of this, Morgan. We are all celebrating you starting barber school. Life is good for you kid." He smiled as he handed her the joint.

The joint reminded Morgan of the last time she had smoked weed. It was in the motor home with Betty three years ago. She quickly shook the thought away. Today, all she wanted to do was be a part of the group for once. She took the joint she inhaled deeply and coughed deep. The guys laughed.

"Easy baby, just hit it lightly." Dean took the joint to demonstrate. Then she smoked it again.

After small talk with the people, Dean said, "Let's go set up our camp." He found them a spot away from the crowd. It was a cozy spot against a tree trunk with branches for shade.

For next two days, all the friends enjoyed fishing and cooking under the stars. Dinner was the fish they caught with cans of pork and beans and canned fruit. Breakfast was hot coffee, stacks of buttered pancakes, and piled up bacon.

On the last day, Morgan felt lazy after breakfast so she snuck away so that the men could clean up the mess from their cooking. Grabbing a low beach chair and towel, she went down to the river beach to wash her body. She kept her white bikini on. The water was freezing but she felt refreshed. After she forced her body to leave the water, she plopped down in her chair and pulled on a tank top over her swimsuit. She sat there facing the rivers and her thoughts were immersed in silence and peace.

"Good morning, baby!" She looked up and was surprised to see her husband standing at the water's edge wearing only his Levis. The sunlight hit the outline of his strong and powerfully built body. He bent over and washed out his white tee-shirt and the muscles of his back and shoulders showed off his stunning, manly presence.

"Take off your shirt," he ordered. "There's no one here; they all went for a bike ride."

Playfully she threw her tank top to him. He rinsed it and laid both their shirts on the rocks to dry.

"It's beautiful," he said as he took in the peaceful view. Then he unzipped his Levi's and pulled them off. He jumped in the water and came out laughing. "It's freezing cold!" With his hair wet and dripping, he walked over, took her hand, and pulled her up. "Come with me."

She followed him inside their tent. A cool breeze flowed through the tent window as they sat on top of the sleeping bag and shared a joint. Dean stroked her hand and then he held it and played with her wedding rings. "I'm going to be the best husband to you. I'm going to be Mr. Mom and take care of Noelle and Cathleen. I'm going to help them do homework. I'm going to stop being a dick and going to the low-life bars. And I won't force you to do cocaine with me."

She hesitated, weighing his words. "You are stoned. You won't remember any of these promises once we're home."

He grabbed her with his masculine arms and held her. "You're wrong this time, Morgan. All I want is for you to be happy. You did so goddamn much for my mother and you're such a good mom to our kids. Damn, you deserve to have your barber career."

They kissed and devoured each other's mouths.

Dean broke their embrace. Unsmiling with a solemn voice, he said, "Baby, I'm just a son of a bitch jerk, I've always been afraid of losing you to the men who are going to fall in love with you when you become their barber."

There was a silence between them. Dean had never said such words to her before. She trembled.

"You take my breath away," he whispered.

She was silent. He took her face in his hands. "I give you my word; I will never disrespect you ever again."

Tears of happiness were in her eyes. She whispered to her husband, "The beach will run out of sand before any man will take my heart from you."

Tenderly he whispered, "The world is going to get one foxy lady behind the chair." Gently she kissed his lips.

"Take off your bikini please," he said.

She did.

"Lie back," he commanded.

She did.

Everything outside the tent disappeared as she lay there naked, outstretched, and waiting. He descended down on her body kissing and licking her like a cat licks its wounds. Gently and fiercely then patiently, he continued until he heard her one last loud moan. Her body quivered in satisfaction.

Turning on her side, she pulled herself up to her knees and said, "It's your turn."

Without hesitation, gently she pushed his muscular legs apart. She kissed, licked, and tenderly caressed every part of his thighs as if she had found a lost treasure. His powerful legs trembled.

Dean purred. "Baby, it's been so long. Oh that tickles."

She whispered, "I will never wait this long to please you." She watched as his manhood rose up to greet her lips in a full salute and she skillfully welcomed his arousal with a deep firm rhythm that continued until she heard him scream in desire.

After their immeasurable pleasure, Dean said, "Baby, this is our new beginning."

That afternoon after packing up their stuff they made a stop at a hamburger joint and ate. Hours later, they drove up their driveway and Isabel, Barney, Noelle, Cathleen, and Ann hurried out of the house to greet them.

"Daddy and Mommy are home!" Cathleen screamed with excitement.

Dean bent over and scooped her in his arms. "Were you a good girl for Grandma and Grandpa?"

"Oh yes Daddy, I was a good girl, and we made cookies and Grandpa swam in the pool with us."

Dean shook Barney's hand and said, "Hey Dad, how's it going?"

Barney snickered. "I'm glad to see you guys. These girls are exhausting. They have kept us busy."

Noelle hugged her mommy tight. Then she put both her arms around her daddy's leg and said, "Daddy, I'm so happy you are home."

Dean put one arm around Isabel and another one around Ann and said, "How are my two best girls?" Arm and arm they all walked into the house together.

Barney and Morgan hugged. "Daughter, it looks to me like you two had a wonderful vacation."

"Oh Daddy, we did. It was so good to get away. I love my husband more than ever before."

Everyone was light-hearted as they made their way into the huge kitchen area and they stood there chatting away.

"So what are we having for dinner? I'm starved." Dean looked at Ann with a grin.

Ann's face turned red. "Oh my goodness, Mr. Dean, I'm so ashamed I have nothing prepared. The grandparents promised the children Jack-in-the-Box for supper."

"Yes, I'm afraid these daughters of yours have been begging us the last two days for fast food and we finally gave in." Barney smiled. "I was just about to leave. Let me change out of my slippers and put my shoes on."

"Don't worry about changing your shoes Dad, the bike is out front so I'll do the food run," Dean offered. He put his leather jacket back on and zipped it up.

Morgan followed him out to the bike. He got on and she kissed him hard. "Hurry up, I miss you already."

"I miss you more," he told her.

Standing on the driveway, she watched him leave and stood there until the sound of the Harley was out of range.

Thirty minutes later, Morgan looked up at the clock above the dining room table. "The fast food place must be busy tonight," she thought.

Then a whole hour had passed.

A chill came over her shoulders and neck while she rocked back and forth on the front porch. She looked out over the lake and watched two ravens in flight. Her bones felt cold. Something was wrong; she felt it in her heart. She went in the house for a sweater.

The telephone rang in the office-study where Barney was watching a baseball game. Morgan watched her father from the doorway when he reached over and turned the volume of the television down, then he reached over and picked up the phone.

"You have his wallet? The eyewitness was a kid..." Barney's voice trembled. "What do you want us to do now?" Then he listened and slowly hung up the phone.

Barney had a frightened expression on his face. He stood up and stared at his daughter. "Morgan." He grabbed both her hands. "I need to tell you something."

"What, Dad?"

Barney swallowed hard his mouth quivered. "My darling, there's been an accident. It's concerning Dean."

"What kind of accident?" she asked.

Barney held on to his daughter and said nothing.

Morgan began to get flustered. "Well, let's go to the hospital, what hospital is Dean at? Daddy, where is my husband?"

Barney's eyes watered. "No, he's not in a hospital. There was a bystander. Some kid named Warren White saw Dean try to beat a red light. A truck hit him head on. Dean was killed instantly."

"NO!" She collapsed to the floor, dragging on her to her father's pant leg. "I want Dean! I want my husband!"

Chapter 64

Four months after Dean's death, Jan. 1, 1980

Morgan laid in hospital emergency room. She watched groggily as a young nurse checked her IV.

"Come here," Morgan whispered to her.

"What do you need?"

"It hurts."

"What hurts? Does the IV needle hurt your arm?"

"I want to die. Kill me."

The nurse left the room in a hurry.

A doctor rushed into the small white room. "How are you feeling this morning, Morgan?"

Morgan glared at him. Then she screamed, "I want to die!" as she stripped the IV from her arm. With a gust of energy, she shoved the tray of water and food against the wall and mirror. She climbed out of the bed, reached down, grasped a sharp piece of glass and held it to her neck. The doctor grabbed her arm and wrestled her to the ground. The glass shard fell away and shattered and the doctor lunged forward to slam his hand down on a red knob. Several more staff attendants rushed into the room to restrain and help Morgan. The last thing Morgan saw was the doctor sticking a needle in her. She passed out.

A few days later, Morgan's eyes were closed as she lay on her back facing a window. Her arms were held down to the side of the bed railing by leather straps. She listened helplessly as Barney, Isabel, and a woman social worker discussed her situation.

"Your daughter would have been dead before the New Year if the housekeeper had not found her. There was more than enough cocaine and alcohol in her system to kill her. When the paramedics arrived to her house, they found her psychotic, violent, and delusional. It's a miracle that she did not suffer a heart attack or stroke."

With his head faced down, Barney's voice was low. "Our girl has been through hell the last nine years with family deaths, as well as the early tragedy of her siblings." Worried, he looked up at the woman. "I think her husband's fatal accident has pushed her over the edge."

"She asked us to take the children. We should not have left her alone on New Year's Eve. What can we do?" Isabel voice was strained and trembling.

"Well, she tried to kill herself with the overdose," the social worker said matter-of-factly. "From what you have told me I understand she has had to deal with extreme trauma through several situations. For now she will be moved to a psychiatric hospital, then from there she may be fortunate enough to go to the Canyon Recovery Home. It is the best center in the country for survivors of childhood and adult trauma."

Chapter 65

Morgan showed no emotion when she arrived at the busy psychiatric hospital. She was first interviewed about her medical history then afterward she created a fuss, screaming, throwing anything within her reach, and refusing to walk. Someone in a white coat shoved her into a padded harness to restraint her, stuck her onto a wheelchair, and pushed her into a room.

Two hours later, two hefty female nurses came into the room. One nurse removed the harness and the other nurse said, "Get up and take off all your clothes." Without a struggle, Morgan stood up and took everything off. She stood with her legs far apart and arms stretched out while the nurse then searched her body for drugs, weapons, matches, or anything that could cause harm to her or others. The nurse finished conducting the physical evaluation and made notes on a chart about any marks on her body.

Morgan was given a shot in her arm then the nurse gave her oral medication and she swallowed it without a struggle. Next, she was wheeled into a white, dim room with several other patients. Morgan stared at a plain white wall and found peace as the meds began to calm her twisted mind. At meal time, she refused to eat and acted more anxious as her chaotic mind started churning. After she was given more medication, her mind calmed down again.

Seventy-two hours later, she was released from the psychiatric hospital. She was put in a white van with bars on the windows that took her to the Canyon Recovery Home.

Three months passed, but Morgan still had no reason or need to speak to anyone. On occasion, she would be polite and say thank you to an attendant. She tried to eat but really had no appetite. She had no enthusiasm and she refused to walk around the grounds of the center.

Every morning, she was routinely placed into a wheelchair and wheeled outside to a spot that overlooked the ocean. She sat in various classes throughout the day and heard but did not listen to the counselors teach about grief and healing. Every class began with a prayer, which she did not participate in; instead, she stared at the floor. Morgan heard the counselor say to the class, "The first thing to accept is that your pain is real. You need to own your pain. Your life will never be the same after a tragedy. Allow yourself grace. This means you can still love your loved ones who are gone and continue to live in this world on your own journey."

Morgan did not believe she could ever get over the pain.

The other class she sat through taught about the dangers of prescription drugs and street drugs. "You cannot numb your pain," the counselors said. All that went through Morgan's mind was that she *wished* she could numb her pain.

Morgan sat in the wheelchair one breezy day, hypnotized by the ocean view.

A Carmelite nun dressed in a long full black habit and black veil with a long white cloak walked over to her. The nun knelt down on one knee in front of Morgan's legs and placed white roses in her lap. She looked up into Morgan's face. "Hello, my dearest friend. I have missed you very much."

Morgan looked at the angelic face that was framed by the wimple that covered her head, forehead, and neck under the black veil. She looked down at the white roses and with one hand; she rubbed her eyes because she feared she was hallucinating. Then she mumbled, "Lucy?"

The nun took Morgan in her arms and rocked her back and forth like her own child. In a soothing voice she said, "Yes, Lucy is here for you. Everything will be all right."

"How did you find me?"

"Your brother Peter found me and called me from Ireland. I

received special permission from my superiors to visit you."

The two best friends sat and talked the rest of the afternoon in Morgan's small bedroom. Eventually, it was time for Sister Amelia to leave.

"Why did you pick the name Sister Amelia?" Morgan asked.

"I choose that name from a saint I admire. Her patronage was against demonic possession." Sister Amelia took her hand. "This is something that you have to overcome. No more will you be easy prey for the devil. Remember Morgan, only heaven is free from problems and heartaches. With God in your heart you can accomplish peace in your mind."

Morgan stood up from the wheelchair with all the strength she could muster and took steps toward Sister Amelia. "Blood sisters forever."

The nun smiled and caught Morgan in her arms. Sister Amelia whispered, "Yes, blood sisters forever." The best friends shared an understanding hug and then Sister Amelia said, "Next time, you come to see me at my convent."

Chapter 66

After the visit from Sister Amelia, Morgan slowly began to make progress. She listened to the counselors in the classroom and learned how to cope with loss. She learned how not to numb her brain but instead to embrace feelings. She became friends with the wife of the pastor who came to the recovery service on Sundays. Her name was Gail. They talked about baptism and the Lord and joy.

"You told me that you were baptized in the Catholic Church when you were an infant?" Gail asked Morgan one day.

"Yes, that's right," Morgan answered.

"You're an adult now. I would like you to be baptized again."

Morgan looked at Gail. "I would love to get baptized again. It would give me a fresh start, except…"

"Except what?"

"I can never stop praying with the holy rosary and I can never abandon my relationship with the blessed mother Mary. My feeling has changed toward the Catholic Church but not my feeling toward my beliefs."

"Morgan, I have been a pastor's wife for more than thirty years. I have known women of all religions and beliefs. No one can tell you how to pray. I believe the earth is all one people and we have only one God."

Morgan agreed. "Thank you, Gail."

Early the next morning, Morgan wore a white cotton dress. She was barefoot and held her blue rosary beads in her hands that Isabel had given her years before. When she walked down the winding staircase to the beach, she felt calm as the sun shined on her face.

Pastor Larry, along with his loving wife, were waiting for Morgan in the ocean waters.

"Do you believe that Jesus Christ died for your sins?" he asked.

"Yes."

"Do you accept Him into your heart as your Lord and Savior?"

"Yes."

"Do you promise to follow Him the rest of your life?"

"Yes."

Pastor Larry smiled. "Upon your confession of faith I now baptize you in the name of the Father, Son, and Holy Spirit." He completely submerged her in the ocean water and said, "Buried with Christ. Rise and walk in new life."

At that very moment she felt an unexplained calmness and joy enter her heart, mind, and body. Most importantly, she felt that she wanted to live.

One week later, she applied make-up for the first time in months and she finished dressing. Morgan sat on her bed looking out the window across the street to a park and watched a man push two swings. The little boy and little girl laughed joyfully as they swung higher and higher. Morgan talked to herself aloud. "Okay, I can do this as a single parent. I will go back into the world and create a wonderful life with my daughters." She heard a knock on the door.

"May I come in?"

"Oh Daddy, it's you!" Barney took his daughter in his arms and they held on to each other.

"How's my favorite girl?"

They both sat down on the small bed. Morgan looked into Barney's eyes. "Thank you for taking care of my girls and our home. I'm sorry I put you through all this. I just couldn't wrap my head around everything starting with Casey and Emma, then my pregnancies, and the O'Donnells, and then Dean. I just caved in. I wanted to die, too."

Barney looked away. He took something out of his pocket and handed it to his daughter. "This is from Luke." Morgan unwrapped the little packages to reveal two elegant spoons from Japan.

"So beautiful. My very first collector spoons!" she said.

She hesitated. "It's time for me to go forward in my life, wherever it takes me. I'm going to follow my dreams and become the best lady barber and raise my daughters to be strong, confident women."

Barney's eyes twinkled like stars. "Daughter, you have just put the sun back in my heart."

Chapter 67

Back in the barbershop, the rainstorm subsided.

Morgan wiped the last tears from her eyes and unfolded her legs that had become stiff from being crossed as she let the memories overtake her. Her heart ached just as much as it had 24 years ago. She got up and stretched, then went to the cupboard and grabbed a dusty bottle of Jack Daniels. She poured it into a small glass and poured it half full. "This is for you Dean, the love of my life," she said aloud. She gulped down the whiskey.

Then she walked to a closet and took out a yellow folder that was hidden under several sweaters on a top shelf. She plopped back on the bed and looked through the file that was full of old photos. There was a small black and white picture of Isabel, Barney, herself; Peter, Noah, Emma, and Casey standing in front of their modest home. The next picture was of Morgan standing with her arms around Lucy as they both made funny faces. Then there was a picture of Morgan with the high hairstyle and the thick black eyelashes, a pink miniskirt, and black thigh-high boots.

Next was the wedding picture of her with Dean and Betty, Rick and Luke. Next was the baby photo of Noelle. Behind that was a picture of Noelle when she had become a lawyer, holding her degree. Another was of Noelle and her husband on their wedding day.

Next, there was a picture of Cathleen as a baby and behind that was her wedding picture. Cathleen was an elementary teacher. Her husband was a songwriter who made a lot of money. Then they both quit their professions and became missionaries. They traveled all over the world and finally they settled on an

Apache Indian Reservation in New Mexico to teach.

At that memory, a thought crossed Morgan's mind. She rushed into the bathroom and quickly removed her nightgown. She grabbed the large hand mirror, determined to admire the tattoo that covered most of her back. She looked in the mirror and saw a beautiful African elephant that held one leg up to show the diamond bracelet that Dean had given her so many years ago. The tattoo artist Sun had helped her decide on this. "You remind me of an elephant," Sun had said to her. "You are highly intelligent and compassionate and you never forget a face. And when you are nervous you dance in a circle around your barber chair."

Morgan stared close at her tattoo and aloud she whispered, "I love my wise elephant and I will always love you, Dean." She slipped her long white nightgown back on.

Still restless, she walked over to the front room and to the tall filing cabinet. She inserted her key into the slot and turned it, taking a deep breath as she pulled one long drawer open. Her mind stepped into another world. These files were arranged in alphabetical order by career.

For years, Morgan had been handing each new client a card to fill out with his or her personal information. After performing their haircut service, she would jot down what type of haircut she did as well as the price and the conversation they had so the next time they came into the barbershop she would remember how their last visit was.

Searching through these files, she indulged in reading some of them to reminisce the times she had shared with these very special men.

She searched the file for famous men she knew. She went to the back and lifted up one card from the "P" file.

'Priest.' Governs the Catholic diocese in Los Angeles.

Name: Archbishop Michael MacKay.

Note: Priests should be allowed to marry!

Deceased.

Morgan has learned so much about that wonderful,

compassionate man. She knew he suffered with some of the church rules. Morgan closed her eyes and remembered him in her chair and their conversations.

The file behind "Priests" read "Politicians." There were several clients there. Morgan smiled and laughed to herself, thinking these people were such drama kings, full of good intentions in the beginning but unfortunately their best ideas get derailed by corruption. Politicians loved to get their hands in the cookie jar.

Next, she pulled out the file "Sports." This file contained names of a few of her city's most gifted athletes, trainers, coaches, and owners. Morgan felt privileged to know that most of these men were real heroes and dedicated professionals.

Many of these athletes suffered from identity crises because they had come from humble beginnings and were launched to super fame. It was challenging for a few to cope with super-stardom. For years, she had stood silently behind her barber chair as groups of them came into her shop and discussed among themselves the problems the public never saw. She closed her eyes and saw the elite football group talking about their troubles, the epidemic misuse of prescription narcotics like Percocet, Vicodin, Xanax and lots of alcohol and sex. The gifted few discussed the deadly word: "retirement."

She opened the file labeled "Event Stubs." It was full of ticket stubs given to her by a handful of athletes who had presented the lady behind the chair with free tickets to events in the best stadiums of southern California. For more than 23 years, she had attended professional baseball, football, hockey, and basketball games and never once paid for a seat.

She inched up to another file and pulled the "I" slim file out, it contained "Inventors." The file had four names. She smiled when she saw the name of one and she remembered the day she had just hung up her fresh new barber license proudly on the wall and Justin cruised into the barbershop with a long skateboard under his arm. He sat down in the barber chair and just jabbered away. He had been a sweet teenage boy with a head full of ideas and the most difficult hair. Justin's strawberry blonde hair was course and straight with the most stubborn cowlick. She had been his barber since that day. Justin had created wonderful outdoor Snow Toys for people to ride on. Twenty-four years later, Justin the genius was now a billionaire and still a friend to her.

Her fingers grazed again to the back and stopped at "Mexican Workers." The waiters and the dishwashers worked at the famous restaurants that surrounded her business. She remembered how she would open the shop two hours early one day a week for them and charge only five dollars for haircuts. Each man was particular in having a perfect haircut but they were courteous and always tipped her one dollar with pride.

Morgan saw the name "Francisco" and immediately remembered when she was 35 years old. He was an extremely handsome 22-year-old waiter from Mexico City and there was no denying the chemistry between her and the caramel-skinned, six-foot-tall young man with the dark bedroom eyes and beautiful smile. Without restraint, she had broken all the rules and spent three delicious months having a passionate fling with him. He spoke no English and she spoke very little Spanish. Instead, they shared the language of love and laughter.

Morgan remembered the day when his Aunt Carmela came into her shop.

"Morgan, I want to talk to you about my sister's only son. Francisco is in love with you. But you cannot have him. It is all planned; he goes to Spain with my rich cousin. My nephew Francisco will study to be a doctor!"

"What do you want me to do?" Morgan had asked.

"Promise me you will let him go," Carmela had begged her.

It was a very challenging day when she broke it off with Francisco. He cried into her arms. They made love for hours in the morning and that evening they said good-bye at the Los Angeles International Airport. Morgan did not get out of the car; she left him at the curb.

Years later, Morgan had received a precious love letter from Spain which was written in English from Dr. Francisco. She never answered him back. Gently she put the card and his letter back into the "Mexican Workers" file.

Overtaken by the sentimental longing for clients, she spiraled over to another filing cabinet filled with information on skilled middle-class workers and white-collar workers. They had shared stories about life in the real world. Morgan's fingers slipped through the pages. Her face lit up with a smile. She knew she had a good reputation with the bartenders, truckers, mailmen, and teamsters because she had given special price cuts to these hard workers.

Reluctantly, she pushed the cabinet closed and noticed the rain had stopped. She stood up, peeked through the blinds, and was blinded by sunshine. Tightness gripped her throat as she realized that this was the last part of a rare and privileged time.

She went back to her makeshift bedroom and began to tidy up, folding and putting all the bedding away. In her usual meticulous way, she dressed for the day, then she looked over to the entire spoon collection and said aloud, "Thank you for comforting me through the storm."

The electricity came back on and the telephone began to ring.

Morgan answered, "Hello, Mustache Barber shop, may I help you?"

"How's my daughter? Did you make it through that damn storm?"

"Yes Daddy, I did. It was quite a long two nights and three days in here." She smiled.

A hard knock came on the door, startling Morgan.

"Who the hell is knocking on your door at 6 o'clock in the morning?" Barney asked.

"I don't know Dad, let me go see, don't hang up." Morgan put the phone down on the desk, walked to the blinds, and peeked out. "It's Sam!" She grabbed her keys and unlocked the door.

"Oh my God, what in the world are you doing here?"

He grinned. "I came to see if you are okay. I know you need my help after this rain."

Morgan hugged him. "Yes, I need your help."

Morgan hurried back to the telephone. "Dad it's all good,

Sam is here."

"Yes, I heard. He was worried about you. When can I expect you?" Barney asked.

"Tonight."

"Perfect."

"Daddy, I love you until the beach runs out of sand. Goodbye."

Sam looked at the pile of pictures that were stacked on her desk. He picked one up and studied it. "Boss lady, is this you?"

Morgan looked down at the picture that showed dozens of motorcycles lined up beside a coffin that she was standing next to. "Yes Sam, that is me."

"You look very young and sad."

Her forehead wrinkled and her eyebrows drew together in a frown. "It was one of the saddest days of my life, and yes I was a young widow at 26."

Sam looked at her with questioning eyes. "I never knew you liked motorcycles!"

She looked at the photo again. "I never rode the bike wanting to go somewhere on it, I rode the Harley wanting to be with the rider. After my husband died I never had the desire to ride again."

"Was the motorcycle fast?"

"Yes, Sam very fast." She grinned. "In fact it was so fast that my eyes watered and my hair stood up like this!" She pulled her long hair straight up from her head and they both laughed.

Morgan sat down, serious. "Sam, please sit down." She patted the seat of the chair next to hers. He sat. "I want to explain to you what is going on with the barbershop and I want you to help me with some packing." Her eyes locked on the file cabinets then to the racks of spoons and then back to Sam while she fidgeted with the button on her blouse.

"Sam, how long have you worked for me?"

"Seven years," he answered.

"Do you do know that I have never traveled outside of California except for once and I have never been on an airplane or a boat?"

"Yes boss lady, I know this," he replied.

"Would you like to do some traveling with me? Our first country will be Vietnam so we can find your mother. Then I would like to visit China to say hello to my friend Mr. Fang, the businessman. Then we will go to Japan to visit Luke, my dear brother-in-law. I have not seen him in 27 years. Then we will go to Singapore to visit my tattoo artist friend Sun. And then we fly to Ireland to visit Peter and Noah. I have not seen my brothers in 31 years."

Sam stood up from his seat. He walked and stood in front of Morgan and knelt down at her feet and bowed his head. Respectfully he answered, "It would be my honor to travel with you and protect you, boss lady."

With a warm smile she said, "From here on, you may call me Miss Morgan."

The End

Catholic Nuns:

Sister Margaret~Mean Nun at Grammar School
Mother Bernadette~Loving High School Principal
Sister Helen~Untradional Modern Nun no veil
Sister Agatha~ Lovely Carmelite Nun at Retreat House
Carmelite Nun~ Escort at Retreat House to visit Mother Bernadette

Catholic Priests:

Father Alexander~Mean Priest at Grammar School
Father Paul~Wonderful Priest at Grammar School and Wedding

Christian Pastor:

Pastor Larry~ at Recovery Home Gail~Wife of Pastor Larry

Best friends To Morgan:

Sam~ Vietnamese employee at Barbershop and Loyal Friend

Sun~Chinese Tattoo Artist

Josephine~ Lovely Black Plump Woman Bakery worker at Donut Shop
Ann~German Housekeeper and Nanny and also Personal Assistant at home Mr. Kennedy~ Lawyer

Best Friend to Betty:

Nina~Apache Indian-Spanish Friend in Pecos New Mexico

Neighbors of Rick and Betty:

Shirley~Lovely Jewish Neighbor
Mr. and Mrs. Stevenson~Senior Neighbors

Extra Characters:

Secretary at High School
Heinz~Old Man Barber in town
Man in office that looked like a Smurf
Crabby nurse in Dr. Wilcox office
First Young Unkind Nurse during Noelle's birth
Second Young Unpleasant Nurse during Noelle's birth
One Unlikeable Lady Visitor to visit Betty's bedside

Second Distasteful Lady Visitor to visit Betty's bedside
Emergency room Doctor for Morgan
Social Worker at hospital
One Lady Nurse at Psychiatric hospital
Second Lady Nurse at Psychiatric hospital
Candy Stripper at Hospital after Noelle's birth
Camera Lady filming during Cathleen's birth
Nurse in charge of Cathleen after her birth
Nurse assisting Morgan in wheelchair before Cathleen's birth
Several hospital Staff watching Cathleen's birth
Men lining up at Donut Shop
People that attendant The Wedding
People in hospital rooms near Rick
People that attendant Funeral for Rick
Bus driver to Donut Shop
Bus driver to visit Mother Bernadette
Bus driver to Psychiatric hospital
Biker people and Club People at Tootsie home
Biker people at Kern River
Two people 'Hippies' at house party

Barber College:

Mr. Steinway~Owner and Famous Barber himself
Mr. Gable ~ Studious Barber Instructor
Young man for student haircut

Doctors:

Doctor Wilcox~Old Man Traditional Family Doctor who delivered Noelle
Doctor Madison~Young Woman revolutionary Doctor who delivered Cathleen
Doctor Olson~Betty O'Donnell's Cancer Specialist Surgeon

And last but not least:

Nurse:
Head Maternity Black Nurse~Mrs.Bessie Kane assisted at Noelle's birth and breast feeding first time.

CPSIA information can be obtained
at www.ICGtesting.com
Printed in the USA
FSOW01n1225161214
3929FS

9 781941 069196

The Instant Upgrade

Book design by Rita Ester

www.theinstantupgrade.com

ISBN 978-1-943784-60-8

This book is dedicated to my many clients over the years. Working with you is the reason why this book has come to fruition.

Author's Preface

I have designed this book to be a multi-media experience with the intention of maximizing its impact and to offer you, the reader, as much support and benefit as possible.

I would recommend going to www.theinstantupgrade.com/webinar to watch a free webinar I created that accompanies this book. On this website you can also opt-in to my email list to get ongoing tips, insights, and inspiration that will expand upon and deepen the insights you gain from this material.

At the end of this book you will see an invitation to explore the Instant Upgrade Tools on a deeper, more customized level. Whether you feel inclined to do this or not, I do recommend that we stay in touch and that you reach out to let me know how this material impacts your life.

While I have a large online audience, I love building personal relationships with people and welcome your feedback and insights. Because you've made it here, I now consider you family. You can also go to my Facebook fan page at www.facebook.com/kevindohertyonline and engage there in any way that inspires you.

Writing this book has been one of the great joys of my life. May the ease, fun, and creative flow that went into this project benefit you as much as the actual words.

CONTENTS

The Instant Upgrade

An intentional shift into higher frequencies of reality where you immediately upgrade your human experience and performance level throughout all areas of your life.

Welcome to the new, upgraded version of your life. This book is designed to help you naturally and easily shift into higher frequencies of reality where you have access to all of the exalted states that you long for–love, freedom, abundance, peace, happiness, and confidence. In the pages that follow, I'm going to show you how to reinvent yourself using a unique and highly potent toolkit that is both immensely practical and deeply mystical.

We are going to start this journey based on the exact stage of life you find yourself in right now. Wherever you are and however you made it here, you have arrived in perfect time. No matter how stressful your current situation is, how difficult your past has been, how worried you feel about your future, or how many problems are piled on top of your daily life, you are in the perfect place to receive what this book has to offer. If you're already doing pretty well, we are going to work together to optimize your performance and go to an entirely new level of success and fulfillment. If you feel stressed, overwhelmed, alone, or stuck, the nine tools I'm going to share are exactly what you need to turn things around. Whatever you most genuinely desire to create and experience in your life, this book is designed to take you there in an accelerated fashion.

While I'll be covering nine unique tools, I consider this book to be its own potent tool you can use anytime to tap into a higher frequency – you'll learn what this term means in the coming pages–but for now, see it as a way to upgrade your thoughts, feelings, and circumstances in a way that reflects how you really want to be in the world. Anytime you feel stuck in a less than optimal situation or emotion, simply open this book randomly and read a few pages. After a few minutes, you'll likely notice that your frequency lifts and you'll feel instant relief and forward progress.

All nine tools I'll be sharing are essentially reiterations of one core teaching:

You are already free. You are already enlightened. You are already whole, complete, and fully alive. Whatever you want in your life, it's already done.

Because the core message of this book tends to be counterintuitive for most of us, given the fact that we are deeply conditioned to believe the opposite is true, I have intentionally created nine different tools so I can say the same thing to you over and over again, but with different nuances and from different points of view. You'll notice a kind of methodical repetition in the language I use and the ideas that I share. This is done to help you ingrain these principles on a deep, instinctual level. Repetitive learning for this kind of material will help you make the all-important transition from conceptual to experiential learning. Consider this book to be a big experiment you're going to implement in your life. You're not just going to read over these ideas, put this book down, and go on with your life as normal. You're going to test these tools on a regular basis. This book has the potential to help you make radical, profound, and permanent shifts that will benefit you in ways you likely can't imagine right now. The key is to be willing to take the leap from keeping all of this in your head to applying it in your direct experience.

Here's what has happened to me over a two-week period when I committed myself to applying what I'm about to teach you:

- I have lost ten pounds without any willpower or force.
- I am performing at a much higher, more confident level in my tennis.
- The chronic anxiety I have felt about the uncertainty of being an entrepreneur has dissolved.
- My energy level is at an all-time high.
- I have been able to make peace with a relationship that was previous-

ly causing me a great deal of hardship.
- I have been willing to explore with curiosity and openness some previous life themes that I found highly distasteful and unsafe.
- I spend far less time checking out TV, Facebook, and so on.
- All of my addictive behaviors have been cleared. My 'old' self latched onto all sorts of vices.
- I have much greater insight into my purpose and the meaning behind my existence.
- I feel about 98% less stress.
- My personal level of happiness is at an all-time high.
- I feel confident talking with people, whereas before I was extremely introverted, even isolated.
- This very book you're reading now was created. This could not have been possible without implementing the tools I'm going to detail in later chapters.

Honestly, I could go on. What I'm about to share with you has transformed my life in all ways.

I know what you're thinking: That's great for you, but there's no way I can do that. I've tried before and I know for a fact that I can't have these wonderful breakthroughs in my life.

I get it. I was the exact same way for most of my life. I read just about every self-help book on the market. I got my B.A. in Buddhist studies and meditation. I tried all the tips and recommendations. I felt that I was trying my best, yet nothing seemed to touch my suffering. After all of the meditation, personal development, exercise, dietary changes (and I have tried just about everything), I still felt that I was struggling in my life. I was at a loss as to why this was happening.

This is why I'm so confident that what I'm about to offer you will finally be the solution you've been longing for. You see, I'm about as stubborn as they come. I spent most of my life locked in a battle with depression and anxiety. I felt isolated, insecure, worried, alone, and afraid, year after year. Everything I tried to heal, cure, or fix my suffering only seemed to lock the pattern in deeper, further solidifying the belief that

I was not capable of any real and lasting transformation. I have had some incredibly dark moments in my life. I have spent entire days, even weeks of my life wondering why I am here at all… and why I felt the way that I did. I know what it's like to dwell in immense uncertainty and fear, to feel invisible and invalidated by the world, to be locked inside the confines of my thoughts to such an extent that it was like a 24/7 prison. I've tasted the depths of hopelessness as a human being. I know what it's like to feel entirely exhausted by the simple process of living, to feel overwhelmed by the necessity of functioning.

Now I know I had to experience all of this so that I could have true empathy for the struggles that normal people face, which has made the teachings in this book immensely more powerful. To some degree, you likely feel similar emotions swirling through you every day. Maybe your story isn't as dramatic as mine; maybe it is. Either way, you're here because there's a part of you that is weary and wants to cut to the chase. As cliché as it sounds, I know for a fact that if I can do this, you can do it too. Whether your current situation is such that you feel stuck in mediocrity, or you're dwelling in more extreme forms of suffering, I want you to know that there is indeed a way out. It's not hard. It doesn't take time. You don't have to sacrifice anything. You don't need to change anything about your current circumstances. You're perfectly primed to transform your life starting right now. You only need a willingness to experiment with the tools I'm about to share.

The Instant Upgrade applies equally to all facets of your life. Our work together involves shifting you into a higher frequency of reality that creates a systemic ripple effect through all dimensions of your existence. After all, you've likely already fallen into the pitfall of thriving in one area of your life to the direct sacrifice of another. This commonly manifests as creating a high level of success in your work only to find that your spouse feels alone and neglected. Maybe your career is full of stress and unhappiness, but you feel pretty fulfilled in your relationships. Whatever the case is for you, the focus of this book is to create a new paradigm that you live from, one that is highly practical and always available, and simultaneously upgrades your life in a holistic fashion.

Please know that this book is not just another self-help book full of neat ideas about the law of attraction or mindfulness. I've personally read hundreds of these books, and I'm sure you have as well. I am highly sensitive to the fact that you already 'know' a lot about how to change your situation. You understand some of the fundamental principles of transformation. You've heard Oprah and Eckhart share their insights about the spiritual path. Don't get me wrong, much of this information is useful.

The problem that 98% of us have is in the direct application of various self-help techniques to our daily lives. Regardless of how much we agree with the points of view we assimilate, we are inevitably stumped by the question of 'how':

- How do I actually do this?
- How do I make this relevant to my crappy job, excess weight, loneliness, debt, depression, and so on?
- How do I perform at my best when it really matters?
- How do I finally get to the root of my suffering?
- How do I cross over from understanding to direct experience?

These are the questions that the personal development industry is so often at a loss to answer. I understand that you don't want more theories. You don't want to read about more studies to prove a certain point of view about happiness or optimism. You've heard enough of that already. What you want is a practical set of tools to transform your life starting right now. That's exactly what this book is designed to do–support you in creating a new reality for yourself regardless of your current circumstances, your past, or any seemingly unworkable conditions in your daily life.

I should also state the following word of caution before we move forward: This book will test you. It will challenge you. It will stretch your thinking. It will expand your viewpoint on what's possible. I fully expect some of these ideas to be controversial. You may violently reject some of the principles I'll be sharing. If you're not ready to shake up your definition of what reality is and who you are, then put this book down right now. Please know I am not joking about this. If you're fine with the status quo and you really have no interest in changing your life, this book is not for you.

Now, I know you wouldn't be here if there wasn't a part of you that is completely ready to experience this new paradigm that will be laid out for you. However, I also know that every single one of us has a tendency to defend what we think is right and to resist change in whatever way we can. Trust me, I still have this part of me too, and I'll be talking a lot about how to relate to this aspect of our identity in following chapters.

My best advice is to simply be open to what you're about to learn. Test it out in your own life. Be curious and inquisitive rather than skeptical or defensive. This book is designed to shake you up in magical and profound ways. To do that, there needs to be a little controversy. After all, you've embraced a very specific and solid view on reality (as we all have) that this book will likely challenge in highly meaningful and positive ways.

If you're willing to 'play' with the information I'm about to share (and I use that word intentionally), what awaits you is indeed an upgraded version of reality, where you likely won't even recognize your previous self in a few short weeks from now. Play with these tools in your daily life. Take action. Don't just treat this like yet another personal development book that gathers dust on your shelf. The value of this book lies in its practical application. Yes, the ideas are inspiring and may make you feel a little better. Gathering more ideas, however, is not going to lead to the upgraded life you deeply desire. Implementation is the key to unlocking the potential this book has to offer you.

This book is not designed to delve deeply into philosophy, psychology, or various spiritual traditions. I am going to intentionally keep the language as free of dogma and rhetoric as possible. Whether you're Christian, Buddhist, Hindu, Muslim, or an atheist, you can benefit from this book. These tools are designed to be universal in nature. Nobody is excluded. As long as you have a desire to change, you will benefit in profound ways regardless of your religious upbringing. With that said, there will be a few philosophical principles that I cover that will empower you to realize your full potential in relation to these tools. If you're holding onto fundamentally distorted or inaccurate viewpoints on the nature of reality, we need to shift your perspective in order for you to benefit from this material. In The First Instant Upgrade Tool, we will cover these principles as a foundation that we need to lay to reap the most benefit from the other eight tools.

If at any point, you feel confused or overwhelmed by the philosophical components of this book, simply take a deep breath and keep reading. Let it go. As long as you're not noticing strong resistance to what I'm sharing, you can still benefit greatly from the tools. You'll also likely notice that as you apply the tools in your life, the philosophical underpinnings of this work naturally become more clear and understandable.

Most people think that they 'know' a lot about who they are and why they are here, but few people on this planet are genuinely happy and fulfilled. Obviously, there is an enormous gap between knowledge and experience. This book will fortify your knowledge base only to the degree that it supports you in directly experiencing an upgraded reality.

While the concepts explored in this book can definitely be seen as radical, and perhaps even a bit 'out there', I consider myself in no way to be a 'woo woo' kind of person. I like to focus on what works and I tend to be highly practical about this. I have included in this book only what I have observed works in my direct experience. If the tools feel highly metaphysical or esoteric that's only because you live in a culture that has convinced you that you exist in a one-dimensional physically based world, and that your power is derived from the material plane of existence that you see all around you. If you look carefully at your situation, you'll clearly see where that archetypal construct has gotten you–usually to a place where you're banging your head against your circumstances–and wondering why it feels so difficult to change.

In order for real transformation to occur, you have to be willing to embrace a relatively counterintuitive, even irrational way of relating to your life. Most conventionally based, rational approaches that are designed to make you more successful and fulfilled tend to backfire. You'll learn why as you go through this book. Even if this material is out of the boundaries of your comfort zone and context for your normal way of life, I invite you to be open. As you'll hear me say time and again, be willing to play around and experiment with these tools in your daily life. Do this even if there's a part of you that feels cynical or skeptical about the content.

In the pages that follow, I'm going to show you how to shift into higher frequencies of reality using your own internal resources. Of course, there are a variety of external triggers that can shift us into higher frequencies such as hallucinogenic drugs, holotropic breathwork, meditation, Tantric sexual practices, yoga, acupuncture, alcohol, fasting, and energy healing. This is not going to be yet another book about these approaches. While these external substances and techniques can all be powerful catalysts, they are commonly used as crutches where the only way we feel we can 'go to a higher level' is through such external assistance. If you don't know how to wash your dishes or pay your bills from a higher frequency, the overall purpose of using external aids becomes convoluted. Many people find that if they rely on external triggers to gain insight and clarity the integration into daily, practical reality is highly challenging. This is not to diminish in any way the value that these approaches have to offer; it's simply a pattern I've noticed in my own life and in my coaching work. When you know how to activate your own innate resources to induce higher frequencies, you can relate to any situation you find yourself in from an elevated perspective, one that is the highest, most inspiring representation of how you want to be in the world.

In this sense, it's helpful to think of the tools I'll be sharing more as triggers that naturally activate your innate power rather than externally practiced techniques that seem to induce change from the outside in. All of The Instant Upgrade Tools are innate to your make up as a human being.

As a business and performance coach, you'll notice that my way of describing the tools is largely centered around helping you perform better in your life, whether that means getting more clients or customers, making more money, creating a higher level of fitness or athletic performance, or enhancing your relationships. I am passionate about helping people perform at higher levels and I will use whatever means necessary to get you where you want to be. If you're an entrepreneur who wants to upgrade your business, or an athlete who wants to tap into the next level of your potential, or a stay-at-home mom who wants to parent and manage the family at the highest level possible, this book is for you. I see these tools as capable of helping just about anyone, but in particular, they are ideally suited for those who want to take the leap into higher levels of performance in business and life.

Before we jump in, I want to take a moment to let you know how much I appreciate you being here with me on this journey. Maybe you and I don't know one another on a person-to-person level, but I believe that it's in no way random that you've made your way here. Buckle up and enjoy the ride! Upgrading your reality is by far the most exhilarating, entertaining, and meaningful step you can take as a human being. I'm thrilled to be your guide as we enter a higher dimension of existence, one that frees you up to perform at your best, face all adversity with grace, and confidently create a life without limits.

The 4 Low Frequency Tools of Our Modern World: The Real Reason Why People Don't Change

"Everything is the way it is because we've all agreed that's the way it is."
Charles De Lint

I'm going to say something right up front that may shock you: Change isn't hard. Even more so, you don't have to work for it or make all kinds of sacrifices. Change can indeed be an easy, fun, and enjoyable process. In fact, it really should be. Why? Because in every single moment, life is changing all around you. Nothing is static. Whether you like it or not, you are constantly changing and there's not a thing you can do to stop that from happening. Everything in the phenomenal world that you can perceive through your senses is in a dynamic state of constant change. This includes the cells in your own body, the neurochemicals in your brain, and the thoughts and feelings that present themselves every 1/60th of a second.

With this said, the real issue isn't that you're not changing; it's that you don't feel empowered with the process of change. You don't feel like you're 'running the show', which translates as feeling a lack of control and power in your life. This is how the vast majority of people live. Circumstances show up and we react to them. We get locked into a reactive cycle of dealing with what we see in front of us. We try to change from this place of reactivity, where we never quite feel clear on what it really takes to transcend this chronic cycle of disempowerment.

Indeed, all forms of what we call 'stress' are ultimately caused by this habitual feedback loop of disempowered reactivity to our circumstances. When we don't feel in control, we will inevitably default to feelings of force, willpower, and anxiety to get through life. We will impose a false sense of power that almost always stems from a fundamental insecurity in who we are and why we are here.

I'm sure you've come up against your fair share of stress. Maybe you have been through a corporate layoff that jeopardized the safety of your family. Perhaps your business feels like a roller coaster ride of ups and downs that is sapping your energy and slowly but surely exhausting you. It could be that you've lost a loved one either through divorce or death, and it seemed to deal you a blow that you just can't recover from. As you well know, there are infinite stress-based scenarios that can potentially plague our lives and undermine the quality of our health and well-being.

Most people are chronically locked into a painful cycle of generating stressful circumstances. They do their very best to cope with or fix these circumstances, only to find that they are continuously creating the same patterns again and again. Many people spend their entire life in this cycle. Some realize it, some don't.

You're likely here because you do indeed realize that you've been doing this to some degree or another for many years. You see the problem; you just don't know what the actual solution is, or even if there is a solution. In your darkest moments, you've encountered the demon of hopelessness where you convince yourself that you are destined to stay on this cycle of struggle and mediocrity until the day you die. You've tried everything. You feel like you've done your best… and still, it doesn't change.

If you're at all like me, it's not necessary to paint a more vivid picture of the problem. You know it all too well. In fact, billions upon billions of human beings have also known this same problem throughout human history. In various Eastern spiritual traditions, this is typically called the wheel of suffering. The basic idea is that we continually create circumstances that are less than optimal, and we have no idea why we are doing this, in spite of our best efforts.

I want to take a moment to emphasize the importance of this particular discussion and to highlight the gravity of this ancient truth. Most people suffer every day they are alive. It may be a quiet or subtle kind of suffering; It may be much more extreme. This has always been the case throughout human history. You and I are both highly vulnerable to this truth. Indeed, our default setting as human beings is to struggle with this life we've been given, as is evidenced by the widespread difficulties that people have had through thousands of years of human existence.

The purpose of this book is to end your suffering. First, we need to acknowledge the truth that suffering is indeed a prevalent, if not dominant experience of the human condition. This may sound heavy or solemn to you right now, but by the end of this book you'll have an entirely upgraded understanding of the human condition. Right now, I simply invite you to feel the gravity of what I am saying. In this sense, the intention is to amplify your intensity in applying the tools I'll be sharing in later chapters. Connect with the part of yourself right now that isn't casual about this. If you're perusing these pages in a kind of unfocused, superficial way it's not going to lead to transformation. You don't need to feel bad or heavy about what I'm saying. Instead, just cultivate a kind of focused intensity where you get really engaged with the process of ending your suffering.

Whatever your current struggles are in your work, relationships, health, spiritual life, or finances, I want you to know all of this is a byproduct of a core problem that really gets to the heart of why people suffer.

Ready? Good. Pay close attention, as what I'm about to share with you serves as the core premise of our work together and is the foundation of creating a new life, one where you finally transcend this painful cycle of creating and reacting to limiting circumstances.

The real problem (and in fact, the only problem) is that you are stuck in a low frequency of reality and have never learned the tools that will shift you into higher frequencies.

Once you solve this problem, everything in your life changes in a magical, deep, and lasting way. Everything.
Until you know how to change your frequency, you will always, 100% of the time continue to generate beliefs, thoughts, feelings, behaviors, and actions that feel limiting, painful, mediocre, or stressful. This is why so many of your previous attempts to change your life have felt like utter failures. When you try to change your circumstances without shifting your frequency, you are setting yourself up to struggle. You will endlessly bang your head against the wall, baffled as to why you can't create lasting change, no matter how hard you try.

I'm sure you're already intimately familiar with how this plays out in your life.

You try to go on a diet, lose a few pounds, feel initially excited and optimistic, and full of hope that you're finally going to go all the way this time. Then, sometime in the not-so-distant future you find yourself exactly where you started with the scale showing you the same frustrating number, and an overbearing attraction to certain foods and lifestyle choices that make it feel impossible to do anything about it.

You set all kinds of new goals for your business after listening to the latest motivational guru. You muster up excitement and hope. You take massive action and get some really great results. For some reason though, you can't sustain it. Your enthusiasm wanes, profits drop, and you find yourself back at ground zero. On top of this, your spouse is giving you a not-so-gentle reminder that, at the height of your excitement, you basically neglected your family and other important aspects of life.

You finally meet a partner that treats you well. You fall madly in love and are absolutely sure that 'this is the one.' You map out your life together and are so relieved and excited to finally have true love. A month later, you find out that your partner has been seeing someone else on the side. You are back where you started, feeling alone, convinced that you'll never taste the joy of real love.

You invest thousands of dollars in private lessons and the best golf equipment, you practice as best as you can over and over, but you just can't go to the next level in your game. You are stuck. No matter what you do, your game seems to stagnate at your current level of performance.

Obviously, these are only generic examples that point to the struggle that so often defines the human experience. Take a look at your own life. Where do you feel stuck? Hopeless? Like you've tried everything and can't get that aspect of your life to change. Take a look at the big picture of your life. Assess the degree to which, in general, you feel that you're flowing, evolving, engaged, connected, and fully alive.

Whatever your current story is, here's the core idea that I want you to reflect on:

Whatever is causing you distress, struggle, or suffering is ONLY due to one cause–you are stuck in a low frequency of reality.

Because of this you can't change no matter how hard you try. Even more so, the harder you try without having the right tools at your disposal, the more frustrating and hopeless your situation feels. Nothing seems to work. Maybe you get temporary results and breakthroughs, but you always seem to default to the same limiting set of conditions and feelings that have been there for as long as you can remember.

I could write an entire book on why people don't change and the various trappings that keep us stuck. I want to give you just enough of a context so you can clearly see why your life hasn't been all that you hoped it would. I've distilled this down to four low frequency tools we've been taught to use that keep us stuck in life. We have all been indoctrinated with all four of these tools as our primary way of functioning and living in our modern world. From the moment we entered this world, these tools have been essentially drilled into us from all kinds of sources–our parents, teachers, religious figures, coaches, media sources, and political institutions.

Part of our work together involves helping you wake up from the collective cultural trance that these four misguided tools reflect. We live in a world where following these tools is the norm. Deviating from them is a surefire way to get raised eyebrows and expressions of concern from people who care about you. As you upgrade your life and break free from cultural conditioning, don't be surprised if you start baffling a lot of people around you. This is a positive sign that you are indeed shifting into higher frequencies and leaving behind the cultural trance of mediocrity.

Laying out these four low frequency tools will help you see why you've been stuck in your life and by virtue of contrast, how to activate the power of The Instant Upgrade Tools with greater conviction and clarity.

Low Frequency Tool #1
The Safety Trap

The overarching directive given to us by various centers of influence is to aggressively and constantly seek safety above all else. The conventional mantra that sums up this way of living is:
Go to school. Get good grades. Get a good job. Save for retirement.

Our entire modern culture is still entranced by the pursuit of safety and security. We are taught to avoid uncertainty, to minimize risk, to take care of our own. Have you noticed how much an aversion you tend to have to uncertainty, change, and risk? I certainly have. It's like we are wired to be vigilantly on guard against the horrors of the unknown.

When we choose safety above all else, what we will inevitably end up with is a life that may feel comfortable, but that lacks excitement, adventure, true joy, and constant learning. If security is our highest value, then fleeting pleasure and flickers of true connection is the best we can hope for.

Here's the deal: There's nothing inherently safe about being alive. At anytime, anyone of us can die, get terribly injured, or endure violations of our basic human rights. You may call this a morbid or pessimistic outlook, but it's simply the truth. This human body we have is fragile. This world we live in is full of current and potential calamities. Whatever we think we are doing to minimize or remove our exposure to the unsafety of life is nothing more than a fallacious game we are playing. Once again, safety as we typically define it doesn't really exist. It's a myth, yet we are deeply conditioned to chase it.

Why do we do this? Well, as long as the illusion is intact, it can be pretty convincing. We can create a life that appears to be safe and secure, and for periods of time we can totally buy into the belief that we have indeed achieved a life that wards off danger and uncertainty. That is, until something happens that instantly dismantles this belief. And it always does.

You feel safe until:

- you are laid off from your job.
- your business experiences a drastic decrease in revenue.
- a loved one gets cancer.
- your spouse tells you they want a divorce.
- your child overdoses.

Obviously, we can conjure up countless scenarios that show up in all of our lives that reveal the ultimate illusion of safety.

Is there anything wrong with seeking a stable, safe job? Planning for the future? Putting money into your 401k? Of course not. What tends to be problematic is the belief you have around why you are doing this and how it's protecting you from the rawness of your human experience.

On a deeper level, we prioritize our lives around safety because we are conditioned to believe that death is a highly unpleasant, unwanted, and terrifying experience. Ultimately, our quest for safety is an attempt to deny the reality of dying. We are wired to survive, to keep our identity intact as best we can. We will do whatever it takes to preserve our sense of self, our body, and our mind. As you well know, this is a game that none of us can possibly win as the death of our physical body is an inevitability.

As you shift into higher frequencies of reality, you'll come to realize that there is no such thing as safety. Even more so, you can never actually be unsafe. I'll explain why this is the case in future chapters. For now, do an honest assessment of your current life and determine to what extent you've chosen safety over all else.

This can manifest in many ways, including:

- choosing a job that in no way reflects your passion or potential.
- choosing a spouse or partner who looks great on paper, but whom you aren't in love with.

- holding a vision for your life that is small, uninspiring, or average.
- making just enough money to survive without ever 'going for' your fullest financial potential.
- holding onto an extra twenty pounds as a way to ward off intimacy and being seen.
- denying yourself a truly meaningful experience in the name of responsibility.
- procrastinating on a passion, such as playing music or writing a book.
- allowing routine to deaden your spirit.
- pushing away true love and intimacy (being commitment phobic).
- allowing labels such as introvert or highly sensitive to keep you from connecting with people and being confident.

Whatever your current version of playing it safe looks like, all that it means is that you've bought into the collective cultural trance of seeking security over freedom. You've fallen into the safety trap.

For the sake of clarity, it's important to point out that the opposite of safety in this context is not recklessness. When you escape from the safety trap you don't become a wild, irresponsible person. Quite the opposite. What it means is that you prioritize your life around new values such as creativity, connection, curiosity, and love. When you choose the safety trap, you are stuck in fear. Your creative resources and intuition will largely be blocked. You'll be vulnerable to anxiety, depression, and other unwanted states. Why? Because you're basing your life on something that doesn't actually exist. You're chasing a phantom. When you structure your life around something that is untrue, you're opening yourself up to all kinds of distorted beliefs and experiences. Stress will be your constant companion.

Low Frequency Tool #2
Externalizing Your Power

Do you remember exactly when you were taught that 'the power is out there'? Whether it's a God that exists outside of you, the government, teachers, bosses, corporations, doctors, or a domineering spouse, we are bombarded by the belief that we don't innately possess the power to create and change our life.

As you can see, this tool is intertwined with the first low frequency tool, the safety trap. If we believe that 'the power is out there', we will be forced to seek out safety at all costs. We will sacrifice our passion and excitement in the name of stability and certainty.

When we externalize our power, our only choice is to be a victim to our circumstances. We will feel lost in a random world that is giving us a chaotic array of situations that we do our best to deal with. We become magnets for limiting beliefs, fear, and all kinds of unwanted feelings and perceptions.

When I work with clients in my coaching business, I can usually tell within a few seconds if someone is externalizing their power. They describe their life as if it's happening 'to' them, as if they have no control over the experiences they are generating. They describe the conditions of their life as if they are randomly generated events that show up without any contribution from their end. Because I work mainly with entrepreneurs who want more money and success, here are a few statements I commonly hear from people who are externalizing their power:

- The economy is killing my business.
- There's too much competition.
- I wish I could get more clients.
- People who are successful got lucky.
- I hope I can save enough for retirement.
- I'm afraid I won't make enough to pay my rent.

• I can't afford it.

Can you see how these statements reflect the belief that 'the power is out there'? There's a distinct energy of lack, fear, and worry emanating from each of these statements.

As you implement the Instant Upgrade Tools into your life, you'll no longer feel any inclination towards these kinds of statements. They simply won't be uttered from your mouth. Why? Because you are literally dwelling in a reality where these states of mind don't exist.

Indeed, shifting into higher frequencies is very much a process of reclaiming your power, wherever it has been stripped from you. You'll come to see that not only do you have the innate power to create and change your life based on your ideal design, but even more so, you have the infinite creative power of the entire universe dwelling within you. You are THAT powerful!

Low Frequency Tool #3
The Motivation Misnomer

Most attempts at transformation are short-sighted and set up for self-sabotage. We normally feel compelled to change due to two primary causes: Desperation and motivation.

Most of the time, when we try to change based on these two factors, the results are temporary. When you are desperate to change, you've become so exhausted or disgusted by your current situation that you'll do whatever it takes to alleviate the suffering it is causing. When you just can't take it anymore, you become willing to suspend your fear of the unknown and relinquish your tight hold on your routinized way of living.

There are times when desperation can lead to a shift into a higher frequency, when we become permanently immune to a previous habit or behavior. When we feel desperate we often will experience flickers of heightened states of consciousness. Our normal safety net is temporarily eradicated and we are put in touch with a rawer, more truthful, and fearless dimension of our being. We contact a kind of primal energy to transform our situation that has a lot of raw power to offer. I'm sure you've heard the old Chinese saying that in crisis lies great opportunity. Essentially, every time we feel desperate, we have a unique ability to reclaim our power and forge a new path and identity.

The problem is that unless we have the right tools to work with, we will necessarily default back to our comfort zone once the crisis we are in subsides. In that comfort zone we dwell in the same low frequency of reality that may have a slightly different form.

In my experience working with people, it's much more common that we simply transfer our low frequency behaviors into a new form while creating a more tolerable version of the situation that caused us to feel exhausted or in crisis.

Motivation occurs when we get injected with a newfound enthusiasm to reach for something higher in our life. Most forms of motivation are born out of desperation or a more subtle sense of discontent with some aspect of our current situation. The problem with motivation is that it's an extremely fickle state of mind. It can disappear just as quickly as it arises. You can arouse an intense motivation to lose twenty pounds, but the odds are that this motivation will eventually crumble when you come up against an inner demon like a limiting belief about yourself, or an external circumstance that generates stress for you.

Motivation is a highly conditional and fragile phenomenon. It is like the wind. When it blows in your direction, you'll find yourself asking, "Why don't I feel like this ALL of the time?" When it blows away from you, you are left despondent wondering how you ever conjured up the energy to change in the first place.

If motivation is the only tool you have to change your life, you're in for a rough ride as a human being. One day you're motivated to go to the gym. The next day it's the last thing you want to do. One day you're fired up to implement a new marketing strategy and generate revenue for your business. The next day you find that you'd rather get a root canal than have to think about money and marketing for another second. Why is this? How could it be that your desire to take care of yourself and perform at a high level vacillates so dramatically?

We Have It All Backwards: The Real Problem with Motivation

Most of us use motivation as a tool to upgrade our lives. We want motivation to serve as a bridge that will take us to more positive feelings and experiences. As you'll discover moving through The Instant Upgrade Tools, this is backwards thinking.

We convince ourselves that when we lose twenty pounds, make more money, or find our soulmate we will then feel better about ourselves. We will have more energy, confidence, purpose, and so on. In this sense our motivation so often comes from a place of lack. We believe that sometime in the future we will be able to have better feelings and experiences, and that motivation will take us there. Our launching point for change however, is steeped in the (largely unconscious) idea that I am not enough in this moment, that something is lacking, and that I need to get motivated in order to fill this void.

As counterintuitive as it may sound, using motivation to try to make yourself a better person is exactly why the typical mechanism of motivation is rigged for failure.

If you're trying to go on a diet so you can feel better about yourself, or to make more money to become more abundant, or date more people to build your confidence and experience true love, you've fallen into the motivation trap. If you try to eat more vegetables and stop your sugar addiction yet you do nothing to shift into a higher frequency, it will backfire. If you try to make more money without tapping into the frequency of abundance first it will end in disappointment. If you meet a beautiful woman or man and feel validated and confident as a result, without having first shifted into a frequency to support that experience, your heart will get broken. Simply put, anything you do to try to improve your situation must begin with upgrading into a higher frequency. Otherwise, you are bound to create the same patterns of struggle throughout your life. You will exhaust yourself going through repeated cycles of motivation and disappointment.

When you use The Instant Upgrade Tools what you are essentially doing is upgrading your thoughts, feelings, perceptions, and attitude right NOW regardless of your circumstances. Nothing needs to change outside of you. With this powerful toolkit, you'll naturally have the energy and clarity to focus on the things that bring you the most joy, excitement, and well-being. You don't need to force any of it. You don't need to try really hard. You simply generate the feelings that you desire in this moment and allow that to naturally catapult you into a new level of motivational fuel upon which you base your life.

In this context, it will be helpful to differentiate between the terms inspiration and motivation. As I define it, inspiration is the natural state of mind that arises when you apply the Instant Upgrade Tools. Motivation is the typical, conventional process we use to impose will power to create change. Inspiration is born naturally out of a high frequency state and is steeped in abundance. Motivation is born naturally out of a low frequency state and is steeped in lack.

Inspiration is:

- natural, organic, and effortless.
- sustainable and solid.
- available in all circumstances we face.
- generated from a state of wholeness.

Motivation is:

- manufactured and hard to maintain.
- unstable and precarious.
- highly conditional.
- generated from a state of not being good enough.

Once again, the key is to induce the state of Being you most desire, starting right now. If you can do this, it will change everything for you.

To my bias, this is the most important skill you can develop in your life. It far supersedes all other skill sets, as it is the greatest factor in determining how much fulfillment, freedom, and happiness you experience while on this planet. Ironically, very few of us are taught this skill growing up. We are instead taught how to survive and function in society, do our best with what we have, and get by as best we can. Why is this the case? Why aren't we taught the single most important skill that will set us free in this life right from birth? Hang tight–I'll explore that question in the first Instant Upgrade Tool.

The skill we are going to cultivate is both radical and simple. It is profound and practical. In essence, I am going to show you how to become fully alive in this very moment and to live your life from a place of innate fullness. I am calling this a skill as it truly is something you get more masterful at with practice, just like playing a musical instrument or picking up a new sport. The instrument or game in this context is your existence. When you know how to upgrade your life in any given moment, you'll become immune to the suffering that plagues people at lower frequencies. You'll finally break free from the painful cycle of using will power and short bursts of motivation to improve your life.

To be blunt, there is nothing in the future, nobody outside of you, and no external circumstance or condition that will ever make you feel better than you feel in this very moment. How does it feel to take that in? The raw truth is that getting more clients and making more money really won't make you a happier person. Losing twenty pounds may give you a temporary confidence boost, but it means nothing for your long-term happiness on this planet. Finding your soulmate can't make you feel more complete or connected.

I know that can sound pretty devastating to the part of you that is attached to the future and external conditions as the basis of your happiness. To the Real You however, these words will come as a relief. Your happiness, fulfillment, and joy is entirely 100% up to you. This moment is the only time EVER to access these states. You don't discover these states, or hope for them, or try to wish them into existence. Instead, you proactively create them into being.

Low Frequency Tool #4
Analysis Paralysis: The Tremendous Gap Between Understanding and Experience

Our modern world is infatuated with the intellect. We are taught from a young age to use our left brain, analytical mind as our primary weapon against an unsafe and uncertain world. In essence, we are told time and again that we can 'think' our way through all of our problems. This may very well be true when it comes to relative challenges we face in daily life. It doesn't hold up well at all however, when we try to think our way to a happy and fulfilling existence.

In my professional career as a holistic health practitioner and coach, I can't tell you how many people I've worked with who could write an encyclopedia about their current problems and predicaments. Most of us are very clear on the details of our struggles. We've put a lot of thought into why we are the way we are. Most of us have gone to therapists to understand the connection between how we were raised and who we are today. We can make all kinds of connections between who did what to us and why we feel the way we do.

The problem is that most of us are trained to believe that analyzing our problems is a powerful way to solve them. If we see things clearly enough in terms of why we struggle in the way we do, that will naturally lead to a solution. We have been duped into believing that understanding leads to freedom.

Having a clear analytical framework of why you are the way you are can indeed be a helpful tool. The big roadblock is that most of us stop there. We have a conceptual understanding of our situation, but we still don't know how to transform at a core level. Instead, we compensate by over-developing our thinking mind to the point that it becomes more of a block that hinders our growth rather than an asset.

Your thinking mind may serve you very well in your career or other areas of your life. If it becomes the sole tool you use to be happy and fulfilled however, you will inevitably get locked into a limited, struggle-based life.

When you apply the Instant Upgrade Tools you'll come to see that true transformation is a holistic experience that includes your mind, body, energy, beliefs, behaviors, and actions. The totality of who you are is included when you shift into higher frequencies of reality. Your mind can not get you there on its own.

This was a big one for me prior to discovering these tools. I spent most of my life trying to better understand, negotiate with, and analyze my suffering. I lived very much from the chin up and unconsciously assumed that if I could just understand my situation better, it would lead to the change I so badly wanted.

As a result, I waited and waited, and waited some more. As you likely know, waiting for things to change is a painful way to exist. By living in my head for so long I was hitting the pause button on my life. It wouldn't be an exaggeration to say that this process of waiting for clarity almost made me go insane. In fact, many people live in their heads to such a degree that it becomes a form of neurosis, sometimes even leading to complete mental breakdown.

Being obsessive about understanding yourself, your purpose, and your struggles, is ultimately a defense mechanism that protects you from the rawness and enormity of your existence. You can't take in the wonder and incomprehensibility of the universe you live in when you're stuck in your head. You can't be vulnerable to the infinite mystery of the cosmos when you're constantly analyzing, judging, and filtering your experience.

The human mind can be a wonderful servant or an unbearable tyrant. The Instant Upgrade Tools will ensure that you are using your mind as an ally rather than an enemy. This doesn't mean at all that you need to stop trying to understand your human experience. It simply means that you welcome other tools to support you in directly experiencing higher states of reality.

What you'll discover is that as you have more direct experiences of The Instant Upgrade your ability to serve, guide, and help others will go to an entirely new level of potency. If you've felt powerless to change the world, or that your impact isn't as meaningful as you would have hoped, this is likely because you've been stuck in concepts rather than having the transformational experience of freedom. When your work or mission stems from the direct experience of entering higher frequencies, you'll inevitably impact people in more potent and profound ways.

To reiterate, you can know a tremendous amount about yourself, this world, spirituality, and human potential and still be miserable. In fact, this happens all of the time to people. What you know does influence your state of being to an extent, but it will be quite limited if you don't integrate that knowledge into your actual experience.

Yes, knowledge is power. It can help you become more functional, successful, and respected in the conventional world. If not harnessed in the right way however, it can also block you from accessing higher levels of power that reflect states of being such as wisdom, grace, connection, love, and abundance.

When you upgrade to a higher frequency of reality you get to do away with the shackles of motivation, will power, lack-based beliefs, wishful thinking, analysis paralysis, and feeling like a victim to your circumstances. Keep in mind, at lower frequencies this is impossible to do. The nature of that particular frequency can only generate those particular states of consciousness. When you apply the Instant Upgrade Tools you'll be amazed by how swift your mindset can shift out of these limited states and into an entirely new world of emotions, beliefs, and experiences. I know this may sound far-fetched right now, but here's what I want to tell you:

There is really no such thing as a 'big' change. Change is just change. When you upgrade your reality you can access entirely new dimensions of being in an instant. This can feel both earth-shattering and completely relaxed at the same time. This is how fluid and open your human experience is. It's only our insistence on our rigid points of view that makes this sound absurd or impossible. As you access higher states, you'll come to see that what's really absurd is the rigidity and limitation that you used to impose on your life. Indeed, you'll come to see it as comical how you used to adhere so stubbornly to your beliefs and behaviors.

Let's summarize the main problem you've had up until this point, then we'll dive into each of the Instant Upgrade Tools in depth.

From a young age, you've been deeply conditioned to base your happiness on what is happening outside of you. You've been told time and again that you should seek safety over all else. You've been taught that you lack power to create and change your life. You've been trained to change your outer reality as best you can, using motivation and analysis as your main transformational tools. You've tried your best to improve and fix your life, but you always seem to land in the same quality of life, one that never quite feels as amazing as you want it to be. You've used your mind to attempt to get into deeper levels of understanding, but that hasn't really led to any kind of lasting transformation.
You often feel like nothing works for you.

This has all happened in the way it has because you've never been given the tools that shift you into higher dimensions of reality, where inspiration and flow become the natural mode of being. This all changes, starting now.

The First Instant Upgrade Tool
Filter Cleansing

"Through our eyes, the universe is perceiving itself. Through our ears, the universe is listening to its harmonies. We are the witnesses through which the universe becomes conscious of its glory, of its magnificence." Alan Watts

Our first tool to help you instantly upgrade your life is called Filter Cleansing. This tool is designed to support you in seeing the Truth of your human experience and remove any distortions or inaccuracies in your way of perceiving things. The power of the subsequent tools can only be activated when we have a truthful conceptual framework about who we are and how life works. If we are holding onto limiting beliefs and misguided viewpoints on the nature of reality, our ability to leap into new, upgraded versions of ourselves will be drastically limited.

We want your mind to be an asset–not a liability–in how you grow as a human being. The cleaner the filter is through which you see reality, the faster and more profound the leaps forward will be. You don't need to completely understand or master all of the concepts outlined in this tool in order to instantly upgrade your life. The main thing right now is to be open to exploring new ways of seeing your reality and who you actually are.

My goal is to keep these concepts as simple and actionable for you as possible. I am going to purposefully avoid going too deeply into the mind-bending theories of quantum physics or the philosophical tenets of various spiritual traditions. Deep intellectual learning of this nature can be very helpful, but only if it naturally inspires you and feels engaging and useful to your everyday life. You can go as far down the rabbit hole of studying physics and mysticism as you'd like. My personal experience is that this kind of learning is supportive up to a point, but can easily lead to excessive analysis, confusion, and headiness.

It should also be said that my goal is not to prove these concepts by turning this into an academic discussion with all kinds of evidence, data, and studies to support what I am suggesting. Countless books have been written on each of the main principles I'll be covering. My purpose is not to defend the merit of these tools by proving to you that they are 'real' or useful to you. Instead, I simply invite you to test out everything that I am saying in your daily life. You don't have to believe all of this right up front, as I know some of these concepts can feel radical if you're relatively new to them. A small dose of skepticism can be healthy, as long as your mind is still open to using your life as a laboratory to test each of The Instant Upgrade Tools.

We want to get you to a place where you can use your mind in a constructive way that naturally guides you based on an accurate way of seeing. The most effective way to do this is to give you a simple set of reference points that will continually keep you anchored in a truthful relationship with yourself and your life. The Truth sets you free in a seamless way. The more accurately you see things, the more you'll feel confident, empowered, and joyful without any effort whatsoever. If you have to strain or use willpower to feel good about your situation, it means you're telling an untruthful story about what's happening. When your filter is clean you automatically feel amazing, expansive, light, playful, and solution-oriented. This is true even when 'bad' things happen, or you are inundated with challenges.

I'd like to share this simple set of reference points with you so that you have a tangible guidance system in place that can always navigate you back to a healthy way of seeing your reality. I call this guidance system The Nine Principles of High Frequency Living. Let's go ahead and jump in.

The Nine Principles of High Frequency Living

1) You are an infinite being having a human experience. Who you really are is so far beyond the limited confines of your thoughts and your body that it is literally mind-blowing when you get a direct glimpse of your actual Self. There is nothing static, fixed, or solid about your identity. The 'real' you is a wide open, ever-changing, dynamic, infinitely

powerful Being that can't be adequately described in words.

Most of what you've been taught about who you are has only locked you into a limiting definition and experience of yourself. All of the ideas, beliefs, and societal rules that you've been exposed to have certainly created a highly convincing illusion that you have a fixed and solid identity, but it is an illusion nonetheless. Even more so, your past isn't you; that too is an illusion. To this point, it seems as if there's no doubt you've been a certain person with distinctive personality traits and behaviors, right? And that, because you've been a certain way for so long, it's unrealistic to expect things to change overnight? And it seems safe to say that the odds are overwhelmingly stacked that you'll continue to go on with your life as you are now, with only slight variations in your reality? After all, this is just who you are.

What if that is not the case at all? What if you've been telling yourself a quiet falsehood year after year buying into a mistaken belief about what's really going on here? What if the 'real' you created all of this so you could completely buy into the limited appearance of things, and when you were ready, discover that there's a lot more to this life than you've allowed yourself to perceive? Could it be that you're here to play this fun game of pretending like you're a solid, limited person who comes to discover that you're actually infinite in nature?

I say yes! You are an infinite being who is simply pretending to be human for a while. You are pretending to buy into all of the normal human feelings, dramas, and experiences that make for an epic story. You are wearing different costumes, assuming and acting out different characters that appear to be highly convincing in their solidity, yet are nothing more than fun roles that you can fluidly move in and out of.

When I tell you that your identity is dynamic, how does that make you feel? If you're really hearing me it will likely come as a profound relief, and trigger a feeling of excitement. After all, carrying around the baggage of being a solid, separate, fixed self is a highly limiting and usually painful experience. If we believe that who we are is set in stone, we repel any potential for real transformation to occur. When we see how fluid and dynamic our identity actually is we come to see with total clarity that things can change fast. Even if we've been 'a certain way' for thirty years, when we see the reality of who we are, we can shift into a new role or character in an instant. Life feels open and exciting.

Since we don't have any inherent limits on who we are we can create ourselves as we want to be. We can create our lives as we want them to unfold. We can take ownership of our lives, and instead of waiting around for the universe to tell us why we are here and what we should be doing, we can proactively create whatever excites us the most.

The Infinite, Real You will often be termed The Higher Self or Ultimate You throughout this book. This higher dimension of who you are is always there behind the scenes, guiding and creating your human experience. Everything you see around you is being generated for you in the precise way that will support and affirm the story of your life. As you'll see, learning how to consciously tell your story is one of the most empowering practices you can use to become more intimate and aligned with your Higher Self. The more expansive and inspiring your story is, the more you're seeing life as your Higher Self sees it, which is as a wide open field of potential with no limits.

When you activate the power of the Instant Upgrade Tools, the intention is not to think more positively, improve yourself, or 'fix' your life from your normal human point of view. Instead, the ultimate intention is to access this field of limitless potential through seeing reality clearly. You're not going to be manufacturing new states of mind that feel forced or fake; you've likely tried that already and bumped up against the limits of conventional self-help tools. Instead, the Instant Upgrade Tools help you see how fluid and open your experience is. When you shift into higher frequencies of reality through the use of these tools, you are quite literally morphing into a new being. The 'old' you no longer exists. Each frequency upgrade on the path to full alignment with your Higher Self collapses the reality of the previous 'you' in the lower frequency. As you upgrade, you see that you are not really improving or fixing anything; you are simply morphing into a new state of consciousness, one where your previous problems and stories no longer exist. If this is at all confusing, don't worry about it. We will explore this life-changing concept throughout this book in great detail.

To summarize, the 'you' that you've taken yourself to be is entirely made up. Regardless of your past, what's happened to you or your current circumstances, you can choose to invent yourself however you want. Many of the great wisdom traditions throughout human history have said the same thing; this is nothing new. What WILL be new is how we apply this understanding to your daily life

2) You came here to live out the most epic story possible. Many people spend decades of their life, endlessly trying to figure out what their real purpose is. For many the question, "What should I do with my life?" becomes a prison sentence that confines them to a painfully limited understanding of their human situation. This describes me for most of my teenage and adult life. I was someone obsessed with figuring out what in the heck I'm doing here and how I should be spending my time. I felt constantly restless and unsettled, never feeling like I was 'doing the right thing' with my time.
Now I see the 'old' me with a great deal of humor. I now realize that I was playing a character who acted out the role of being confused about his purpose in life. I was fully invested in that role and thought it was highly compelling. I tried for years to find the solution, not realizing that the entire time I was unconsciously assuming that everything I was struggling with was actually real. I didn't know that I was playing a character and that my identity was fluid.

As you'll learn throughout this book, we all do this to one degree or another. The character we play can be consumed with a spiritual path, incredibly depressed, passionate about making a ton of money, a health and fitness nut, incapable of having true love… the possibilities are endless. The most loaded question if you want to transform your life is, "Do you realize that it's all made up and that you can play any character you desire?"

Based on this question, we could distill down the purpose of human life to three key points. You came here to:

- play a fun game of pretending like you're limited.
- come to the clear realization that you are indeed just pretending.
- consciously invent yourself in any way you desire through shifting into new frequencies of reality.

The way I see it, my purpose is to experiment with how far I can expand while in human form. How much power can I reclaim? How much can I see through my limited sense of self? How much can I live in alignment with what I know to be true? How epic of an experience can I create while I'm here?

I now see this as my purpose. The clarity that I have developed in this way of seeing has come directly from the tools I'll be sharing with you. If you still feel locked into a story such as, Yeah that's nice for you, but I still feel like I don't belong here and there's no point to my life, all this means is that you are stuck in a low frequency where you believe that this is 'you' saying this. You have mistaken who you really are for the character you're playing. When this is the dynamic at hand it's like the dog chasing its own tail; your understanding can only go so far as the current frequency you're in. As you shift into higher frequencies, this limited way of seeing your life will naturally dissolve and give birth to a completely new way of seeing things.

Could it really be this simple? That the main reason you're here is to live out an amazing story? Yes. In my experience, so much of the heaviness and seriousness around these big questions of life has been completely eliminated as I have activated The Instant Upgrade Tools. From a lower frequency point of view, we tend to either be oblivious to our purpose in life or consumed by it. As your frequency rises you'll likely come to see as I have that you are here to play around. Honestly, there's not much more to it than that. Does that sound ridiculous? Or insulting to the topic at hand? Or superficial? I assure you it's not. When you see that you're here to play, life becomes a lot lighter. There's more natural, causeless joy to draw from which makes you more available to help, serve, and inspire others.

I very much look at writing this book, my coaching business, and all of the 'serious' stuff I do to help my clients and make money as a form of play. The more I see it this way, the more naturally everything flows in my intended direction. Resistance and stress melt away. The potency of my work goes to new levels. When I am open and light in my way of seeing things my clients tend to be deeply impacted by our work together. Miracles happen. No matter how badly I wanted this I could never access these wonderful ideals as my 'old' self given how serious and rigid I was about my purpose.

Please know that as I am sharing this, it's not meant in any way to dismiss the hardship you may be up against in your life. Trust me, I have had my fair share as well. The advice to 'just play' could be taken as a kind of immature or even demeaning suggestion, but I assure you there's more to this than meets the eye. What I am going to do is break down the actual mechanics of how to open up to more joyful, light-hearted ways of being. This is as profound as it is simple. Right now, you may have to take a leap of faith with me when I say that true transformation isn't really what you thought it was. As you enter higher frequencies you naturally feel more playful, inquisitive, and open-ended. I, for one, can't even tell you how much more I enjoy creating myself in this way as opposed to battling with my problems and endlessly spinning my wheels.

3) This universe is a holographic illusion, the seemingly solid, dense reality you see around you is not what it appears to be. Nothing is 'real' as we have conventionally defined it. The 'real world' does not exist. What we see and experience is more like a dream than solid reality. You are inextricably interwoven with the entire universe. What we experience as 'out there' is essentially all happening within the sphere of our own consciousness. We are generating our entire experience within our own awareness.

Outer objects and circumstances have no inherent power or meaning on their own. They show up as nothing more than a reflection of our current state of awareness. In this sense, the universe is always providing you with the exact dynamics that support and reinforce what you believe to be true. If you believe that 'life isn't fair' you'll generate all kinds of experiences within your reality that make this appear to be true, from not getting what you want to seeing worldwide inequality and injustice. If you believe that 'love isn't safe' you'll create a reality where you continually repel the possibility of experiencing genuine intimacy and connection. Life is always mirroring back to you what you are telling it. In this sense, nothing is random. You are being shown the precise dynamics that reflect back to you what you are telling the universe.

Many people initially find this idea that everything is an illusion to be unsettling and destabilizing. For some, it provokes a deep existential fear where they come face-to-face with the reality that nothing exists as they thought it did. These feelings are normal if you are new to this way of seeing your life. As you apply The Tools covered throughout this book, that initial feeling of fear or disorientation will gradually transform into one of sheer exhilaration and excitement. After all, if things are solid in the way we've been taught there is very little room for rapid growth and change. Things are as they are and we are powerless to do much about it. When we see the holographic nature of reality however, we tap into the infinite openness of our situation. We can create ourselves in any way that we desire; we can bend reality to align with our highest form of expression. We can renounce our past and any detrimental habits or behaviors in an instant. The illusory nature of things opens us up to experience the magic that life has to offer.

While my intention is not to prove the validity of this claim that life is a holographic illusion (there are countless books you can read on this subject), I will share a few quotes by prominent physicists and philosophers to help you consider the implications this has on your life.

"Reality is an illusion, albeit a persistent one." Albert Einstein

"The cosmos is within us. We are made of star-stuff. We are a way for the universe to know itself." Carl Sagan

"Multiplicity is only apparent, in truth, there is only one mind." Erwin Schrödinger

"Every living being is an engine geared to the wheelwork of the universe. Though seemingly affected only by its immediate surrounding, the sphere of external influence extends to infinite distance." Nikola Tesla

"There is no out there, out there." John Wheeler

"The doctrine that the world is made up of objects whose existence is independent of human consciousness turns out to be in conflict with quantum mechanics and with facts established by experiment." Bernard d'Espagnat

Now let's be clear, the point of sharing this with you isn't to make your head spin with all kinds of abstract ideas about quantum physics and the nature of reality. My goal is to keep this practical and help you directly apply these truths to your own life. Our modern world has largely forgotten what these great thinkers are telling us and the consequences have been profound. If you are telling yourself that this all sounds either crazy or irrelevant, that's only because you've grown up in a culture that is so geared towards materialism that you've never considered the deeper truth beneath the surface. As you'll see when we apply other tools, knowing that everything is an illusion has immense practical benefit. Not only will you have a deeper understanding of who you are and why you're here, you'll be able to relate to everyday things like money, work, people, and tasks in a new, refreshing way.

4) Our reality is made up of different levels of frequency.

"If you want to find the secrets of the universe, think in terms of energy, frequency and vibration." Nikola Tesla

You've already heard me mention this term 'frequency' a few times and you will hear it repeatedly throughout this book. Instead of thinking that this universe is comprised of linear time and space, it's more accurate (and helpful) to think of it in terms of different vibrational frequencies. A frequency is traditionally defined as the rate at which a vibration occurs that constitutes a wave either in a material (as in sound waves) or in an electromagnetic field (as in radio waves and light), usually measured per second.

To keep this as simple and practical as possible, you can think of a frequency as a certain quality of energy that you vibrate or emanate, which in turn matches up with other frequencies that share a similar vibratory pattern. We could say that who you really are is a vibrating mass of subatomic particles continuously floating in and out of existence. These particles vibrate at a certain rate and density which creates a specific set of appearances that match that rate of vibration. The faster you vibrate, the less dense is your frequency. As your frequency becomes less dense, you start to exude a higher quality of energy that creates a new version of reality around you.

Describing this process in the English language is a bit clunky, but hopefully you get the idea. What's important to know here is that you can shift into higher states of frequency. The Instant Upgrade Tools are entirely geared toward helping you do exactly this. As your frequency becomes heightened you'll likely notice some general themes showing up in your new reality. Let's describe a few possibilities so you can crystallize your understanding of how true transformation occurs.

At higher frequencies of reality you'll experience:

- a greater sense of connection with all that is.
- a heightened quality of self-love.
- greater appreciation for whatever shows up in your life.
- deeper relaxation that is premised upon trusting what is.
- a natural perception that your entire life is steeped in abundance.
- greater conscious power to intentionally design your life.
- heightened clarity around your life purpose.
- the ability to accelerate with greater ease in the direction of what you want.
- a heightened state of presence that keeps you anchored in the Now.
- deeply fulfilling work, relationships, and circumstances.
- a natural excitement about being alive.

Let's contrast this with a description of what typically occurs at lower frequencies, where you'll experience:

- high vulnerability to stress, worry, and low self-esteem.
- being stuck in addictive patterns from which you can't break free.
- constantly attracting people who weigh you down or add negative drama to your life.
- doing work that feels unfulfilling or mediocre.
- self-sabotage and continual negative self-talk.
- being judgmental, defensive, or always needing to be right.
- constant struggle with money and survival.
- confusion around how to solve your problems.
- a constant feeling that life is full of problems.
- feeling bored, disengaged, or stagnant on a regular basis.

The goal of our work together is to help you naturally shift into higher frequencies. I see this as the missing link in so much of the self-help literature out there. Without a clear understanding of how to easily shift into new realities, you'll inevitably find yourself endlessly banging your head against your current reality. You'll try desperately to fix what appears to be wrong, only to end up in the same place over and over again.

Suffering results from staying locked in low frequencies of reality which results from telling limited stories about your life.

Suffering, limitation, and struggle are all caused by being stuck in a low frequency of reality. The meaning you impart to your experience is the main factor that determines your level of frequency. The constellation of beliefs, thoughts, feelings, and behaviors that you've grown accustomed to identify as 'you' is what determines the quality of reality you see around you. Throughout this book I'll refer to this constellation as the story you are telling about your life.

You are always telling a story. That story may seem very real, but it is always just that–a story. Shifting into higher frequencies and ending your struggle begins by becoming aware of the stories you are telling.

From there you can consciously tell new ones as you'll discover in the next Tool we'll be covering called Empowered Storytelling. When you tell yourself, I am a perfectionist and have a really hard time getting things done, you are telling a story. The repeated telling of that story creates a vibrational imprint on the universe that keeps you anchored in a specific frequency of reality. Until you change the story you'll continue to create circumstances that validate your belief that this is true.

We continue to tell the same stories over and over because they do indeed appear to be real. Part of becoming an empowered person is being able to separate the story you are telling from reality itself. Is it really true that you are a perfectionist who struggles getting things done? Only if you say so. There is no inherent reality to that story; it is entirely made up. Just because it appears to be real does not mean that you have to keep feeding it and basing your identity around it. If you'd prefer to tell another story, you can start doing that in this very moment.

As you'll soon discover, the realization that you can change your story in an instant can be both astonishing and immensely gratifying. You can transform your web of beliefs and behaviors in any moment you want; the key is to be clear that you are always seeing your life through a subjective lens that is in no way 'real' in the way you think it is. You can shift into a new reality right now where you are no longer a perfectionist, an addict, someone who struggles with their weight, or someone who worries about money.

It really can (and should) be that easy. We have largely been duped into believing that we need to work really hard on ourselves, have all kinds of discipline, and continually make tiny baby steps on the long, arduous road of self-improvement. Have you noticed how this doesn't seem to work all that well?

There is one mind-bending principle that I want to mention here as it is relevant to your ability to see things accurately and change quickly. When you enter a new frequency of reality, the 'old' you that was part of the lower frequency no longer exists. You are quite literally entering into a new portal of reality where 'you' are completely new, as is everything you see around you. In this way, as your frequency shifts, the people and objects you see around you are no longer the same. They take on a new reality that has a new imprint based on this shift of frequency.

The 'old' dog, husband, or friend you had in a lower frequency no longer exists in your new one. You will still see the appearance of these things as similar, however they are in actuality completely different configurations of reality. The lens you see through is constantly creating the reality outside of you, and it is always fluid and fleeting.

In this way, you can enter new portals of reality without anything on the outside appearing to change at all. You don't have to go to Tibet or sit on a mountaintop to do this. You can if you want, but it's certainly not necessary. New dimensions can be accessed without having to change a single thing on the outside. From this perspective, as you shift into new frequencies, there is literally no such thing as your past. The 'old' you existed in a field of reality that has collapsed and is nowhere to be found.

Don't get too twisted up by this concept, but do take a moment to consider the implications. As your frequency changes, you are creating a new universe all around you. The 'old' universe you identified with has collapsed and you are born into a brand new reality. If this sounds 'out there' keep in mind that quantum physics along with the great spiritual traditions of our world are generally in alignment with this way of viewing how things are. Our modern culture has by and large estranged us from this truth which is why we often feel so limited, stuck, and confused.

5) Who you really are is already perfect, whole, and enlightened. You are merely pretending that this is not the case.

On an ultimate level, there's nothing that you need to change, fix, or improve about who you are. True transformation occurs when you recognize this innate perfection. This fundamental part of you is always there and can never be damaged by life events. As you go through your life you play various roles based on the assumption that you're a limited human who has all kinds of issues and stresses. You often feel far from perfect. No matter how much it appears to be the case that you are anything but whole as you are, this is always the actual truth.

Low frequency living occurs when you are convinced of the illusion that you are indeed flawed and full of problems. You buy into the appearance of things. You've forgotten your real nature. The more you remember who you really are the higher your frequency becomes. You don't have to 'do' anything or be a new person in order to heighten your frequency; you simply have to recognize the truth of who you are which is a wide open field of potential that is always free, always aware, and always present.

All efforts to force yourself to be better, to figure things out, or to fix your problems only make the illusion that you are limited more convincing. When you can relax into the openness of who you are you no longer need to force anything. You can deeply and fully accept all that you see about yourself while simultaneously inventing yourself in whatever way you desire.

Because your natural state is already complete and perfect as it is, any attempt to change yourself is only effective when met with ease, flow, and simplicity. If change feels painful or hard it's because you've forgotten who you really are.

6) Now is all that there ever is. Because there is no past you can invent yourself anew whenever you desire.

Many people never change because they become convinced by the illusion that their past defines who they are. Because they kept telling the same story and creating themselves in the same way year after year, they unconsciously assume that this is just who they are and that's the way it is. The truth is that you can quickly set yourself free from patterns that have limited you for many years.

Linear time does not exist as we think it does. There is no yesterday and the day before where we continually repeat the same stories and patterns. There is only now. You either shift into a new reality in the now or you do not. You always have a choice. If you buy into the illusion that you are who you are because of many years of repeated personality traits and behaviors, you are missing the fundamental truth of your human situation. In this very moment you are a spontaneous, dynamic being who can invent yourself however it suits you. There is no mandate that states you need to keep creating yourself in the same way over and over. All that is happening is that you are not conscious of the power you have to shift frequencies.

Consider for a moment the implications of what I am saying. If linear time doesn't actually exist and there is only now, can you see how this frees you up to relate to this moment in a new, dynamic way, to enter a new portal of reality simply by shifting your focus toward a more elevated state? All of the forthcoming tools will help you do exactly this. Even though it appears to be otherwise, your life is an open-ended invitation to continually create what you most desire–not sometime in the future, but NOW. It is always now.

When you drop the attachment to linear time, life is seen through a new lens. If now is all that there is, how you are relating to this moment solely determines how you live. There is no such thing as a future where things might get better. Wishful thinking goes out the window. It's literally now or never. There is no time–ever–in the future where you will be a better person or your situation will improve because the future does not exist. It is only ever now.

From a lower frequency perspective, this may sound like bad news. I assure you, however, that from a higher frequency this is the best news possible. When you live only in the now, you are free. You drop all of the limited illusions and games that come from being attached to the past and the future. This is the only way to become fully alive.

7) Your circumstances can NOT make you happy. That is entirely up to you.

Nothing outside of you can ever, on its own, make you feel more love, peace, confidence, or happiness. All circumstances are empty of meaning. They are only mirrors for your current state of consciousness. It is up to you to create the feeling states that you desire, then allow life to mirror back to you what you have chosen to focus on. If you look to your circumstances for constant validation that you can be happy, worthy of love, or confident, you're in a for a long game of spiritual and emotional malnourishment.

Once again, at a lower frequency this may sound harsh or like awful news. As you see things in a clearer, aligned way, you'll come to deeply appreciate the reality that the outer world is a mirror for your own mind and is empty of inherent meaning.

8) When shifting into higher frequencies becomes your number one priority and passion in life things can change very quickly, and there's no end to how much you can grow, learn, and become.
Most of us wouldn't naturally think of shifting frequencies as something to be passionate about, but I assure you there is nothing more exciting in life than mastering the ability to enter new portals of reality where you are a new person, with new opportunities and circumstances. If you can become deeply curious about this process and bring a lot of your daily attention to it, that is a great start.

When you are stuck in lower frequencies you don't even realize that this is happening. You become locked in a solid character who is convinced that everything you see and experience is real and is separate from you. You might be passionate about all kinds of things, but probing into the nature of reality is not on your bucket list. You are basically going through the motions, taking everything at face value. Nothing gets challenged or penetrated.

The most direct way out of this mode of living is to train yourself to become highly invested in the process of managing and shifting your frequency by using The Instant Upgrade Tools. The greater your passion is for using these Tools the faster you'll accelerate into upgraded versions of your life. If this is all new to you, just start using the Tools and having fun with them. As you start to see some shifts, your excitement will likely increase on its own and you'll come to value the mastery of this skill set more than anything. This has certainly been my experience.

9) You can trust every single thing that shows up in your reality because it is being created within the sphere of your own consciousness.

Your Higher Self is continuously creating experiences for you that perfectly support your evolution and learning during your time here. Nothing ever happens to you that is inherently unsafe; you may tell a story about it that makes that event appear to be so, but on their own all life events are neutral and devoid of meaning.

As such, you can begin to trust your life on increasingly deeper levels. Even though things will happen that you wouldn't necessarily prefer, you can still choose to relate to those things in a highly empowered and constructive way. If you continually choose to relate to unwanted experiences with resistance or avoidance you are choosing to stay locked in a low frequency. From this place you can expect more of the same to continually show up, usually in more stark and extreme ways to the degree that it will break through your stubbornness and help you consider a different way of being.

To simplify what I am saying, the universe always, 100% of the time has your back. The universe is you. You are it. There is no separation. As you use The Tools you can experiment with living in increasingly fearless ways where you test out what I am saying. You can't screw it up. You can't do it wrong. Your core nature is always steeped in perfection. Because of this, you can relax and settle into your life and have some fun creating whatever the heck you want.

The Second Instant Upgrade Tool
Empowered Storytelling

Let me ask you a simple question, "What is your current story?"

By this I mean what story are you telling yourself day in and day out about who you are and why you're here? What thoughts are swirling through your mind that support and solidify the story you're living?

Now let's go deeper. Is your current story serving you? Is it helping you consciously design the life you most deeply desire? Or are you telling your story based on being stuck in the four low frequency tools? It's one or the other. If you're not sure it's likely the latter.

Nearly all of us have a default story taking place in our mind about who we are, what our life means, and what we should be doing about it. The story we are telling ourselves, the script we are writing, is literally creating the pages of our reality on a moment-to-moment basis.

If you're not aware of your story, chances are that it's not serving you. When you're unconscious of the story taking place in your mind that story is almost always replete with feelings of fear, concern, stress, and all kinds of other low frequency states of mind.

To clarify, your story is:

- your beliefs about who you are and why you're here.
- the thoughts and feelings that are generated as a result of these beliefs.
- the behaviors and actions that are generated as a result of these thoughts and feelings.
- the circumstances that are generated as a result of these behaviors and actions.

Every day that you wake up in the morning there is a story that is about to unfold on that day. You are painting a certain shade of reality based on the beliefs, thoughts, feelings, behaviors, and actions that you focus on. This story is either set to default mode or is consciously created. The purpose of this tool is to wake up to your incredible power to tell a new story and then observe the miraculous shifts that occur in your life as a result.

Consciously creating new stories is truly one of the most powerful ways to shift into higher frequencies of reality, thereby generating new experiences and circumstances that are more aligned with what you truly desire in your life.

The beauty of this tool lies in its simplicity. If this tool feels complicated or confusing in any way, just take a moment to let it go and return with the intention of keeping it as simple as possible.

You can start to unlock the power of this tool by writing down all of the juicy details of your current story. Get out pen and paper, or open up your laptop and start typing. Write down all of the current circumstances in your life and how you feel about them. Write down how you feel about who you are as a person. Write down what is working well, what you feel challenged by, and where you are deeply struggling. Get it all out.
This is your story.

Let's take a look at a snippet of the old story that I told about my life for many years. I recommend doing this in a stream of consciousness way, where you just write without editing or judging anything you're saying. Write your story in the third person; it will be that much more powerful to gain a new perspective on your current situation.

> *Kevin is someone who feels a lot of concern about his future. He has a lot of great ideas and is highly creative, but he often feels invisible like he doesn't really matter. Kevin often struggles with feelings of meaninglessness. His life feels like a big question mark. He doesn't really understand why he is here. He feels frustrated and bored with life. He often doubts his ability to provide well for his family and take care of daily responsibilities. This makes Kevin feel sad much of the time even*

though he tries to put up a good front.

Kevin has a hard time letting go of these feelings of fear and confusion. He often gets motivated to do new things or perform at a higher level, only to be crushed with the disappointment of not being able to follow through. His life feels unstable and inconsistent, like he is always trying to patch things together in a haphazard way. He feels unsafe. Alone much of the time. Lonely. Isolated.

Kevin is pissed off that he feels this way about his life, but he has no idea how to change it. He tries. He really does, but always feels like he comes up short and can't find the key to happiness and prosperity. He wants so badly to tap into these qualities, to be purposeful and confident.

Even though Kevin has enjoyed some unique successes in his career, he often feels unstable and conflicted about his work. He can't stop thinking about this and is obsessed with figuring out what he's really meant to be doing with his life. Money is scary. Kevin doesn't value money as a top priority, but he is always concerned about not having enough.

Because Kevin can't figure out his survival issues, he has a hard time offering love, care, and validation to others. Because of this, he has struggled to maintain friendships. Kevin doesn't mean to be self-absorbed. It's not how he wants to live; he just can't seem to find another way. He is paralyzed by these issues of survival and purpose. He feels that life can't really be lived until he figures this out.

Yup, that was the old me in a nutshell. This was the story I was telling myself year after painful year. I tried all kinds of things to heal and fix this. It wasn't until I mastered the art of storytelling that I was able to create an entirely new reality.

When you read my story you'll notice that it is a combination of facts and feelings. This is how you want to write your story. Here's what has happened to me… And here's how I feel about my life… Be real with yourself. Don't hide from the real story unfolding in your life right now. How do you really feel? What do you really believe? Get it all out.

You'll also notice in my story that it sounds a bit dramatic like I've been through a lot of hardship in my life. To be honest, that is indeed the case. I believe it is for all of us until we unlock the power of these tools. When you write your story feel free to amplify it a little bit. Be dramatic. Be bold. Write down what's really going on. Uncover the stuff that you keep hidden, that feels unsafe to share with others. Unearth your suffering and get it out on paper. Also feel free to write down all of the things in your life that have gone well and feel positive. Get it all out.

You don't need to write an entire book unless you feel inspired to do so. If you can get a couple of pages out on paper, that's a great start.

Here's why I had you do this exercise: I want you to see that your life is indeed a story. What you just wrote down is truly the story of your life. It's the epic adventure you came here to experience. I want you to take this concept of storytelling and make it literal to your direct experience.

Your life is nothing more than a story. You are the author. You can script your story however you'd like.

Whatever feels limiting, stressful, or that generates suffering in your life is due to the fact that you've been unconsciously telling a story that doesn't serve you. You've had the same beliefs, thoughts, feelings, behaviors, and actions dictating your life year after year. You've been telling your story in an unconscious manner, allowing a 'default' story to dominate your experience, one that is steeped in habit, cultural conditioning, fear, and low frequency states of mind.

Your story is unfolding on both a micro and macro level. You are constantly telling a 'big picture' story about your life, along with a more focused story on whatever you are doing right now. If you're about to eat lunch, you're telling yourself a story about why you need to eat lunch, what you should have, if it will be healthy for you or not, and how you'll feel about yourself after you eat.

Storytelling is interwoven into every moment of your human experience. We could say that the primary purpose of our human life is to awaken to our ability to become a master storyteller. This entails actively creating the reality that we most deeply desire.

You were never taught how to become a master storyteller. This means that you take ownership of your creative powers. Even if you've never thought of yourself as a creative person, that's about to change. You can start to awaken your creative faculties right now through the simple act of telling a new story.

What I'm going to have you do now is write down in detail the new story you want to tell about your life. This is the story that most excites and inspires you, that makes you come alive, that feels exhilarating, engaging, and meaningful.

Allow me to share my new story in a stream of consciousness fashion. I'll take about five minutes to share the first thoughts that come to mind about the story that most accurately captures who I really am, why I'm here, and how I want to live.

> *Kevin is a multi-dimensional, ultra-creative, and resourceful man who feels deeply empowered and confident in his daily life. He uses his time productively and fills his life with meaningful and fun activities. He absolutely loves his business and considers it a privilege to serve his clients in the unique and powerful way that he does. Money flows into Kevin's life with ease and consistency. Kevin feels deeply aligned with the energy of money and is grateful that his work feels so meaningful and allows him to enjoy all kinds of interesting activities and relationships on a daily basis.*
>
> *Kevin truly enjoys people. He enjoys meeting new people and is confident in initiating conversations with just about anyone. He feels confident and attractive when he is in social situations. He has fun being in new environments and he enjoys the spotlight.*

Kevin is an exceptional dad who cares deeply about his kids and is excellent at showing them a high level of care on a daily basis. Every day, his kids feel how much he loves them. He truly enjoys his time with his kids and is grateful that he is able to guide and nurture them in ways that truly serve them.

Kevin thrives under pressure. He considers pressure to be a privilege and welcomes the challenge, whether it's a tennis match or a business decision. Kevin enjoys being a high performer and always comes up with his best stuff when it really matters. Kevin is ultra-confident in these situations and trusts his instincts.

Kevin is elated to feel such a high level of inspiration and purpose in his daily life. He lives courageously and enjoys the small moments.

As you see, I could go on and on, telling this story in as much detail, with as much creative flair as I'd like. This is what I'm going to suggest that you do. Write down your new story with as much detail as you can. Even if it feels completely absurd, write down the life that you really want as if it's already happened. You are only allowed to do this exercise in the present or past tense. Instead of, I will be so happy when ___ occurs, you would write, I am so happy that ____ has already occurred.

I invite you to make a daily habit of this, even if it's just for ten minutes a day. Every day, write down the story you want to create as if it's already come to fruition. Write about specific themes or aspects of your life. Write about the big picture of your life. It doesn't really matter what the content is, as long as it feels inspiring and paints an accurate picture of the ideal life that you want to experience.

Can you do that? Make a commitment to yourself to give this at least thirty days. Every day, just ten minutes. If you feel inspired to write more, do it. If not, no worries. Keep in mind when you do this, you are only writing down the most exciting and uplifting version of reality that you'd like to experience. You are not writing out your problems, trying to understand or come to terms with your struggles, or negotiating with your fears. You are not documenting your current circumstances. All of that is your old story. For the next 30 days, you're writing a new one.

In thirty days, you'll be amazed by how much more developed this creative skill of storytelling becomes. Even more so, you'll likely be amazed by what's happening in your inner and outer world. The main thing I noticed as I started doing this on a daily basis is that I simply felt better. It's as if I can almost feel my neurochemicals shifting as I focus on new stories. Personally, I derive tremendous enjoyment from this daily practice.

At this point, you likely have a couple of objections to doing this. Let's see if I can sell you on the power of this practice.

Objection #1 – I hate to write/I am no good at writing/ I have no idea what I'd even say.

Are you having this thought right now? Great! You are telling a story. Now, let's tell a new one. Your first new story may start with these words:

> *Because I can see the value and potential power of this practice, I appreciate my innate ability to develop any skill that I desire and to practice it with passion and purpose. I am grateful that I am an amazing writer who has endless creative ideas. It's fun and easy for me to get my ideas out on paper. I am excited to document a new story based on the life that I desire to experience.*

When you are telling yourself that you are not a good writer or that you can't access your creative faculties, all that is happening is that you are buying into a thought. You are giving it a power that it doesn't really have. You are telling a story that does not serve you. All that needs to happen to change this is to write out a basic paragraph similar to what you see above, then start telling that new story repeatedly until it becomes reality.

Objection # 2: This has no bearing in reality/this is pure fantasy and delusion/I don't see how this is relevant to changing the actual pains and challenges I'm going through right now.

Stuck in this particular thought right now? First off, can you see that it's a story you're telling yourself, one that might not be all that true? Can you be open to considering this? Cool.

Now let's deconstruct this objection. First of all, the story you are currently telling yourself is nothing more than a fantasy. The new one will also be a fantasy. Your story isn't 'real'; it's just that–a story. You can either tell a story that keeps you stuck in suffering, or you can tell a story that feels epic, fun, and abundant. That's entirely up to you. Either way, all that you're doing is telling a story.

I know what you may be thinking, But my current thoughts and feelings about the circumstances of my life don't feel like a story. It all seems very real, very solid.

Let's return for a moment to the first Instant Upgrade Tool. You live in a holographic universe that is in no way as solid or real as you think it is. Not only are all of your beliefs, thoughts, and feelings a vast illusion, but so are your circumstances. You are essentially 'dreaming' this entire experience of your life. There is no outer world that is separate from you; it is entirely a projection of your own consciousness. Everything you see around you is devoid of any inherent meaning. It is all empty aside from the meaning that you impart. The entire framework of your life, from your friends to your job to your feelings and beliefs, all of it is a wide open experience. The only limits are the ones you impose onto your reality.

Quantum physics along with many of the ancient mystical and spiritual traditions throughout history verifies that this is true. Your existence has no inherent meaning or solidity; it is only reflecting back to you what you are telling it. This universe is like an infinite mirror that is showing you the reflection of the story you are telling.

Yes, your story is that powerful. When you keep iterating the same story, you keep generating the same frequency of reality thereby creating the same quality of feelings and circumstances. When you train yourself to become a master storyteller you are taking creative control of your existence. You are stepping into the driver's seat of your life by consciously choosing how you desire the story to unfold.

Still don't believe me? If you feel skeptical about the truths revealed by modern physics and many ancient wisdom traditions, try this on for size:

Ask yourself, "How's my current way working for me?"

If you're not as happy or fulfilled as you'd like to be, what do you have to lose by writing down a new story for thirty days? The worst thing that can happen is nothing, right? Have a little faith. Do something different. Be willing to shake up your life. Drop your insistence on your particular point of view. Be humble and childlike in your willingness to try a new way. After all, there's no risk and tremendous upside potential.

Yes, this may feel absurd. It may feel out of touch with reality. It may feel like it has nothing to do with your current situation. I get it. Do it anyway.

As you enter higher frequencies of reality, you'll realize how absurd it was to deny the power of telling new stories. You'll find it humorous that your 'old' self believed that there was no link between your imagination and your reality. You'll be blown away by the fact that you spent so darn long telling your story in an unconscious manner, and didn't see how doing this was generating all of the stressful emotions and experiences you've had.

There is nothing 'woo woo' or esoteric about this particular tool. It is simply leveraging the simple principle that what you focus on expands. In fact, there is actually a part of your brain called the reticular activating system that is a diffuse network of nerve pathways located in your brain stem that will cause you to see more of what you are focusing on. If you are focusing on acquiring a blue Audi for instance, this part of your brain will cause you to notice more blue Audis in your environment.

Writing a new story helps you shift your focus so that you can become more alert and sensitive to what you want in your life. As you do this repeatedly your circumstantial reality will start to mirror this shift in focus back to you. You'll become more clear and confident about what you want. You'll start to see your life through the lens of innate wholeness rather than lack. You'll ease into your present moment reality however it looks.

What is one thing that is causing you struggle or stress right now? Can you see that it's not the 'thing' outside of you, but the story you're telling about it? Tell a new story–even if it doesn't feel real. Remember, your current story isn't real either even if it feels like it is.

Go deeper. What is your 'if only' excuse for not living the life you really want? We all have one. It goes something like this:

I would totally be on board with all of this if only I didn't have _____ to deal with in my life.

What's the deepest, most ancient story you've been telling yourself about why you can't create the life you really want? Is it centered around self-worth? Safety? Never being good enough? Being stuck in a specific circumstance?

Whatever it is, it's time to tell a new story about it.

> *I am so happy that I now feel totally at peace with ____ (your 'if only') and have all the tools I need to accept and transform it. I appreciate the presence of _____ because it has given me a new level of insight into my life that I could have never had otherwise. It has allowed me to live out a more epic story.*

Storytelling is so powerful because it can be applied to literally anything in your life. Whatever challenge you're facing, you can always choose to impart a new meaning to it, cultivate a new attitude around it, and develop a different perspective in relation to it. Isn't that amazing?

When you tell new stories your intention should not be to push away or avoid your current challenges. You're not using storytelling as yet another tool to avoid yourself and the discomfort you feel. Instead, you're going right into the heart of the things that scare you the most, cause the most resistance, and undermine your power with the greatest force. You are using storytelling to become more intimate with you who are. This entails facing your demons, but doing it in a creative, playful way that neutralizes the typical stigma we feel in facing our deepest fears. When you tell a new story about your darkness you are instantly shedding more light on it, extending more love to it, and welcoming it into your human experience.

When you become a master storyteller, it doesn't mean that the darkness disappears or that you won't have challenges. It does mean that you are taking ownership of your life and savoring the process of intentionally designing your experience. You will still face challenges, fears, and darkness. Any good story has a challenge, right? In fact, the best stories are the ones where the main character must overcome a challenge that feels nearly insurmountable.

As the main character of your story you're not here to avoid challenges or make them go away. You're here to restructure the plot so that you are indeed the hero of your story. By consciously writing out a new script you are proclaiming to the universe that you are ready to be a hero rather than a victim. The challenges are welcomed into your daily life as you can now relate to them in a way that doesn't generate unnecessary suffering or struggle. When you write the hero version of your story you know that in the end the hero always emerges victorious. No matter what happens you can always choose to paste a meaning over your experience that is triumphant, solution-oriented, expansive, and creative.

Remember–you are always either the hero or the victim in your story. The hero consciously creates their story by activating the power of their imagination. The victim lives out an unconscious story that feels random and unclear. The hero welcomes any and all challenges, as any good story is full of drama, friction, and pushing the edge of what's possible. The victim gets buried in a habitual cycle of reacting to their circumstances, never sure why they have the life they do or how they got there. The hero intentionally maps out the most creative story possible. The victim offers little creative input into their story as they operate in default mode, which is full of narrow and limiting viewpoints and archetypes.

Storytelling can be used as a powerful manifestation tool. If you want to look at it as a way of creating 'things' that you desire, that is totally fine. For instance, you could tell a new story about how awesome it is to have that brand new blue Audi. You can describe in detail what it feels like to drive that car, how the leather smells, how the engine sounds, and how you look driving it around town.

You can tell new stories to help you create new things and experiences in any area of your life. You can write down the story of finally meeting your soulmate and how amazing it feels to experience true love. You can tell the story of making all kinds of money. There are no limits aside from how developed your creative faculties are.

Here's the point about storytelling that I want to make sure you are extremely clear on:

Don't get attached to any of your stories.

In other words, don't treat your story as if it's real. Simply have fun telling new stories. You see, there's a common pitfall most people fall into with manifestation techniques. They tend to forget that what they really desire is the feeling that the thing they want will generate for them. As a result, most people get attached to having that 'thing', so they can then feel better about their life.

The blue Audi isn't going to make you any happier than you are right now. It may induce a feeling of pleasure or accomplishment, but you can easily produce those feelings inside yourself right now. How? By telling a new story, of course. You can write out in great detail how amazing it feels to drive this car. By writing in this way, you are actually feeling the exact same feelings you would if you owned the car. There is no difference.

What makes for a great story is not acquiring all kinds of material possessions. Have you ever been to a movie where the entire plot centered around somebody who acquired great wealth and could have whatever they wanted… and that was pretty much it? I didn't think so. Such a movie would be boring and devoid of any meaning. Great movies trigger powerful feelings. Similarly, your life is meant to be an epic story that produces the most vivid feelings that you can access. You are here to feel. So, whatever you desire in the way of material possessions, tell a story that is fun, freeing, and unattached to those things.

Pay close attention when you are telling a story that is fueled by lack. When this happens it won't be fun to tell that story. Instead it will feel heavy and obligatory. It won't flow. You want your story to flow. The best way to do this is to create the feelings you want to experience through your new story. Focus more on creating epic feelings rather than acquiring things. If storytelling ceases to feel playful and light-hearted, it's likely the case that you've become attached to a lack-based belief that is pumping low frequency energy into your story.

Spontaneous Storytelling

Along with formally writing your story for ten minutes a day, you may find it helpful to spontaneously think or say a new story randomly throughout the day. Whenever you have alone time, consider saying a new story that feels highly empowering. You can do this in the shower, while driving, mowing the lawn, washing dishes, pumping gas, or any other daily task. Pick any topic that comes to mind. You can tell a new story in relation to a challenge you're facing at work, or about your body, or your confidence level, or a friend who is pressing your buttons.

The more consistently you are telling new stories about your life, the more you will accelerate in the direction of your dreams. Instead of just going about your day in default mode, choose to wake up and narrate your adventure. Does driving normally feel boring and mundane? Spice it up by telling a new story about your life. Activate your imagination and learn how to play again. The little moments make up most of life. Don't miss them by checking out. Be awake. Engage your mind by consciously choosing a story that makes you come fully alive in the moment.

After taking a minute to review the stories I've told today, I recall that the 25 minute drive to my tennis match was one of the highlights of my day. I could have easily gone into unconscious thinking which usually entails low grade worry and tension. Instead, I chose to tell a fun story about the writing of this book–how many people it will impact, how easy it is to write, and how enjoyable it is to create new ideas and weave all of the content together. I was talking to myself the entire time about this, and before I knew it I was at the courts. I couldn't believe how quickly the time had gone by as it seemed like about 30 seconds.
I have noticed time and again that when I am lost in a fun story the time just blazes by, even when I am doing something that would normally be perceived as slow or painful such as standing in a long line. Wouldn't you rather be immersed in an empowering story rather than resisting standing in a line? After all, you're just as alive standing in that line as you are doing anything else. You can surrender to it and enjoy life in that moment or you can fight it. Another example comes to mind. I recently took my son to a huge water amusement park that I could have easily resisted as these kinds of environments have historically made me feel bored and tired. Instead, I chose to tell a story about how amazing it is to simply witness my son having a blast and how that was more than enough to thoroughly enjoy the day. Telling a new story can be as simple as that. You simply shift your focus to a more aligned, enjoyable way of seeing things.

When you upgrade your experience through storytelling, the most immediate and important upgrade is in your attitude about who you are and why you're here. How you feel about yourself is by far the most important focal point. External accolades, material possessions, and circumstances will all come as a result of anchoring in a new attitude that aligns with a higher frequency. Don't worry about acquiring outer things as you begin this practice. Make your new story mostly about your new attitude, your new feelings, your new relationship with your life. You'll notice that you have a much more immediate sense of control over your inner world and can choose to shift it in whatever way you desire. Your outer world will mirror this back to you, but don't be attached to how long that takes or what form it takes. Stay open and unattached.

I want to leave you with a final example of storytelling to anchor in as deeply as possible the power of this tool.

As I sit here writing these words alone in my living room at 11pm on a Sunday night, it is apparent to me that there are two vastly different stories I could be telling myself. The old, unconscious story would have gone something like this:

> *Ugh. Being alone is kind of flat, but I still prefer it over being with people. I don't see the point of any of this. I guess I'll just do what I always do–have another beer, eat that last piece of pizza, and tune out watching TV. It doesn't matter either way, right? Nobody cares if I take care of myself. I could die tonight and nobody would even notice. Oh well, at least I can enjoy some idle pleasures before falling asleep and doing it all over again tomorrow. Hopefully I can find a better way. But I doubt it.*

Yes, this is a bit dramatic, but the frequency of my previous story was set to a pretty low point. As I sit here now I realize that if I really wanted to I could still choose to tell this story. That potential field of reality is available to me. I would need to lower my frequency considerably to access it, but I could do it.

Instead, I am choosing to tell a different story:

> *Wow. I am so grateful that I had the majority of this day to focus on*

this writing project. I am absolutely LOVING it! I deeply appreciate being immersed in my passion and having the time and freedom in my life to support my vision. It has been such an enjoyable day, using my time wisely, doing what I love, and feeling in the flow. I feel so nourished by following my creative excitement that I haven't been hungry much at all today. I'm continuing to create new levels of focus and productivity and I'm blown away by how much I can get done in a day. I'm so excited to keep going higher and deeper tomorrow.

Whether I choose to dwell in the lower or higher frequency story, each is equally valid and accessible. I get to choose what meaning I impart to this moment. There exists the potential to tap into either one of these frequencies. By choosing to stay conscious and intentional, I find it much more exciting and entertaining to dwell in the higher frequency.

While the high frequency story is more or less documenting what appeared to be my actual experience of this day, keep in mind that I started telling this story of writing a new book and being plugged into my purpose before anything came to fruition in the physical world. I was anchoring in this new story before seeing anything change whatsoever in my outer world.

Start telling a new story. Write it down. Say it aloud as you're driving to work in the morning. Think about your new story as you're taking a shower or walking your dog. Express your story as if it's already happened. Have fun! You are waking up to your creative power and training your mind to enter a higher dimension of reality. There's nothing more exhilarating than that.

The Third Instant Upgrade Tool
Ultra Focus

How focused are you in your life as it currently stands? What percentage of the day are you 100% engaged with the activities at hand, aware of what's happening in your mind, and consciously designing the story that you want to unfold?

The opposite of being ultra-focused is what I call 'default mode', which can be defined as living in a habitual, reactive, and unconscious way. When you're stuck in default mode your life is unintentional, uncreative, and lacking a kind of precision that comes from paying close attention.

The purpose of this tool, becoming ultra-focused, is to help you completely transcend default mode so that your life becomes a highly intentional, carefully designed, creative, and empowered process. When you're stuck in default mode, you are locked into lower frequencies of reality. It's impossible to make genuine and lasting changes. You'll be driven by unconscious desires, false motivation, will power, and fear. Your life will feel like a continual cycle of mediocrity and limitation. You will attract people and circumstances into your life that feel random, less than optimal, boring, and stressful.

As you go about this day, pay close attention to how focused people are around you. Assess the degree to which people are entranced by the default mode of living. Notice how they seem distracted, fragmented, and not fully present. No need to judge anyone for dwelling in this state; simply observe with great sensitivity the degree to which our modern world has become lost in distraction. We are all vulnerable to this way of being. Using this tool, I'm going to show you how to fundamentally operate at a higher frequency that makes you impervious to attention deficit disorder (which most people have), constant overwhelm and distraction, and the nagging feeling that you are being spread too thin in your life.

After all, this is what's going on to some degree or another, right? You feel like you have no time to focus on the important things in life. Your energy is pulled in a million different directions. You are constantly putting out fires. You're so busy taking care of others that you feel it's impossible to put yourself first in a genuine way. Or, on the flip side, you may have too much idle time. You feel bored and disengaged with your life. There's a restlessness always brewing beneath the surface that blocks you from feeling fully relaxed and at ease with your life.

That's the old story, and we all have been victims of it to one degree or another. Using this tool, you'll come to discover that the solution is incredibly simple. The root cause of these issues is being stuck in default mode. You feel that life is happening 'to' you and you're stuck in an endless cycle of reacting to what shows up. What this boils down to is that you lack focus. You've never been taught how to harness the incredible power of your attention to generate the feelings and experiences that are most aligned with who you are and what you value. You didn't learn this growing up in school. Nobody ever sat down with you to cultivate this uniquely powerful skill.

Perhaps you have tried various meditation or mindfulness practices in the past. Of course, many people benefit a great deal from meditation as a way to enhance focus and keep our attention on present moment reality. The problem with meditation is just like anything else, if we try to use it as a motivational tool to feel better about ourselves it will backfire. Meditation becomes yet another prop that justifies why you can't improve or fix your life.

In my coaching business I hear this all the time, "I tried to meditate, but I could not get my thoughts to quiet down".

So many people who turn to meditation end up feeling confused and conflicted about what's it's supposed to be doing to help them. Why? Because they didn't shift their frequency to a higher level first, which would then make meditation a very simple and accessible practice. When you become ultra-focused, the goal is to make your life a continuous meditation. That may sound like a far-fetched ideal right now, but when you enter higher frequencies you can absolutely access this state of heightened awareness and attention.

When your life becomes a continuous meditation you'll notice that:

- your resistance to what's in this moment drops away and you surrender to a natural state of flow and ease that guides you at all times.
- your mind calms down or becomes more stimulated as a natural response to what is happening in your outer reality.
- you get way more done, with a much greater sense of ease and purpose.
- time expands; you create yourself having more time to fit everything into your day.
- stress dissolves. You come to see that stress is always a result of being stuck in the past or the future. When you are present, there's nothing to stress about.

The more skilled you become at heightening your focus, the more you see that you can bend reality in whatever way you desire. You become more empowered in the way you perceive things. You naturally choose beliefs, feelings, and behaviors that are the most meaningful, entertaining, and fun for you to engage in. Without focus, you will be a victim to your thoughts, feelings, and circumstances.

I could go on and on about all the benefits of being ultra-focused but I think you get the idea. You likely already understand how vital focus is to your well-being. The question of course, is how?

My intention is to keep this discussion highly practical. I want you sharpening your focus in this very moment as you're reading this book. The development of this skill begins now. No need to analyze or think about it. Just do it.

Sharpening your focus is simple. If it starts to feel complicated or confusing put the book down, take a few breaths, and return with a fresh mindset. Please be aware that as you practice these tools there is no right or wrong, or good or bad. Intense focus is not a heavy, serious practice. It should feel playful and fun as much as it feels like discipline. If it starts to feel too serious simply shift your focus to where this is coming from–what thoughts or feelings are you having that are causing you to judge yourself or pigeon hole your experience in a limiting way? When you start practicing heightened focus you are welcoming the totality of who you are. The part of you that is discursive, unfocused, and pretty much all over the place is going to come along for the ride. Don't expect this part of you to magically disappear. When you practice becoming ultra-focused you're simply choosing–over and over–where your attention resides. You're choosing which part of yourself you are feeding, which story you are writing.

You always have a choice. Where your attention goes is entirely up to you. Nothing outside of you is dictating what you focus on. There's no other entity or person within you who has control over your thoughts and feelings. This one is on you. Owning this sets the stage for rapidly accelerating your ability to heighten focus throughout your daily life. If you are convinced that you don't really have any power over what you focus on, then it's time to tell a new story. Actually, this is the first experiential practice that I want you to play with for the next few minutes. I'm going to cover three simple techniques you can use to become ultra-focused and turn your life into a continuous meditation. The goal is to become as intentional, deliberate, creative, and dynamic as possible in the way that you live your life. That's what focus does. It helps you tap into your amazing internal resource base to quickly transition from the low frequency default mode of living into a new, conscious way of being that is infinitely more enjoyable.

The two kinds of high frequency focus

When your focus takes you into a high frequency state of consciousness, what you'll notice is that it feels like a unique blend of being deeply relaxed and ultra-alert. Your mind feels both intensely engaged and calm. This state of relaxed intensity may sound paradoxical, and it actually is from the perspective of lower frequency states. We are generally either too intense, where we are vulnerable to manic states, impatience, or aggression, or we are too relaxed which can manifest as passivity, depression, or creative inertia.

When I describe the ultra-focused state of high frequency reality it may sound similar to a manic state. The difference is that there's a quality of poise, calmness, and restoration that accompanies your ability to produce at higher levels. You're living from an unattached, spacious point of view where you don't lapse into unconscious behavior or addiction as is typically the case with mania.

To create this unique blend of ingredients into your high frequency life, it's important to acknowledge and practice both of these kinds of focus.

Let's take a look at each:

1) Stimulative Focus: This is a heightened state of engagement and present moment attention on whatever task is at hand, whatever you are doing in any given moment. Stimulative focus has a forward-moving efficiency that fuels it, where there's no room for B.S., clutter, or excuses. Many high achievers and successful business people are experts at using stimulative focus to accomplish their goals. They have a 'do whatever it takes' attitude and will not allow any obstacle to get in their way. They are intense about this pursuit, often to the point of becoming obsessive about it. Stimulative focus also tends to govern the lives of stay-at-home moms who have an endless to-do list and are always multi-tasking. This kind of focus allows us to get a tremendous amount done in a short period of time.

2) Regenerative Focus: This is a heightened state of relaxation and composure that you consciously sink into as a way to restore yourself on the deepest level possible. Regenerative focus is a powerful way to recharge your batteries, boost your adrenals, and create a Zen-like tranquility that permeates your life in the face of all circumstances.

In the above examples, most high achievers and stay-at-home moms are deficient in this type of focus, which is the main reason why they tend to suffer from fatigue and overwhelm. Regenerative focus makes everything seem workable. You are able to perceive reality as fluid, malleable, and easy.

At a certain point in your development into higher frequencies, you'll notice that these two types of focus merge into one harmonious approach to life. You can dance between the two at will and no longer see any separation in how you use them on a daily basis. Along these lines, you can work incredibly hard on a big work project using stimulative focus, while simultaneously being deeply relaxed and attentive to the moment using regenerative focus.

A great example is how I am choosing to write this book. I can feel both of these types of focus interweaving into a heightened state of productivity that feels simultaneously energizing and peaceful. I certainly feel that I create my best work from this place and I'm sure you'll find the same to be true. Merging these two types of focus is how you get into what's called the zone, or a state of flow. All resistance drops away. There's no effort or willpower. You become a vessel for whatever wants to be channeled through you and you simply allow it to happen.

Merging these two types of focus also greatly heightens your intuition. By developing a simultaneously relaxed yet alert state, you'll be open to the subtle signals you get from a deep place within yourself that can skillfully navigate you through life and help you make decisions. When we enter higher frequencies, this 'deep' place is no longer seen as deep or mysterious at all; it's a state of being you can access by implementing all of these tools into your daily life.

The following three exercises will help you develop both of these types of focus. Pay attention to how you are feeling. If you're getting impatient, edgy, or urgent, it's time to implement regenerative focus into your present moment. If you're feeling bored, confused, dull, or you're procrastinating, it's time to implement stimulative focus into your present moment. Use these practices spontaneously on an as needed basis to apply the antidote to whatever current block or struggle may be showing up for you.

Experiential Practice #1: Tell the Story of Being Ultra-Focused

We are going to use the second Instant Upgrade Tool to immediately activate this third tool. Get out pen and paper or open up your laptop. Spend the next fifteen minutes using stream of consciousness writing to map out your new story around the topic of focus. If your old story was that of being spread too thin, feeling scattered, or struggling to slow your mind down, you are going to script a new one that is basically the exact opposite. Your new story might go something like this:

> *I am so grateful that I have heightened my focus in all areas of my life. I truly feel that my life is a continuous meditation and I'm finding it easy and fun to stay engaged and present with what's happening in this moment. My mind feels sharper and more clear than it ever has. I have total power over where I put my attention. When I slip into default mode, I'm able to snap out of it quickly and can easily refocus.*
>
> *I love being focused. It's one of my great passions in life. As a result of becoming ultra-focused, I am experiencing some incredible shifts and it really didn't take long at all. My stress level has decreased significantly. I worry less than ever. I have more time in the day than I ever have–plenty of 'me' time to take care of myself and build my energy to take care of others. My business/career is skyrocketing, as my productivity is now through the roof. It's so fun for me to be a high producer. Every day, my focus continues to sharpen. I can clearly feel that I'm in a new reality and that what I see around me is reflecting back my heightened state of presence. I thoroughly enjoy inhabiting my life and being present to what's here now.*

This is my stream of consciousness story on becoming ultra-focused. I must say, that everything I wrote here is true in my life. Because I have been telling a new story about my level of focus, I am able to write this book in a period of time that most people would consider absurd (less than one month). I can incorporate plenty of exercise, time with my kids, and attending to various responsibilities with ease. I now have a story that there is an abundance of time in my life. No need to be urgent or frantic. Being at ease always generates better results. This is my story and I'm sticking to it!

You may want to write a new story about your level of focus on a daily basis until you can feel it really sinking in. Keep writing down new ideas about how you're able to create and sustain intense levels of focus while also being relaxed and at ease. Write this down as if it's already happening. Even if your current reality seems like the exact opposite of your new story, write it down anyway. Be willing to be a little bit absurd. Push the edge of your comfort zone. Use your imagination in ways that you haven't since you were a child.

Experiential Practice #2: The Five Breath Process

The Five Breath Process is particularly useful for developing regenerative focus in your life. Whenever you feel overwhelmed, scattered, urgent, or off center, use this simple technique right there in the moment. I also recommend that you use it three to five times a day as an ongoing practice. Do this for the next thirty days and observe what happens.

The Five Breath Process is incredibly simple. All that you need to do is stop whatever is going on in the moment and take five deep, slow breaths, allowing your mind to empty. Feel the breath moving deeply through your diaphragm into your lower belly. Simply observe any thoughts or feelings without identifying with them. If it feels supportive, you can also count the number of each inhale. As you inhale, you can say to yourself '1', then exhale. Inhale again and say '2', then exhale. Be sure to inhale and exhale in a slow, deep, deliberate fashion.

I've also found it quite useful to smile when I do this. I have noticed that the simple act of smiling immediately lightens my mood and elevates my frequency. The 'old' me would have judged this as cheesy or stupid, but I assure you, it works. As you smile, you can also visualize what's called an inner smile. In this sense, you imagine your inner world lighting up with causeless happiness. Keep this simple. Just do what feels right.

The Five Breath Process is extremely powerful for cutting through negative momentum in your life. Have you noticed that when you think a negative thought, it immediately leads to a bad feeling which then causes unwanted behaviors? When you use this tool you are cutting through the habitual momentum of this cycle and creating a pattern interrupt for your nervous system and psyche. Instead of allowing this negative momentum to dominate your mind, you choose to take five deep, slow breaths, feel the space around your situation, and smile.

Do this anytime you are struggling, but also do it spontaneously throughout your day. I tend to use this when I'm driving, washing dishes, and very often on the tennis court when I'm feeling tense. I've found it to be quite useful for inducing a state of instant relaxation that helps me perform at a higher level. Try it out in your life and see what happens.

Experiential Practice #3: Waking Up with Focus

Let me ask you, when you wake up in the morning, on a scale of 1-10, how alert are you? 1 being you're in a zombie state, 10 being totally alert with a crystal clear mind.

If they are honest, most people will rate themselves as a five or less on this scale. When we wake up feeling foggy headed with all kinds of random thoughts bombarding our minds, we are setting the stage for a day of more of the same. With this practice, we are going to play a fun game.

Tomorrow morning when you wake up I want you to notice how quickly you can pay attention to your breath. Can you notice yourself inhaling within three seconds of waking? Or does it take you several minutes before you remember that you had an intention to do this?

Playing this game will help you see with total clarity how alert you are upon waking. Do this for the next thirty days and see if your ability improves. Can you get to a place where you can bring razor sharp focus to your breath the instant you awaken? Now that is focus! And it's an extremely powerful practice. The better you get at this, the more of an impact it will have. Upgrading your frequency from the moment you open your eyes creates an undeniable tone of inspiration and present moment awareness for the day.

Here's a more advanced game you can play once you get really good at this first one: After you are able to bring attention to your breathing, immediately tell the story of how this day is going to unfold. Do this before you get up to go to the bathroom. Lay in bed and take two minutes to tell a deliberate story. Flood that story with gratitude, excitement, and confidence as best you can.

Here's an example of a story I might very well tell myself upon waking:

> *I am thrilled to be alive for another day. I know that this life is a gift and I'm excited to use this day to its fullest potential. By the time my head hits the pillow tonight, I will be able to close my eyes knowing that I took full advantage of all of the opportunities that were presented to me. I deeply appreciate that I landed three new clients today and made ___ amount of money. I'm excited to be ultra-focused today and to spread my energy through all themes of my life, taking exceptional care of my kids, my business, my body, and so on. My life is amazing. Let's get this day started.*

Can you see how telling this story instead of allowing a randomly generated, unconscious mess of thoughts to dictate your day can help you create a new tone of power and clarity? If you can develop this ability, you'll no longer think that making your life a continuous meditation is that big of a deal. After all, if you can be conscious right when you open your eyes, you certainly can for any other moment of the day.

Practice this for the next thirty days and observe what happens. Yes, it is a challenge. With a little practice it gets much easier and the ripple effect it creates through your day will be immensely positive.

As an extension of this practice, if you are able to create a morning ritual where you inundate your consciousness with the most inspirational and uplifting practices possible, I highly recommend it. Spend the first hour of your day doing whatever lifts you up the most. In your current story you may be too busy to pull this off. Start telling a new story about freeing up this time in the morning–that's my first tip. Secondly, do what you can, even if it's just ten minutes. This could be time that you write, exercise, meditate, do yoga, or use the other tools in this book. Whatever excites you, do it. One of the Instant Upgrade Tools is all about excitement, so I'll leave you with this for now and we will expand on this conversation when we discuss that particular tool.

$5,000 in Five Minutes

I'd like to share a rather uncanny experience from my own life that reveals the incredible power that being ultra-focused can activate into your life. I had this experience several months ago, when I was tapped into an elevated state of consciousness for a prolonged period of time. I was more focused than I had ever been in my life during this phase. My mind was crystal clear, I was anchored in the present moment, and I was intensely working on new stories. I could feel the simultaneous energies of intensity and tranquility washing over my being from the moment I woke up until the time I went to bed.

I like to use my business as a laboratory for testing out different manifestation techniques. Given that my old character was deeply invested in fear around money and survival, business serves as a wonderful symbol to reclaim power and invent myself as I desire. During this period of my life, I wasn't really focused on my business at all. In fact, I had more or less taken a two-month sabbatical, as I was focused on healing other aspects of my life that deserved my attention. One day however, I got a spontaneous desire and decided to run with it.

I wanted to apply my heightened focus directly to the theme of making money. Here was the simple exercise that came to mind:

For the next five minutes, sit on your couch and visualize with as much relaxed intensity as possible that a $5,000 payment will be made by a new client. Give yourself exactly five minutes to actualize this into physical reality.

So, I plunked down on my couch, closed my eyes, and started to write a new story about how awesome it was that this just happened. I imagined my phone dinging with a new notification that I had made a sale. I anchored in the quality of absolute certainty that this was my experience. Every single second, my mind was locked into this imagined state. I generated feelings of appreciation for the transaction and told myself how fun it will be to help this new client.

About four minutes into this exercise, I got a sale for $5,000.

Yes, this sale literally came out of nowhere. I wasn't expecting anyone to buy anything at that particular time. The actual truth, however, is that it didn't really come 'out of nowhere.' The sale was with me all along. I was simply using the power of heightened focus to anchor it into my physical experience.

So, you tell me–was this mere coincidence? Luck?

I will say this, in the moments after it happened, I was 100% sure that it had nothing to do with coincidence or luck. Through that elevated state, I could see that human beings have access to all kinds of invisible powers that are largely lying dormant within us.

To be honest, I have tried this experiment a few others times and it has been hit or miss. Does this mean that we can only manifest randomly? Sometimes the universe will give us what we want; other times not? Not at all. During that five-minute window where I created a $5,000 sale, my focus was at an all-time high. Seriously, I have never been that dialed into a high frequency in my life. It was as if I entered a completely different portal of reality where the absolute certainty of making this sale that I was imagining somehow merged with physical reality. My imagined state of certainty was so powerful that I was able to bend reality in a super accelerated fashion.

I believe that this kind of manifestation power resides within each of us. To activate it requires not only tremendous focus (both stimulative and regenerative), but also, from my experience, a boldness and courage to completely transcend the collective cultural belief system that says this kind of experience is absolutely impossible. Heightened focus enables us to break free from all of our unconscious assumptions that inevitably limit us. You have to be at least slightly delusional (from a conventional point of view), a renegade, to be willing to enter this kind of inner terrain. It's not for the faint of heart, as you are literally leaving behind the entire collective agreement we've all bought into about how this universe operates and our place within it.

I recall that about an hour after this experience, after the initial awe and excitement had subsided, I was struck with a deep, raw anxiety about what I had just experienced. I could sense the implications of being able to pull things into my reality in this way. It blew my mind. The part of me that wanted to hold onto my convenient belief system and solid sense of self had nowhere to turn, and for a few moments a feeling of terror erupted within me. That passed and what was left was mostly excitement about the staggering possibilities.

Danger: Don't Try This at Home

As I mentioned, this kind of experimentation is not for the faint of heart. You have to be ready for it. If you DO manifest what you're focusing on, you'll likely have a similar experience as I did. Your worldview will be largely shattered. It may scare you to your depths. It may cause you to feel that you have no ground whatsoever to stand on. If you DON'T manifest what you're focusing on, the typical reaction would be to judge your experience as a failure by telling yourself that you're no good at this, or maybe other people can do this, but not you, or this is all just a bunch of metaphysical hocus pocus. It's easy to buy into cynicism.

If you want to experiment with bending reality, go into it with humility and openness. If you don't get the 'result', that in no way means it doesn't work. What it does mean is that you are developing a new skill of becoming ultra-focused, and there's still a gap in your ability to anchor new things into your physical experience in a rapid way. Never allow your typical assumptions about reality to get in the way of staying open to possibility. It could also mean that what you are trying to manifest isn't relevant to your story at this time. In the case of the $5,000, it was apparent that this experience was meant to be a part of my story. Trust whatever happens; it's always perfectly designed.

What I have discovered is that the degree of heightened focus I have is directly proportional to the speed at which I can pull things into my experience. The more focused I am, the more likely it is that I can manifest something fast. Along these lines, if you're new to this practice, you may want to give yourself a longer window rather than five minutes. Give yourself the next month to gently and playfully practice focusing on what you want as if it's already here. Be super intense about it, but also completely spacious and unattached. Remember, attachment to it showing up directly blocks and undermines the power of your focus. Too much attachment means it's time for more regenerative focus. Relax. Drop the urgency. You're already perfect as you are. Nothing is missing. You're just having fun.

This experience from my life demonstrates why focus is your most powerful acceleration tool for creating the life you want. The more focused you are, the faster things can move in your life, both in terms of clearing out the old, unwanted elements and anchoring in the new elements that most excite you. Unfocused people have stagnant lives. Focused people have dynamic lives. Start to think of focus as a dynamic skill you can develop that has no end point. For the rest of your life, you can commit to achieving higher and higher states of focus. The higher your level of focus, the higher your frequency of reality becomes and the faster you can manifest and intentionally design your life.

I'd like to share one last insight about this experience. I've read all kinds of books about manifestation, and to be honest, most of the material that I've read only fortifies the ego and solidifies attachment. I believe that manifestation can be one of the most powerful catalysts for spiritual growth. On the contrary, it can also be used in a misguided way to lock in our limits and take ourselves out of present moment reality.

Part of regenerative focus is the ability to self-reflect and consider why you want to manifest the things you do. If manifestation doesn't seem to work for you, it's only because you're trying to get something 'out there' that you think you don't already have. You're using manifestation as yet another prop to justify feelings of lack and not being enough. People who are highly skilled at manifestation would never look at this practice as a failure if they don't get what they want within a certain timeframe. There's no agenda, so there can be no failure. If you have an agenda, it's coming from lack, and you will be disappointed.

When you practice manifestation, your only agenda is to have fun and play around. You're delighted when you actually 'get' the thing you're focusing on, but you're also completely fine with not getting it. Be sure to use regenerative focus to step back and consider what your agenda is. Do you need that thing to show up? Or are you just having fun with experimenting? Your job is to simply be ultra-focused, then let your Higher Self take care of the rest in terms of what actually shows up.

The reason I was able to anchor in the $5,000 into my physical reality is that I was just having fun. Yes, my focus was incredibly intense. I was actually sweating because I was so concentrated during that five-minute window. But I did not need that money to show up in that window. I had zero expectations. I was basically saying to the universe, "Hey, I'm already whole in my life… let's have a little fun and create something new."

This is by far the best attitude to embrace in relation to all of these tools and towards your life in general. Write your story so that you're already there. Nothing is missing. There is no lack. Then, have some fun and use your life as a laboratory to see what you can create. Doing this keeps you deeply humble and supremely confident, and that is a winning combination in my book.

The Fourth Instant Upgrade Tool
Character Acting

If we revisit the universal truths outlined in Filter Cleansing, the first Instant Upgrade Tool, it becomes apparent that our identity is in no way solid, fixed, or permanent. Nothing is set in stone about our thoughts, feelings, personality, behaviors, or actions. Because we exist in a holographic universe that is constantly changing we must consider that we too are part of the hologram. What this means is that whatever we 'think' we are is nothing but an illusion. We are making it up just as we make up the seeming reality of there being a coffee table that we can prop our feet up on.

From a quantum/mystical perspective our feet don't exist. The coffee table doesn't exist. The separation between our feet and coffee table doesn't exist. It's all a holographic illusion. We've simply pumped ourselves full of ideas about who we are and what this universe is. Our ideas give us a feeling of standing on solid ground, a reference point we can use to understand our lives.

The problem is, most of the ideas we have formed about who we are and what life means are deeply limited and misguided. The accumulation of various beliefs that form our self-image prevents us from tapping into our higher potential, accessing more exalted states of reality, and having more fun while we are here. When we believe we exist as a solid, separate entity we are going to feel weighed down by a lot of baggage. Change will feel hard and slow. Life will feel more mundane than magical.

Let me ask you, "Who are you?" Really give this some thought. Are you your thoughts? Feelings? Are you your body? Your personality? I assure you whatever answer you give me that appears to be solid can be deconstructed back to a point of absurdity. All of your thoughts and feelings are changing constantly, flickering into and out of existence. When you're not thinking, are you still you? If you are your body, what happens if you lose a limb? Are you a lesser you at that time? What happens when your body dies? Do you just go away?

Since the beginning of human civilization people have grappled with the BIG questions of life. Who am I? Why am I here? What does all this mean? What should I do about it?

As you've learned from our exploration of various universal truths in the first Instant Upgrade Tool, we can develop a high degree of conceptual clarity in relation to these questions. Ultimately though, we are not meant to 'understand' these answers on a conceptual level. We can't 'think' our way into an accurate understanding of how this universe operates and why we are here. The only option is to experience the mystery of these questions and have a blast doing so. That's what I'm going to recommend for you.

How do we do this? Character acting.

The premise of character acting is that because your sense of self is in no way solid or real to begin with you can literally invent yourself in any way that you please. You have a unique ability to morph into different characters which gives you the opportunity to play various roles and try on different costumes during your human experience.

You've already gotten a taste of this from the storytelling tool. By virtue of changing your story and activating your creativity and imagination, you are inventing yourself into something new. Character acting takes this a step further. Now you are going to act as if you are already the person you most deeply desire to be.

This may sound like the 'fake it until you make it' approach I'm sure you've heard from various self-help and positive thinking circles. My take on this is more subtle and I believe, more accurate. The truth is that you're not faking anything when you're character acting. Why? Because you're making up who you are and the story of your life all of the time regardless of what you do. In a sense you are faking it right now. If you're suffering a lot in your life you're simply playing a character who suffers. That's the script you've been writing, the screenplay you've chosen to act out.

To go further, I don't think it's accurate to say 'until you make it'. The truth is, 'making it' is an illusion. You never make it. You simply play around with various frequencies of reality to create the most ideal expression of yourself in this world. You're not faking it. You're not making it. You're just experimenting with new roles, new scripts, and new plots that feel interesting and exciting and that inspire you to reclaim power.

This conversation could easily turn abstract and pretty heady. There are incredibly complex schools of thought especially in the ancient Buddhist traditions, that go into great detail about the mechanics of No Self and the emptiness of the world we live in. You don't need to know 99% of that in order to apply what I am saying to your life. As with all of the tools, I'm going to keep this highly practical and actionable for you so you can benefit from this tool starting today.

One simple way to access character acting is to look at the new stories you've been writing and intentionally choose to play the leading role of that story for that particular day. Instead of keeping the story confined to your head you're going to activate it into your daily life (if you thought the storytelling tool was absurd and far-fetched you're going to LOVE this one).

After reviewing the new, inspiring story you've written for that day you simply ask yourself:

> *Alright, how would I act if I was this person already? If I was already experiencing all of this in my life, who would I be?*

Then you start honing your actor's skill and you do your best to become that character.

- How would this person dress?
- How would they carry themselves in space?
- What would their posture look like?
- How would they manage their time?

- What would they think about?
- How would they handle challenges?
- What would they eat?
- How would they take care of their body?
- How would they view the world they live in?
- Who would they hang out with?
- What would their home look like?
- How would they treat their environment?

Get the idea? Your job is to play that new character in the most vivid and fun way possible. Nobody else has to know you're doing this; it can be your own private little game.

Character acting launches you into higher frequencies with incredible speed, as you're literally re-inventing who you are in a playful and light-hearted manner, without attachment. This practice is one of the greatest catalysts for personal evolution.

Let's start with your physical appearance. When you look into the mirror do you see an authentic version of yourself staring back? Does your appearance capture your power, radiance, and presence? Does your body feel like it's a strong, healthy vessel? Do your clothes represent the level of quality and care that most optimally showcases who you desire to be?

If you've often felt unattractive, invisible, or ordinary for much of your life, it's time to play out the role of a new character who acts in a way that represents your most desired expression of how you want to show up in the world. First, write out the new story of how you appear in the world. Remember–there are no limits and it's entirely up to you. Have fun painting a new picture of the image you'd like to convey. Be open to new ways of presenting yourself.

Then, start taking small steps toward inventing yourself in the way you've written. Try on new clothes. Adjust your posture to reflect this new character. Determine what's in your immediate control and have fun making these micro shifts in who you are. Whatever feels out of your control (like being twenty pounds lighter), simply act as if you are already that person. When you look in the mirror choose to see the ideal body you want to have. Paint that perception over whatever is looking back at you in your reflection.

In the introduction to this book I mentioned how I lost ten pounds within two weeks of applying these tools. What I'm sharing with you now is the main reason this happened. I created a clear story in my mind about the ideal body that I desired, then chose the perception that I was already inhabiting this body. I imagined this body looking back at me the mirror. It was fun, light, and unattached, not coming from a place of lack whatsoever. You can do the same.

Now let's take a look at how your new character manages their time. What do they do when they wake up? Do they have a morning ritual that energizes and inspires them? Do they drink a cup of coffee? A smoothie?

Keep in mind, whatever your old character was doing that felt uninspiring, routinized, or stress-based, this new character is basically going to choose the opposite path. Does this new character spend much time on the computer? Watching TV? Do they like to spend their time mostly around people? Alone? How much do they want to work? Play? Rest?

Does your new character thrive from having a lot on their plate? Or do they like simplicity more? What do they do before bed? What feels most meaningful for the new character before they close their eyes?

Create some structure for your new character in how they manage their time. Have fun with it. It's all wide open.

Now let's look at what your new character likes to think about. Since you're now becoming ultra-focused you know that you can choose your thoughts. You can make thinking a highly deliberate process. Whatever thoughts caused your 'old' character to feel out of alignment, bad, or stressed out, your new character is going to consciously think in a way that generates more happiness and empowerment. Remember, you're acting. Even if this doesn't feel real, that's fine. The old stuff you were thinking about wasn't real either; it's all made up. You are simply living out the story of your choosing. There's a fine line between fantasy and reality. In fact, there really isn't a line at all.

My 'old' character used to think about:

- how hard life is.
- how separate I feel.
- how scary the future is.
- how uncomfortable I feel in my body.
- how people feel threatening and unsafe.
- how life feels futile.

My 'new' character prefers to think about:

- how excited I am to work on creative projects.
- how fun it is to perform at my highest level.
- how I am sowing amazing seeds for my future.
- how attractive I feel in my body.
- how confident I am around people.
- how magical life is.

I am consciously thinking about and acting out this new story as best I can for as many moments of the day as I can. You can do this too.

Does this sound hard? Unrealistic? Like a lot of work?

There's your old story kicking in again. Care to let go of that now? In your new story, character acting is some of the most fun you can have as a human being. What could be better than constantly playing with your identity, inventing yourself anew as you see fit? Engineering the ideal version of your being into existence?

Being a static character who never changes is a recipe for a dull, limited life. Haven't you had enough of that way of being? Your sense of self is not solid. Stop pretending like it is!

You can write and act out all of the juicy details of your new character in all of its vivid glory. People will likely start noticing a difference in you. At first, they can't pinpoint it, but over time it becomes increasingly overt. Some people who master the art of character acting seem to literally morph into a new being. Their appearance, personality, voice, posture–all of it is upgraded to such an extent that the old person is barely recognizable.

For a moment I'd like to invite you to step back and consider just how powerful this tool is. Can you see how much potential it has to upgrade your life? And do it in a way that is fun, effortless, and creative? Can you see how it can work on literally any aspect of yourself or your life?

Perhaps you're like my old character. You struggle a lot with your purpose in life. You wonder why you are here, how to do something meaningful with your livelihood, and how to contribute in a way that makes a lasting impact.

In my work as a business and life coach, I hear this particular story all of the time. People come to me with all kinds of angst about their mission and purpose. They feel like they are wasting time, sinking in a quagmire of conflicted thoughts about what they should be doing and how they should be living. So many people feel like they are failing to live up to their potential. They feel restless, bored, and frustrated. Deep down they feel that they are letting God down, or their spouse and kids. This is actually an epidemic in our modern world. It's a pretty heavy way to get through life.

If this has been your struggle, can you see now that you've simply been playing a character who believes all of this to be true? Can you see that it's all a story that you're living? And that the story can easily be changed? Can you see that perhaps your purpose is simply to tell a new story? Could it be that simple? YES!

If you want to go on playing the character who struggles to figure out their life, be my guest. Keep beating your head against the wall, reading from the same script, acting out the same role day after day. If on the other hand, you decide that you're sick of this low frequency reality, you now have the precise tool you need to instantly shift out of it. How would it feel to never, ever have to play the character again of someone who struggles with their purpose? My goodness, if your experience is at all like mine it's a relief beyond measure.

Write out your new story of being someone who loves what they do, is plugged into their purpose, and is having a blast impacting the world using their unique strengths. Then, start character acting and role playing that story. Invent yourself as that person. It really is that simple.

Do you believe that finding your purpose needs to be hard? That it couldn't possibly be this easy? That it's your destiny to struggle with the problems of your existence until the day you die? How's that story working for you? You do see it's just a story and that you're simply playing the character who believes all of this, right? If your identity is in no way solid, why not choose to play a new role, one that is a heck of a lot more fun and enjoyable? And yes, the irony rings true that doing exactly this IS a major part of your purpose as a human being. You are here to have fun, to play, to experiment, to invent yourself as you desire, to give your highest excitement a tangible form through your work. That IS your purpose.

Can you see the absurd fun of unconsciously playing a character who is trying to discover their purpose in life, only to now know that your actual purpose is mainly to see that you're acting and that you can shift into whatever role you desire? Being human is such a blast.

Apply character acting to any aspect of your life that you want. Stuck in a dead end job? Write out your new story of how you were able to easily transition out of that job into your dream livelihood. Write out how it all just happened without any force. Now, start acting out that role as the new character. What is this new dream livelihood? Start acting as if you're already doing exactly that. Talk about it. Bring it to life in your daily experience. Activate your imagination as fully as you can around it.

Want an amazing man or woman in your life? Write out the story in vivid detail as if it's already here now. Start acting out the role being in a beautiful, amazing relationship. Talk about this person as if they are already here with you. Anchor their presence into your reality through your imagination. Play out the role of them already being part of your life. Do this without any lack-based belief or attachment. Have fun and play with it.

Remember, you are here as a human being to feel in the most vivid way possible. That's all that your Higher Self really cares about. When you are character acting you are feeling the dynamic array of emotions available to you just as a real actor does in a movie. When you can activate the feeling of what you desire as if it's already here it becomes apparent that you don't' actually need that new job, partner, or body in order to be happy and whole. You can play the character who is already fulfilled. Doing this diminishes the attachment to having that new thing which greatly optimizes the possibility of it showing up in your life in actual physical form.

When you are stuck in your old character all you can really do is project lack-based beliefs out into the world based on the endless feeling of not being good enough. If you don't know you're a character playing a role you're never going to feel like you're enough. Why? Because it's true! You're greatly limiting your human experience by attaching to solid, fixed points of view about who you are and why you're here. You're insistent upon maintaining the identity of that character. The truth is that you are a multi-dimensional being who is highly capable of creating yourself in a variety of dynamic and refreshing ways. When you tap into this power, you'll finally feel like you're enough as you'll taste the incredible depth and infinite possibility that lies at the core of who you really are.

Intentional Practice

At first, character acting may feel awkward, like you're not quite sure if you're getting the hang of it. The simplest way to see this is that you are practicing the new stories you are telling in your daily life. Just as any actor needs to practice their lines so they can truly master the role they are playing, you are now doing the same thing. You are writing out and telling new stories, then intentionally practicing your new role repeatedly. Don't expect to nail it right away. You can't screw it up and it's all meant to be fun. The practice is just as fruitful as the end point of mastery.

What you'll notice is that the more intentional you practice anything the faster your progress will be. In my life I have written a new story about how I relate to all forms of practice, whether it's practicing tennis, writing, or playing a new character. The typical cultural belief system is that developing any skill or changing anything substantial is a long, hard, slow process. I was never inspired by that story. One big area of purpose for me is testing out various ways of practicing speed in my life and annihilating commonly held beliefs around our potential for change and skill progression. The goal for me is to make my practice come alive. It doesn't feel rote or redundant. If you bring ultra-focus to your practice in this way, you can often make enormous strides in a fraction of the time it takes most people. Master coaches realize this. They train their students to master the art of practice. Whatever talents or skills you want to develop in your life, start telling a new story that you can do so in an accelerated fashion. Then bring a heightened quality of presence to your practice. Don't go on autopilot; make it come alive. On a bigger scale, practice character acting in the same way. See yourself as fluidly shifting into new roles in whatever way inspires you. Intentional, repeated practice helps you stabilize higher frequencies so that the new reality you create becomes you.

Redefining Performance

Take a moment to review the subtitle of this book. In particular, I want you to think about optimizing performance. What does this term now mean to you? As a character you are always performing. Your life is the stage. Everything you see around you is part of the set. Your friends, family, and colleagues are all other actors in your script. Optimizing performance means choosing the character you play and the script you write with great care. It means choosing to live out the most epic story that you possibly can.

Isn't this a more meaningful and expansive definition of performance than simply getting more done or achieving at a higher level? You can do that of course if you write it into your script. But now you know that optimizing performance means taking ownership of your role as the main character in an amazing story. Carefully craft your character. Perform like you mean it.

The 5th Instant Upgrade Tool
The Radical Reframe

A more extreme and cathartic form of storytelling, The Radical Reframe is specifically applicable to any and all challenges you face in your life. Whenever you tell a disempowering story about a challenge you are facing, you will solidify the patterning around that state of frequency, thereby guaranteeing that you'll continue to experience life events that challenge you in an undesired way.

I was recently working with a new client on Skype for the first time and, during our initial call I had her share her story of her current situation. She spent a good thirty minutes detailing the agonizing frustration of trying to build a chiropractic practice and feeling bombarded by stress, health problems, and continuous ups and downs. She had been on the verge of quitting a couple of times, but knew this was the work she wanted to do. While admirable, her persistence was causing her blood pressure to skyrocket. She had lost the ability to relax and constantly felt overwhelmed trying to keep up with the demands of her practice.

The most difficult aspect of her situation was that she could not find a way out. She gave it her best and was doing everything she could to manage her life, but no matter what she tried she always felt stuck in the same prison of financial instability, overwhelm, and stress. She tried meditation, prayer, and various relaxation techniques. She went to a variety of doctors and healers to figure out what was going on. No matter what she did she felt stuck in her situation.

Her life had turned into an ongoing challenge that was slowly killing her.

This is her story:

> *My practice is constantly stressful. I can't seem to get a grip on my life. My patients love what I do, but there are never enough of them*

to give me a financial cushion. I can't stop worrying about this. I feel overwhelmed and like I am doing this all alone. I really want to start a family, but I can't, given how unstable things are. I barely have any energy left to keep this all going.

Upon hearing where she was at, I could sense the urgency of helping her reverse this downward spiral. It was clear to me that she was locked in a low frequency of reality and had never been given the tools to shift out of it. It was time for an Instant Upgrade.

I gave her the homework assignment of ten minutes a day of empowered storytelling as a baseline for helping her shift into higher frequencies. Because she was inundated with challenges, I also gave her this tool, the Radical Reframe. I consider this to be a potent means of alchemy, where you transmute the most damaging and painful feelings or circumstances into their exact opposite. In the Vajrayana Buddhist tradition this is called turning poison into medicine.

The practice is very simple to execute. Here's what you're going to do: The next time you feel stuck in a certain challenge, you're going to stop whatever you are doing and use the Five Breath Process. Start by neutralizing any negative momentum you feel around the challenge at hand. As you take five breaths you're going to assess what your current story is that is causing you to struggle. Next, you're going to tell a new story that has the exact opposite point of view and corresponding feeling.

See if you can create an immediate shift in your frequency right in the face of the things that cause you the most difficulty. This tool is one of the most effective ways to reclaim power in your life and tap into higher frequencies. The premise that we are operating from is that all challenges we face are nothing more than:

- Opportunities to evolve and reclaim power.
- Catalysts that can immediately propel us into higher frequencies.

Every time you use The Radical Reframe, this is the philosophical backbone of the practice. Pain and discomfort are only showing up so you can reclaim power, learn about yourself, and go to a higher state of consciousness. This alone may be the only story you need to say to shift you out of struggle.

After using Empowered Storytelling and The Radical Reframe for less than 24 hours, my client emailed me letting me know that this was the best she had felt in years. She couldn't really understand it, but she didn't really care. A feeling of profound relief had washed over her that was deeply healing and restorative. Simply by reframing her situation in a way that served her, she was able to tap into a higher frequency where the emotion of relief was now accessible. She had struggled every day for years, groping for this feeling, but never able to access it. This alone will set the stage for a variety of outer changes to develop in her practice and life.
Let's take a look at another client I recently worked with who I will call John.

John is a corporate executive who has enjoyed a successful career. He has a beautiful wife and two kids. He has a great life by all accounts. Lots of nice material possessions, a big house, fancy cars, and expensive vacations. John's big challenge is that he has never managed his money very well and just got laid off from his job. The layoff came out of nowhere with very little notice.

Even though John has made six figures for years, he lives on the edge with money. He likes to spend more than he likes to save. John assumed it'd never be a problem as he expected to have his job until he could comfortably retire. Now John finds himself in one of the most difficult situations in his life. He has $15,000 of monthly expenses and just lost his only way to keep his family afloat. John has four months of savings and then there will be nothing.

When John came to me he was having panic attacks. His blood pressure had shot up and he couldn't sleep well. He felt like life whacked him upside the head. He couldn't stop worrying about his future. In a nutshell his story was as follows:

Oh my God. What have I done? How could I have been so irresponsible? How could my boss have done this to me after all I've done for that damn company? It's not fair. What am I supposed to do? I'm going to run out of money and my family is going to be on the street. I'm a terrible father and husband. How could I do this to my family? There are no jobs out there that will pay me what I make now. The best case scenario is we'll have to downgrade our lifestyle to a point that will really be awful for my family. I can't believe this.

Most people in John's situation would likely react in a similar fashion. They would rotate out various low frequency emotions such as guilt, shame, anger, and anxiety. They would panic. They would lose their composure.

The first step with John was helping him to gain an accurate perspective. I helped him see his situation as a story or an adventure he came here to experience as a human being. His Higher Self created this happening so John could learn how to reclaim power and shift into higher frequencies. Getting fired was the perfect development in John's plot as it gave him just enough juicy emotional content to work with to stay engaged with this life.

I helped him apply The Radical Reframe to the challenges he was up against. He created a new, empowered version of the story of getting fired:

How amazing is it that I created this exact situation to show me where I've been hiding and unconscious in my life. What a wakeup call! I now see that I've used money as a crutch to stay pretty numb and that I've become stuck in a routine that doesn't serve me. Losing my job is the perfect opportunity to get myself back. I am already becoming more conscious of my relationship with money. I see why I overspend and I'm really excited to clear this pattern.

I now realize my job had become a security blanket that made me feel half alive. I'm so grateful to feel excited again! I choose to see my anxiety as excitement in disguise. I know that I can trust myself and that

I can create an even better opportunity for my family. This experience will help me clarify what my real purpose is. I choose to see this as a blessing.

Can you see how John losing his job is an inherently neutral situation? The default mode would be to react with fear, aversion, and a lack of trust. That's the unconscious story that most people would form. Using The Radical Reframe however, John chose to impart a new, empowering meaning to his experience that carries the exact opposite frequency of the fear he would get locked into from focusing on the unconscious story. John can literally use an event that most people would label a crisis to reclaim tremendous power.

Amazingly, John is now quickly building a performance coaching business that centers around helping executives create higher levels of success and fulfillment in their work. After shifting his story he realized that he had the perfect built-in network to quickly start getting some new clients. Life never would have opened up in this way had he stayed stuck in the story of being a victim to getting fired.

You can use this tool with anything, from minor annoyances to the most earth-shattering, devastating events in your life. Stuck in traffic and feeling irritated? Is that how you desire to feel? If not, choose to paste a new meaning over that experience that carries the polar opposite frequency of irritability. When I'm stuck in traffic, I get excited! It gives me time to practice singing (another passion of mine). Yes, you'll often find me wailing at the top of my lungs when I'm stuck in rush hour traffic. People around me think I'm nuts I'm sure, but I find it crazy that most drivers choose to be unhappy just because their car isn't moving.

Write down one of your BIG challenges that you're facing right now. Then, write down the story you're telling that makes it feel challenging. Now, tell the opposite story. Observe how you feel.

Remember, with all of these tools, the whole point is to have fun and experiment. There is no right or wrong. If you find yourself saying,

'I must be doing this wrong' or anything of that nature, realize that it's just another story that is keeping you stuck in a low frequency of reality. It is impossible to do this wrong. You simply practice, observe, and then modify your practice based on what happens.

What to Do When Nothing Seems to Work

I'd like to explore the use of this tool a little bit deeper. Do you believe me when I tell you that this is your reality and you can choose however you want to feel? Do you sense the truth that you are creating this entire experience? You're creating this book in front of you right now. You're creating the challenges you're facing. You're creating the story you enact in relation to those challenges. It's all part of your unique experience and it's all being generated from within the sphere of your own consciousness. Nothing outside of you is happening 'to' you. You're not a victim in any way. There is no impostor in your mind who is forcing you to think and feel a certain way. It's all your own creation. When you practice a tool like The Radical Reframe, you'll likely notice significant shifts in your energetic and emotional state. This tool has the potential to quickly liberate you from years of suffering and limitation. When it 'works' it produces a palpable sense of relief and if immense power has been reclaimed, bliss.

But what happens when it doesn't seem to work? You tell a new story that is the opposite of the one causing you to struggle but you feel the same? When this happens it's helpful to step back and ask yourself, "Who is running the show here?" If this is all your creation then you have power over how you want to feel. When you tell a new story yet you still feel the same your innate power has not been activated. You're more or less going through the motions. In order to activate the transformational power of this tool you have to choose to feel the instantaneous shift in your energy and emotions. It's up to you to activate the desired feelings that reflect the most accurate, empowered, and inspired version of your new story.

This is your reality. You can feel however you want. Nobody is in control of that aside from yourself. If you try this tool and don't feel any different, the issue is that you haven't chosen to activate the feelings you're looking for. Do you want to feel different from using this tool? Then DO it! Don't buy into the story that some mysterious force outside of yourself is responsible for how you feel. In any given moment you can choose to feel however you want.

My goal in sharing these ideas with you is to do everything I can to ensure that you don't use this or any other tool as yet another way of feeling bad about yourself. Of course, I can't force you to want to change. If you don't have a genuine desire to experience new emotions and stories then literally nothing can help you. You're simply being stubborn and insistent that being closed down is the right way for you to live. If you've made it this far however, I know that you want to change. You desire new, fresh states of consciousness.
If you're struggling to 'own' your innate ability to create whatever stories and feelings you want, tell a new story about that. Write out the old story:

I struggle to implement these ideas into my life. I like everything Kevin is saying, but I just can't seem to figure out how to do this. I feel stuck. I don't understand why it's so hard for me to change. I try to change my story and I still feel the same. Now I really know that nothing will work for me. I'm a lost cause.

If this is your story, great! A lot of people share a similar version of this. You are simply playing a character who is insistent upon generating a reality where you can't change. Want to play a new character? Cool! Let's do it. It's that simple. Let's create a new story around this:

I am so grateful that I know without question that I am the author of my own existence. I can choose to feel however I desire. I can choose to impart any meaning to my reality that most excites me. I love how open I am to change. It's easy for me to shift out of disempowering stories, often in the blink of an eye. I LOVE knowing that I am an Infinite Being who can choose whatever frequency of reality I desire to dwell in. Life is good!

Let that new story sink in. Did it shift anything? Yes? Great! Onward and upward. No? Alright, let's get even more creative with it.

> *Isn't is vastly entertaining and humorous that nothing I do works? That everything I try lands me in the same place over and over? How amazing is it that I have the power to create myself as a character that can't change! How much power must I have by absorbing every single self-help tool under the sun only to still feel the same crummy way? Not many people could pull that off. I am thoroughly entertained by my stubbornness. I seriously think it's great. How entertaining it is to create myself not being able to change! I choose to deeply appreciate the unchangeable character I've created.*

The more stubborn you are to allowing in and creating transformation in this moment, the more creative you can be about the story you're telling and the character you're playing. There is always a way to shift up stagnant perceptions even if they have been there your entire life.

Use The Radical Reframe in any way you feel stuck. Keep stretching, bending, and shaping the story you're telling until you can tangibly feel a quality of lightness and relief wash over you.

When you activate the power of this tool it's an instantaneous shift into a lighter, more expansive frequency. Literally a lifetime of holding can dissipate in a moment. That's not to say the residue won't return; it likely will. That particular challenge or trauma will never have the same power over you though. You've broken free from the low frequency that the event triggered in your life. **You're free.**

The Radical Reframe is a super-charged tool because it more or less forces you to come right up against the edge of your comfort zone, excuses, and unwillingness to change in this very moment. Anytime you are suffering, it's 100% optional. As you apply this tool you'll come to see how you actually choose suffering over freedom so much of the time.

There is a presence within each of us that is violently opposed to change and will do whatever it takes to maintain the status quo. True transformation connotes the death of what's familiar. This presence wants to ensure our survival and our ability to stand on solid ground. It will fight to the bloody end to protect familiar ground and ward off uncertainty.

When you use The Radical Reframe and to a slightly lesser extent, all of the other tools, you are willingly inviting this wily little devil into your conscious awareness. You are coming face-to-face with your own insanity. After all, to ward off freedom and choose bondage **IS** insane! To act as if you're a victim and have no free will to think and feel and create reality as you desire is pure delusion.

Inviting the part of you that has zero interest in change into your conscious awareness is an incredibly powerful practice. The only way that this presence can exist is through unconsciousness. It lurks in the shadows of default living. When you shed light on your experience and choose to be intentional and awake this part of you has nowhere to hide. It evaporates when exposed to the light of awareness just as a vampire does to the light of the sun. It is a phantom that can only exist when we are asleep to life.

This can be yet another creative story to tell if you're feeling that nothing ever works for you:

> *I'm so grateful to expose the part of myself that actually does not want to change. I see that the only reason that nothing works is because I've been allowing this presence to linger within me year after year. I'm excited to shed light on this presence and evaporate it through simple awareness. When I'm aware, change is fun and highly desired. Because I'm the author of my experience I now see that I can transform simply because I want to. It is simple.*

Using The Radical Reframe to Clear Limiting Beliefs

From the time we are able to think we are indoctrinated with all kinds of beliefs about who we are, how life works, and what we need to do to stay safe and be successful. As our conceptual mind forms, we develop a primary lens that we see the world through that informs the character we invent ourselves to be. Our beliefs serve as reference points that give us a feeling of solidity and familiarity.

The subjective lens that we see reality through is primarily colored by a particular belief that tends to dominate our worldview. Many people spend their entire life unconscious since their life is being filtered by their own subjective viewpoint. When it comes to inventing yourself as a new character, part of the work/play involved entails shedding old, limiting beliefs so you can consciously choose which lens you want to see life through. Let's take a look at some of the most common limiting beliefs that tend to serve as the core source of our struggles:

- I am not enough.
- Life has no value/I don't matter.
- I am powerless/The power is out there.
- Life isn't fair.
- Love isn't safe.
- I can't trust life.
- I must give to the point of exhaustion in order to be a good person.
- Life is meaningless.
- Hard work is all that really matters.
- I have to fight for what I want.
- Success always comes at a sacrifice.
- Caring for myself is selfish.

Can you identify with any core beliefs on this list? My old character had a core belief that life is meaningless and I have no value. I created a frequency of reality that perfectly supported and validated that belief to be true.

Whichever one stands out for you, use The Radical Reframe to transmute that belief into its corresponding virtue. For instance, if you were indoctrinated with the belief that you're never good enough, it will likely be readily apparent how that belief has undermined your life on many levels. Through all different stages of life, you've been carrying around this heavy baggage of never feeling like you've arrived. You can never relax. There's always more to do. You'll never feel complete.

You can see how a whole story of life forms out of this one core belief. Now you're going to write out and continually focus on the exact opposite point of view. You're going to start acting as if you're already there, you're always whole and complete as you are, and that you can live your life from a place of fullness rather than lack. If the core belief of never feeling good enough has made you set unhealthy boundaries, constantly worry, over think things, overeat, and try to nourish yourself in misguided ways, you're going to act out the opposite behaviors. How would this new character eat, think, and set boundaries if it was good enough?

In this way, you can go right to the heart of the core wound of your old character and reclaim power from a belief that has kept you limited. When you are no longer enslaved by that belief you quite literally become a new person. You see life through a new, more conscious and empowering lens. You enter a higher frequency. You instantly upgrade your life.

If it feels hard to let go of your core beliefs use The Radical Reframe on that challenge:

> *I'm thrilled by how easy it is to instantly shift out of this belief and turn it on its head. I now see that this can happen in an instant and that it doesn't need to be hard in any way.*

By doing this, you are reclaiming your power from the belief that change is hard.

On an ultimate level, all of our beliefs are empty. It can be helpful to occasionally focus on this ultimate state where you renounce any and all belief systems and hang out in a state of pure, open awareness. This was the practice that I was fervently committed to in my early spiritual life. I was always trying to empty my mind and let go of attachment to any particular belief or subjective lens. I now see that it's more fun and helpful to consciously choose new beliefs and allow myself to play a character who is fueled by those new paradigms of reality.

As humans we are here to experience the dynamic range of feelings that existence has to offer. It's hard to do this if your entire focus is on being empty. That was my experience at least. As long as you are aware that any belief you choose is empty, you can pick and choose what serves you the best.

The Sixth Instant Upgrade Tool
The Breadcrumb Trail

Every single day you are being given cues by the universe as to where you should put your focus and how you should prioritize your life. The question is, are you paying attention to those cues? Because you've been conditioned by the low frequency tools of our modern culture, you're often led by misguided input as to what values you should base your life around.

Using The Breadcrumb Trail you are going to train your mind to get highly attuned to the signals you get that feel the most exciting, inspiring, and uplifting. When you are genuinely excited by something, this is not a random event that comes out of nowhere. This is your Higher Self letting you know that you're onto something meaningful. As a human being the feeling of excitement separates lower frequencies from higher ones perhaps more than any other state of mind. Your work is to follow your flickers of excitement, no matter how subtle, absurd, or mysterious they may be.

Many people in our modern world have lost their natural connection with the feeling of excitement. They go through life feeling a rather confined spectrum of emotions–not too high, not too low. The Breadcrumb Trail opens us up to a much more vivid and dynamic emotional experience. After all, we are here to feel not just to function.

How often do you feel genuinely excited about your life? My 'old' character was barely ever excited. Life felt too heavy and there was too much to worry about. I had a perfectly arranged arsenal of limiting beliefs that I could use at anytime to justify why being excited was not an appropriate or accessible state of mind. I also used to have a story that I couldn't trust life and therefore wouldn't allow myself to get very excited about the cues and signals that were placed before me.

Now I experience extremely fun swings of excitement every day. Even this morning I was excited to drive to Starbucks, grab an iced coffee, and set aside an hour to write this particular section. To be honest, nothing could excite me more. I feel blessed to have this time to do exactly this. I appreciate beyond measure the combination of writing and iced coffee. I can consciously generate whatever level of excitement I desire around what I'm doing.

As you go through your day, your job as a human being is to simultaneously generate states of excitement while also being attuned to the universal signals you're being given. You can start right now. In this moment, what excites you most? Go do that. The more you can base your life around your highest excitement, the more rapidly you'll be able to shift into higher frequencies of reality. Most people have a few blocks come up in relation to doing this:

- I have no clue what I'm excited about.
- I would do that, but I have too much else to do.
- I will be unsafe if I do this. It's irresponsible.

Let's focus on each of these so we can get you to a place where you have no excuses left in terms of why you can't start following your excitement right now.

If you're at a loss as to what excites you in life, all that's happening is that you're telling a story that blocks you from tapping into your natural connection with and passion for living. So, my first tip for you is to start telling a new story that would go something like this:

> *I love inventing myself as someone who radiates enthusiasm about my life. Excitement is my natural state. It's fun for me to generate all kinds of passion, even about little things like what I'm having for lunch. Every day, I see all kinds of opportunities to follow my bliss. I am getting more attuned to the universal signals that help me navigate through life. I am fearless about following my excitement.*

You are capable of experiencing excitement just as much as you are depression, numbness, or anxiety. It's simply a matter of heightening your focus and shifting frequencies where new emotional states can be accessed. Your sense of self is fluid, not static. Even if you've lived your entire life feeling unexcited that can literally change in an instant. Tell a new story. Start playing a new role. Assume the character. How would you act if you were excited? Start talking like that. Start walking like that. Hold the space of being an engaging, passionate human being. If it feels made up, no problem! The unexcited version of you is equally made up even if you've been doing it for fifty years!

The more you can generate unconditional excitement for your life as it is right now, the more rapidly things will change. Even if your current circumstances appear to be antithetical to high frequency states like passion and enthusiasm, you can still choose to generate the emotional state that most accurately reflects how you wish to be in the world. It all depends on where your focus is. As you know, most of us convince ourselves that our focus must be locked into one particular narrow dimension, as it appears to be the most rational and appropriate response to what we see happening around us. We largely base our emotional state around what we did yesterday. Whatever our most recent feeling state was, we'll basically continue to do more of that. The only way we typically snap out of that one dimensional feeling state is if life whacks us upside the head with a pattern interrupt. Something happens that forces us to feel in a new way, whether positive or negative.

When we wait for life to show us why we should change our frequency, we are being victims. We are basing our feelings around our circumstances. We are stuck in reactive mode. This is the trap that many of us fall into:

- I'll feel better when I finally get a girlfriend.
- If only I could lose this weight, then my confidence would increase.
- If my boss would only validate my performance, then I'd feel worthy.
- I wish my business would get more clients, then I'd feel safe.

Get excited for the fact that you can feel better now, you can increase your confidence now, you can feel worthy now, you can feel safe now. Nothing whatsoever needs to change outside of you in this moment to generate these feelings. Even more so, nothing outside of you is ever responsible for how you are feeling. Isn't that exciting? Can you appreciate that?

As we discussed in our first Instant Upgrade Tool, there is a higher dimension to who you are that is really running the show of your life. Your job as a human being is to merge as closely as possible with this higher intelligence so you can see your life as it does. This part of you views existence as an infinitely open, playful, miraculous expression of divine energy. When you allow yourself to feel excited, you are generating feeling states that come as close as possible to how your Higher Self sees life. You always have a choice–do you want to pretend you're this limited human character who has a bland, mundane existence? Or do you want to lean in closer to this mysterious, mind-blowing, infinitely powerful presence that is the Ultimate You? As a human, you're always going to be playing a character. You get to decide if that character is excited or bored, engaged or checked out, passionate or numb.

The more you choose higher frequency states such as excitement, the more intimate you are becoming with the Ultimate You. You are starting to see existence itself for the wide open miracle that it is. You are no longer imposing the limiting viewpoints of your old character on the enormity of reality. As such, you can structure and engineer your life in a way that aligns with the impulses of this Higher Intelligence. The more you do this, the more fun you have. You'll start to see abundance in everything. It becomes apparent that going out and getting a cup of coffee can indeed be a thrilling, miraculous experience.

As Einstein said, "There are only two ways to live your life. One is as though nothing is a miracle. The other is as though everything is a miracle."

Which do you choose? One connotes staying locked in a lower frequency, one connotes dynamically shifting into higher frequencies. Many people in our modern world have grown cynical about what Einstein is suggesting in this quote. They believe that if people choose to see life as a miracle, they are just being delusional and living in a fantasy world. What they don't realize is that they are being just as delusional in their cynicism. Their insistent point of view is keeping them locked in a low frequency and preventing them from accessing the most life-affirming and wonderful emotional states that they have full access to as a human being. When people genuinely see life as a miracle, they are simply dwelling in a higher frequency of consciousness. They are more aligned with their Ultimate Self.

Keep in mind that from the point of view of the Ultimate You, if you choose to be stubborn or cynical about following your excitement, you are perfectly supported in doing that. There is nothing 'wrong' with that choice; it's simply a low frequency. Either way, it is still a way of seeing reality that is highly entertaining to the Ultimate You. Being locked in struggle and pretending like you're a limited being offers enormous entertainment value to the part of you that is infinite. What a fun game it is to be infinite in nature, yet be so convinced of limitation. Humans are masterful at pulling off this farce.

If you'd like to break free, simply start generating and following your excitement. Pay attention to what lifts you up the most and start boldly moving in that direction. Choose to make this your top priority in life. Even if there's a lot of clutter in your current circumstances, you can still bring your focus to what excites you. You can generate new feeling states regardless of your outer world. Start to tell a story about how much openness and free time you have to dedicate to your passions. Put your focus there as much as possible.

Will you be unsafe if you follow your excitement? Many people feel that it's irresponsible or self-indulgent to acknowledge their passion as it will take them away from their daily responsibilities. You likely know what I'm going to say to this: It's time for a Radical Reframe:

> *I now see that NOT following my excitement is irresponsible, that I am here as a human being for the exact purpose of following my bliss, and that I'll be of much greater service to my family, friends, and the world at large by staying plugged into my Ultimate Self, and seeing life as it does. Following my excitement is the purest form of safety.*

When you're following the low frequency rules of our modern culture, are you ever really safe? Can you see that it's a big lie? Are you willing to test this?

This doesn't mean that you have to quit your job and leap into uncertainty today. Start by taking small steps. What can you do right now to follow any exciting impulse within you? Does it mean taking up a new hobby? Writing a book? Making new friends? Joining an online dating site? If it feels supportive to you, make a High Excitement List where you write down in detail all of the things that would thrill you–big and small. Start implementing the small things and choose to create a reality where the small things naturally propel you into higher frequencies, which then makes the big things way easier and more accessible. All change can be easy and fluid.

If you feel stuck in a mediocre job that makes you feel bored and dead, inundate your life outside of your work with inspiring activities. Surround that job with as much excitement as you can. Write out the story of how easy it has been to shift into a much more meaningful career, and it all started with taking the baby steps of following your excitement in your hobbies and extracurricular activities. Become ultra-focused on that new story all of the time.

Whatever excuse comes to mind as to why you are not able to generate or follow your excitement, do you now see that it's an illusion? That you created all of this? That you're playing a fun game of pretending like you're blocked and that your situation is actually wide open? That everything is workable?

I'd like to share a couple of vivid examples from my life that perfectly showcase the power of following The Breadcrumb Trail.

Writing this Book

After I finished my last book The Purpose Principle, I had no interest in pursuing another book project. Many years went by and it was the farthest thing from my mind. I was convinced that I'd never put another book out into the world as I knew the daunting nature of the task at hand and opted for easier ways to get my message out.

One day I was hanging out with my son in San Diego, driving down one of the congested California freeways, and was spontaneously overtaken by the vision for this book. It seemed to come out of nowhere and it was intense. In a flash I saw the entire outline, the core premise, the ideal reader whom it could help, and how to structure it into my business.

My first thought was, uh oh.

Like I said, I had been resistant to writing another book, but this impulse was so clear and powerful that it felt like it was choiceless. I had to write this book. Once I let go of the story that writing a book is hard the excitement for this project welled up inside of me and overtook me. I couldn't wait to get started. To be honest I actually tried to put it off for another few days while I was in San Diego, but I couldn't stop thinking about it. I followed The Breadcrumb Trail and surrendered to the process of bringing this book out to the world.

Hopefully, it is evident to you as you're reading along, but there has been almost no resistance to the writing process. I've been ultra-focused on my excitement above all else and the words have just poured out onto the page. I've been shocked by how easy the process has been.

Making My First Music Album

Ever since I was a little kid, I had a quiet dream of being a singer in a rock 'n' roll band. I've also been deeply passionate about music. Since I was a teenager I've enjoyed the thrill of envisioning myself on stage singing with thousands of fans clapping along and loving the music. Playing the character of being a singer has always excited me, but I kept that dream locked up inside of me believing that it was silly and ridiculous.

On a recent trip to Portland, Oregon I was hanging out with my brother who happens to be an amazing guitarist. We were jamming in his basement with me hacking away on the drums, doing my best to accompany his riffs. Colin said something along the lines of, "I wish we had a vocalist" and before I knew it I found myself saying, "Oh I'm pretty sure I can sing. Let's mess around and see what happens." I think that the couple beers I had gave me some liquid confidence that normally would not have slipped out. So, we took the riff that Colin created and I played around with writing some lyrics and experimenting with different melodies. Within a matter of minutes I hopped on the microphone, had him play the riff, and sang my vocals. Boom. We looked at each other and knew we were onto something. In one take we nailed our first song. We were shocked by how easily it came together. Colin laid some drum tracks over it and we were blown away by how cool it sounded. So we decided to do a few more songs. Within a couple of months we had our first album of eight tracks. I must say, it's been one of the most fun things I've done. I am still shocked that we were able to do this with such little effort. Yes, there has been a lot of work that has gone into getting our CD out there but overall, it has flowed without any strain or force. Awesome. (FYI, you can pick up a copy of the CD at www.ubiquitystrain.com).

Making the CD has been enormously entertaining and fun. It would also be fun to sell lots of albums and build a cult following around the world. I'm writing a story of that happening. Who knows if that will unfold in physical reality. I don't really care. I'm just having fun and following my excitement. Wherever it goes, that's what's meant to happen.

This experience clearly taught me a couple things:

Any excitement that we have as human beings is not randomly put there. It is a signal from the universe that there is potential to create something meaningful, fun, and helpful. When you're excited about something, there's energy in that for you and you are being nudged to explore it. You likely have a talent or natural potential that would benefit you to develop it.

We are multi-dimensional beings capable of creating a diverse array of things. I now see that we need not be limited to one passion in life. If you ever find yourself feeling confined by having to only focus on one thing, my life is evidence that it's simply a limiting belief that you are buying into. My work as a coach enables me to engage with a pretty multi-dimensional skill set. On top of that, there's no reason I can't do anything else that feels exciting–writing books, playing tennis, making music, you name it. You don't need to limit yourself in any way. Create a story that supports you in exploring your multi-dimensional nature and enjoy the process of expressing and offering your many talents and passions to the world.

The Seventh Instant Upgrade Tool
Appreciation Amplification

I'm sure you already know how helpful it is to express appreciation for your life. Most self-help books go on and on about the amazing benefits of gratitude. Yes, I do think it can be tremendously helpful to write down all the things you are grateful for in your life and to focus on appreciating all of the small details of your daily experience.

If you feel inspired to keep a gratitude journal by all means do it. If you want to tell yourself three things you appreciated about the day before you fall asleep, fire away. There is a ton of scientific and anecdotal evidence that validates the benefits of gratitude.

I'm going to talk about appreciation and gratitude in a new way. This conversation is going to be a little more subtle, but has the potential to activate the most profound benefits that these qualities can offer you. You see before I knew about these tools I tried to focus on gratitude. I really did. And you know what? It felt totally fake most of the time. There was no power behind it. I was forcing myself to see the good in life, but I didn't really feel it.

In my coaching work I see this on a regular basis. Clients come to me and say they are trying to focus on gratitude. They are doing what all of the books recommend but it's only making them feel worse. Why? Because they don't really appreciate their actual circumstances. They can't muster up gratitude for feeling depressed, being in debt, in a struggling business, or being stuck in overwhelm. It feels forced and contrived. They are basically faking it but not making it. Nothing is really shifting and in fact, they are only feeling like more of a failure as gratitude practice becomes yet another prop that convinces them that nothing works.

If you're honest with yourself, you've likely come up against this as well. I used to get really frustrated hearing all of these incredible testimonials on the power of gratitude and how it led to miracles in so many lives. Why couldn't this happen for me? Ugh. All it did was make me feel worse.

Some people do benefit greatly from conventional gratitude practices which is great. If that's you, keep doing it. Most that I have worked with however, haven't been able to tap into the real power that gratitude practice has to offer. Let me explain why:

If you don't know you're a character playing a role that's entirely your own creation, you can't unlock the true power of gratitude.

What most people do is try to use gratitude to fix, change, or improve their life from the perspective of being a fixed, solid self. They don't know they are playing a character. They assume that they can use a tool like gratitude practice to feel better, but all that happens is the practice becomes yet another reinforcement of lack and not being enough. Because they don't know that their sense of self is wide open, they don't shift into a higher frequency that would support doing gratitude practices. They expect the practice to do that for them. In essence, it's no different than trying to change your diet to feel better, or trying to meditate to calm your mind, or going to therapy to heal your past.

If you don't know you're playing a character you're going to be locked in a certain frequency of reality. Within that frequency nothing can really help you. Everything you're using to improve your situation is merely a prop that upholds the density and reality of that particular frequency.

What could be more frustrating than trying your best to feel gratitude, only to have it mirror back time and again your inability to truly and deeply change? Honestly, this is the norm. When people are unaware that they are simply playing out a character in a holographic universe, they will be locked into the confines of that character's energetic frequency. Nothing can change. Nothing outside of you can work.
With that said, here's how you're going to amplify appreciation in your life and unlock the incredible power that this tool has to offer:

Focus on appreciating the fact that you are a character playing a role in a dynamic, wide open story.

You can experience genuine appreciation in this way, regardless of what is happening in your life. You don't have to try and force yourself to appreciate the unwanted circumstances that you're currently up against. You don't have to manufacture positive thoughts about how great your life is. Simply appreciate the fact that who you are is infinitely open, dynamic, and adaptable. Appreciate the immense openness that this truth brings to your life. You are surrounded by infinite space and potential. You can morph into new characters at will. You can invent yourself anew every single day. Can you appreciate that? Can you appreciate how nothing needs to change right now in order to appreciate that?

Recognizing the power you have to play new roles creates genuine, unconditional appreciation. Anytime you're up against an unwanted circumstance, instead of trying to force yourself to feel good about it, simply step back and realize that you can tell a new story about it and play a new character in relation to it. You can completely shift out of the old character's contracted way of seeing that situation. Isn't that incredible? Nothing deserves appreciation more than that.

When you wake up in the morning, focus on the appreciation you have that the day you're about to live is in no way set in stone. It's empty, open, and free. You can choose to perceive anything that happens to you however you desire. You have free will to act out the character you wish to be.

Can you feel appreciation welling up within yourself right now? I mean, it truly is amazing that we humans have this kind of power. Let it in. Savor the experience of being able to shift into a new role with ease. Enjoy the fluidity of your life. Allow yourself to feel deeply enriched by how much creative power you can impose on your reality. This is the basis of genuine appreciation.

As you begin to see the truth of your situation as a human being, that you are playing a character in an epic story, and you're beginning to appreciate the infinite freedom built into this truth, you'll now be able to feel gratitude for whatever shows up in your life. Why? Because it's all fake. You are creating all of it. It's all part of your unique script. As a fluid character, you can invent yourself feeling immense appreciation in relation to anything–paying bills, dealing with debts, confronting a difficult marriage, dealing with an illness, being overweight. The appreciation stems from seeing the emptiness that permeates all of your thoughts, feelings, and circumstances. In this sense, you're not appreciating the bill you're paying as if it's a real, solid thing outside of you; you're appreciating the emptiness of the bill, the fact that it's made up, a prop in your story.

Do you see the difference? And the radical implications of amplifying appreciation in this way?

What if you don't have enough money in your bank account to pay that bill? From the perspective of the solid, stuck character who doesn't see the emptiness behind it all, the best you could do is try and manufacture a positive thought or feeling about this situation. You'd try to tell yourself all kinds of affirmations to get through it and feel a little better. Most likely, it would feel forced and it would lack power.

From a higher frequency however, you see that you are simply playing a character who is living out a story of not having enough money to pay a bill. The bank account isn't real. The lack of money isn't real. The bill isn't real. You're not real. It's all made up. It's simply a story. Knowing this, you have infinite power to relate to this situation however you want. If you want to feel anxious and bad about it, awesome! If you want to spin your wheels and spend all day trying to strategize about how to fix it, go for it! If you'd rather drop all that and instead tell a completely new story and act out a new role, by all means do it! You have the power to do whatever you want with that situation, and that is exactly why you can amplify appreciation around it.

As you amplify appreciation you can choose to feel amazing about not having enough money to pay that bill. You can see that it's simply a story you've written and that you can start writing a new one by neutralizing the momentum of the old story and choosing a new character to play. From a higher frequency perspective, you can treat that unwanted circumstance with as much fun and playfulness as you would anything else.

Does this sound crazy to you? Impossible? Delusional?

I get it. When you're stuck in lower frequencies where you believe that who you are is real and solid none of this seems possible and it likely sounds a bit ludicrous. From a higher frequency point of view, please know that being stuck in suffering around not having enough money and believing that you're a one dimensional person who has limited options is also considered to be insane. Believing that it's all real and that you don't have choices is the purest form of delusion. Buying into your limitations is the highest form of self-deception.

How do you feel as you are reading this right now? If these words are hitting home for you, you'll likely notice a feeling of profound relief. You may also feel a bit disoriented if this is the first time you've been exposed to this way of seeing your life. Pay attention to what's coming up for you. If you're feeling defensive or contracted around what I'm sharing, what story are you currently holding onto that makes you feel that way? Is that story working for you? Are you choosing to be right rather than to be free? As you're reading, allow the impact of what I'm saying to go beyond your conceptual mind. Let it impact you on a heart level. Be open to testing out what I'm saying in your direct experience.

You're already free. You're already enough. You're already everything that you need to be. There's nothing to fix, change, or improve. Nothing outside of you will make you happier. You can access your innate freedom by choosing to see that your sense of self is not solid. You can choose to feel tremendous appreciation that as a human being you have the free will and power to recognize your innate freedom. You are free to invent yourself in any new way that feels inspiring to you. You can relate to any circumstance of your life from the point of view of that new, inspired character. You can choose to fall in love with your ability to do this.

Do you feel it? The relief that this brings? The openness and appreciation that it sparks within you? Do you see how you can extend this foundational appreciation to literally anything in your life? Do you see that you can choose to dwell in causeless happiness?

Are you blocked anywhere in owning this truth? Can you choose to shift into a new story where integrating this kind of appreciation into your life becomes a fun practice rather than something that is confusing or that requires a ton of analysis?

Amplifying Appreciation Through Surrender

As you become more anchored in this foundational form of appreciation, you'll likely notice that it naturally extends to all areas of your life. From a higher frequency everything that shows up in your daily life is welcomed and accepted. Why? Because on an ultimate level you put it there. Whatever shows up is part of your script and is relevant to the theme you're meant to explore. Because of that you can trust it–even if it's not something you'd prefer.

Whatever you've experienced in your life up to this point, every single detail has been strategically designed to help you live out the most epic story possible. There hasn't been one thing that has happened to you that has been inherently unsafe, problematic, or stressful. All life events are completely neutral. What has caused you to feel unsafe or stuck in problems is the story you are telling. Most people can't separate life events from stories. They don't know they are telling a story and playing a made up role in relation to those events. They think their circumstances are the cause of their problems. They are banging their head against the wall of their very existence. Because of this, most people feel that they can't trust the universe. They can't relax into whatever shows up because it seems to be randomly generated, unstable, and unsafe. They can't surrender.

If you can't surrender to what is, you can't appreciate your life.

I'd like to invite you to join me in an experiential exercise. From a low frequency point of view, this would likely be labeled as highly challenging and difficult. From a high frequency point of view, allowing yourself to 'go there' will help you reclaim power in your life in the most cathartic and accelerated way possible.

I want you to write down the worst thing that has ever happened to you in your life. Was it the loss of a loved one? A betrayal of intimacy? A violation of your boundaries? A crippling illness? Losing a job? Going bankrupt? Witnessing a violent act? Being neglected by your parents? Being ridiculed and ashamed?

Now assess the degree to which you've surrendered to this experience. Have you accepted it? Forgiven it? Does it still haunt you? Are you still holding onto it? How much is it impacting your current life? How much of the residue continues to undermine your happiness?

What story are you telling yourself about that experience? Is that story actually true?

To the extent that this life event is causing you to suffer and not trust life, you are telling an inaccurate story of what happened. Can you see that?

How would it be for you to shift into a new character around that event? To impart a meaning to it that would allow you to be liberated and reclaim your power from it? Write down the new story you want to tell.

Hang in there with me, we are going to go deeper.

Now can you feel a basic quality of appreciation well up within you that you have the ability to shift your story and relate to that event in a completely new, more empowering way? Can you feel the relief this brings?

If this is as far as you want to go right now, you've done great. Let's keep digging though.

From this foundation of amplified appreciation can you extend a feeling of gratitude to that event?

Keep in mind for now, I am not talking about feeling appreciative for the solid feelings of trauma that occurred in relation to that event. I am asking you if you can feel appreciation for the underlying emptiness of that event, the fact that it was an illusion, a storyline in your movie, empty and devoid of inherent meaning.

Now if you're still with me you can explore extending appreciation to the actual trauma you experienced. How could this be possible? Because even the trauma is made up. It's simply part of your story. You have the power to shift into a higher frequency of reality where that trauma no longer exists. From that higher frequency the event never happened, at least not in the way you think it did from a lower frequency point of view.

This is the beautiful thing about exploring new frequencies. As you enter higher ones the previous reality you were in no longer exists. And I don't mean that as some nice, metaphysical thought to make you feel more comfortable. It's actually true. From the higher frequency, whatever you experienced as the old character in a lower frequency never actually happened. That field has collapsed and is nowhere to be found. As you enter new frequencies you are literally a new being with a new reality.

Can you appreciate that?

Using the Instant Upgrade Tools you'll come to see that your past never happened as you thought it did. The future also doesn't exist. Linear time is a massive illusion. Instead of healing or letting go of your past it's more accurate to say that you are collapsing patterns in a field of potential realities. When you collapse old patterns they no longer exist. It never happened. There is no past. There is only now.

Can you appreciate that the past doesn't actually exist? That whatever happened to you can collapse into non-existence? That you can invent yourself anew and completely shed the residue of previous traumas by entering new frequencies of reality?

Hopefully you are starting to get a clear picture of what genuine appreciation looks like. The more accurately you see the Truth of your situation the more you'll naturally appreciate everything that has and will ever happen to you. You'll be able to trust whatever shows up, intuitively knowing that it's always there to help you learn and to support you in reclaiming your power.

If you get fired from your job, if your business has a downturn, if your partner leaves you–whatever shows up–it's only there to help you live out your epic story and make contact with your infinite nature. When you are telling new stories you are using your creative faculties to connect with your power source. In this sense there's nothing 'out there' that could possibly hurt you or threaten your safety. When you tell an accurate, empowered story, it's all workable.

Can you appreciate that?

The Eighth Instant Upgrade Tool
Circumplanting

Have you noticed that you tend to base your feelings around your circumstances? Whatever is happening 'out there' determines how you feel about yourself and your life. If your circumstances are not going well you feel bad. If they are, you feel better. If you run a business and are getting more clients, you feel relief. If your client base decreases, you feel stress. If someone tells you that you look attractive you feel positive about yourself. If they tell you that you look ugly your self-esteem suffers. If your boss gives you a promotion you feel excited. If you get fired, you feel afraid.

When we buy into the collective cultural belief that our circumstances should determine how we feel, we are locking ourselves into low states of frequency. We will continue to cycle through the same quality of reality, never able to escape the patterning that makes us feel limited, lost, stressed out, or lacking abundance.

Let's not underestimate the gravity of this dynamic and the profound impact it has on us. Many people spend their entire life stuck in a reactive cycle of basing their sense of self-worth, daily thoughts and feelings, and behaviors around what shows up in their outer world. When we are stuck in this cycle of reactivity, daily life feels random, chaotic, and usually either subtly or incredibly frustrating. We can never seem to crack the code on what it really takes to improve our situation. What we don't realize is that the code we are looking for is always staring us in the face.

As you've learned throughout this book, the key is to be enough of a renegade in your life to boldly proclaim how you want to feel regardless of your circumstances. You now know that you can choose causeless happiness by simply tuning into a new frequency of reality where there is abundance, connection, peace, and creative insight. Not only can you enter a higher portal of reality anytime, but there is no limit to how high your frequency can go. It truly is infinite.

If we are locked into our circumstances, we are blocked from higher frequencies. We will continue to react to what we see happening to us, thereby endlessly creating more of the same. Life will have its way with us. We will feel powerless.

Not only does our power get stripped from us when we get locked into circumstances, it also drains from our being when we are attached to our past. Many of us buy into the belief that because we've been a certain way for so long, we either can't change at all, or it's going to be extremely difficult. Being attached to this belief is a surefire way to lock yourself into the same low frequency over and over.

What's amazing about using this Instant Upgrade Tool–Circumplanting–is that you come to realize that you literally can shift into higher states in an instant, regardless of how long you've been a certain way. It all depends on your desire and how willing you are to explore. If you've been a certain way for most of your life that is not working for you, yet you're open to wearing new hats and experimenting with new ways of creating yourself, then you can absolutely upgrade in a moment. If you're insistent on the belief that you can't change and that's just the way it is, all that you are doing is repelling any form of assistance and denying the very power that makes you an infinitely unique, amazing being.

If you'd rather be right than be free then by all means keep doing that. It's a perfectly valid way to exist. Many people unconsciously prefer to keep beating their head against their circumstances, endlessly waiting for life to change, or resigning themselves to this being all there is. As I mentioned in the introduction of this book, I used to be as stubborn as a mule. I had every excuse in the book why I couldn't choose to feel good about my life. From a higher frequency point of view, I now see how insane it was to deny myself the joy and freedom that comes from simply choosing my feeling state in an unconditional way. I'm sure you've heard the definition of insanity as doing the same thing over and over again and expecting a different result. That is what we are all doing when we base our feelings around our circumstances. I would define insanity as 'staying in the same low frequency repeatedly without being willing to change it'.

Circumplanting is the tool we use to stop the waiting game. Waiting for things to change or to feel better is a painful state to be in. Have you noticed? With this tool we are going to strip away the power that our circumstances have over us. Think of this tool as a formal declaration to take your power back anytime you notice that you are giving it away to your circumstances. Every time you find yourself locked into a circumstance you're going to consciously choose the feeling state you'd prefer to be in for that moment.

You can see the relevance of Ultra Focus for this tool. In order to activate the power of Circumplanting you have to be aware of how you're relating to things. You can't be asleep at the wheel. This is why it's important to train yourself to become ultra-focused. Make your life a fun game where you stay constantly aware of your thoughts and feelings along with your tendency to latch onto your circumstances as the basis of how you should feel. Choose to make this a top priority in your life, something you're deeply passionate about.

The reason this tool is called Circumplanting is that every time you cut through the cycle of habitually reacting to what's happening outside of you, a new seed is planted that inevitably germinates into circumstances that reflect higher frequency states. You come to see that you have a natural power to generate high frequency circumstances just as you generate high frequency feeling states. When you consciously choose a new feeling in spite of whatever circumstance you're facing, you are planting a new quality of potential circumstances into your field of reality. When you feel contracted and stressed you plant seeds for the same quality of circumstances. If you keep reacting to these new circumstances with the same input of contraction and stress the cycle repeats itself and will never change. That is, until you plant a new feeling state that collapses the pattern.

This may be one of the empowered stories that you'd find helpful to write into your life:

I now see that I have the power to feel however I want regardless of what is happening outside of me. I no longer base who I am around my circumstances. I proactively create who I want to be, and I allow life to mirror back to me this proactive, purposeful way of living. I now know that my circumstances are only ever reflecting my chosen frequency. I can accelerate the creation of joyful, abundant, and fun circumstances anytime I want. I do this by consciously choosing how I desire to feel and activating my power to paste any meaning that is most helpful over what's currently happening. I can always tell a story about any circumstance that allows me to feel empowered, clear, and confident. Nothing outside of me can take my power. It is easy for me to detach from my circumstances and take ownership of my life.

Take this statement in for a moment and really let it impact you:

Your circumstances are always nothing more than a mirror for your current level of consciousness. If you want to fundamentally change your circumstances, the only way to do this is to elevate your consciousness.

In a sense, you could say that your circumstances have no energy or life in them. They are only mirrors, apparitions of the phenomenal world. What's happening around you in this moment is purely the result of the frequency of consciousness you've been dwelling in. This is why trying to change, fix, improve, or understand the external world is usually a recipe for disappointment and ongoing struggle. It's like trying to put makeup on the reflection you see looking back at you in the mirror in order to look better.

When you shift frequencies, things around you don't necessarily appear any different. Amazingly, you can enter entirely new portals of reality, yet things on the outside appear to be the same. Everything around you bears a resemblance to how it did in lower frequencies, but in fact you are now in an entirely different universe. The reality you see outside of you is not static. When you shift into a higher frequency, what you see outside of you instantly shifts as well, even though it appears the same. You still see the same desk, car, or person. There is however a marked difference in your relationship to what you see and because of that, whatever object you see is actually, in reality, a completely new thing.

There are endless realities within the reality you see. You access new realities by shifting frequencies. When you do this, outer appearances can carry the same resemblance, but they are in fact part of your new reality. They have a different energetic configuration and vibrational pattern.

So in this sense, your circumstances actually do change instantly every time you shift into a higher frequency. What you see around you is literally no longer the same stuff. You literally have a new husband or wife, computer, or dog within your new frequency even though they appear to be the same. As you anchor in new patterning and collapse old fields the changes occurring in your circumstances will become increasingly noticeable.

Let's stop for just a moment. I know that I'm guiding you into some pretty heady stuff here. Take a breath. If your mind feels a little wobbly, get yourself centered again. Learning how the quantum world operates can be disorienting. After all, the notion that we can slip into new realities at will rightfully comes as a surprise to say the least, when you've been repeatedly taught that the world is a one-dimensional, physically based reality with clear laws of cause and effect and linear time.

As you become more skilled at detaching from circumstances and fluidly shifting into new frequencies you'll likely find this to be highly entertaining and fun. That has been my experience. It can still be disorienting for me at times when I really consider the enormity of what I'm laying out here, but mostly it just makes life a million times more interesting. I for one, got really bored in my old character, pretending I was bound to the limiting laws of the physical world and that my power was locked up in my circumstances. That became a total yawn fest and actually caused me to lose almost all interest in being human. Now I see that the most fun we can have as human beings is to see how far we can go on the path of reclaiming our infinite power while still having a human body. Isn't it something to know that you're an unbounded spirit with limitless power who can slip in and out of various frequencies at will and create new realities as you please? To my bias, that is a heck of a lot more interesting than pretending that I am a limited human who is stuck in a cut and dry material plane of existence with very few options.

Start playing with this tool. Consciously plant new circumstances. Tell the universe how this is all going to go down and start living accordingly regardless of what's showing up outside of you in this moment. You can start planting new circumstances even if your current ones have kept you stuck for years spiraling in the wrong direction, attracting all kinds of unwanted things to yourself. Your past literally does not matter. Once again, this tool is about drawing a line in the sand and fundamentally reversing the reactive cycle of basing your identity around your circumstances. You can start by formally declaring for yourself that you are ready to reverse this cycle. Proclaim this to yourself every day.

If you've watched Spider Man 3, there is a scene toward the end where Spider Man is hitting the poles to create a vibration that pulls the monster (Venom) away from the person (Eddie). As the poles vibrate louder, Venom is violently pried out of Eddie's body. This may be a slightly more dramatic depiction than what actually occurs in our lives, but I've always found this scene to accurately capture the process of becoming unglued from our circumstances. We must be willing to vibrate at a higher frequency as a way of detaching from the incessant reactive cycle of basing our entire life around what's going on 'out there.'

It will likely be helpful to continually remind yourself that the outer world is only ever a mirror for your inner state. Life is waiting for you to tell it what to do. The universe is reflecting back to you the signals you're putting out to it and always validating the story you are telling it with the perfect circumstances that match that chosen story. It's never random and it's always 100% accurate.

If you are telling the universe that you feel terrible about a current dilemma you're facing, all that the universe can do is respond with 'if you say so', and give you more of the same. When you use Circumplanting, you are ensuring that the universal mirror of your life circumstances is deliberately created instead of randomly generated. You know that you can plant new seeds anytime you desire (I recommend doing so many times a day), and that those seeds will inevitably develop into the outer reality that reflects your greatest excitement.

If it sounds or feels hard to detach from your circumstances, tell a new story. It's not hard. Just be willing to experiment. What's hard is being glued to your circumstances and basing your self-worth on external factors. What's hard is staying locked in lower frequencies. What's hard is carrying around the baggage of resisting change and surrendering to your natural state. Changing all of this is great fun. At least that has been my experience and that of many of my clients who have been actively working with The Instant Upgrade Tools.

How to Understand and Benefit from Unwanted Circumstances

As you upgrade into higher frequencies you'll notice that as you stabilize higher quality feeling states, your circumstances begin to reflect this back to you in increasingly vivid and obvious ways. For a period of time it can feel as if your life is on cruise control, as you're feeling more in the flow and enjoying the ride of intentionally designing your life.

Now we get to one of the most important points of the book. As you access higher frequencies this does not mean in any way that all of your circumstances will be 'positive' or desired. You will still generate situations in your life that your conscious mind labels as unwanted. For instance, all of your focus could be on how amazing a new job will be. You tell a story of that ideal job falling into your lap and how easy it was to transition out of your current job. To your surprise you end up not getting that job. Even more so, your current boss offers you a raise. You are creating a set of circumstances that appears to be contrary to what you've been focusing on.

How do you make sense of this? To be honest, when this happens many people give up on themselves. They start telling a story that goes like this:

> *I guess all of this stuff about shifting into new frequencies is fake or simply does not work for me. I did what I was told to the best of my ability and ended up with a situation that is pretty much the opposite of what I wanted.*

This is actually a story I used to tell myself. I'd put a little work into shifting my focus but when I didn't get what I wanted or I got the opposite of what I wanted, I gave up and became pretty cynical and angry.

Here's what you need to know about this dynamic:

Your main purpose as a human being is to consciously choose the desired feeling state and story that is as close as possible to how your Higher Self sees life. What matters most is the quality of feelings you are generating during your time here. When unwanted things occur, consider it your job to trust whatever shows up and still tell the most empowering, uplifting story that your imagination can access in that moment.

After all, you have two choices when you face undesired events:

- Use it as an excuse to allow your frequency to sink and become a victim.
- Dig deeper into the circumstances at hand, recognize the inherent neutrality in it, and tell a more creative story about what's happening.

If you choose option one, you are pretending that the event is real, that it's happening 'to' you and that the story you're telling about it is indeed real. You're not able to separate the meaning you're giving it from the event itself. Whenever you find yourself saying 'this shouldn't be happening', you are basically denying the relevance of what your Higher Self is creating for you and imposing your own limiting viewpoint over it.

You can use all of these tools with utmost dedication and skill and you'll still find that your Higher Self creates experiences for you that feel surprising, unwanted, or seemingly burdensome. Why does this happen? Why can't we just tap into a higher frequency and poof! Every outer situation we find ourselves in is completely desired and makes logical sense as to why it's there?

Not getting what you consciously desire can simply be seen as a test from your Higher Self. This higher level of intelligence is directly asking you, "Are you sure you want to continue elevating your frequency?" When 'bad' or unwanted things happen we are being guided to surrender to what is and see it in the highest way possible. It doesn't matter what the event is; if something shows up that you feel is a mismatch for your current frequency, you are being nudged to stabilize that frequency. Unwanted events always have the potential to destabilize our focus and shake up our conviction of who we are and how we want to live.

Your Higher Self is prompting you to come to the ultimate realization that your circumstances don't matter. You can choose to feel amazing regardless of what's happening in your outer world. When you can still keep your focus on empowerment and telling creative stories in the face of unwanted events, you have passed the test. You have stabilized the higher frequency you're in. If you choose to see that event as truly problematic, as separate from you, and if you fail to recognize that it's completely up to you to impart whatever meaning you want to it, your frequency will downgrade and you'll find yourself in the same familiar, limiting patterns.

My purpose in spending some time on these concepts is to do everything I can to ensure that you don't have any wiggle room to make excuses and downgrade your frequency. It can be quite a pitfall when you are coasting along, feeling better than you ever have, finally holding your power and designing the life you want from the inside out, only to have a seemingly counterintuitive circumstance show up that feels dense, difficult, and causes you to say, "Oh crap, this is the last thing I wanted to happen."

Circumplanting isn't about gaining full control over the circumstances of life. There is always a Higher Intelligence at work that is really running the show giving you exactly what you need to support your evolution into higher frequencies. Whenever you feel frustrated or disappointed by what's showing up in your life, recognize that you are telling an uncreative, inaccurate story that could easily be shifted into your preferred state and way of seeing. It's not hard. It's a choice based on your desire to do so.

You don't have full control over your circumstances, but you can certainly align with the exact science and art that makes your outer world exponentially more intentional, uplifting, and positive. What you always have full control over is your relationship with what's here now. Think of life as a dance of simultaneously surrendering to 'what is' while consciously creating what's coming next. Whatever shows up is exactly what's meant to be there–it's never random, inaccurate, or inherently untrustworthy.

Whatever shows up in your reality, your Higher Self is always asking the question of you, "Can you enjoy the ride and trust what's here?"

Think about it this way: As a human being you will always have to face the reality of taking care of your body and ensuring your survival. At the same time, your body will die. Other people you care about will die. You can't hold onto anything. This is the basic truth of our human situation. When you shift into higher frequencies you are still vulnerable to the truth of impermanence. Your conscious mind would likely never prefer or desire the death of a loved one or other situations that are rooted in the basic foundation of human reality. Yet, these things happen. We can't avoid this reality by virtue of shifting into elevated states of awareness. In this sense, don't expect Circumplanting to help you bypass the baseline reality of being human.

As I mentioned, many people get caught up on this point. They expect complete smooth sailing in their circumstances as they evolve into higher frequencies. You'll still have all of the diverse, contrasting experiences that are inherent to being human. Your relationship with all of it is however, upgraded and seen from higher, more truthful perspectives.

What I am describing here is a pretty subtle dynamic on our path of personal evolution. From your current perspective it may appear to be highly paradoxical that you can focus on your highest expression of reality, yet generate contrary and limiting experiences, and still choose to see those experiences through the lens of being exactly what you need to continue your growth. It can be easy to buy into the notion that if the Instant Upgrade Tools don't continuously lead to highly positive circumstances, it's all a farce and for nothing. Cynicism plagues many people who feel that they give this way of being an honest effort, only to find they are still having to face situations that appear to be out of alignment with the work they are doing on themselves.

To reframe and summarize this conversation, we could say that the highest level of being human is to be completely open to whatever is here by virtue of telling whatever story you want about it. Your ability to create and manifest new circumstances with higher levels of precision and power is directly associated with how much or little attachment you have in relation to what actually shows up.

This statement carries within it the ultimate paradox and riddle of our human experience. The more you can surrender to and trust whatever is here now, the more accelerated your ability will be to create whatever you want. As you practice Circumplanting in your daily life you'll quickly come to realize just as I have, that it's one of the most revealing, provocative, and potent tools we have as humans to accelerate our spiritual awareness.

The 9th Instant Upgrade Tool
Quantum Flashing

My son Ezra recently asked me, "Dad, where does the universe end?" In that moment he was using our next Instant Upgrade Tool, Quantum Flashing. As with many of the other tools kids tend to naturally ask the 'big' questions of life and be plugged into their imagination. They don't see themselves as static, separate beings. They are in touch with the playful nature of existence, the openness that underlies all experience.

Quantum Flashing helps us to instantly expand our perception of what is happening. Anytime you feel small, limited, or stuck in your life, I recommend using this tool. You can use this on both a macro and micro level. On a macro level, you're going to flash on the enormity of the universe a few times a day. That's it. Simply drop whatever else you're doing or thinking about and deeply consider the notion that this universe is both infinite and eternal. There is no place where it begins or ends. There are trillions of galaxies, dimensions, planets, stars, and beings. Your conceptual mind can't even come close to fathoming the enormity of the world around you.

On a micro level, you're going to look at any object around you until you can see that it contains the entirety of the universe within it. You can do this by visualizing the quantum nature of that object. Go ahead and grab a pen right now and take a few moments to deeply consider the Truth of that pen. Is it really a solid object that is separate from you? Are you a separate being holding something outside of you? If the answer appears to be an obvious 'yes', then keep going deeper. Where does that pen end and you begin? Where you do end and the pen begins? The pen may appear to be a solid object, but in truth it is a vibrating energetic field of subatomic particles continually flickering in and out of existence. It has no actual solidity; it is empty. It only appears to be solid and separate from you because your senses are not developed enough to see its quantum nature. That pen carries all of existence within it. It is in no way separate from all that is.

Same goes for you. Your body is also an energetic field of subatomic particles that is inherently connected with everything you see around you. There is no barrier where your body ends and the outer world begins. That way of seeing things is an illusion. You live in a holographic universe that has no solidity.

When you're reflecting on the enormity of the universe or the quantum truth of a pen, the point is to recognize that you are in no way separate from what you are perceiving. Most people look at the staggering size of the cosmos and feel miniscule, like a useless speck of dust that is here for a flicker of time, then perishes. That's a pretty depressing (low frequency) worldview. When you use this tool, the whole purpose is to flash on the truth that you ARE the cosmos. Everything you see around you and all the visions you have of the infinite galaxies that you can't even come close to comprehending, all of that is you. You're not using this tool to feel even smaller and less empowered than you already do. Instead, you are allowing yourself to consider the profound paradigm shift that occurs when you acknowledge the Truth of your situation as a human being. You are all that is. You are the awareness that underlies all that you see. Infinity and eternity are interwoven into the very fabric of your core identity. You are in no way separate from the outer world. It's all the 'real you.'

I'd like to share a more subtle description of this tool. This way of seeing my life has been a powerful catalyst for shifting my frequency. This practice may start off as a visualization that feels imagined, but you'll soon come to feel the truth of this exercise and directly experience the freedom it brings.

Take a moment right now to put aside all distractions. As best you can, bring yourself to a state of ultra-focus. Now, reflect on how you normally perceive yourself–an individual with a separate body and a separate sense of self that is clearly distinct from the outer world. Consider how you normally function in the world, continually seeing other people as separate entities with their own unique identity and signature that is completely removed from your identity and body. Contemplate how your thoughts continually feed into your sense of self, how your thoughts appear to be so real, and how they convince you that 'you' are what's happening between your ears. Recognize how your typical sense of self is steeped in separation, how you assume as your baseline way of living that you are indeed your own self that is clearly divided from the outer world.

Now, visualize that the opposite is true. See yourself as all that you are conscious of. Everything that you see around you is the real you. Your body is simply another appearance floating in the space of your own awareness. Your thoughts are nothing more than flickers of energy, coming into and out of existence. They do not define who you are in any way. The real you is pure awareness. This book, the couch you're sitting on, the room you're in–all of this is you. Feel the spaciousness that this way of seeing generates. Allow yourself to open up and breathe into the openness of who you really are. You are not your thoughts and feelings. You are not your body. The experience of having a separate body with thoughts that give you a concrete sense of self melts away. You are the vastness that is all around you.

Did you feel a shift? Quantum Flashing welcomes space into your experience. The more spacious your perspective, the higher frequency you're in. We could say that the highest frequency you could be in as a human being is a complete experiential merging with the cosmos so no individuated sense of self remains. Your moment-to-moment way of seeing is that you are All That Is. On the contrary, the lowest frequency we are capable of is when there is absolutely no space in our perspective. We are suffocated by our unconscious assumption that we are a separate being with a very limited identity who is powerless to impact the world.

Another way of framing this tool is that you begin to see that life is happening 'from' you instead of 'to' you. Since the Ultimate You incorporates all that you are aware of, all experiences are being generated within the sphere of your own consciousness. That boss who is reprimanding you for being five minutes late for work is 100% your own creation and is in no way separate from you. That unexpected bill you got in the mail has been strategically created within your own field of awareness. It is never random; it's all happening from within your own self-generated hologram of reality.

Can you see how this paradigm shift naturally leads to a more elevated, empowered, and truthful relationship with life? When you buy into the belief that life is happening 'to' you, your only option is to be a victim and do the best you can to manage the randomness of life events. When you consciously shift into realizing that ALL of this is the Ultimate You and it's being created within your own consciousness, now you are in the driver's seat of your existence. You realize that your physically based character self is continuously co-creating reality alongside the Ultimate, Higher You.

Life becomes a lot more interesting and entertaining when you can see the quantum nature of reality in your direct experience. Your experience is seen as fluid and easily changeable, with infinite possibilities. The notion of feeling stuck pretty much dissipates, as that illusion can only be upheld from a lower frequency point of view, where you believe that you exist as a solid self in a physical reality. You start to understand the quantum nature of any problem you have, meaning that you see that it doesn't actually exist. All problems are stories. From a quantum perspective, we can shift into new stories instantly and at will. The only thing that causes a problem to persist is our belief that it exists and is solid.

The deeper you explore quantum reality, the more open you become to what are called transcendent or mystical experiences, which can be defined as highly elevated states of frequency. We all have access to experiences such as merging with Oneness, or a complete cessation of all thoughts and openness to all that is, or a direct realization of the emptiness of our personal identity. These experiences can be profound and deeply transformational. They can also be quite destabilizing, sometimes to the point that one loses their grip on reality to such a degree that they have a spiritual emergency or psychosis.

When you use Quantum Flashing, I'd recommend simultaneously telling a story that you are shifting into higher frequencies in a way that your nervous system is equipped to handle, and is supportive to your psyche. Use regenerative focus as needed, as Quantum Flashing can stimulate us to the point where we take sudden leaps into a higher frequency, but we aren't ready for what we experience there. We have such little context for that new reality that it completely throws us for a loop and our entire sense of who we are and what life is becomes so radically altered that we can't integrate back into a functional way of being in the world. This experience is quite common amongst those who use psychedelic drugs, but can also happen if we use this Instant Upgrade Tool in a reckless way.

When I use this tool my intention is always to stay centered. My way of seeing is now such that I can only view life from a quantum perspective. I naturally perceive everything as an illusion that is being generated within my own consciousness. There are times where the direct experience of this can be so energizing, even thrilling, that I need to use the Five Breath Process to ground myself and relax into stillness. I appreciate very much the sense of not being a solid, separate self. If you're new to this way of seeing things, all of this may sound quite scary and even threatening to your survival or safety. I assure you, as you start diving in and choosing to see reality in this way, you'll be amazed by how much enjoyment there is waiting for you as a human being. Being stuck in a flatland worldview, where what you see is what you get, is the actual reality that you should feel threatened by. This is where most people dwell, and it seems quite apparent that it doesn't lead to high levels of well-being, abundance, and joy.

As I've said repeatedly, be a renegade. Use this life you've been given to explore. Tell the most creative story you can every single day. Flash on the wide open nature of your situation as much as needed. Use this as the basis of becoming a highly resourceful person who can always adapt and shift into whatever version of reality feels inspiring.

When you're out and about living your life, choose to see everything as a dream. See that other people are in no way separate from you. See them as part of you. Determine if you can feel the interconnectedness you share with everything around you. Every moment of your life gives you ample opportunity to flash on the quantum nature of things. Step out of your own thoughts and skin and expand your awareness to include all that is around you. Expand your definition of who you are.

Doing this is an instant cure for boredom and mundanity. Even boredom can be perceived in a fascinating way. Who in here is bored? What story am I telling myself that generates this feeling? Is that story real? Is it how I'd like to show up in my existence right now? What power do I have to shift out of boredom in this moment? Is it set in stone? Could I choose to replace it with being excited and engaged?

After all, it's pretty amazing that you can invent yourself being a character who gets bored, when you are in fact an infinite being with unlimited capabilities. Isn't it funny that out of all of the myriad feelings and expressions we could choose, boredom is the one we favor?

You can only relate to a seemingly 'stuck' emotion like boredom in this way if you're tapped into the quantum realm. You see that boredom is actually just as fascinating as any other state of mind, as within that boredom the entire universe resides. Most people become bored with life for the sole reason that they buy into the myth that this is a limited, one-dimensional universe. They are disconnected from the quantum nature of reality, which carries within it all fields of potential. When we use quantum flashing, life becomes a fluid dance in and out of a variety of dynamic emotional states. Nothing feels static. Everything becomes interesting. Whatever exists is perceived for the infinitely fascinating symbol that it is.

Now that you've learned the nine Instant Upgrade Tools, you can see how they are all interconnected and feed one another. You'll be able to tell more empowered stories if you recognize the quantum nature of your life. You'll be able to play more compelling characters if you have heightened focus. You'll be able to follow your excitement with greater ease if you understand the mechanics of how you create the circumstances that you do, and how to relate to whatever shows up with grace and surrender. All of these tools are meant to be used in a simultaneous fashion and continuously applied to all themes of your life.

Resonance: The Outer World is a Mirror for Your Chosen Frequency

Before we transition into a discussion of how the Instant Upgrade Tools can be used to enhance the main facets of your life, I'd like to spend a little time on the topic of resonance. Understanding this concept will help you clarify why you have the exact circumstances that you do in your life. I would define resonance in the following way:

Resonance is the synchronous vibrational relationship between consciousness and the outer world.

Whatever your current level of frequency is will attract specific events, people, and circumstances that share a similar frequency. You'll likely notice that you tend to be attracted to people who you feel a common bond with, where you share a mutually felt sense that you can relax and be yourself. If you stop resonating with a friend, they will eventually be cleared from your reality. The same is true with your spouse. To the degree that you share a similar frequency, you will likely continue to create one another being there in the role of husband and wife. If one person raises their frequency and the other does not, then eventually the foundational integrity of the marriage will weaken and there will be no choice but to go separate ways. This is quite common when one person in a marriage has a sudden spiritual breakthrough. They are no longer in the same frequency that drew them to their partner. If their spouse doesn't join them in that new frequency the marriage can't persist in a harmonious way for long.

Whatever you feel drawn to in your life is due to the resonance you share with that thing. If you crave doughnuts, then doughnuts are a perfect match for your current frequency. If you love a certain band it's because their music resonates with your frequency. As human beings, everything that we are attracted to is due to resonance.

As you'll see in the coming sections, resonance is why people struggle to change chronic habits and patterns, whether that means giving up foods they like, breaking bad spending habits, or going to a new level in their business. The only way to create lasting changes is by first changing your frequency. In this way, you can then create a new resonance with people, objects, and circumstances that will naturally cut through old habits, addictions, or limiting behaviors. If you try to change something on the outside without first shifting your frequency, you will still resonate with that thing and inevitably be drawn to it again and again. Or, you can shift the object of your desire to something new that shares the same frequency. For instance, you can quit smoking, but then transfer the same low frequency energy onto a new habit like gambling, junk food, or compulsive exercise.

Most people live as slaves to this all-important concept of resonance. They try and try to change their outer world without understanding how to first change their inner world. This is of course why The Instant Upgrade Tools are so powerful. You can now use resonance to your advantage as you are empowered with the knowledge that a higher frequency always brings with it new circumstances, opportunities, and people that will be reflected back to you.

Let's go ahead and explore the issue of resonance across a few major life themes while also laying out a practical overview of how you can instantly upgrade these themes in any way that serves you.

How to Instantly Upgrade Your Business

I'd like to spend a little more time on the subject of business and entrepreneurship given that my coaching work focuses primarily on helping business owners perform at higher levels using the tools outlined in this book. I love being an entrepreneur and I love helping other entrepreneurs.

Over the years, I've had the good fortune of working with thousands of entrepreneurs, mostly people who are committed to positively impacting the world through their business. I've helped a lot of business owners make more money, get more clients, and create higher levels of outer success. What really excites me however, is helping my clients become new characters by shifting out of a victimized, fear-based relationship with their business and into true empowerment and confidence.

My first several years of owning my own business felt scary, unstable, and stressful. I could not relax into it and enjoy the ride. I also felt that I couldn't quite access my fullest potential to help my clients on the deepest possible levels. I always sensed that I was missing something in my approach, that I could or should be doing more to get them better results.

If you're an entrepreneur I'm sure you've already come face-to-face with similar challenges. You know how easy it can be to slip into the many potential pitfalls that cause most businesses to fail. Our widespread cultural conditioning suggests that building a business is a difficult, risky path, fraught with hardship, sacrifice, and high levels of risk. If you're going to do it, you better have thick skin, a high tolerance for failure, and a strong ability to manage risk.

But does it have to be this way?

I'm not going to sugar coat the challenges that entrepreneurs face. I know firsthand that every day when you wake up there is the potential to look at the reality of being 100% responsible for your survival and spiral into negative feelings and victimhood. I have done it many times as my 'old' self, as have many of the clients I have worked with over the years. It is possible however, to fundamentally upgrade your business. Doing this will radically transform both your big picture vision and your daily operations.

Let's start by taking a look at six of the most pervasive entrepreneurial obstacles that I have witnessed time and again in my coaching work, then apply The Instant Upgrade Tools to each of them.

The Six Biggest Business Obstacles

1) Playing Small

As a business coach, this is one of the biggest blocks to success that I see for so many entrepreneurs. What this boils down to is that we are constantly telling ourselves a story that keeps us stuck in a highly confined reality, where we never access higher levels of our potential. If your goal in business is to just get by then I recommend getting a job instead. This is what a job is designed for–to keep you comfortable at a baseline level where you have just enough to function and live your life. If you're going to willingly take on the challenges of entrepreneurship where you will be forced to face your fears, manage risk, and become highly self-reliant, why not hold a standard for yourself that makes it all worth it?

Playing small doesn't serve you, your family, or your clients. Think about it. You're actually an infinite being who can create whatever you want while you're here. Why settle for a vision that reflects a mere sliver of your actual potential? Why sell yourself short?

Playing small means that you are pretending that you're really a limited human who doesn't deserve more than just the basic necessities to keep on going. When your vision is small you'll keep telling the story of struggle and limitation. Money will be seen in a negative light. You'll exude an energy to prospective clients that actually repels them from working with you. You'll continually create circumstances that validate the feeling that playing small is all you can ask of this life.

Let's keep this practical and bring the focus to where you are right now. Take the next five minutes to write down the current vision you have for your business. This may be the first time you've done this and if it is this first step will instantly set you on a better path. Some entrepreneurs aren't even sure what their vision is. They don't know if they are playing small or not. They just try to keep up with the demands of each day, doing the best they can, putting out fires, and trying to stay afloat. This is also an example of playing small. When you play BIG, you are VERY clear on your vision. You know exactly what you want out of your business and you are not afraid to declare it to the world.

When you write down your vision you can include all of the details that feel relevant in terms of your ideal income, how many hours a week you work, how your business fits into your lifestyle, how many people you help, and any other factors that are meaningful to you.

After you're done I want you to assess on a scale of 1-10 the degree to which this vision inspires you. If 10 is through the roof passion and inspiration, anything less than a 9 is in need of an upgrade. Go ahead and write out another draft of your vision, but this time let's take it up a few levels. Let's raise your income significantly. Let's get you helping way more people. Let's dramatically increase the quality of life you have around your business. Keep writing until you can feel a shift into a higher frequency.

Where would you absolutely LOVE to be six to twelve months from now? What is your imagination telling you that feels the most exciting, that triggers the most inspiration possible? Write it all down.

Welcome to the new, conscious story of your business. This is the story you are going to be telling yourself every day from now on as if it's already here. Forget the old story. No more selling yourself short or playing small. Even if you don't have a clue as to how you'll get there yet, don't worry about it. Right now I want you to get comfortable with being bold in your vision. Take a stand for what you really want in your life even if part of you is full of judgment that it's irrational, preposterous, or that it will never happen. Do it anyway.

Your Higher Self created you being an entrepreneur to experiment with how far you could take it, to use your business as a vehicle for morphing into the highest, best expression of yourself that you can create, to think and play as big as possible.

Does this mean you have to be a multi-millionaire? Of course not. But I will say that I rarely meet an entrepreneur who is truly thriving with anything less than a six figure salary.

Your new vision should challenge you in a healthy way. It should help you step up your game, intensify your focus, and stay naturally motivated to keep going in the face of all setbacks. Your vision is the backbone of your business. If it is small, your business will be built on a flimsy foundation. If it fills you with genuine inspiration, you'll be able to hang in there through all challenges you face.

If your business feels stuck on a regular basis your vision is too small. With a big vision your creative instincts are engaged. You can see new perspectives that prevent you from getting ensnared by stagnation. You are so clear on what you want out of your business that nothing can stop you from moving forward. This book is actually a great example. The intensity of my vision is propelling this book to completion. Every time I sit down to write I could buy into the voice of confusion, overwhelm, or self-doubt. Because my vision is so big I simply don't have time for any of that. There's no room in my psyche to feed those mental states. Every time I feel a flicker of hesitation my vision swoops in and picks me up. My frequency will not allow for those lower states of conflict any longer, at least not for prolonged periods of time. You want to run your business in the same way. Make your vision so big that it's all you see. It suffocates all the clutter that keeps things moving at a snail's pace and makes it all look really hard and difficult.

2) Fighting with Money

I'm going to dedicate an entire section of this book to upgrading your financial life, so I'll keep this short. As an entrepreneur what is your current story about money? Do you see it as a problem? A source of stress? The main reason why you can't be happy and at peace right now?

Carrying around all sorts of heavy baggage around money is not going to work for long if you're trying to build a business. Money is to your business as blood is to your body. It is your lifeline, the most essential nutrient that feeds your business. Without it, you won't be in business for long. Let me ask you: Do you treat your own blood like it's a problem? Is it greedy to desire healthy blood coursing through your body? Money is no different. Wanting more of it doesn't make you greedy. Telling a negative story about it only causes disease in your business.

Want to hear my current money story? It goes something like this:

> *I think making a lot of money is awesome. The more I make, the more people I'm helping. The more I make, the better lifestyle I can offer my family. The more I make, the healthier my business is. I know that money is neutral, but I choose to see it as a highly positive symbol in my life. Money is a fun game to play, a way to keep score with how I'm doing in actively creating my chosen frequency and living up to my potential. Money comes easily to me. I make money from a place of deep integrity and creativity. I feel complete harmony with giving and receiving money. It's entertaining and fun for me to pay bills. It's rewarding for me to receive money for my talents. I am thrilled to make seven figures. If I lost it all tomorrow, I'd still be thrilled because I'm completely unattached to it. And I know exactly how to make another million quickly.*

This is the meaning I choose to impart to money. Telling variations of this story consistently has completely transformed both the outer success of my business and my inner relationship with it.

The point is to start telling this story now regardless of your current financial circumstances. Plant new circumstances into your reality through the fun process of acting as if you already are in complete harmony with money and see it as an ally in your life.

3) Undervaluing Yourself

Your business is a mirror for your self-worth. To the degree that you believe that you deserve success and money, your business will accurately mirror this back to you. Many service-based entrepreneurs tell themselves a story that there's always so much more to learn so they can't feel good about taking money from clients or customers. They never feel complete in their skill development or knowledge base. The story they are telling is repelling people from investing in what they offer.

If your current beliefs reflect low self-worth, it'll likely show up in a few ways:

- Undercharging: You feel that you have to set your rates on the lower end because there's either too much competition or you believe that people just don't have the money to afford a higher rate.
- Giving too much: Many service-based entrepreneurs try to do every single thing they can within their power to help each and every client. They end up draining themselves and are unable to work with more than a handful of people at a time, which causes their income to suffer.
- Worrying constantly: Entrepreneurial worry is an epidemic. Whether we admit it or not, most business owners quietly worry about their situation all of the time. They worry about their future, if they will ever be able to feel safe, how they will provide adequately for their family, staying ahead of their competition, and offering the best services and products possible to their clients and customers.

Can you see how all three of these symptoms of low self-worth lead to burnout? Many entrepreneurs finally go out of business because they never free themselves from the crippling story they are telling about their own worth. They end up stuck in a rut of constant worry, endlessly creating circumstances that validate that worry.

How about we change this right now? After all, worry is optional. You can shift out of it in any moment and it has nothing to do with your circumstances. You can choose to perceive yourself as highly deserving and as capable as anyone else in your industry. Worry and low self-worth are simply low frequencies that you've been locked into based on years of conditioning that have convinced you that you are indeed 'less than' or undeserving.

My 'old' story around self-worth was a doozy. I struggled for years to feel like I had a place in the world and that I was worthy of having meaningful work that paid me well. I believed I had to make all kinds of sacrifices, force the issue, and impose my will in order to keep my family safe. I had very little trust that the universe would always guide me in the right direction and that I simply had to stay open to what showed up. Based on this, I made all kinds of forceful decisions, such as moving my family across the country to live in a place we did not want to be so I could start a business with someone who was already successful. I was so convinced that this person would make all the difference in my success that I was willing to sacrifice everything to work with him. After uprooting my family and trying to settle into a new area, it turned out that this doctor wasn't even close to being ready to start a new business. He was so busy in his current job that he was a couple of years out from even getting started. I gave all of my power away to outer circumstances, believing that they would save me and keep me safe. Now I see that this always backfires. The power is always 100% of the time, within ourselves. Same goes for safety, stability, and security. It can really only be found within.

When we are telling a story of not being worthy our thinking gets cloudy. We can't find a deep reservoir of wisdom within from which to make skillful decisions. We either act recklessly and impulsively, or we become so cautious that we refuse to take any risk and we stay paralyzed in our current situation. Before you jump in and tell a new story be sure that you are clear with the overarching theme of self-worth in your life. What were you taught about how much you deserve, what you are capable of, and how worthy you are of receiving money, love, recognition, safety, and fulfillment? How have these beliefs impacted your life? Your business? Can you see the clear relationship between your current self-worth story and the state of your business?

Keep in mind that upgrading your self-worth does not need to take a long time or be all that difficult. Your natural state is one of infinite worth so all that you are doing is shifting into a higher frequency where you can clearly see that this is true. Indeed, it's much more work to stay stuck in a low frequency where you carry around the baggage of pretending you're not worthy. Continually activate the Instant Upgrade Tools around your self-worth until you can tangibly feel that you've entered a new frequency. This is an effortless shift into a 'new you' that happens whenever you are ready for it. Tell a new story, play a new character, heighten your focus, and amplify your appreciation that you have the power to do this. Even if you've been stuck for thirty years in a story of 'I'm not worthy', use quantum flashing to realize that there is no past and that who you are is in no way solid. It can all change in this moment.

With that said, take a few minutes right now to write down your new story around how worthy you are. Write down variations of this story over the next thirty days. To help you generate ideas, I'll share a portion of my new story. You can use this as a springboard for your own ideas.

> *I now see that I am an infinite being who came here to pretend that I am limited. How amazing that I've used self-worth as a powerful prop to convince me that my limitations are real! I now know that I am as deserving as anyone. I welcome meaningful things into my life and am wide open to receiving what life has to offer, whether that comes in the form of money, love, nourishment, ideas, or opportunities. I now know that I am generating all events within the field of my own awareness.*
>
> *How could I not be worthy of what I, myself, am creating? The fact that my Higher Self is creating what I see makes it ludicrous to assume that I don't deserve what this world has to offer. I believe anything is possible and that there are no limits to what I can create. I am worthy of it all.*
>
> *The more I am willing to receive, the more I have to give. The more I allow in help, the more I can help. It now feels arrogant to deny my own worthiness. I love being open to receiving the bounty that this life*

has to offer. It is immense indeed. I know that my Higher Self is always giving me exactly what I need. I have become highly skilled at staying open and allowing myself to be guided by this higher intelligence. Life flows in a perfectly orchestrated fashion and I am worthy of experiencing anything that arises. Since I now know that I am infinitely worthy, my business is thriving. Money flows in with ease, people naturally pay me what I'm worth, and attracting clients is as natural as breathing.

You can see in my story that quantum flashing and filter cleansing play big roles in the way I perceive self-worth. It's quite helpful for me to remember who I really am and to see things accurately as the basis of having a high level of value. What works for you? Write down your new story and become ultra-focused on it as you go through your day. Keep your focus here even if your outer circumstances don't change right away. What matters most is that you are choosing to be happy now. You are not basing your inner state around your circumstances. Doing this on a daily basis will end your feelings of worry, instability, and lack once and for all.

4) Overvaluing Hard Work

The story that 'hard work creates success' is one that I bought into in my first phase of business. I was told to hustle and keep grinding at all costs until I got the desired result. After a couple years of pounding the pavement all I had to show for it was a mediocre business and a high level of exhaustion and frustration. I discovered there's a lot more that goes into business success than just hard work.

As an entrepreneur I'm sure you've been exposed to similar stories that inflate the value of hustle. Hustle doesn't always lead to our desired outcomes. When it does, it's because hustle resonates with someone's frequency and is a truly inspiring way to build a business. If you love to hustle, it will work well for you. In my case however, I really don't like to hustle. It doesn't inspire me to spend most of my life working. I tried and tried and was constantly being shown that I was off track. My family let me know that I was putting my business before them. My health was mediocre. I didn't have time for tennis and other hobbies that are meaningful to me.

I know it may sound illogical but I have come to see that you can create whatever level of success you want based on what feels naturally inspiring to you. If you love the grind, then go for it. In my case what has mostly created my success is:

- The creativity and innovation I bring to my industry.
- My ability to articulate my message in a way that resonates with people.
- Using strategic marketing such as Facebook advertising that is not time-consuming or labor intensive.
- Packaging my programs in a way that leverages my time.

I am far more inspired by creativity, communication, and time leverage than I am by hard work. Yes, I do enjoy working hard but not all of the time. I like to go in spurts. Sometimes I'll even take several weeks at a time to do everything but work. My business can still run itself and generate consistent revenue whether I'm present or not.

What are your seven figure attributes? Become intimate with them. If you can outwork everyone in the room, then awesome! That quality has been given to you for a reason. Just don't fall into the trap of believing that hard work is the ultimate difference maker in your success. It's one piece of the puzzle but in my experience there are other factors that are actually far more important.

5) Being Attached to Outcomes

One of the greatest pitfalls that entrepreneurs face is their continual focus on future outcomes. They base their happiness around getting to that next milestone or achieving the next breakthrough, all the while forgetting that this moment is all they have. They tell themselves a story that goes something like:

> *When I land that next contract or make that next commission, then I can relax and feel some peace about all of this.*

I used to fall into this trap on a daily basis. I was always trying to get to that next rung of success. It felt impossible to settle into and enjoy the moment, as there was always so much more to do and achieve. It felt very real in my mind that being present was actually irresponsible. If I didn't continually focus on future results, my business would be jeopardized.

This is why so many entrepreneurs struggle in their marriages and friendships. Their ongoing attachment to future outcomes prevents them from being present, which causes the people around them to feel like the business comes before they do. Even when they are with their family or friends, their mind is on their business. They just can't let it go.

Here's what I have learned in my own entrepreneurial journey: Getting more clients, making more money, hitting new milestones, none of it actually makes me happier. Does it provide some enjoyment? Sure. Does it give me a temporary feeling of satisfaction? Yes. Is it ever the source of my actual happiness? Not even close.

If you feel stuck in future outcomes, it's important to know that you're locked into a low frequency that likely isn't serving you well. You may want to use The Radical Reframe to create a more abrupt stop to this momentum, as I know how seductive it can be. Every time you feel fixated on a future outcome, stop what you are doing and tell yourself something along the lines of, Even if that happens, it won't make me any happier than I am now.

You'll likely need to do this repeatedly until you can feel the new story taking hold. Another Radical Reframe might be, If I can allow myself to be happy now and not be attached to ___ happening, the odds of it happening will increase significantly. I choose to let it go. Whatever my Higher Self creates for me, that is always what is meant to happen.

I've found this to be true in my business and all facets of life. Letting go of any attachment to what I want optimizes the potential for it to show up. When I am fixated on it, I am blocking it. Have you ever noticed that when you really need to get somewhere and you are feeling the urgency and impatience mounting, every single traffic light turns red just as you arrive to it? This is how life works. You'll continue to get red lights if you're attached to outcomes.

Tell a story that frees you up to be happy now, to be present with your family and friends, and to enjoy the process as much as the result. Use filter cleansing so you can see the actual truth of this new story. Your business will be more successful if you are present in this moment and unattached to future outcomes.

6) Getting Lost in Overwhelm

One of the greatest complaints I hear from my clients is that they feel overwhelmed by all of the tasks of running a business, let alone balancing their business with their personal lives. They are trying to wear too many hats, constantly putting out fires, managing people, details, projects, and daily challenges. They are spread too thin and can never seem to come up for air. The more 'successful' they become, the more overwhelmed they feel. More money brings with it more demands on their time and greater responsibility.

Can you relate?

Most of us end up feeling overwhelmed as business owners because we have been taught from so many sources that overwhelm is a given as an entrepreneur. Because we accept this as fact, we create a reality that makes it appear to be a foregone conclusion. I'd like to share three insights about this based on many years of entrepreneurship that have completely transformed my relationship with overwhelm.

• Overwhelm is a story that can serve you or imprison you. Just as with any dynamic or event in life, the meaning we impart to it determines how it shows up and whether it is a symbol of freedom or bondage. Rather than trying to manage overwhelm or make it go away, I recommend seeing it in a new way. I used to hate feeling overwhelmed. Now, I have a new story about it that goes like this:

Overwhelm is a sign that I am active in my business and that a lot of people desire my attention. This is a GOOD thing! I appreciate that there is so much interest in what I do and that I have so much to attend to in my daily life. It keeps things interesting and purposeful. Overwhelm means there is momentum gathering toward a positive breakthrough. The more overwhelmed I feel, the more opportunity I have to become ultra-focused, tap into a high frequency, and invent myself as a more powerful, capable, and resourceful person.

As you can see, I welcome overwhelm because I choose to see it as a positive. I would far prefer being overwhelmed rather than being underwhelmed. What's ironic is that the more I see it this way, the more space and freedom has opened up in my daily life.

The writing of this book serves as a powerful metaphor for what I am saying. Writing a book tends to be an inherently overwhelming process, as you have to not only create but then organize thousands of concepts into a coherent whole that flows well from beginning to end. At any point, I could easily choose to see the overwhelm in a negative light. If I did, the entire process would be stalled and my vision would be delayed, halting my momentum and causing me unnecessary stress and frustration. Instead, I choose to tell a story that serves me. I see the book as already complete. I focus on the excitement of bringing it out to the world. I raise my focus whenever the details feel like a lot to handle. I flood my mind with appreciation that I can even do this in the first place. I allow my heart to open to the excitement of both the process and the end result.

• Overwhelm is care in disguise. Just as anxiety is excitement in disguise, I see overwhelm as a sign that you care and have a strong conscience. You are attentive to details. You are vigilant about taking care of things so that other people don't have to be burdened. Instead of telling yourself how problematic it is that you are overwhelmed, focus on how amazing and wonderful it is that you care so much about your life. Bring ALL of your focus to this and amplify appreciation around this highly positive attribute. Have you noticed that you can't really feel overwhelm and appreciation simultaneously? They reside on different frequencies. Whenever you feel overwhelmed choose to flood that moment with gratitude for how much you care about your life and how committed you are to helping others and ensuring that things go well.

• Overwhelm stems from believing that you exist and that there is a solid world outside of you that is real. Overwhelm creates a kind of frenetic momentum that prevents us from having the space or perspective to question what's really going on underneath the surface of things. What a wonderful prop to use to lock us into our current frequency! In order to liberate yourself from overwhelm you have to see that you alone created that pattern in your life, and you did it for a clear reason. You actually desired to play a character who is spread too thin, tired, anxious, scattered, and takes on too much.

Does that creation no longer serve you? Great! Start shifting into a new way of being starting now. It's not hard. It doesn't take time. YOU are running the show here and YOU get to decide who you want to be. If overwhelm doesn't serve you, choose a new costume to wear. Use the tools to shift into a new frequency and invent yourself how you want to be. Does that mean the appearance of overwhelm is going to magically vaporize the moment you do this? No. But it does mean that your relationship with what you see around you is radically different. You can relate to the seeming overwhelm of your circumstances from a new level of frequency, one that carries the resonance of space, peace, and clarity. As you stabilize this frequency, your outer world will over time, mirror it back to you.

So much of the time you don't need to 'do' anything to manage or fix your overwhelm. You just need to see it in a new light. Create some space around it and recognize that it's a totally subjective state of mind based on the character you are playing. Is there a payoff for staying overwhelmed? It can, after all, be a wonderful prop you use to convince yourself that you're a limited human with real problems. If you created it within your own reality, you can just as easily uncreate it. You can collapse the pattern using the Instant Upgrade Tools.

Quantum Selling: A New Way to Upgrade Sales and Convert More Clients

"We convince by our presence." Walt Whitman

If you're a coach, consultant, or service-based entrepreneur, you already know that your sales skill will largely determine your income. The better you are at selling your offers the more clients you'll get and money you'll make. Many people have a strong aversion to selling, believing that it is a disingenuous, loathsome process that they have to put up with in order to stay in business. I used to feel this way too. Now I actually enjoy selling. I see it as a fun game much like everything else. The Instant Upgrade Tools can help you create a huge paradigm shift that makes selling more effective and fun.

In particular, let's look at the Quantum Flashing Tool and apply it directly to having sales conversations with prospective clients. Based on the principles of this book you now know that other people are in no way separate from you. Every prospective client that shows up is being generated within the field of your own consciousness. Before you get on the phone with that person, take a moment to see them as an extension of yourself. Whatever objections they have to working with you, whatever fears or challenges they express, all of this is coming from you. They are mirroring back to you yet another way of expressing your infinite nature.

When you see your clients in this way it will immediately put them at ease. Instead of trying to get something from them you can now relax and deeply enjoy the process of helping them during the sales conversation. You don't need to coerce or convince them into buying from you. Instead, extend an energy to them that lets them know that you totally understand and are present to their challenges. After all, on a quantum level they ARE you, so you have full access to whatever they are thinking and feeling. The better you are at dispelling the tension of there being an agenda to make a sale, the more sales you'll make. If people feel like they are being sold to they often won't buy. If they feel they are being deeply listened to and empathized with they will often buy. It really is that simple.

You can choose to have that sales conversation in a way that very much feels like you are talking to yourself. Another part of you is mirroring and sharing some challenges. You don't need to convince yourself to buy your products or services, right? You can relax, drop the agenda, and just listen. If you use Quantum Flashing for your sales calls, I can virtually guarantee that you'll enjoy them a lot more and have higher sales conversion.

Resonance and Your Business

Any business has its own frequency that is primarily influenced by the CEO/owner, but also by the employees and overall community within the organization. How would you describe the frequency of your business? Does it exude a high quality of energy?

Your business will attract clients and customers based on its frequency. If you are upset by the quality of clients you get, it's time to upgrade your frequency. Do you often complain about money, feel like you can't afford things, or wish that you could get things for free? Expect your customers to do the same. Do you feel wishy washy, unclear about how to move forward, or paralyzed in making decisions? Expect your customers to have a lot of objections in working with you. Do you feel a lot of doubt about your abilities and your worth? Expect your customers to mirror this back to you.

I have seen time again both in my own experience and with my clients, that when we upgrade our business frequency, we naturally start attracting higher quality clients or customers. Your goal is to make sure that your upgraded frequency emanates through your website and all other marketing materials. From the moment a prospect hears about your business, they will get hit with an immediate energetic impression that either repels them or attracts them to you. If getting customers feels hard, it means the energy that you are emanating leans toward the repelling side of the spectrum. As you upgrade your frequency, review the process that you use to take people from initial exposure to a sale. Does every detail of that process exude a high frequency? Does it cause people to be highly attracted to what you offer?

This all starts with you. As you use The Instant Upgrade Tools you'll likely notice that your business naturally upgrades and as a result, you attract customers who are ideal for what you offer. Good marketing happens when you can strategically position all elements of your business in a way that feels highly inspiring and attractive to your audience. When I review marketing materials for a client I can usually tell within a few seconds what kind of frequency the business is dwelling in. In fact, every person who visits your website or sees an ad for your business is left with a similar impression. For me, the process is a lot more conscious given the nature of my work. Most prospective customers don't really know why they do or do not buy, unless there is something overtly guiding them in their decision. The underlying reason why they choose you over your competition is that they feel a resonance with your business. As you now know, there's an awful lot you can do to ensure this happens to your advantage. No matter what your current circumstances are, spend the next thirty days consciously raising the frequency of your business. I have seen time and again that doing this alone can cause profound changes in revenue, client conversion, and the overall ease with which your business grows. This is especially true if you strategically design all of your marketing materials to reflect higher frequencies. This is a big subject that is outside the scope of this book. If you'd like to learn more, I'd recommend applying for a free call with my team at www.theinstantupgrade.com/apply.

10 Wealth Generating Stories You Can Tell to Upgrade Your Business Frequency

To close this section on business I'd like to share ten new stories you can begin focusing on and acting out in your daily life. These are stories that I've found particularly useful as a business owner and use for many of my clients with great success. As you likely know by now, these aren't just affirmations; these are new ways of being. You can choose to upgrade your business right now by implanting these perceptions of outer reality. Have fun creating your entrepreneurial identity in whatever way serves you and your clients or customers best.

1) I go from idea to implementation with incredible speed. Million dollar ideas are continually being created in my mind with little to no effort. I know intuitively which ideas I need to move on fast and I am masterful at executing those ideas in a clear, efficient way. My business is so successful because I take massive action on my best ideas. I know that money always springs out of ideas and I am totally empowered in this process of accessing new ways of seeing that are quickly monetized.

2) Nobody is offering what I offer. Even though others may appear to do what I do, I don't believe in competition. The level of innovation and uniqueness that I bring to my business helps me stand apart in a crowded marketplace. Nobody can do what I do. My clients/customers feel this unique power that emanates from my business. We easily get new business because we are positioned in such a compelling way. We are like a breath of fresh air in our industry. People rave about how out of the box we are in the solutions we offer and how creative we are in the way we package our products and services.

3) I have seven figure attributes that come as natural to me as breathing. What I love about my business is that I can simply be myself and the money flows in as a natural result of who I am. I have innate strengths that I bring to the table that make me a lot of money. I have so much fun being able to express my gifts in a very natural way. My business is the perfect fit for who I am. Out of all the potential business models and industries I could have chosen, I deeply appreciate how I chose the one that perfectly fits who I am. This is why I generate wealth so easily.

4) I can delegate all of my weaknesses. I create wealth from amplifying my strengths. I have an amazing team around me who supports me in all ways. I know exactly how to hire and train staff who are the ideal fit for my business. They fill in the weak links and always know exactly what needs to be done. My team supports my lifestyle freedom. They love working for me and are passionate about the mission of my busi-

ness.

I can simultaneously enjoy making more money and having more time. As I become more financially successful, I am so grateful that I have structured my business to simultaneously free up my time. I have a truly abundant lifestyle around my business. Since I started with the end in mind, I intentionally created a structure that would support my highest values. I can work as much or as little in my business as I want and still do incredibly well. It is like a well-oiled machine.

5) My clients and customers spread the word about my business like wildfire. Because we offer products and services that are of such high quality and we have a culture that truly cares about people, word of mouth has skyrocketed. I am delighted by how we have a natural, very powerful sales force in our clients and customers. They love helping us grow. We love them for doing this and let them know how much we care. Our audience is extremely loyal to us which is the basis of our long-term stability and growth.

6) I love to promote my business. Because I have such a clear mission and vision, I am always excited to get more visibility. I can always choose to market in a way that is genuinely helpful to people. I embrace being in the spotlight, as I know that the success of my business relies heavily on the incredible exposure we get. Out of everyone in my industry, my business gets the most attention and notoriety. There is a tangible energy of expansion that we generate from our passion for promotion. Promotion equals prosperity and I embrace this wholeheartedly.

7) I thrive when there are challenges. While others might collapse in the face of setbacks, this is when I am at my best. I actually enjoy when things don't go the way I want. I see business as a fun game and I know that obstacles make the game more fun to play. I become a stronger, wiser business leader every time I overcome a challenge. Therefore, I welcome the opportunity to grow in this way. Whatever challenge the day brings, I am always up for it. I am unstoppable in the face of all adversity. My resiliency makes my business bulletproof against external

factors like the economy.

8) I can make more money when the economy is in decline. As a savvy entrepreneur, I know that there is always a fortune to be made during times of recession. My job is to become even more creative in the way I promote and package my services and products. There is always a way to increase profit during economic downturns. While my competition is freaking out, I am quietly increasing profit by solving problems in new ways.

9) I know that my Higher Self is giving me exactly what I need in every moment. Whatever shows up in my business, I can trust it, simply because it's there. If for any reason it becomes clear that it's time to let my business go, I can do so with grace and ease. After all, it was never really mine in the first place. I see that it's all an illusion, a fun game. Therefore, I am not attached to any of it. This is why I can be so fulfilled and content with its day-to-day operations and growth. I enjoy the process as much as the outcomes.

10) All other important aspects of my life are thriving just as my business is. My family feels great about my success and I appreciate that I can give them my fullest self as my business grows. I have plenty of time and energy to focus on my health, my hobbies, and my relationships. My business perfectly supports my ideal lifestyle.

How to Instantly Upgrade Your Financial Life

Let's talk about money. Without question, the most helpful thing you can do right now to completely transform your relationship with your finances is get very clear on the story you are telling. How do you feel about money? What does it symbolize to you? What thoughts go through your mind every day in relation to money? Write down in detail what your current money story is and remember, it's just a story that can easily be changed.

My old money story went something like this:

> *I am really concerned about my financial future. I just don't see how I'll be able to make enough to put my kids through college, support my family, and retire comfortably. It's scary being an entrepreneur, where money feels so unstable. It might run out soon. I better work harder to try and make more. If only I didn't have to worry about money, I'd be happy. I don't see the point of taking care of my health and other aspects of my life. After all, I'll never have enough money to make anything else worthwhile. I just wish I didn't have to deal with it. I guess I'll just spend what I make whenever I get the chance. It'll be gone soon anyway. I just don't understand how I'll ever feel safe with money. It doesn't make sense to me.*

You get the idea. My 'old' self was writing a pretty limiting and disempowering story about money. I created a reality where I put excessive drive and focus into making money, but would not value managing money all that well. I felt that making it meant I should also quickly spend it. Because I didn't feel safe with money, I spent many years living on the edge. I somehow always made enough to make ends meet, but it was constantly a source of anxiety.

In my coaching business I get to hear people's money stories on a regular basis. Without fail, the clients who are telling an empowering story about money are the ones attracting and making it. The ones who see money as a problem are usually broke or barely getting by. They think this is the case because money really is 'the problem.' They don't see that the real problem is the story they are telling about it, and the lack of awareness. Yet, they could choose in this very moment to tell a completely different story.

Just so we are clear, money is a completely neutral force in your life. As with all other objects in the phenomenal world it has no meaning on its own. It will show up in your life purely as a symbol based on the meaning you give to it. If you think money is evil, you'll repel it and it will logically be seen as a problem. There will never be enough, making it look like a burden and source of stress. If you don't value money much and see it as beneath you, it will likely show up just enough so that you can barely get by. People who think money doesn't matter end up with very little of it. If you see money as a way to expand your options while helping more people, including your family, you'll likely have more of it. The amount you make and hold onto is directly proportionate to the story you are telling about it.

Want more money? Start telling a new story. Rewrite the meaning of money in your life. Choose to see it as a fun game, a way of keeping score on how much of your value you are offering to the world. In fact, if money is your biggest trigger that seems to keep you locked in a low frequency, use Empowered Storytelling every day for the next thirty days and see what happens. Write down in detail what your ideal vision for money is as if it's already happening. Heighten your focus around this story as you go about your day. When you feel stress coming up around money stop whatever you are doing and identify the story you are telling.

Do you notice that money triggers your stress worse than anything else? Use the Radical Reframe. Clearly identify your current money story, then choose to focus on the exact opposite story. Keep your focus there at all times. You are no longer allowed to verbalize your old story. You are collapsing that pattern and upgrading to a frequency that supports you, where money is no longer perceived as a problem. Keep in mind this has little to do with how much money you currently have or make.

This tends to be one of the biggest challenges we have when it comes to permanently transforming our relationship with money. The illusion that money is real, that it is the very basis of our safety, is so convincing that it can feel downright delusional to not see money as a problem or something that we need to be very serious and heavy about. Remember that we all came here to play a fun game of pretending like we are limited. What better prop than money to thoroughly convince us of our limitations and lack of safety?

Just as your very identity is fluid and dynamic, so can be the presence of money in your life. If you've played a character who has struggled financially for many years, this can easily be transformed starting right now. The first step is to realize that you have indeed been playing a character. You've been acting out a specific script around money that has given you the exact financial circumstances you see in front of you. There is nothing inherently wrong or problematic about that script; it's just a story you've been immersed in. If on the other hand, you are convinced that who you are is fixed and solid and that money is a phenomenon that is separate from you, the only natural reaction is to boost your defenses, lead with fear, and do your best to protect yourself in the face of something that you feel has power over you. Money is very often seen in a way that causes us to go to war with our own reality.

Take a moment right now and look at your current financial situation. Can you feel in your heart that it's simply a prop based on the story you've been playing out? Can you feel the space around it? The truth that there is no problem? That money is neutral?

If money has been a continual source of stress, can you now see how the lack of space and unconscious fear you have about your survival and safety is a choice? Making more money is not the solution. That is the rabbit hole that most people fall down. They believe that if they could just make more money they could finally be at peace. As David Geffen says, "Anybody who thinks money will make you happy, hasn't got money."

How much money you have or don't have is never the real issue. You have to choose to be empowered in your relationship with money now, regardless of your financial circumstances. Even if you've gone bankrupt several times, have massive credit card debt, or are barely making ends meet, realize that you're simply playing a character who is locked into a low financial frequency. You can certainly try all kinds of conventional budgeting and money management strategies, but until you realize that it's all fake you'll continue to create and live out the same patterns and quality of circumstances.

Many people try to use affirmations such as 'I am a money magnet' to improve their financial situation. They repeatedly tell themselves how prosperous they are and how money comes to them easily. As with anything else, you can tell yourself whatever you want, but if you don't understand the actual mechanics of transformation, affirmations become yet another tool of self-sabotage. Repeating positive statements to yourself has no innate power on its own. You activate the power of new self-talk when you realize the emptiness that underlies your entire human experience. Instead of manufacturing positive thoughts around money (that you don't really believe), the purpose of The Instant Upgrade Tools is to fundamentally create yourself in a new way that supports a more empowered relationship with money.

Money is showing up in the way it is right now due to resonance. Your current frequency is causing money to appear in the exact way that it does–as a problem, a source of limitation or stress, or a symbol of abundance and freedom. Instead of forcing yourself to feel good about money, you can cleanse your filter, see the Truth of the situation, and invent yourself anew as the fluid and dynamic being that you are.

If you currently make $50,000 a year, this exact amount is showing up because you resonate with money in a precise way that reflects that specific dollar amount. If you want to make a million dollars a year, ask yourself what level of frequency would naturally support that? Who would you need to become in order to easily create that amount of money? If you believe that it's impossible to make seven figures a year, then of course it won't happen. Realize however, that it's just another limiting story that appears to be true. In reality, there is actually no difference between you and people like Richard Branson or Bill Gates. The only difference is that they have a different money story than you do and therefore dwell in a higher frequency. You can access that frequency as long as it's something you genuinely desire and it's relevant to the story that your Higher Self wants you to explore.

Why Do So Many People Seem to Go Without?

One of the common questions people have around the topic of money is, 'If money really isn't a problem, then why are so many people in poverty, starving, and denied of basic human needs? If this was true, wouldn't every single person have everything they need to be comfortable and healthy on this planet?'

Because this question is often used as a barrier to becoming more financially empowered, let's explore it through the context laid out in this book. While this point of view may challenge you, the main idea here is to realize that you are creating the reality you see around you based on the level of frequency you are residing in. The collective world you see around you is showing up only as a mirror to reflect back to you what you believe to be true. If you see a lot of lack, suffering, and injustice, this is because your current frequency supports that way of seeing. What you see outside of you is always empty of any kind of inherent meaning. You can overlay whatever story you want on the outer world.

As you enter higher frequencies you no longer see the outer world through the lens of lack and fear. You see that all outer phenomena are generated within your own awareness; nothing is separate from you. As such, you can choose to perceive all outer events in any way you desire. From a lower frequency perspective, it seems 100% logical to assume that witnessing starvation or lack in our world automatically carries within it the truth that suffering and limitation do indeed exist. As your frequency elevates, you become more skilled at separating events from the meaning you impart to them. This is no longer an automatic, unconscious process. You become impervious to the tendency to use outer circumstances to justify any preconceived notions of what life means and who you are.

If this is at all confusing to you, don't worry about it. Have a little faith and keep it simple. Even if it feels fake to do so, start to see your current financial situation through a more creative, empowered lens. Cut through the need to get things to change 'out there' before you can feel better. Be a little bit rebellious. If 98% of the people you see around you seem to have a disempowered relationship with money, choose to be in the 2% who relates to things in a radically different way. Instead of telling the story that you should feel a certain way about money because everyone around you seems to feel that way, radically reframe your perspective: 'Because everyone around me seems stuck in a money rut, this is exactly why I choose to be in the small minority who creates an empowered relationship with money starting now. Whatever the masses are doing, I now know that doing the opposite is often where the freedom is found.'

What Feels Better: Making More or Spending Less?

There is no one right or wrong way to become financially free in your life. The key is to make sure that your behaviors resonate with the ideal version of how you aspire to be in this world. When it comes to making and spending money, follow The Breadcrumb Trail. I have seen time and again in my own life that money follows excitement. If I am genuinely passionate about a project or program I am offering, it naturally generates more money. From a business perspective your level of excitement is directly felt by prospective clients. If they feel your passion they will be much more likely to ride that wave and invest in what you offer.

As an entrepreneur I have come to realize that I am far more uplifted by the goal of making more money rather than spending less. I put a lot more focus on increasing income rather than reducing spending. If your current income level has a ceiling on it and it appears that the only way to create prosperity is to spend less, just make sure that this is a condition that truly serves you in life. As a dynamic, fluid being, remember that you can create new circumstances gracefully and easily if you choose to write this into your script. Nothing is set in stone.

Most conventional financial advice focuses on saving for a rainy day, putting aside 1% of your income for forty years, and denying yourself the daily cup of Starbucks as the best way to ensure financial security. If this resonates with you then go for it. Save and budget to your heart's delight. The problem is that this way of relating to money tends to be largely driven by a fear-based, scarcity mindset. There is only a certain amount you have access to and therefore, your only option is to deny yourself certain things in life in order to secure your financial future. I have never resonated with that way of perceiving money.

My chosen way of relating to money is that it is in infinite supply and that I can create as much as I want as long as I enter a frequency that supports that creation. I don't need to restrain or deprive myself in any way. I get much more entertainment value out of perceiving money in this way. It works for me.

In order to help you get totally clear on your current financial frequency I'd like to share a few statements that tend to reflect more of a scarcity mindset. As a rule of thumb, I recommend that you refrain from verbalizing and solidifying these kinds of statements into your reality.

- I can't afford it.
- It's too expensive.
- I would do that, but I don't have the money.
- I wish money didn't exist.
- Rich people are greedy.
- If I focus on making a lot of money, I'm being selfish.
- Money doesn't matter.
- The only reason I do this is for the money.
- The more money I make, the less time I have.
- It will take me years to get out of debt.

You get the idea. Verbalizing statements such as these may appear to be entirely logical and justified. You may feel that it actually is true that you can't afford something you want. The idea here is that you don't solidify around that feeling. You don't use the statement 'I can't afford it' as a proclamation that makes your reality seem limited and solid. It's just a story even though it appears to be real. You are imagining the experience of there being an outer object that you desire that you can't afford. You are playing the character of someone who doesn't make enough money to pay for that thing. Do you get it? None of it is set in stone; it only appears that way if you believe that it is so.

Taking Empowered Action

It should also be noted here that shifting into a higher financial frequency does not mean that you can then just passively kick back and wait for the wealth to come pouring in. Once you're in that higher frequency you'll naturally resonate with specific action steps that generate the income you desire. You will restructure your business or career in a way that best reflects the inner shifts you've made. There will always be a new, corresponding set of action steps to engage with that align with the changes in your inner world. Many New Age philosophies make this sound like a passive process, where you can shift into a higher frequency and poof! the money magically shows up in your bank account. While there are rare occurrences where this can happen (refer to my story in the section on Ultra Focus), most of the time it's a much more practical process. The inner shift to a higher frequency leads to new behaviors and action steps that inevitably generate new circumstances. It's quite ordinary actually.

The use of these tools is meant to be a highly proactive process. As a business coach I am a huge proponent of getting all of the right systems set up to ensure maximum financial growth. I am not in any way suggesting that you can just kick back, make some inner changes, and expect a whole new set of circumstances. Empowered action is an integral component of the tools. If you want to use character acting to create yourself as someone who is financially successful, there will be daily action steps you'll take to make that happen. The inner shifts and the outer action steps are part of the same congruous process.

I'd like to leave you with five new empowering money stories that may help you write a new script that supports you in breaking free forever from your current financial limitations. Use these in whatever way helps you tap into a higher financial frequency.

Money shows up in the exact way that I need it to. If I want to do something and don't seem to have the funds to follow through, it simply means that the timing was off or that thing wasn't really relevant to my story. I always have the funds to experience exactly what I need.

I am having so much fun being generous with money. It is highly fulfilling for me to give money away just as easily as I receive it. I have an open, unattached, fearless relationship with money that helps me serve this planet in a more powerful way.

Making money is just as easy for me as spending it. I appreciate both sides of the spectrum equally. The more I spend, the more I make.

The more money I make, the more freedom and options I have to live on my terms. I see money as a symbol of freedom that opens new doors of possibility. Increasing my income frees up my life in fun, meaningful ways.

I no longer see any difference between making \$50,000 and \$5,000,000. The dollar amount is empty of meaning. If I desire to, I can choose to shift into higher frequencies, then play the character who takes specific actions to make the ideal amount of money that I envision for my life.

How to Instantly Upgrade Your Athletic Performance and Talent Level

I am in love with the game of tennis. After taking a twenty year break from playing I picked up a racket about five years ago and have been playing a few times a week ever since. I am by no means a world class player but I can hold my own at the recreational level.

To be honest it would be more accurate to say that my old character had a love/hate relationship with tennis. I was often deeply frustrated by my lack of progress and the tension I would feel before matches. My nerves would overtake me and I usually found that I played to about 40% of my capacity in any competitive environment.

I often found myself straining to improve my game. I would try really hard and do all the right things, but found my development to be painstakingly slow. Most of the time when I practiced I would force the issue, demanding that my mind and body succumb and do whatever it takes to get better.

With this force-based mentality I ended up creating two pretty intense injuries–tennis elbow and a bulging disc. I was forced to take prolonged breaks. I got cortisone shots and tried all kinds of healing modalities. Nothing really helped. I was pissed off and ready to give up, not only with tennis but with all of the pursuits of my life that I deemed meaningful yet were not progressing. As my old character, that was a pretty long list.

I was stuck in a low frequency around my tennis and many other elements of my life.

One of my wake up calls was when I went out to practice with a friend one day and could barely walk around the court. My back was so flared up that I had lost nearly all mobility. Yet there I was, still giving it the old college try. That experience helped me to surrender to a new way of relating to all of this.

Since that happened I have been telling a new story about tennis. My old story went like this:

> *This sport is so damn frustrating. I can't figure out why I'm not getting better. I'm doing everything right. I'm sick of putting in the effort and not seeing results. It's not fair. I get too tense to play well and feel suffocated by pressure in a match. I know I'm capable of more than this, but I can't figure out how to activate my potential.*

The new story I've been telling goes like this:

> *I love this sport. It's so fun to get better every single time I step on the court. Even when improvement is subtle, I simply enjoy hitting the ball. It's a privilege to be out here. I feel relaxed and sure of myself when I play matches. I enjoy the pressure and thrive when it really matters. My body feels at ease on the court. I am a tremendous player and am winning tournaments.*

I have chosen to become the character who lives this way in relation to tennis. I upgraded my frequency and haven't looked back since. So what has happened to my game?

Well first of all, I feel way better about it and that's what matters most. I am way more confident that I can beat players at my level. I look forward to the challenge of playing tournaments and am more engaged with the process rather than the result. My serve and forehand have spontaneously undergone mechanical improvements that I struggled to achieve for many years.

I made it to the final of the most recent tournament that I played, which is the first time I've done this at the 4.5 level.

Amazing, right? Yes, it is. And you can do the same in whatever way you compete or perform.

It could be said that the five greatest catalysts in life to help us wake up and transform are parenting, marriage, health, death/loss, and business.

I would argue that competition is right up there as well. When you compete in a win or lose environment it's like a magnifying glass for your current state of consciousness. You see yourself so clearly. It becomes obvious what frequency you're dwelling at and what story you're telling yourself. This is why I love tennis. It's not just about hitting a ball over a net; it's a mirror that shows me where I'm at in my life.

Along these lines, my first competitive match several years ago was a huge catalyst for me. I was playing a guy that I felt I should have beaten in my sleep, yet I was so nervous that I could barely get the ball over the net. He ended up winning in the third set tiebreaker. I drove home disgusted with myself. When I walked into my house I chucked my tennis bag across the living room, dropped to the ground and spontaneously let out a huge amount of emotional baggage. Basically, I lost my shit.

As you know, this emotional upheaval wasn't really about the match; it was a mirror that was showing me about myself and where I was at in my life. I hadn't wailed like that in years. I knew I was onto something useful for my life.

If you're a competitive athlete you already know how your chosen sport is a powerful metaphor for the way you live. How you approach competition is the same way you approach life. Where does fear, timidity, and self-doubt show up? How do you relate to pressure? How do you perform in the most crucial moments?

If you've been living in default mode in relation to your sport, I can assure you that using these tools will instantly upgrade your athletic performance. Talent alone can get you to a certain point. What takes your performance to an entirely new level is how you are using your mind. Just as with anything else, if you continue to tell the same old story you'll continue to be stuck in the same low frequency that can only generate a narrow set of outcomes. You can't improve all that much if you don't shift your mindset.

Let's start right now. Write down your current story in relation to your sport. How do you feel about your current level of performance? About the progress you are making? About how you handle pressure? About your confidence level? How much do you allow yourself to enjoy being out there doing your best? How much does your inner critic show up to undermine your experience? When do you get frustrated? Does your sport ever make you want to go ballistic?

You've likely been stuck in this story for some time just as I was. You've seen how challenging it is to make substantial progress. Remember that true (and rapid) progress comes from shifting out of any low frequency state that you're in, where the patterning you've created can only generate the results you're getting.

Take the next thirty days to write a new story that expresses the most optimal, inspired version of who you'd like to be in your sport. What does your new identity look like? Don't hold back. Write down the ideal 'you' in relation to competition, pressure, and how you handle winning or losing.

Before your next competitive event, anchor this new story into your mind. Allow the new meaning you're imparting to naturally induce a state of happiness, confidence, and relaxation. Next, assume that character. Act as if you are already that ideal version of yourself. Become ultra-focused. Use the Radical Reframe when you're feeling stuck, negative, or anxious. Amplify appreciation. Use all of the tools you now have at your disposal to optimize your performance.

One of the most helpful stories I now tell about tennis is that I care far more about the process rather than the results. When I play a match I look for what is going right during the process. What am I doing that's working? Can I do more of that? Can I have fun with it and not take it too seriously? Amplifying what is working rather than trying to fix what isn't working often helps me perform better. The underlying attitude is non-attachment. I choose to tell a story that I don't really care if I win or lose. If I really allow this in, I always play better. At least for me, being attached to winning causes a suffocating layer of expectation over the experience that undermines my performance. If I know I'm always doing my best, then I can allow myself to be curious about the process–what's working and what may need adjustment.

If you want to optimize your performance, what matters most is the quality of presence you bring to your sport. You're either going into competition in default mode where you're going to blindly react to whatever happens, or you're going to be intentional and awake to what's happening. You'll be cued into the subtleties, the shifts of momentum, the details that often get overlooked. You'll be able to detect how present your opponent is. You'll see with more clarity where their weaknesses are and what you need to do to exploit those weaknesses.

Another story I tell myself is that there's always a way to win. Even if the other guy is technically a better player, my story is that the quality of my presence puts us on equal playing field. I can use creative insights to figure out how to win. When I'm present my mind is able to problem-solve and propose solutions with much greater efficiency.

Does that mean that I will always win? No. I am however, optimizing my chances by choosing to perceive that there is always a way to come out with the victory.

One of the radical reframes I use is that losing is highly valuable. My 'old' character was highly competitive and hated losing. I'm still competitive and I do enjoy winning, but I choose to see losing as a valuable learning experience. Whether I lose to a player that I should have beat or I lose to someone who is simply way better, I choose to impart a meaning to it that feels like a win.

When I feel like I'm losing my composure on the court and tension or anxiety is mounting, I will ask myself some simple questions: Am I present? Am I choosing to have fun? Do I need to win this match to be happy? Can I be just as happy if I lose? Am I trying to impress anyone by winning?

These questions often help me regroup and loosen up. If I still feel more tense than I'd like, I'll use a radical reframe such as I appreciate this tension. It's helping me to perform even better. Pressure is a privilege.

The greatest athletes use the power of their mind just as much as their body in order to perform at their highest level. After Novak Djokovic won the 2016 French Open I read an article where an interviewer asked him if he believed he could break Roger Federer's record of seventeen grand slam titles. Djokovic's response went something like this:

"I don't mean to sound arrogant, but I've come to believe that anything is achievable in life."

Muhammad Ali was one of the greatest boxers and humanitarians that ever existed. Ali was quoted as saying, "I am the greatest. I said that before I knew I was."

Can you see how these world class athletes achieved such astounding success because they wrote a story and played a character that supported those accomplishments? Sure, they practiced incredibly hard as well, but many athletes practice equally hard and never reach that level of glory. Empowered storytelling is the difference.

Focus on What's Going Right

My 'old' character was obsessed with trying to problem solve and fix what was wrong with my strokes. I really don't do that much at all anymore. In any kind of competitive environment it can of course be helpful to identify weaknesses and try to improve them. From a low frequency however, we tend to fixate on and judge our weaknesses, especially during a competitive situation. This is often what makes us feel tight and prevents us from getting in the zone. When we are in the zone we are focused on what's going right. Our attention is on our strengths, what's working, and how to amplify these strengths to the point where that's all that grabs our attention.

In one of my recent tournament matches, I walked off the court after a pretty routine win and could easily identify several things that felt 'off' about my game. They were pretty minor, but my old tendency would have been to hyper focus on those problems and try to figure out what I should do to fix them. Instead, I consciously chose to focus on the many details of my game that went right. I told a story that listed out all of my strengths during the match. As I was doing this I could feel such a greater sense of confidence and ease wash over me.

Of course, this basic tip can be applied to any aspect of your life. Amplify your strengths way more than trying to fix your weaknesses. Instead of trying to improve or even figure out your weaknesses, instead tell a new story that those weaknesses are already new strengths. For instance, if you're a tennis player and you have a historically weak serve, instead of spending most of your time racking your brain about how to fix it, you'd simply start seeing your serve as a weapon. You'd use your imagination to anchor in a new reality where your serve is amazing. Of course, you can still work on your mechanics through regular practice, but your overall focus is on the new reality of your serve already being fantastic.

Making Peace with the Worst Case Scenario

In any competitive environment we know going into it that there is always a chance we will lose or not perform well. Sometimes it's helpful to experience this. If we always won and performed at our highest level, it would cease to be a challenge. If you feel tense or anxious prior to competition, the underlying psychological trigger is nearly always attachment to winning or performing well.

I'd recommend experimenting with telling a story before your next event that you're totally at peace with losing or not performing well. Whatever happens out there you're going to choose to accept it. You're unattached to any particular outcome. Sure you're going to do your best to win and compete well, but if it doesn't happen, you're totally okay with that.

This doesn't mean that you stay focused on losing or resign yourself to a negative outcome. Instead, you're simply making peace with all possible scenarios. This way of seeing things frees you up to perform your best. To the degree that we are attached to the outcome, our performance will suffer.

Living at a higher frequency doesn't mean you're always going to win or perform at your peak potential. It does mean however, that you impart a meaning to whatever happens that serves your highest good and frees you up to feel peaceful regardless of the outcome. With that said, you will likely win a lot more using these tools. Your confidence will skyrocket. Your performance level will go to a much higher level. Just don't be attached to any particular outcomes and enjoy the process.

What About Talent?

Many people would argue that super athletes such as Novak Djokovic and Muhammad Ali are born with their greatness already inside of them. Their talent is woven into their DNA. They were destined to become great. It's obvious that people are born with a predilection toward certain gifts and strengths that come very naturally to them. We all have strengths that we wrote into our story before we were born. The highest expression of our talent however, comes through practice, mindset training, and commitment to developing new skills. In my experience, I don't think I actually have much innate talent for tennis. Some people seem to 'feel' the ball quite naturally and have impeccable hand skills. Through repeated practice however, I've been able to develop a talent for the sport. I believe we can do this with anything that feels inspiring and relevant in our lives.

Most experts in the fields of athletic and human performance focus primarily on how to practice in a way that accelerates skill development. My personal and coaching experience suggests that the Instant Upgrade Tools offer an equally (if not more) powerful way to accelerate talent and optimize human performance. When you practice in a conscious, deliberate way and you combine that with Empowered Storytelling, Character Acting, and the other tools, you can likely maximize your talent in the shortest amount of time possible. My sense is that a lot more research will be done in the coming years on the power of the mind in affecting all areas of performance.

You don't need to have a scientist verify that any of this is true or untrue. Simply test it out in your own experience. You may want to start telling an empowered story of how much fun you're having accelerating your talent level and making enormous progress in short periods of time. This is actually, another story I have been telling to myself:

> *Every time I step on the court, I'm a better player than the last time I was here. My game makes greater leaps in improvement in three days than most players make in three months. I love being able to activate my talent and potential in such powerful and effective ways.*

I'd like to reiterate a point that I've made throughout this book, given its relevance to the topic of athletic performance. Many performance coaches tell their students to think positively and to use affirmations. Hopefully you already see how The Instant Upgrade Tools are radically different.

When you try to manufacture positive thoughts within the confines of a low frequency of reality, it can only lead to temporary results at best and self-sabotage at worst. When you upgrade, you are going into a new frequency of reality where you are not using any kind of artificial tools to try and feel better. When you're telling new stories, you're doing so from the perspective that who you are is a wide open, dynamic, constantly changing field of energy that can be altered in any way you desire. When you compete or perform, you're not trying to force yourself to believe that you feel good or that you're confident. You're quite literally choosing to embrace the openness of who you are and actually become what you envision through the power of your imagination. There's nothing fake, forced, or contrived about it. It's as real as you acting as if you're struggling and not making progress. Normally when we use positive thinking we are doing so from the belief that we are actually a pretty screwed up person. We try to introduce new thoughts into our low frequency which can only lead to more of the same limiting patterns.

The Truth is that you're already enlightened, complete, and perfect as you are. You're just playing a character that is pretending that it's limited. You can morph into a new character at will, one that is equally as real (or fake) as the old character. Who you really are is a wide open field of potential.

This may sound like a pretty deep or mystical way to approach playing a round of golf. It's also highly practical. Test it out in your own experience and see what happens. Keep in mind there is no such thing as doing this wrong. I'll likely fail at this is the same old story you've been telling yourself. Choose to have a great deal of fun inventing yourself in whatever way feels most inspiring as an athlete. Be that person now. If you can imagine it, you can start living and embodying it in this very moment.

How to Instantly Upgrade Your Health

"You replace every molecule of every cell within your body within the course of one year. I am not being flip when I refer to the 'new you.' It is quite literally possible, no matter how bad you are feeling or eating today, to be utterly transformed in just 365 days. But it won't take you that long. You can be feeling significantly better in just a couple of days and make lasting changes to your health within a month."
Woodson Merrell

Take a moment to reflect on your answers to these questions:

- How do you define health?
- What does ideal health look like to you?
- What is the main cause or source of ideal health?

The conventional definition of health is that it is the absence of disease. You likely already know that there's a lot more to true health than simply not being sick. You may define health as the ability to thrive in life or having ample energy to function at a high level. I'd like to stretch your version of what health really is based on the context of the tools you just learned about.
Here's how I would now define health:

True health is the ability to consciously invent yourself in whatever way you desire based on recognizing the open, fluid, and limitless nature of your human experience.

I don't define health based on the presence or lack of various symptoms; it's much more about the degree of consciousness you have and the clarity with which you see who you really are and why you're here. All health and well-being stems from this core source.

From this point of view you can have perfect blood pressure, the ideal weight, high energy, or excellent digestion and still be profoundly unhealthy. Why? Because if you don't know that it's only the character you've created that appears to be healthy, and that it's not really who you are, you will necessarily get attached to the 'perfect' health that you have, which is, from this perspective, quite unhealthy.

On the contrary, you can be dying of cancer and still enjoy a state of perfect health. If your relationship with cancer is premised upon experiencing the space and illusion that underlies the illness, you are healthy. Health can be accessed and magnified in any moment; it's not based on the outer conditions we have.

When I was locked into my 'old' self I often felt unhealthy but could not put my finger on why. It just felt like something was off. By all normal markers, I was in perfect health, but my feeling was always one of being out of balance or fundamentally lacking in some mysterious factor that would help me heal and feel well. From this place of lack, I tried all kinds of things to make myself feel better–vegetarianism, gluten free diets, yoga, acupuncture, jogging, herbs, massage, psychotherapy, fasting, meditation, and on and on. You name it, I likely tried it. Yet nothing really worked.

Many of these approaches actually made me feel worse about myself as I either ended up using too much willpower to make lifestyle changes, or the techniques just wouldn't put a dent in my feeling of being 'off', which made me feel like a failure, or like something was definitely more wrong with me than I could have imagined. I saw plenty of other people around me benefitting greatly from these approaches. Why couldn't I? It was frustrating to say the least.

Now I see that I was simply locked into a low frequency.

When we try to make lifestyle changes with the goal of feeling better yet we continue to stay stuck in the same frequency, we are setting ourselves up for self-sabotage. Some people spend their entire life trying one diet after another, exploring yet another healing technique, or looking to doctors, gurus, or experts to fix their situation. They ride the roller coaster of constant ups and downs, making some improvement then returning to their normal behaviors and ways of feeling.

To be clear, what I am talking about here is what it really takes to make long-term, permanent changes in your life. Of course if you eat organic vegetables instead of cookies for a week there's a good chance you'll feel better. Food does have a strong effect on our frequency. The point is that it's up to us to change our frequency first before we expect food or anything else to do it for us. This is a critical distinction to make when you go about initiating new lifestyle patterns. First create the inner shift to support the outer changes you intend on making. If you want to eat organic vegetables as a way of life, first upgrade into the frequency that would reflect that change. You can do this by using all of the Instant Upgrade Tools. When you do this, eating more vegetables will be a completely natural, desired experience. There will be no force or willpower involved. You now have a resonance with vegetables that you didn't have before.

Are you starting to see more clearly how this works?

In my story I could never create long-term changes as my 'old' character. I would be really 'good' about exercising, doing yoga, and eating well for a period of time, but it would always backfire. At some point I would inevitably find myself saying, F__ it. What's the point?

I would then return to the same behaviors that locked in my current frequency which were abundant with cravings, addictions, and pretty extreme patterns. I'd get locked into those limiting behaviors and habits for another few months, get fed up again, then make some new lifestyle changes, feel better temporarily, get bored or frustrated, then revert to the old patterns. Like most people I spent most of my life on this painful cycle.

The diet industry is a multi-billion dollar cash juggernaut. The question arises, why do so many books need to be written on what to eat? After all, it's pretty simple. More fruits and vegetables will make you healthier and help you lose weight. Processed sugars and refined carbohydrates will cause inflammation, weight gain, and fatigue. Just stop eating that stuff and start eating leafy greens, healthy protein, and whole grains and you're good to go. It's so simple, right? Yes, but why can so few people pull it off? Most of us are aware that we should eat this way, but few of us actually do. What is going on here?

Consider once again the issue of resonance. You'll be attracted to specific foods based on your current frequency. We could safely generalize and say that if you're stuck in a low frequency state, you'll likely feel a gravitational pull towards cookies, candy, cereal, muffins, bread, pizza, fast food, soda, and fried foods. There will be a resonance with these foods which causes an overwhelming desire for them that you feel you can't escape from. If this is the case, you can read every diet book in the world and they will all backfire and make you feel like more of a failure.

The quality of your frequency determines how foods taste as well. If you absolutely love the taste of sugar, flour products, and fried foods, it means you have a resonance with them. If you are repelled by the taste of healthier foods such as kale, wild salmon, quinoa, blueberries, and so on, it means that your frequency is not aligned with these foods. If you try and force yourself to eat them, all that happens is you feel a high degree of deprivation. A lack of satisfaction dominates your experience of food. Trying to change your diet from a place of deprivation never works. Yes, you can get temporary results. If you have a lot of willpower you could even make it a whole year. But at some point it will backfire. You will return to the foods that resonate with you based on the frequency you're in.

Fascinating, isn't it?

The 'old' me loved sugar and bread. I always said that bread was my favorite food on the planet. I thought it tasted amazing. It turned out that my body actually hated the sugar and bread that I loved so much. I had a clear allergy to these foods as I would get bloated, feel puffy and lethargic, and even more depressed if I indulged too much. I believe that my 'old' character had a chronic case of candida due to taking too many antibiotics as a kid (I was on tetracycline for over two years straight for bad acne, another perfect prop that I added to my story to lock in my suffering). The constant craving for sugar and carbs and the accompanying physical discomfort caused by these foods was a perfect reflection of my frequency at that time. I was masterful at using food to lock in the patterning that perfectly supported that reality.

The 'old' me was also highly skilled at using exercise as another form of self-punishment. From that level of frequency I never naturally enjoyed or felt motivated to take exceptional care of my body. I never felt inspired to do things like yoga, jogging, or other forms of exercise. It all felt like 'work' in the derogatory sense of the term. I could sometimes induce a runner's high from jogging, but it was short lived and still mostly a painful experience. I never felt interested in being embodied. Yoga made me really uncomfortable, as my body was unusually stiff from having severe knee problems as a teenager (another layer added by my Higher Self to lock in the belief that I was limited). I grew up with pretty severe knee pain that eventually migrated into my hips and lower back. While everyone was telling me that yoga was the cure for this, every time I did it was extremely uncomfortable and I felt constant resistance. I even forced myself to do Bikram Yoga nearly every day for a year straight (yes, I can muster up a fair amount of willpower at times). Did this cure me of my ailing body? Quite the opposite–my improper use of this practice led to the beginning stages of degenerative disc disease.

You already know why this happened. There was no resonance between me and yoga. It was a forced fit, an energetic mismatch for the frequency I was dwelling at. I couldn't access the practice in a way that was genuinely inspiring and healthy.

Take a step back and assess the degree to which you see this cycle playing out in your life. Have you noticed a long-term trend of having temporary breakthroughs in your health and well-being, only to come crashing down again a few weeks or months later? Have you found yourself endlessly perplexed as to what it really takes to create permanent change? Now you know why.

The solution is always to shift your frequency starting in this very moment. Do that first, then go ahead and initiate any lifestyle changes you want. Since applying The Instant Upgrade Tools some interesting things have happened in my life.

I now naturally enjoy and desire healthy foods in a way I never did before. My experience of food is so radically different than it used to be that I still find myself in shock at times as far as how easy it is to eat well. Ultimately, there's no right or wrong way to eat. When you shift into higher frequencies your experience with food and other lifestyle factors may look vastly different from mine. We are all unique and there's no one way that things need to look. In my experience I now naturally desire foods that I used to be repelled by. Without even thinking about it too much or planning in advance, I find myself choosing an organic, whole foods diet that is mostly gluten, sugar, and dairy free. With the same amount of ease that I used to chomp down a muffin and/or scone with a latte for breakfast, I now prefer green smoothies and Chinese herbal tea in the morning. Just as I used to feel a strong aversion to most healthy foods, I now feel the same aversion to sugar, wheat products, and refined carbohydrates.

This more or less just 'happened' as I shifted into a higher frequency. I wasn't really expecting it nor planning it. As I upgraded my experience I found myself eating new things that reflected that inner shift. Honestly, I don't feel attached to any of it. If I want to have a muffin, a beer or two, or some ice cream, I'm totally cool with that. I have felt a few occasional impulses to have these foods, but I have pretty much avoided almost all of them as they genuinely don't sound appealing. I also used to enjoy regular red wine and have lost all interest in that for the time being. It no longer resonates.

Can you see how none of this feels forced, dogmatic, contracted, or rigid? Based on our new definition of health you can have the purest diet on the planet and still be unhealthy. Food is just a prop. Without the right awareness of what it is (a prop you're placing in your hologram of reality that has its own frequency), even the healthiest foods can add to your suffering. Anytime you get caught in a righteous, preachy, black and white, or deprived relationship with food, it's a sign that you are using food as a prop to keep you stuck in a low frequency.

I remember that when my 'old' self would have some success making dietary changes for a period of time, I would feel a certain degree of judgment about people who were 'unconscious' about their food intake. I felt like my way was better. I would cycle through feelings of righteousness as if I had finally cracked the code, only to have it come crashing down, leaving me feeling the exact opposite–like I didn't have a clue and everyone was doing a better job than I was.

Many people use food as one of their primary forms of bondage. They tell an unconscious story about food that strips the nourishment and joy out of their life. Of course, anorexia and bulimia are on the far end of this spectrum, but millions upon millions of people struggle with ongoing feelings of deprivation, guilt, shame, and powerlessness in relation to how they nourish themselves.

If this describes you to any degree, can you see the way out now? That in this moment you can choose an entirely new story, become ultra-focused on that story, and start playing a new character whose new, higher frequency in no way matches up with the previous pain you put yourself through? It IS possible. Play around with it. It doesn't have to be hard and I don't say that to undermine the intensity of your struggle. I just want you to see the way out.
I encourage you to look at exercise in a similar way. If you feel absolutely zero desire to move your body it means that your current frequency is out of resonance with exercise. As with food, there's nothing inherently wrong with not exercising. It is possible that you can upgrade your frequency and still choose not to move your body.

In my experience I have noticed a constant desire to move, stretch, breathe deeply, get my heart rate up, sweat, and work at my edge. I find that I crave this on a daily basis. Since upgrading my frequency, I exercise pretty much every day and only do things I find highly enjoyable. Exercise is fun for me. Before I pretty much hated it. Every day I do some combination of tennis, yoga, walking, and weightlifting. I still don't feel inspired to jog, go on long hikes, or take up new sports. Whereas before yoga always felt like torture, now I really enjoy it. The sensations it produces in my body feel as pleasurable as they do painful. Before, it was always one-sidedly uncomfortable. I now find that I can ease into various postures for longer periods of time without any resistance. Before, my mind was always racing, pretty much resisting it to the end. I now get a little bummed when I have to quit doing yoga and move onto something else as I often find it to be deeply satisfying. Before, the last thing I wanted to do was get up in the morning and relate to the stiffness in my body. Now I often spend twenty minutes stretching before I jump onto the computer to work.

Since I changed my lifestyle patterns I have noticed that I look and feel much better. My energy has increased dramatically, I have lost ten pounds and my body feels more radiant and youthful. I feel more at ease in my own skin than ever before. My mind feels alert and stimulated yet also calm and relaxed. It wasn't the yoga or the dietary changes that caused all of this; it was the upgrade in my frequency. The lifestyle patterns simply mirrored this internal shift and have helped me to establish a new kind of momentum that feels exciting and lasting.

What I find interesting is how these kind of changes can simultaneously be perceived as life-changing substantial, and not that big of a deal. From my current perspective I very much feel like the changes I've made are as natural as breathing. They don't feel earth-shattering at all even though in a sense, someone on the outside looking in would likely say that they are. From the outside looking in, making lifestyle changes can feel overwhelming, daunting, and scary. There's an intelligence behind these feelings as they truly are difficult, let alone impossible, if you're not shifting your frequency to support the changes. Once you're there however, it's not scary or intimidating at all. It's easy. Actually, even saying it's easy isn't quite accurate. It just 'is.' Just as my 'old' character always found it easy to eat sugar, my new character finds it equally easy to eat kale. No difference.

Just in case you're curious, here's a quick list of some of the main 'high frequency' foods that I'm finding that I naturally desire:

Blueberries
Raspberries

Peaches
Kale
Spinach
Beets
Salads
Flax Seeds
Chia Seeds
Coconut Oil
Coconut Water
Spirulina
Probiotic Fiber
Adaptogenic Herbs
Organic Lean Meats
Wild Salmon
Quinoa
Brown Rice
Sweet Potatoes
Nutrition Bars (I like Vega, Larabars, and EcoHemp)

I am also finding that I naturally desire staying hydrated way more than used to be the case. I am constantly drinking water, herbal teas, and electrolyte drinks. I still feel drawn to my morning cup of coffee but I don't desire any cream or sugar in it. I used to hate black coffee and could only drink it if it was pretty doctored up. Now I only want black coffee. I used to hate the taste of Chinese herbs, now I thoroughly enjoy a cup of strong herbal tea. I have no idea why except to say it's entirely due to resonance.

I want to reiterate that my diet and exercise patterns are in no way what you should do. The whole point is to discover for yourself what you're naturally drawn to, experiment, and refine as needed. It also should be clear by this point that I choose foods and exercises in a spontaneous fashion. None of this is regimented or planned out. I just do what feels right on any given day. I don't feel excited by the idea of regimenting my lifestyle choices. Instead, I see every day as wide open with possibility. Who knows, tomorrow I may decide to eat a pint of Ben and Jerry's for breakfast. If that resonated with me I'd be all over it! Spontaneity seems to be one of the hallmarks of high frequency states, at least in my experience.

A Few Thoughts On Liberating Addictions

As you can imagine, my take on addiction is going to be radically different than the conventional wisdom that says, once an addict, always an addict. From the point of view that this book is coming from, buying into that kind of statement is a surefire way to lock yourself into your current frequency. I know what this statement is getting at, that in order to prevent addictive behaviors in the future we have to own the fact that we will always be vulnerable to succumbing to our vices.

When you shift into a new frequency you are literally a new person. The old person who was bound by specific habits no longer exists. The deeper issue isn't if you'll be vulnerable to your vices again; it's if you will create yourself downgrading your frequency again to generate the illusion that you are the same person you were before, with the same resonance toward specific substances or activities. You do have free will to upgrade and downgrade your frequency as you desire. Once a higher frequency becomes stabilized however, it becomes increasingly unlikely that you would downgrade, as there would be no relevance or benefit to doing so. Since you have full control over that, you'd simply choose to stay in the higher frequency, as it's more supportive, fun, and useful for your life.

The Instant Upgrade Tools can be extremely powerful allies in cutting through the resonance you feel with your chosen addiction. Just as you would with any other life theme, go through each of the tools and apply them accordingly. Start writing down and telling a new story about being a person who is in no way aligned with the addiction and how easy it was to end that phase of your life. Start playing around with acting out that new character. Start seeing the addiction as a prop you've generated within your own hologram of reality to convince you that you're limited. Tell a new story about reclaiming power from that prop. See that since you created it, you necessarily have the power to uncreate it. You can collapse that field just as swiftly as you opened it up.

On the contrary, realize that if your frequency doesn't change, you'll continue to have a resonance with that addiction and the pull toward it will be unbearable. It's helpful to know this so that you don't feel like a failure when you're trying to quit the addiction. If the resonance isn't addressed, there's no other coping mechanism or strategy you can use that will actually work on a permanent basis. Also, keep in mind that you may still have to endure temporary physical and emotional discomfort even if you shift into a higher frequency. You'll likely notice however, that you have a lot more space around the sensations that arise during withdrawal than you normally would. The discomfort may be there but you're not struggling against it. I've seen it happen both ways. Some people are shocked to find that quitting the addiction was way easier than they expected. Others still notice discomfort, but find that they can handle it in a new, empowering way. When you break the resonance that you have with an addiction, you'll notice an immediate shift in the way you feel about it. You become repelled by the exact same quality that made it previously attractive. When you notice a desire for it, it is tinged with an accompanying feeling of aversion.

From the conventional point of view, quitting an addiction is an inherently long, hard, and demanding process. When you use the Instant Upgrade Tools however, you see that it doesn't have to be that way. Any kind of change will be perceived as hard if we stay locked in the same frequency. While I've never struggled with a full blown drug addiction or anything of that nature, my 'old' self had a highly addictive personality. I can safely say from my own experience that it is possible to renounce an addiction in an instant. That doesn't mean the impulse or residual momentum of that addiction won't resurface; it likely will. What it means is that you are able to reclaim power from the addiction in a moment and that you can create your reality so that it never has power over you again.

There is only one real addiction and that is the addiction we have to a false sense of self that keeps us stuck in the same constraints of our current reality. All other outer addictions are a byproduct of this main issue. When we go to the source and upgrade our frequency we are annihilating the root cause of why the addiction was created in the first place. Many people have done this and they are no longer addicts in any way whatsoever.

How to Instantly Upgrade Your Relationships

As you likely know by now upgrading your relationships begins and ends with the relationship you have with yourself. If you are using these Tools on a regular basis, it's a sign that you care about yourself and your life and want to experience the vast amount of goodness that this universe has to offer. We are heavily conditioned in our modern world to put ourselves last, to deny our own worth, and to hide from our innate greatness. Expressing a deep level of self-care so often feels foreign to our sensibilities. Many feel that deep self-care automatically connotes narcissism or arrogance. Somehow we believe that it's more responsible or upstanding to deny ourselves the immense benefits that come from choosing to care for ourselves.

One of my favorite mentors growing up was a meditation teacher named Stephen Levine who mainly works with people in the context of death and dying. I heard him say something at a seminar I attended when I was seventeen years old that still sticks with me to this day. It went something like this:

If we were at a restaurant and we heard two people having a conversation at the table next to us in a similar manner to the way we talk to ourselves, we wouldn't be able to get through our meal. It would make us sick.

Using the Instant Upgrade Tools helps us to fundamentally change our self-perception. We talk to ourselves in a new way, hold ourselves in space in a new way, and invent ourselves to radiate the kind of love and joy that reflects the highest version of who we want to be. As we shift into higher frequencies we lose interest in self-abnegation, judgment, punishment, deprivation, or any other belief or behavior that denies our basic right to feel worthy and loved. It becomes our natural tendency to show ourselves just as much appreciation and care as we do our children, parents, close friends, or anyone else we love.
Let's examine a few general trends that you'll likely notice in your relationship to other people as you apply The Instant Upgrade Tools. As

I share a few potential outcomes of upgrading to higher frequencies, feel free to use these descriptions as new stories you are writing into your life. As you write new stories, Character Acting is the next tool you'll want to experiment with as you transform your relationship with people. Start by choosing a new role to play in environments where it doesn't feel like a big deal. For instance, play the character you wish to be when you're interacting with the checkout clerk at the grocery store. Engage with them as if you're already embodying the qualities below:

• **You feel more comfortable and settled in your own skin.**
As you write a higher level of self-love and care into your script, you'll notice that you feel more at peace within your body. You feel at home in who you are. Your posture, movements, facial expressions, and gestures all begin to reflect this greater sense of ease. There is a sense of grace in the way you carry yourself in the world.

• **You can relax around other people.**
As you settle more into yourself and become more embodied this naturally extends to others. You feel at peace and secure with yourself in any social environment. Because you are relaxed you put others at ease. The energy you emanate makes people feel safe. They quickly feel that they can trust you.

• **You become a deep listener.**
Because you don't always need to fill the space by talking and expressing your view on things, you can now listen on a deeper level. You hear what people say but more importantly, how they say what they say. You can glean subtle cues from people that makes them feel validated.

• **You exude a high degree of empathy.**
Because you've renounced self-consciousness you can now step into someone's situation and vividly relate to what they are going through. You can see them for who they are because you have a clean filter. You can recognize someone's true colors within seconds. There is no wiggle room where they can hide or use typical facades.

• **Your sensitivity works for you instead of against you.**

You come to enjoy being a highly sensitive person who is attuned to the subtle dynamics at play in any human interaction. You see this as a huge positive in your life, as you can easily set boundaries that prevent you from getting overwhelmed by people's energy. You feel on a deep level but you are in no way cursed by your ability to do this. Because you are imparting an empowering meaning to being sensitive it has become one of your greatest assets.

- **You care less about what people think.**

You come to see that people's opinion of you is nothing you need to take seriously. You have a lot of humor and space around judgment directed at you. Because you don't take yourself so seriously there is nothing inside of you that can get offended. You're not holding onto any rigid viewpoint on who you are so there is no territory or belief to defend. You see clearly that someone's opinion of you is nothing more than a projection of how that person feels about themselves. Instead of feeling terrible when there is negative judgment directed your way, you feel compassion for the person whose filter is distorted enough to project negativity onto others. The only way they could do that is if they are suffering.

- **You feel more attractive.**

As you upgrade your frequency the general energy you emit to the world will feel clear, uplifting, and light. People are naturally drawn to you because of this. While you're not as attached to physical appearances, you can humbly see the person looking back at you in the mirror as a highly attractive, radiant being. This is more of a chosen perception than concrete physical attributes that typically reflect attractiveness. While your physical appearance will likely go through some alteration to reflect new frequencies, you feel more attractive overall simply because you are at home in yourself.

You can see how these new shifts into a more relaxed, confident, altruistic version of yourself describes what many would call charisma. As you upgrade your frequency you'll naturally become a more charismatic person. This doesn't mean that you are always a people person or the center of attention. You can simply be yourself, feel at home in your skin, and create an energy around you that is accepting and peaceful. Although it is often more of an unconscious dynamic, people feel this very deeply. I invite you to come up with your own definition of charisma and play that role accordingly. I used to believe that I had to be like Tony Robbins or Zig Ziglar in order to exude charisma. The term always felt kind of annoying and inaccessible to me as it seemed to only apply to extroverts who love being in crowds, leading the way. Now I define charisma as just being myself as fully as I can.

Transcending the Labels of Introversion and Extroversion

My 'old' self was highly identified with the label of being an introvert. I was convinced that I was far better off being alone most of the time and that I rejuvenated myself when I was away from people. I often felt drained by social interactions and avoided them as much as I could. I simultaneously craved alone time and felt lonely when I was by myself for prolonged periods.

As my 'new' character, I now see that labels such as introvert or extrovert are mostly useless. We are all dynamic, complex creatures who can invent ourselves in whatever way we want. As such, it is natural to choose a balanced blend of social interaction and alone time. Because I choose to be at peace with myself I now enjoy both equally. I can derive just as much energy from interactions with people as I do from being alone.

I have noticed that many introverts use this label as a way to solidify the character they are playing and not challenge the elements of it that aren't serving them. For instance, I often get asked a lot, How can I grow my business if I'm an introvert? Given that just about any business entirely consists of serving and interacting with people, it doesn't serve a business owner to get locked into the belief that they are better off alone than with others. My suggestion is to make your identity more fluid, to invent yourself in a way that would serve your business and potential customers. If you are attached to being alone it's probably better to just get a job that would support that goal.

When I've made similar suggestions on my Facebook pages, some 'diehard' introverts have retaliated by saying something to the effect of, That's easy for you to say. You have a big audience and it's obvious I enjoy the spotlight. You don't understand what it means to be an introvert and lack sensitivity to the challenges we face.

I understand why someone highly identified with the role of being an introvert would feel this way, but the truth is that my 'old' character was as introverted as they come. I spent long periods of time on my own, pretty much isolated from the world. I consciously chose to re-invent myself as someone who enjoys the spotlight and thrives from having a large audience. Why? Because as an entrepreneur, it's far more helpful to my bottom line and the people I serve. I still enjoy alone time and need a fair amount of it to stay on my game, but I am open to whatever life presents, whether that entails being with people or not.

I am not saying that you need to completely renounce being an introvert. Instead, just be sure that you are telling a story about this role that is actually helpful and feels inspiring. If that label is locking you into a limited framework that is based on fear or lack, then it may be wise to use the Instant Upgrade Tools and start playing a new character. Write down a new, empowering definition of what being an introvert means to you. Focus on all of the amazing attributes you have as an introvert that enable you to thrive in this world. Or, simply do away with these kinds of labels altogether as I have. You may be more inclined to one side of the spectrum or the other but at some point, you stop buying into labels and categories.

If you identify yourself as an extrovert, the same ideas apply. If you tend to resist alone time, look at your resistance in a new light. After all, the relationship that you have with yourself is always paramount to your happiness and fulfillment. If you can't be with yourself without distraction, what story are you telling that causes it to be this way? Can you impart a new meaning to being alone that helps you befriend yourself?

Just as many people are playing characters who are deeply challenged by being in social settings, others have the same challenges with being alone. Either way, the tools can be applied to reclaim your power and invent yourself in a way that feels most helpful.

Resonance and Relationships

The people that you create being a regular part of your reality are there because you share a similar frequency as them. If you don't feel very fulfilled by the quality of your relationships, shift into a new frequency and allow the magic of resonance to work to your advantage. Your ability to upgrade your relationships with others is based entirely on your ability to upgrade your relationship with yourself. This is true in the context of both platonic and romantic relationships. You can only ever attract people who share a similar frequency. If you find yourself longing for more love and connection in your life, looking for these qualities outside of yourself is a pitfall that can only lead to continued longing. You first have to know how to generate these states within your own experience before you can expect them to show up outside of you. The universe is only a mirror for your frequency.

Denying yourself love is like stripping away a core form of nourishment in your life. In my work, I've seen so many people who are masterful at pushing love away. They have a highly trained army of defenses that stand guard against the vulnerability that true love entails. The stories they are telling typically go something like:

- I don't deserve love.
- I will never have someone who loves me the way I am.
- Love doesn't feel safe. I can't trust it. People always betray me.
- All that men care about is sex. They will say anything to achieve their selfish motives.
- Conscious women are so high maintenance. Their demands are unrealistic.
- I have a lot of work to do on myself before I can have love in my life.

What is your current 'love' story? Do you unconsciously deny yourself the joy that comes from both self-love and being receptive to the love that others have to offer you? Are you using your past as a way to stay guarded and ward off vulnerability?

As human beings our love story tends to make our experience here that much more dramatic and interesting. From the Higher Self's point of view, ALL feelings we have in relation to love are supported. Even if we choose isolation and the constant denial of love, there is an equal amount of drama and juiciness in that as there is in being heavily immersed in human relationships. You are supported in whatever way you prefer to exist; the point is to make sure that your preference is actually conscious. If you've denied yourself love as a self-protective mechanism to ensure you don't get hurt, that would be a useful story to examine and then re-write. As the hero of your own story, what does love look like to you? You get to invent your own definition. Just make sure that your definition is consciously created, as opposed to unconsciously handed to you from your parents, the culture you are immersed in, or your past.

We are deeply conditioned to believe that having a soulmate who loves us unconditionally is necessary in order to live a fulfilling and happy life. Millions of people long for this kind of connection with another human being, yet never seem able to attract it into their life. When they do meet someone who feels like 'the one', they often get their hopes up and invest themselves fully in the relationship, believing that they have finally found someone who can make them feel whole. Eventually however, the chemistry or compatibility declines and they are left disappointed.

As ironic as it may sound, the best way to attract true love from another person into your life is to be completely okay without it. The more you come to see other people as projections or emanations of your own consciousness, the clearer it becomes that they can't offer you anything that you can't offer yourself. You don't 'need' another person to make you feel whole, validated, or worthy of love. These are all qualities that you generate within yourself. The other person is simply a mirror showing you the love-based lens that you are seeing your life through. If you long for love from another, it's a sign from your Higher Self to generate that exact feeling state within your own field of awareness. What you are looking for is found within yourself. As you embrace this truth and start using the tools to re-invent yourself as someone who has a high degree of self-love, because of resonance, you will naturally create another person showing up to reflect that back to you, as long as it's relevant to your story.

How to Gracefully Transition Out of Relationships That Don't Serve You

The beautiful thing about upgrading your frequency is that you don't need to force anything. If you find yourself in a relationship that is no longer reflective of who you are the first thing to realize is that, due to the issue of resonance, that person will naturally fade out of your life in whatever way your Higher Self scripts it. You don't need to try to control the situation or impose your will in a way that feels urgent or desperate. Instead, start focusing on how appreciative you are to be in a new place in your life, surrounded by people who completely support you and resonate at your chosen frequency. Tell a story of how easy it has been to transition out of this relationship that is no longer serving you. Instead of seeing that person as a burden or a shackle that keeps you tied down, see them as a reflection of your past self that is gradually fading out of your life. In a compassionate way, cut your energetic and emotional ties with them and consciously see them being more free and open to new possibilities within their new reality (which no longer involves you).

In this way you can actually be free of any limiting aspects of that person even if they are still showing up in your reality. They have no power over you. Now that you know how to use resonance to your advantage, you can actually have fun collapsing the pattern that caused them to show up in the first place. Instead of it being a struggle to get them out of your life, you can see it as a game you're playing to test your skill at shifting into new frequencies and collapsing the patterns of old circumstances. You don't take them personally or get enmeshed in the drama of their emotions. Instead, you see them as a holographic image that can evaporate just as easily as it was created. This in no way denies the feelings of that person. In fact, it's just the opposite. You are taking a stand for what is in the highest good for both people, and you're doing it from a place of space and compassion.

Obviously a whole book could be written about applying The Instant Upgrade Tools to love and human relationships. My intention here is to keep it practical and ensure that your top priority in life is to love yourself in the deepest, highest way possible. This is the ultimate game you came here to play. In a world that appears to be full of conflict, violence, and hatred, where fear and defensiveness feel like perfectly rational ways to live, can you see through it all? Can you penetrate the illusion of the outer world and be a renegade who chooses love above all else? Can you live from a place of simultaneous vulnerability and strength, where you are open to whatever life brings you, whether it's the love of a soulmate, the kindred connection of a new friend, or the guidance and wisdom of a new mentor? If you choose to stay open, life will always give you experiences that support and feed you on the deepest levels.

How to Instantly Upgrade Your Spiritual Life

While the Instant Upgrade Tools are designed to be highly practical, you've likely already noticed the profound impact they can have on your spiritual life. These tools change the way you see yourself and this life you're living on a core level. They open you up to recognize the natural fluidity and infinite potential of your life. Although I haven't stated so explicitly, one of my goals in this book has been to integrate ancient spiritual teachings into the daily life of the average modern person. All too often, there remains a distinct schism between theory and practical application. I have witnessed this frequently in various spiritual communities where it was obvious that people were unable to integrate the teachings into the practical matters of daily life. They may be able to sit on a cushion without moving for hours on end, but their relationships, finances, or career was by all accounts a total mess. In my coaching work, I've seen many deeply spiritual people struggle immensely with their finances, largely due to the unconscious stories they are telling. The way I see it, spirituality is a process of becoming awake to how we perceive life in all of its nuances and themes. The Instant Upgrade Tools are designed to help you bring awareness to any theme where your power is locked up right now.

After making it this far, you are hopefully not only clear on how to integrate these tools into your daily life; you're also seeing how to apply them to your deepest beliefs and the core perceptions you've formed around who you are and why you're here. Since we've spent a fair amount of time focusing on the practical matters of life, let's discuss some of the BIG topics of life and death within the context of The Instant Upgrade Tools. As I mentioned in the introduction, my intention is not to share any particular philosophical or religious point of view, or to engage in a debate around what God is, why people die, and other deeper questions. I'd simply like to share what I've discovered after shifting into higher frequencies in my own life.

Who or What Is God?

Yes, I'm going to jump right into the fire. Now of course the English language is grossly inadequate at conveying the subtlety necessary to truly describe who or what God is. I'll share some of the main insights I've discovered and leave it up to you to do with this what feels relevant and inspiring. I am only using the term God because it's the one most familiar and accessible to our Western culture. Keep in mind that you can use any term that works for you.

There is a common saying that goes something like this: The main thing that prevents you from directly experiencing God is the many beliefs you've acquired around what God is or is not.

From a higher frequency perspective, God is beyond beliefs. Any belief we use to try and capture the essence of God is inaccurate and limited. We could say that God is the infinite openness we experience that is beyond all beliefs. This includes the belief that God does or does not exist, God is inside or outside of us, God is loving or wrathful, and so on. We basically need to do away with all of this in order to have a direct experience of God. No belief system or logic-based philosophy can ever encapsulate the Truth in this sense. All religious traditions can point the way, but it's up to each of us to shed our own light on what is True and have the courage and willingness to keep penetrating our beliefs.

God never 'goes' anywhere. The Presence that we call God is within and outside of every single thing. You are God. God is you. There is no separation. What I mean by this is that you are a unique yet inseparable expression of the infinite nature of existence itself. You are creating existence moment-to-moment. You do this simultaneously as a 'person' who appears to be a certain way, and also as an infinitely powerful, all-intelligent Presence that is the basis of all that is. You can't really 'understand' this on a purely rational level. It is inherently paradoxical to the conceptual mind. The only way to know God is through direct experience.

No matter how much you know and even after you've mastered the tools in this book, God will always remain a mystery that can't be fully comprehended. Our job as humans is not to understand this mystery; it's to live 'as' the mystery without resistance. We can unite with this infinite intelligence and allow it to guide us naturally through life. We do this by dropping our attachment to things being a certain way, and by cutting through the tendency to impose our will and limiting stories on the natural flow of things.

As you tell more empowering stories about your human life, you are upgrading into higher frequencies of reality where your perceptions become more accurate and precise. This doesn't mean you fully understand the mystery of life; it means that you increasingly live from a place of non-resistance. You become aligned with and plugged into this mystery and you know that this is where all creative power stems from. I've come to define spirituality in exactly this way:

Spirituality is the connection I have with unseen forces that enables me to intentionally and simultaneously create and surrender to my life.

Is Enlightenment Hard?

Many religious traditions throughout history share a commonly held belief that knowing God or becoming enlightened is the hardest thing to achieve as a human being. Some traditions adamantly state that you have to sit on a mountaintop for twenty years, meditating without pause, foregoing sleep and food, and sacrificing every human comfort and desire in order to become enlightened or experience God. Perhaps this is why we are highly influenced by the belief that change is hard and takes a long time.

My 'old' self created a reality where I fervently bought into this way of seeing things. I used meditation and spirituality as a prop to convince myself that I was indeed limited and imperfect in this moment, and had to use all kind of purification practices and rituals in order to even come close to accessing a deeper understanding. I played 'the good

student' and meditated an hour a day, went to retreats, and devoted my life to my quest for the truth.
The problem I came up against is that this entire way of 'being spiritual' felt forced and unnatural. In the back of my mind I always wondered what the point of doing all of this really was. Usually these practices just made me feel worse about my situation. The more I tried, the worse I felt.

Now I see that this was all a highly effective prop I created to pretend that I really was a limited human who had to work extremely hard to get somewhere on the spiritual path. My very ideas of spirituality were exactly what was preventing me from accessing my spiritual power. As it is for many, my fixed way of seeing spirituality was the final, most convincing hurdle that I had to overcome in order to actually experience true spiritual clarity and power.

Now my new story about spirituality goes something like this:

> *There is nothing that I need to change, fix, or improve about who I am. Enlightened energy is always accessible. I can tap into an awakened, more intelligent perspective at anytime. I have just as much access to the enlightened state in this moment as I would through another thirty years of meditation. I'm already completely awake; I just need to choose to see myself in this way. I have immense amounts of fun experimenting with accessing my spiritual power. I thoroughly enjoy pretending to be a physically based, solid human who is really something much more mysterious, vast, and powerful.*

At this point, you may want to ask yourself if your current definitions of God and spirituality are supporting or hindering your life. Depending on your religious background, this may require courage, but I know that you can do it. Be sure to consciously create a reality where you are attracting people who can support you in your new definitions.

If you don't resonate with any spiritually based terms like God, the divine, Atman, and so on, don't worry about it. Create your own way of describing your path. I often relate much more to terms like reclaiming power, high performance, removing limits, and clearing blocks as opposed to traditional religious or spiritual terms. There is no right or wrong way; just use whatever feels constructive for you. Just be sure that you're not subtly telling a story that welcomes cynicism about spirituality into your life. If you're jaded about what I am describing in this section of the book, carefully examine the story you are telling and make sure that it's actually true and not just another subjective perception that is limiting your point of view. Being jaded or cynical about spirituality can only result from being locked into the belief that the physical world is either all that there is or all that can be accessed. It's a sign that your filter needs to be cleansed.

Ending The Quest: Waiting Vs. Creating

What would happen if you stopped seeking for answers, clarity, to discover yourself, or to find God? Our seeking is often what keeps us locked into a low frequency. If you find that being a spiritual seeker is a genuinely inspiring process, by all means keep doing it. I for one found it exhausting. Now, my intent is not to seek for anything, but to shift into increasingly higher frequencies where new insights and perspectives naturally arise. I have immeasurably more fun doing this than playing the character of a seeker who struggles to know what life is about. Instead of waiting or asking the universe for answers, I now see it as up to me to create the answers. Whatever answers I am looking for are always present within the field of my own consciousness; they are not outside of me. The more I use the Instant Upgrade Tools, it becomes clear to me that I far prefer creating myself as already being what I seek, rather than constantly looking for answers outside of me. Test this out in your own experience and see what resonates. You may be surprised to discover that shedding the label of spiritual seeker frees you up to tap into higher levels of clarity and confidence.

From Doubting to Trusting to Knowing

If we view the spiritual path as a process of becoming increasingly empowered, we could say in a general sense that the evolutionary process tends to go from doubting to trusting to knowing. When we are in a victimized state where we are not owning our innate spiritual power, we tend to doubt ourselves and the universe at large. We feel that we can't trust what shows up and that we have to impose our will on reality in order to stay safe. We make decisions from a place of force, which continually attracts the same quality of circumstances. As we shift to a higher frequency, we go through a fundamental paradigm shift where we begin to trust life in an unconditional way. Even if we have circumstances that we don't prefer, our insight is deep enough to realize that we have a Higher Self that is generating the exact experiences we need in order to grow, learn, and reclaim power. At an even higher frequency, our trust shifts into pure knowing. There is no longer any separation that we see between our inner and outer world; we know that we are generating all of it within our own sphere of awareness. As such, we are totally clear that whatever shows up is always there to support us. Trust connotes a slight degree of separation. Knowing connotes complete unity. We no longer need faith in order to navigate through life; we are aligned to such a degree that all resistance has dropped away.

Most of humanity lives in the 'doubt' end of this spectrum. I heard one teacher say that 95% of human beings are currently in a victimized state of consciousness, where they unconsciously believe that they are separate from life and that it is happening 'to' them. In my experience, I'd say that is pretty accurate. Keep in mind however, that we create people around us appearing to be at a certain level of awareness in order to support our long held point of view or as a contrast to help us break free and see the Truth of our situation. If you are a victim, you're going to create a reality where you see victims all around you, as this will perfectly support and justify your belief that your current way of being is indeed the way things are.

I'd say that less than 1% of humanity lives in the 'knowing' end of this spectrum. Most highly empowered people are in a state where they deeply trust life, but there remains some degree of separation. When we fully 'know' that we are inseparable from existence, being human is no longer relevant. You've 'won' the game. The story has ended.

Death and Loss: A New Perspective

We take it as a collectively agreed upon truth that we must mourn the loss of loved ones and suffer when they die. Many people never recover from losing a son, daughter, parent, close friend, or spouse. These life events can appear to be permanently damaging, as we can never seem to gain a perspective that allows us to let that person go and move forward with our lives.

Of course it is human nature to grieve and experience deep sadness when we lose someone that we love. This is a completely normal response and carries as much meaning and beauty as any other emotion that we experience as human beings. There is also nothing wrong with being permanently impacted by death. When someone close to us dies, it changes us forever. We see the world in a different way.

What I'd like to address is the prolonged suffering and unending grief that so many people feel when someone close to them dies. While grief is a natural human reaction to loss, suffering that endures year after year is unnecessary. If you've had a hard time letting go of a loved one and are carrying a deep heaviness in your heart for many years, let's apply a few of The Instant Upgrade Tools and see if we can get that to shift.

First, let's apply The Radical Reframe. Ask yourself this question:

> *Would this person want me to suffer in the way that I am? Is this really the best way to show them that I care? Could it be that I'm showing this person the opposite of true love by holding onto them?*

If you are honest with yourself, it becomes clear that the person you lost would only want you to be happy and view them in a peaceful, light-hearted way. They would never want you to use their presence as a source of suffering or bondage. They would want you to set yourself free and by virtue of doing that, set them free. In no way does this mean that you stop caring about them. Actually, it means that you are showing how much you care by being willing to let them go. You are honoring their wishes. If you're holding onto that person out of loyalty but it's causing you to suffer and not move on with your life, hold in your mind what that person would say to you in this moment. On a quantum level they are here with you now. Just because their body dies doesn't mean they go anywhere. You can talk to them and even listen to them through activating your imagination. Can you see them telling you that you need to move on? That it's safe and that they know you still care about them? See if you can allow that in.

Here's another Radical Reframe that you may find useful:

Death is in no way a 'bad' thing or a problem. When people die, they are surrounded by love. They don't actually 'go' anywhere.

When you consider the quantum nature of reality you start to sink into the truth that the physical world is a vast web of illusions and myths. Death isn't anymore real than life. Both are simply labels we give to consciousness. When someone dies in your hologram of reality they don't actually 'go' anywhere. Your entire experience of them as a separate being from you was only an imagined perception that had no inherent reality. You can continue to talk with them, feel their presence, and imagine their 'beingness' with you even after their body dies.

Now I know this may sound a little 'out there', but hang in there with me. In many indigenous and shamanic cultures throughout the world people have long realized what I'm sharing with you. They would see our modern culture's views on death as completely delusional. These cultures don't have nearly the same stigma associated with the dying process. They see it as a natural unfolding of the process of creation and dissolution, all of which happens in the infinite dream of consciousness.

Even though it seems contrary to our modern point of view that death is inherently problematic and replete with suffering, you can choose to tell a new story about it. This will help you when loved ones die, and it will also help you see your own death in a completely new light.

When you tell a lighter, more empowering story around death it will have a wonderful byproduct of freeing you up immensely in your life. You'll naturally have an interest in exploring what it means to be fully alive. When this interest is muted, it's always a sign that we are trying to ward off death and therefore are telling a disempowering story about what it means to live and die.

Here's the story I now have about death:

> *Nothing actually happens when people die, aside from immediately shifting into a higher frequency where they are no longer bound by a physical body. Their presence is just as accessible as it was when they were here on this physical plane. Just as with life, death is ultimately a playful, light transition into a new mode of expression. When people die, they are surrounded by the most expansive love they have ever experienced. Why would we be afraid of that or treat it like it's a problem? Of course I feel grief when 'bad' things happen in the world and when loved ones pass on, but I always see the ultimate Truth underlying that grief. My Higher Self enjoys experiencing the entire spectrum of human feelings and the incredible contrast of dark and light that occurs in the human realm. I can accept it all because on an ultimate level, it's all being generated within my own awareness. Whenever death happens I welcome it, as I know that it's nothing more than a natural expression of existence. I choose to be fully at peace with death and impermanence.*

Can you see how imparting this meaning to death can free you up in your life? How so much of the fear and anxiety and low frequency emotions you have are directly related to a fear of death and a driving need to survive and sustain your body?

I want to state again that my suggestion to see things in this way does not in any way invalidate the pain people experience when a loved one dies. I am spending some time on this because I have seen time and again that our collective cultural belief system around death is largely erroneous and damaging, and usually goes unchallenged. We assume that death really is a problem and that prolonged suffering is a natural, even responsible, way to handle loss. My main advice is to make sure that your beliefs and assumptions are accurate and serving you and your loved ones in the most freeing way possible. After all, if we believe death really is a problem, then we will inevitably believe that life is a problem too. If life inevitably funnels into an unwanted, painful endpoint, then our days will always feel limited and problematic.

Feeding Your Frequency: Creating Stability and Preventing Downgrades

In my personal experience there have been a few sudden and dramatic leaps into higher frequencies where I could tangibly feel that my entire sense of self had gone through an upgrade. Until recently I found it quite challenging to stabilize these leaps, as they often felt like a temporary glimpse into a new way of being, only to be followed a short time later by old patterns that locked me back into a lower frequency.

Just as you can upgrade your life, you can also downgrade. The instant shifts you make into a new portal of reality aren't initially stable and permanent. In my experience I would leap to a new level, then end up telling a story that it was okay to more or less go in default mode and that I didn't have to do anything to maintain that new frequency. What I discovered is that we should not underestimate the part of us that is intent on checking out and maintaining what is familiar.

Now I see that it is possible to sustain a new frequency permanently without needing to experience a kind of teeter totter between the old and the new. The main tip I have for you is this:

Don't ever stop.

Seriously, that's all there is to it. If you base your life around these tools, you will not only sustain a higher frequency than you are at right now, you'll continually leap into even higher dimensions. There are no limits.

When I have downgraded, it's because I bought into a limiting belief that it's okay to stop and that I didn't have to be proactive about using these tools. I convinced myself it would all take care of itself. Downgrades can also occur because you latch onto some residue from your old frequency. A fleeting thought passes through your mind that is steeped in an old, limiting belief and you decide to identify with it and give it power. Or, a circumstance pops up that tests you and you decide to tell a negative story about it. Before you know it, you've lost access to the new frequency you had entered and you feel like the same old person with the same old life.

The whole point of these tools is to not look at them as foreign, external 'things' that you use to feel better. Think of them instead as power switches that turn on the power source of who you really are. In this sense they become your life. You don't use them for a period of time then stop using them. You want them to become an integral part of your daily life.

You can build the use of the tools into your story:

> *I enjoy using these tools every single day. I don't look at them as separate from me. They are now the foundation upon which I live my life. I value them so much that I have chosen to make them a continuous, ongoing part of how I live. Just as I eat, sleep, and breathe, I use these tools in the same way.*

Whenever you experience a downgrade, the key is to catch this happening as quickly as possible. The more skilled you become at Ultra Focus, the more sensitive you will be to your feeling state and the more aware you will be of the lens you are seeing your life through. If this tool is developed, you won't be able to go for very long without noticing that your frequency has downgraded. Your emotions, desires, and actions will feel more cloudy and conflicted.

Many people have an initial breakthrough then downgrade for a prolonged period of time, even years. They aren't focused enough to realize that this has happened. The trance of lower frequencies can be quite hypnotic. It's up to you to become passionate about using these tools as much as possible so that you prevent prolonged periods of malaise, inertia, mediocrity, or disengagement from life. I'd rather see you being hyper vigilant rather than casual about this. Even if initially it feels a little too intense or obsessive, this shows you care and are taking this seriously. Eventually you'll find the perfect balance between stimulative and regenerative focus. If you're new to practicing these tools, your main job in life is to train yourself to constantly remember them first and foremost. As I've said a few times, there is a part of you that likely doesn't want to do any of this, and that part of you is quite skilled at making you forget that any of these tools exist.

Don't let that little devil dictate the course of your life any longer. You have power over that part of you and you can choose to make these tools a top priority.

While I've made it clear that outside factors are never the cause of you entering a higher frequency, they can certainly support you in sustaining a new way of being once you've made a leap. This is very much how I view food, exercise, meditation, healing techniques, and conscious lifestyle choices. I can tell that the high frequency food I eat helps me to maintain the momentum of continual growth. That is not to say I couldn't maintain it if I was living on pizza and beer, but I think based on my current level of development it would certainly make it more challenging.

I enjoy meditation and yoga now because I can tell that these practices support the momentum I have generated and help me to stabilize higher levels of reality. I see acupuncture and Chinese herbs in the same way. Continually moving my body through tennis and walking also feels very supportive. Same with reading books, listening to music, and being outdoors a fair amount. Minimizing TV, mindless internet browsing, and most forms of conventional media has also felt helpful.

All of these activities and techniques can be used as props to stabilize new frequencies and feed the positive momentum you've generated from using the tools. If you're ready, you can definitely make the Instant Upgrade a permanent transition into a 'new you.' You alone are responsible for both the upgrades and the downgrades.

You now have nine tools you can use to shift into new realities, create the life you want, and invent yourself as the infinitely powerful and amazing being that you truly are. Nothing is blocking you from the freedom, love, and abundance that you have always longed for.

What's most important now is that you take action on what you've learned. Proactively use these tools in your daily life. Make this your number one passion. I know how easy it is to collect information but do very little with it. There is tremendous power within these tools; it's your job to activate them. All that you need is a willingness to explore and a desire to be the empowered creator of your existence.

Upgrading your frequency is very much like flipping on the light switch of your inner self. You become plugged into a new power source that shines light on your experience regardless of what shows up. Have you felt this light switch turn on yet? Are you excited about your life and the potential you have to create new stories?

Before you put this book down for a final time and go on with your life, I invite you to feel any degree of appreciation that wells up within you that you care enough about your life to have made it this far. You wouldn't have made it here if you didn't value yourself on a deep level. Now it's time to go out there and intentionally design your life on your terms. It starts in this moment. It's not hard. You don't need to force anything. If you ever feel confused, just revisit the nine tools as laid out in this book and practice each one as I have described. Each practice is designed to be simple and highly accessible.

The upgraded version of yourself is already here with you. The tools are like a chisel that carves away anything you've accumulated along the way that has caused you to forget this. Relax into who you really are, have fun, and create the most epic story that you can imagine.

The Next Step...

In my coaching business, my main focus is helping people integrate the tools covered in this book in a customized fashion. I work primarily with entrepreneurs who want to use these principles to optimize performance, reduce stress, increase revenue, and create a more abundant lifestyle around their business.

Most of my clients are healers, health practitioners, coaches, and authors. I've had the good fortune of helping thousands of people over the years in my group coaching programs and through my online community.

Whether you're an entrepreneur or not, if you've been impacted by the message of this book, chances are I can help you deepen your experience using these tools and accelerate your results. I am deeply inspired to help my clients use these tools to heighten performance in any area of life. If you're an athlete looking to up your game, or a corporate executive who wants to upgrade your career, chances are I can help.

If you'd like to explore working with me in a more customized fashion, go ahead and follow these three steps:

1) Go to www.theinstantupgrade.com/apply
2) Fill out all of the forms there with as much detail as you can
3) Look for an email within 48 hours to let you know if you've been accepted

If you are approved, either myself or one of my team members will do a free phone call with you where we will look at your current situation, what challenges you're up against, and where you'd love to be in your business and life. We will then discuss a plan that details how we can help you.

Because there is such a high demand for strategy sessions, our team can only do calls with people who are in an ideal position to receive what I have to offer. If you feel inspired to do so, I'd love to have you apply.

Kevin's Websites

To deepen your exploration of the Instant Upgrade Tools: www.theinstantupgrade.com

To listen to the accompanying webinar for this book: www.theinstantupgrade.com/webinar

For alternative health practitioners: www.buildyourdreampractice.com

For coaches, speakers, and experts: www.intentionalwealthinstitute.org

To check out Kevin's band Ubiquity Strain: www.ubiquitystrain.com

To follow Kevin on social media:

www.facebook.com/kevindohertyonline
www.twitter.com/kevin_s_doherty
www.instagram.com/kdohertycoach
www.youtube.com/kevindohertyonline

Advance Praise for Barbara Rapaport's

reimagined

Barbara Rapaport's struggle to finally put to rest her childhood demons – at age 65 – has given rise to one of the most brave, honest and emotionally true memoirs I've read. Her psychological insight, her deep understanding of her lifelong struggle, provides a roadmap for all adults who still wrestle with false and damaging internal beliefs."

Robert Kegan
Meehan Professor of Adult Learning
Harvard University

"Told in captivating prose, Reimagined takes the reader on an emotional roller coaster in which Barbara Rapaport recounts the complexities and implications of her own doubts and self-limiting thoughts. Whether the reader is dealing with personal challenges or serving in a leadership role, much can be learned from Barbara's experience."

Rick Baker
President/CEO
Grand Rapids Chamber

"Barbara Rapaport's story is an intimate reminder that although our early experiences shape who we are, doing the hard work of uncovering how they define the future is a battle worth fighting. She isn't afraid to ask tough questions; her candor, her wisdom, and her will to persevere is inspiring."

Meredith Bronk
CEO and President
OST

"Barbara Rapaport's memoir, Reimagined, is a coming-of-age experience caused by a perilous cancer surgery and the recurrence of damaging childhood memories. Rapaport, a talented writer, tells of her development into an emancipated adult through vivid instances of family interactions, hospitalization traumas, her father's narcissistic and suffocating authority. Throughout, we witness the growing acceptance of her need to discover who she really was. The memoir is very personal, a wonderful read and inspirational for readers of any age who are still aspiring to uncover who they are."

Georgia Everse
Co-founder and CEO
BravoEcho

Reimagined

Print ISBN: 978-1-7363420-0-8
EISBN: 978-1-7363420-1-5

Library of Congress Control Number: 2020924862

Names: Rapaport, Barbara A., author.
Title: Reimagined / Barbara Rapaport.
Description: Includes index. | Grand Rapids, MI: Real-time Perspectives Press, 2021.
Identifiers: LCCN: 2020924862 | ISBN: 978-1-7363420-0-8 (pbk.) | 978-1-7363420-1-5 (ebook)
Subjects: LCSH Rapaport, Barbara A. | Rapaport, Barbara A.--Childhood and youth. | Bone--Cancer--Patients--Biography. | Cancer--Patients--Biography. | Cancer--Psychological aspects. | Self-actualization (Psychology)--Biography. | Women executives--United States--Biography. | Executives--United States--Biography. | Businesswomen--United States--Biography. | BISAC BIOGRAPHY & AUTOBIOGRAPHY / Personal Narratives | BIOGRAPHY & AUTOBIOGRAPHY / Survival | BIOGRAPHY & AUTOBIOGRAPHY / Medical
Classification: LCC RC265.5 .R37 2021 | DDC 362.1/96994/0092--dc23

Cover and Interior Design: Cindi Yaklich Epicenter Creative, LLC

To Stuart, Jay and Leigh
– you are the wind beneath my wings.

contents

About the Author

Barbara Rapaport is an executive coach and leadership development consultant whose clients span more than twenty countries worldwide. She is the author of the *Leadership Coaching Toolkit,* a four-part series of self-administered workbooks intended primarily for rising leaders. A resident of Grand Rapids, Michigan, Barbara is closely aligned with the Grand Rapids Chamber where she facilitates workshops for local leaders who are keen to engage in deeply transformative personal and professional development experiences. In addition to her executive coaching practice, she hosts a podcast, *The Answers Are in The Room*, in which local leaders are willing to share a difficult challenge and be coached real-time on the air. Barbara has been married to her dedicated spouse, Stuart, for thirty-nine years. Together they raised two awe-inspiring children, Jay and Leigh. *Reimagined* is her first book.

realtimeperspectives.com

facebook.com/barbara.rapaport.39

linkedin.com/in/barbara-rapaport-429113

Introduction

In 2017, at the age of sixty-five, I enjoyed a strong marriage, two kids who had grown into wonderful adults, a successful consulting practice, a beautiful home and enough financial security to travel overseas or bask in the delight of Broadway musicals. Like many people, I'd experienced traumatic moments in childhood that stayed with me on and off through mid-life, but I was confident they no longer haunted me.

In my career as an executive coach, my work focused primarily on guiding my clients to find fulfillment in their work. Even when our conversations revealed some painful personal truths, I was able to help them discern when these truths seemed to be catalysts for self-sabotaging behaviors and then help them discover better pathways forward. I'd effectively reached a point where I parlayed my own capacity to reframe events – ones that for years triggered doubts about my own self-worth – into meaningful growth opportunities for my clients. I encouraged many of them to follow a path that often mirrored my own. By then I'd learned to be

purposely intentional, assuming complete ownership of my choices and their consequences, and I followed a strict policy of no blame, no debilitating feelings of guilt or regret.

I shared with my clients the stories and rationale behind why and how I had stopped beating myself up, hoping my experiences would motivate them to do the same. I explained that when we revert to outmoded, negative beliefs about ourselves in response to the words or actions of others we are abdicating way too much of our right to show up as *who we really are*. I felt I could speak this way to clients because I had matured into an emancipated adult. I'd done the work, and I tried to show my clients how they could deem themselves worthy of staking a similar claim for themselves.

But a singular event that fall crippled my confidence. It thrust me into deep anxiety and revived my old belief that I was inherently bad. It made me question whether this myth was true after all, and whether the confident worldview I had developed as a mature adult was the illusion.

Prologue

I spent much of my childhood and young adulthood believing that everything that happened was categorized in terms of "either/or." Either you were a rule-follower or a rule-buster, smart or stupid, right or wrong, worthy or undeserving. I had no concept of a middle ground.

The imprint of such a polarized way of thinking came early. I was five years old. This particular weekday in 1957 had started like any other. I woke up, got ready for school and had my usual good time as a kindergartener. I loved school. The teacher was nice. I made friends easily and enjoyed doing fun things with them. I liked rest period even though I never napped. Instead, I lay on my carpet square and let my imagination run free. I don't remember specific thoughts. But I do remember being at peace. I was enveloped and protected by a loving family. I was free to be me, still naïve enough to live as if the world was full of unrestricted adventure and utter delight. I hadn't yet been on the receiving end of adult behaviors that left me frightened and defenseless.

In the afternoons, I got to hang out with my mom. I was her special helper, doing some of her housekeeping chores alongside her, sprinkling water on the laundry so she could iron using the steam setting, watering the menagerie of plants clustered in a sunlit corner of the family room, dusting furniture or setting the table for dinner. Being included in her daily routine made me feel important. On days she was busy doing something beyond my interest or abilities, I'd occupy myself. Sometimes I played with my Betsy Wetsy doll, mirroring the same care and attention I received from Mom. Betsy Wetsy had a unique design. You gave her a water-filled bottle, and it flowed down an interior tube, resulting in a "wet" diaper. I soon realized that dealing with soaked diapers, on an ongoing basis, wasn't so much fun after all. But because Mom so efficiently navigated her day-to-day responsibilities as a housewife and mother, I quickly learned to follow in her footsteps. It wasn't long before I opted for "pretend" liquid in the doll's plastic bottle. There was no "mess" to clean up, I had more time to do other fun things with Mom after she had finished her housework.

Other times, I'd work in my coloring books or flip through magazines. Even at that early age, I couldn't wait for *Look* magazine to arrive in the mail. I'd marvel at the photographs, imagining what life was like for the people in them. I knew I was getting a glimpse of a world that extended beyond mine because the clothes and geographical backdrops were so foreign. The notion of a foreign culture was still too abstract for me, but I remember feeling an intense desire to explore things outside my own world.

This particular weekday in 1957 turned out not to be normal at all. Our usual routine was shattered when after school, someone (I can't remember who) told me, "Dad's in the hospital and he's not going to be coming home for a few days." This made no sense to me. In my brief life, neither he nor my mother had ever gone away

overnight. There was no explanation, just the statement of fact. No one thought to ease my anxiety. But given the sense of foreboding that immediately filled the house, I didn't dare ask any questions. They were telling me Dad was okay, but I sure wasn't getting the impression they were telling me the truth. If he was fine, why was he in the hospital, and why couldn't I see him? Something terrible must have happened. If something terrible could happen to him, seemingly out of nowhere, why couldn't the same be true for my mother, one of my two older sisters or me? I was too afraid to ask because I was petrified about the answer I might get.

A week later, Dad came home from the hospital. He went back to work. Just like before his absence, he still came home every weekday at 5:30 PM, and we ate supper at 5:45 sharp. As a family, we continued to go to synagogue most Friday nights and Saturdays. My older sisters and I went to school, did our homework and watched our favorite TV programs with our parents. But while many of the routine activities of daily life continued as before, my home life was anything but the "normal" I had known.

Under pressure from my Dad's doctor, Mom got the message she needed to assume full responsibility for taking care of him. Years later, I learned the doctor was a psychiatrist, treating Dad for what, in those days, was referred to as a "nervous breakdown." It was the 1950's, a time when many people viewed doctors as godlike creatures. If my mother was overwhelmed by the prospect of assuming this responsibility, she wasn't about to speak up and question such a revered, male authority figure. Acknowledging she couldn't give sufficient attention to Dad *and* me, she enlisted my sister Stephanie, fourteen, to be my surrogate mom. Stephanie played that role, on and off, until she went to college.

We lived across the street from our synagogue, in Fair Lawn, New Jersey, a suburb near Manhattan. Almost everything we did socially

revolved around the synagogue. For a few months following Dad's breakdown, I was instructed to tag along with Stephanie when she went there for her Jewish youth group activities. Her teenage friends were always nice and friendly to me. They considered me something of a mascot. When I was around them, I sensed I had better be a cute and compliant little girl, blending into the background just enough so as not to get in the way. I didn't want to bring attention onto myself by doing anything that would embarrass Stephanie. I surmised early on that being in the spotlight probably wasn't a good thing.

Because the rules around where I'd be spending my time and who'd be watching over me were new, I couldn't rely on the comforting daily routine I had developed with Mom to guide my behaviors. I loved Stephanie. But being with her and her friends, instead of being at home with my mom, left me feeling untethered.

My five-year old brain couldn't comprehend why this was happening. If bad things happen out of nowhere, with no accompanying logical explanation, I concluded that I was somehow to blame. After all, life had been grand until suddenly it wasn't. In the aftermath of Dad's breakdown, it stood to reason that Mom's decision to cede my care to Stephanie must have been the result of having done something very bad. Why else would the person I trusted most in the world to keep me safe leave me to cope without her?

My five-year-old brain concluded that I was to blame for having sufficient power to make people sick, and that I must be inherently defective. There was no claim to any benefits of having such a mighty super power. My destiny, therefore, was to do penance for this irredeemable character flaw. If I didn't live a life of penance, I'd be abandoned and doomed to one filled with loneliness. My specific penance would involve me pretending to be good, so no one would find out the opposite was true. It was an "either/or" proposition. I wasn't going to tempt fate and risk causing another family trauma.

But sometimes when I exhibited this pretense of a selfless, devoted daughter, I felt a warrior-like instinct to rebel. Somehow, I found the courage to dare and imagine that I actually was a good person, rather than a bad person *pretending* to be good. A devoted fan of wholesome TV shows, like *Leave it to Beaver* and *Father Knows Best,* I wished I could have relationships with my parents like the ones portrayed in those idealized and sanitized versions of family life. I concluded that the lessons June and Ward Cleaver or Margaret and Jim Anderson taught their kids were proof that children deserve to be cared for and protected by their parents. No matter what.

I moved through this mental tug-of-war beginning in elementary school, then through college and into early adulthood. Through a series of life events that broadened my understanding of the complexity of human relationships, I freed myself from this constant tension. Or so I thought. I made a choice to let one side of the tug-of-war prevail, the one which personified my internal rebel. I didn't follow my mother's wish that I go to law school. That was her dream, not mine; she hoped I'd fulfill what had been a lost opportunity for her. The sole daughter, among three brothers coming of age in The Great Depression, she was the only child who wasn't allowed to get a college education. Even though I felt sad for her, and angry about the gender disparity she was forced to endure, I found the courage to be selfish. I wasn't going to follow a career path I wasn't at all interested in just to satisfy her.

I disappointed my mother again when I moved away from my parents to start a life in Boston, fulfilling my desire to settle in a cosmopolitan East Coast city. I loved my life there. I functioned wholeheartedly as an independent, single woman, establishing my own community of friends and building a career in business. No one there saw me as having powers that could make people sick. In

fact, the opposite was true. I developed a whole network of friends and colleagues who only respected and cared for me. I felt liberated.

When I met Stuart, I took a chance on building a life with him in Grand Rapids, Michigan, where he was in business with his father and brother. We married, had a son, Jay, and three years later a daughter, Leigh. I navigated three different career paths, each stretching my skills and intellectual capacities beyond even my own expectations. First, I served in administration at a state university. Next, I navigated a twenty-year corporate career at a Fortune 500 company, and I eventually served on the executive management team, a personal success story I never imagined was possible. Ultimately, I resigned to start my own executive coaching and leadership development consulting practice, and I've been thriving in that role ever since.

Even though my dad's extreme self-centeredness dominated my formative years, forcing me to subordinate my needs so his could be met, I slowly but consistently found the courage to stay the contrarian course, stubbornly surviving my rebellion's losses and triumphs. Living on my own, as an adult, I reckoned that *no one* had the power to define me or my destiny. I discovered there always was another way to reframe my thinking so that seemingly insurmountable obstacles became conquerable. By the time I reached the age of sixty-five, I was confident the tug-of-war was behind me. I had developed a no-blame stance, assuming complete ownership of my choices and their consequences. I was a full-fledged emancipated adult until September 14, 2017, when the courage and conviction I'd spent years cultivating suddenly vanished into thin air.

CHAPTER 1

Disruption

I was getting ready for my sixty-fifth birthday party the following evening. I was particularly grateful that I had reached this milestone, because my mother and her mother, Grandma Olga, had both died young. Mom was fifty-nine and grandma was sixty-two. Since I share their genes I, too, imagined I would be destined and doomed to die young. It weighed on me the most the year I turned fifty-nine and my daughter, Leigh, was twenty-five, the same age I was when Mom died. But I had beaten the odds and wanted to celebrate this milestone birthday in a particularly meaningful way.

A few months earlier I had learned that Stuart was planning a surprise birthday party with our local friends and family. But that wasn't what I wanted. I had one wish, and that was to celebrate this "special" birthday with Stuart, Leigh, Jay and a diverse group of female friends whose lives had intersected with mine over the span of six decades. I intercepted Stuart's plan and asked him, and Leigh to help me plan a different type of celebration. We'd host a dinner

party at our home on Friday night and extend the celebration into the weekend, since some of my guests would be flying to Grand Rapids from both coasts.

I carefully handpicked the guest list, imagining a sea of faces around our dining room table representing multiple generations, each having a connection to one or more important stages of my life – my older sister Doris, from Long Island, the person in the room who has known me the longest; my dear friend Hannah, from New Jersey, who I've been close to since junior high; Mindy, a former colleague who lives in California; Ellie, a former coaching client, from New York; and Robin, our onetime nanny and a second mother to Jay and Leigh. I'd round out the table with Grand Rapids women, as young as thirty and as old as sixty-five, who I'd come to know and cherish in the Jewish community or in various phases of my career path.

I could hardly contain my excitement over the fact that soon I'd be surrounded by all of these nurturing souls. Their willingness to celebrate me affirmed my self-actualization. I felt deserving of the love they showered on me because they had told me the meaningful ways I had impacted their lives. I started out the day feeling an energy like no other I could recall. I sensed that the best time in my life was still ahead of me. As David Brooks describes beautifully in his book, *The Second Mountain,* I was at the stage of life where I could leverage all I had accomplished to give back to the generations that would succeed me.

I tingled with anticipation as I drove to pick up Mindy at the airport. Because she lives in California, we rarely get to see each other, and I was particularly thrilled to have precious one-on-one time with her before other out-of-town friends arrived the next morning.

My friendship with Mindy dated back about thirty years, when we both worked at a global manufacturing company headquartered in

Grand Rapids. When we met, she was the team leader for the Western region's sales team. Because I coordinated many of the sales support systems back at headquarters, I interacted with her frequently and we became fast friends. I was drawn to her immediately because of her striking ability to put strangers at ease, an attribute I admired and wished I could cultivate. I mostly was too shy to put myself out there confidently with people I didn't know. I could hold my own in conversations with strangers, but I rarely was the one who initiated them. Whenever we were together, I was awed by how graciously Mindy made anyone we encountered feel visible. It didn't matter whether they were a parking attendant, a restaurant server or a stranger in an elevator. She chatted them up in ways that always resulted in them laughing or smiling. She had that effect on me, too, which was one of many reasons why I loved being around her.

In Mindy's presence I feel swaddled in a blanket of love, warmth and security. Yet, there's always enough give that I can ease out of her emotional embrace when I'm ready to go back out on my own. I can tell her anything about myself. She encourages me to laugh about my foibles. She's nonjudgmental when I cry about my disappointments and setbacks. She lifts me up when I disclose raw, painful truths. She often tells me that I do the same for her. This is the kind of mutual acceptance I yearned for as a little girl but didn't get to experience very often.

When I drove up to the airport terminal, I jumped out and gave her a huge bear hug. This was always the best part of our visits, a way to savor the physical sensation associated with being connected to a truly precious friend. I had planned the day's schedule. We'd do girl talk over lunch then make a quick stop to pick up something for the party I had printed at Staples. Dinner would be with Stuart and Leigh; Jay wasn't arriving until the next day. The schedule gave us license to revel in the amount of private one-on-one time we'd have throughout the day, a perfect way to start the weekend festivities.

It was a warm September day, so I was wearing a crewneck tee-shirt and a light jacket. It was great to be unencumbered by the heaviness of a winter coat, gloves and hat. Mindy was thrilled. She tolerates cold weather but, being from Los Angeles, doesn't relish it. After we picked up the printing at Staples, when we reached the parking lot, Mindy naturally made her way to the passenger side of the car. For no apparent reason, I stopped for a moment and put my hand on my chest. I felt an unfamiliar, circular, hard mass just below my collarbone. In spite of the warm temperature outside, a chill went through my entire body. I had an instantaneous intuition that my life was going to change dramatically, just like it had when the aftermath of my father's breakdown changed how I made sense of the world and my role in it. As I looked at Mindy across the car, my friend's warm, comforting presence couldn't extinguish the same sense of disruption I had back then.

I was utterly confused. The mass didn't feel like it belonged there. It was large, so why hadn't I felt it before? I thought and heard myself say out loud, "What is this?" She looked back at me with a quizzical expression. I asked her to come closer to see if she could see and touch it. She could. We were both somewhat perplexed about what it might be. I hurriedly said something about how it probably wasn't anything to worry about. I also asked her not to mention it to anyone else for the rest of the weekend. There was no point in raising an alarm when we had no facts to inform us that anything was actually wrong. Translation: Buck up and pretend this terrible thing isn't really happening.

To the outside observer, the weekend was only filled with joy. The party was full of reminiscences and affirmations about how I had made a difference in each person's life. In turn, I shared how much each one had contributed to me becoming the best version of myself. The extra time I had with the out-of-town guests was as

fun as I'd hoped. But to say I was preoccupied is an understatement. The night before the party, after everyone had gone to bed, I investigated the mass more carefully, hoping it was my imagination playing tricks on me. But it wasn't. I looked in the mirror, slowly and gently fingering the mass. It was very rigid. A quick Google search validated my recollection that benign tumors tend to move around more freely, while cancerous tumors are more static. In that moment, without any doubt, *I knew I had cancer.*

I moved into a state of compartmentalization in an effort to calm my fears. Was I standing on the precipice of a future filled with suffering, painful treatments and agonizing surgeries, only to die in the end? Would I have the fortitude, or even the will, to fight for my life? In spite of this internal turmoil, I soldiered through the party and the rest of the weekend. I stood by a belief I had developed when I first understood that there could be fatal implications to a cancer diagnosis. It was more than twenty-five years ago, after reading *First, You Cry*, by Betty Rollin, an NBC news correspondent. The memoir described her self-transformation in the wake of a breast cancer diagnosis and mastectomy. Hearing Betty Rollin's story made me realize how naïve I had been about the disease. Until that point, I thought that the only trauma associated with breast cancer was the disfiguration associated with the loss of a breast. It had never dawned on me that cancer could cause people to die prematurely. Ever since, I'd equated cancer with death.

Over the next twenty-five years, I maintained an unwavering belief: If you think you may have cancer, don't waste your breath praying that you don't. If cancer is ravaging your body, it's already too late. Keep the worry at bay until you get a firm diagnosis. Then be smart about the choices you'll need to make. If you're going to pray, focus your prayers on being granted the wisdom to make the right choices moving forward.

This defense mechanism served me well during the birthday weekend. I couldn't reach out to my internist until Monday anyway. For the rest of the festivities, I lived a double life. I was the strong, courageous warrior who had weathered all the battles, which had ended with me being victorious in authoring my own life. This was the persona that I showed my immediate family and guests. The other persona was the fearful Barbara who went into hiding, a persona I had developed when I was a young child, a persona I thought I had outgrown. I silenced my fears, pushing them down and pretending they didn't matter. I didn't want to take the chance that if I expressed them, I'd be shut down with well-meaning platitudes like, "Don't worry, you're going to be fine." What if my years of penance had failed me, and the truth – that I didn't deserve to be supported or comforted – was the actual reality after all? It wasn't until Sunday night, after everyone had left, that I finally told Stuart, Leigh and Jay about the mass.

It wasn't difficult for me to hide the internal inferno that raged that weekend. The act of living a double life was all too familiar to me. I learned to hide my true feelings back when Stephanie and her friends got used to me tagging along where I really didn't belong. I didn't want to give her any reason to think I was ungrateful for her care, because I was afraid I wouldn't survive if she, like my mother, chose not to look after me.

If Stephanie did resent me, she didn't show it. In fact, I became very close to her, purposely looking to her for some of the nurturing I missed from my mom. After Stephanie left for college, if Doris wasn't home when my parents went out, Mom found a babysitter – usually one of my cousins who lived in the next town and were only a few years older than me. When Mom couldn't find someone, my parents took me with them when they socialized with their friends.

There I was once again, being pushed into situations where I didn't fit.

I think my parents' friends accepted my presence because I was an unobtrusive and polite kid. My father's illness had given me a college degree in how to show up as a pleasant and likable child. Acting otherwise could fuel his anger at having his sense of equilibrium destabilized. Now I was on my way to acquiring a Master's in how to fade into the background. In some ways invisibility suited me. It allowed me to live a rich, imaginative life in my head without any risk of saying or doing something that would upset anyone else. I never knew when Dad would cast a disapproving glance or chastise me for some minor offense, like slurping my water or interrupting the conversation to ask my mother for help with something when he felt her attention should be focused entirely on him.

By the time I was nine years old, I'd had enough of tagging along where I didn't belong. I announced I was mature enough to stay alone since the babysitters didn't really watch over me. Instead, all they did was sit in the same room and watch TV. Surprisingly, Mom and Dad didn't put up too much resistance. How could they argue when their friends talked about how grownup I was for my age? I rejoiced in my ability to take control and privilege my need to stay home, safe in my own company. Not being under the constant scrutiny of adults, whose rules of proper decorum inhibited me, would be a relief.

The next time my parents went out when Doris wasn't going to be home, I stayed on my own – but spent the entire night riddled with anxiety. Any creak in the floor, walls or ceiling caused pangs of distress. The same thing happened if I heard unfamiliar sounds outside. Even though I ended up being sorry about getting what I asked for, I remained stubborn and defiant. I wasn't going to let the anxiety win because I vowed not to give my parents the opportunity to know how vulnerable I was feeling. I didn't want to give up what little control I had marshaled. I made up my mind to suffer through the night and silently vowed never to tell my parents how much I didn't want to be alone because I was

afraid someone might break in. I concocted a mantra that I repeated over and over in my head, "I can do this."

Mantra or no, I couldn't relax. I wrapped myself in one of mom's hand-crocheted afghans and nervously kept vigil. My mission was to show my parents I could be independent and didn't need them. When they came home at midnight, I was still sitting in Dad's recliner watching TV. Perry Mason and the Defenders had kept me company. When they asked me how it went, I said "great" and nonchalantly sauntered off to bed. But inside I was relieved they were home so I could relax, secure in the company of adults, no longer intent on proving my capacity for independence to them or to myself.

Similarly, on the Sunday night of my sixty-fifth birthday weekend, I finally relaxed into knowing I could stop putting on a brave front because I trusted my family. I knew I could share my concerns with them without having to worry about proving how strong and independent I was. Although the discovery of the mass in my chest triggered similar childhood feelings of wanting to hide from painful circumstances, I wasn't that child anymore. I was confident the family would rally around me once they knew what was going on.

Chapter 2

Impatience

First thing Monday morning, after the birthday weekend, I emailed my internist to tell him about the lump. I reached out to Dr. Gary first because he had always guided me when I needed to navigate any medical challenge, especially those associated with my immune deficiency disease. Diagnosed when I was a teenager, ulcerative colitis is a chronic inflammatory bowel disease that causes ulcer-like sores in the digestive tract. Fifty years of coping with the symptoms meant that I was no rookie when it came to pain. A relentless adversary, the illness has occasionally rendered me seriously anemic and depleted. Over the course of my career, I made it through three medical leaves and multiple surgeries to replace joints ravaged by arthritis, a secondary effect of the disease. Dr. Gary advocated for me through every one of those challenges. I trusted him and his team implicitly.

The next day, I met with Dr. Gary's nurse practitioner, Joyce, because he couldn't squeeze me into his schedule. Joyce's immune system is compromised, so she always wears a surgical mask. This

stands out because I had never met her before, and while I was waiting for her to come into the exam room, I was reading a sign taped to the door which explained why she would be wearing a mask. She had survived her own life-threatening medical challenge and, to remain engaged in her work, she needed to protect herself. Even in my state of anxiety, I admired her straightforward assertion of what she stood for and what she required to keep herself safe.

While I was waiting for Joyce to join me in the exam room, the threat of a cancer diagnosis was eating away at my capacity to move forward with the same kind of resolve. Finally, she came in and, as she palpated the mass, I looked intently at her eyes and forehead to see if I could discern any specific level of concern. She crinkled her forehead, which I took as a sign that she was puzzled. I read that correctly. She indicated she'd never come across anything like this before. But her voice didn't reflect urgency. In a calm and matter-of-fact way, she said she was referring me for an ultrasound to learn more.

Even though I also appeared calm, I was feeling impatient. If this was cancer, as I suspected, I knew that much more aggressive diagnostic procedures would be required. Why waste time with an ultrasound, which would give us very limited data? Why not go straight to the scans that inevitably would be required anyway? But protocols, mostly dictated by insurance requirements, would ultimately drive the process. I had no choice but to defer to the medical system's timeline. While I was grateful for Joyce's quick action, I was frustrated by my powerlessness to make things happen more quickly. Given my childhood distrust around whether authority figures had my best interests at heart, I had become an adult who, in challenging situations, didn't relish sitting on the sidelines while other people called the plays.

Three days later, I was at the hospital for the ultrasound. The technician rubbed my chest with cold gel and then she moved the

probe, called a transducer, back and forth. When she was done, she told me to stay positioned on the table until she returned, without explaining why I couldn't get dressed. I remained lying on my back, shivering in the hospital gown, for about ten minutes. In those ten minutes, I didn't catastrophize about the outcome. I had already self-diagnosed cancer. What tormented me was having to wait without the benefit of an explanation. I wasn't looking for the technician to share any specific findings; I knew that wasn't hospital protocol. Perhaps if I'd asked what was going on, and had gotten a reasonable answer, I would have felt less invisible. But something stopped me. It was a memory of what good girls do when they're in situations where authority figures have complete control.

The memory was from a time when I was fifteen, sequestered in a small exam room at a doctor's office in Philadelphia. I had been exhibiting inflammatory bowel symptoms for months until finally, my mother's friend, a general surgeon, referred us to a renowned gastroenterologist. The goal was to get a firm diagnosis and set up a treatment plan. My father took off work, and together with my mother, we woke up very early in the morning to make the 100-mile drive in time for the appointment. We had been told to plan on being there for most of the day.

The diagnostic procedure was a barium X-ray. It necessitated undergoing an enema to cleanse my bowel and then drinking barium dissolved in water. Barium is a thick, chalky, vile-tasting liquid that shows up white as technicians trace its movement on X-ray film; it highlights abnormalities of the digestive tract.

Several times during the procedure I had to take gulps of the barium. I had been subjected to similar X-rays back in New Jersey, so I knew exactly what I was in for.

Each time I took a gulp I gagged. It took all the willpower and concentration I could muster to keep from hurling it back up. In anticipation, I initiated what would become a persistent coping mechanism for how to get through grueling and frightening medical procedures. It was a variation on the "I can do this" mantra I had created the first night I babysat myself six years earlier. I intentionally put myself in a state of mindfulness around being present in the moment, meditating over and over on my new mantra, "just get through it."

Roughly thirty minutes after the procedure was over, I was told we had to go through the entire process again. A piece of stool had shown up on the film, and my intestinal tract needed to be totally clear in order to make an accurate diagnosis. I wasn't given a choice. Alone in the exam room, after hearing the news, I wanted to scream. I couldn't fathom why all of the preliminary testing, plus what I had just gone through, wasn't sufficient for a diagnosis. At fifteen years old, I was uncomfortable wearing hospital gowns that revealed intimate parts of my naked body to strange men, medical professionals or not. I was repelled by the thought of having to go through the humiliation of being subjected to yet another enema. I was convinced I would hurl back every ounce of barium they forced me to swallow. I couldn't bear the thought of how ashamed I'd be if that happened. I hadn't learned yet that sometimes we have no control over our bodies.

But I also knew that even if I actually screamed, my voice wouldn't be heard. My father had very strong views around what children do and don't get to decide. My experience up until then had been that when I asked for something that was important to me, if it didn't jive with his view of how the world is supposed to work, he'd usually look me straight in the eye, and with a determined, no-nonsense frown answer emphatically, "no." When I asked for a reason, he'd claim that "Children want to be told no." He likely had heard or read that perspective from someone with expertise in child psychology. The problem was, he hadn't ever demonstrated

the capacity to decide whether a given situation warranted that stance. He also was perpetually unable, or unwilling, to explain things to me in a way that I could comprehend, and more importantly, that I could trust.

Medical histories of family members on my mom's side were fraught with illnesses that had often resulted in cancer – Crohn's disease, ulcerative colitis and stomach ulcers. Even before this visit to the specialist, I had been quietly obsessing about whether this set of symptoms meant I already was suffering from cancer. But I held these thoughts at bay, remembering the dictum that dominated our family life: "Don't upset Dad."

Even though I was filled with anxiety, wondering if my illness was that serious, I couldn't imagine a scenario where the attention Mom had been bestowing upon Dad since his breakdown would be diverted to me. In a battle between his needs versus mine, past experience dictated that in spite of her efforts to be a neutral mediator, I'd be the loser. Keeping Dad's moodiness at bay always took precedence, probably because she feared the implications on the family if he had another nervous breakdown.

I wished I could muster the courage to tell my mother how afraid I was that I had cancer and if so, ask her what would happen as a result. I had a strong preference around what I hoped could have transpired. I wanted to be evaluated by someone I *trusted.* That person was my pediatrician, a good-humored, unassuming and kind man. But I wasn't given an opportunity to even voice my wish to ask him if he'd be able to figure out what was wrong. If I had spoken up, perhaps the spell cast by my father, to protect himself from dealing with his own inability to establish healthy boundaries between his emotions and the emotions of others, would have been broken. Dad would twist my words, making it about how I was at fault for not trusting his judgment. I stayed silent. It was much safer not to risk the recriminations I'd face since it was pretty likely I'd lose the argument in the end. So before, during and after the visit to the specialist, I commanded myself to "just get through it."

Now, fifty years later, I found myself repeating the same mantra when the ultrasound technician left the room without giving me permission to get dressed. After about ten minutes, she returned with the radiologist. Despite having been subjected to a lifetime of diagnostic procedures because of my ulcerative colitis, I had never experienced a radiologist being called into the room in real time. He approached the table and said something about the technician not being able to "get all the views" needed.

The radiologist's poker face, as he rolled the transducer around my sternum, didn't surprise me. I understood why he wouldn't want to reveal anything that could be construed as a diagnosis; the rules are that the prescribing physician always informs the patient of the results of any tests. I knew I *"shouldn't"* ask. But that didn't sit well. By now I had developed a strong conviction, one I often shared with my clients, that we should be wary whenever we utter or think the words I "*should*" or I "*shouldn't*." For many people, those thoughts represent a tendency to act in accordance with the standards of others, instead of with their own, or to please others instead of doing what would please themselves. After all, why do they feel they don't have permission to ask any question they wish? It's my contention they always have that right. Along with that notion, I encourage my clients to be prepared for any answer they might get. Yet in this moment in the procedure room at the hospital, I couldn't follow my own guidance. Suddenly, I felt I was no longer the emancipated woman I'd been assuming I was.

A few days after the procedure, I learned that a "mass-like" structure was evident in my sternum. Whether it was benign or cancerous was inconclusive. This launched a seemingly endless series of scans, laboratory studies and doctor visits. Within ten days I was scheduled for a CT scan and an MRI. Things were moving relatively quickly, but not quickly enough to distract me from the

constant worry around how I would find the strength to navigate what was to come. I couldn't shake my previous worldview that a cancer diagnosis equals death.

Before undergoing the CT and MRI, I attended synagogue services in observance of the Jewish new year. *Rosh HaShanah* is a very important holiday in Judaism. It commemorates the creation of the world and marks the beginning of the ten "Days of Awe," culminating in *Yom Kippur*, the "Day of Atonement." It's generally a solemn period of time, a chance to beseech God to inscribe you in the "Book of Life" for one more year. The ten days, in essence, provide congregants with a last-ditch opportunity to repent for any past wrongdoing and commit to being better in the future by performing good deeds.

I've always appreciated the solemnity associated with the high holidays. It's a reminder to take time out and reflect on a purpose that reaches beyond the routine activities of day-to-day life. That doesn't mean I relish sitting through the long services in synagogue. While seated among the congregation in the sanctuary, I've often allowed my mind to wander, experiencing the chanting of the Hebrew prayers in the background similar to the way I've benefitted from instrumental background music when I allow myself to go into a state of mindfulness. The chanting of prayers on the high holidays is especially soothing, since Stuart is the one doing the chanting. He serves as the lay cantor of our synagogue and each year, his constancy in reciting prayers on behalf of the congregation is very calming. Watching him fulfill what, for him, is purely a labor of love, has always been one of my personal signs that all is as it should be.

But this year, I was agitated. My attempts to experience the service as a forum for quiet contemplation were unsuccessful. I couldn't join in singing any of the prayers or concentrate on the

Rabbi's sermon. I was obsessed with the notion that my name had already been entered into the "Book of Death." Nothing could change the fact that I already was destined to die before achieving everything I had set out to accomplish.

During the simple repast following the service, I watched as congregants and friends mingled easily amongst each other. They smiled as they shook hands and conveyed the traditional wish for a *Chag Sameach,* meaning "Happy New Year." Many who hadn't seen each other during the year caught up on their respective lives. They noshed on the sweets, cookies and pastries laid out on the table to represent hope for a *Shanah Metukah,* a "sweet" year. It was like watching a slow-motion film, where everyone else was part of a special community, and I, the protagonist, was an outsider observing from the sidelines. I couldn't be like them; I had cancer. I felt excluded from this state of belonging. A wave of utter isolation washed over me.

A mournful sob worked its way up from deep inside, then escaped into the air within earshot of Leigh. Without hesitation, she quickly grabbed my arm and ushered me out of the social hall into the empty lobby. With that simple gesture, I recalled what it was like to have someone focus attention on me in a completely nurturing way. She let me cling to her tightly as I sobbed, "I'm so scared." My daughter's nurturing gesture offered a tiny ray of hope. I might not be able to trust that I'd be able to take care of myself right now, but I could still trust that my immediate family would watch out for me. Relying on people didn't need to be an all-or-nothing proposition – either only relying on myself or only relying on others. Could I find a path toward surrender that would allow me to hold onto a "both/and" stance instead?

A few days later, the results of the CT and MRI came in and Dr. Gary sent me the following note: "Dear Barbara, the reports do

indeed look concerning for a tumor arising from the sternum. There is a team of bone tumor specialists in town. I will see if we can get an urgent consultation this week. An actual tissue diagnosis will be the initial step. We will contact you later today." The word "urgent" provided another indication the tumor was cancerous. His quick effort to advocate for me with this team of specialists gave me some temporary peace. He had always looked out for me in the past and wasn't abandoning me now.

I was scheduled to meet with this multi-specialty care team right after the holidays. I knew I'd finally get the absolute confirmation I was seeking then. More importantly, I'd be able to learn about treatment options. My ten days of repentance, which tradition dictates should include reflective moments focusing on self-forgiveness and envisioning how to renew my commitment to Judaism, became more of a constant stream of rumination around "what if" scenarios.

What if the tumor was inoperable? What if I'd have to undergo radiation, chemotherapy or both? What if I couldn't trust myself to make the right choices for me and my family? What if I couldn't work? I was our family's primary breadwinner. As a consultant who works on a "fee for service" basis only, there'd be no medical leave or disability benefits if I had to be out of commission for months, or more. I couldn't relax, because the stories I was making up in my head about my prognosis were all dire. I needed, at least temporarily, to silence the storyteller's concerns about which player in my internal tug-of-war would be up to the challenge of keeping me alive – the rebellious warrior-princess, or the quiet, deferential little girl.

In preparing myself for the meeting with the bone cancer specialists, I followed my instinct and determined that some knowledge was preferable to total ignorance. I took action by logging into my

health system's patient portal and reading the reports from the CT and MRI. One of my computer monitors was open to the portal; the other was open to an online medical dictionary. I was going to read every word and translate the findings into language that a non-medical person could understand.

I didn't have to read very far. The last line of the MRI summary at the top of the page said it all: "This is favored to represent a chondrosarcoma, given the appearance on MRI and prior CT. Orthopedic oncology consultation is recommended." Although I had never heard the word "chondrosarcoma" before, I knew that a "sarcoma" meant cancer. Further reinforcement appeared in the phrase "orthopedic oncology." Only people diagnosed with cancer sought the expertise of oncologists. It had been three weeks since I first felt the mass in my chest, and I now had confirmation that my intuition had been right.

I told Stuart, Jay and Leigh about the test results. They recommended what, under different circumstances, would have seemed to me to be a perfectly reasonable perspective. "Let's stay optimistic and wait to see what we learn from the multi-specialty care team." All three were going to join me at that initial meeting. But since I was the primary victim of these circumstances, I knew their upbeat perspective wouldn't carry me through. There were plenty of moments when anxiety entered my consciousness, reigniting my fear of mortality. Each time that happened, I braced myself by relying on my trusted mantra to "just get through it."

I also continued learning about what surgical removal of a chondrosarcoma usually entailed. A few days before the scheduled visit with the care team, I sequestered myself in the room that served as my home office, the one space in the house where I felt totally comfortable. Every time I walked into the room, the pale-yellow walls lifted my spirits, like being in the sunshine. Because light is so

important to me, I had never put up any window treatments. Choosing to infuse the room with light was an act of defiance against the dark, foreboding atmosphere that permeated my childhood home.

Growing up, I lived under a constant worry that any wrong word or action might cause Dad to revert to one of his self-protective modes. He'd complain when there was too much noise in the house, the simple, youthful chatter that naturally ensued when I dared to bring friends home to play. He'd glare at us in a way that made my friends uncomfortable, so I decided to frequent their houses instead. If I was acting in any way that created some type of emotional trigger in him, he'd say, "Stop it, I can't take it." The habitual use of this phrase eventually silenced me, reinforcing my belief that I must be an innately bad person to cause him to be overwrought with such intense emotional frailty.

My home office was where I conducted my executive coaching sessions. It had the usual assortment of practical equipment – two computer monitors, keyboard and printer. The shelves and worksurfaces, however, were lined with my treasured books and *tchotchkes* (the Yiddish word for trinkets). These included my favorite photographs of Stuart and the kids, as well as a diverse assemblage of memorabilia, reminders of the friends who had given them to me. For years, Leigh had teased me that for a woman who detested clutter in the rest of the house, the *tchotchkes* in my office told a different story. But I stood by this contradiction. The *tchotchkes* were symbols of nurturance. I felt comfort in their presence. The order in the rest of the house meant I could rely on a predictable home environment. This was in sharp contrast to my childhood home, where the emotional chaos wreaked by my dad's moods left me feeling unsafe much of the time.

As I educated myself about chondrosarcoma of the sternum, I assumed the role of objective researcher. My job, in the moment,

was clearly defined. I had to absorb and comprehend as much as I could in order to avoid any chance of being sucker-punched when I heard the multi-specialty care team's assessment of my condition. I sat at my computer for a few hours, searching the internet until I found a series of case studies detailing the surgical procedure used to excise a tumor of the sternum. These papers were published by the National Library of Medicine, a branch of the National Institutes of Health, so they were expert and reliable.

As I read the case studies, I began to absorb the enormity of the surgery I'd *likely* have to undergo – and it was overwhelming. I'd be in surgery for hours with my heart and lungs exposed. My sternum would be cut to whatever degree necessary so that the tumor could be removed, implants put in to replace the sternum and muscles repositioned to protect the implant. I couldn't imagine how anyone could survive such a complex set of procedures. I also couldn't fathom that I would be the one lying helplessly on the operating table, having this done to me. The fact that I had cancer was no longer an abstraction. It was a stark and cruel reality. I couldn't fabricate any type of protective armor to shield me from the brutality of this onslaught. I was standing face-to-face with my own mortality, feeling nothing but emptiness and hopelessness. I never felt so alone in my entire life. Even my *tchotchkes* failed to soothe me.

Chapter 3

Choosing Me First

The purpose of sitting down with the multi-specialty care team was for me to meet the orthopedic oncology surgeon, Dr. Joel and the numerous people who would support me through this. I was prepared for them to share specifics about my tumor and the surgery I'd require. The goal was to leave with enough information to decide whether I wanted to proceed with their recommended treatment plan. I resolved, in advance, to remain composed, no matter what transpired. I was afraid if I lost control, the medical professionals wouldn't take me seriously. I dreaded being rendered voiceless, which is how I felt growing up countless times when I tried to express what I needed to feel safe and genuinely cared for. In spite of how many times as an adult I *was able* to assert myself, the enormity of what was at stake *now* threatened to reduce me to this child-like state of powerlessness.

After my ulcerative colitis diagnosis, at age fifteen, a day came when I finally mustered the courage to explicitly rebel against our family's unspoken norm to not upset my father. I had always avoided him as much as I could, finding sanctuary in my room and stifling any expression of anger, frustration or unhappiness when I had no choice but to be around him. I knew from experience when I tried to be honest about my feelings that I could predict what would happen. He'd tell me to stop because he "couldn't take it." So, I kept my real emotions simmering quietly under the surface and got away with it, until the day when I didn't.

It was a quintessential spring afternoon. The delicate breeze that came through the open windows had its usual calming effect. I have always loved the sense of renewal that accompanies spring. The beams of light that sneaked in through the curtains created mysterious shadows on the floor and furniture. The movement between light and dark, without any apparent structure or limitations, engendered a sense of playful boundarylessness. Normally, it would have been a moment to relax and enjoy being touched by the spirit of possibilities that often accompanies spring. Instead, I boldly told my father about something I wanted to do, even though I already knew he didn't agree and it was unlikely he'd sanction it. I can't recall specifically what I was asking for, but I do remember being emphatic about why his point-of-view was wrong. Whatever it was, he came back at me hard, "Don't you dare question me on this." he said. This single, punctuated statement ignited a firestorm.

My usual "suffer-in-silence" strategy failed me. I screamed back at him, "You never give me a chance to tell you about what I need. You're always too focused on yourself." Suddenly, almost unwittingly, I'd turned the tables, and now there was no holding back. It was as if every grievance I harbored since age five regarding my dad's chokehold on the family dynamic spewed out uncontrollably. My tone was high-pitched, frenzied, bordering on hysterical. "You don't care about me. You

never did," I screamed. "You just want to shut me up because you can't handle *your* feelings." After years of walking on tiptoes around him, I had had enough. The longer I maintained my combative stance, the more furious and flustered he became.

He countered, "You don't know what you're talking about. You're the one at fault here. This isn't the way children are supposed to treat their parents."

I wouldn't let him off the hook, why should I? I came back swinging. "You never acknowledge what I'm going through. You never acknowledge my pain." I paused, then I hit him with my coup de graçe. "It isn't always *about you.*"

My hope, that my mother would intercede and defend me, was immediately dashed. She briskly ran around the house shutting the windows while saying, in an urgent voice, "Shush, the neighbors will hear." I couldn't fathom why both of my parents couldn't put aside their own vulnerabilities and recognize the intensity of the pain that had gotten me here. Instead, Dad did what he always did. He claimed I was being unfair to *him.* I suppose that my mom, unable to mediate a truce, defaulted to feeling shame, or perhaps even guilt, for her powerlessness. If Dad and I were on opposite sides of the tug-of-war, she was helplessly trying to hold onto the middle so neither side would have to lose. Amid my numbing disbelief, the fighting match came to a screeching halt when Dad screamed at me, "*Stop! You're making me sick!*"

I didn't hear anything after that; I was too shocked by the brutality of his statement. He was finally validating what I had surmised ever since his breakdown: that he believed I had caused it. When Mom didn't correct him, I felt as if I had been sucker punched and wondered if I'd ever recover. I contemplated fighting back by refusing to accept such an absurd notion. Instead, I chose to retreat to my room, sensing that if I confronted him, I'd pay too big a price in the end. I vowed to never again bring up how his words and actions left me feeling worthless and unloved. I soon developed a new personal mission – to

go along to get along, until I was old enough to leave home and live on my own.

During the drive to the care team appointment, I completely withdrew into myself, fully concentrating on containing my anxiety about the impending prognosis. By allowing my emotions to simmer under the surface, I lowered the risk of taking out my trepidation, anger and grief on the care team members. It was as if I was fifteen again, afraid that if I triggered anxiety or anger in any of the team members, then I risked being discounted in some powerful way.

Silence filled the air. I imagined that Stuart and the kids were trying equally hard to contain their own fears. I appreciated that no one tried to offer platitudes. We were far from knowing if everything would turn out all right. Putting up the pretense would have been laughable given what we already knew about my condition.

I also knew that today was a day of reckoning around the different points-of-view my family asked me to consider in terms of the best treatment options and locations. Stuart's view didn't present a challenge. He said he would support any decision I made. Jay and Leigh each did have specific views they were willing to share with me. When Jay heard about the cancer diagnosis, he responded with pragmatism. A lawyer by profession, he exhibited his quintessential skills, advocating hard for seeking a second opinion. Initially, he lobbied for Stanford, near his home in San Francisco. When I said I absolutely wanted to be close to our support system in Grand Rapids, he asked if it would be okay for him to investigate options at the University of Michigan in Ann Arbor.

Leigh, on the other hand, encouraged me to trust what my soul was telling me to do. She put forward another possibility that no one

else had dared to either imagine or state – that refusing treatment was also an option. She hoped I'd choose what was best for me in my estimation, even if it meant feeling as if I'd be letting the family down. She didn't want me to make a choice motivated by guilt.

My daughter's stance was an extremely courageous one to take. Only a few years earlier, when Leigh had worked in my consulting practice as a marketing specialist, she had heard me, on multiple occasions, tell workshop participants about the importance of assuming their own "agency" – exerting personal power to take actions on their own behalf. Now I was humbled by her wisdom, realizing that in this situation, the mentee had become the mentor.

The lid of my emotional container flew off as soon as we arrived at the hospital's cancer pavilion. We were about to drop off the car with the valet when I realized I had forgotten to bring the forms I had been told to complete in advance. It had taken an unusually long time to fill out the ten-page medical questionnaire, and I had left it on the kitchen table. I mercilessly berated myself for my stupidity. Devoid of any compassion for myself, I easily could have descended into an even deeper place of self-loathing. But Jay interrupted this dubious descent. He immediately volunteered to drive home to retrieve the forms. I was worried he wouldn't get back in time to hear what the doctor would say. Still, I was grateful for and took comfort in his take-charge attitude. I sensed that I was witnessing the first of many instances, in which each family member would take turns being the level-headed decider. They must have been grateful as well. No one argued with him.

I willed myself to put on a protective shield before entering the waiting area. I immediately told the receptionist that I had forgotten the questionnaire and that my son would be bringing it soon. With just a hint of trepidation, I asked whether we would have to reschedule the visit. She reassured me that I could send in the

questionnaire later. But her reassurance wasn't enough to stop me from ruminating on how I wouldn't have been able to cope if the visit had to be rescheduled.

It had taken every bit of focus I could summon to prepare myself for the hard facts the team would present. I didn't have any inclination to allow that intensity to dissipate. If I had, it would mean relinquishing the protective armor I had donned for the occasion. The armor was a precious defense mechanism. I needed it to deflect the harsh truth that might be revealed – the probability of me dying from the cancer itself, or from the surgery required to exorcise it from my chest cavity. When a medical assistant brought me to a tiny room to check my vitals, my "just get through it" mantra reverberated through my consciousness.

Next, I was escorted to an extremely large examination room, where I was joined by my family. Jay had made it back in time. In addition to the usual furnishings I expected to see – examination table, medical cabinet, stool – there was enough space for four chairs, arranged in a semi-circle. I instantly took in the layout, imagining the examination table as a stage where I'd be the star attraction. The audience, comprised of my family, were seated in the semi-circle facing the stage. The rest of the cast was unknown, but the orthopedic oncologist, Dr. Joel, would serve as the director. It was a disorienting image, since there was no script to study in advance and I didn't have any idea as to the director's style and approach.

The first player who joined us was the team's physician assistant, Anne. She was friendly and polite. The first thing she had me do was get undressed and put on a gown. Since my family was in the room, she pulled together the curtains that surrounded the examination table in an attempt to provide a measure of privacy. I instantly felt uneasy. It was so awkward undressing in a room where my family was separated only by a thin curtain.

I felt myself being pulled in two different directions. My strong, courageous and tenacious self hoped to take full advantage of the expertise and support that the care team could offer. I wanted to listen without judgment, giving Stuart and the kids a chance to be heard as well. Then, I could bravely assert my final decision, assuming a modicum of control over my own destiny.

At the same time, something more insidious was at work. I craved the relief I'd experience by relinquishing my personal agency and letting the hard decisions be made for me. That way, if I didn't survive this ordeal, I'd be released from any personal accountability for the outcome. I was suspended in an either/or scenario – either my family and the medical experts would assume responsibility, or I would. I couldn't imagine any way the two scenarios might intersect.

Anne completed a basic examination, asked a series of questions, then opened the curtain and invited me to sit with my family. Dr. Joel would be in shortly. I was terribly self-conscious, being the only one in the semi-circle wearing a hospital gown. Not wearing my own clothes created a feeling of separateness and physical vulnerability. The protective emotional armor I had donned that morning cinched even tighter.

Dr. Joel came in, smiled and thanked us for coming. I began judging him from the instant he reached out to shake our hands. Would he treat me like an intelligent adult, or as an older woman dependent on her children to intervene for her? Would he be straightforward in sharing the facts, or would he come across as sugarcoating the truth about my condition? Would he look me in the eye to gauge my state-of-mind? Would he coax me to express my concerns and fears, or basically just tell me what I had to do?

I was relieved when, from the start, Dr. Joel demonstrated genuine empathy for what we all were going through. His empathy came through in his words and gestures. He looked directly at me

when he asked me questions, trying to assess not only my literal understanding of what he was conveying, but my emotional reactions as well. He exhibited patience, making sure that every question we posed was answered. He offered the same degree of attention to the family that he extended to me. And he met the single most critical criteria I respected in medical professionals; he wasn't condescending.

He explained that this was a very rare form of cancer. He also confirmed that by the time today's visit was over, we'd have a good understanding as to how the care team he was assembling would be poised to do everything they could to ensure a successful outcome. Initially, as I expected, the list of questions he asked me was long. I was focused, clear and concise in my responses. Despite the fact that I was terribly antsy to get to my big question – How likely was I to die from this? – I managed to hold back. Perhaps he would just tell us, eliminating the need for me to ask. I could wait until the very end of the visit to pose the question, if it still made sense.

There was another reason I refrained from being too assertive during the early part of the meeting: I wanted to avoid creating a highly charged emotional atmosphere. Instead, I intentionally chose to be a polite and obedient patient, listening respectfully with intense concentration. I didn't want to be held accountable for missing important information, misunderstanding that information or wasting anyone's precious time. I didn't want to lose my cool for fear that Dr. Joel might be so annoyed that, even though he'd help me, he would only do so begrudgingly. Given how many times in my life when so-called caregivers couldn't be trusted to see *me*, in spite of Dr. Joel's compassionate bedside manner, I still was waiting to see if he deserved the benefit of the doubt.

After all his questions were answered, Dr. Joel presented the treatment plan he and his colleagues had developed. It truly required a multi-specialty team. It included a nurse facilitator, a specialist

in cancer radiation, a specialist in chemotherapy, a cardio-thoracic surgeon, a plastic surgeon and a social worker. I would have a chance to meet with some of them today and others over the next few weeks. Dr. Joel indicated that the only option available to us was surgery to remove the tumor. When he explained the steps that would be taken during my surgery, I remained calm and in control. I wasn't blindsided because of the preliminary research I had done about this type of surgery.

What I couldn't have prepared for was my reaction to *specific details* of my case. Because the size of the tumor was quite large, he anticipated having to remove my entire sternum and parts of my ribs, a "radical resection." The stage of the tumor couldn't be known until it was removed. The exact location of the tumor was a concern as well. Images showed that it was reaching into the mediastinum, a large cavity between the lungs that houses the heart, esophagus and trachea. The tumor also was in close proximity to my main pulmonary artery, which meant that the cardiac-thoracic surgeon might be called upon to address any heart-related complications.

The list of risks was staggering – infection, neurovascular, cardiac and/or pulmonary injuries, prolonged intubation, chest tubes and drains, local tumor reoccurrences, wound healing delay, potential subsequent surgeries and blood clots. There would be no definitive prognosis until after the surgery. At that time, the doctor would be able to gauge whether the extraction of the tumor had left clean margins, i.e., no evidence of cancer cells sloughing off the tumor onto nearby tissues; there needed to be a clean margin of four centimeters. If any cancerous cells had been left behind, eight weeks after the surgery I'd have to go for radiation treatments every day for six weeks.

Overall post-surgery recovery would be extremely difficult. This was, in his words, "big" surgery. After listening to all this, I realized I wouldn't be getting an answer to my question about

how likely I was to survive. Even if I came through the surgery and recovery without any life-threatening complications, I'd still be at risk for cancer cells metastasizing somewhere else in my body.

I was told I should expect to be in intensive care immediately after the surgery. I would have limited use of my arms for weeks, with one immobilized in a sling, because there was a risk that I'd tear the protective muscle flaps the plastic surgeon would have sutured together from my breast tissue. After being released from the hospital, I'd likely have to spend time in a rehab facility.

The emotional protective armor that had gotten me through the earlier part of the visit slipped away. It offered no protection for such a monumental invasion of my chest cavity, which housed most of the vital organs necessary to support life. I suddenly could visualize the tumor, recognizing its power to invade those organs and end my life. I felt its heaviness, its authority, its prowess. It was the enemy, and I was a warrior fighting for my life.

Dr. Joel posed his final question, "Do you want a second opinion before agreeing to the treatment plan?" He had colleagues in other institutions who he believed would provide an expert assessment. At first, Jay's thoughts about seeking a second opinion at the University of Michigan and Leigh's efforts to release me from feeling I had to accept treatment were dancing around in my head. I avoided looking directly at Stuart, Jay and Leigh. In that brief moment of silence, I gave myself permission to listen to the only voice that really mattered. "I don't want a second opinion. I want to go ahead with the treatment plan you presented." The family raised no objections. I trusted that their silence, whether they were relieved or disappointed, was evidence of their respect for and devotion to me. They honored my right to choose.

This decision didn't come easily. From the moment Jay and Leigh were born, I had been vigilant about keeping them safe; I

never expected it would ever be the other way around, where I'd be on the receiving end of their efforts to keep me safe. I suspect Jay would have felt more comfortable if I decided to seek a second opinion. But doing that might have led me toward a path where I'd feel less safe, putting myself in the hands of a hospital system I had no experience with and recovering in a city that wasn't close to home. To outside observers, this may have seemed like a decision based on practicality, but in my mind it was much more than that. It was a defining moment in which I chose to be utterly selfish, an assertion that if I had to focus on *anyone else's* needs, I wouldn't have the strength or resilience to fight the good fight, the one I needed to win if I wanted to survive. I made this choice on my terms, relinquishing any guilt I might naturally have assumed for choosing my needs over my family's.

Chapter 4

Self-Sabotage

I spent the five weeks between the multi-specialty care team meeting and surgery arranging to put my coaching practice on hold and attending to numerous medical appointments, including more blood draws, a total body bone scan, visits with the cardio-thoracic and plastic surgeons who'd be assisting Dr. Joel and a pre-op physical with Dr. Gary. During the consults with the two surgeons, what I heard from them was mostly a repeat of what Dr. Joel had told me. Still, I appreciated the opportunity to meet the other two people who literally would be holding my life in their hands.

The rest of the time I followed my normal routine as much as possible. Having even a slight semblance of normalcy helped distract me from thinking about the surgery. I dressed, showered, brushed my teeth, met with clients and did routine chores around the house. But if I appeared patient on the outside, it was an act. My "just get through it" mantra had been replaced with "get this thing out of me."

In spite of my impatience and rigid focus on routine, I didn't allow myself to fall into a depressive state. That is something my father would have done – swallowing up everyone's energy in an attempt to elicit sympathy for his suffering. In direct contrast, there were quite a few moments when I intentionally used my capacity for empathy to support my family. They were having their own reactions to this trauma and I didn't want to make things worse for them. Instead, I actively contributed to their planning efforts, offering suggestions about ways they might feel supported *by me* post-surgery. It was a way to convey, at least to myself, that my own fears hadn't left me completely oblivious to their needs. Translation: I wasn't my dad.

We decided that Jay would come back to Grand Rapids for the surgery. Remaining in San Francisco would have left him isolated and separated from the comfort of being close to family. Because we imagined that the burden of keeping people informed would fall primarily on Leigh, we decided to use CaringBridge as our primary communications vehicle. This is a website that allows you to share health updates with friends and family while eliminating the energy-drain associated with responding to individual phone calls and emails.

Before we began to use CaringBridge, I made a list of everyone I wanted to telephone personally before the surgery. They had all been cheerleaders for me during the last ten years, when I had my previous hip and back surgeries. Pre-surgery calls always left me feeling more positive about going under the knife. They were a reminder of how important my relationships were to me – what I meant to this select group of friends and relatives, and vice versa. This time, however, there was a more serious intentionality behind the calls given the type of surgery this was. Simply being under anesthesia for the better part of a day was dangerous in its own right.

The volume and magnitude of the risks Dr. Joel had warned us about meant the stakes, overall, were much higher. What if these conversations were the last ones I'd ever have with these individuals? Obsessed with the possibility that I might not live through this surgery or its immediate aftermath, I felt compelled to let them know how much I appreciated, loved and cared for them. I owed them so much. These were the people whose nurturing throughout the various stages of my life provided counter-intelligence to what my dad had always led me to believe – that I only had value if I subjugated myself to others.

The hardest call I made was to my friend Hannah. We had known each other since junior high school and had stayed close ever since. With Hannah, I trusted that I could express my fears about not surviving. She'd understand that I didn't want to put such a heavy emotional burden on my family. I trusted she wouldn't try to lure me into a false sense of optimism. During the conversation, I couldn't choke back tears, and instead sobbed as I revealed how afraid I was that I was going to die. In the most confident, matter-of-fact and utterly believable way possible, she said: "That isn't going to happen, *not on my watch.*" The sheer force of her will filled me with an optimism I could hold onto. There were countless times, during the long months of recovery, when her words got me through some of my darkest moments.

Dr. Gary was the other person who touched me in an equally poignant way. In the more than thirty years he had been my internist, he always checked on my emotional well-being as part of any assessment of medical conditions. In spite of me knowing him as a loyal advocate, I initially found myself holding back from revealing my fears around possibly having only a short time to live. I didn't want to risk his disappointment because I was feeling weak and powerless. What I wanted was for him to nurture me and offer

to protect me, with no strings attached. I was embarrassed that even at my age, I still found myself yearning for a compassionate father figure to make up for the one I never had.

While Dr. Gary was completing the brief pre-op exam, he asked me how I was holding up. As always, he watched and listened intently. He must have sensed I was holding back because even though I said I had complete faith in the multi-specialty care team, I teared up and wouldn't look him in the eye. I worried that if I let down fully and told him the truth, I'd be opening a floodgate and there'd be no stopping the rush of raw emotion. My fear was if I couldn't retain my composure, I might jeopardize my relationship with him. What if it turned out I was too much for him to handle? He would be, after all, the person I'd need most to have on my side once the frenzied aftermath of the surgery had dissipated. I knew from previous surgeries that the surgeons usually have little to do with managing the longer recovery process. That job always falls to the internist or family doctor.

Every experience I had ever had with Dr. Gary told me that my childhood fears of irreparably disappointing him, for being needy in my own right, were ridiculous. Even so, I remained caught up in an amygdala hijack. This is a term coined by Daniel Goleman in his book *Emotional Intelligence: Why It Can Matter More than IQ*. It refers to an emotional response that is immediate, overwhelming and out of measure with the stimulus that triggered the threat.

The intensity of the hijack matched one that occurred when I was in second or third grade. One of my earliest dreams was to become a dancer. I loved dancing because it took me out of my head and into my body. When I danced, I wasn't distracted by thoughts of keeping my father happy or hiding out when he was home. I got lost in the

rhythm and grace of the finely coordinated movements. I experienced what it felt like to balance myself no matter what position I held. It was the part of my childhood where I truly felt at peace.

I vacillated between wanting to share this deep yearning to dance with anyone who might encourage me, and keeping it buried in the depths of my soul. Even though I had plenty of anxieties around being good enough to compete as a professional dancer, I wanted something of my own that others could see and value enough to encourage me to pursue it. But even one of my closest friends discouraged me. She said I didn't have a dancer's body type; my frame was too large and I wasn't thin enough. I desperately wanted to challenge her view and find someone who would support me in following my dream, *no matter what.*

The opportunity finally presented itself when, along with a few of my girlfriends from the neighborhood, I participated in a ballet class conducted by a young woman in the basement of her home. I don't remember much about the experience except that the teacher was nice to us and we focused on learning and refining the five basic ballet positions. At some point, the moms must have had a confab and decided to enroll us in an after-school ballet class at a bona fide dance studio. The first day, the instructor told us to demonstrate a series of ballet moves. She wanted to assess our respective skill levels. I had no idea that the purpose of the assessment was to determine which of the class offerings would be most appropriate for each of us, given our respective competency levels. So, I was totally unprepared when the instructor abruptly pulled me and my mother aside right after class to tell us I was too advanced to remain at the same level as my friends. She asked my mother to consider moving me up to a more advanced class.

Her words triggered a duel between two critical conflicting desires. I wanted so badly to follow my dream, and here was an adult who was offering to support my dancing. But I also felt trepidation. Along with this opportunity to succeed came the possibility that I might

fail. At the same time, I couldn't shake the idea that my friends, the girls who up until this point had been the foundation of my social life, would reject me if I moved ahead without them. I pictured myself alone in my room comforted only by the company of my books and my dolls.

That evening I felt restless and agitated as I attempted to calculate the losses I'd incur, no matter what decision I made. I played out the alternatives in my head. In the end, the uncertainty associated with following my dream overwhelmed me, and I settled for the safety of the belonging I had cultivated with my friends. I told Mom I wanted to stay in the same class as my friends. She took it in stride, and I don't recall her asking why I was making that choice. In her defense, she didn't know the depth and intensity of my yearning. I had, after all, become quite shy and introverted following my dad's illness. She hadn't observed too many occasions when I took risks or sought the spotlight. How could she possibly know about my internal torment if I didn't tell her about it? I had the discomforting realization that even in situations where I might benefit from being honest about what I wanted or needed, the only person stopping me from trying was *me*. Self-sabotage became part of my make-up because I didn't have the courage to handle the visibility that comes with playing big.

Dr. Gary woke me out of my hijacked state, not aware I had been debating on whether I had the courage to tell him about the magnitude of my internal torment. He caught my gaze and asked me straight out: "Barbara, are you afraid you're going to die?" The floodgate opened, with tears filling my eyes and then, uncontrollably, running down my face. I took off my glasses and wiped my face with the palms of my hands, but couldn't stem the flow, "I'm terrified I'm not going to make it." He quickly fetched a

box of tissues. I dabbed at my face and blew my nose several times. Without hesitation, he reminded me of how he had always seen me – strong, courageous and worthy. A fighter. He made no promises about my prognosis, but he did make the only one he knew he could keep. He would not abandon me.

Chapter 5

Holding On

Early the morning of November 10, 2017, the four of us piled into the car for the twenty-minute drive to the hospital. Just like when we drove downtown for the visit with the multi-specialty care team, we sat in silence. Everything we could possibly have anticipated had been discussed. Time for further speculation had run out. When we arrived, I deferred to the family to point me in whatever direction we needed to go. I recognized how fortunate I was to be on the receiving end of their strength. I scanned their facial expressions, wondering if they'd reflect any fears that they were struggling to contain. I knew this day was going to be terribly difficult for them. But when their faces didn't indicate any undue stress, I felt both relief and sadness. The relief came in knowing they weren't indicating that they needed me to put any effort into keeping them safe. The sadness came in knowing I wasn't able to be there for them, even if they did need me. They would have to keep themselves as safe as they possibly could.

I knew that the best strategy for me during the pre-op phase was to be polite and comply with any requests. I steeled myself to "just get through it." Quite soon after arriving at the hospital I faced a major disruption to that strategy. It blindsided me in a way I never could have predicted. Immediately after completing the registration procedure and finding a seat in the waiting area, a young man and woman approached me, calling me by name. They explained they were representing the major medical research institute in town and asked if I'd sit with them for a few minutes. I was totally taken aback. How did they know who I was? Why were they bothering me right before the surgery? Later, I figured out that they must have asked the receptionist to alert them when I had arrived. So much for honoring my right to confidentiality.

Stuart and I joined them at a small table only a few feet away from the other people in the waiting room. They made a single request. Would I be willing to donate my tumor for medical research? It took about five minutes for them to explain the purpose of the research and reassure me that I would be an anonymous donor. But it seemed as if they droned on and on. I didn't listen to any of the details. I was too furious.

My fury emanated from my disbelief at their incredible insensitivity. They had cornered me. How could they have such *chutzpah*, the Yiddush word for shameless audacity, to disturb me and my family at such a critically difficult time? The multi-specialty care team had known about this surgery for weeks. Why didn't they have these people contact me before today?

This interchange opened a deep wound. It brought to my consciousness the rage I associated with countless other frightening times I had endured in the past, with people who were thoughtlessly ignoring my fears and pain. I wanted to shout at them to stop. But my "good" self wouldn't dare do that. How could I create a scene at

a time when everyone else in the waiting room was facing their own potential trauma? I felt like an outside observer, passively watching my own victimization at the hands of two people who appeared totally oblivious to my vulnerability.

The day my dad's mom, Grandma Newman, died stands out as one in which my father taught me, yet again, that my feelings didn't matter. Grandma had been in the hospital for a few days when, one afternoon, my parents were summoned to come quickly. I could tell by how suddenly they dropped what they were doing that things had gotten serious. I vaguely remember Mom telling me and my sisters that Grandma didn't have long to live.

A few hours after my parents left for the hospital, they were home. They came in the back door, which led directly into the family room, where my sisters and I were watching television. We didn't know what we were supposed to do while our grandmother was taking her last breaths; it was a situation we hadn't encountered before. Dad came in first, went straight to the TV, turned it off, beelined for my parents' bedroom and shut the door, all without uttering a word. A chill filled the air. Mom must have said that Grandma had died. But after that, my sisters and I were left totally to our own devices. Clearly, distracting ourselves by watching TV was unacceptable. But no one explained what children who had just lost their grandmother *should* do.

I wasn't given a chance to console Dad. Even worse, Grandma's sudden death reinforced my belief that bad things happen out of nowhere, and I shouldn't expect to be comforted when they do. Dad was so self-absorbed that he didn't even consider that an eight-year-old kid, who hadn't experienced the death of anyone close to them before, might *also* have feelings of sadness or anxiety. I remember sitting quietly in the family room wondering what came next. What would her funeral be like? When would it be? Would

> I be allowed to go? Did I even want to go? The lesson I took away from this was that when people were myopically focused on their own agendas, there was no room for my voice to be heard.

When these two strangers asserted their agenda at the hospital right before my surgery, the fighter in me wasn't present. I looked at Stuart and said, "I don't know what to do." He jumped in without hesitation. "Go ahead and sign the release." He knew me well enough to ascertain that the quicker I got away from those two individuals, the better. Here was another example of someone in my family jumping in, without hesitation, to be the level-headed decider. I don't know what would have happened if he hadn't come to my rescue. His unconditional love was always with me, but I clung to it more aggressively in this moment. I signed the forms, got up abruptly and went back to where Jay and Leigh were sitting. Stuart was right behind me. I wanted to nestle into whatever little bit of comfort being in their presence might provide before my name was called and I was whisked off to the pre-op area.

When it was time go, we were told that only two people at a time were allowed to be with me. That meant Stuart, Jay and Leigh would have to rotate. Leigh volunteered to stay back initially. But neither Stuart nor Jay went back to the waiting room to give her a chance to be with me. She later told me that sitting alone with her thoughts, she grew increasingly anxious and frustrated. She feared that no one would bring her back in time for her to give me a hug. I was panicked as well at the thought of not seeing her. As we got closer to the actual surgery, I prompted Stuart to ask someone in the pre-op area to bring Leigh back to see me. I felt terrible that she had to be alone, without support, for all that time.

Having had previous surgeries, I was used to the protocols that the nursing staff followed, and I was a good patient, reverting to my timeworn strategy of polite compliance. I was grateful for the sincere, caring attitude they showed me while efficiently going about their business. It was touching to see how attentive they were to me, a complete stranger. I made a mental note to myself: If I make it through this ordeal, I will intentionally get better at remembering to engage with strangers in a way that builds connection, even if just for a few moments. Being rendered visible can mean a lot to people who feel invisible much of the time. Without making the effort, I realized I may have missed opportunities to make life better for those who do.

Since my surgery was first on the list that day, it wasn't terribly long before I was wheeled into the holding area, the last stop before going to the operating room. Stuart and the kids were allowed to be with me. Dr. Joel came by so I could sign the final authorization for surgery. In my peripheral vision, I could see that the two people who had asked me about donating my tumor were hovering nearby. One of them was holding a small cooler. I imagined them as two vultures, taking cover in the shadows, waiting to swoop down on my carcass to strip it bare of the tumor. The image repulsed me. I averted my attention away from them.

Suddenly it struck me that I was just minutes away from the moment I had been dreading for so many weeks. As that reality set in, I found myself becoming more anxiety-ridden. I craved a few minutes of alone time with my family. I selfishly wanted to look at their faces, praying I could be part of the next twenty to thirty years of *their* lives. The intensity of their attention on me was devoid of any reciprocal demands. I experienced a brief sense of calm and a tiny bit of hope that, through their strength, I'd harbor the resilience I would need to come through this. The truth that there might not

be a "when this is behind us" for all four of us remained unspoken. It was an absolute and undeniable awareness of my own mortality.

I wasn't thinking at all about whether or not I had lived a meaningful life. I knew that I had made a difference for family, friends and business associates, by helping them give voice to their deepest yearnings. I had built a personal brand around the following intentionality: "I believe that the answers are always in the room, and my purpose is to create a context for those answers to surface." I knew there was more that I wanted to do in fulfilling that purpose; I simply wasn't ready to die. I would go into the surgery determined not to surrender peacefully.

In the minutes before the anesthesiologist came by to give me the sedative that would pull me away from consciousness, I took charge. In the last precious moments with my family, no rules or protocols were going to stand in my way. I had asked Stuart to bring a Hebrew prayer book so that he could read a prayer that's often chanted in the face of a serious health challenge. He opened the prayer book and began reciting it. But too many tears welled up. He became too choked up to continue. I can almost always read him like a book; he couldn't imagine the pain of a life without me. He gave the prayer book to Leigh, signaling her to continue reciting the prayer. Somehow, she mustered enough of an inner strength to continue reading in his place. I could hear her choking down the sobs.

By this time, the entire medical team was huddled nearby, taking in the scene. I noticed them, which distracted me from the prayer. I thought how odd it must be for them to witness this. It would have been so foreign to them. Given the predominance of Christianity in Grand Rapids, medical staff were used to patients, families and even doctors bowing their heads and saying a prayer to Jesus before surgical procedures. But now they looked puzzled. They couldn't understand the words because they were in Hebrew. When someone

from the team inched towards us, probably in an attempt to get things underway, someone else in the huddle held them back. She intuitively understood that we were engaged in prayer and signaled the others to give us the time and space to complete it.

My attention returned to my family, and I felt grateful that I had been granted this one wish, to have this private moment with my family, in the spirit of our Jewish tradition. By the time Leigh closed the prayer book all four of us were letting the tears flow freely. They each gave me a hug, clinging just a bit longer than normal, in case this was goodbye. It was a last attempt to cling to my life as I knew it.

Chapter 6

The Miracle and the Macabre

There were three stages to the surgery, each one contributing to the brutal beating my body had to endure. Initially, all standard elements of a major surgery were initialized – anesthesia, intubation, arterial line. The incision went from the base of my trachea down to the lowest part of my sternum. The dissection of five ribs and the removal of the entire sternum was facilitated by a combination of medieval-sounding instruments – a reciprocating saw, chisels designed for cutting bone, rib cutters and electro-cauterization probes. These were tools you'd expect to see in a horror film.

Next, once the sternum was removed, the surgeons built a prosthesis to replace it. It was fabricated on the spot to ensure a precise fit. The material used, bone cement, had to harden and cure before the prosthesis was secured through a series of screws. Both sides of my clavicle were also plated together to ensure stabilization of the portions of my ribs that remained. Finally, the plastic surgeon created the muscle flaps required to cover the sternal reconstruction.

Breast muscles were cut away from the skin, positioned over the reconstruction site and secured via attachment to other muscles and my clavicle. The surgery lasted around eight hours, a testament to how a living being can endure trauma of such extreme magnitude for a prolonged period of time.

Meanwhile, I later learned, my family spent the same eight hours living a different type of trauma. Stuart couldn't concentrate on anything other than the minutes ticking away on the clock in the waiting room. Leigh, normally impatient when she has to sit for long periods of time, knew to come armed with things to do. But once she had completed them, she became antsy and found it nearly impossible to distract herself. Jay wasn't able to share with anyone what he was feeling and mostly withdrew into himself.

All three were anxious about the unknown, and there was no relaxing until they finally were given an update after the first phase of the surgery. The tumor had successfully been removed. The surgeons were mostly confident they had achieved the margins needed to prevent the spread of any cancer cells. However, they cautioned the family that we wouldn't know that for sure until the pathology reports came back in about a week.

Hearing this news, they felt a temporary sense of relief. But only one part of the surgery had been completed. There was still a long way to go before any of them could imagine relaxing. The kids broke up the monotony by taking a long walk to a nearby coffee shop. They needed some fresh air, as well as the change of scenery. Because hospital waiting rooms are not conducive to private conversations, the walk also gave them a chance to talk about what they'd need to do to help me and Stuart in the weeks ahead as well as after I came home.

When the surgery was over, I was transported to the ICU. Naturally and thankfully, the anesthesia had left me oblivious to what I had been subjected to. But as soon as I came out of it, the

horrific nature of the assault on my body became immediately and mercilessly apparent. Despite the high dosages of pain medications, I was in relentless, excruciating agony. I momentarily took in the miracle that I had survived the surgery, before, within seconds, becoming overwhelmed by the intensity of my physical suffering. It consumed me in a way I didn't think was possible. The pain flowed through every cell in my body, without a single moment of relief. I finally surrendered to the truth that the only control I had was the choice of whether or not to continue breathing.

In the ICU, every breath I took was agonizing, causing the medical staff and my family considerable concern. Things got worse when I began to purposely hold my breath in an ill-fated effort to make the pain stop. Even though everyone urged me to stop, I couldn't listen to reason when all I wanted was for the agony to be over. In the weeks before the surgery, I had worried that I might not have the resilience to get through this degree of suffering. Would my warrior-self have the strength and fortitude to keep going? Now, for the first time, I wondered if I wanted to. I didn't have the capacity to make a conscious choice about this because my body simply took over. It focused all of its attention on getting me through the next breath, the next and the next.

Simultaneously, there was a continuous stream of medical protocols being followed and vitals being monitored. The interventions seemed endless. It had been determined that five departments would be involved in my post-operative care. Chest tubes would be managed by the cardiovascular team, drains would be maintained by the plastic surgery team, pain control would be handled initially by an anesthetist, with ongoing maintenance by palliative care, and the orthopedic oncology team would monitor post-surgical healing. More than a dozen people from these various disciplines came and went at all hours.

By continuously trying to hold my breath, I only made things worse. Medically, I was in hypoxemic respiratory failure, which meant I didn't have enough oxygen in my blood. To help push air into my lungs, someone placed a BiPap mask over my entire face. Between that and the extremely heavy doses of pain medications, I fell into a dreamlike state. My family and the people who were caring for me floated in and out of the room like apparitions. Their voices were muffled and often unintelligible. I observed their actions as if they were movements in a ballet. I hovered above it all, as if in a parallel universe. I was nothing more than a mass of body organs, bones and soft tissue struggling to breathe. I felt nothing other than the constant, excruciating pain.

To help alleviate and manage the pain, a decision to insert an epidural was made. This was done to continuously intercept and block pain messages. But this wasn't enough to secure my release from ICU into the general hospital population. Attempts to get me to sit up in a chair to lower the risk of pneumonia induced more pain and severe nausea. My left arm was in a sling to keep the stitches that held the muscle flap in place from tearing loose, but I wasn't coherent enough to remember my precautions around not moving that arm. I refused to eat.

The one night I was supposed to spend in the ICU turned into four. There were a few instances when I recognized how fortunate I was, in spite of being so disconnected from my real life. My family had communicated to friends and other relatives that visiting was not possible until I improved significantly. But one evening, while I was still in the ICU, our friend Isaac, who lives in Vancouver, Canada, didn't know the rule and surprised us with a visit. He had been in an all-day business meeting in Connecticut and commandeered the company jet to bring him to Grand Rapids so he could see me for a few minutes. Through the fog of my BiPap mask, I remember

feeling utterly touched, recognizing that I must be worthy of this demonstration of affection because no one would go to this extreme if they didn't really care about me.

Another incident that stands out is when the ICU nurse and Leigh were coaxing me to eat. They didn't care what I consumed, they just wanted me to take in some calories. I wanted no part of it. The pain left me with no appetite and, given the limited mobility I had in my arms, it was challenging to even lift a piece of silverware. Finally, the nurse said: "I'll make you a deal. If you always eat one bite from everything on your tray, I won't bug you anymore." She had taken time to figure out a way to help me move toward gaining strength without robbing me of my right to have some degree of personal choice. I forced down each tiny bite because I didn't want to let her down. Through the haze, I recognized she was rooting for me.

Toward the end of my stay in the ICU, these types of gestures meant a lot because even though I was detached from my normal life, they reconnected me to what mattered most. Instead of the ballet of apparitions floating in and out of my field of vision, I saw real people acting in ways that privileged human connection. Someone from my family was present for every intervention. Stuart often answered the medical staff's questions when I couldn't effectively respond. Jay and Leigh kept a low profile but interceded whenever they sensed I needed help. Leigh diligently kept everyone in our circle aware of my progress by posting summaries on the CaringBridge website.

The housekeepers tiptoed in, always asking if it was an intrusion if they took a few minutes to clean the room. When the food service staff delivered or picked up my tray, they never left without checking if there was anything else they could do to help me, like moving the things on my tray table closer so they'd be within reach. Even the seemingly endless number of medical providers who interfaced with me each day treated me as an intelligent adult, deserving of respect.

They directed their questions at me, offered me opportunities to provide information that would inform the decisions they'd make on my behalf and patiently explained the reason behind any decisions they did make.

I was aware enough to be both amazed and abhorred by the medical technology that was being wielded in this monumental effort to save my life. On one level, I was absolutely humbled by how medical science had evolved to a point where life-saving measures of this magnitude and complexity were possible. This truth only enhanced my respect and admiration for the many practitioners who worked in collaboration during the surgery, and after, on my behalf. Some only knew me superficially and others were total strangers. Yet, they all demonstrated they cared. I wasn't ever inclined to take this for granted.

At the same time, discovering the abuse my body had endured left me keenly aware of every individual's unqualified fragility. I saw my body as a delicate flower that had barely survived a heavy downpour, still threatened by an ominous sky filled with dark clouds portending another deluge. But in spite of my instability, my caretakers were able to stave off any immediate onslaughts. They conferred daily and successfully diminished the pain enough so that I could be transferred to a regular hospital unit. This was an incredible milestone. It was day five after my surgery and, for the first time since then, I felt a tiny glimmer of hope that if I'd gotten through the worst of it, I might just make it.

Chapter 7

The Show Must Go On

The day I transferred to a unit in the general hospital, the social work staff began preparing us for my release. Given my medical condition, it seemed absurd to be contemplating that so soon. But I was grateful, in the end, because it put in motion a medical evaluation process that turned out to be to my benefit. The next day, I looked up and saw a tall, dark-haired gentleman standing at the foot of my bed. I remember him smiling at me as he said "This was a big surgery, Barbara. You will get well. We can help you." For a moment I wasn't sure if he was real or if he had appeared in a dream. Perhaps the pain medications were playing tricks on me.

The next day, he returned and repeated what he had said the day before. This time I was lucid and knew that he was real. Dr. Sam was one of the department chairs from a well-respected rehabilitation hospital in Grand Rapids, and he was there to evaluate my case. On his recommendation, I either would be accepted or rejected for admission to their acute rehab unit. I hoped to be allowed to go there after being

released because it was a premier rehab facility in our community. His words seemed to imply that I was a viable candidate. I was comforted and extremely grateful, knowing that not everyone who is assessed gets admitted. I felt a measure of relief from my anxiety, given the certainty that my next stop would be there, rather than going straight home. I couldn't imagine that I'd rally quickly enough to manage my own mobility and selfcare. I was determined not to put the burden of that on Stuart and Leigh.

We had been told that my release would come as soon as my pain was effectively managed. Given the continued high doses of medication, I got through most of the next week toggling between moments of lucidity and fogginess. I still couldn't find adequate words to describe the magnitude of my suffering. But I tried to remain as upbeat as possible because I didn't want to come across to anyone as being ungrateful for all they were doing to support me. The empathy meter I had installed in my work as an executive coach remained in working order.

I also knew that a more positive state of mind would have a positive impact on my healing. In our family, the way that shows up is through teasing. Stuart and I have a long history of making fun of our respective foibles. He loves to tell jokes that, in nearly forty years of marriage, I probably have heard more than a hundred times. So, when he started repeating them to the nursing staff, I'd teasingly roll my eyes, shake my head back and forth and ask them not to encourage him by laughing. In the most deadpan, sarcastic voice I could muster, I would say "He's *so* much fun to live with." This made everyone laugh even more. It was the kind of back-and-forth teasing that wasn't unusual for a couple who'd been happily married for so long. It made the staff feel good about coming into my room, which made me feel more upbeat.

The daily interventions by the medical staff became increasingly predictable. The incremental improvements they observed weren't

as obvious to me. For the majority of the first ten days after the surgery, I was tethered to an oxygen tube and an IV pole. Multiple times a day, staff members came in to facilitate the management of the temporary valves and test tubes. Since I wasn't allowed to use my arms to move from a prone to a seated position, or vice versa, I required assistance for every change in body position, whether in bed or in a chair.

Rather than press the call button every time I needed something, I often waited for more than thirty minutes until someone on the nursing staff was in my room to take my vitals or bring me medications. Only then would I ask them to do the small thing I needed and couldn't do on my own. I overcompensated by being super thoughtful and polite – always saying "please" and "thank you" for every action they took on my behalf. I did this because I had made up a story that "good" patients don't bother the staff and risk negative consequences.

I had absolutely no basis for this narrative. In fact, nearly all my previous hospital experiences had proven I could rely on the genuine support of the nursing staff. But it still was distressing to be so completely dependent on others – while also keenly aware that I had no choice. I harbored the fear that this time, my needs would be too much, just like they had been too much for my father, and I'd be left to fend for myself.

Small efforts by physical therapists to get me to sit up or walk left me overcome with nausea and increased pain. Additional medication was always the response to that, keeping me in a back-and-forth swing between lucidity and fogginess. Initially, the occupational therapists couldn't effectively help me initiate the most basic aspects of self-care, like washing my face or putting on a clean T-shirt. As a result of the anesthesia, my bladder wouldn't empty properly, meaning that, a few times a day I was subjected to

what's called a "straight cath" procedure, where a tube is inserted into the bladder to empty the build-up of urine. Each time felt like a tiny violation because it was impossible to maintain any measure of modesty. Then, when the amount of urine indicated I still wasn't capable of urinating on my own, I felt defeated.

We finally received some good news on the eighth day. The surgeons had gotten clean margins and the actual stage of the cancer they removed was lower than they had anticipated. I wouldn't need any radiation. I was relieved about the margins being clean. The news soothed my fears about the cancer metastasizing in the future. Being released from this particular obsessive worry, I rallied. I was determined to approach this phase of my recovery the same way I'd approach learning a new skill, like when I learned to scuba dive. My therapists would be my trainers. They'd start by teaching me fundamental methods and principles. Then I'd do practice drills over and over, appreciating their feedback so I'd know what to focus on in order to improve. If I kept at it, I'd be rewarded by achieving a level of mastery. By breaking down the challenges that I faced into these logical and sequential steps, they didn't seem so overwhelming. I would show myself, and everyone around me, my bad-ass "can do" attitude.

I began to understand the rhythm of my recovery. Moments of unbearable, relentless pain would be interspersed with sudden bursts of absolute conviction about what I was capable of overcoming. My current optimism was inspired by the doctors, nurses, nurses' aides, physicians' assistants and therapists who were generously giving of their time and expertise in service to my rehabilitation. All I had to do was hunker down, get past the pain and follow the guidance of these expert helpers. I'd be rewarded for my courage and fortitude in fighting the good fight. I held onto an expectation that the trauma of this experience would dissolve into a distant memory. At various

moments each day, I messaged to everyone around me, "I've got this." When my family saw me acting more like myself – chatting informally with the nursing staff, responding optimistically to reports about my progress and exhibiting my typical exaggerated fake annoyance with Stuart's attempts at humor, they too began to believe that I meant it.

Then something unforeseen caused a disruption, and I was thrown back into my other persona, the one where I reverted to finding comfort in hiding rather than taking the risk of voicing my fears.

It was the eleventh day after surgery. Because my pain was finally under control, I was soon to be discharged to the rehabilitation facility. But the morning I was supposed to leave, I coughed up blood. Within twenty-four hours I was diagnosed with a hemothorax (blood between the chest wall and the lungs) and a herniated lung (a tear in the chest wall). After attempts to drain the blood didn't work, I was scheduled for surgery two days later.

When I heard the news, I realized that my "can do" attitude had been camouflaging worries I'd been hiding, around not *being enough* or not *having enough* of what it would take to survive this deep, extended trauma. Questions raced through my mind on a continuous loop. How could I possibly live through the effects of more anesthesia? Where would I find the resilience to endure even more pain and suffering, on top of what I already was coping with? Would I ever regain my independence? I became totally preoccupied with these thoughts, buried in an unrelenting state of agitation.

That's when the sense of profound abandonment crept in. Finding out I needed another surgery came just a few days after Dr. Joel had told us he was moving away from the area and no longer would be able to manage my care. His partner, Dr. Matt, would take over. Dr. Matt introduced himself to me during his rounds the day after Dr. Joel's departure. As I looked up at this stranger,

now suddenly my post-cancer caretaker, I wondered if I'd default to being a model, compliant, good patient, or if I'd have the courage to show up as I really was, grappling with a question that kept circling around my brain, "Was it time to let go?" I had a strong desire to voice this yearning to surrender, to verbalize without any reservation that I had had enough. I didn't have the will to fight the good fight anymore. Even more compelling was a proclamation that only I could hear. I didn't want to survive if I had to endure much more suffering and a dubious quality of life.

The idea of relinquishing the will to live actually brought some relief. It would free me, finally, to give up my life of penance – even though I thought I had done that years ago. The magnitude of my suffering revived the tug-of-war between my great pretender and my valiant warrior. Choosing to be the pretender meant I was two-faced. When that side of me prevailed, I believed, I used subterfuge to keep my evil, self-serving proclivities at bay, an imposter play-acting selflessness. Choosing the valiant warrior path meant I was proudly selfish, taking a courageous, authentic stance, on my own terms.

As much as I wanted to free myself from this internal struggle, I reverted to old habits and didn't share these roiling thoughts with anyone. I was convinced that I couldn't trust anyone to understand; this was too much for anyone else, especially my family, to have to deal with. It didn't dawn on me that expressing what I was feeling could have been recognized as a call for help and might have been answered with compassion and respect. I resigned myself to performing, an actor playing a part that had no understudy. I owed it to everyone I loved to make sure the show would go on.

Chapter 8

Long Days and Nights

The night and day shifts in the hospital had different cadences. The days were noisy. Visitors passed by and chatted in the hallways. Patients on gurneys and in wheelchairs squeaked through the corridors, toward other parts of the hospital for diagnostic tests. Nurses and aides huddled around their mobile computer stands, coordinating their efforts. Since I couldn't concentrate enough to read or watch TV, observing these activities was my main form of diversion. The daytime hum reminded me that there was life beyond my room's four walls.

There were countless interruptions, starting before dawn, when the technicians came to do a daily blood draw. Most were kind enough to only put on the light near the entrance to my room. I appreciated that they didn't turn on the bright overhead light; I could remain drowsy enough to fall back to sleep.

The din of the daytime routine brought comfort by keeping me distracted from my darker thoughts. I was particularly grateful

for the care given by the nursing staff and enjoyed my interactions with them. They took a personal interest in me as someone who was more than just the woman with cancer who had gone through this uniquely complicated surgery. In fact, because my surgery had been so rare, a few nurses told me that colleagues in other units had asked them about it. Apparently, word had spread about the surgical team's success with such a rare procedure, and people were curious. I didn't enjoy or crave this kind of attention. It left me feeling like a case study, not a human being and didn't take into account the prolonged pain and suffering I was enduring now.

Still, I felt tremendous gratitude for the nursing staff. Each one of them advocated for me when things got too hectic, like when I was too exhausted to follow the regimens that the physical and occupational therapists assigned me. The nurses ran interference, telling them to come back later, or the following day. They also interceded boldly when it was obvious that my pain medication "cocktail" wasn't doing its job. One night I had a horrific hallucination in which I was screaming for help but no one could hear me and I couldn't escape whatever traumatic event was unfolding. When I finally woke up, exhausted and terrified, the nurse immediately contacted the key players responsible for managing my pain meds and didn't let up until they ordered an alternative concoction.

Dr. Matt also played a key role in helping me modulate my mood swings. My trust in him quickly became incontrovertible. The first time I met him, when he stood at the foot of my hospital bed and told me he was taking over responsibility for my care after Dr. Joel's unanticipated departure, he recognized I was feeling extremely vulnerable. Translation: I felt like I had been abandoned. Earlier that day, unable to control my bowel movements, I had another accident in bed. When he asked what was on my mind, I began to cry, telling him how frustrated and ashamed I was about my incontinence. It

was a constant reminder of my dependence on others for everything related to my physiological needs. He looked me straight in the eye and in a tone that was not at all condescending said, "Barbara, it's a small problem overall given everything you're dealing with. The staff is here to take care of that for you. You don't need to worry about that right now."

This and other interactions with Dr. Matt positioned him as a good guy, as far as I was concerned. I took his consistent invitation, to speak my truth, as a sign he believed what I was experiencing truly mattered. If he was confident that I had a long, cancer-free future ahead of me, I could trust him. I'd use his confidence and encouragement as springboards for my own positive actions moving forward. While Dr. Joel had orchestrated the technical fixes that ultimately gave me a chance to survive, Dr. Matt often gave me the impetus to thrive.

There were moments of intense frustration as well. I understood that each member of my recovery team needed to make their own daily examinations, updates or reports about my progress. But there seemed to be little if any coordination among them, and I soon got impatient with the constant stream of traffic in and out of my room. It seemed like each person asked the same questions, and I repeated the same responses. I kept wondering why my answers weren't entered into my chart so I only would have to answer each question once. My family pointed out that the answers likely were being charted, but it probably was easier for the staff to ask me the questions real-time, rather than take the time to review the chart. I wondered how "coordinated" my care actually was, and it wasn't just me. I admired the nurses even more as I watched them assume oversight for what could have been some serious redundancies or omissions among this entourage of caregivers.

The best part of each day was late afternoon and early evening. Stuart and Leigh were always with me at dinner time. Leigh took on

the responsibility of bringing a home-cooked meal to the hospital every night. She was concerned about my lack of interest in food, which was compounded by my repulsion at the hospital's cuisine. Each time the food service staff brought in a tray, the smells and tastes made me nauseous. To coax me to eat, Leigh exhausted herself making sure she always brought a delicious hot meal for the three of us to eat together, my daughter's daily expression of her love.

She mostly cooked healthy, nutritionally balanced meals, but once in a while also brought comfort food, like macaroni and cheese. She had purchased a zippered case that was specially designed to keep food hot, large enough to contain an entrée and a couple of side dishes. She'd dish out each item, gently coaxing me every evening to eat just a bit more. This one hour of family time, with her and Stuart, was another element of my daily routine that provided some comfort and a few moments of normalcy.

The night shift's rhythm was completely different. The hallways were mostly quiet unless there was an emergency or a patient, recently out of surgery, was moaning and crying out from pain. Sleep was my only escape from all the reminders of how damaged my body was and how totally dependent on others I'd continue to be. But to stay ahead of the pain, the nurses needed to wake me every few hours to give me medication and check my vitals. In between, if I needed to go to the restroom, I had to sit patiently while the aides put a strap around my waist. They would cling to it as I stepped forward, preventing me from falling while I navigated the short distance to the bathroom. Often, I'd get frustrated when I'd have to be the one to remind them that I couldn't use a walker because of the pressure it put on the reattached muscle flaps. But I also made sure to make my reminders gentle; I didn't want to give them any reason for not answering the call button right away. I was scared I might have an accident in bed.

This anxiety came and went countless times during my hospital stay, rooted in my childhood notion that if I did have the power to make my dad sick, perhaps I also had the power to do equivalent damaging things to those I relied on for my medical care. Constant surveillance of their body language, tone of voice and gestures gave me clues as to whether they saw me as a force for good or a force for evil.

When my sleep was interrupted, my inner thoughts often turned dark as well. My obsession with wanting to let go took over. I desperately wanted to silence the constant mental chatter, but the interruptions were constant, preventing that peaceful escape into sleep from happening with any consistency. Yet, it also didn't escape my notice that throughout the night, the nurses also were my angels. Each time they came in to give me my meds, I knew at least a few hours of respite would follow, submerging my dark thoughts until the next check-in.

After three weeks, I was stable enough to be discharged to the rehab hospital, where the rhythms were similar, but the degree of medical oversight diminished and the amount of physical and occupational therapy increased. During my one-week stay, the therapists pushed me toward functioning much more independently. Even though dark thoughts still plagued me in the quiet hours of the night, the staff's optimism and steadfast belief in my capabilities boosted my spirits. While dragging my oxygen tank alongside me, they encouraged me to walk the halls and do strengthening exercises in the gym, each time going beyond what I had done before. I felt each staff member's joy in seeing my gradual progress. Once I was in rehab, I was *all in.*

As my discharge day neared, a single medical issue kept me anxiety-ridden: nearly every minute of every day I was still dependent of oxygen. Any time I engaged with the medical staff, I voiced this concern, asking outright if I'd ever be able to come

off oxygen. Their responses were always non-committal. But realistically, how else could they respond? It was too soon to know if I'd ever get back to normal oxygen levels on my own.

In the tug-of-war I'd experienced over the previous months, between choosing life over death, I had privileged life. If, after all I'd been through, it turned out I'd have to be dependent on an oxygen tank for every breath, I wanted no part of it. I disliked having been beholden to an external source of oxygen source while I was in the ICU, but that was the ICU and it was to be expected. I detested the idea of needing the tank once I got home. Whatever control I'd surrendered to this point – concerning my mobility, my self-care and my personal modesty – would only have been worth it if I could get back to living a normal, independent life.

By the end of my stay in rehab, my oxygen levels were satisfactory during the day, but still too low at night to risk sleeping without being hooked up to the tank. Stuart had arranged for a medical supply company to deliver tanks to the house, and they delivered three: the heavy main tank, a backup and a small portable one.

I felt terribly fragile as the tanks were set up in my bedroom. They looked like immovable boulders, a bit too comfortable where they were positioned, seemingly ready to take up permanent residency. I realized that including a portable tank was precautionary, in case I needed to leave the house when my oxygen level dipped too low. But to me it was a constant reminder that I might actually not be able to breathe fully on my own, ever again. I was haunted by the image of complete dependency on a device that would significantly interfere with and curtail my activities.

But I also was ashamed of how my reaction could be seen as an arrogant disregard for anyone who is lucky enough to survive because of such life-saving appendages. Even so, I made it my mission to get rid of these boulders. My iron will must have paid

off; about two weeks later, my nighttime oxygen levels were back to normal. As soon as Dr. Gary gave his approval, we called the medical equipment company and arranged for the tanks to be picked up. I felt liberated.

Chapter 9

Façade

For the next nine months, a series of unanticipated medical challenges kept ping-ponging me between optimistic and pessimistic views about my future. The first was on a Saturday in December, ten days after leaving the rehab facility. I was alone, lying on the family room couch, experiencing severe pain in my chest and hardly able to move. I was scared. I couldn't reach Stuart because he was at Sabbath services and no one at the synagogue would answer the phone. Leigh was having brunch with a good friend visiting from California. I hated to interrupt their visit, but I needed someone to help me figure out whether we should go to the emergency room or call an ambulance. The pain was that severe. I called her and she rushed home.

Stuart arrived a few minutes later and we decided to call an ambulance. I was in so much pain, Stuart and Leigh were afraid to help me off the couch. The EMTs arrived, assessed the situation and put me in the ambulance for the short ride to the emergency room.

Lying on the stretcher, looking up at the ceiling, I kept thinking about how odd the motion felt. It wasn't at all like being a passenger in a car, where you can anticipate turns and stops. My body simply leaned in whatever direction the driver was steering. It reminded me of my recent hospital stay; I couldn't prepare myself for most of the turns and stops that happened there, either. It also reminded me of being on a train, but without any visual orientation afforded by having windows. This feeling of being separated from the real world had become an all-too-familiar experience. During similar moments of detachment, I had become adept at numbing myself against any possible bad news. I used the time in the ambulance to prepare myself by reciting my old, familiar mantra, "just get through it."

The EMTs indicated they were concerned I might be having a heart attack, and the ER staff acted quickly and efficiently, conducting a series of diagnostic tests right away. In between interactions with the staff, I concentrated on willing my body to have the fortitude and resilience to get over yet another unanticipated hurdle. Within a few hours we knew my heart was fine. The pain was a result of my oral pain medications not doing their job. They prescribed a new combination of pain meds and I was released.

For the next few months, I progressed in a way that brought a much-needed sense of calm to everyone, including me. The physical and occupational therapists motivated me to push just far enough so that I'd exceed our collective expectations, but not so hard that I'd overdo it and lose momentum. Given their help with daily living skills and mobility, I felt a little more normal every day. After a few weeks of looking back on the progress I'd made, most mornings I woke up optimistic. I had emerged from the worst of it and proven that I could get past the challenges that still lay ahead. Finally, I was able to see the value of the doctors' admonitions to "give it time."

Stuart and I started to socialize again. This was a big step forward, given that in the hospital, I hadn't wanted any visitors. In that environment, my total reliance on aides for my personal hygiene and mobility left me feeling extremely vulnerable. My friends knew me to be capable, strong and independent. If they saw me in such a state of dependency, how could I be sure they wouldn't always see me that way from now on? This was a totally irrational fear; that's simply not what good friends do. But that awareness didn't stop me from establishing a firm "no visitors" policy until I returned home.

Once I loosened these reins, I was cheered, not exhausted, by the opportunity to reconnect with cherished friends and extended family. It didn't matter if the connection was in-person or by phone. Just knowing I was alive to hear their voices brought me joy. These mini-reunions also gave me a chance to share my gratitude for their love and support. But they also let me reinstate my role as a friend who, once again, could provide love and support for them with equal devotion.

During this same period, I felt a rebirth of my enthusiasm for reengaging in my coaching practice, helping individuals develop or enhance their leadership capacities. I figured the smartest approach would be to start with a part-time schedule, coaching only from my home office. Virtual coaching was commonplace for me anyway since my practice includes clients from more than twenty countries. Fortunately, I didn't have to worry about the group workshops I facilitate since none were scheduled for a few months. By the time they started up again, I felt strong enough physically and emotionally to return to a full-time schedule. These interactions resurrected my sense of purpose – to help others discover their own self-imposed hidden barriers, define their authentic selves and be guided in their efforts to be heard. Slowly but surely, I began to stop identifying myself solely as a survivor of a life-threatening, traumatic illness.

In reclaiming myself I unexpectedly awakened to fresh, new truths about the power of human connection by reading the comments people had posted on the CaringBridge site in response to Leigh's frequent progress reports. During the four weeks I was hospitalized, seventy people posted more than three hundred comments. The posts came from my sisters, stepmother, in-laws, nieces, nephews, friends, colleagues, clients and coaching partners. They represented relationships I had developed in the U.S., Canada, England, Ireland, Israel and Chile. Many of the comments referenced my "strength," "courage," "toughness" and "tenacity."

Some were expressions of tender humor, "I feel sorry for that poor tumor that decided to mess with Barbara Rapaport." Others were tinged with admiration, "You are taking this challenge on in the 'Barbara way'... careful thought, solid problem-solving and consideration of the path forward! I would expect no less." I also was reminded many times of how much I meant to others, "We are ALL impacted, touched, changed, improved, enhanced, challenged, stretched and loved by you." Statements by those who know me best acknowledged the struggle I was facing, "It sounds like you're doing a grand job of managing the polarity of scared and optimistic."

Many of them became cheerleaders when I was going back in for the unanticipated lung surgery, "Just another bump in the road. Barbara is a fighter, so I know she'll get through this; she is a strong lady, with an iron will, so she will come through this with flying colors." Perhaps most touching was the way so many of them expressed equal concern for the well-being of Stuart, Jay and Leigh, "It's good to be alongside Barbara, from a distance, and appreciate what a tough journey it is. Respect to you all for how you are handling it. Thinking of you all." The offers to help them get through this were countless.

When I finally sat down to read the entries, these expressions of unconditional friendship and love nearly overwhelmed me and ignited an internal spark to increase my own capacity for human connection. But I found that I couldn't fully act on this impulse because, despite how genuine the comments were, I felt like I was reading about some other stranger, also named Barbara. She, not I, was the one who deserved such love, care and support. How was it that I could be aware of these sentiments expressed by people I trusted and cared about, yet still couldn't *hear* them?

Here I was, decades later, finding it difficult to shake the idea that maybe my father had been right all along. If, in his eyes, I'd failed to be a good daughter, that meant I couldn't possibly have grown up to become such a good person. In his telling, anyone who felt otherwise probably had only been duped by my deviously well-crafted façade – the façade I'd constructed as a child living with a father who was incapable of seeing, hearing or understanding anyone else. But I began to restore my confidence that this "crafted" façade wasn't an illusion. My friends and family were telling me, in ways impossible to deny, that I really was a good person.

Chapter 10

Detachment

Two months after I returned home from rehab, the results of my CT and MRI gave me a renewed appreciation for life. Each successive quarterly report showed that I was free of cancer, reducing the likelihood of a recurrence. After my third set of scans, Dr. Matt was able to say with confidence, "You can move forward without worrying anymore, Barbara."

The first obvious, forward-moving action I took related to my consulting practice. My forced hiatus from work had given me an opportunity to confirm a suspicion I had been harboring for a while. When I turned sixty-five and became eligible for Medicare, I naturally started thinking about retirement. But all that time unplugged from work convinced me that any effort to acquire hobbies, any commitment to complete my reading list or any increase in coffee chats with my friends couldn't replace the satisfaction I derived from helping clients discover their hidden barriers. My work is what gives me a purpose to get up in the

morning. Once I returned to a full-time work schedule, several times a day while in the middle of some work activity, I'd hear a voice in my head whispering, "This is amazing. I wasn't supposed to be here." Translation: I was nowhere near ready to retire.

With renewed enthusiasm, I hired Sarah, a consultant who tweaked my social media presence to attract rising Millennial and iGen leaders. We linked my future business success to the leadership development needs of these younger generations. They seemed most in need of the kinds of services I offer because so many of them have been thrust into supervisory and management positions prematurely. I wanted to use social media to communicate with them in ways that demonstrated how well I understood their unique development challenges. This was my intentional and sustained effort to remain relevant.

Then I started making arrangements to travel again. Stuart and I are fortunate in that our kids still like to travel with us. Each time we visit someplace new together, even before the trip is over, we usually start planning the next one. At the time of my diagnosis, we were just a few weeks away from putting down a deposit on a family trip to Italy. The itinerary covered all the major cities – Rome, Florence and Venice. When we asked Jay and Leigh what would make the trip extra special for them, Jay said Pompeii and Leigh chose Cinque Terre. It was supposed to be the trip of a lifetime. But the possibility evaporated once we knew I had cancer.

Now we held a family conference call to discuss rescheduling the Italy trip. We settled on June of 2020. Meanwhile, Jay and Leigh started musing about mother-son and mother-daughter trips. Given all the angst I've had around whether I would ever be a good enough person, deserving of love, there's nothing more validating than having my children say they wanted to spend time with me doing something we all enjoyed – exploring the beauty of foreign

countries and experiencing other cultures. The message I took from this was this, even though I may have been a disappointment to my father, I certainly made up for it by being a good mother.

Leigh and I settled on Paris; ever since she was a girl, when we read *Linnea in Monet's Garden,* she had asked if the two of us could visit the garden in Giverny. Jay wanted to go where neither of us had been. He was partial to South America, given its natural beauty and his fluency in Spanish. Although he and I didn't land on a particular location right away, we kept sending ideas back and forth. Because I wasn't strong enough to travel yet, we didn't schedule either trip. But it was still fun to do the research and create possible itineraries.

Even though I'd resumed most normal activities, I still found myself occasionally seeking to be detached. In the past, this had been a way to protect myself from Dad's neediness and his demand that I focus all of my attention on alleviating whatever was troubling him. My detachment then was avoidance of having to deal with his insecurities. This was a different form of detachment, informed by my preoccupation with the belief that cancer is always lurking in the wings, and that if you don't detach from superficial distractions, you may be relinquishing your commitment to vigilance. Then cancer will sneak up and catch you unaware.

A few weeks after the meeting with the multi-specialty care team and before the surgery, Stuart, Leigh and I went out for dinner at a local restaurant. On the surface, I was present. We chatted with each other and the staff like anyone would. No outside observer would guess that we were in the midst of a family trauma. This was in stark comparison to my perception of everyone else in the room, who appeared as untroubled as we did, as if everything was normal and as it should be. At first I was envious. How could they go on as if nothing was wrong when my life was turning upside down?

In between feeble attempts to be present with my family, my gaze fixated on the sea of faces. I wondered if any of them, like me, were in a battle with cancer but intentionally hiding it from the world. Societal norms don't usually tolerate any expression of such fragility in public. When the server asked, "How are you doing tonight?" the only acceptable response would be, "Fine, how are you?" The first part of the answer wasn't true. The second part was me deflecting attention. It gave me cover so I could avoid saying what I really felt because my fear of being dismissed was always lurking just below the surface. Amidst all the chatter and laughing around me, I felt lonely and isolated, the way I did so many times in childhood when in desperation, surrounded by people, I went mute instead of expressing my physical or emotional pain. Perhaps some of the people in the restaurant that night had a similar history of having been left behind without a voice.

I also pondered whether they might be going about their usual business, totally unaware that cancer was surreptitiously wreaking havoc on *their* bodies, just like I was doing the weeks before my sixty-fifth birthday party. I mused about grabbing each of them by the shoulders and shaking them to get their attention, to warn them not to be so nonchalant. That's what a genuinely good person would do. I imagined having the courage to shout at them, "Don't take this carefree moment for granted. You might already be following in my footsteps." I knew, of course, that this would be seen as crazy, not courageous. They wouldn't listen to me anyway, and I'd just end up profoundly disappointed in myself for having failed them.

After the surgery, even though I was outwardly living my "normal" life, I remained leery, constantly maneuvering through the mental gymnastics that helped me discern when, and when not, to keep an emotional distance from others. I was haunted by the subtle daily reminders of cancer, such as the swelling and numbness

whenever I touched my chest, or the neck-to-abdomen scar I saw in the mirror whenever I got out of the shower.

At one of my many follow-up appointments with my internist, Dr. Gary, I voiced one of my many concerns. "Does being without my sternum mean that my heart will be unprotected if I fall or I'm in a car accident?" He responded in his usual steady, calm way, "Quite the opposite. Your implant is much stronger than your sternum was!" In spite of all his assurances, I remained preoccupied with the notion that no one is immune from cancer's insidious intrusion. What if I hadn't paid enough dues yet and mine would return?

Chapter 11

When Selfishness Tugs at Your Heart

While the outside world observed me grabbing onto life with a renewed zeal, my family was privy to my darker moments as I fought against the relentless worry about cancer striking me again. Quite often, in the middle of a seemingly carefree interaction, I'd feel a hint of anxiety unconnected to what was going on right then. A single thought would echo over and over, "This may be the last time I will ever do this." My facial expression remained neutral, giving the appearance I was still engaged. But my mind wandered off into a hopeless view of the future, an assertion that if I ever had to battle with cancer again, I wouldn't be able to endure the suffering. This was a far cry from my more recent and optimistic perspective of, "This is amazing. I wasn't supposed to be here."

Swinging on a pendulum between hope and despair became emotionally draining enough that I eventually decided it was time to get outside help. I called Gilda's Club of Grand Rapids, a nonprofit organization providing emotional support for anyone impacted by

cancer, or grieving the loss of a loved one. I trusted it would be safe to go there because my friend, Deb, was one of the founders. After her first bout with cancer, Deb and two of her friends, also cancer survivors, established the Club. All three wished they could have had a place like the Club to go to for social and emotional support when they were grappling with their own respective challenges.

I scheduled an orientation for a Saturday in early February and asked Leigh, "Would you mind coming with me? I'm afraid to go by myself." I couldn't anticipate how I would react, being in a space where most people had cancer and likely would suspect that I did, too. My apprehension about everything I had been through simmered just below the surface, and I knew it wouldn't take much to break through my protective armor. The whole point in going to Gilda's was so I wouldn't have to hide my internal angst anymore, but I wasn't going to jump in without a lifeline, and I thought my daughter could help me vet the program before I committed to it. For the few hours we spent there, I remained tethered to Leigh, monitoring her facial expressions for signs of concerns with the program. I trusted that she would have an intuition about whether the environment would be safe enough for me to safely reveal my vulnerabilities, or if it felt like I was pushing myself too far out of my comfort zone.

Gilda's Club is housed in a big, old, renovated farmhouse. From the moment I arrived, its homey atmosphere radiated safety and comfort. In the large front room, the furniture was upholstered in colorful floral patterns. Kids were crawling on the couches while their parents sat nearby, engaged in relaxed conversations with other "members." There were smiles on nearly every face in the room. The sound of laughter drifted towards me as light poured in through large-paned windows. The attitudes of the people I met that day weren't mired in darkness and despair. Whatever burdens they were

carrying, they appeared to be on a par with their sense of optimism. They exuded joyfulness in being alive and present.

After a brief overview and tour with one of the staff, we were invited to stay for a simple brunch. The smell of the coffee brewing lured us into the warm, inviting atmosphere of a bright and airy country kitchen. The meal had been prepared by one of the volunteers, another survivor who had found the club during her own struggle with cancer. I was touched when she said, "I try to do this as often as possible. I shop for the groceries and prepare the food because this place is special. I just like being here." She didn't need the club's formal services anymore; she simply wanted to have a reason to hang out. She loved the feeling of belonging. I allowed myself to hope that, if she felt that way about the place, maybe I eventually would, too.

This volunteer served us a beautifully presented plate of homemade quiche, a colorful array of fruit and a fresh pastry. We perched on stools at a large island with a few other people visiting for the first time, gabbing like old friends catching up. Staff members and other volunteers, lured by the comforting aroma of the pastries, wandered in and out. The established members and first-timers bantered among each other. Even though I wasn't yet convinced this was a place where I could work through my anguish, at the very least I'd sensed that I'd be surrounded by genuine people who had the capacity to fully grasp what I was going through.

Gilda's Club proved to be a tree of life with many branches. While I began to participate in a support group every other Thursday, Stuart attended a parallel support group for family members that dealt with the challenges they were facing as caregivers. Because there were so many activities going on at the Club on these evenings, members and their families were invited to enjoy an early dinner at no cost, catered by volunteers. People sat together at communal

tables and unabashedly shared their stories about what had brought them to Gilda's Club. I was surprised by how many people weren't dealing with cancer themselves. They were taking advantage of the support groups so they could more effectively walk alongside a family member who was battling the disease.

Stuart always insisted on coming with me. This wasn't because he felt so in need of the support from his group, although he certainly was willing to benefit from the experience. Rather, it was a tangible way for him to be there for me, a manifestation of his steady and unconditional love. We'd rush there after work, grab a bite with the community and then go off to our respective groups. On the ride home, we usually talked about any new insights or epiphanies. Stuart was always touched by how many family members were struggling and on the verge of utter despair. Hearing their narratives helped him enhance his own empathy muscle. Before this, he mostly would take people at their word. This experience showed him something I always focus on in my coaching practice, which recognizes that what an individual says may not actually be an accurate expression of what they mean. There often is something deeper they meant to reveal. It helped him better understand my purpose, as a coach, and why my work has been so meaningful and rewarding.

The first time I participated in the group, I gingerly walked into the cozy meeting room. Being the new girl, I was feeling nervous and a bit shy. I looked around the room at the different faces. It was like the first day of kindergarten or junior high when I wasn't sure if I'd fit in. What if I was the only new girl? Would they like me? Since some of them had been meeting for a long time, would they already have formed cliques that I wouldn't be allowed to join? Even in this supposedly safe space, I had doubts about whether I'd be deemed worthy.

A large basket of handmade shawls was right next to the door, under a sign indicating they had lovingly been crocheted by

generous volunteers. A staff member encouraged me to choose one. I carefully rummaged through the basket and selected one made of soft beige and white wools, soothing in both color and texture. I imagined this shawl would envelop me if the anxiety got to be too much and I needed to nurture myself back to a state of calm. An array of cottage-like furniture – a small sofa and enough upholstered chairs to seat about a dozen people – felt warm and inviting. I beelined for a comfy-looking chair that had a short seat, so my feet could rest on the floor. From then on, I always tried to grab this same seat as if I was staking my claim at this table. It served as my home base during the time I would spend in that room.

Each time we met, the facilitator set the tone by welcoming everyone, whether they were first-timers, occasional participants or regulars. The message was clear – we accept you for who you are, wherever you are on this journey. She reminded everyone of the guidelines. When it's your time to speak, introduce yourself, give some background on the status of your cancer and respond to a question posed by the facilitator. No "bashing" of specific health care providers is permitted since someone in the group may be under the care of that person or medical group.

The questions were always open-ended: "What is one thing you wish you could get back to that you've had to put on hold?" Or, "What in your daily routine gives you joy?" They were structured to help everyone ease into whatever topic was most on their mind.

"I'm feeling guilty about not spending enough enough time with my children."

"Most of my friends and even some of my siblings are avoiding me now. They aren't comfortable being around me. They don't know what to say or do. I feel completely alone."

"At first, when I couldn't get through an entire workday because of being exhausted from chemo, my boss was very understanding. Now he seems to have lost patience with my situation."

"I hate having to be so dependent on my spouse for just about everything."

For anyone with a shred of human compassion, it would be impossible not to feel the sadness and pain behind these revelations. I was deeply touched by how the others in the room responded after someone else shared their story. No one, besides the facilitator and me, had any formal training in counseling or coaching. Yet, they all demonstrated the capacity to respond to one another without trying to "fix" anything. They were keen listeners, vulnerable in sharing their own challenges, while remaining optimistic about the wonderful things life still had in store for them. For one participant, a doctor, that meant traveling on a medical mission to a developing country. For another, it meant being able to take care of a grandchild again. All were confident enough not to blur boundaries, only tuning into the suffering revealed by the speaker, without any inclination to upstage them. I felt like a devoted disciple, trying to capture every bit of sage-like wisdom they bestowed upon me and one another.

The sharing of stories in this way clearly wasn't meant to be a competition. This was not a situation where only those who suffered the most deserved compassion and respect. Even so, the first few sessions, I found it difficult to reveal my innermost fears to the group. Initially, I focused on listening with my coach's ear, wondering what I might say to validate and uplift everyone else. I would rush through a description of my cancer status, briefly answer whatever question was posed and quickly say, "I'm good," signaling we could move on to the next person. Because many in

the group were dealing with a recurrence or metastasis of their original cancer, I was reluctant to reveal how scared I was about a recurrence. How could I possibly be worthy of the same support they deserved, when their suffering was more heightened and their courage extraordinary compared to mine? In spite of my resolute belief that Gilda's Club was a safe zone where I could express this fear, whenever it was my turn to speak, I held back.

After a few sessions, these sages caught onto my strategy – and they wouldn't let me get away with it. They gently pushed and probed, until I finally let down my guard. and revealed some of my fears. One member of the group in particular strengthened my resolve, giving me courage to acknowledge some of my fears out loud. He was a young man with a wife and small kids. From the outside, he appeared to be a picture of health – tall, good looking, with bright eyes and a knowing smile. There were no visible signs of the physical and emotional turbulence he dealt with every day. He had been fighting his cancer for years, ping-ponging between remission and recurrence.

He was keenly aware of his vacillating moods and how terribly distressing they were to his wife. He recognized that his children were feeling a range of emotions, from frustration that their lives kept going in and out of a state of "normal," to fear that he might not survive. He fretted over how he could help his children cope. Even though he acknowledged the cancer wasn't his fault, this admission didn't mitigate his guilt over being the cause of his family's suffering. He was anxious not only about how much they could endure, but also about how little he could do to alleviate their burden. He bravely and unapologetically shared his story.

His story also got me thinking about the impact my illness had, and continued to have, on my family. It unnerved me. My diagnosis, surgery and recovery hadn't damaged my family in a similar way,

given that my children were adults when cancer invaded their lives. But I hadn't reckoned that it likely had changed my relationships with Stuart and the kids forever, in ways I might never comprehend. What happened to me also happened to them. They too had to cope with constant uncertainty around whether I was going to live or die. If I survived in the short term, would their feeling of relief quickly be upended again by a recurrence?

They each had to find a way to cope, at least for a while, without the same degree of guidance, nurturing and empathy they normally could count on from me, their mother and wife. If I acted in ways that didn't take their pain into account, was it possible the bonds that previously had kept us inexorably linked would be broken? Would they become so emotionally self-sufficient that they'd no longer rely on me?

I knew what it felt like to reach out to my mother when I was frightened, only to be dismissed. During a thirteen-day period in October of 1962, when I was ten, the world hovered on the brink of a nuclear disaster. In what became known as the Cuban Missile Crisis, the Soviet Union tried to assert its military dominance over the United States by building a nuclear arsenal on the island of Cuba, a mere ninety miles from Florida. The United States responded by establishing a blockade around the island. After a tense standoff, the Soviets agreed to dismantle the missiles and the United States agreed not to invade Cuba. The crisis had been averted.

At the time, I didn't understand the global implications of this; all I knew was that a potential disaster of tremendous magnitude loomed on the horizon. My parents watched the news constantly. The reporters and anchors spoke in unusually solemn intonations. The headlines revealed the seriousness of the standoff between President Kennedy and Premier Nikita Khrushchev.

The New York Times: "U.s. Imposes Arms Blockade On Cuba On Finding Offensive-Missle Sites; Kennedy Ready For Soviet Showdown"

The Miami News: "Russia Warns U.S. Of Nuclear War As First Test Of Blockade Near."

Both Kennedy and Khrushchev became household names associated with the possibility of bringing the world past the brink of destruction. During the crisis, the atmosphere in our house was solemn and tense, and our communication – never free-flowing to begin with – was even more perfunctory and devoid of any humor or light banter.

One day, without warning, our school held an air raid drill to prepare us for the possibility of a nuclear attack. The drill was called "duck and cover" because school children were instructed to get under their desks and put their arms over their heads for protection from the radioactive fallout. In my elementary school, we did a variation on the theme. Everyone lined up in the hallway. Then we were told to sit with our backs to the wall, heads bent down, covered by our arms. I don't know if our parents had been given advance notice. But if they had, mine hadn't prepared me at all; I was totally blindsided by the activity and how frightening it was. Even with my limited understanding of what would actually occur in a nuclear attack, I was savvy enough to know there was no way we'd be protected from it, crouched in a school hallway. Duck-and-cover struck me, in that moment, as totally absurd. I remember being terrified that something so devastating could happen without warning, and that I'd be trapped in school, unable to be comforted, in some way, by the presence of my mom. By this point, she had resumed being my primary caregiver after Dad's breakdown, ceding my care to Stephanie only on rare occasions. I had come to trust, once again, that she'd be there to comfort me when I was scared or deeply troubled.

That night, I couldn't sleep as images of devastation and suffering portrayed on the news raced through my head. My mother must have felt sick that night because she had gone to bed quite early. Overwhelmed with anxiety, I

tiptoed across the hall to my parents' bedroom. I stood at the side of the bed where Mom was sleeping and whispered just loud enough to wake her, "Mommy, I can't sleep. I'm afraid there's going to be a war and we're going to be killed by a bomb." She opened her eyes, sighed and responded, "Can't you talk to Dad about this right now?"

I was stunned. Suggesting I go to Dad for nurturing, when even I, at ten, grasped his limited capacity to connect on an emotional level, was shockingly out of character. I turned around, went back to my room and got back into bed, unable to soothe myself to sleep. I decided then and there I never would do anything to cause my kids to feel as alone as I felt that night.

Yet here I was at Gilda's Club, wondering if I may have been doing exactly that to my children. Listening to the poignant stories of my support group companions left me grappling with a truth I had never considered before, until this memory surfaced: Parents can't always do what's best for their children, and themselves, simultaneously. Selfishness, despite its connotations, isn't necessarily good or bad. Context determines whether a specific selfish act will have negative or positive consequences, and there are times when being selfish is the right choice, such as it was when I chose to have my cancer surgery locally, in Grand Rapids.

I began to allow myself to wonder. Was it possible I had *unfairly* cast Dad as an out-of-control narcissist because of the attention he demanded and received after his nervous breakdown? Had I been the selfish one, demanding attention be given to me, when he was the one who actually deserved it? I found the courage to accept the possibility that my criticism of Dad's diminished capacities may have been too unforgiving. But even so, I remained steadfast in my despair that Dad chose to use his illness as

justification for protecting himself *over me.* As I coped with the demons that descended upon me as a result of having cancer, I made a different choice: to safeguard myself in ways that nurtured my children as well.

Chapter 12

Wrestling with Bullies

In spite of the validation I received from the support group, sometimes I still felt undeserving of their kindness. It didn't matter that I often asked my clients, "Why are you so sure everyone else deserves to be treated with compassion, but you don't?" The irony in not being able to walk the talk didn't escape me, but recognizing this apparent double standard and hypocrisy only added to my heightened self-loathing. This was especially true after my most recent scans confirmed that I remained cancer free. I felt guilty even sitting alongside the others in the group who weren't in remission. When I blurted that out in one of the sessions, there was a rapid and unanimous rebuke: "Barbara, don't you see that your good news gives us hope?" I didn't.

When they coaxed me to share my story, they didn't know that being cast in any limelight was utterly abhorrent to me. Even if the degree of suffering I endured following the cancer surgery warranted attention from others, the clock had run out on me

being worthy of such consideration. Angling for their attention by continuing to play the "victim card" was something my dad would have done. If my support group even suspected I was a reincarnation of him, they might have withheld their kindness and compassion, my fear of not being worthy of belonging would have been realized.

At the same time, the irrationality of my reaction was obvious. As someone who is always open to contemplating a wide range of perspectives, I became determined to put my skepticism aside to see if I could broaden my point-of-view. I began to pay closer attention to messages others conveyed about my worthiness, more readily acknowledging the messages I had been discounting, including the CaringBridge entries and the support group's encouraging feedback. I considered how I might be deserving of these expressions of love and compassion, since I was confident none of the messengers had hidden agendas. They had no expectation of a quid pro quo, building up my ego so that someday I might do the same for them. They simply were my cheerleaders, rooting for me not only to survive, but also to thrive.

This shift in my thinking about being a good, deserving person became evident in my moods and behaviors. In everyday activities I was experiencing more joy than sadness, not sweating the small stuff as much. Most things that in the past had set me off, like people not showing up for a scheduled coaching session, paled in comparison to the challenges I had overcome since November. With each successive scan being clear of cancer, I faced each day with more optimism about the future. I even mused about the possibility of finally being able to take that family trip to Italy. I assumed a growing appreciation for the resilience human beings can draw upon in spite of incredible pain and suffering. I even tentatively began to see myself as a hero.

Then, without warning, the unbearable suffering returned. One morning in March, four months after returning home from the rehab

hospital, I woke up with excruciating back pain. Hospitals use a one-to-ten scale to rate pain, with ten described as, "unimaginable," "unspeakable" or "worst pain possible." Mine was a ten plus. Having had two previous spinal fusions, I immediately recognized the source of this particular pain as the result of nerve compression. I was ninety-nine percent sure I'd need another surgical fusion to get any relief.

Over-the-counter pain medication hadn't helped at all. So, the next day, Stuart took me to the emergency room. A staff neurosurgeon ordered the standard scans. According to his assessment, the results indicated it was too soon to do surgery. He could, however, justify admitting me to the hospital for pain management. We didn't really understand his rationale for holding back on surgery, but we couldn't get the second opinion we wanted from my regular neurosurgeon, because he was on vacation. My internist, Dr. Gary, couldn't help either. The hospital system no longer allowed private physicians to manage patient care, that responsibility having become the domain of hospitalists, general care practitioners who supposedly coordinate overall inpatient care. We felt we had no choice but to listen to this particular neurosurgeon. I was in so much pain, I submitted.

The neurosurgeon told us he was transferring me to the hospital campus where I had undergone the cancer surgery. That facility houses a renowned heart center, and given my recent history, he wanted to have thoracic surgeons nearby as a precaution, in the event surgery ultimately would be required. This increased our confusion given that he had been clear that surgery was not an option. But we allowed him to maintain control of my care: I was transferred by ambulance and assigned a room.

For the first few days in the hospital, they managed my pain with intravenous doses of Dilaudid. As grateful as I was for that relief, my frustration with some of the medical staff intensified. The

surgeon's PA conducted the daily rounds. Normally I would have accepted this, knowing that PAs have specific expertise in their chosen discipline. But in my experience, that expertise usually comes into play after surgery, when they handle patients' routine follow-up care. In my case, there still wasn't a confirmed diagnosis or treatment plan indicting surgery was needed.

I felt this particular young man was out of his league. I couldn't tolerate his arrogance, as evidenced by a swagger that had me imagining how much he thought of himself as a doctor. He rubbed me the wrong way every time he opened his mouth, usually giving me perfunctory answers to questions that seemed to come from a script he had memorized. Even though I had previous experiences with nerve compression and a reasonable knowledge base about back injuries, he either didn't listen to or discounted what I had to say. I cringed every time he walked in the room. Even Leigh would roll her eyes if she happened to be visiting when he was on his rounds.

Prior to my cancer surgery, I had experienced my fair share of blunders perpetrated by so-called medical experts. After my second complete hip replacement five years earlier, I came out of the general anesthesia, stunned at the severity of my *back pain*. The next day, the pain was at a level ten. By late afternoon, I told the nurse it was excruciating, and I needed a different form of relief. Having had my other hip replaced five years earlier, I knew this wasn't normal post-operative pain. The nurse said she would let the hospitalist know so she could come by, assess what was going on and recommend how to address it. I waited patiently all day for the hospitalist to arrive.

That evening, around 6:00 PM, she sashayed into the room. Without stopping to introduce herself or ask how I was doing, the first thing she said was, "I've had a terribly long

and hard day today." Shocked, I rapidly jumped into self-protection mode and asserted what I needed her to hear: "I'm experiencing excruciating pain in my back. This isn't normal pain associated with a hip replacement. I know because I had my other hip replaced and nothing like this happened after that surgery." She did a perfunctory check of my lungs, and when she was halfway out the door, looked back at me and said, "Don't worry. This is perfectly normal. It will be better tomorrow." Translation: It was late in the day and she simply didn't want to be bothered with my problems. I was just a name on a list she could check off.

This brush-off triggered memories of my dad's flagrant indifference to my needs. Furious and desperate, I called Stuart and asked him to come over right away. When he arrived, we talked things over with the nurse. I asked her if she would advocate for me to be discharged so that I could get back under the care of Dr. Gary. The irony of my request didn't escape her. Here I was, supposedly in the most prestigious hospital system in the region, asking to be released so I could access appropriate care.

Without hesitation, the nurse jumped in. She reached my orthopedic surgeon, Dr. Kevin, explained what had happened and passed along my request to be discharged early. Dr. Kevin was angry about the situation as well but unable to intercede given his limited privileges at this particular hospital. He told us he suspected that during the surgery, one of the nerves in my spinal column had been nicked. His expectation was it likely would settle down with the right pain management. Given my disgust over the inept treatment at the hands of this hospitalist, he agreed I could take care of myself just as well at home, especially since I would be able to enlist Dr. Gary's support. I was out the door the minute the discharge papers were signed. I found out later that Dr. Kevin had lodged a complaint with the hospital's medical director, citing what he believed was "a clear example of poor medical practice." I did as well and the hospitalist was eventually fired.

Back then, when I asserted my right to leave the hospital after my hip surgery because of poor medical care, it was with an air of confidence. I believed I deserved respect that wasn't forthcoming. Being on the receiving end of such disrespect motivated me to act swiftly on my own behalf. Why, in that situation, did I rebel against being bullied, demonstrating the capacity to advocate for myself, while in this one at the hands of the staff neurosurgeon and his PA, I was passive and submissive? All I could fathom was I had lost my will to fight these injustices. Over the last few months, there were just too many situations where I suffered indignities that had rendered me powerless. I was too exhausted to fight the system. It was easier to submit.

On the fifth day in the hospital, I still languished in bed, tied to an IV tube, with no discernible resolution on the horizon. Confusion remained around why there still was no plan for a surgical intervention. The lack of a treatment plan made no sense to us. After all, I had been transferred to this particular hospital campus because five days earlier the staff neurosurgeon stated he wanted me to be close to the heart center.

While the pain remained under control, I was single-mindedly calm, attentive and overly solicitous. I hoped that by being a "good" patient, the neurosurgeon and PA would take notice quickly, then get the surgery scheduled and over with. Still, nothing. My frustration reached a fevered pitch just after midnight on day five. It was time for the Dilaudid to be injected into the IV tube, when a nurse told me the hospital had run out. The plan was to replace it with high doses of Ibuprofen or Tylenol, because the hospital's supply of Dilaudid, a very powerful painkiller, was manufactured in Puerto Rico and Hurricane Maria had shut down the facility that produced it.

I was astonished. The hospital staff had to know this was coming. Why would they wait until the middle of the night to tell

me I was affected instead of working out an alternative beforehand? How could a medical facility of such stature have no viable alternatives other than over-the-counter analgesics?

At first, even though the nurse talked to me in a calm voice, my inner rebel snapped to attention. My response was emphatic; I was not about to accept this news without being offered a suitable alternative, "This isn't acceptable. The only reason I'm here is for pain management. If you can't help with that, why am I here?" Her response was equally dogmatic, "You have to *calm down*. There's *nothing* I can do."

I couldn't believe she was chastising me for not being "calm" instead of advocating on my behalf. She had, at her disposal, resources she could call on to address the real issue – my legitimate need for a viable alternative to Dilaudid. For about ten minutes we engaged in a shouting match. The upshot was neither one of us was feeling heard. I was sobbing so hard I began to hiccup uncontrollably, "Why can't you call someone and identify an alternative?" Over and over she repeated the same mantra, "It's not my fault. Hurricane Maria caused this devastation. There simply isn't any Dilaudid in the building. All I can give you is something over-the-counter."

In those wee morning hours, I felt totally alone and frightened, aware I couldn't bear any more of the excruciating pain and utterly frustrated by the nurse's callous attitude. I decided not to call Stuart or Leigh to see if one of them could come over and run interference for me. I didn't want to wake them up; they were already stressed enough watching over me in the daytime. I felt I should be able to stand up to this bully on my own. I had plenty of things I wanted to scream at her, but they all basically would have conveyed the same notion: "Don't you dare mess with me given what I've gone through the last five months. I don't deserve to be treated this way."

Although I held back from screaming at her, I was determined not to abdicate. After all that had happened and the amount of excruciating pain I was in now, I'd reached the end of my capacity for empathy and patience. I dug in for a long skirmish, knowing there wasn't anything the nurse could say that would get me to give in. As she watched me getting more and more worked up, hardly being able to catch my breath between each sob, she finally began to show concern over what might transpire for me medically if we didn't resolve this impasse.

At last, she agreed to contact an on-call physician who could prescribe something else. It turned out to be a simple solution: Dilaudid can also be administered in pill form and wasn't in short supply at the hospital. All that needed to be done was to switch me over. It's fortunate that nurse was no longer assigned to support me during my stay in the hospital. If she had, I would have had her barred from entering my room.

But that wasn't the end of my troubles. The next day, the same staff neurosurgeon who admitted me to the hospital for pain management ordered another set of scans. This time he said that the scans confirmed I had a herniated disc; that's what was causing the nerve compression. Surgery was the only option. Late that evening, a week after I first went to the emergency room, I agreed to the surgery. I was relieved the waiting was over but concerned that this particular doctor was my designated surgeon. But by then I was in too much pain and too caught up in the hospital's bureaucracy to object.

The next few days were relatively uneventful. I was used to hospital routines and went along with them. But right after I was discharged, I called the staff neurosurgeon's office and told the receptionist I would not come back for the first follow-up appointment if I had to see the same PA who had been so dismissive to me in the hospital. She obviously told the PA what I said because,

to his credit, he swallowed his pride and called me back. This time, he listened to my concerns about how his interactions with me had come off as very condescending. He didn't cast blame, nor did he try to make excuses. He seemed to accept the feedback graciously. When he asked if I'd reconsider meeting with him, I told him I would. My capacity for empathy and patience, no longer diminished by unrelenting pain, had returned.

At the follow-up appointment, I told the PA that I had been falling quite frequently. He immediately followed protocol and sent me to be fitted for an ankle-to-thigh leg brace. I had to wear it, every time I went out, for the next couple of months. I hated it. It was another reminder that I wasn't free of immobility and pain. After I got fitted for the brace, I decided not to go back to that neurosurgeon's office for any additional follow-up care. I had an entirely different mindset around my capacity for taking control of my destiny when I wasn't feeling defenseless in the hospital.

I called my neurosurgeon, Dr. John, and got permission to transition my case over to him, if any follow-up care was needed. I didn't have a premonition that anything else would go wrong; I was just being prudent. But a month later I was in Dr. John's office because the pain in my back had returned. Following yet another series of scans, he told me I needed surgery *again*. This operation would be a spinal fusion to stabilize three discs, including the same disc the other neurosurgeon had worked on plus two more. I would stay in the hospital three to four days and would have to wear a back brace for eight weeks. He also confirmed that because the other neurosurgeon had waited so long to operate, I likely would have permanent nerve damage in my left leg. He said it would be a year before we knew. A year later, that turned out to be true.

I couldn't stop thinking about whether I ever would be free of these recurring medical traumas and all of the collateral implications

– the frequent sessions with physical and occupational therapists, the constant repetition of CT scans and MRIs, maneuvering amidst all of the implants and prosthetic devices that interfered with my ability to move about unencumbered – it all was simply too overwhelming.

By the time we got to the hospital for this second back surgery, I was feeling defeated. It was my fourth surgery in six months. I had become convinced that my body wouldn't make it through one more major surgery. I felt sure one of my major organs would fail me; my luck had run out. Before I was wheeled into the operating room, when Stuart bent over to give me a kiss, I whispered to him, "If anything happens and I don't make it through this one, it's okay. I had a good life." I didn't want Stuart and my kids to be left wondering.

Chapter 13

Despair

It turned out I came through the second back surgery with only a minor hitch; my blood pressure was distressingly low. Once again, a nurse advocated on my behalf. He showed visible concern, keeping Dr. John informed about my BP readings until a blood transfusion was ordered. Even though I had to stay in the hospital a few days longer, I was extremely grateful I didn't have to resort to yelling before I could get the staff to take me seriously. But even though I didn't have to ingratiate myself to get the attention I needed from the staff, I remained unconvinced I was resilient enough to get through another post-surgical recovery period. I couldn't commit to fighting the good fight, one more time, because I seriously doubted whether I had any fight left in me.

I wasn't intentionally seeking death; I was questioning whether I wanted to be alive. I skulked around my family and friends, desperately trying to keep them from finding out I was harboring such dark thoughts. I was afraid of how they'd treat me if they

knew the truth. Would any of them find me abhorrent and not want anything to do with me? Would some consider me a danger to myself? Would their efforts to intercede and keep me safe make my ability to cope day-to-day even harder?

When I was a teenager, still living at home, a painful incident ultimately led me to harbor a similar fantasy of being released from the struggles of my daily existence. It came as a result of my mom not being able to successfully mediate disputes between me and Dad. With the best of intentions, she had arranged for me to see a psychologist. She genuinely wanted to help me find a way to cope with my increasingly vocal, negative feelings toward my dad. Also, my doctor had told her that emotional stress could contribute to a flareup of my ulcerative colitis symptoms.

Dad would bring me to the weekly therapy appointments and wait in the outer office. After I had met with the psychologist a few times, I told her how I didn't feel safe enough to express my deepest needs to my father. She abruptly stood up and said, "Okay then, let's bring him in so you can tell him that." I was startled at first, and then panicked, going from zero to a hundred miles an hour in about ten seconds. Here was another adult, someone I had just begun to trust to protect me, pushing me to confront my father, with no prior discussion about whether I felt ready, or even wanted to share my innermost feelings with him. The psychologist made no effort to help me develop skills or safe strategies to manage the response I could expect from Dad. The image of a stop sign popped into my head, but I ignored it – or more likely, I was too young and naive to know I had sufficient agency to dig in my heels and refuse to participate in the conversation.

The psychologist opened the door, invited my dad into the office and asked me to repeat what I had just told her. I complied. Speaking in a monotone, I alternated between

gazing directly at my father, looking down at my hands and pulling at my cuticles, a nervous habit I had developed. Dad, probably as shocked as I was about what was transpiring, nervously looked back and forth between me and the psychologist. I didn't hold back. I told my father how afraid I was to express myself when he was around, how he always loomed large, cutting me off any time I expressed anger or frustration because it made him uncomfortable. I said I constantly worried he'd blame me for his discomfort, when all I wanted was to be heard. I had come to believe that he not only wanted me to suppress my feelings; I surmised he didn't want me to feel anything at all. I admitted I felt invisible.

Dad's facial expression was one of disbelief – wide eyes and furrowed brow. All he said was, "I didn't have a clue. I'm doing my best. I don't really understand what she's talking about." I felt like a cigarette butt, nonchalantly thrown on the floor, with the flame slowly burning out, waiting for him to press it out with his heavy leather shoe. I panicked even more. If I gave him further cause, he might initiate a final, firm push downward, and the flame – my flame – would be extinguished forever. On our ride home from the session, he kept repeating some version of "I don't understand what you're saying" while I sat rigidly silent, barely breathing, looking straight ahead, not daring to say anything that I knew would only make things worse.

Not too long after this incident, I was holed up in my bedroom, the one safe space I had created for myself. Late one afternoon I reached my lowest point of hopelessness and despair. I didn't believe I could spend another moment being subjected to my father's demands, or to his lack of accountability for his contribution to our negative interactions and relationship. I wanted to call one of my close friends from overnight camp and tell them how, in his presence, I felt like my true self was being suffocated. I was seeking a lifeline, someone who'd validate that I wasn't crazy, that my rage toward him was justified and, most importantly, that if he were to get sick again, it wouldn't be my fault.

But I hadn't asked for permission to make the long-distance call. In those days, it was expensive to call long-distance and Dad used to time my calls to make sure I hung up before or right at the three-minute mark. I was forbidden to incur any overtime charges. I stood in the corner of my room where there was an extension phone perched on the bookcase. The proximity of the phone, and knowing it was against the "rules" to call one of my friends without his permission, thrust me into the deepest level of despair I had ever experienced.

For the first and only time in my life, I contemplated suicide. I imagined how things would be better for everyone if I simply was out of the picture. I'd be released from the invisible shackles my father had used to restrain me every time we had a test of wills. Mom would be free of trying to perpetually negotiate peaceful resolutions in no-win situations. There would be an end to my internal tug-of-war. On one hand, I'd be released from my guilt around not being good enough to keep my father from getting sick. On the other, I wouldn't have to keep fighting so hard to prove my innocence in the first place. I realized I had enough agency to let myself off the hook.

During this period, I was taking a medication to reduce stress and anxiety. It was what today we would call a "controlled substance." It had been prescribed at the lowest dosage possible. I held the recently filled bottle of pills in my hand for about ten minutes, twirling it between the thumb and forefinger on my right hand. I was staring at the bottle, in a reverie around what would transpire if I swallowed its contents. Would I be frightened or at peace as the medication took effect? Were there enough tablets to do the job? Would my parents appreciate that I hadn't chosen a more violent and messy way of taking my own life?

I was abruptly shaken out of my musing when it crossed my mind that if I wasn't successful in my effort to kill myself, my life would likely get even worse. Not only would all of the issues with Dad still be there, but now my most important protector, my mom, couldn't trust that I

wouldn't try to harm myself again. To keep me safe from myself, she'd institute more oversight on my comings and goings. I also realized my sister Stephanie wouldn't be able to trust me to babysit my nephew Josh, whom I adored.

Acknowledging that stark reality was all it took to get me past such a potentially devastating fantasy. I vowed never to contemplate the act of actual suicide again, although the notion of wanting to be detached from life would probably repeat itself. But I also promised myself to pay serious attention whenever I found myself feeling such a desperate desire for detachment. I would use that longing as a wakeup call to find a constructive way forward.

When I began to have a similar yearning to withdraw from life after the four surgeries and recovery periods, I remembered the commitment I had made to pay serious attention to my feelings of despair. I knew I had to take drastic action when I began waking up every morning and the first thing that came into my head was, "I don't want to do this anymore." I didn't know what "this" meant, but I knew I had to find out. In my coaching practice, I had always shared my philosophy that the answers are typically in the room, and my role is to create a context for those answers to surface. Yet here I was, inhabiting a "room" in my head, but the answers weren't forthcoming.

I couldn't articulate any single thing that was getting in my way; the "this" that I didn't want to do anymore was a vague feeling of discontent. I did recognize that something in my work had changed, and it was weighing heavily on me. I was beginning to experience my role as a coach as being that of a receptacle for all the loss and despair my clients were feeling. I felt like that container was going to burst open at any moment, strewing the contents haphazardly in all directions.

The actual interactions with my clients hadn't changed in any discernible way. What did change was my own protective shield, the one I had previously deployed to limit how much I allowed myself to feel their pain. It was as if when my sternum was removed, the natural buffer between my clients' heartfelt needs, and my heart's capacity to absorb them, had also been removed. Now, when they told me about their sadness or despair – around failing to meet expectations, finding it difficult to handle conflict or being anything less than perfect – I conjured up more than simply empathic responses. I actually found myself sharing their experience of suffering so much that I started to be haunted by how much of their pain comingled with my own, and I became depressed about my powerlessness to fend off their suffering.

Another new medical challenge added a dimension to this powerlessness. A fragment of one of my molars had broken through my gums and, because of my recent cancer diagnosis, the oral surgeon was concerned it might be bone cancer. It took several agonizingly long weeks before the biopsy results came back. Until I got the report, I wasn't able to be fully present in anything I was doing, at work or at home. I was distracted by thoughts of another cancer diagnosis leading to interventions that were radical in their descriptions – surgery to remove the cancerous bone, jawbone reconstruction and the possibility of facing death head-on once more. The thought of going through such drastic procedures again was too devastating to contemplate.

My family history also cast a pall over the situation; my paternal grandmother had survived cancer of the jaw and my father was diagnosed with squamous cell carcinoma of the ear, the same type of cancer typically seen in the jaw. So, naturally it was a relief when the biopsy results came back negative. I'd experienced all that worry for no reason. Okay, for *some* reason. But it still

took a toll on me and left me wondering if I had enough resilience to fight rather than follow the temptation to surrender.

Finally, a business decision by one of the organizations I had contracted with for more than a dozen years added to my angst around not wanting to accept "this" anymore. I'd been serving as an instructor and coach in a program designed to certify other professional coaches in a particular coaching model. My annual responsibilities included coaching eight of the twenty participants for a year and participating in two on-site residencies. I always felt indescribable joy when I engaged in these on-site sessions. I got to mingle and learn from an amazing cohort of likeminded professionals and a few world-renowned thought leaders. In my mind, those six days a year were a uniquely precious development opportunity; they brought me to a place where I felt I belonged.

A few months into my recovery from the second back surgery, the program administrators announced to all the coaches that for business reasons, we no longer were invited to be present in the residencies, although our coaching services were still required. I was initially grief stricken, feeling the loss as if someone close to me had died. Shock waves reverberated inside me – emotional, intellectual and physical. Having been with the program since the original pilot, suddenly I felt relegated to the role of business contractor rather than an integral member of the team.

I understood the business reasons for the shift, the primary one being that by eliminating the expenses associated with having the coaches attend the residencies, they could be paid more for their coaching services. But this rational decision didn't take the sting out of being left out of the residencies. I found it difficult to sleep, obsessing over the chance that somehow, I must have been perceived as not good enough to remain a full member of the team.

I recalled a brief email exchange with one of the program's founders a few years earlier, when the program was put on a temporary hiatus for a year to determine if and how it might be offered in the future. At that time, I was feeling anxious about the possibility it wouldn't be revived, and I wrote to him, "I can't imagine never being in the same room with you, not being able to learn with and from you ever again." He wrote back reassuringly, "Barbara, I can't imagine a scenario where that would happen," which left me feeling confident that I was an integral part of the team, that what I brought to the table, in many aspects of the program's design and delivery, still really mattered. That's why, when it did happen, the betrayal felt profound. For months, any time I thought or spoke or about it, I was reduced to tears.

But over time I became attuned to a competing force against this despair. It was signaling me to grieve the loss and find my way past it. In an unexpected moment of clarity, I recognized that just because my colleagues' decision had significantly impacted me, it actually wasn't *about me.* This was a notion that my father could never have comprehended, and when I identified it, I felt incredible relief. My deepest fear would not be realized; I *was not* like my dad. This simple but profound revelation enabled me to begin reframing my sense of self-worth, liberating me from the false narrative I had fought my entire life – that my inherent unworthiness was why I had been cast aside. I knew then that it was time to stop beating myself up.

Chapter 14

Waiting in the Wings

One thing that always distracted me from feeling powerless to ward off feelings of sadness and despair was delivering my leadership development workshops at the Grand Rapids Chamber of Commerce. While interacting with the participants, focusing on their growth as leaders, I was able to compartmentalize. I found myself in a state of flow – energized, fully present and enjoying each moment. In the summer of 2018, after my second back surgery, I was doing a facilitation for the Chamber when the program coordinator asked if she could stop by for a few minutes. She wanted to invite the participants to an annual fundraising event during which an award is given to someone who is recognized for their lifetime of service to the Grand Rapids community.

The program coordinator joined the workshop midway through and enthusiastically encouraged the participants to attend the fundraiser. Then she looked at me and said, "We're especially excited to tell you that this year's Distinguished Community Trustee

Award honoree is Barbara Rapaport." The people in the class grinned and applauded; I stared back, utterly dumbfounded. The previous recipients were, in my estimation, community movers and shakers who impacted the region in significant and obvious ways. How could an unassuming, behind-the-scenes player like me, be worthy of such an honor?

When I was seven years old, I had a similarly bewildering experience. My parents belonged to a local swim club that offered a day camp for school-age children. I took a bus to the camp each weekday morning. Later in the day, my parents would drive to the club and spend a few hours lounging at the pool with their friends while I entertained myself by swimming laps, diving off the diving board or pretending to hunt for underwater treasures. My parents would have to drag me out of the pool when it was time to head home.

On the last day of camp, the counselor had all the girls in my group sit in a circle for a closing ceremony of sorts. She asked us to think about the following question: "Who in our group do you think is the most all-around camper?" A few names were shouted out, none of which were Barbara. When the group input was exhausted, the counselor turned to me with a smile and said, "Actually, it's Barbara." I was totally blindsided, having had no idea what I had done to be considered so deserving in the eyes of my counselor. I must have been having an impact in ways that were more subtle than obvious. My young camp friends didn't realize this, but my counselor did. I reveled in being center stage, at least for a single afternoon.

This event set the stage for me to find ways, as an adult, to be recognized for operating behind the scenes. It helped me understand that in my own quiet and deliberate way, I'd be able to make a difference and effectively help others shine, precisely because I deflected attention away from

myself. In my career as an executive coach, I had always told my clients, "I'll never be the one winning awards. But I'll be in the audience watching individuals like you, who I've had the privilege of coaching, get theirs." So, when it was my turn to be the award recipient, I almost couldn't process it.

As I pondered what I wanted to convey in my acceptance speech, I recalled how many clients over the years had told me I had "changed their lives." Without fail, upon hearing this, I would immediately deflect their attention by saying, "I was only walking alongside you. You did all the heavy lifting." In my estimation, to do otherwise would have been a reflection of arrogance. I held to the belief that my job was to help them identify any areas of self-sabotage that interfered with their capacity to lead from a place of authenticity rather than from externally imposed dictates.

While writing and polishing my speech I suddenly realized that, by helping my clients fulfill their goals and dreams, the sometimes profound insights we uncovered had led to my own self-actualization. These individuals had taken what they learned in our sessions and shared that with others in their companies and our community. For the first time, I recognized that my professional and personal commitment to uncovering "the answers in the room" had a cumulative, ripple effect beyond my wildest dreams. The notion of me leaving a legacy of this magnitude, however, had never entered my consciousness.

I shared these musings with the audience the night I received the award. I also told them that what mattered to me most, in the end, was the reinforcement that I had been living in a way that was true to myself. And even if I had never received any formal recognition

for what I had done to create this ripple effect, it had occurred anyway. The impact would be the same whether or not I was aware of it. The whole rewarding episode left me pondering: Had I spent too much of my life yearning to be special enough to deserve the spotlight, when my real calling was to remain in the wings?

Chapter 15

Incongruity

After living through the cancer experience, childhood fears about my intrinsic unworthiness came back in full force, decimating my confidence. Thinking I had left this childhood trauma behind years ago, I was blindsided and mystified when it resurfaced with such vengeance. I had stood up to my father many times, beginning with that emotionally charged encounter years ago when I screamed, "Everything isn't about you!" And there were many subsequent events where I refused to let him bully me into believing I was egotistical and self-centered. I'd spent much of my adult life dismantling these youthful misperceptions, but the cancer and its aftermath made these old feelings of unworthiness rise again.

When I was twenty-five, my mother died of viral encephalitis. It was an extraordinarily difficult time for my family because we no longer had a home in New

Jersey. The funeral service was to take place there for a few reasons. We wanted our former Rabbi and neighbor to conduct the service. The majority of my parents' New Jersey friends wanted to attend, and if we held the service close to the cemetery, in Long Island, New York, most of them wouldn't have made the two-hour drive.

My dad, who had been walking around in a daze, bemoaning how he couldn't live without Mom, put us all on edge. We defaulted back to our childhood norm of, "Don't do anything to upset Dad." But it was hard to do that since my sisters and I were navigating totally new emotional territory. We were feeling our own immense loss, but true to form, Dad continued to put his needs front and center. When one of us reminded him that we also felt deprived of our mother's love, his immediate response was, "You girls don't understand. Men have *certain needs*." I was disgusted and appalled at his insensitivity.

In the days before the funeral, my mind went back to the time, a few months earlier, when I got a call at work advising me to rush down to Florida because Mom was slipping into a coma and we might not get another chance to say goodbye. My sisters and I coordinated our flights so we could rent a car at Miami International Airport and drive straight to the hospital. When we finally got to see her, she couldn't converse with us, but I will never forget the joyful look that lit up her face when we arrived. There isn't much that can trump a mother's genuine love for her children. Just before a staff member wheeled her out of the room for a diagnostic procedure, she mouthed the words, "I love you." That was our last interaction before she fell into a coma that preceded her death a few months later.

I also couldn't stop thinking about another incident that occurred while Mom was in the coma. I was at the hospital with my father. I entered her room and saw that he had pulled down her hospital gown and was fondling her breasts. I backed away, nauseous, feeling the violation as if it was happening to me and sickened by the fact that she had no agency to stop it. I fled to the hallway and stood by a window,

softly crying, when a nurse approached me and asked me if I was okay. I wasn't. But I couldn't reveal the repulsion I felt about my father's total disrespect for Mom. It would serve no purpose. But I also vowed that I wouldn't tolerate any further offensive behavior from my father toward her while we coped with our impending loss.

I made good on this promise the day of the funeral. My sisters, Dad and I walked behind the casket until it was placed in the front of the funeral home's chapel. We were directed to seats in the first row. Before we could sit down, my father flung himself on top of the casket, bellowing that he couldn't live without her and wanted to be buried along with her. Unlike so many other times in my life when I was resigned to playing my part, allowing everything to center around him, this time I fought back.

To me, this day was not only about what he or my sisters had lost. It also was very much about what Mom had lost. She wouldn't get to see her grandchildren grow up. She wouldn't walk down the aisle when my sister Doris or I got married. I wasn't going to let him take her losses away from her. I reacted immediately, instinctively and with all the strength my five-foot, one-hundred-and-ten-pound body could muster. I grabbed one of his arms, pulled him up and whispered in his ear, "You are going to pull yourself together and get through this."

About ten years later, when I was married and had children, two similar repulsive episodes led me to finally distance myself physically and emotionally from my dad. At my nephew's wedding in Cleveland, after I had greeted Dad with a harmless peck on the cheek, he approached me a few minutes later while I was talking to a couple I knew from Grand Rapids. Without any warning or hesitation, I heard him say, "Why don't you ever kiss me on the lips?"

I felt the same revulsion I had experienced watching him disrespect my mother in the hospital. Not wanting to create a scene at a family celebration, I fixed him with a quizzical expression and quietly walked away. But I didn't forget, biding my time until the right moment presented itself.

A few years later, when he and my stepmother were visiting us in Grand Rapids, Dad hugged me, wrapping himself around me so that his hands cupped my breasts. The revulsion was instantaneous; I also felt a momentary panic that someday he might do something inappropriate to Leigh as well. I had to keep her and myself safe.

I pulled away, telling him he had made me uncomfortable, and that I felt it would be best if we had limited contact. We ended up having an exchange similar to the one we had that day when I let out all of my childhood grievances in a nearly uncontrollable tirade. Only this time, I set the rules. We could talk on the phone, but I didn't want to be around him physically anymore. I was done pretending that I owed him anything, no matter how that made him feel. If he had a problem with that, I told him, he needed to work it out himself. In our first phone call after he left, he started up again, asking why I was so aloof and seeking to distance myself from him. When it was clear he wasn't actually trying to understand or empathize, I ended the conversation, "If you're having problems with this, maybe you should go see a therapist."

These moments of self-determination bolstered my confidence to stand up for myself in professional settings as well. At one point during my tenure at the Fortune 500 company, I spoke up and demanded equity when I discovered I was being paid less than my male counterparts, a battle that ultimately took three more years to resolve. Another time, during a six-month review, a manager spent ninety minutes deriding my performance. It was 5:30 PM and I stood up, went to the door and told him I wouldn't remain a passive recipient of his abuse any longer. Later in my career, I convinced a different manager, who was considering bringing in an outsider to run a function parallel to mine, to agree to my recommendation that we integrate both functions and let me manage them. When I turned fifty, I took a huge risk and banked on the likelihood I could optimize all my skills and experiences as an independent practitioner, on

my own, without the benefit of role models or mentors sponsoring and supporting me.

This was the woman I had become – strong, self-assured, emancipated. Yet, these attributes became illusive when cancer invaded my chest with a violence I couldn't have anticipated, and shook me for months without letting go. The courage to speak out that I'd developed over many years was suddenly no longer second nature when I felt misunderstood or disrespected by the doctors or medical staff. I seemed to regress back into my tormented youth, afraid I might not be deserving of support and compassion. I neglected to credit others whose values gave rise to genuine acts of kindness and compassion towards me. Much like during my childhood episodes of self-doubt, I allowed myself to wonder if my inherent bad nature had destined me to experience such a severe degree of physical and emotional suffering. I could hardly remember whether the emancipated woman I had become ever really existed.

Chapter 16

Forgiveness

Winning the Distinguished Community Trustee Award validated my intuition that being a behind-the-scenes player didn't render me any less deserving. But that realization still didn't help me figure out what it meant when I woke up every morning thinking, "I don't want to do *this* anymore." I reached out to my friend Christine, one of the most spiritual and soulful people I know, and I confessed my doubts. Here I was, a bona fide coach who helped others discover their hidden barriers, yet I couldn't do the same for myself.

I knew Christine would embrace me with a compassionate and loving heart, as she had done so many times in the past. We had been close friends for more than thirty-five years, ever since we were colleagues at the Fortune 500 company and were in a sales training class together. We had seen each other through troubling and deeply satisfying career transitions, as well as heartbreaking and joyful family moments. I knew if I told her the truth about my uncertainty, she would engage her deepest self in trying to help me move past it.

Because I was still recovering from back surgery, we had this particular conversation by phone while I was sitting in bed, propped up against the pillows, my proper posture being maintained by my back brace. After the usual check-in about our husbands and kids, Christine asked how I was coping. I immediately told her about my fixation on the phrase that ran through my mind as soon as I opened my eyes every morning. Then I blurted out, "I'm stuck."

"What do you mean?" Christine probed.

"I don't know what my purpose is anymore. I'm not sure I even want to be a coach anymore. But when I think about giving that up, it leaves me feeling empty."

She didn't respond right away, which was her way. Whenever we had earnest conversations like this, she almost always knew immediately what she wanted to convey, but she usually paused for a few moments to thoughtfully choose her words.

"Barbara, I think your struggle is grounded in something spiritual rather than concrete. Maybe it's time for you to focus on connecting with your soul and letting go of everything else you already think you know about how to fix things." She knew that traumatic life events can trigger emotional setbacks throughout adulthood. But she also knew that old forms of problem-solving wouldn't necessarily be useful now. A nurturer at heart, she was coaxing me to find the courage to self-discover a way out of this suffering.

I took from our chat a desire to focus on finding a path that would redefine my professional purpose – something that would bring me joy and satisfaction during this last pre-retirement phase of my career. It took a few months of researching before I found a blueprint that seemed to totally hit the mark. It was a four-month, virtual "Purpose Discovery" program. I signed up, committing to engage fully even though some of the practices—including daily

meditations, a death lodge ceremony and a spirit-guided soul quest in a remote natural setting – were definitely out of my comfort zone. It would have been easy to find excuses to pick the practices that were easiest, or shortcut the required journaling of personal reflections. But I was determined not to sabotage the one process that might lead me to discovering what the "this" was that I didn't want to do anymore.

My perseverance paid off. I benefitted most from two aspects of the program. One was the small group sessions where five of us met weekly, with a mentor, to share our experiences at a level of vulnerability that wasn't possible in the larger group sessions. This group helped me interpret the exercises and practices I engaged in by suggesting a variety of different lenses through which to view the outcomes. They treated me with good humor, compassion and tremendous patience. They met me where I was ready to be, without imposing expectations about how they hoped I'd progress. I reciprocated, finding tremendous joy in being valued both for what I was able to give and receive. In the journal I kept about these discussions, I uncovered more expansive ways of thinking about how to identify the next iteration of my purpose and any hidden barriers I might, unintentionally, be allowing to intrude.

I reflected on how my old ways of making sense of the world had often steered me in the wrong direction. Instead of assuming I could only find purpose by actively seeking my purpose, I began to see the power in opening myself up to having my purpose *discover me.* Meditation, it turned out, was an important element. In one particularly compelling reverie, I saw myself separated in the middle of a circle of stick figures. Then a few minutes later, the image gently shifted and I ended up where I belonged: in the circle, with everyone else.

I found myself admitting that there could be meaning for me in both images, and letting go of the belief that I could only exist in one

of the images or the other. I began to accept a notion that, until now, had been foreign to me. What if I didn't have to choose between being *either* in the spotlight *or* remaining in the wings? I allowed the idea of living with such cognitive dissonance wash over me. I began to recall times when I was meant to be in the spotlight, in the middle of the circle, offering my gifts and talents to individuals who valued them. I also remembered when I'd happily been on the receiving end of what others had to offer to me. There could be joy, not just obligation, in reciprocity.

For much of my life, because my dad had unjustly forced me into the disingenuous role of "pretender," I hadn't ever imagined there could be more than one dimension to how people actually are in the world. If I didn't deserve to be typecast into a singular version of myself, then I had to admit I owed the same respect to my parents. Dad may have had a softer, caring side that I never got to see. Why else would Mom have married him? Perhaps she, too, experienced dissonance over when to be my advocate with him – maybe she was just navigating the tradeoffs between doing so in the spotlight, or privately, in the wings.

The other aspect of the program that impacted me greatly was called the Circle of Trust. I was tasked to invite individuals in my network of friends to serve as a sounding board as I sought to uncover my soul's deepest needs. Their role was to give me space to grapple with my personal revelations and insights throughout the course of the program. It was a critical role, helping me interpret what I was uncovering as my understanding of self revealed increasingly greater depths.

I picked three friends to invite into my circle, each of whom I'd met at different points in my corporate career. They knew me well and I trusted them completely. Even so, I was anxious about asking them to participate. I was afraid the time commitment would

be a burden given their busy schedules. Even though I experienced a momentary panic that they wouldn't deem me worthy enough to devote the time, I stood by my commitment to push forward and do whatever I could to engage in every program offering. I sent an email to all three explaining what I was up to and what role I was asking them to play along the way. Without hesitation, all three agreed to participate.

My friend Christine, who had been the catalyst for me beginning the program in the first place, joined in. So did Jeannie, who I'd met when she was a contract writer and we had an opportunity to work together. Deb, one of the founders of Gilda's Club, was the third person to agree. We had met twenty years earlier when our workstations were positioned next to each other. Besides being the most upbeat, life-loving person, I had ever encountered, Deb also was navigating her fifth challenge with cancer. When she got my invitation, she texted me back, "I'll be there as long as I can get up from my sofa!"

For ninety minutes, once a month, they patiently sat around my dining room table, laid bare except for glasses filled with water and a box of tissues. Cell phones stayed muted and tucked away. This distraction-free environment made it easy for my friends to focus on coaxing me to transform my perceived negative self-image. Snow or slippery roads were never an excuse for bailing out. Deb always was able to "get off the sofa." One time, Christine even took an Uber to my house because her son needed to borrow her car. They were totally committed to making my growth a priority. And like the support group at Gilda's Club, they challenged me whenever I attempted to shy away from the spotlight by deflecting the topic of conversation away from me.

During one session, I mentioned that I wasn't sure I wanted to continue in my coaching practice. I shared another image that had

surfaced during a different meditation. In this one, I was a receptacle for other peoples' pain and suffering, and there was no room in this container for mine. I suspect this was based on the same tired and illogical premise I had been fighting for years – focusing on me meant I couldn't simultaneously focus on others, a zero-sum situation.

Jeannie has a knack for introducing tangential perspectives that are useful in interrupting obsessive thoughts. This typically opens up a pathway for more spacious perspective-taking. In two sentences, she offered an entirely different way of tackling this quandary around my identity as a professional coach. "I think you're limiting yourself when you think about whether you still want to be a coach," she said. "Whatever you end up calling yourself, it might be useful to stop seeing your work as *making a difference* for others in the world; maybe it's about *being a difference*."

Her assessment instantly lifted a fog that had been clouding my judgment for my entire life. There would never be enough acts of penance to make up for my supposed evil nature. The good person I pretended to be was the good person I had become. All I could reasonably hope to do now was show up as I already was. I felt as if a huge weight had been lifted off me.

I sat quietly at the table, saying nothing for a few minutes. I stared at a piece of paper where I had scribbled some notes to remind me of what I wanted to say at the beginning of the session. I was using this pause to be sure whatever I did say in response would be genuine and heartfelt. I wanted to catch myself before responding in a way directed only toward what I suspected would make Jeannie and the others feel good about their insights. They weren't in this with me so that I could soothe *their* egos.

While contemplating Jeannie's advice, I recalled other comments these women had made during previous discussions. When asked what gifts I bring to the world, they told me I'd exhibited the

capacity to build genuine connection by being profoundly present. They cherished my ability to see into and reflect back the essence of what was difficult for them to articulate. Most meaningful to me was their belief in the depth of my empathy and compassion. They confirmed, if indirectly, that the Barbara I had always feared was "bad" was an illusion; she never existed.

The work I did around discovering my soul's purpose didn't result in a huge "aha" that would dramatically change how I interacted with others. It didn't leave me feeling as if I had been utterly and instantly transformed. It was more like what Christine, Jeannie and Deb had predicted – a "ripening" or "untangling" of my current purpose. This purpose had been defined back when I started my consulting practice, deliberately setting out to help others recognize the power they *already had* to fix what troubled them. I saw my job as creating a context in which they could accelerate identifying, and then letting go of, self-sabotaging behaviors. This ultimately had become my way of *being* with my family, friends, colleagues and clients. But in that effort, I had always seen myself as totally separate from others, clinically removed, vigorously protecting their boundaries and mine, thinking that I couldn't risk contributing to their suffering by tainting them with "Bad Barbara's" nefarious powers.

Now, I recognized my desire to continue helping people uncover hidden barriers, but only if I could be wholeheartedly connected to them during the process. What would be new for me was an intentional dismantling of the protective shield that had kept me from embracing the suffering that binds all human beings. The receptacle that I thought had no more space for other peoples' pain and suffering disappeared. I realized, instead, it actually had been a vessel of my own creation, a refuge that I used to maintain a safe distance from others.

In reexamining and redefining my purpose, I concluded that from now on I would listen to others with a different openness. I'd strive to be acutely more aware of how often, and for how long, early traumas impeded my clients' determination to be a *difference in the world.* I would do this by revealing my own efforts to forgive myself for all the wrongs for which I'd unfairly accepted responsibility, and for the times I had chosen me first, when the alternative meant I'd be succumbing to the belief that I didn't matter. And I'd dig deep, finding the energy and resilience to help others do the same.

Chapter 17

At Peace

Two parts of myself had been battling against each other for the better part of my life. I'd always feared, maybe even assumed, that standing up for myself would put me at risk of becoming self-centered and selfish, like my father. When I finally was able to leave this tug-of-war behind, it felt like I was letting go of a constant, lifelong companion. We had endured a love-hate relationship for sixty years, one that alternately nurtured my intrinsic goodness and chastised me for being inherently unlovable. It took such a long time to give up the fight because I thought doing so would have to be precipitated by declaring a winner and a loser. If "Good Barbara" won, it would be at the expense of "Bad Barbara," and vice versa. Because they had been unambiguously intertwined for the majority of my life, I couldn't imagine living without either one.

There was no single remarkable event signifying the end of the struggle, no grandiose funeral or period of mourning. Rather, it was a gradual awakening to what I already inherently knew but hadn't

previously been able to fathom in a tangible way. The catalyst for pursuing this awakening likely wouldn't have come without my frightening duel with cancer and subsequent quest to define the "this" I didn't want to do anymore. That hard work had actually begun the September day in 2017, when I put my hand on my chest and discovered the mass that would change my life forever.

In the intervening months, I couldn't ignore all the messaging coming my way that countered my previously held belief about not being "good enough." These messages came to me in a barrage of separate and distinct instances, in:

The boundless, unconditional love from my family patiently cheerleading me on, even when I wondered whether everyone would be better off if I simply wasn't here.

The words of love, support and hope shared by my extended family, friends and colleagues on CaringBridge.

The phone calls from my childhood friend Hannah, to Stuart, every day, for the four weeks I was hospitalized.

The fact that all of my clients and business partners waited patiently for me to recover so we could resume our leadership development efforts right where we left off.

The honor of being named a recipient of the Distinguished Community Trustee Award, a recognition of how my good work had an impressive rippling effect community-wide.

The friend sitting behind me at synagogue, after I hadn't been there for a year, tapping me on the shoulder whispering, "You are a warrior."

The truth that complete strangers, like my support group at Gilda's Club and my small group in the Purpose Discovery program, not only cared for me unconditionally, they also cheered me on as I got stronger, generously allowing me to reciprocate by helping them discover their hidden paths.

The incredible six days in 2018 I spent in Paris with Leigh when, finally well enough to make the trip, she grabbed my hand to keep me from falling every time I stepped on and off the sidewalk.

The chill that ran through my entire body, when attending the Bar Mitzvah of a relative in New Jersey in 2019, and I heard my Hebrew name announced during the blessing for those who are ill, unaware that for two years there had been a sustained effort, in a community seven hundred miles away, to pray for my healing.

The shared wisdom of my dear friends in my Circle of Trust, whose tenacity in challenging me to accept my inherent worthiness culminated in Jeannie's wise words, "Barbara, you never were bad. You just were standing in a shadow that cast you in a different light."

When I absorbed the volume, frequency and consistency of these messages all at once, they reflected a truth I no longer could evade. From the age of five, my view of myself was ingrained with the notion I had sufficient power to make people sick. Acceptance of this shadow side was impossible for a five-year old. Even worse, however, was how it plagued me on and off for sixty years. When the idea that I was able to perpetrate such evil in the world first surfaced, I concluded that I had no choice but to continually seek penance for being such an abomination. My coping strategy was to always demonstrate selflessness towards others. Doing so over and over would be proof of my unwavering commitment to provide value, to deserve to be in this world. I'd vigorously deny my self-interests to glorify the interests of others.

This strategy worked for quite a while. But eventually, a different side of my persona stepped up, no longer content to wait quietly in the wings while my shadow side took center stage. Experiences with people outside my nuclear family revealed how much goodness I brought to the world, just by being me – teachers who told me I was

smart and talented, friends from the neighborhood, school and camp who sought out my company because they found me interesting and extremely creative. It took being diagnosed with a chronic illness, in my teens, to even begin to reverse course on the life of penance I had chosen. That's when I began an alternative coping strategy, also aimed at survival. I acknowledged and allowed my inner rebel to surface. I was a warrior who had the energy and resolve to fight just as hard for my right to demand equal time for my needs to be met.

The numerous emotional ups and downs I faced following the cancer diagnosis and its aftermath were these warring factions engaging in one final battle royale. Because both were predicated on enabling me to survive, I couldn't let go of either one. Subsequently, I lived day-to-day swinging back and forth between both extremes. A third alternative – the possibility of living a life encompassing *both* the selfless and self-serving parts of myself, in tandem, had never entered my consciousness.

The constant battle was eating away at my resilience and will to live another day. While I endured each subsequent medical trauma, an intense weariness enveloped me. The fight was no longer about which side of me would prevail in the end; it was about whether I had the conviction to be in the fight at all. I may have hung on because I was a warrior. But truth be told, I was a wholeheartedly reluctant one.

In engaging in the Purpose Discovery program, I'd start my day sitting in my living room, quietly seeking to commune with nature. It was energizing to experience myself as part of a greater and bountiful natural universe. My ego took a back seat as I saw myself *of the earth* rather than *on the earth.* When I'm alone in the house, the living room has become the perfect place to find peace and solace. On sunny days, floor-to-ceiling windows invite constant bursts of light. Because a variety of trees stand just outside these

windows, I have come to appreciate how much trees can teach us if we simply take time to notice them. I observed that when the wind blows, the leaves sway with more or less intensity, depending on the tree's species, height, strength and rootedness in the ground. As I watched the wide range of movements, I imagined the trees were whispering to each other. If I listened very intently, perhaps I could learn a sacred mystery of life.

One particular morning, the leaves and branches of some nearby firs were shuffling briskly, as if they had something on their mind that needed to be resolved immediately. A strong wind bobbed the branches up and down, helter-skelter. The sunshine maneuvered its way between the moving branches. Its rays reached the windows in flashes of light that cast dynamic shadows on the floor and furniture. The vision made me think about how trees often demonstrate tremendous agility and adaptability, even in the face of challenging weather conditions. Through it all, many stood tall and strong, for centuries, generously inspiring the peaceful coexistence between light and shadow.

I held this image in my heart and soul. It touched me in a way I couldn't fully comprehend in the moment, until I was in a therapy session a few weeks later. I was telling my therapist, Chuck, that I recalled a session with him many years before, when I was in my forties, seeking to understand how I could show up as my best self when parenting Jay and Leigh. The image I had then was of two Barbaras, standing across from each other, divided by a gated, white picket fence. Their facial expressions reflect deep concentration. Neither one feels safe enough to open the gate and join her counterpart on the other side. Being separated is causing them a level of despair and to alleviate it, they had hoped to break down the barrier and become one. But becoming one was fraught with the danger of annihilation. One Barbara would have to be subsumed

within the other. Although I had been living with these two "dis-integrated" selves since the age of five, this was the moment I finally was able to acknowledge their coexistence.

Twenty years later, two years after the cancer diagnosis, and I'm back in a therapy session with Chuck. This image reappears, only it has evolved into something quite surprising. The two Barbaras are facing each other again, but suddenly the white picket fence disappears. The girls move closer to one another. They grasp each other's hand and begin walking together, their faces beaming with delight. They are inextricably connected to and supported by the other; neither one losing herself in the other.

In that moment, I realized my internal tug-of-war was finally over. Both sides were now living side-by-side in peace. Both had forgiven each other – and themselves – for the suffering they had caused one another. I reveled in the fact that both of them shaped who I am – the unassuming helpful woman who makes a difference behind the scenes and the strong, courageous and resilient warrior who allows herself to stand in the spotlight when she deserves to be the focus of attention. Most important, I was ready to embrace both Barbaras and celebrate their coexistence – eager to live my life *Reimagined.*

And so now, I am at peace.

Epilogue

When I set out to write this memoir, I had one goal in mind – to understand why my cancer experience continued to haunt me long after my body had healed. I was plagued by my inability to come to grips with the immense suffering I'd endured. I couldn't stop the voice in my head that was pushing me to find a way to let go of two crippling beliefs – that I somehow deserved to suffer this much, and that I didn't deserve this second chance at life.

Determining whether, or how much, either of those beliefs were true was hard enough. What followed was equally difficult – finding the words, sentences and paragraphs to bring the unembellished truth to light. Fortunately, the process of writing *Reimagined* allowed me to end the internal battle, claim that I was worthy of life and find joy and comfort in simply *being me.* For anyone else suffering from crippling beliefs, I hope my story will motivate them to identify ways to reframe those beliefs sooner rather than later. I wasted too many years allowing myself to be victimized by my own false narratives. My hope is that others

won't wait until a life-threatening event serves as the catalyst for exorcising the demons that hold them captive.

Two years after my diagnosis, I admit to still feeling on edge about whether cancer is looming in my body and simply hasn't revealed itself yet. It doesn't take much to elicit a feeling of panic because nearly every time I have some type of medical appointment, I am questioned about my illness. What kind was it? What long-term effects have you noticed? Have your scans remained clear? These questions are catalysts for reliving, if only for an instant, those dark days.

Recently, I was on the phone with Linda, one of my friends from my childhood with whom I've remained close. I was telling her about the results of a recent blood workup. The report caused my gastroenterologist to be concerned enough to have me repeat the test, this time looking for tumor markers. Linda asked me what I imagined it would be like for me, if I discovered I had another form of cancer. I answered without hesitation, "I'd fight, kicking and screaming to get the disease out of me; there's so much more I still want to experience. But I'm also confident in one thing. I wouldn't suffer in the same way."

I've come to understand that my suffering was due more to emotional rather than physical pain. As I healed physically, I noticed I also was liberating myself from an even greater trauma – a lifelong belief that my survival depended on one of my two personas eradicating the other. If faced with cancer again, I'm confident my physical suffering would either be mitigated or extinguished through the administration of palliative medical care. Any chains left over from the shackles of self-annihilation that have held me captive in the past would have been cast aside, forever.

It has also become apparent that the anger I had harbored against my father for nearly my entire life wasn't only about what had transpired during my interactions with him; it also was directed

at what *hadn't* taken place. I'd been robbed of what my kids have been blessed with, an amazingly caring, compassionate, kind and fun-loving dad. In coming to terms with the anger I carried for so long, I inadvertently uncovered a gaping hole that should have been filled with a father's love. I have yet to fully mourn that loss.

I have begun to wonder if my understanding of my relationship with my dad has been somewhat flawed. Perhaps it had never been about me falling short of being "good enough," which implied there was something inherently wrong with me. Instead, maybe it was about me being "too much" for him. This interpretation offers a potentially broader perspective around why my dad, more than fifty years ago, may have felt compelled to scream at me, "You're making me sick." The simple explanation could be that, like many of the clients I work with in my coaching practice, he simply lacked emotional intelligence. For the first time ever, I can feel some empathy for his deficiency. I'm able to conjure up how vulnerable he must have felt by not being able to adequately assess, take responsibility for and overcome the emotional barriers that kept him from establishing more loving relationships with his wife, children and extended family.

While *Reimagined* is primarily the story of my relationship with my dad, in the aftermath of its completion, I find myself thinking deeply about my relationship with my mother. I can appreciate her commitment, unwittingly thrust upon her by Dad's psychiatrist, to assume full responsibility for taking care of him. He was our sole provider and I suspect Mom feared for our safety and security if he suddenly couldn't hold down a job. In hindsight I think she did the right thing. She assessed the situation and identified the resources she had on hand. She figured that Doris was mostly old enough to fend for herself and Stephanie was mature enough to watch out for me. In spite of Mom briefly ceding my care to Stephanie, apart from

the few incidents noted here when I felt invisible in her presence, I knew the truth: Mom had never stopped loving me.

My mother was the one person who, in spite of my dad's overbearing presence, ultimately took responsibility for mediating the stresses and tensions that inevitably erupted between him and me. She walked that tightrope, keeping herself nearly perfectly balanced, until my junior year in high school, when I was hospitalized for a serious case of anaphylactic shock.

I think of that as the time when my mom came back and took me under her wing again, just as she had before Dad's breakdown. From then on, whenever she witnessed me being the object of his selfish demands, I realize now that she was steadfastly trying to tip the scales in my favor. I suspect this was because she had finally mustered the courage to cast off her own demons, letting my dad know she'd only continue to bestow compassion on him if he did the same toward me. In so doing, she taught me that parents are human; they always have the choice to rectify their mistakes.

For years, I closely and quietly observed my mother demonstrating attributes I hope I've displayed toward my own children – encouraging me to be who I was rather than someone else's preferred version of me, advocating for me when I didn't have the strength or know-how to advocate for myself, providing wisdom and counsel when others might not have my best interests at heart, demonstrating the value of self-care and, when I was particularly lonely, taking on the role of best friend. Since writing my story, I've let go of the pain I felt around perceiving that she had abandoned me to my sister's care. Instead, I feel tremendous gratitude for her unassuming mentorship. I've even come to identify her as my earliest protector, making it my mission to follow in her footsteps and do everything in my power to keep my children safe, or more importantly, help guide them so that they can keep themselves safe.

It's important to note that *Reimagined* was written during the COVID-19 pandemic. For me, there was no escaping a comparison between the real-time suffering of others I was hearing about in daily news reports, and the nature of my own suffering. This comparison revealed a stark reality that hadn't been obvious to me before. While the personal suffering I recounted in the memoir was real, I also recognize that it was conceived within a framework of white privilege. Such privilege gave me things I took for granted – comprehensive health care coverage, a safe and affordable home within which to recuperate and a cohort of family and friends who were free to carve out time to watch over me and focus their attention on keeping me safe. These privileges didn't negate the fact that my physical and emotional pain were excruciating. They did, however, mitigate the intensity and duration of what I ultimately had to cope with.

I've also realized that releasing the demons that held me captive throughout much of my life hasn't been a remedy for the stresses associated with everyday living. In spite of my profound gratitude for the peace I was able to find in writing this memoir, I still experience my fair share of worries – moments when I obsess about whether or not I'm being good enough for my family, friends and colleagues, and when I beat myself up for failing to meet my own exacting standards.

What I am able to do now, however, is fall back on my newfound appreciation for human connection. It is the only constant that I can rely on when I am feeling completely alone, vulnerable and too overwhelmed to tend to myself. The countless individuals who stood by me during this dark period of my life have inspired me to find solace in the knowledge that a temporary retreat isn't destined to end in a permanent defeat. They coaxed me into viewing my world through a lens of optimism. This memoir is my gift to them.

Acknowledgements

Writing *Reimagined* was a labor of love. It came to fruition in the span of a year because of the guidance and wisdom of my memoir coach, Shari Caudron, the stylistic savvy of my editor, Luc Hatlestad and the creative intuition of my designer, Cindi Yaklich. Their collective talents helped me convey my story in a way that has the potential to uplift and inspire others. My gratitude to them knows no bounds.

I received feedback on the first draft of the manuscript from Kati Boland, Lizzie Williams, Sarah Cavanaugh, Rick Baker, Georgia Everse, Meredith Bronk and Bob Kegan. Because they validated that what I wanted to convey represented some universal truths, I had the confidence to see the writing through to final publication.

My dear friends, Hannah Butensky, Mindy Danna, Christine Albertini, Jeannie Hosey and Deb Bailey (who sadly succumbed to her fifth bout of cancer prior to publication) were instrumental in seeing me through the emotional ups and downs of my Purpose

Discovery journey. Along with my sisters, Stephanie Goldsmith and Doris Kleinman, countless other friends and family members (too many to mention by name) and the devoted individuals I came in contact with at Gilda's Club, they have been my cheerleaders throughout every stage of my illness and recovery. Their love and support never wavered.

The medical marvels described here could never have happened without the skill, dedication and compassion afforded to me by Gary Humphries, Joel Post, Matthew Steensma, Genevieve Waldron, Steve Naum, Charles Willekes, Sampson Ho, John Keller, Brian Gilbert and Chuck Grayson. They all contributed to making me whole again, in body and spirit.

The twists and turns of my career path have led me to establish deep connections with academic and business professionals in more than twenty countries. I will always be grateful to the teams at Minds at Work and the Grand Rapids Area Chamber for giving me opportunities to enhance my perspective-taking and expand my capacity to think creatively.

My husband, Stuart, never complained during the countless hours I spent squirreled away intent on forming sentences, paragraphs and chapters that I hoped would be meaningful to the young professionals I work with every day. He remains the epitome of unconditional love. My son, Jay, continuously expressed pride in my tenacity to push beyond my comfort zone. My daughter, Leigh, inspired me daily to stay focused, courageous and joyful when moments of doubt seeped into my consciousness. I stand on their shoulders.

Made in the USA
Monee, IL
10 April 2021